The City

Markus Naerheim

The City

Copyright © Markus Naerheim, 2008

AUTHOR'S NOTE

This is a work of fiction. Names, characters, places and incidents either are the product of the author's imagination or are used fictitiously, and any resemblance to any actual persons, living or dead, events, or locales is entirely coincidental.

To order additional copies of this book, or to learn more about the author, please visit www.markusn.com.

Cover design by TNBD

www.tnbd.net

ISBN 978-1-60530-956-9

Printed in the United States of America

The City

Part I

1

Jack Wild came to the city at night, and when he saw the lights in the darkness, San Francisco seemed to answer his hopes for a great change in his life. It took him a day and a half to come out from Arizona. He had grown up in Casa Grande and gone to school in Tucson. He was twenty-four with a BA in Business. Jack was the only member of his family with a university degree. He preferred sports to business, but listened to his father who said, "If you want to make money and have a future, you have to deal with money. You're a good ball player, Jack, but there's no future in entertainment. Sports is entertainment."

Now Jack sat on the bus full of thoughts of the future: of corporations, projects, meetings and profits. He imagined himself seated behind a large desk typing on the computer, or talking on the phone to clients; he imagined marketing, selling and climbing up the ranks. Discipline was his great strength. With discipline Jack would prove himself indispensable; with hard work he would be successful.

These selfish, arrogant thoughts protected him from the unknown landscapes of California and the strangers that surrounded him. Jack was nostalgic for the past and hopeful of the future. The present was the stink of alcohol from a neighbor's breath, the grease and filth of the man's hair, and the wrinkles of worry that time had carved into his face. For this present Jack felt only revulsion. He felt revulsion for the crying baby, the banter of foreign languages, and the people of all shapes, sizes and colors different from his own. He realized that only money could spare him contact with the filthy, tired and deranged of that bus. Jack felt fear and panic at being one of them: faceless, foreign and unimportant. Still, that hadn't stopped him from drinking with the old man out of Fresno.

"Going to the city, boy? I remember the first time I gone to the city. I was full a' money from construction and I went and had me some girls. They gave me a massage and I gave them money and they gave me the rest. Ha, ha. I wish I was young like you so I could go do it all over again. The city, they's some good times. Say son, you wouldn't have a few dollars to help out an old man? Times ain't as good as they once was. What's a young fella with a future like you need with a couple a' bucks?"

Jack reached into his pocket and gave the man some money to shut him up. Then he searched the bus for an empty seat. The man was a living, breathing failure and waste of human life. Jack thought with sincerity that shooting him would be a favor. The world would function better without such misery. Christ, it made him sick to see a human being turn that way. It made him sick to think how greatly men differed in character and fortune. Fortune or no fortune, Jack believed that ruin was a man's own doing, and that even a poor man could live with dignity.

When he thought about the city, girls came to mind. Jack imagined strange and interesting girls, and how he would like to meet and be with a great many of them. It didn't occur to him how these girls might change him from who he was. Jack was strong and would not allow any part of the city to break him like it had broken the old man. He would take the city and shape it to his character and not the reverse.

Jack was sure to find success in the city. After all, wasn't he the star pitcher for U of A, an honors graduate in Business, and a notorious womanizer of sorority girls and impressionable freshman? No, he was not just any Arizona boy.

Jack's life was packed into his gym bag. He thought it best to travel light, contenting himself with a few changes of clothes and a suit handed down from his father. It was a brown suit, outdated and ill-fitting, but he had a nice tie and good pair of leather shoes that would serve him for a job interview. What he did not bring he could go back for. What he did not have he would buy when he had stable work.

The bus roared toward the city. Jack could finally see the skyline and the bridge, not the Golden Gate but another lesser bridge that connected the lights on the other side of the bay. He was no longer tired, but tense and eager to hit the streets and find a hotel where he could have a hot shower before going out on the town.

Jack got off the bus oblivious to where he was in the city or where he should be. The streets were blurry with lights. Here and there was a bar or restaurant, a man sleeping in a doorway, a shopping cart full of cans covered with blankets and the smell of urine burned into concrete.

A young beautiful woman walked leaning into her cell phone while some men on the corner drank from paper bags and rap thumped on the boom box. Jack felt far away from home. The romance of distance was gone now, and he thought about where he could go to relax and digest the novelty and swallow his own sense of loneliness and alienation. Jack didn't know where to go, so he thought it best to hail a cab. He stuck his arm out, and the cab stopped for a couple up the street and took them off into the night. He tried again, and this time the cabby drove past without slowing down or looking his way. Jack noticed someone in the back seat. You have to be more aggressive, he told himself.

Down the road Jack saw another cab marquee, and he stepped into the street and whistled. The cab came to the curb, and he got in and told the man to drive. Jack didn't know where he was going, but thought the best way to see the city would be to take a ride. He was tired of buses. He had saved some money and could afford a night of fun before he went looking for work. With his education, Jack didn't think work would be a problem. The internet economy was booming in the city. Every day he read a new success story in Business Time: of twenty-somethings turned millionaires with one good idea. With such news, he couldn't help but feel that tickle of excitement before success. Jack had never failed in his life. He had a deep fear of failure; it had made him stubborn and relentless. He knew he could support a lot of hardship until times got better.

"Where to mister?"

"I need a room. Take me to a hotel that's close to the bars."

"There's lots of bars in this city. Bars for all sorts of folks. I know bars where you have to take your clothes off to get in. The guys, they pay to be horse-whipped and walked on with high-heeled shoes. If that's not your thing, then I know a great piano bar where they dress up in drag and sing show tunes. I know bars with electronic bulls in the back. That's a bar for guys that like dicks."

Jack heard him out. He was not one to shock easily. Sure, he hadn't traveled much, but he had read plenty of books and seen pictures in magazines.

"Listen, I just want to go to a place with some nice girls. I'm a regular guy. I just want a beer and some good scenery."

The cabby smiled.

"I've seen a lot in this job. Sometimes I wonder if regular exists. I tell you, people get bored and when they're bored they do strange things. That's what happens when people live on top of each other. They try to escape themselves."

What are we listening to," Jack asked.

"Rai music. It's from my country. I am from Algeria. Do you know it?"

"No," Jack said. He knew nothing of the history of bombing and killing in Algeria or the startling vocals of Rai. He sat entranced by the errant rise and fall of the Arabic. There was no question that there was great feeling of either love or pain in that music.

They fell silent and Murshid, the cabby, drove casually, making a turn here or there at leisure; it was pleasant change to have no destination and still be on the clock. He had met a good many people in his job, and they all had a different story to tell. Murshid was glad that people weren't all the same, or like himself. Without the kaleidoscope of humanity that entered his cab, work would be boring. There were better and worse jobs, certainly, but he made enough to feed his family.

Murshid had one night off a week for the bowling league, and sometimes he would drive to the beach. The ocean was something he respected but feared, because he had never learned to swim. He had nightmares of drowning in the ocean; he could not imagine a worse fate then to have his lungs fill with water as he gasped for life-giving breath.

Murshid's journey to America had given him great status with his family abroad. He received letters from distant relatives in such quantities that every Sunday he was obliged to sit down at his desk to respond. Many of them wrote of sending their children to visit, perhaps in hope that they would find a good job so they could send money home. To such letters he would reply that it would be an honor to receive this niece or nephew in his home, for they were certainly hard workers, though it was an honor that he could not accept due to unnamed difficulties. Truthfully, he could not afford another mouth to feed, they did not have enough room in the apartment and he could provide no work for the new arrivals. He was the textbook successful immigrant who could not help his own family. He knew his refusal meant an uncertain and challenging future for his young relatives.

Unfortunately, the subjects Murshid most wanted to discuss he could not name to his passengers. That was the cabby's burden: to know more than others but be condemned to silence. That was repression, and he had learned it in America. Do your job, be polite and shut your mouth because people don't want to hear the truth, especially if you can prove it.

"I know a good hotel downtown. From there you can get a cab anywhere. North Beach is a nice place. It's for the tourists. Also, there's the Mission, that's better for you. There are many bars and young people."

Murshid stopped in front of the hotel. Jack paid and thanked him for the ride. He slung his duffel bag over his shoulder and walked past the uniformed doorman who gave an ever so slight nod of the head.

Maybe he couldn't afford the place. Still, it was his first night in the city, and he wanted to look out at the skyscrapers from his window and feel warm and safe in a way that only money could make a man feel. He was glad to have a credit card. He got a suitable room for eighty dollars: a third of his monthly rent in college. He told himself not to think about the money.

Jack took the elevator to the twentieth floor. Once inside, he collapsed on the bed. He pulled up the sheets and jumped up and down on the mattress. He opened the curtains and looked out at the skyline of his new home, savoring his newfound freedom. Jack was glad to be away from his parents. Comfort had returned, and he was no longer nervous or afraid. Now he craved music, loud delicious music, alcohol, and a pretty girl to laugh and roll in the sheets with, skin to skin.

The exhaustion of the trip took over. The novelty faded and Jack went to take a shower. He stood a long time under the hot water feeling layers of emotion fall way. His mind raced with memories. He remembered the time he had hit a baseball into a pitcher's face breaking all his teeth, and how the young man gaped at him -a black hole in his mouth- as the blood ran down his chin. What was once shock had turned to laughter. Jack laughed out loud and his voice echoed on the tile. How that young man must have hated him. He wondered if the day would come when someone damaged him in a way that he would never forget.

2

Jack changed his clothes to go out. He wore his favorite jeans and a plaid collared shirt tucked into his belt. He shaved and combed his hair. He pointed at himself in the mirror and gave a wink. You go, lady-killer.

The cabby dropped him on the corner of Sixteenth and Mission.

"They are plenty of bars here, kid. Just take a walk."

Jack had a hundred in twenties in his pocket. He didn't want to be short on cash if he invited someone to a drink. Even so, he didn't plan on spending more than fifty.

The Mission was not like he expected. It was run-down and everything was written in Spanish. Jack walked up the street and looked in the shop windows. A Latino wearing a cowboy hat, boots, jeans and a belt with a silver buckle in the shape of a horse, passed by with his arm around his girl. Jack thought of Mexican revolutionaries, and how the man must have been very proud and sure of himself judging by the size of his hat and mustache. Jack didn't think men looked good with mustaches; it was an outdated style. Jack didn't need any facial hair to protect himself from the ills of the world.

The neighborhood lacked the vibrant bar scene and beautiful women he had imagined. The streets were abandoned and lonely, and Jack thought of the *vaquero* clutching his girl close to keep her safe. A cold wind blew trash by Jack's feet, and he wondered how long it would take for him to find a group of friends that he could laugh with, talk big, and close out the bad and ugly of life.

Passing a *taquería*, Jack looked in at the sterile light, the neon of the beer signs and the Latinos eating with their families, and thought how he wanted to be in a dark bar pressed tight with people. He imagined the heat and music mingling with the conversations he would eavesdrop for lack of company. He longed to hear a good story like his father used to tell. He wanted to meet someone who would make him laugh, and he knew that the woman he married had to have a sense of humor.

Down the street, Jack noticed some girls outside a bar smoking. Approaching, he met their eyes and stepped inside to join the crowd. The décor was something out of his grandmother's house, but that didn't bother him. There were many girls, some of them beautiful in a way that was very unlike the girls he had known in college. They seemed elegant and reserved, not sporty and vulgar like he was used to. He could not imagine any of them in bikinis or sports bras. Mostly, they wore black. They were works of art with their dyed, bleached and styled hair, fashionable clothes, and arrogant posture.

Jack wondered what sort of bar it was. Outdated cosmetics advertisements for nail polish and skin cream covered the walls. The man painting nails and the old-fashioned salon seats with the hairdryer helmets put him off. He felt out of place, so he did the only reasonable thing and went to bar to order a beer. Beer in hand, Jack felt safe again and he leaned on the counter to watch the crowd.

Seeing all those people, each unique, all of them strangers, made Jack feel distant from himself and what he thought to be wholesome, which was a good pair of jeans, a plain t-shirt and a fresh haircut. Fashion was secondary to Jack and he wondered who these people were that tried so hard to be different in dress and appearance. The women were strange and exotic, and he couldn't judge them properly to single one out. It maddened him to be distracted and deceived in such a way. Suddenly, nothing was familiar. Jack ordered another beer and drank it down as quickly as the first. He was shy and didn't want to stand out; he preferred to fade to the background where he could watch and judge the crowd.

Jack wouldn't allow himself to be intimidated. He had the charm in him; he liked to socialize and had always been well-liked. Honesty had gotten him far in life; paired with loyalty, it had earned him many friends. He didn't see why it should be any different in the city.

A girl came and stood next to him at the bar. Jack had noticed her before. She was one of the many versions of beauty that fit his taste. In particular, he liked the contrast between her black hair and blue eyes. He was a man for contrasts and exaggerated features. Beauty to him had always been about new and unusual combinations.

She ordered drinks and ignored him.

"Hi, I'm Jack. This is my first night in the city. I'm from Arizona."

"Hello, Jack."

After paying the bartender, she gathered her drinks and pushed her way through the crowd. "Have a good night," she said.

"You didn't tell me your name."

"Elizabeth. Listen, I've got some friends waiting. I'll see you later."

Jack watched her go. She was neither friendly nor hostile. No, she was ambivalent. He would take ambivalence over hostility, and he felt good for his initiative. He would watch and wait for a suitable moment and approach her again. Patience, Jack, patience. You don't have to do it all in one night.

After his second beer, Jack made his way to the bathroom. He was the kind to hold his piss, and now in the urinal a relief not unlike good sex flooded through him as he emptied his bladder. He went to wash his hands in the sink.

"I saw you standing alone at the bar."

Jack looked into the mirror and made eye contact with the man. They were alone.

"Yes. I'm new in town. I haven't had the chance to meet anyone yet."

"This town can be pretty lonely without company," the man said.

"Yes, I suppose it can," Jack said.

"You know, I'm not much for the game. When I see something I like, I grab it. Most people, they're afraid to make a move."

"That's sounds like good advice," Jack told him. "Otherwise, you could spend all your time standing around."

"Listen, you seem like a nice guy. I bet you're out to have a little fun tonight. Am I right?"

"Well, if something comes my way, sure," Jack said.

"How about I help you out?"

"Oh yeah, how's that?"

"Why don't you just come into the stall with me and I'll show you."

"Excuse me?"

"I'll give you the best blow job you've ever had," the man told him.

"I think you've misunderstood," Jack said, feeling queezy. Images of prison and rape filled his mind. Smiling, the man closed his hand around Jack's bicep and steered him toward the stall.

"Don't you want to have fun? All that out there is bullshit. A good-looking guy like you should take advantage. Just give me five minutes. You won't have to do a thing. Just shut your eyes and think of a pretty girl, if that's what you like. You won't even know the difference."

Jack felt the blood rush to his face.

"Get your fuckin' hands off'a me. I told you you've made a mistake," Jack said, shrugging him off. The man was about his size and stood between him and the door. I'll knock this son of a bitch out if I have to, Jack thought, holding up his fists to defend himself. The man stepped back with his hands out.

"Hey, take it easy buddy."

Jack lowered his arms.

"It's a shame, you know. People should be free with themselves and their bodies. You're just afraid you're going to like it. That's what everyone's afraid of. Wouldn't that just turn everything upside down?"

Jack ignored him and pushed past him out the door. Though he was not the sort to lose his temper, Jack was flushed and his heart beat fast in his chest. He thought again of prison and being forced to do things against his will to please others. Sex: it was about power and control, and he wanted to be in control of women. With some that was possible, and with others it was not.

Jack did his best to forget the incident. It was a fiction he liked to keep at a safe distance. He was not one for perversion of any sort, though he wouldn't deny that there were individuals who would abuse themselves and others for pleasure. The thought made him ill. He considered leaving, but then he remembered the girl.

He ordered another beer. Elizabeth was sitting on a couch in the lounge. He went and sat down next to her.

"Hello again. I just got propositioned in the bathroom. A man came asking if he could do me a favor," Jack said.

Elizabeth looked at him. "And did he do you a favor?"

"No, of course not. I refused. It was all very ridiculous. Probably one of the strangest things that's happened to me."

"I know plenty of men who go both ways," she said. "I don't go with guys who go both ways. It's unsafe."

Elizabeth sipped her drink and looked him in the eye.

"I don't like to get picked up on in bars," she said.

"I'm not picking you up."

"What do you do to keep from being bored, Jack?"

"Well, back home in Arizona I'd hang out with friends, go to parties, drink beer and play pool. For vacation and on the weekends, me and my dad would head out into the desert, camp and go hiking or rafting. The rest of the time I'd be playing ball or working in my dad's shop. To tell you the truth, I've never really had time to be bored."

"Once I climbed the Golden Gate Bridge during a full moon," Elizabeth said. "No ropes or anything. It was a stupid thing to do, but I wouldn't trade the feeling of being up there looking out over the city, gripping the cold cables with the wind in my face and whipping at my clothes, for anything. When I was up there I couldn't help but think how it was the same bridge that people jumped from to their death, enough so that they had to put in nets to catch them."

"You must be an adventurous girl. I've never done anything like that," Jack said.

"So what is it you like about Arizona," she asked.

"A lot of things. The sunsets, the stars at night, the rocks and hidden canyons, the open space and solitude. The desert is a spiritual place. Growing up there it becomes a part of you."

Jack imagined Elizabeth climbing the Golden Gate Bridge. He thought she must have many other stories besides and he wanted to hear them. He was attracted to her and wanted to be with her, but was content to get her number and pursue her to the extent that she wanted to be pursued.

Elizabeth liked men a great deal. She liked touching their bodies and how, as a woman, she was at liberty to do so without reprimand. Men were funny in that they loved to be touched and held, though it was at odds with their masculinity and they'd never admit it. She remembered times when the men were tense and nervous under her touch, though they pretended to be in control as she allowed them the favor of moving from one stage of intimacy to the next. She was a patient girl.

Elizabeth drew men to her with blunt words and the fact that she wasn't afraid to pursue a conversation wherever it might lead. She was known for her crude sense of humor and didn't believe there was anything dirty or shameful in sex. Mostly, she didn't like to be with men who were inexperienced; that was a waste of time, though it was impossible to know how a man would perform based on his conversation.

Elizabeth did not appreciate a man who came without getting her off. So long as he got her off at least once, then he could put on his clothes and leave. She was not one to need company in bed. She was young. Fear of being left alone was five years off at the least, and children perhaps another five after that.

She had been with naive men who told her they loved her. Whether they were sincere or not, she was put off by such sentiment, believing that true love was something one didn't talk about. The men that loved her she used for sex, and those she lusted after she might have loved if she could have caught them. Elizabeth knew that love had something to do with people slipping away.

So what was she to do with the young man staring at her in that way? He was handsome enough: the sporty, all-American type that looked good in a pair of briefs, but she was unsure about his intellect. He was, after all, an Arizona boy and that was the sticks. He wasn't stupid, just uncultured.

Elizabeth hadn't been everywhere but she had traveled enough to know that you couldn't escape yourself. She had backpacked around Europe on a whirlwind, one month, ten-country tour; she had taught English in Mexico and taken a road trip up the east coast of Australia from Sydney to Cairns. She did not see the point in sharing her travels with others. Those experiences were hers to keep even if she could not remember them correctly, covered as they were with the magic dust of nostalgia.

"So what is it you do," Jack asked her.

"I work for a wireless company. I'm an analyst. I do research for new products."

"What sort of products do you sell?"

"We're merging the internet with telecommunications. Soon you'll be able to do everything via a small computer in your phone."

Jack didn't know anything about it, but he imagined she made good money and that made him embarrassed to be unemployed. He told himself that he would find a good job, one that he wouldn't be ashamed to talk about.

"It sounds challenging. I'm sure you must love it," he told her.

"No, not really. A lot of it deals with gathering consumer information. We buy and trade data, find out buying patterns and spam email. My job isn't interesting at all. It's a competitive market. I don't know if I'm gonna have a job from one day to the next. The only people they really need are the programmers."

"What was the name of your company again?"

"Listen, Jack, it's been nice meeting you but I gotta go. Here's my card. We can talk more another time."

Elizabeth excused herself and Jack shook her hand noting how the soft smooth skin contrasted with her vice-like grip.

Jack was drunk. He leaned back in his seat, took a slug of his beer and studied the card: Conscious Net Alternative Communications. Elizabeth Brown: Market Analyst.

Well, it was a start. Perhaps they needed someone else to work at the company? Maybe he could get into sales and work his way up? Maybe he would ask her to dinner. Elizabeth was straightforward and sincere, she thought for herself and she had climbed the Golden Gate Bridge. In other words, she was a catch.

Jack checked his watch. It was just past midnight and he wasn't ready to go to bed. No, he wanted to hit another bar. Elizabeth aside, if he met another girl of similar beauty who could speak, then he would be satisfied. He didn't feel there was anything insincere about playing the field. After all, he was just trying to find a match, even if it was only for a night. A more permanent set up would take some doing, and he was in no hurry.

Jack stopped in numerous bars and drank until he couldn't speak straight. The more derelict his condition, the more confidence he had to talk to the girls and touch them. He was sloppy and thinking in results. The girls turned from him or humored him; they told him to get lost or that he was drunk. Some conned him for drinks, and others left him alone with himself.

Of all this Jack remembered little. He spent his twenties and stuffed the change in his pocket. At one bar, he bought drinks with his card and left it behind. When the bars finally closed, Jack got into a cab with a smuggled cocktail, and the cabby protested.

"Settle down. It'll be all right. Want a drink? You must get thirsty driving all night," Jack said, holding the glass up to the driver's face. "Go on, have a drink, it'll make you feel better."

The cabby hated drunks and all the nonsense commentary he had to put up with from kids half his age. It was with a force of will that he kept his mouth shut. Many times, he wanted to stop the car and tell them to get out and walk. In this case, he pulled the car to the curb.

"I'll take you where you're going. But you gotta drink up first. We're not moving until you finish up."

"Fine, then. Yes sir. I'll just drink up. This one's for all the assholes and bitches in this world. Cheers!"

Jack drank and threw his glass on the sidewalk. He was not a pretty drunk. He was not feeling pretty. Instead, he felt bitter for going home alone. Sometimes drinking made him violent and angry. He remembered getting into fights in the frat house with his friends: how he had woken up several times with bruises, and once a missing tooth with his mouth crusted with blood. Often he didn't remember how he had gotten to bed. Yes, it was hard being the life of the party.

3

Jack woke up inside himself: the all-American boy next door who worked hard, was kind to women and could not talk about his feelings. He was dressed, his head pounded and his mouth was cotton. He sat up and the pounding increased. If he had to describe it, he would call it a blue cactus ball bouncing around and pricking the soft gray of his brain. He wanted to cut a lid for his head, fold open his skull, take that cactus out and stick it in the wall. He wanted to stay in bed all day but he remembered his obligations. He felt the guilt inside himself for being a good-for-nothing and that forced him into the shower. When he was done he told himself he felt better. When he opened his wallet and saw there was no money and also that his credit card was gone, Jack felt very much alone. It would take him time to get a new one, he had no fixed address and his bank account was almost tapped out. In the pocket of his jeans he found twenty dollars in assorted bills, and that was when he packed up his things. He had spent beyond his means and he would have to find more humble lodgings. It was noon and he gave the maid a guilty smile on his way out. Her almond eyes seemed to look through him. He was startled by the power of her four-foot stature, the brown of her skin and her pear-shaped body.

Jack's first stop was at McDoogle's for a combo meal breakfast. He ate his two-patty cheeseburger and fries, licked his greasy fingers, and washed it all down with the brown syrup soda. Customers sat hunched over in the molded plastic chairs with their rolls of fat and mismatched clothes, bags at their feet, sweat pants and sport caps with teams from this city or that on their heads.

Jack felt ill. He told himself it was the hangover, and not the people or how they lived and ate, or how he was eating, that made him feel that way. He liked fast food for its convenience; he could eat in five minutes and be back on the street again to digest. He didn't like to think about eating. If he could have a door to his stomach where he could put in a chunk of gray, malformed matter to give fuel to his system, he would. Jack didn't know how to cook for himself. He had never put anything in his refrigerator besides soda and frozen snacks, and sometimes meat to barbecue. He never bought vegetables or fruit.

Walking down Market Street, Jack wondered how long it would be until he had a place of his own. He longed to make some friends, have phone calls to look forward to, and not be faceless and an obstacle to be pushed and shoved in the street. He saw many men and women with their hands out asking for help, but he did not help them. He had himself to worry about.

Jack found a suitable hostel and paid for a room with his dwindling funds. It was a small, single room that smelled of cigarettes and stale beer. He was depressed by the sight of the broken bed, the tacky and threadbare floral comforter, the bare ceiling bulb and the suspicious red stains on the walls. A small institutional desk and a chair, the kind he remembered from grade school, were located in the corner by the window. Jack thought how filthy the room was compared to the sterile comfort of the previous night. He thought about business trips, and how in sterility one had no dreams, while here one wouldn't be able to sleep from fear.

Having spent too much on alcohol, and having lost his credit card, Jack decided to look for work immediately. He had some resumes handy and an outdated laptop at his disposal. What he needed was access to the internet. The public library seemed the best place to get it without paying. Jack had already done some research and sent several electronic copies of his resume to promising companies. For the past two weeks he had checked his email dutifully and in vain for a response. Perhaps it was foolish to come without something certain in hand. Still, without risk there could be no reward.

Jack was inexperienced and any change good or bad would make him wiser. He needed to check his email and comb the listings for some entry-level work with the larger and more important companies. He changed and put on a collared shirt, a conservative tie, a pair of slacks and some dress shoes. Later, after the library, he would stop in a few places and ask for work face to face. He wasn't sure how it would go, or if he could get past the secretaries, but he would try.

In the back of his head a voice said: you need work now, you don't have more than a few hundred dollars in the bank. Then he thought: you don't know anything about the internet economy. You don't even know what most of those companies do. You don't understand web design or on-line sales or marketing. All you know is that the internet is a virtual store linking producers and consumers in new and innovative ways. You also know from reading Business Time and Tech Planet that many on-line companies don't actually sell anything or make money. They exist out of pure speculation; they are strong on the stock market because people believe in them.

Above all, it was an exciting time to be alive. The internet was a democratizing and creative force that was fundamentally changing the way human beings communicated and interacted with one another. The challenge was in finding truth, utility, value and innovation in the sea of knowledge and opinion that formed the content of the virtual world. What was necessary was the ability to both discriminate and synergize new and often disparate ideas.

Jack felt fortunate to have been born at such an opportune period in history; now all he had to do was find his niche. It was the Wild West in hyperspace: the gangsters were there and the cheats and the frauds and the visionaries, too. It was a lawless, unregulated domain, and anyone with a good idea, just an idea, could make millions and retire. People were paying for the rights to the theory that a new service would be the business of the future.

Jack thought about those who had lived through the Great Depression, or had come of age and fought in World War II or Vietnam. In the midst of such adversity, Americans had managed to progress both socially and economically. Because Jack remembered this history, he felt an added obligation to take full advantage of the current climate of prosperity. The internet was the key to the future and he wanted to be a part of it at any cost. Jack did not care which part so long as he could work his way into a position of influence.

4

Elizabeth was tired of sitting at the desk in her cubicle without seeing daylight five days a week. She hated processing endless orders and payments for cell phone service, keeping updates on the clients, and dealing with the constant phone calls and email when there were problems with that service. "Analyst" was a nice term, and it looked good on a resume, but beyond that it wasn't much. Some people mistakenly believed it to be synonymous with "consultant," except that most analysts studied data and searched for patterns or trends and emerging opportunities for sales and business expansion, while consultants talked ideas and told clients how to transform their business so that it would be successful. Not that being a consultant was easy, just that consultants got paid disproportionately well for telling people what they were doing wrong.

There was very little that was creative in her work, and she envied the designers and programmers who found new and creative ways to improve communication and make products more efficient and pleasant to the eye. Still, they had a long way to go with customer service and infrastructure with all the broken connections and the fact that a phone would receive a signal in one neighborhood or room and not the next.

The truth was Elizabeth did not care for any of it. The titles of the job positions lent a false sense of importance to what had always been a static profession: sales. Elizabeth thought how the names "analyst" and "technician" masked the true tedium of such work. She thought that to call programmers, artists, was morally wrong. During one job search she had looked under "artists, writers, and related professions" and found only web designers, programmers, and data managers. That seemed to be a clear sign of the decline in creativity of the nation, and the streamlining of all professions into one universal role related to maintaining and improving the web of communication for sales. True art, she thought, can never be married to commerce; it was a dark time indeed when people such as herself, sitting in their cubicles, were given to believe they were creative. Her job and most of the jobs in the dot-com industry were about managing something that most of them as yet did not fully understand. If ever there were time for failed, half-baked ideas it was now, she thought. She wondered how long she would last working as an overpaid secretary and salesgirl with a fancy title. In social situations she heard people name off their titles and their companies, and it was difficult to distinguish one dot-com from the next. Most of them sold net real estate, storage, advertising space, business to business services such as billing, all of which was nothing new and dependent on other companies actually producing something of value: a real product or piece of information that someone was willing to pay for. The most profitable e-business was without a doubt entertainment: music and images, but not books or words unless spoken because people no longer had the attention span to read or the capacity for critical thinking. Instead, they had grown accustomed to being patronized like children.

Elizabeth only used the net to buy plane tickets. Music and information she could get for free, and if they charged for what she wanted, she would find it somewhere else. What was happening with the net, she thought, was the homogenization of society. It signaled the subjugation of individual character by material universality. Soon everyone would be able to make their own music and star in their own movies. The internet would be clogged with so much information and creativity that everyone would slip back into obscurity in spite of their new-found individuality. When everyone became an artist the value of art would be downgraded to a hobby. And certainly with the global reach and constant borrowing and sampling of ideas, it would become increasingly difficult to find some original meaning or context in which to orient one's life independent of others. So while everyone was busy becoming more of an individual, they were becoming more uniform.

You have too much time to think about this stuff, Elizabeth thought. The truth is you don't work very hard; you're overpaid, bored and lonely. You haven't gotten laid for a long time, because you're a cold and superior-acting bitch, and that's because you're afraid of being hurt. Because you have no trust. How much of that is you and how much of it is the environment you live in: the current culture of convenience and individuality, and the lack of communication between people? How much is it the fact that since you don't know who you are anymore, you're afraid to speak to anyone for fear that they will take away or alter the identity you are searching so hard to find? In the end, everything comes back to the search for identity, she thought.

Elizabeth had finished all her tasks, and since she couldn't get away with sleeping on the job, boredom had taken over. Unfortunately, she had forgotten her book at home, and she didn't feel like sending any personal emails because now anything to do with the computer felt like work.

Soon she would do something crazy again like jump out of plane or buy a motorcycle. That was the usual result of her panic attacks caused by urban, repetitive living.

Later that day, Elizabeth was called into the manager's office. He told her that sales were down and the economy was suffering, and now there was a need to cut unnecessary expenses. Elizabeth knew then that she was unemployed and thought: if anything the managers are unnecessary since they get paid for doing so little. She knew that the industry was due for collapse given the strata of managers. That was a clear indicator of excess and waste and the eventual decline of empire. Some thought it was the expansion of the arts, but no, it was the increase in mindless, repetitive jobs for the many to benefit the lazy few, coupled with the erosion of art into entertainment, a national obsession with sports, and the degeneration of film into violence. Great achievements and personal integrity were hard to find in a society of fat, comfortable sheep.

"Fuck you," she told him. "And just remember you're next. I've also been reading the paper and watching the news, and with this new president we're all in for a rough ride. Anyway, if you don't write code these days you're out. You and I both know that."

Elizabeth didn't dislike him as person; she even remembered going out for drinks with him and her colleagues (how she shuddered to use that word), and having a good time in the total oblivion of alcohol. Still, while packing her bags under armed supervision, Elizabeth realized that she had been tense and worried about such an outcome, and though she had ignored it, she had seen the empty desks and also the nervous way everyone worked as if they didn't know what to expect from one day to the next. The company wasn't making any money, nor had it ever made any money. Venture capital, debt and speculation could only go so far.

Elizabeth was being watched because they didn't want her to damage any files or steal any information. When she left, they took her pass key so that she wouldn't come back like that executive on the fifteenth floor that had gunned down ten of his co-workers and then shot himself in the face. No, she wasn't gonna go out like that. Such a display of emotion was beneath her. She would not set fire to anything or be dragged out. She would walk away and thank God for her freedom. Mostly, she wanted to get drunk and do nothing for a while. That was no way to deal with her future, but she didn't care. As far as her parents were concerned, she was still employed and happy and making a life for herself. Hell, she might even call them and say she had met a nice guy. That would get them off her back.

5

There was a two-hour wait for the internet, but first Jack had to get a library card. Hadn't someone said you could judge a man's culture by the number of library cards he had? Well, this would be Jack's third as soon as he made up a fake address and phone number.

"This is provisional until you return with some proof of residence, a bill or letter, or something of that nature," the librarian said.

Jack promised to return. There was nothing dishonest in what he had done. So long as he returned his books everything would be fine.

Jack took the polished elevator upstairs. The sterility of the library reminded him of a prison. On the third floor, Jack leaned over the rail and looked below. He imagined jail cells surrounding the central courtyard. The library was a prison for books, except that the books could leave with an escort but only for two weeks before they had to return next to the same neighbors in the same alphabetical order.

Jack wandered through the stacks looking for some reading. He remembered all the times books had been recommended to him by this or that person, but he couldn't remember the names of the books or their authors. How frustrating it was to stand there with infinite choice and not know the great from the mediocre. He thought about the cereal isle and bars. There was truth in that about not judging by a cover. He plucked down several volumes and read them in fragments. Sometimes the writing matched the title and sometimes it did not. Eventually, Jack found what he thought was a good book, and he took it with him and sat down to read while he waited.

The first few lines of the novel transported Jack away from the library to a small Czech village know for its brewery. In that village there lived a young, pretty, long-haired girl famous for her ability to drink more beer than the men. Now that his hangover had subsided, the image of the girl drinking on a hot afternoon made him thirsty. He thought again about work because he needed money to drink.

Jack checked his messages and saw with dismay that he had received no response to his numerous emails. The discovery made him lonely. He thought again about the beer-drinking girl with red hair so long that she had to hold it her hand so it wouldn't drag on the ground or get caught in the wheel of her bicycle. Then he thought about calling Elizabeth, the only person he knew in the city. He hoped she would be able to help him with work. He was attracted to her and the work served as an excuse to call.

This call was the procrastination of his need to show up in person in various offices in town to state his case. Jack was not a fast-talker and he disliked people who were, though he could see the value in it. Especially now when he had to secure a place for himself. Soon he would have to give it shot, even if he failed and looked foolish or got tricked into a less than advantageous agreement. The trick was to make himself appear greater than he was and not show just how eager he was for work. He would work for forty thousand a year: that was only normal for a recent graduate. But he wanted to hold out for sixty or fifty-five or even fifty. Not that any of it meant anything to him. He had never worked for salary but by the hour; he did not understand lump sums or how much more fifty was than forty, in terms of quality of life. No, he would have to puff himself up like a frightened kitty for them and pretend competence and experience he did not possess.

Jack dialed the number on the card and stood looking out at the library crowd: the strange, downtrodden vagrant crowd that it was. He smelled more than a few men from a distance and saw their long, ratty hair and beards and the wild staring of their eyes.

"Hello, yes, may I speak to Ms. Brown please?"

"Ms. Brown? Hang on just a moment."

"Thank you."

Jack always felt that the public phone was an exposed place where strange ears could catch intimate words and appropriate them; it was the vulnerability of sleep in an exposed place, or of a public show of affection. It drew unnecessary attention, and he found that he held the receiver close to his mouth, curled in on himself, and spoke quietly with his hand over his mouth.

"Sir, Ms. Brown no longer works here."

That was unexpected. He had been counting on her; she was his trump card. How could she not work there anymore? He had met her just last night.

"Are you sure?"

"Sure am."

Jack saw no point in arguing with the woman or putting the blame on her or pretending she was against him.

"It's important that I speak with her," he said. "I have very important news. Do you know how I can get into contact with her?"

"I'm sorry, sir, I can't provide you with that information."

Damn and double damn, he thought. I'm not an insane or dangerous person; I just want to talk to her. I should have gotten her cell number the night we met. That was an oversight on his part. Still, he had to think of it from the secretary's point of view. She had no way of knowing if he was a psycho or not. It was easy for him to forget that women had to be concerned about their safety, and that meant not giving out personal information to strangers. But Jack didn't want to be a stranger to Elizabeth. He wanted to ask her for some help and advice, and she was his only contact. But then came the thought that he wanted more for her than that, and that if they did get to know each other better it would have a permanent impact on both their lives, for better or worse.

If Jack had been comfortable with a room of his own and a job, he wouldn't have worried so much about her. He would let her slip away like the memory of that phone call. But now, alone as he was, it was as if a lifeline had been severed. He knew she could have helped him.

"You can always send her an email," the voice said. "Have a nice day."

Jack found Elizabeth's email on her business card. He had used up his internet time for the day and felt like kicking himself. When he got the chance, he would write her a nice message. Hopefully, she would still use that email and not forget about it. Thank you wonderful secretary. Jack wondered why no one had ever written a song for all the secretaries of the world who kept order in the universe and tended the lines of communication. He thought of the importance of timely and accurate information. In the past, empires had collapsed on misinformation, false reports and delayed communication. He thought about insider trading, and how the right tip at the right time could make a millionaire on the market. He thought of the messengers to the Incas, and how they ran for days and nights and often died on arrival. He thought how many people had lived and died in the truth or lies of correspondence. His problem was that he didn't know where to go for work or who to talk to. He needed to work on getting connected.

What was his important news, then? It was the second time that day that he had bent the truth. If he had been able to speak to her what would he have said? Elizabeth, hi this is Jack, do you know where I can get a good job? Oh, and when I have a good job and some money can I take you out? Or, more sincere to himself and less to her: how could he charm her into letting him stay with her? He had very little money left, perhaps only enough for a few more nights in the hostel. Even if he got an interview it might be weeks before he heard word, a week or two before he was hired, and then another few weeks to get paid. His was not a realistic plan, and he knew it. He would have to find something in the meantime. He also needed a place to live.

Jack thought again of the email he sent to his mother, guarding her from this reality:

Hey Mom. The city is great. The bridge is still there and it's very impressive in person. I've been getting to know my way around town. Soon I'll have a job and a place to live. I know several companies that are interested in hiring me, but I'm still not sure which one to choose. There's so much to do here, and lots of interesting people to meet. Also, it's nice to live by the ocean. I miss you guys and I promise to write again soon. Say hi to dad and Carol for me.

Love, Jack

Well, it wasn't all true, but what wasn't could come true. A little optimism never hurt; it would help put his mother at ease so she wouldn't worry so much. She hadn't wanted him to go. Why did he want to leave when he could keep managing the hardware store? San Francisco was expensive, and he would never see his family or friends. Still, she let him go hoping that he would see his error and return. Jack was determined to prove her wrong.

That afternoon Jack took a walk through the Financial District and found the address of a company he had applied to the week before. The building was large and imposing, and he was shy about going in. He felt awkward and out of place. Jack thought people were staring at him and he wanted to appear like he knew what he was doing. An attractive woman in a pantsuit brushed past him in the doorway. Finding the courage, Jack went inside and walked straight by the reception to the elevator. Still, he must have hesitated because when he passed the desk, Colby, who had worked there for seventeen years, called him over.

"Can I help you, son?"

Colby could tell a young man looking for a job a mile away. He could see the nervousness and guessed it was Jack's first time in the city.

"Where is it that you're goin'?"

"Suite 1240," Jack said. "I have an appointment."

Whether or not the kid had an appointment was no business of his. Colby just wanted to make sure he didn't get lost. Suite 1240 would have its own reception to screen the clients.

"Twelfth floor. The elevators are to the back."

"Thank you."

Colby sat back in his chair and thought about all the people he had seen come and go with their tight faces and brisk pace, dressed in identical suits with cell phones at the ready. The cell phone reminded him of the pacifier you gave to babies when they cried. Colby had the paper out and he looked to the sports section to see how the Giants were doing.

"Hey Carl," he said, addressing the security guard standing by the door. "Giants beat St. Louis 5 to 4."

"Did Tarry hit any out of the park?"

"Two-run homer to win it."

"That guy's on a roll. We're lucky to have him. He does us proud."

"Damn straight," Colby agreed.

Carl was a good guy, if not a horrible poker player. Colby almost felt guilty for taking his money at their weekly poker nights. Though Colby had never asked anything of his friend, he felt Carl was someone he could count on in a crisis.

On the job, Colby met all kinds of people, and when he had a feeling about someone, he was usually right. Like the guy that worked up on the fifteenth with the nervous hands who came and went always alone with his head down looking at his feet. Colby couldn't help but notice something disturbing in the man's eyes. It was not the disturbed look of a man who'd had a bit of bad luck, but that of a man whose brain wasn't quite right. What did you expect for a code writer, he thought. That kind of job would drive anyone crazy.

Colby was familiar with most of the employees and what they did, and he had heard plenty of gossip, too. He imagined that something would go wrong with the man, but not that he would kill ten people and then himself. Since then, the office managers had kept him posted on who was fired and who was not; it had been their mistake to not take his ID away. Two of his security guard friends had lost their jobs over it, and he had been called in for questioning.

Well, it was a large building with many offices, and it wasn't his job to screen people, but to direct them where they needed to go and give them information. Even if he had known the man was dangerous, what could he have done? Perhaps one of the guards should have seen the bulge under his coat where he had taped the automatic rifle to his body. Perhaps it was right that they had been fired; perhaps times were changing like the schools had changed with their metal detectors. Was that any way to live? Yes, the world had changed plenty in the last twenty years and who was he to keep up with it? Mostly, his kids kept him from losing touch completely. A good thing to have kids; it kept the boredom away.

In the elevator a video screen streamed facts and figures, sports scores and bits of news, and a funny story about a man dressed as a cartoon character from McDoogle's arrested for assault against somebody who had provoked him in a strip mall parking lot. A sad story, Jack thought. Imagine the humiliation of being in that suit and having to stand in front of a fast food joint and clown around all day? A humiliating job with a necessary serving of anonymity. It was the kind of job where you came to work then put on your uniform. There were many ways to make money from the back-breaking to the humiliating to the violent, Jack thought. The drawback of most work was that you had to be away from home doing things you wouldn't normally do on your own time. At least most people. The trick was to find work that suited one's skills and character. Work that one did not hate. Some people loved to work as clowns dressing up and playing games with children. Jack could respect that, though it wasn't a job he would choose for himself.

Jack arrived at his floor, went inside the office and approached the secretary.

"Hello, I'm Jack Wild. I'm here to see Mr. Brandt about a marketing position. I contacted him a few weeks ago and I wanted to talk with him in person."

At that moment the phones were ringing off the hook and the girl looked stressed.

"Hello, yes, could you please hold?" She pushed a button and the phone rang again. "Hello, I'm on the other line. Please hold."

The phones kept ringing, and Jack felt sorry for the girl and her repetitive job. He stood and waited for her to be free.

"Yes, I'll transfer you over. One moment, please. No, I'm sorry, he's in a meeting. I'll direct you to his voice mail. That would be a question for customer service. Please hold while I get you connected."

"I'm sorry," she said. "Usually there are two of us, but Marie called in sick. How can I help you?"

"I'm here to see Mr. Brandt."

"Do you have an appointment?"

"No, I don't. I just need to talk to him for a few minutes. I've already contacted him about a job position."

"If that's the case then I'm sure he'll get back to you to make an appointment."

A man came into the office and stood next to Jack. The girl's eyes shifted from Jack to the man and back again.

"If I could just see him today I'd really appreciate it."

"Why don't you make an appointment," she said, looking in her book. "The first opening is two weeks from now on Tuesday at ten."

"Don't you have anything sooner?"

Liana looked at him. She didn't understand why people thought that secretaries lied and screened people. She had a list and it was full; if she said the first appointment was next Tuesday, then it was. She understood the young man wanting to come earlier, but it wasn't possible. She knew there weren't any openings in marketing but she wouldn't tell him so. He might take it wrong and personally, and that was why she didn't talk straight. He could see Mr. Brandt in two weeks and hear it from him. Normally, she wouldn't schedule such an appointment, but she liked the young man for his face and felt bad discouraging him.

"I guarantee you'll see Mr. Brandt the Tuesday from next. That is the most I can do for you."

"That's fine," Jack said, doubting that Mr. Brandt was so busy he couldn't take time out in his day for a five-minute meeting. Jack knew a bit about the company and was hoping that with enthusiasm and a few facts about his background and experience, he could win him over. He was a big boy now, and if Mr. Brandt said no, well then he would thank him and wish him a nice day and look elsewhere.

The secretary was nice enough. He knew that she didn't have much power, and that probably she didn't like her job and wanted more from life. He did not see the sense in arguing with her. She took down his name and wished him a nice day. Jack left thinking the only thing that made one man different from the next was not who he was or what he could do, but who he knew. After that, Jack didn't have the grit to try it again the same day. He had an appointment and that was enough.

In the early evening, Jack walked down to the wharf and Pier Thirty Nine. He marveled at how quickly the skyscrapers and glass and steel ceded to the ocean. He saw the low-lying wooden docks, the chipped paint and rust on the ferries, the white phosphorous-covered moorings and sidewalks, the bright lights and signs, and the shops full of t-shirts and stickers and the rest of the consumer mess that went along with tourism.

Jack smelled the fish stands and watched the steam rising over pots of boiled crabs. Men in aprons stood behind troughs of ice and gray aquariums full of lobster. Jack realized that he hadn't eaten since breakfast and that his hunger was making him irritable. He bought himself a bread bowl of clam chowder and a bottle of beer and sat on the stool shoulder to shoulder with the other tourists. He thought from that day on everything would only get more familiar because this was now his home. After he scooped the bowl empty, Jack ate the wet sponge-like bread and washed it down with the rest of his beer.

Jack walked down to the edge of the wharf and stared out across the bay to Alcatraz. He thought of the men that had died swimming to freedom in that icy water, and he wondered just how cold it was. What a shame he couldn't stick his hand in the water from where he stood. Standing there, he looked back on the city, on the modest bulge of skyscrapers in the center and the houses that crept up the hill. Already it seemed small and accessible, not at all like he remembered when he arrived.

Jack continued on toward Ghirardelli Square and dropped down to the shore by the aquatic park. The still water was interrupted by a solitary swimmer, his arm hooking above his head and knifing down, as he moved forward in the water. The man did not wear a wetsuit. Jack imagined going for a swim until he put his hand into the water. He was used to the lukewarm water of Lake Havasu and water skiing there. He thought of the boats crammed into Copper Canyon for spring break, so that you could walk from one to the next with your beer in your hand. He remembered the time he had climbed the cliff and jumped into a narrow gap of water between the boats. He was very drunk, and it was luck that he didn't lose his footing on the jagged rocks. He jumped and dropped his cup simultaneously to watch it fall beside him. His stomach filled his chest and he braced for the water. He continued to fall much longer than he wanted with his stomach stuck in his throat. Before impact, he tucked in his arms and kept his legs tight together so he wouldn't dislocate his shoulder or rupture his groin. He had never been hurt jumping, but later that day a kid hit the cliff as he fell and ended bloody in the water. He was in bad shape when they got him on the boat. When the paramedics came he was pasty white and bleeding badly, his blood thinned from the alcohol. Whether he had died, Jack wasn't sure.

Lingering on a bench, Jack watched the man swim in the fading light. The wind kicked up, a biting wind nothing like the heat of the afternoon, and he jammed his hands deep in his pockets and thought about going back to rest. He didn't want to go back to the dingy hostel but it was all he had. In any case, he could shut the door on the world and be warm and safe.

6

The hostel had one communal bathroom per floor. Jack stood in the hallway with a towel around his waist, bare feet in his tennis shoes and a shaving kit under his arm. He tried the door and found it locked. He had been looking forward to a hot shower and now he stood in the draft of the hallway bare-chested and looking to the traffic on the street below.

The bathroom was strangely silent. There was no sound of running water, or urine or flushing of the toilet. When Jack finally put his ear to the door, he could make out a faint sobbing. Christ, he thought, it could be hours before I get in there. Jack walked back to his room and lay down with a creak in his metal army cot that curved his body like a banana. He drifted in and out of sleep until a voice brought him abruptly back to the present.

"Come on, Hal, come on out. I didn't mean anything by it. Sometimes I get irritable and say things I don't mean. I ain't sick'a you. You and me, we're good friends. We've made it far together, and I didn't mean it about splitting up and going our own way. We've been good together, Hal, and I want you to know that."

There was no reply from the man in the bathroom. The voice in the hallway continued.

"Listen, I've got a few dollars I've been saving. Why don't we go get ourselves a good meal for a change. My treat."

Still no answer.

"Hal, you can't stay in there all night. That's not a solution. You ain't a loser like I said you was. You're a hell of a guy, Hal, and our luck will turn around, you'll see. Now come on outta there and let's be friends."

Andy banged on the door and thought to himself: I wish he would stop acting like a baby. He's sure got thin skin. He's a good fella and he's never done me wrong, but boy is he sensitive. And I know it's not Hal, it's me. Sometimes I get so tired of people I just wanna be alone. But it gets lonely all right coming into a new city with no one to talk to, looking for a place to bed down for the night and a hot meal. I'm glad we went to work on the farm, though. That was nice. Hard work, but it sure was peaceful sleeping out in them fields, and we got all our meals and enough cash to make it to the city. We had a few good nights on the town, and I guess I'm just nervous now that the money's almost gone. Hal don't know how to keep care of his money and he's been living off me. But I can't abandon him now. He doesn't know how to take care of himself. Poor guy's got a broken heart with life and he suffers.

"Hal, this is your last chance or I'm going out alone. You ain't had nothin' to eat all day. You'll see how with some food in your stomach everything'll be better. Then we can figure how to get outta here. We gotta get south before the rain starts. I ain't never been to Mexico. Imagine Mexico, Hal, just sun and tequila and *señoritas*."

Hal didn't answer.

"All right, I'm going to the room to get my coat. This is your last chance."

Stubborn, sensitive fool. How did I ever get mixed up with him? He sure has changed since I known him. The man has no stamina for this sort'a life. He shoulda been a doctor or a lawyer, Andy thought, snorting to himself. Imagine Hal, a big-time lawyer. Hal's the sort that 'ud be sad in any kind a' life. Some people is just born that way.

Hal leaned over the sink and felt the fear of not having any money and being abandoned by the only friend he had. He was so bloody hungry his hands shook and he thought: this is how it feels when your stomach starts to eat itself. He looked at himself in the mirror: at his sunken cheeks and the wrinkles in his face and his bony callused hands. Once I was a boy and my body didn't hurt and I could swim in the river and run through trees. I was happy then, and now I'm dying.

Hal loved Andy more than he had ever loved any woman, except his mother who he hadn't seen for many years. Sometimes he imagined crawling into bed with Andy, who would run his fingers through his hair and tell him a funny story, and he would feel okay again. He would do anything for Andy and was hurt and scared when Andy said to leave him alone and that he was tired of supporting him, and sick of his whining and sadness. He remembered when Andy had said, "Can't you see, Hal, you're a loser. No one wants you in this world. You're a loser and you're never going anywhere in life because you can't take care of yourself. Be a man and stop that whining. Christ, as if money was anything to worry about. Listen, maybe you should go back where you got family. This ain't the life for you, Hal. I reckon you're all used up."

Hal felt the truth of those words and he wasn't strong enough to carry it. If he had been, then maybe he'd stop running away and face himself. If he'd done that ten years ago, then maybe he could have been somebody. As it was, he had burnt all his bridges and abandoned women who had loved him in search of adventure and truth. Once he had been a strong young man with a destination. He had despised his home, his town, and his people and the simple life they led. And now, twenty years later, he was decaying in a lonely city with a man he loved who could take care of him and help him when he couldn't help himself.

Hal didn't want to be a burden on Andy. He knew Andy had meant what he said about him being a loser, and it didn't matter what he promised now because it had been said and there was no taking it back.

Hal looked down at his wrists and watched the blood leak from the cuts of the razor. He watched with a sort of selfish indulgence that was not the desire for death, but a cry for help. He had cut across the veins, instead of straight up and down, because he was incompetent even in death. Still, to be able to mutilate himself and see that there was a way out, and that it was close, gave him a renewed desire to live. It was for Andy's sake that he kept on living, and Andy was waiting for him. So, it was with the panic of wrongdoing and punishment that Hal washed himself, wrapped his wrists in toilet paper, put on his sweater and wet his hair. When he stood up from the sink, his vision clouded over and he lost his balance and fell to the floor. He thought he was dying then. He couldn't see and his ears rang, and then the room came back into focus and he stared up at the cracks and crumbled plaster of the ceiling. He forced himself to his feet and whispered to himself, "I'm coming, Andy, wait for me because I'll be there."

"Come on, Hal," Andy said through the door, "tomorrow is another day and you'll see how our fortune will change. I got a few dollars so let's go and get something to eat."

"I'm thirsty, Andy. I'm so thirsty I can't tell you."

"We'll take care of that, too, don't you worry," Andy said.

Nausea filled Jack's mouth. He had never been close to poverty or misery, and now he heard it in the strain and false strength of the men's voices. He thought about the relationship between the two men and how they must have been forced together by circumstance; it saddened Jack how sometimes life forced people to be together against their will. That went as much for the two miserable men outside his door as for husband and wife. When circumstance decided friendship and love it became nothing but mediocrity, sadness, conflict and finally hate. He thought of women that went with abusive men and men who went with plain or ugly women; women that married for money and men that married for looks; it seemed just about anyone would tolerate someone they disliked for money or a favor. The whole of it made Jack sick. A man alone might be lonely, but at least he wouldn't have to support the burden of others.

Jack waited until they were gone before leaving his room. He didn't want to see their faces or be an accomplice to their shame and degradation. All he wanted was a hot shower and the softness of his bed. He went into the bathroom and saw the bloody razor in the sink, the red handprint on the mirror and the vomit in the toilet; it was an image Jack would not forget. He showered infected by the sickness of that faceless man. He tried to make his mind hard and tight and told himself: I am different from those men. I know how to stay safe and free in this world. That is not my blood and will never be my blood. Jack scrubbed his body thoroughly with soap, hoping that the cleanliness would go beneath his skin and into his mind to wash away the images of defeat and loneliness and misery and death to which he had given no consideration until that moment.

In the middle of the night, Jack was torn from sleep by a pounding on the door.

"Fucking whore," a voice shouted in Spanish. "Open the goddamned door! I'm gonna teach you some respect. You think I'm gonna let my girl go around with my best friend?! I've seen you with Cesar and the way he touches you and how you smile at him when you think I'm not looking. I see everything, Maria, I know everything and there's nothing you can hide from me. When I'm finished with you I'm gonna have a talk with Cesar. I'm gonna knock his teeth out, and there's a friend for you. And God help me if he's in that room then I'll kill you both and with good reason."

Jack lay in silence. The pounding on the door grew more forceful. Jack could understand bits and pieces of the man's Spanish and thought: there is no way I'm opening that door. I'm not taking the fall for Cesar anybody.

"If you don't open the door, I'm gonna knock it down."

Christ, Jack thought for the second time that night. Christ, and who the hell is Maria? Why this Maria could fuck anyone she liked for all he cared. Still, he was glad he was not Maria. Jack imagined the large, angry man outside his door and hoped he wasn't armed. The man was slurring and out of control from drink. His imagination was getting away from him, probably, picturing Cesar on top of his girl sliding his dick in and out of her hot red pepper cunt, while she clung to him like the whore she was. Poor guy, what an imagination can do, especially when a man is small and insecure with himself.

Jack heard the man throw his weight against the door. He's going to break in, Jack thought. He's worked himself up and he's going to come in fast and violent, so I'd better turn the lights on so he knows I'm not Cesar and that this isn't Maria's room.

After turning on the light, Jack searched around for a suitable weapon to defend himself. The room was bare. There was no other option but the chair. It didn't occur to him to talk with the man. No, Jack felt he was beyond talking and perhaps would mistake him for another of Maria's lovers.

Jack turned the lock as quietly as he could. The body crashed against the door but it stayed shut. Luis was doubled over panting in the hallway. He was out of shape from too much drinking and his gut made him gasp and wheeze for breath. That whore, he thought. I'm going beat that whore black and blue. God, he loved Maria and her thick legs and the way the sweat poured off her body making her slippery in his hands when they made love. He wanted her so badly that he would beat her to keep her; he would beat her until she gave in. He did not feel worthy of her and it made him jealous the way the men looked at her in the bar, especially Cesar. He had suspected something between them for a long time and then Cesar had said, "That Maria, she is very beautiful. You are lucky to have a woman like Maria." Luis knew then that he had been given the horns. He saw it in Cesar's contemptuous smile and the hungry whiteness of his teeth.

With that thought in mind, of Cesar drinking with him and fucking his girl and pretending nothing, Luis threw himself again at the door. This time it gave unexpectedly and he lunged stumbling into the room before a chair smashed down on his head and knocked him unconscious. When he came to, a young man stood above him.

"I don't know any Maria or Cesar. You've made a mistake. This is my room. There's no Maria here, so you'd better leave."

Luis held his head and stared at the young man standing there wary and tense. I've made a mistake, he thought. I'm a fool and I wish to leave this room now and forget this has happened. The situation made him sober and clear-headed. The man had heard him wail over a woman and lose his control, and Luis felt terribly embarrassed.

"I've made a mistake," Luis said, lowering his head. "I'm very sorry. I apologize for disturbing you. Please forgive me."

Luis got up slowly and walked carefully backwards into the hall and shut the door behind him. He walked quickly down the hall, hoping the man wouldn't call the police. When he was drunk he did things he wouldn't normally do and often couldn't remember. Still, why wasn't Cesar at the bar and where could he have gone if not with Maria? Perhaps Maria was not on the third floor but the second? Luis had a bad memory for places and numbers. He went downstairs and stopped at 203 and knocked on the door.

"Maria, my life. It's Luis. Please let me in. I don't have anywhere else to go."

The bastard, she thought. Bastard that goes out drinking and leaves me here alone. Bastard, but I love him and he is a baby and cannot take care of himself. Bastard with the deep sad eyes and that moustache to be tough when he is like a little boy.

Maria rubbed the sleep from her eyes and opened the door for him. Luis stood in the hall and forced a smile through his guilt.

"Well, come in then. There's no use standing in the hallway. Sit down and I'll make you something to eat."

Luis felt the hate disappear. He looked around the room and it said Maria, beautiful Maria, and no Cesar, and he knew that no man had been there. How could he have doubted her and also Cesar who was his good friend from the same city in Mexico and lover of the same football team? Why, they were practically brothers.

"You are much woman," he told her and tried to touch her, but she moved away to the stove.

Jack was no longer scared. When the man was on the ground looking up at him, Jack saw the shame and embarrassment he never wanted for himself. He couldn't recall a time when he had been in such a position with a woman and hoped that time would never come. He had been rejected but never betrayed. He had shared women he didn't care about with friends. He had treated women badly but none had or ever would betray him. The truth was Jack didn't know much about women and couldn't imagine that women like men were curious and that, in fact, he had friends that had been with his girl behind his back. If he had known he might have taken it personally, though it was not any shortcoming on his part but just a desire for variety on hers. He didn't understand that few men could give a woman everything she wanted.

Jack lay in bed wondering how he would feel if betrayed by a woman. Even if he loved that woman greatly, he wouldn't get violent. Violence was desperation and fanaticism, and these were attitudes that were shameful and best not adopted, no matter how strongly they were felt. Jack believed in appearances and he was glad that the intruder was not his friend and that he would not have to see him again, because then it would be hard to look him in the eye.

Jack had trouble getting back to sleep, and when he did, he dreamt about being with Maria and the man coming in on them and their eyes meeting and the man attacking him in a blind rage. Jack didn't want to find himself in such a position. No matter how beautiful a woman looked or how appealing she was, he would not fall into that trap. Since he had never been in such a situation, he couldn't be sure how he would react. His thoughts were only speculation: optimistic, safe speculation at that.

7

Jack tapped his dwindling bank account and paid for another night at the hostel. During the day, he sent emails to companies he knew nothing about, edited his resume to suit what he assumed were their needs, and cut and pasted portions of the job description into his cover letters so that perhaps his application would stand out in a key word search. Then he sent an email to Elizabeth on the pretext of finding work but with the hope that she would want to see him again.

Later, Jack made some phone calls and was prevented from speaking to anyone of importance. He knew that finding work was about speaking to people face to face, and after many weeks of sending resumes on the computer and making cold calls without result, he grew more realistic about his prospects. He couldn't wait until next week for an interview. He needed immediate work, and it would likely be something other than what he wanted, and he would console himself with the fact that he would only have to do it until something better came along. Still, he couldn't afford to work full time for eight or ten dollars an hour. After tax that wasn't much money, and it would leave him little time to get ahead. He didn't want to be stuck on a survival wage.

Then Jack thought about restaurants. He had known many friends who had worked in restaurants in Tucson where they earned a decent living on tips. When they came to the bar after work, their pockets fat with twenties, they would sport drinks for their friends; they had their days free to study or play sports, while Jack had to work at the chain home repair store doing stock and sales. Jack never had money to sport drinks and he didn't have much free time either. Because he was putting himself through school, Jack worked almost full-time. When he wasn't in class, he was at work; when not at work, he was on the field pitching. He was used to sleeping four or five hours a night, and now that he was unemployed, he didn't know what to do with himself when he woke up in the morning. It was better to have a job than to have nothing to do at all. It was no good to wander around town, watch the hours pass and not get paid for them. Yes, he would work in a restaurant, though he didn't have any experience. How hard could it be to serve food? Such a job took no thought at all, and it would give him time to look for other work. In the city people had money, and he was certain one could make good money waiting tables. There were many restaurants and Jack didn't think it would be hard to find a job.

<h1 style="text-align:center">8</h1>

Elizabeth was completely fed up with work, so perhaps it wasn't so bad after all being laid off and unemployed with six weeks paid.

Now she sat in a bar on Haight Street drinking martinis in the middle of the afternoon. The bar was nearly empty. It was dark inside and she could see the street through the open doorway and that rare bit of sun shining down on the city. Though it was sunny, the wind blew cold. She liked to sit inside and imagine the heat like she remembered from Southern California where she grew up. There were many things she liked about Southern California; the longer she was away, the more she liked it, because she had forgotten the bad. She didn't realize how much she liked the sun and the heat until she moved to San Francisco where there was little sun and plenty of cold and rain. She knew many people who pretended it wasn't that way and dressed to defy the weather. That was something very Californian, especially in Northern California, which lacked the climate that made California famous. She knew many foreigners who had been disappointed by the weather in Northern California and also the temperature of the water. It was a shame to live by the ocean and not be able to swim without a thick wetsuit. She was lonely and Southern California was home, like it or not.

Unemployment was making Elizabeth negative and pessimistic. She found herself more disturbed by the beggars on the street and their ragged dogs. She understood why they were there; it was hard work finding a job one didn't want that paid enough to live decent. Her rent was too high and each month she threw her money out the window to support other people that had been lucky or clever enough to buy a house or an apartment or inherit one. She knew that she would never live that way, at least not working her old job. Most Californians would never own the home they lived in. Though she had been overpaid in her job, Elizabeth was still underpaid compared to the cost of living, like most people were underpaid though they worked hard. These thoughts made her want to drink until she couldn't see straight or stand on her own two feet.

She had made an appointment to meet her friend Jeff at the bar. All throughout the industry people were getting their pink slips and packing up their desks with same-day notice and being escorted out and forgotten. Jeff had also been laid off.

When Jeff got there, Elizabeth was slurring to the bartender.

"You know it wasn't worth it anyway. I was a drone. I punched numbers and collected data on people I never met. There was nothing creative in it. Though I'm not creative anyway. Even if I was creative, there wouldn't have been a place for it. I tell you, I should have been a designer."

The barman Sam nodded to her. He was in his forties and had raised his kids working in the bar and was now putting them through college. He had lived in San Francisco most of his life. In the last few years he had watched the city become increasingly superficial with all the internet brats with sixty-grand plus salaries straight out of school with no experience. He considered them posers and felt no pity for the girl. In fact, he disliked her; it was because of her and others like her that the rent had gone up in his apartment. The girl who sat in front of him didn't know hard work and struggle like he did. She hadn't fought for her country, worked on the docks or in construction, or tended bar. She knew very little about real life, and he didn't feel sorry for her lack of creativity and overpaid boredom. Sam couldn't imagine having a job where he would be paid for being idle and bored. In his case, when it was slow, he made no money. Still, he liked being there in the afternoons because he could be alone.

Jeff was a typical computer geek who didn't have to worry about money. Upon graduation he had been hired by Conscious Net, who gave him a large signing bonus and even found him a place to live. After he lost his job, he began to suffer from insomnia. Derailed from his routine existence and stripped of the security of a steady paycheck, he became anxious and afraid of the future. Jeff had been unemployed for two weeks and still hadn't found the motivation to look for work. Mostly, he wandered around in a daze, wondering at the meaning of life. Life to him had been work, and without work he didn't know what to do with himself. When Elizabeth called him up, he jumped at the chance to meet her for a drink. His prompt and solicitous attention to her tech support needs at work had evolved into friendship. He was attracted to her and secretly hoped she shared his feelings.

"Elizabeth, hi. Am I late?"

Elizabeth felt sorry for Jeff. He was the typical nice guy who women found utterly unattractive because he was polite, kind and helpful. Since they were in the same boat, and because she didn't want to be alone with herself, she thought to call him. She wanted someone to talk to her and tell her stories so that she would forget about her own life. In spite of two years in the city, she could think of very few unique and interesting stories about her own experience. Jeff wasn't exactly the right person for entertainment, but everyone else she knew was at work.

"Hi Jeff. No, you're just in time. Come have a drink. I'm already ahead of you and you gotta catch up."

"I don't know about drinking in the afternoon. It makes me feel guilty," he said. "I've always thought drinking in the afternoon was wrong."

"Drinking in the morning is wrong. After twelve, it's open season. Anyway, I asked you to come meet me at the bar. Why did you come if you don't want a drink? If you wanna stay, you have to drink. Nothing's free around here. Sam, get him a martini, please," she said.

"Why is half the bar roped off," Jeff asked.

"Shhh," Elizabeth said, putting her finger over her lips. "That's the VIP seating," she whispered, leaning into him. Sam was at the other end of the bar.

"But there's only one person sitting there and the rest of the seats are empty. VIP seating at two in the afternoon?"

"Keep it down would you? He'll get upset."

Sam only served martinis. It was his bar and he only served martinis because there was no other drink that could match it, and it made him angry when people ordered beer or some stupid mixed drink with a fancy name that tasted like fruit juice.

"I'll take a beer," Jeff said.

"The lady ordered you a martini," Sam said.

"I don't drink hard liquor."

Sam felt the anger build inside him. Goddamned poser bourgeois brat. He would be damned if some jerk came into his bar like he owned the place thinking he could order whatever he wanted. Sam leaned close and his face changed to horrible grimace:

"You're embarrassing me, you're embarrassing yourself, and you're embarrassing everybody in here. Now get the hell out. And I'm not gonna tell you twice. I refuse to serve you. I don't serve beer, understand? It's a martini or nothing. And now nothing because you blew it."

Jeff was wide-eyed. He realized the man was serious the way the veins bulged on his neck and by the spittle that sprayed his cheeks and forehead when the man leaned forward and grabbed him by the shirt. Jeff sat there dumb, and then Elizabeth started to laugh.

"What's so goddamned funny," Sam asked her. "You think this is funny? Go on and get the hell out! You brought him in here now you can both leave. People like you make me sick. Can't even order a decent drink. I only serve martinis here. This is the best damned martini bar in town. You wanna ruin my reputation?"

Elizabeth knocked back that last swallow of what was admittedly a very good martini and took Jeff by the arm.

"Come on. Let's get out of here. Don't take it personal, it's just an obsession of his. He doesn't serve anything but martinis. I tried to steer you clear. Let's go get some forties and go to the park. God, I have this unbelievable urge to smoke a joint."

"What kind of a bar is that," Jeff asked. "How does he stay in business acting that way? I don't have to be treated like that. I should go back and punch him in the nose."

"That's not a good idea. If you resist, Sam gets violent. I've seen him fight a man and kick and stomp on him until he's out of breath. He's got a lot of anger inside."

Sam leaned back on the counter and felt the pulse of adrenaline shoot through him. The truth was he loved his job. He had worked a long time to have his own bar, and now that it was his, he could do what he damned-well-pleased.

Sam looked down the bar to one of his regulars.

"Can you believe these kids, Mike? They think the world revolves around them. I've been here for twenty years, and they still don't know that a martini's all they're gonna get."

"Go figure, Sam. These kids have no sense of history. Go on and gimme another."

"Sure thing."

Sam mixed up the martini with great care and attention. He poured one for himself and one for Mike and they toasted and drank them down in the dead of the afternoon. Christ, the martini was good drink, Sam thought. A fine drink, a noble drink. The American drink. Nothing but gin and vermouth in a good martini, and maybe a twist of lemon or an olive for kicks.

Jeff was still shaken up from the bar. He felt reckless with Elizabeth and he wanted to say something or do something to impress her, but instead he kept quiet. He had many things to tell her, but he thought she would laugh at him like she had laughed in the bar. Elizabeth had a vicious sense of humor. Always when he was with her he felt vaguely inferior, as if he didn't know how to live.

Elizabeth was drunk and thought: what if I kiss him? I'm not attracted to him, but it would be fun to see his reaction. I never do anything like that anymore. He's a little awkward but I could hook up with him. That's the alcohol talking, she told herself. It's the alcohol and the fact that your values and beliefs have been turned upside down. You wanted to make money, but now you know it's meaningless. So you want to experiment, and that's meaningless, too. You're twenty-six; you have two maybe three good years left before things start to go downhill. So you might as well enjoy yourself.

Elizabeth wasn't sure if she was attractive anymore, and she was proud and choosy about men. She wanted a man to surprise her and be funny and not afraid to make a fool out of himself. A man who didn't mind looking stupid for a woman was just the kind she wanted. In the bar she had made Jeff look stupid and now he was quiet. Jeff took things too seriously.

They came to the liquor store, and Jeff remembered her request.

"Hang on. I'll just be a minute."

Elizabeth waited for him outside and watched the street; everything was easy through the vision of a couple martinis, and she was no longer worried about the future.

Jeff stood in front of the glass doors and looked at the beer. He didn't know what kind she wanted and thought: why don't I just get a bottle of something stiff and we can take turns drinking? Elizabeth's a tough girl and she might like that. He pointed to a pint of whiskey on the shelf, and the man took it down. Jeff paid and stuck the liquor in his coat pocket.

Walking down the street, they were accosted by a disheveled young man.

"Why don't you give me some change so I can get drunk?"

"Sorry, man, another time," Jeff told him. That was his token response. That and, "Sorry, I don't have any change," or "I'm broke." Still, why should he lie? Why shouldn't he say, "Fuck off and leave me alone. Fuck off, get a job like everyone else, and leave me alone."

Jeff didn't like to be touched in public or confronted, and it seemed they always singled him out. He hadn't figured out the trick to walking past the beggars unnoticed. He tried not to look them in the eye, but sometimes their filth and misery was so curious that he couldn't help himself.

Jeff thought of car crashes and other calamities, and how few things were as attractive as death to a third party. He remembered when he was young a bus had gone off the road and he and a friend had come upon it hiking. It was turned on its side and they had climbed through the shattered windows, sat in the seats and imagined what it would have been like to die there. It made him think of another story that he related to Elizabeth.

"Once I was on the bus downtown late at night and there was a bum sitting in the back next to a woman," he said. "She was dressed-up and all for going out, and the bum had his head in his lap and was swaying back and forth with his hair over his face. The woman had her mirror out and was fixing her make-up when the man leaned over and threw up on her. I watched the spray hit her in the face and pour into her lap; he must have been well-fed because it was a lot of vomit."

Elizabeth turned to him.

"And what did she do," she asked.

"What could she do? She screamed and said, 'Oh my God,' over and over again. You should've seen the shock on her face, but the man was so far gone that he paid her no attention. I was mesmerized. The other passengers stared, too, but no one said anything or did anything to help her. Not that she could have been helped, I mean, what she needed was a hot shower and a good laundromat. She had to sit on the bus like that for twenty minutes. I wonder if that changed the way she thought about the world. You know there are some things you never forget."

Jeff didn't know why he told her the story, or why the memory had come to him. Perhaps it was inappropriate, but sometimes he spoke without thinking. He couldn't stand to pick and choose his conversation with people, and if she didn't like it, she would be the sort to say so. Elizabeth was forthright and that was what he liked about her.

"Sometimes I think I'd like all those beggars to disappear," Elizabeth said. "I don't like them because they remind me of how people can become if they are very lazy or very unlucky. I don't like to look at them because I think of myself like them, and perhaps that's the only impulse for charity. I suppose now there's little difference between us and them. We don't have any work either."

"The difference is in the mind. We have an education," Jeff said. "I'm sure some people on the street also have an education, but not the kids on this street, many of whom aren't real beggars but middle class brats from the suburbs like Alameda, Dublin and San Jose. A lot of them are just here to slum it for a while and sell some drugs. I've got no respect for kids like that throwing away their privilege."

They crossed into the park and the city faded away. Elizabeth felt the comfort of the trees around her. Golden Gate Park made San Francisco superior to other cities. Hadn't she heard somewhere that it was the largest urban park in the world? Well, whether it was or not, without it the city would be almost unbearable. Without the park and the ocean, the city wouldn't be San Francisco and she wouldn't live there. She wondered what other cities in the world could compare and Rio de Janeiro came to mind with its beautiful beaches at the foot of those green mountains. She had never been there but she imagined that the natural landscape was what made it, and certain other cities, great.

They came to Hippie Hill, and though it was a Wednesday, the place was crowded with young urban kids beating drums, playing Frisbee and soccer, and hanging out on blankets smoking dope and drinking.

They found a place on the hill with a good view of the crowd and sat down in the grass. Jeff took the bottle from his pocket and took a swig. It tasted terrible and he tried not to make a face when he passed it to her. She took it without comment and tilted it to her lips. It burned nice going down and she thought when they finished it would be time to take a walk.

"You like whiskey," he asked.

"It does the job," she said.

"If I had a dog I would teach it to catch a Frisbee," he said. "A dog is a good animal. When I get settled I'm gonna get one."

"This is the first time I've had nothing to do in a long time. Maybe I should take a trip? Dogs aside, I'd like to go away for a while," Elizabeth said.

"Where would you go," Jeff asked.

"I don't know. It doesn't really matter. Anywhere but here, I guess. I'd like to go somewhere where it's warm and I could just wear a bathing suit all day, every day."

"Then you should go," he said, missing her already and feeling the jealousy build inside him. He didn't want her to go unless he could go with her.

Yes, she just might go. In fact, she could be gone in a couple weeks if she got motivated. Elizabeth hadn't left the country in over a year. She was feeling reckless and in need of new experience.

They passed the bottle back and forth. Soon there were only a few swallows left, and she said, "Let's get out of here."

They walked on the path past the tennis courts and then down through the ferns and palms and the neatly landscaped paths by the small lagoon with its sinister water. A couple of kids came toward them and when they were close one of them said, "Buds." Elizabeth stopped and he pulled out a bag. She studied it and smelled it and asked how much and the kid said, "Sixty. Straight from Humbolt. This stuff is the bomb."

Elizabeth nodded that she understood and pulled out fifty, two twenties and a ten. "This is all I have," she said. The kid took it. "Peace," he told her, before he and his friend disappeared up the path.

They found a secluded place to sit, and Elizabeth took out her pipe. Jeff didn't usually smoke, though he had done it before and been around it enough with friends. He told himself it was a special occasion like smoking a peace pipe and that it would create a bond between them. They smoked and he no longer felt tense or nervous.

"I've been thinking of going back home," he told her.

"Go back home? And do what -live with your parents? Back home is no different from here. You're gonna have to find a job anyway, and since you've got a nice apartment, you might as well stay put. Going back home is like quitting."

"Yeah, I don't know, it's just been hard for me lately. I'm not used to being out of work."

"You're a programmer," she said. "You can have work tomorrow if you want it."

Jeff thought about programming and how no one understood what it was and that he was ashamed of it because people thought: computer geek. The way she said programmer made him think: alien. *But you're an alien! You can find work tomorrow with your special powers that no one understands.* Well, there was nothing special about it, just the desire to work out problems and get systems to function based on formulas, and he had actually enjoyed what he was doing before the company let him go. Imagine the luck of getting paid well to do something enjoyable. It had seemed and was, too good to be true. And now he was thinking of finding work in some other field. He had romantic notions about driving big rigs across America. He imagined being on the move and watching the landscape go by, sleeping in his truck and never having to return to his cubicle again. While he enjoyed programming, he felt that sooner or later it would drive him crazy. He spent entire days without speaking to another human being and that was no good for anyone.

"I don't know if I can handle the work I'm doing," Jeff said. "Often I can't sleep at night because I'm solving formulas in my head. And I know these formulas don't mean anything. Sure, they can be used, but no one appreciates them. No one can understand them or share my ideas. Sometimes I wish I was good at something besides putting numbers together. I know it's futile and there's no point to any of it. Still, it's nice when formulas work. There's a precision there and everything has its assigned value and there's no confusion. I can't handle confusion," he admitted.

And you're confusion Elizabeth, he thought. I don't know what to do with you or how to act and sometimes I listen to myself and sound stupid, and what is the formula to get you to like me?

These were the things Jeff thought and was incapable of expressing. He hated how his statements came out like apologies or complaints. He wished he could be positive but that was hard since he had lost faith in himself. Yes, he was low and it was nearly unbearable to sit with her under the tree and be unable to reach her. He thought: I could touch her right now if I had the courage. I could do anything I wanted if I had the courage. Then again, if I had the courage I wouldn't be living this life. No, my life would be better.

Jeff was aware that he created his own melancholy just as some produced their own honey. He felt that melancholy was a beautiful emotion and that only a man who thought about his mistakes and failings could ever grasp at some deeper meaning to existence. The numbers were easy, but melancholy was his true defense against life. Ah, that life is as such and that I was born in this way, he thought.

Elizabeth didn't hear him about his obsession with mathematics. Or rather she heard him but failed to listen. It's his style, she thought. He needs a new haircut and different clothes. His glasses are cute and also his nervous intelligence. He's much better than most of the men I've met in bars. What if I kissed him? I'll kiss him and it will be just this time and now because I want to and I can. Men are very simple, she told herself.

"I sure needed a smoke to relax," she said, turning to face him and opening her mouth slightly to pass her tongue between her lips. "I really don't see anything wrong with it. A joint now and again can do wonders for stress, and it gives me the strangest ideas."

Like all men, he can't read the signs. You know he won't make the first move and you're gonna to have to do it all yourself. Elizabeth thought to herself: if only he knew I would let him do whatever he wanted with me. No you wouldn't, her mind protested. You're not that kind of girl and you wouldn't do it right here. You're a tease and you're cold and dead inside and you like to play with men. You feel sorry for him, is all, and you know he won't force you or surprise you. Remember, you're in control.

Yes, Elizabeth thought: I am in control. She ran her fingers through her hair and sighed. "It sure is a nice day," she said, casually putting her hand on his leg.

Jeff tried to think clean. He knew clean-thinking was part of being a man and he would think clean and not imagine anything that did not exist, such as her hand on his leg. That was a friendly gesture, nothing more. Nor would he imagine her lips or her breasts straining at the fabric of her sweater or rolling in the leaves with her. He would imagine none of it because he liked her and didn't want to be rejected or slapped or thrust out of the comfort of the dope and the smell of her. No, he was lonely and sad, and if he could just sit with her, it was enough.

"Jeff, we're friends, aren't we?"

"Yes, I'd like to think so," he said.

"And friends tell each other things, right?"

"Sure."

"Do you find me attractive, Jeff?"

"Very much so," he said, feeling his cheeks go hot.

Elizabeth was drunk and she felt confident now, but even though her mind was confident, her words betrayed her. She said, "Sometimes I don't feel pretty. I'm getting older and I worry about wrinkles and I wish I could be eighteen again and think like I do now."

"Don't talk nonsense," he said.

"What?"

"I said you're talking nonsense. You're pretty and intelligent and lots of guys would love to be with you."

Jeff said it with passion and he meant it. For once he wasn't afraid of the words or how she would react. Elizabeth noted how he turned to her when he spoke and looked her straight in the eye when he hadn't before. On impulse, she leaned in to kiss him. After the shock and novelty of it passed, Jeff remembered to kiss her back; then he put his arm around her and they sat together for a time in silence.

"Let's go, it's getting late," she said.

"Yeah, we should probably head back," he said.

It was Brian Cole's fifth year at Amerika. He was one year into his thirties, that is, one year closer to his death, and the more he thought about it, the more he realized that his twenties were the best years he would ever see and that life could only get worse.

The last five years waiting tables had made Brian bitter about life and arrogant with others. In that way, he was no different from other headwaiters in the city. He was a professional who had grown comfortable and lazy with his work, and who lacked the courage and ambition to find a career that would provide him with both status and enjoyment in his life.

Brian had seen many people younger than himself come and go from the restaurant. Many were musicians or artists of one sort or another who worked only enough to get by so that they might spend the rest of their time pursing their creative dreams. They were young arrogant men and women without patience who thought themselves destined for greatness, and with some of them this attitude would prove to be a self-fulfilling prophecy. When those young men and women quit, Brian imagined them stepping into a bright future. Except for those that he saw as a threat and had fired, he knew they wouldn't remember him. Brian didn't have a future, though he did have responsibility. He wrote the staff schedules, did the purchasing and kept inventory. He was a waiter and manager without being decidedly either. After working his way up from busboy, Brian had locked in the big money nights, Thursday through Saturday, for himself. He worked three nights a week and spent a month in Hawaii every year in the slow season.

Amerika was one of ten restaurants of any worth in the city. It was located on the border between Italytown and the Financial District and catered mainly to businessmen. Tuesday through Saturday, four waiters worked five-table stations in each of the five "theme" rooms.

The entrance to Amerika was designed according to the palace of a certain Saudi sheik. It contained a bar and lounge with a stage where imported gypsy belly dancers performed and a particular elephant named Matilda catapulted them into the air and caught them with her trunk. It could be said that Matilda was one of the luckiest elephants around; she wasn't doomed to have her waterhole run dry, or to be hunted and stripped of her tusks. Matilda had also been trained to serve cocktails but she had to be given a drink to do it. There were many men who envied that elephant that grabbed half-naked gypsies around the waist and tossed them in the air to their delight.

The main dining room was furnished with low tables and chairs with cushions embroidered in gold thread, mosque-like pillars engraved with Arabic script, latticed archways, fountains with fish spouting water, statues of mermaids with bared breasts and little boys peeing. The illuminated domed ceilings, pleasant gurgle of flowing water, and checkerboard polished marble floor gave one a sense of being close to God. Here, the window seats were reserved exclusively for the important faces of the city: the mayor, dotcom millionaires, movies stars, designers, politicians and prominent businessmen all sat there. Ornate partitions were placed strategically between tables to provide the necessary privacy for insider trading, hostile takeovers and the great cash flows of venture capital.

From the splendor of Moorish architecture the restaurant curled like a nautilus. Through red velvet curtains lay Victorian England with its large gilt mirrors, durable lacquered furniture and fat cushioned couches, suits of medieval armor and weaponry, traditional coats of arms, and the reproduced portraits of immortal kings, queens, dukes, and barons. The bookcases were filled with leather-bound volumes of classic literature, and the fireplace was crowned with a stuffed boar's head. There were vases replete with roses, silver tea services and tapestries of historic battles.

Next came the colonies and the charms of the East Indies with carved teak and mahogany furniture, colorful batiks, statues and paintings of Shiva and other deities, gamelan music, and humidifiers to keep the dense rainforest foliage healthy and the poisonous frogs and occasional gibbon content. Here the bussers wore loincloths and were referred to as the Untouchables. The waiters wore slippers, loose white tunics, bright red sashes and light canvass breeches that tapered at the ankles; the waitresses dressed the same, except that the tunics left their bellies exposed. Both sexes were adorned with jewelry. When they walked one could hear the pleasant jingle of metal that announced the arrival of food and drink. Here the curious sounds of the sitar and the tablas combined to create a sufficiently seductive environment.

Through the beaded curtain, Japan beckoned with the simple black ink of calligraphed kanji and hiragana on the white walls and the red rising sun of the East painted on the ceiling. Patrons sat on tatami mats at black lacquered tables bedecked with minimalist flower arrangements. Food was presented in handmade ceramic bowls and served on bamboo trays. Bridges arched over miniature streams linking tandem ponds filled with rare and colorful koi. One pond contained an island with a miniature Shinto shrine complete with a zen garden decorated with red lanterns, carefully placed stones and gravel raked to perfection. Ronin war armor dangled lifelike from the ceiling, and samurai swords bought by G.I.s after World War II were displayed in racks on the walls. White rice paper lanterns were strung across the ceiling from one corner of the room to the next. A Japanese sushi chef sliced and diced top-grade seafood at a rotating bar in the center of the room. The waiters and waitresses wore kimonos; the women dressed like geisha and the men wore wigs with bald skulls and ponytails, as was the fashion in feudal Japan, with scabbards on their hips and costume swords. Every hour on the hour, the spotlight hit the stage and the Taiko drummers gave a performance.

The restaurant went full circle and connected behind to the entryway via the Wild West Saloon. Yes, straight through the double swinging doors with a man silhouette cut from them like a comic book bar fight, was that slice of Americana with the neon beer signs and the jukebox playing America's favorite country music that took up the first ten spots on the Billboard charts now and forever. There was sawdust on the floor and the gum-smacking waitresses went topless in their daisy dukes, vests and cowboy hats with breast implants that gave their tits all the resilience of any member of the squash family. The waiters dressed like cowboys with stubble on their faces and cigarettes dangling like a challenge from their lips. On the walls were license plates from every state of the Union as well as plaques of barbed wire samples from ranches across the West. The walls were decorated with Confederate and Union army uniforms under glass, political rally posters with donkeys and elephants from past elections from both parties, American car logos, as well as World War II propaganda posters, including Rosie the Riveter flexing her arm with the caption: We can do it! The American flag and the flags of every state in the union hung proudly from the rafters.

Amerika was a place where one could get a bloody Texas steak, fresh pufferfish sashimi carefully prepared to avoid tetrodotoxin poisoning, shepherd's pie as salty and terrible as any from a British country inn, Indian curries to make a man die from spice, baked lamb heart and Arabic pastries like delicate dead sugar spiders in your mouth. This unique and eclectic combination of cuisine and culture created an environment unlike any other anywhere in the world.

However, in Amerika the rules were strict and one had to wear the appropriate uniform. Some men disliked the samurai wigs, while others disapproved of cowboy boots and Stetwood hats. Certain women did not like to spend an hour on make-up to be a geisha, and many were embarrassed to go topless. But they did it regardless, because that's what the job called for.

To Brian it didn't matter. He was an Arabian prince holding vigil over the cool and pleasant Moorish palace. He could wait tables with dignity and the security of the curved dagger tucked in the sash of his robes. Here the bussers wore djellabas and their faces were not seen. They ran around like brown mice on the slick marble and disappeared into the corridors that connected every room to the hidden kitchen. Only the sushi chef had the pleasure of brandishing his knives for an audience.

Brian remembered working at Amerika as a Page, an Untouchable, a Jawa and an Army Private. He had hated such work because it made him a slave to people more powerful than himself. But he had swallowed his pride because at Amerika one made better tips than anywhere else, that is, if one could make it to the exalted position of server.

Amerika was a humiliating environment. Many people gave up in their first week when they discovered that being a busser meant living inside the walls of that place and not being seen, dressing up in degrading uniforms, having only a fifteen percent discount on food, submitting to a drug test every month, and collecting good behavior stars like in kindergarten for showing up on time, not making mistakes and accepting extra shifts. Only after four stars could one learn to wait, which meant a week of watching a waiter and also doing their job and not getting paid for it.

That afternoon found Brian in the staff locker room, donning his sheik robes and admiring the blade of his dagger. Unbelievable that it's a real dagger, he thought. I'm glad Carlo doesn't give these to the bussers. They couldn't handle the responsibility.

After paying his dues, Brian was making more than most people in their nine to five office jobs. He had his pick of the tables with the eye of five year's experience to identify the big tippers. He liked to think he could perform mind tricks on the customers.

"You will give me a big tip," he said, curling his fingers toward his face in the mirror.

Brian had a job where he didn't have to think and he got paid between forty and fifty an hour to do it. Only in New York does it get better than this, he thought. I wonder what they make at the Four Planets?

10

They were in a garage in the Marina district. The girl Karla sat on the floor in her underwear on a piece of cardboard with a young man standing over her. His name was Arnold Kazinski, and at that moment he felt the first stirrings of an erection as he studied her. He was sweating and he took off his horn rim glasses to wipe them on his Hawaiian hula print shirt.

"It's hot in here. Do you mind if I take my shirt off, he asked.

"No, not at all," she said.

Arnold removed his shirt and threw it on the nearby workbench. Karla noticed him staring at her again, and to break the silence, she asked, "So what do we do now?"

"Okay, so I'm gonna take this wet plaster and make a mold out of your body," he told her, replacing his glasses and pushing them up on his nose. "But first I need you to take off your bra and underwear and rub some of this oil between your legs and cover up with this piece of gauze. Take as much as you need, it keeps things from sticking later."

Arnold was nervous and his palms were damp. Though he had done it a thousand times, each time was like the first because no two women were alike. To put her at ease, he explained the casting process.

"After that, we'll have you lie down while I rub plaster onto your body. I'm going to add pieces of fiberglass mat to help the mold hold its shape. You'll feel the first layer start to dry and it'll get hot; that's when I'll add the second layer, which will cool you off some. Then I'll add a third and fourth layer until it's thick enough. When it all dries, I'll remove it and we'll be done. How does that sound?"

"Sounds easy enough to me," Karla said.

"It is. The only thing you have to remember is not to breath too deeply or you'll crack the mold. So, are you ready?"

"Sure."

Karla lay down on the cardboard in the heat of the lamps. Because of the glare, she couldn't see Arnold clearly until he came close. Then she felt his hands smearing the cold, wet plaster on her breasts and skin and snaking it between her legs. She thought: I don't know why I'm here, but it's my day off, and what else would I do in the middle of the afternoon on a Thursday in the city? Arnold felt her tense up with the contact of the cool plaster.

"How does that feel," he asked.

"Good, it feels good," she said. His hands were strong and Karla liked the way they felt on her body.

Arnold continued to rub her breasts through the thin layer of wet plaster. From time to time, he looked at her face. Her eyes were closed and her breathing had increased. Arnold liked the feel of her body in his hands. All women are beautiful, he thought. And all of them want to have fun. It's just a question of taking them out of their routine and showing them something new. Thank God for these glasses, he thought. Thank God for these glasses and my voice that's a couple octaves too high. Because I've learned to use this image to my advantage. They think just because I'm big, I'm clumsy; and because I have glasses, I'm shy; and because my voice is high and squeaky, that I'm insecure. But I'm a man, except I'm smarter; who else can get women to take off their clothes and consent to being fondled in the privacy of a garage? How many is this now, he asked himself, knowing exactly how many and remembering each one distinctly from the rest.

"I'm gonna put on some swim trunks," he said. "Just stay still or you'll crack the mold."

Karla lay there with the sweat pouring off her face from the lamps. She felt exposed and vulnerable but also extremely sexy and beautiful. He had made her feel that way. She was a model now. Her body was immortalized forever in plaster and soon people would stare at it on the wall of a gallery.

Hers was not the body of fashion magazines, television or the movies. No, she had big hips, rolls in her stomach that hung slightly over her waist and large breasts that slide to the side from gravity. She was not tall and thin, but she was a woman, and Arnold knew how to appreciate a woman.

Arnold was an artist and he was shy and kind, and she thought: God, when he was touching me I wanted him to be on top of me and inside me. He is a boy in a giant's body and what a cock he must have.

Arnold came back in his swim trunks and flip-flops. With great care, he added another layer; this time intimate contact with her skin was prevented by the dried plaster. And so it went for two more layers after that. The heat lamp was effective in speeding up the process.

Arnold flipped the switch to the hot tub and the water started to boil and hum with bubbles.

"It's good for the wintertime or whenever I need a vacation. You know power naps? Well, for me, this is a power vacation," he said.

Arnold was a man of detail. He had built a makeshift gazebo out of dead palm fronds and bamboo. Next to the hot tub were several inflatable palms he had found at a garage sale. He put some reggae on the stereo and the skank of the keyboard and the baseline made all thoughts of the city fade away.

"Let's have a look," he said, testing the plaster with his fingers. It was drying but still too wet to remove.

Arnold wore sunglasses, and Karla thought he was a mirage when he came close. She heard the upbeat music and felt the heat of the lamps and saw Arnold in his colorful trunks and wondered: where am I?

"Sometimes you have to treat yourself," he told her.

Arnold went to the fridge and took out a couple of beers. He cut some limes on the workbench, worked them into the long necks, and pushed them until they fell and fizzed in the yellow.

"Here. You shouldn't move," he said, tilting the bottle to her lips. Karla drank and some beer ran down the white mold of her chest. He took a long drink and told her, "I have my own island paradise right here in my garage."

"You're crazy, Arnold," she said, laughing. The beer was cold and refreshing, and she couldn't wait to be free from the jail of her own body.

"I've thought about building a bar down here and starting my own after-hours club," he said. "Maybe I'll truck in some sand from Ocean Beach and fill in the floor for my own private beach."

"Is it ready yet?"

"Let's see," he said, working his fingers around the edges of her neck and down between her legs. She felt his curious fingers and then he pulled it free and held it in the air. He turned it over in his hands.

"Beautiful," he said.

Karla stood up and he handed her -her nudity. She ran her fingers along the plaster of her breasts and smiled.

"That's neat," she said. "Wow, that's me. That's my body."

"Uh-huh."

Arnold took another drink of his beer and admired her naked body. He took the mold from her and put it on the bench. Karla was looking at the hot tub and the tropical beach poster that covered the wall when Arnold began to fondle and kiss her.

"Oh Karla, what a woman you are," he said.

"Let's get in the tub," she said.

"Not now, no, I have to do something first, it can't wait, I have to do it now."

They lay down on the cardboard, and Arnold grabbed hold of the extra flesh of her waist and her behind and held on as he went in and out of the hotness of her, while she thought: oh God, yes, no, where am I, who am I, what day is it today? She wanted every Thursday to be like that. Thank God for a man who appreciated women. Karla held him tight and didn't want to let him go even when he was finished.

"I can make you another one next week, and you can keep it for yourself," he said, climbing off her slippery sweat-soaked body. "Now let's get in the hot tub."

11

Jack had to have work by the end of the day. He decided the easiest would be to go to any and all restaurants, starting with the ones that looked nice and working his way down until he had a job. He knew nothing about restaurant work or waiting tables except that people made a living at it. Jack wasn't afraid of work and knew that his situation was temporary. You can't ask your folks for money, even though tomorrow you'll be on the street. You're a man now and you've got to support yourself.

Jack went to North Beach and walked past the nicer restaurants trying to work up the courage to go inside. Only the nice restaurants, he told himself. That's where you want to be. In his ill-fitting suit, he entered various establishments and approached the dignified men and woman behind the bar or on the floor in their pressed black slacks, white long-sleeved collared shirts, vests and polished leather shoes, and asked for work. He knew it was important to look them in the eye and he was prepared to lie.

At the North Beach Bistro the man behind the bar asked him without looking up from his business, "Do you have any experience? What kind of work are you looking for?"

"I'm looking to wait tables," he said.

Jack had never waited in his life. The thought of it made him nervous, but he couldn't afford to work as a busboy. Waiting was bad enough but bussing, that was slavery for a man with a college education. Or so he thought.

"Can you bartend?"

"I've done some bartending," he said with hesitation, "but I'm more of a waiter."

"Why don't you leave a resume? We need a bartender to do a few shifts a week."

The man was in his thirties. He was a handsome professional who could have been an actor or a businessman. He must do well for himself here, Jack thought. He must be the manager.

Jack admired the interior, the classy bar with its innumerable bottles and the man's ability to mix drinks. That was a skill, and Jack was out of work and on the other side trying to appear confident.

"I, er, I don't have a resume with me. You see, I've just come into town . . ."

"The boss'll be in later. Why don't you come back then, say around five?"

"Sure. And what's your name?"

"Mike."

"Mike, I'm Jack. Thanks for your help."

Mike nodded and went on about his business. There were no openings for waiters in the restaurant. The young man was polite enough but he didn't have experience and he wasn't professional. Mr. Chang usually hired on sight and he wanted only professionals.

Jack went to Ciao Amico and knew immediately that he had stepped down a level in class when the sixteen-year-old gum-smacking waitress approached him.

"I'm looking for work," he said. "Do you have any openings for waiters?"

"Do you have a resume," she asked. Jack looked at the menu and saw that it was mostly fried food and pizza. There were televisions on every wall covering every angle and he decided that he had made a mistake.

"Yes, that's what I'll do," he said. "I'll come back with my resume. Thank you." Once on the street Jack breathed a sigh of relief and hoped his luck would improve.

Just that afternoon Brian had lost a waiter to one of the boss's epileptic tirades. Brian hated working afternoons because the tips were bad; he preferred to stay out late and sleep in.

The boss, Carlo Marini, was Italian. He had been in the United States for seven years and had married an American woman who kept him like a dog with his tail between his legs. Grace was a large, fat, ugly woman of Italian origin who spoke Italian with a thick American accent. Carlo's English was still bad and without his wife he wouldn't have been able to run the business, especially without the green card she had gotten him. As a legal resident of California, and with some of his wife's considerable capital, Carlo had opened a small restaurant. As business grew he bought surrounding properties, knocked down the walls and expanded according to his inspiration. He was a man with a vivid imagination: an Italian of the exaggerated variety. He was a throwback of Roman decadence from the days of empire and lead plumbing. Now he was one of the richest restaurateurs in North Beach and greater San Francisco. In return for his wife's favor he had given her a child that she raised without restriction. The boy, Nello, was mommy's little angel and had never lacked for anything. He wailed and threw tantrums, and Brian hated when she came in to check up on business with little Nello behind her: Nello, who aggravated the elephant Matilda with a kitchen knife; Nello, who threw food at the waiters when he ate.

Carlo needed his wife but he didn't love her; she had a great sexual appetite that made him sick to satisfy. At work Brian and the other waiters watched as she bossed him around and scolded him. He would say, "Yes, dear. You're right, dear. Right away, dear," and she would say, "Look, you've made Nello cry." Sometimes Carlo wished Nello had never been born and he was still a bachelor. He had such a fear of his wife that he had never cheated on her. The waiters felt sorry for Carlo, though Carlo was a thief, but that was nothing out of the ordinary for restaurateurs.

Sometimes Carlo would pull a trick with the tips and swallow a ten or twenty when giving change. Brian had caught him at it several times. Feigning surprise, Carlo would say, "Oh, that's right, you did give me a twenty. I thought it was a ten."

One couldn't blame Carlo for being a thief, because he was very humble and disliked telling people what to do. But there were two Carlos: one was shy and unassuming; and the other went into the fits of rage until he lost his breath. He had been known to hit waiters and throw customers out.

The law required Carlo to pay his staff minimum wage, and Brian had learned to count his hours before the time cards went in because

Carlo always subtracted a few hours or a day of work to cut his expenses. He was a good businessman.

When Jack walked into Amerika, he felt very small. Seeing a man clad in a sheik's robe, Jack wondered: what kind of place is this? It looks like a Vegas nightclub.

Carlo was sitting at the bar having a drink in his blue and white *Azzurri* warm-up sweats. He had a big baby face, his hair hung in his eyes and he wore a gold chain around his neck. He was forty-three and a millionaire. But inside him was also the poverty of southern Italy and the memory of his days as a *carabiniere* in Calabria when the mafia had shattered his forearm with a shotgun blast and kicked his teeth out. It was in America that he was able to reconstruct his smile, but his arm still hurt when it rained. He could not forget having one set of dishes that everyone shared during lean times when they had survived on fish, pasta and water. That was when he had learned how to steal before becoming a *carabiniere* and a florist; he had always loved flowers.

Jack walked across the marble entryway to the bar. This was the grandeur he had expected to find in the city. He stared up at the domed ceiling and scrutinized the intricate designs on the pillars and archways, unaware that it was Arabic script stating: God is great, God is one. He was mesmerized by the jets of water from the fountain, illuminated by the glow of the skylight. The man in the robe watched him approach.

"Hello, my name is Jack and I'm looking for work as a waiter. I'm a professional and you won't regret hiring me. Give me a try, and if I'm not everything I say I am, you can let me go."

Jack didn't notice Carlo at the bar but focused all his attention on the man in the robe who looked to him like a foreign dignitary. This must be the owner, he thought. Good. It's nice to speak directly to the owner and not a waiter.

"Do you have experience," Brian asked him. He needed to fill the lunch shift so he wouldn't have to work double.

"Sure, plenty."

"Why don't you leave a resume and we'll get back to you," Brian said.

"Well, I'm new in town and I don't have a place yet so I wasn't able to. . ."

"Listen, there are a lot of people that want to work in a place like this. Without a resume I can't take you seriously."

Jack thought to say that he would do anything for the job.

"Why don't you give me a try? You won't be disappointed. I'm a real hard worker," he said.

And I am an Arabian prince, Brian thought, touching the dagger on his belt.

"This is what I was waiting for," Carlo said. He grabbed Brian by the arm and pointed to the door.

"Over here," Carlo shouted happily. "Yes, yes, over here, gentlemen."

The men in overalls wheeled the cart over, securing it on each side with their hands. Jack watched them struggle with its weight and noted the care with which they held the mysterious object so it wouldn't come crashing onto the marble floor. They had to be careful so the cart didn't get away from them.

"Careful. Careful now. We don't want it to fall," Carlo said.

Brian thought without emotion: if it falls I can go look for another job. Brian knew that when Carlo got upset the anger needed a convenient and familiar target. He thought to disappear into the kitchen; when the cart swung precariously from side to side, he felt sick to his stomach. Who knows what it is, but it must be important to him. He doesn't even look at his son that way.

"That's right, put it right there."

Once it was in place, Carlo jumped from his chair and pushed the two men away. "Go on, have a drink. Brian, get the men a drink."

The men went to the bar and sat down.

"How about a couple of beers," one of them said.

Brian tapped the beers and passed them over.

"All right. This is it. Are you ready?"

Carlo felt the excitement tickle inside him. I can't wait to see their faces. I hope there aren't any mistakes. He grabbed hold of the sheet and jerked it away.

Brian tried to keep a straight face. There in front of him were two Carlos: one in his track suit with a foolish grin and flushed face exclaiming, "*Mamma mia*, how it is beautiful, what lines, what noble features"; and the other silent Carlo, frozen in the white marble with the cold stare of power in his eyes, wearing a toga, a sword on his belt and a military helmet under his arm.

The workers exchanged a look. I can't wait to get back in the van and talk to Jim about it, Larry thought. This guy must have spent a pretty penny. Christ, if I had that kind of money I'd get a new truck. This guy is crazy. Only presidents have their own statues, and they only get them after they're dead.

"History is a fiction," Carlo said, holding his arms wide in the glow of the skylight. "It is an invention of the mind," he said, tapping his forehead with vigor. "The imagination of man has shaped the world. And this is just the beginning, because a man, like wine, becomes better with age." Carlo embraced the statue and kissed it affectionately on both cheeks. "He is beautiful, is he not? Brian, get a camera. I want a picture to send home to the family in Calabria. America is a place of dreams, my friends. Everything they say about America is true."

Right, Larry thought. Sure, what a dream to move furniture for a living with a bad back that keeps me up at night while I pop aspirin to keep the pain down to a dull throbbing, and I'm not getting any younger. Still, this beer is good and it's nice to sit down and I know Jim wants to laugh and we'll laugh plenty later. There have been too many days where nothing interesting at all has happened.

Yeah, America, land of the free and home of the brave, Jim thought. The sword is a bit much, the sword and the helmet. A bust would have been enough. What difference is it to me? People have family portraits and paintings of old dead relatives. But they're dead. I wonder if he'll give a big tip. If he tips well then I don't give a damn what he does.

"Thank you, gentleman, thank you," Carlo said.

Jim produced the invoice from his pocket. "We need your signature."

"Brian, sign for these gentlemen, please."

Brian signed everything and read everything for the business, since Carlo could neither read nor write. Education and wealth, it seemed, had little to do with one another; if anything being illiterate had made Carlo more clever, just as blindness improved hearing. Carlo took two twenties from the register and pressed one into each of the deliverymen's hands.

"You're good people, you workers. I've always respected the working class. My father, he was a laborer, and there is no shame in it."

The men nodded, and Larry thought: I'll break your teeth, you workers. I'll break your teeth, you dago son of a bitch. He walked to the door and thought: how is it that one man gets rich and another does not? This work is enough to make a thief of a man. There is nothing noble about work. Those that don't work patronize us and say we are noble, but they don't want our nobility. That I don't understand. Larry checked his watch. One-thirty. They still had half the day to go and then Friday, too.

Every week it was four more days, three more days, two more and so on. He was living his life in a countdown.

"Do you know what I was thinking, Brian," Carlo said.

Cazzo, Brian, a nice guy with no ambition. If I was young and handsome like Brian, Carlo thought, I'd go do something with my life. How is it possible that he stays in this humiliating work? He's a good worker, though, and I wouldn't want to lose him. He's stupid and will never get anywhere, but at least he's loyal and fears me.

"No, what's that," Brian asked.

"I want to put in a swimming pool. Why not? How many restaurants are there with a swimming pool? Then I'll hire some models to swim in it naked. How about that? Why, I'll buy up the office next door. I've heard rumors of bankruptcy," he said, with his hand covering his mouth. "Anyway, it would be sort of a bathhouse with heated pools and massage rooms. Who wouldn't want to go relax in the hot tub after a good meal? We'll just expand the employee changing rooms and showers. What do you think?

I think you're losing you mind, Brian thought. I think when the mafia kicked and beat you they did permanent brain damage. I think that you do too many drugs, and I know that without your import export business and your wife's investing in the markets, you'd be bankrupt.

"Why don't you make a statue of your wife," Brian suggested.

Carlo stopped and the color drained from his face.

"It's true. Grace doesn't know about the statue. She is a very jealous woman. I must make a statue of her, also. She will think my statue a frivolity unless she has one of her own. And of course one for Nello. I must confess about Nello. He does not have traditional values. He is too American, *capito*? When I was his age I was supporting my family working odd jobs."

"He's five years old," Brian said.

"You're right. Perhaps I did not support my family when I was five. But I learned discipline. I did not cry and insult my father with such language. You've heard his language. It's right from the sewer. It scares me to think one day he'll take over the restaurant. Let's hope he has good taste like his father."

Jack was uncertain whether to excuse himself or stay. The other restaurants were not like this. This is grand and ridiculous, and the man is crazy, but I need the work.

"So why don't you come back with a resume and we'll give you call," Brain concluded.

"And this young man," Carlo said, noticing Jack for the first time. "What can I do for you?"

"He's looking for a job," Brian said.

"Excellent, you're hired. What's your name?"

"Jack."

"Right. Now John, help me move this statue into place."

"Not John, Jack."

"Right, Jack. Now I was thinking over by the fountain. Brian, call the sculptor and tell him I will fax some pictures of Grace and Nello. I need them done immediately. In the meantime, we'll keep this one covered with a sheet. Even better that she does not come at night. It would be a shame to keep such a likeness covered."

"Now listen up, Jack. Here everyone wears a uniform. All great cultures have had a certain mode of dress and a system to separate the different classes. *C'e*, also I have always liked putting on costumes. The *carnavale* is, after all, a medieval Italian celebration. It was started by powerful noble families to give the commoners some distraction from their miserable lives. That is what Amerika is about," Carlo confided, putting his hand on Jack's shoulder. "We create an illusion of being in another place or time. People come to this restaurant to escape into fantasies and dreams. Do you understand?"

"I think so," Jack said.

"Now kiss the statue's feet."

"What?"

"I said kiss the statue's feet. I demand loyalty. If you are loyal to me you will do well. But if you break my trust then," Carlo took a finger and drew it across his neck.

So he's a little dramatic, Jack thought. He likes to make things larger than they are. He's a clown. Fine, I'll kiss the statue's feet. Damn, I need this job and I don't have any money or a place to sleep tonight. Just do what he says. It's easier just to do it and not ask questions or resist or fight it in your mind. He is not trying to humiliate you. He's just crazy.

I remember when I was young, Carlo thought. What I wouldn't give to trade places with Jack and be young again. You have forty-three years. You are not old. Yes, but you are married. You are married to a horrible woman and you are not free; you have too many responsibilities and you are not happy. You were happy when you saw the statue, but you are not happy any more. It's like that whenever you buy anything. You got the new Ferrari and you were happy, and then you drove it alone and felt alone in it and thought: if only I was not so alone. Being a *capo* is about being alone. The boy has no responsibilities, he is free. *Ma*, look how he has kissed the statue's feet just like you told him to. This one will be a waiter for the night shift. You like him for no reason. You do not even know him and you like him.

"Tell me what else I should do," Jack said.

"You will need to learn the menu. Take this one with you. And the wines," Carlo said, handing him a thick black book. "Also, you will have to learn to dance. I do not know where I will put you, but each room has it's own dance. The people like a show. People are not serious and they like to laugh. This I know because life is ridiculous. If I could only tell you of the ridiculous things I have seen and done," he said.

"Brian, where should we put Jack? I am going to have him work some day shifts and also the night. The day does not matter because only the front is open. But at night?"

Brian despised Jack; he despised his feigned innocence and his boyish good looks, and he was jealous of him for kissing the statue's feet. It reminded him of the pricking of fingers between friends and mixing of blood to seal a friendship.

"Put him in the Wild West Saloon," Brian said. "He knows nothing about Japanese, Thai or Indian cuisine. He needs training."

"Yes, it's true. He is best suited for the saloon."

Jack thought: Brian is an asshole. He is standoffish and I don't respect him, and what's so great about waiting tables? A monkey could wait tables.

Brian thought: he should have been made a Jawa to start or an Untouchable. I had to work here for a year as an Untouchable and now Carlo gets the statue and is in a good mood and Jack will get to work nights. Once Jack sees that money, he'll resent the days.

Brian gathered his robes and went to take an order. He leaned over the table and looked at the customers with a grave face to ensure they wouldn't take liberties and try to switch one side dish with another, or remove a necessary sauce, or say they were allergic to butter. He nodded and snapped up their menus and marched off. At the bar he made a gin and tonic bribe for the chef, Martino. At one-thirty Martino's eyes were already glazed from drink and he was relaxed and ready to release his violent laughter or start shouting without intent. Only when Martino was quiet and serious was he dangerous. That was when he was sober and the resentment of life filled him up like a tank of gas. He was a proud Mexican with an enormous revolutionary moustache that covered his upper lip and even his teeth when he spoke.

Brian put the drink on the counter. "Just the way you like it, *cabrón*," he said. Brian had been working with Mexicans long enough to spice his conversation with plenty of well-mannered macho insults involving mothers, sodomy and animal slang. Still, he had never had the courage to say, *hijo de puta*. He knew you could call a Mexican anything but a son of whore. They didn't take well to that.

"We have a new waiter. Un *nuevo camerero*. I don't like him. He is arrogant. He thinks he is better. He will walk over you, *buey*."

"We will see the day when a *gringo* walks on me," Martino said, stiffening. "You walk on me I break your legs. This new one should be careful."

"He's big, Martino. Athletic. I'd watch out or he'll kick your ass."

"I kick your ass, *maricón*. This one, that he watches himself or else. You remember Brent? Some people need to be taught a lesson."

"I remember the police coming and pressing your face into the filet mignon and sending you back to Mexico," Brian said.

Fucking Mexicans, he thought. Brian hated to work with the Mexicans in the kitchen with their excessive pride, and also the busboys that were lazy and pretended to be deaf. He hated having to speak Spanish when he was in his own country, and much of that hate came from being lazy himself and believing that he was better for being white and thinking he was too good to work for a living. Brian suffered from a sense of entitlement and couldn't see that his hatred of Carlo and the Mexicans, and now of Jack, who he didn't really know, came from the fact that he was small and insignificant and couldn't keep his insecurities and troubles to himself.

"*Pues*, Brent had the face of pumpkin when I was finished with him," Martino persisted. "I heard his ribs crack when I kicked him like *la migra* to pregnant women on the border."

"Yes, you're very much a man," Brian said. "Now get me table three."

Martino had none of the good humor or relaxed attitude of his younger brother Santos, who made salads and washed dishes. Martino hid his insecurities behind a wall of severity and hostility. He used his size and his impressive moustache and scowl to gain respect.

Martino had always lived in the shadow of his brother. It was Santos that had gone first to the United States to support the family. Only when Santos had gotten him a job did Martino follow after. He had tried not to cry when he left his mother, the village and the many wives he had satisfied behind their husband's backs. He lived in the memories of drinking and playing cards with his childhood friends.

Santos was the smarter of the two. He couldn't cook or do anything artistic, but he was good with money and spoke decent English. Santos told Martino that at their current rate of work, with their collective wages, including those of their cousin Juan the busboy, they would be able to expand their pig farm on the outskirts of Guadalajara. Pork was good business and soon they would build another house on their land where they all would return to live.

The next year Juan was to marry a plain but chaste woman from the village. Juan was a soft-spoken young man of twenty-two. He didn't mind that his wife was ugly, so long as she was a good wife and mother to their children; it was the pretty girls one had to worry about sharing without permission with strangers or even friends. Juan was quiet and easy-going. He avoided any situation in which he might have to raise his voice or fight for something that was his and could be taken away from him. In this way, he hoped to have a peaceful life. I will not be a great man because all great men are thieves, he told himself, but I will have peace, which is all a man can ask. When he saw the waiters give only ten dollars tip of several hundred they had earned, he would bite his tongue and console himself with the thought that if he were a waiter he would do the same. He couldn't argue because he had learned early that in Amerika he didn't exist and for that reason Carlo paid him below minimum wage. To protect himself from the endless repetition of work, Juan had learned to live in daydreams. He moved in the polish and beauty of Amerika and thought only of Mexico, of the dry plains and hills of Guadalajara, of his future children laughing and riding the pigs, and of his wife to be who would care for him.

When Jack finished with work he had nowhere to go.

"You done good today, Jack. We'll see you tomorrow for the night shift, all right? Don't worry you'll be done training by the end of the week," Carlo said, clapping him on the shoulder.

Do I get paid for training, Jack wondered. He was in a tight spot financially and couldn't wait much longer for a paycheck.

"So when do I get paid?"

"The checks come every two weeks on the first and the fifteenth. Today is the eighteenth."

I wish I could stay the night, Jack thought. I could sleep right on one of those couches in the hookah lounge. Otherwise I don't have anywhere to go. Maybe I can go sleep in the park?

Jack had fallen silent.

Carlo smiled. "Don't worry, tomorrow you'll get some tips. Come on and get something to eat. I feed everyone here. You can have anything you want, just no meat or seafood."

Fair enough, Jack thought. Now I don't have to get a burger. He was in no hurry to leave. Still, what if Elizabeth wrote back? He would stop by the library on the way to the park. It was a big park and there had to be plenty of places to lay down unnoticed. He would think of it as camping.

Jack had a falafel pita with hummus, a salad with kiwi lime dressing, and a soda. He wanted a beer but didn't want to give the wrong impression. Carlo sat next to him at the bar and had a glass of red wine and a rack of lamb in a honey mustard sauce with polenta and steamed vegetables. He picked at an antipasto of prosciutto and melon. Jack ate his pita and felt his stomach growl. He and Brian's eyes met looking at the lamb. Brian ate a vegetarian curry with apples and raisins and bits of tofu.

Jack excused himself. Carlo waved with a lamb rib in his fingers and returned to sucking and slurping the bone.

"You come tomorrow at six. Memorize the menu and the wine. Brian, go show Jack his locker and get him a uniform for the saloon."

Reluctantly, Brian got up from his meal. Never get to sit down and eat in peace, he thought. Always a slow customer wanting the bill or a phone call or some other nonsense. He found a Stetwood hat and some Baducci pre-stressed jeans, brown leather chaps, a red scarf, a corduroy shirt, a leather vest and cowboy boots. Then he showed Jack his locker and gave him the combination.

These costumes are ridiculous, Brian thought, but I like the robe and also my dagger. Still, I would never wear a kimono, a red riding uniform for the foxhunt or a loincloth. But you've worn rags. You've humiliated yourself and you don't want to do it again. Perhaps that's why you're always in a bad mood. You resent having to humiliate yourself for a living.

Jack took the clothes and thanked him. He unzipped his duffle bag and sorted through his luggage. The locker was a lucky break. Unfortunately, it was too small to fit much more than his uniform, his blazer, a few shirts and his extra dress shoes. He supposed he could have asked Carlo to look after his things, but then Jack didn't want him to know that he was homeless. For a moment, he considered wearing the uniform out on the street so he could leave his laptop behind but, as it turned out, the computer was either too wide or too long to fit in the locker. Strutting around town like a cowboy, though, that would be a laugh. Probably no one would even notice. How ironic to come to the city from an outpost like Arizona to dress up like a cowboy. Yeah, how ironic.

12

Should she write him back or not? She read the message again:

Hi Elizabeth. Jack here. I called the number on your card and they said you don't work there anymore. Anyway, I enjoyed meeting you the other night. I can't get the image of you on the Golden Gate Bridge out of my head. You're such an adventurous person.

As for me, I have been looking for work. I'm staying at a hostel. Money is tight now and I'm hoping to find something soon or I'll be on the street. The city is very large and I feel lost. I was wondering if we could meet and talk? You're the only person I know here and I would like that very much.

Please send me your number so I can give you a call.

Best regards,

Jack Wild

What stood out most in the letter was the "best regards." She was not sure what "best regards" implied, beyond being a safe and meaningless conclusion to a letter, used primarily for business communication. But best regards in a personal letter? She felt betrayed by that careful statement. Then she read, *"You're such an adventurous person,"* and a smile spread across her face.

I can see right through your best regards, Jack. The city is large, you're lonely and I'm all you got.

The letter was a cry for help. Jack needed her and he wished her much more than best regards, though he didn't have the courage to say so.

That was a man for you. Still, he had found the nerve to call her and send her an email. Do I respond, she wondered. Yes, I'll respond.

Tired of living inside herself instead of engaging with the world, Elizabeth decided: I'll help Jack and be his friend. Then she thought: you don't want to be his friend. You want to bait him and see how far he'll go. You want him to get through all your traps and contradictions to find you, the real you, as you are and don't know yourself. Her mind wandered and she thought: it sure was fun kissing Jeff yesterday. You sure took him by surprise. Remember how hot his ears felt in your hands? Elizabeth stared at the blue of her screen and started typing:

Jack,

Yes, it's true I no longer work at Conscious Net. I was not satisfied with my work. I believe that I can do much more with my life. I have decided to take some time for myself to decide my future. I am planning on taking a trip. I need to dive to the bottom of the ocean, sail a boat in stormy seas, or hike through some wild, empty woods. You understand. It's like the bridge. I need to grab the cables of life and expose myself to the elements. I need to feel alive.

Now she would get down to the business end of the letter:

I understand what it means to be alone in this city. If you need any help or someone to talk to, then I'm here, at least for now. My number is: XXX-XXXX

Good luck,

Elizabeth

Good luck. It could be a goodbye or an invitation. Good luck with your life or good luck at getting up the nerve to call me. In her experience Elizabeth knew men to prefer cowardice to risk. To test his resolve, she considered telling him she had a boyfriend, or that she was a single mom, or that she liked to party and that, even as she was writing him, one of her lovers was lying satiated in her bed. Though it was funny, writing such nonsense would only be a cruel joke at herself and gender relations, so she decided against it. If only I did have a naked man in my bed, she thought, looking to the empty sheets. If only I were more courageous.

If Elizabeth's courage weren't a farce, she would have liked to enjoy a new man every day, no strings attached. She would have spread her legs wide and accepted many men, regardless of social convention and what other women, in particular her housemates, would say. If you had many lovers your housemates would be jealous and that jealousy would turn to hate. They would think you a traitor because some men would take the sex for granted, like a beer after work, and forget that a woman's pleasure matters, too. It would turn gender relations completely upside down, and a lot of people wouldn't be able to handle it. You know this and it weighs on you every day living in this society, so why think about it? It weighs on you with those women's magazines that create ideal women for men with articles like ten ways to turn him on, ten ways to pick up a man, ten ways this and ten ways that. Fuck those magazines and the lie of women's liberties in America. We're not free because it's all about a man's pleasure, she thought. So take a number, Jack, and prove that you're not like all the rest. To Elizabeth, American men had mostly proven to be idiots.

13

Jack stepped out onto the street with his duffel bag slung over his shoulder. He walked a few blocks through Chinatown, caught the 30 down Stockton to Union Square and transferred to the 7 on Market, which would take him to the Haight and eventually Golden Gate Park.

The Haight bus was full and he had to stand. People squeezed on and the driver said, "Everyone move on to the back." No one moved and he said, "Move on back now," and people inched back a token distance and stopped. Jack wasn't used to crowds. His bag was heavy on his arm, and when he turned, he bumped it into other people and had to excuse himself. Eventually, he dropped it to the floor and stood with a leg on either side.

"You get off the bus," the driver said. "This bus ain't leavin' until you get off. Yeah, I'm talking to you. I saw you sneak through the back doors. Well, we'll just sit here until you leave. I know your game. I'll sit here all night if I have to."

Jack saw the man with his long ratty hair, a blanket over his shoulders, the trash bag in his hand with his belongings, and the layer of grime on his face and hands. Then he smelled him, that acrid human stink of filth and degradation, and watched how the other passengers shrank away from him and pretended he wasn't there, while the irritation built that this invisible man was delaying them all.

They sat for several minutes in silence, and the man didn't move but just swayed in his seat and stared to a place that was not the bus.

The bus driver said, "I've notified the police. If you don't wanna go on your own, they'll take you away."

Jack thought about the other men and women he had seen get on through the back doors. Why stop the bus specifically for this man who can't pay his own way and not for others that can but don't? Why not kick that young man with his cell phone and slick neon plastic sneakers off the bus for not paying?

Jack realized then that the city was as much about illusion as reality; it was not a man's thoughts or character that mattered in that place because men related only by appearance. The people on that bus were packages of different colors, shapes and sizes to be judged and labeled by each other accordingly.

"I'm goin' one more stop. Please driver, take me one more stop," the man said. "I ain't got no money, otherwise I'd pay. I'm askin' you a favor. Ain't there any decent folk left in the world?"

There was another of those great silences on the bus that occurred when men and women were forced to face their own conscience, and yet not a single person spoke and said, "Driver, drive on," or "Driver, I'll pay this man's ticket so he can have a ride." Nor did Jack pay. He told himself that it was because he was in a bad way with only a few dollars in his pocket. If he had known, Jack would also have gone through the back doors to save a dollar.

The police came, boarded the bus, took the man by the arms and hauled him out of his seat. The man grew limp with authority. He had learned to fear those men in uniform and be ashamed of himself. They told him, "Sir, you're causing a disturbance. We're going to have to ask you to get off the bus." There was a politeness in those words that was belied by the way they steel-armed him to the door, and by the way his legs were bent slightly so that it was clear that he was moving against his will.

The bus moved again, away from bad conscience, and the passenger's thoughts returned to their preoccupations which filled the void of solidarity between them that they all knew existed either by reason or intuition. Jack thought about the times he had slept in strange places for reason of circumstance. If he couldn't sleep on the bus, or in a car, then how would he sleep on a park bench without a blanket and with the constant threat of intrusion?

Riding on the bus put him in fear. For the first time Jack saw how many people in America had very little or lived for hope of a future that would never come. From those lives that surrounded his own he could see clearly the decline and misery. For some he thought: if I were ever in such a bad way I would kill myself. He wondered vaguely how bad it would have to get for a man to take such action. Ironically, he had heard that there were more suicides of powerful, intelligent men than the poor and miserable. God's joke. Ha, ha. Jack didn't understand the reason for this, except that some men and women had been made so hard by life that they were impossible to kill. They lived on the very edge of death, yet they wouldn't die. They were so far away from being able to create their own world that they had become animals. Never in the country where he lived had Jack seen people living with so little surrounded by abundance. He thought of the half-eaten plates of food that he had scraped into the trash at work that day, of the juicy steaks and filets of fish that he was too proud to eat off those used plates, but that if no one had seen, he would have eaten. He thought of the waste of the city, of broken compasses and himself riding the bus around in circles for the rest of the night until morning when he could go back to work.

The bus driver, Bobby Garcia, no longer saw the humanity of his passengers but considered them to be cargo to be transported from one destination to another. There were certain lines he liked better than others and the Haight line was his least favorite. He was tired of the young white kids in their rags, tattoos and pierced faces on his bus. He was intolerant of anyone who came running to the bus hoping to get a ride after the doors had closed, and of passengers who did not hurry to board. For such people he would shut the doors; it gave him a bitter satisfaction to hear their fists pound on the window and their muffled insults through the glass. It was his bus, after all, and he could do as he pleased. He would transport passengers that were respectful and refuse those who were rude or created a disturbance. How he hated those brats that snuck on the bus, and when kicked off, pulled the cable in the back so it came loose from the electrical wires with a crash, and he would have to stop and climb up in the middle of traffic to put it back in place.

Otherwise, Bobby didn't want the homeless on his bus and made a habit of kicking them off. He didn't respect anyone who didn't work for a living. He was a Mexican American born to first generation immigrants. He was a citizen and he spoke perfect English with no accent.

Bobby had been driving the bus for nearly thirty years and would retire with a small but reliable pension. Some days it was all he could do to think about that pension when he had to shout, "Move to the back," and people did not move, or when there was a disturbance, which was every day, several times a day. As a bus driver, he had learned that there were many types of people competing for a decent life in the city, and he was amazed how they could all get along. It was a theory of his that privilege and comfort led to corruption and decay. Though immigrants worked very hard for success, he felt that one day their grandchildren would throw away the privilege their parents had been given. He thought of how he had done better than his father who had been a gardener. Bobby had put his son and daughter through college; no doubt they would surpass him in success and then his grandchildren would stay the same or decline. He didn't want to believe it, but he knew from studying history that great families came and went and blood didn't transfer will or intelligence, but just a beating heart. That heart could be just or wicked, but in the end a man could only live according to his circumstance, and some circumstances were better than others. He wanted very much to have grandchildren to tell them what he knew about the world: that was the only way he could see to save them from their mistakes. Still, he knew every man must make his own mistakes to learn. Driving the bus, Bobby philosophized about human life on earth. If he were able to record his thoughts, perhaps it would have made a good book.

There were certain professions that led a man to great-thinking and politics was not one of them. If the bus drivers ran this country, Bobby thought, there would be more justice in the world. But perhaps not, he contradicted, with drivers like that racist Jerry who was put on probation when he told a black man to get to the back of the bus. No, not for men like that, but for the drivers who saw people as people and appreciated that each passenger on the bus was lost and trying to find a destination. No one knows it better than me, Bobby thought. I drive this bus in circles and I see the people come and go: some new, some familiar, each of them with a family and friends who love them. And they are all searching for happiness. It's the same happiness I think of when I am on my last circuit and I see one of my brothers standing at the stop in his brown uniform with the orange logo and his backpack with a few goodies for the road, and I hand over the controls to him to steer all those lives where they need to go, so I can lay down with my wife and sleep.

On dark and stormy nights, of which there were many in the city, Bobby Garcia opened the doors to the wet, shivering figures at the curb. He saw the gratitude in their faces and imagined that he was taking them from hell to their salvation. When he heard a "thanks," he would graciously nod his head or touch his cap. That "thanks" would fill him up for a moment and remind him that he did exist and was not just a faceless Charon delivering men from one side of the abyss to the other, but one of them, a part of the living and breathing of life.

14

Jack walked through the park with a growing sense of loneliness as the light faded and the air grew cold. He walked for a long time until he didn't feel as if he were in the city anymore. When the trees blocked out the road and the buildings completely, he daydreamed about camping. It was too early to lie down to sleep, and Jack wished he had something to read and some light to read by. He thought of his own bed in his mother's house and, consequently, the cold seemed sharper than before. He told himself: this is only for one night, maybe two, if you get some tips tomorrow and don't have to work for free bussing and helping the waiter.

Jack walked deep into the park, sat down by a lagoon and watched the ducks with their necks folded backwards in sleep like alien ships. He imagined turning one of those duck bodies on a spit over a campfire and thought: I'm glad to be off of that bus and away from people. It grew dark and he changed into his warmest clothes and used the bundle of his duffel bag as a pillow. Even dressed as he was, the cold wouldn't allow him to sleep. This is California with its sun and surf and blonde girls and palm trees? Bullshit. You had to learn the hard way; if you hadn't blown your money and lost your credit card, you wouldn't be in this position, but at least you have a job.

With such thoughts in mind, Jack finally drifted off to sleep. Some time later he awoke with a light shining in his face. A man leaned down close to him and his first thought was: I'm gonna be robbed. Jack lay still and confused, broken from his dreams, and the man said, "Can I see some sort of ID?" Jack sat up and the flashlight was now down at his chest and he could make out the silhouette of two men in uniform. The police.

"Yes sir, officer," Jack said, fumbling for his wallet.

The man took his ID and studied the picture.

"From Arizona, huh?"

"Yes sir. I've just moved out."

"The reason we're here, Jack, is because you can't sleep in public places in the city: not on park benches, not on the grass, not in the street. Understand?"

"Yes sir."

"What's a young man like you doing out here anyway?"

"I had an argument with my girl and it's a long walk home."

"I understand. But you can't sleep here. A lot of bad things happen in this park. It's best you move along."

"Yes sir," Jack said, standing up.

"Have a good evening, son. Maybe if you're nice, she'll take you back."

"Yes, thank you. Good evening, gentlemen."

The police left and Jack thought: one thing I don't mess with is the police. With police, it's polite or nothing. They tell you to do something, you do it. For all they knew I could have been some junkie. If I'd been a jerk, they'd have put me in jail.

Still, it isn't right that a man can't lie down on public property if he wants to sleep and doesn't have any other place to go. I'm going to have to find a better spot. Where do the men and women I've seen on the street sleep?

Jack walked on alone through the park. The sky flashed and he heard the crack of thunder. There was a dread in him for what he knew was to come. The rain wet his hair and face and soaked cold to his skull; then it began to pour. Jack had an old and heavy laptop computer in his bag, and he had to get out of the rain. He went off the main road onto a dirt trail. His eyes were accustomed to the dark and he peered into the trees and looked for shelter under the branches. Hearing voices, he advanced until someone said, "Who's there?" Jack stopped dead on the trail. He heard the cop in his mind: *a lot of bad things happen in this park, son. It's best you move along.*

"My name's Jack. I'm just looking for a place to bed down. I don't have anywhere to go for the night."

The fear was tight in his throat. You don't know who or how many they are. You have a computer in your bag. Still, you don't have any money, so they can't rob you. Thank God I'm not a woman, he thought. If there's a problem, I can defend myself. I really need to get out of this rain.

"Come on there, Jack, no need to stand in the rain."

Jack stooped low and crept inside the trees. Under the branches was a makeshift fort with a tarp stretched over and tied off at the corners. A small lantern hung from a metal wire and blankets were spread on the ground.

"Go ahead and have a seat. The name's James. We're all prisoners here. Ha, ha."

Jack sat down and saw them, four men and a woman, and one of the men asked, "So where you comin' from Jack? You look nice in them clothes. You sure you ain't lost?"

"I've had a bit of bad luck," Jack said.

"Well, you know what, Jack, then you ain't lost at all. Bad luck, he's right here with us, only he's too rude to introduce himself."

This man, Jack saw, had a few teeth missing and his face was tanned and wrinkled from a hard life spent outdoors.

"This here is Doc. Don't ask me why we call him Doc because he doesn't have any sort of education," James said. "I think he named himself Doc. If you can't be a real doctor, you can be a doctor to your friends, I guess. Every man is famous to his friends. Didn't you know, we're movie stars, Jack, and don't you forget it. It just so happens that we can't write history."

Jack wasn't sure where he stood with the men, what they thought and felt, or how they had arrived at this point in their lives. Still, James was jovial and seemed to take things in stride.

"Is this where you guys live?"

"We live on the street, Jack. There are many reasons for a man to be on the street: for some, it's idealism; for others, genius. Some of us lack love, familial and otherwise, and others are just plain crazy. And drugs, they often lend a helping hand toward a man's destruction," James said.

"We ain't too much for drugs here, except for good ol' alcohol to dull the senses, though that don't make us no different from the rich folks," Doc said. "Without alcohol I don't think men could get through the hard times and loneliness, rich or poor. There's so many excuses for drinkin' and I've drunk for everyone one of 'um. I done drunk for losing my job and my woman, and to forget I'm hungry and tired and cold and miserable. Here you are, Jack. Get the heat in ya'."

Doc held out the bottle to him. Jack took a drink and it burned and warmed his belly. He made to hand it back and Doc motioned for him to pass it to the woman.

"Go on, Doc, that's no way to talk to a young man," James said. "He's liable to get discouraged. Why Jack, when I was your age I thought I could do anything and I did. I went all the way to Mexico and lived on the beach with the *señoritas*. I would have married one if I wasn't such a man for adventure."

"You might look at us and think we're finished, Jack, just a bit of human ex-cre-ment, but we live more in one day than most men live in a lifetime. Modern man, you see, is afraid to live; he is afraid of men like us who have nothing and want nothing from life but a bit of food and a place to bed down at night," Doc said.

"But it ain't all roses, Jack. Even on the street and with men like ourselves, there are rules; some men have been living here a long time like this and there's competition like anywhere else. Maybe you were lucky tonight to find us because there are a lot of bad men and women on the street that'll take whatever they can get from you. I've seen one man kill another over a place to sleep. He stuck the knife right in him like an extra appendage and left him to choke on his own blood. And you think he got punished for it? No sir. A man like that don't exist, so he can't die. They just take his body away and dump it like he was never born and didn't have no mother. Do you understand, Jack? This is an education that I'm giving you," Doc said. "You ain't like us. We can smell it on you. You're just a boy lost in the woods, but perhaps it'll do you good to sit with us for a while."

"Let me tell you something about survival," James said. "A man will do anything to survive. No man is too proud to dig in the trash if he's hungry. No man is too proud to steal from someone who has more than he needs. You see pride is a useless emotion when you get right down to it. It doesn't serve folk like us. Still, I've seen men fight over women, like Mary here, though I don't know who would want Mary 'cause she's demanding, and if you want something from her you gotta give in return."

"Shut up, you old dog," Mary said. "Don't you listen to 'im. These men ain't never gotten over comin' outta their mother's warm insides. When things get tough and men cry, who do you think's there to comfort 'em? They say a woman's weak, but I raised some kids who are out in the world now, and I ended up here, so it just goes to show that being a mother is a thankless job."

"You know what happens to a man on the street, Jack, when he don't have no one to talk to and people walk him by and pretend he don't exist, and he's gotta beg to eat, and instead of eatin', he gets to drinking to survive the day, and every time he shuts his eyes someone comes and shakes him and tells him he can't sleep, and he's gotta cut his hair and clean himself in a public bathroom, and he don't have no money to keep his clothes clean or buy new ones? I tell you it drives a man crazy, and when you're down real low you fight to keep from losing your mind. So you got the junkies and men who don't want to be with society, and men that are lazy and have no sense of worth in themselves because they been kicked too many times, and then you got the crazies. Those crazy men speak a lot of truth, Jack. They are like the great artists of the world, except no one can hear or see them," James said.

"We keep a tight group here to survive, and we survive because we talk to each other and help each other out. When someone has a bit of luck they share it with the others. A man alone on the street sooner later gonna lose his mind," Doc said.

Jack thought to himself: I'm different from them and either tomorrow or the next day I'll sleep in a bed and eat a hot meal. But I do feel badly that they have to live this way, though some have chosen it, while others have made mistakes and ended here, and a few weren't born with the right machinery of reason. These men are no different than me. They need love and friendship, food and a place to sleep like anyone else.

That's a fine and noble thought, Jack. That's fine and noble and you only think of them now because they have given you something, though they have nothing. The truth is you feel each man should take care of himself. You are not them. That's why you have a sick desire to hear their miserable stories and to imagine yourself walking in their world.

"Why you got that look on your face, Jack? I've seen that look before. I've seen it on the street when I put my hand out for change. Man, you look ill. Like we make you sick," Doc said.

"No, that's not it," Jack said. "I'm grateful to you for letting me come out of the rain, and if I could help you, I would. It's just that I don't have anything to offer."

"That's all right. A man helps when he can. This won't be your last chance," James told him.

"Speakin' a' bad luck, you hear what happin' to Crazy Jim," Will asked.

"You mean when he was waving his plastic gun around in the street and the police came and shot him dead," Walker said.

"It didn't even look like a real gun. It was yellow and funny-shaped like an alien gun, and he was standing in the light by the Nordworth Center where he always used to stand and also where he slept, and all them police knew Crazy Jim," Will said.

"That's what happens when you stand too close to the Nordworth Center scarin' off them customers," Walker added. "He shoulda kept to himself instead of raisin' a reputation. You know, like we keep outta sight in the park instead of downtown gettin' hassled by the police for sleepin'."

"How do you guys eat if you don't work," Jack asked.

"Well, there's some shelters in town where they give you food and a bed," James said. "You gotta line up early if you want a bed. Like in the morning. Eatin's all right. There's usually enough food for everyone. It ain't much good, but it fills the belly. I've been living here for seven years like I am now. I know where to get the handouts at restaurants, the good dumpsters to dig in, where, when and who to ask for change, and also the good spots to sleep, like this one, which is better than the shelter when the rain don't get in. I've found a way to live almost for free, and every now and again I get some paying work if there's something I want like a new pair of shoes. I wash my clothes and shower at the beach, and check out books from the library because reading is the only way for a man to save his mind. Aside from Doc and Mary and the boys, books been my best friends. I've had great conversations with dead men in my head . . ."

Doc passed around the bottle of foul liquor and they drank until it was gone. The group unfolded their blankets and got ready for bed. James gave Jack a blanket for himself. It was a cold night and Jack didn't care that the blanket was filthy and that many people had slept with it. He used his jacket as a pillow.

James turned out the electric camp light.

"Good night, everyone. And try to have some pleasant dreams, would you. The one good thing about dreamin' is it's free."

Everyone said their goodnights and the camp fell quiet. James lay awake with his eyes open thinking how they were his family and that they depended on him. It was nice to feel needed and loved. In the dark he searched for Mary and put his arm around her and found her lips. Mary was a plain woman, a bit worn around the edges, but she had a good heart and he felt sorry for her. James needed someone to feel sorry for because he no longer felt sorry for himself. No, he despised himself for walking out on his wife and son, and destroying that stable domestic life. Comfort had presented itself too early in his life, and he had accepted it because it was the right thing to do. In his haste, James realized he had married a girl he didn't love and had a child before he could discover his own character. He had worked a job he hated and had little time for anything else.

The day he walked out, James had stared at himself in the bathroom mirror. He no longer recognized himself. He had become a man without opinion or passion: a man who had never taken any risks and always done what he was told. He couldn't stand it any more to look at himself and see that imposter. So he packed his bags and left.

I feel like I'm in a television commercial. I'm the perfect dad and the perfect husband, and that image is nothing but a fabrication and the suppression of my own desire and will. James was not alone in that sentiment. Everywhere in America marriages were splitting up. But few had chosen the drama of complete abandonment. Somehow they managed to share their children and maintain contact, strained and awkward as it may have been. James wondered what his son, Jesse, would say if they were to meet again, about how he was living and what he had done. He thought the boy would never forgive him. If I were him, I wouldn't forgive myself. I don't forgive myself. Jesse turned twelve in October, and James hadn't sent him a card or a present. He no longer had the right to any contact with his son because he had betrayed him. And though he may have loved Jesse, he would have left him again if given a second chance. Because he was not right with himself and therefore could never be right by others.

You were comfortable, once, James thought. Your life was perfect like a picture, at least from the outside; now look at you. Well, it's not so bad here, anyway. I mean you get used to it and stop missing all the useless crap they tell you to care about.

Like you told Jack, you know how to survive. You have a small bank account, you work some, give what you have to those that have it worse off, and share your company so that people don't feel so damned lonely. Is that a way of atoning for your guilt? No, you feel compassion for these people because you identify with them. They are lost like you, for different reasons, but they are lost all the same. When people are lost they find comfort in each other, and that's why we all stick together, I suppose. Because we can't take it out there alone anymore.

And what about Jack? He'll do all right for himself. The boy's got a lot of courage coming to stay with us like this. Boy, I really gave him a talking to. I really let him know what we're all about. I don't know why, but if anything he'll remember us, no matter what happens to him. Sure, I'm glad he came. It was a nice distraction. That's all you can hope for in life: that one day will bring something different from the next, hopefully not worse but better. Two steps forward and one step back, James thought. That's man's progress here on earth.

Jack couldn't sleep waiting for the day to come so he could make some money and improve his situation. It can't get worse than this, he thought. Remember, you're only here for one night. You may share humanity with these men and the woman, but you don't share their fate. You would much rather work than live like this. Well, forget it. These men are okay, and you're not in any danger. James is certainly a character. I wonder where he comes from and what sort of education he has? He's not like the rest. I wonder why he chooses to live like these men if he's not like them? Is that laziness or cowardice, or perhaps some sort of enlightenment? I don't know. All right Jack, get some sleep. You have to be at work by ten tomorrow for the lunch shift. He pushed the light on his watch. That gave a good eight hours if he fell asleep right then. Maybe you'll only sleep seven and half because you think too much.

Will waited until he thought everyone was asleep. Then he reached for Jack's bag and zipped it open. Jack was facing the other direction and didn't wake up. Will felt his way gingerly through the clothes and found the laptop. How much was that worth and how could he sell it? He searched for a wallet or some money. Then he felt one of Jack's hands close around his wrist, while the other slapped him in the face.

"What's going on? What are you doing in my stuff?"

James woke up and turned the flashlight on them.

"What's going on here?"

"He was getting into my bag," Jack said.

"I was just curious to see what he had in there. I thought he was hidin' somethin' from us. He don't belong with us, and I thought he might be hidin' a gun or some drugs or somethin'. Maybe he's hiding from the law, even. Or maybe he's got some food in there. I'm awful hungry. I ain't eaten since lunch."

James's voice came out flat.

"That's breakin' trust, Will. We may not have much, but we have our dignity, and I want to keep it that way. I've never seen you look in my pockets, and we don't look in yours, so I don't expect you to look in Jack's. Here we still believe in personal property and if people want to share, that's fine, but they're not obliged to. So what do you have to say for yourself?"

Will hung his head. He was young, younger than Jack, and perhaps the life was harder on him because he was new to it. Jack could see he was near to tears.

"I'm sorry, Jack. I was just hungry. I saw you with your big bag and I thought . . . Well, I didn't think and I'm sorry."

"That's fine, Will. I don't have anything in the bag anyway," Jack said.

"'Cept that nice computer."

"Yes, except that. Listen James, thanks for the hospitality, but I think I'm gonna go now. I don't wanna cause any more problems."

"Nonsense," James said. "Nonsense. If you try and sleep out there the police'll bother you. And besides it's raining. I figure you and your computer are safer with us."

Jack stayed and the rest of the night passed without incident. When he woke up in the morning everyone was gone except James, who was reading in the sun.

"Finally up, eh? Sleep well?"

"Well enough."

"Want a banana?"

"Sure. Say, thanks for letting me stay last night. It was raining pretty hard," Jack said.

"I would rather be homeless in Southern California," James said.

"Well, I gotta get going. Thanks again for everything."

"Sure, Jack. And don't be a stranger. Here's a piece of advice from an old man like me. If you ever have to choose between tryin' somethin' new or continuing what you've always done 'cause it's safe, try something new. Even if you fail, it's worth it."

"Uh, I guess so."

"Kid, you've got a lot to learn, but you'll learn it."

Jack felt bad leaving James. He felt that behind his talk James was a lonely man who didn't fit in with the others and probably hadn't fit into his past.

"Say James, if there's ever anything you need . . . I'm not doing well now, I mean I don't have any money, but if there is something I can help you with then . . ."

"No need to get sentimental, Jack. I can take care of myself. You don't need to feel obligated. I just offered you a place to sleep on some public ground. Anybody has a right to that."

"Right. Well, I'll see you later, James," Jack stuck out his hand and James shook it.

"Goodbye Jack, and good luck."

When Jack left, James found he couldn't read anymore. He wondered where Jack was headed and if he would get crushed by life, or if he would be like an ox and bear up under its weight. Jack was honest and polite and kind. He had been like that once; it had given him comfort but not meaning in his life. Perhaps he had thrown his old life away because it was mediocrity?

15

Once a night, in the Wild West Saloon, Jack had to participate in a showdown. A man in black would come into the bar, grab one of the waitresses, usually Candy, who liked the attention, and try to kiss her while she resisted his advances. At that moment Jack would have to drop whatever he was doing and challenge the bad cowboy. He would say, as he always said into the mike on his lapel, "You leave the pretty lady alone."

And the masked cowboy, who was really one of the other waiters in disguise, would reply, "Them's fightin' words," and put his hand on the gun on his hip.

Jack would then back away to the other side of the bar and ready himself for the draw.

"When I say draw, you draw, or you'll be dead, understood partner," the masked man would say.

At first it had been hard for Jack not to smile. But after getting blown away by each and every masked waiter time and time again when he was supposed to save the girl, he learned to take it more seriously. The first night he couldn't get his gun out of the holster before he felt the sting of the red paint that splattered on his vest. It was then his job to die by collapsing on the filthy sawdust covered floor, while the masked cowboy kissed his girl. You could never see if the masked cowboy really kissed the girl, because he dipped her so that their faces were covered by his hat. Some of the guys Candy kissed, but more than anything she wanted to kiss Jack.

After the first week, Candy approached him in the changing room. Jack noted her smooth, tanned behind peaking out from the bottom of her daisy dukes. Her shirt was tied at the waist and still wet from the wet t-shirt contest, and he could see her breasts. That Carlo's a pervert, Jack thought. Wet t-shirt contests and topless night and those half-naked girls in the colonial room. Carlo only hired good-looking women; he would hire them on the spot, but he never touched them for fear of his wife.

"A girl's liable to think you don't want to save her at all the way you shoot, Jack," Candy said. "Don'tcha know the girls like a straight shootin' man?"

When Candy said this, she leaned close so that her breasts brushed against his torso. She looked up at him, and Jack thought about how cowboys were meant to be tough and lonely.

"It's not that I don't want to save you, Candy. I just don't feel right about killing a man," he said.

"Oh Jack, you're silly. You talk like we're in the movies. All I can say is that when you learn to shoot you'll get a big reward."

Jack watched her walk away, hyperextending her back and pushing out her chest to keep his attention. The way she smacked her gum made him think of fraternity girls and how they were easy, and also of Elizabeth, who he was to meet after work on Friday. Candy sure was cute, but he didn't think he could talk to her; and if he couldn't talk to a woman, then he couldn't love her; and if he didn't love a woman, then he felt bad going with her for entertainment. The truth was when Jack liked a girl in particular, the others didn't matter. Even though so far he had nothing going with Elizabeth, he wanted to be faithful to her.

Jack had finally gotten paid and was back at the hostel practicing his draw in front of the mirror.

"Draw!" he would say to the reflection, jerking the gun from its holster. "Draw! Draw! Draw!" And he would keep this up until the action of grabbing for his gun was pure reflex.

Now when the masked rider came he was nervous, and Jack blew him away every time. Then he would grab Candy and give her a big kiss. He told himself it was only theatrics, and that the kiss didn't really matter, though Candy always used her tongue. Jack found that the regulars enjoyed this spectacle and would often buy him shots. They would also bet strangers at the bar so they could take their money.

In addition to the duel, Jack was expected to ride the mechanical bull, along with the other waiters. The first few times he had been thrown on his head. The trick here was that the waiters set the time to beat for the customers. Any customer who out-rode a waiter would get a free drink.

Carlo liked this spectacle very much; he would come to watch from the bar, and when someone was thrown, he would laugh. The novelty of people getting thrown from the bull never died for him. He always laughed in that manic, uncontrollable way of someone who had succeeded in bringing the absurd to reality.

Carlo had always been fascinated by the Wild West. As a child he had seen too many Westerns, and he had always wanted to grow up to be a cowboy. But now he was more than a cowboy; he had cowboys working for him, riding the bull and dueling. Next he planned on setting up a fake gunfight in the bar with stunt men. Carlo was certain there was more fun to be squeezed from life and he would find a way to do it. Because his childhood had been taken from him by poverty, he was determined to enjoy it now. To that end, he had installed a control behind the bar to speed up the bull and the violence of the bucking. The waiters all knew about it, but they had little to fear. It served to keep the customers from collecting free drinks. To keep from being sued Carlo padded the floor for a soft landing.

Being an undefeated gunslinger gave Jack some pride in his work. He liked the weight of the paint gun on his hip, though it was dangerous because there were times that he wanted to draw on the customers and blow them away. But he was a man of self-control, like any good cowboy, and had a reputation to keep.

Otherwise, Jack fell into the routine of bringing people their food, smiling, saying the right thing and laughing at their jokes. If customers were rude, he pretended not to notice. If he made a mistake, he apologized, though sometimes when a customer joked, "There goes your tip," Jack would reach instinctively for his six-shooter, and the joker would have a nervous laugh and not mention it again.

As a waiter, Jack learned a lot about people: he learned that men who talked big in front of women tipped small; that as a waiter it was his job to take crap from people that had had bad days, or did not like their life or their spouse or girlfriend; that being over-polite didn't necessarily increase his tip; and that when he was blunt and serious, the customers didn't take liberties. Finally, he learned not to apologize for things that weren't his fault, such as food being late because Martino was holding plates or letting food burn to make him look bad. Thank God I'm not a cook, Jack thought. Waiting tables can be busy but it's not as hard as being busy in the kitchen and having the waiters constantly placing orders. Jack had learned to not push the kitchen because the cooks were in control and could make his life hell.

Waiting was different for men and women. Candy made her money by flirting with drunk men and sticking her tits in their face. She had been doing it that way ever since puberty, learning early that showing off her body or lying on her back was often the only way for a pretty girl to get ahead in life.

Like any attractive young woman, Candy liked attractive young men, and she had an eye for Jack. When he kissed her the first time as her cowboy savior, she stuck her tongue in his mouth, rolled it around and clung to him. He remembered her whispering in his ear, "You'll always be my cowboy, Jack."

Candy reminded Jack of the sorority girls, and he didn't think it would be too difficult to get her into bed. If that was true, he thought best to just leave off it, because he didn't respect her. She had a high-pitched voice, and he wasn't much for redheads. I bet she's never climbed a bridge or jumped off a cliff into the ocean or roughed it for a week in the mountains. Just look at her nails and that tattoo on her ankle. Isn't that original? Both it being on her ankle and the fact it's a dolphin. He felt sincerely that dolphins were played out, both as tattoo and as a favorite animal. What about a sloth or a kiwi bird, he thought. If I ever get a chance to see an exotic animal, please, let it be a sloth.

That night Jack had a date with Elizabeth. He was to meet her at a club called Brando's in the Mission. Aqueduct Lover was playing. According to Elizabeth, they were a big time jazz band from New York. Jack didn't know much about jazz but he thought he liked it; though when he heard it, it made his stomach knot up with concentration. No, he was more into good old rock and roll, preferably from the sixties. It was his misfortune that he wasn't born in the sixties: that generation of free love and civil protest. No one protests anything anymore, he thought. Unless you dent their car or they fall down and hurt themselves on your property. Then they sue you. That was something Jack didn't understand. Like the burglar that sued for being shot and paralyzed while breaking into someone's house.

The last customers left, and Jack went back to the lockers to change. The men's and women's locker rooms were separate and each had its own showers and toilets. Jack showered, put on a collared shirt, a pair of jeans and some sneakers. He smoothed his hair in the mirror with some gel and shaved off his cowboy stubble. He had two days off and not soon enough.

Jack was satisfied with the money he was making. Still, waiting was hard work. He wanted to do a good job and he tried his best to be polite. When the customers asked for something he told them, "Sure, right away, sir," and brought it immediately. Sometimes the customers were demanding; they wanted their food cooked in a special way or served with a special side. He always told them they could have it, and for that Martino, the cook, had grown to hate him.

"If it's not on the menu, I don't serve it, *entiendes*? These *Americanos* always want things a special way. If they want it like that they can stay at home. This is a restaurant."

"I know, Martino. Yes, Martino. You're right, Martino. Please, Martino, and it won't happen again, Martino."

Jack was still learning how to be firm with the customers. When he was very polite and got a bad tip, it made him angry. There's no need to get angry. Some people don't know how to tip and some are cheap. Even with customers like that, you make between a hundred and a hundred and fifty a night. That's not bad. A few weeks more of this and you can start looking for a place of your own and get out of that hostel. Then you won't have to listen to Maria's man break shit downstairs or deal with their shouting matches.

Carlo sat in his office in front of the video monitors. He had installed cameras in every room, including the locker rooms. Every day, before and after work, he sat down to watch and record the women changing.

"*Mamma mia*, look at those beautiful *tette*. How I would love to sweep her. Red on the head and fire in the bed. That's my kind'a *ragazza*."

His wife, Grace, didn't know about the locker room cameras or the tapes stored by month in the basement. Carlo never thought about what she would do if she found those tapes. He knew well enough that it would mean the end of their marriage and his business. Grace was a jealous woman. When she came to the restaurant she ordered the waitresses around, faulted them on the smallest details of their work and made them so nervous that they dropped silverware, broke dishes, spilled wine and took wrong orders. Once when she suspected Carlo of an affair with a certain girl, she threatened to cut her up and tear her eyes from her skull.

Carlo watched tapes of Candy showering and rubbing soap on her body, and also the other girls: Jenny, Kate, Natalie, Jane, Melissa, Carrie, etc. Some he knew just by their naked bodies and not their names. They were all beautiful: some dark and some blonde; some with large breasts and wide hips; others very thin like runway models. Carlo thought: why don't I sell the videos and make some extra money? *Ma*, these girls are like any I see in the magazines, but the magazines, they are boring. You see a picture once and it does not excite anymore. But to watch these girls and see how they act when the men are not around, this is always fresh and new. Who would have thought that from Calabria I would end here? I didn't even own two pairs of shoes when I was a boy in Calabria. Back then I could play music on my ribs!

Carlo watched Candy leave the women's locker room and go into the men's. She leaned up against the mirror where the new kid Jack was brushing his teeth. She touched Jack's arm so that he looked at her. Let's turn on the speaker, Carlo thought.

"So Jack, you wanna come with me and get a drink? Or maybe we could go back to my place and just relax?"

Jack studied her. Aggressive women made him nervous. They were experienced, which meant he had to be better than the competition; he didn't think he was up to the challenge. Sure, men will tell you they love a nymphomaniac, he thought, but a girl like that will eat a man alive because she can't get enough. No, a nymphomaniac is not what one wants. But maybe she's a good girl? Ha, ha, Jack. Ha, ha.

Candy liked sex, and since she could get it any time she wanted, she overindulged. She would have it for breakfast or lunch or dinner in any setting that suited her. But she also had her standards and wouldn't fuck fat, bald or old men. Fuck friends were her favorite kind and for that reason she was quite popular. Still, she could hook up with old friends any time. Jack was fresh meat, and she didn't like to be denied.

Jack looks like a good lay. Look at that athletic body. And he's so polite and shy. I bet I could do things that would make him blush to the roots of his hair.

"You know, Candy, you seem like a great girl and, gosh, thanks for the offer, but I've already got a date tonight."

"That's fine," she said, running her fingers through her wet hair. "Listen, before you leave could you do me a favor?"

"What's that?"

"Couldn't we just have a quickie, right now?"

"Are you kidding," Carlo said, spitting his wine on the monitor and jumping from his seat. "This is too much." He paced the office, refilled his wine glass and sat down to wait for the big play: the winning goal, so to speak. He nibbled his fingers and sat forward tense with his head in his hands and elbows on his knees.

"I suppose we could," Jack said. "But then how would it be the next time we work? How would it be when I have my duel and come to kiss you?"

"It'll be like always, Jack. I promise. I'm not high-maintenance. I'm not talking love here. This is lust. Lust, lust, lust. I have needs and I want some satisfaction."

"I can't," he told her. "I want to, really, but I've got a date tonight. What would she think if she knew I wasn't sincere?"

"And you think she's sincere? Come on, Jack, just a quickie any way you want, cowboy," she said.

Smiling, Candy stepped closer and grabbed his crotch. "You want me on all fours? You want to do it in the shower? Up against the locker?"

Jack pushed her hand away.

"Is sex all anyone ever thinks about?"

"That and cheesecake," Candy said. "I think an awful lot about cheesecake."

You know it is, he told himself. It's all you think about, anyway. It's your reason for getting up in the morning; it's why you're meeting Elizabeth, because you want to get into her pants and she hasn't invited you. No, this is too easy, he thought. You have to have some standards. Also, you don't know where she's been. You can't just have unprotected sex right here. You don't want it to burn when you pee, do you?

"There's no need to get serious, Jack. You've got your serious face like when you're working or waiting for the draw. If you don't want to have a little fun, no strings attached, fine. Maybe another time." Candy made her hand into a gun, pointed it at Jack and fired with her thumb. "See you later, shooter."

Damn Jack, why are you such a prude? What was that all about? How could you pass that up? Just what are you trying to prove, anyway? Boy, I'm glad I wasn't drinking, he thought. Then it would have been game over. I have no self-control when I'm drunk. I wonder, will I become a drunk like that other waiter, Nick? Nick, he's the typical artist, drinking and waiting tables and playing his music. At least he's got his music. What do I have? A rabid desire to make money and be slave to no one? Man, some people would kill to go with a girl like Candy. You idiot. You and your morals. It's not like you haven't treated girls like fuck cushions before. But down deep you're a romantic. You need a girl that'll stick by your side and take care of you, because you can't handle that responsibility alone.

16

Jack spied the marquee from across the street. It was like an old photograph: Brando's, written in those tall, block letters in a font from a time when San Francisco was a different place. The building itself was outdated and classic. Perhaps at one time it had been a diner or a steakhouse.

Jack heard the music as he approached: the whine, chirp and squeal of the saxophone; the ominous thunk thunk of the bass; and a cascading rain of drums. Yes, that music caught his attention and made him curious. The bouncer, a large black man named Lawrence, opened the door and let him inside. Jack thought the man exuded a thorough, satiated cool. Though not a musician himself, Lawrence was a lover of jazz who had taken the job to be close to the music. He had great respect for the musicians and took his work seriously.

"If you're here for the show you have to get a ticket at the window. It's a ten dollar cover," Lawrence said in his baritone.

"Who's the band," Jack asked.

"Aqueduct Lover. They're outta New York. I would call it jazzy, experimental funk. They play here a couple times a year. Ten bucks is a bargain for these cats. You can go to a club and pay twenty to hear someone spin records, but this here, my man," Lawrence said, leaning closer, "this is the real experience."

Jack bought his ticket, and Lawrence let him in with what Jack thought to be a conspiratorial, speakeasy smile.

Inside there was a long bar with red leather stools screwed to the floor. Asian lanterns hung from the ceiling and a large retro smoked glass mirror with inlaid gold stars ran the length of the room on both walls. In the back was a large electric blue aquarium above black leather booths where couples and friends sat drinking and talking. Through an archway to the left of this alcove was the restaurant, which was closed for the evening. To the right was another room with its own bar where the band was playing. Again, Jack noticed the crowd wore mostly black. There were no jeans or baseball caps, though some women had those tight stretch tops that left the belly exposed like he remembered from home. The women here were refined, or so Jack thought, having come from the sticks in Arizona. He hadn't traveled enough to know the relativity of such opinions. He found the bartenders and the waitresses intimidating: the waitresses were all beautiful and made-up; the bartenders had hip haircuts, were clean-shaven and moved like machines, taking money and mixing drinks. Jack wondered how much they made; though they looked successful, they were probably just getting by.

I have to get some nice clothes, Jack thought, catching a glimpse of himself in the mirror. Once again he felt underdressed and out of place. I can't believe no one wears jeans around here. I love jeans, especially this pair that is worn and feels like a second skin.

Elizabeth was not at the bar or in a booth. Next door, Jack could hear the band performing. Another bouncer, wearing a dark suit like Lawrence, stood in the doorway. Jack showed him his generic ticket, the kind one got at a county fair for the merry-go-round, and the man took it, turned Jack's hand palm up and stamped "VOID" on his wrist.

The adjacent room was small and crowded. The music was loud and smoke hung thick in the air. To Jack, this smoke signaled the interdependence that typified city life. There it was, everyone's life-giving breath mingled together like their dreams, visible yet devoid of substance and structure. Jack felt the heat of many bodies together and was overwhelmed by the concentrated odor of perfume, aftershave, deodorant, hair product and sweat. He watched the smiling, animated faces of the crowd as they socialized and noted the serious men and women that sat in the half-arch counter that rimmed the pit where the band played. The band was so close that Jack could reach out and touch them: their instruments and faces and careful fingers that knew music like other hands connected to minds didn't.

Jack shut his eyes briefly and drifted with the melody. The saxophone spoke of suffering and confusion; it twisted in on itself, contradicted itself and fought to be free of its limitations. Jack opened his eyes and stared at the sax player. He noted the veins bulging in his neck and his light black skin slick with sweat. The man had a reptilian quality about him, and though he was thin and emaciated, Jack could not help but appreciate his singular beauty. He's not afraid to stand in front of all these people and put his passion into that instrument for us to judge. I have judged it to the point of savoring and needing it, and I've only been here a few minutes.

Elizabeth was at the bar talking to a ridiculous-looking man with the curliest strawberry blond hair Jack had ever seen. She wore a purple and red patterned, black silk top that looped over her shoulders and was tied behind her neck. She wore no bra, and Jack thought how easy it would be to file his hands under her garment from behind and hold her breasts.

"Hey Elizabeth."

"Jack, hi, I'm glad you could make it. This is my friend Arnold."

"Jack. Nice to meet you."

Arnold smiled and offered his hand. Jack took it, transfixed by the hideous teeth in Arnold's mouth: those animal-like teeth that stuck out at every angle from thick exposed gums. Those can't be real, Jack thought. Arnold was a large man with the face of a boy. He wore black horn rim glasses and his hair was perfectly permed. In his pinstriped suit he looked hugely successful. Jack liked him immediately and thought: how unfortunate about the teeth.

"Arnold is an old friend of mine," Elizabeth said.

"Oh, where did you two first meet?"

"In a bar. You see Arnold and I are both hopeless drunks and flirts. He's one of the few people that can make me laugh at will."

"Hey Jack, do you wanna see my necklace? You're gonna love this. I mean this thing is custom and I don't mean custom, but custom, like people have died to make this necklace," Arnold said.

Elizabeth watched Jack and tried to keep a straight face.

"Sure, let's see what you're talking about," Jack said.

Arnold reached under his collar and pulled out a necklace made out of what looked like chicken bones. In some places Jack thought he saw bits of dried meat, but the light was bad and it was probably just his imagination.

"Isn't that cool," Arnold said with his hideous smile.

Jack didn't know what to say. It was ridiculous. He looked to Elizabeth, but she gave no reaction.

"I guess so. So where did you get it?"

I need a drink, Jack thought. I can't figure this guy out. They're drunk and I'm not: that's the barrier.

"They feel so real," Elizabeth said, handling the necklace.

"Because they are," Arnold said, his expression serious.

"So what are they, chicken bones," Jack asked, but the music drowned out his voice. "Are they chicken bones," he shouted.

Arnold looked at him. "I got them in New Guinea. In New Guinea they still practice cannibalism. I bought them off some shaman in the jungle. These bones, they're human fingers," he shouted back.

A girl next to them at the bar turned to see the source of the commotion, and Arnold flashed his hideous smile and lifted his drink. She cringed and turned away.

"Look closer and you'll see the knuckles. Those came from real people. Isn't that crazy," Arnold shouted.

Jack noted the way the human fingers flared on Arnold's double-breasted blazer.

"And the best part is they only cost me five bucks. Or the equivalent of five bucks in their currency, the *kina*. I strung them myself," Arnold said proudly.

Jack wondered how they got the fingers but he thought it impolite to ask. Did they cut them off a living man, or a half-eaten corpse? Then he thought: well, sure it's a sin to eat people, but it must be a good source of protein. At least I've never heard anyone say that people taste like chicken. It seems every sort of exotic meat tastes like chicken. Frog tastes like chicken and snake and alligator, too. They say human flesh is more salty, like jerky. I wonder if cannibals dry and salt their meat? They must because otherwise it wouldn't keep.

He believes this is my real hair, Arnold thought. Jack's a nice guy but he's kind of gullible. And these teeth, they're ridiculous. How could anyone have teeth like this? Still, it's all about making a strong first impression. I've picked up women with these teeth. It's because they feel sorry for me. The teeth, the glasses, God, I've got to lose some weight. But it doesn't make any difference; the girls don't care, they just want to laugh. People are too serious as it is, Arnold thought.

"You should see his shrunken head collection," Elizabeth said. "Once he invited me over for dinner and I had to eat looking at those tiny heads floating in pickle jars."

"That's when I knew she was keeper," Arnold said.

"Of course I'm a keeper."

"How about a drink, Jack," Arnold asked him. I'm not going to take off this wig or remove these teeth all night, he thought. I can't wait to see Jack's face the next time we meet.

"Yeah, okay, how about a gin and tonic?"

"Good man," Arnold said, turning to the bar to order. He pulled out a money clip of hundreds, Jack saw, and peeled off a bill. There was another hundred underneath and Jack thought: he's not like some people and their money clips with a hundred wrapped around a fat wad of ones. No, at least he's a two deep guy.

"So how's the restaurant, Jack," Elizabeth asked.

"Well, it's good to have work, and I've gotten pretty good with my six-shooter," he said.

"Your six-shooter?"

"Yeah, every night the bad cowboy comes in and I have to blow him away in a duel. At first he would kill me every time. Nick, this other waiter, usually plays the bad guy. He's had a lot of practice. But it's not good for the bad guy to win. No one wants to see a movie like that."

"No, it's too much like real life," Elizabeth said.

"Not when I'm working, because I'm fast now," Jack said. "Sometimes I wish I could step back in time and take on a real gunslinger."

"It would be easier just to shoot him in the back while he's having a drink at the bar," Arnold said.

"Yeah, sure, but there's no honor in that. A man is his honor; if a man can die honorably instead of living dishonorably, then that's exactly what he should do."

Elizabeth liked the way Jack got flustered when he spoke about honor. He was a nice guy; if that was all, then she wasn't interested, but she liked how he talked sometimes. Imagine, he examined Arnold's human finger necklace without comment. Certainly, that's a sign of potential. Also, he's making a real effort to ignore the teeth. He should see Arnold in women's lingerie, like for Halloween when he had to order away for it from HuskyLadies.com. Arnold is the perfect barometer for a new love interest. If Arnold likes Jack and doesn't scare him off, then he passes the test.

"Well, I wish I could say I miss my job. But I don't mind getting paid for going out and drinking. I've got four weeks severance left before I have to find something new," Elizabeth said.

Arnold handed Jack his drink.

"Cheers," Jack said.

"*Salud, Choc-tee, Kanpai, L'chaim,*" Arnold said, repeating the cheers he had learned drinking around the world.

They walked over and pushed their way closer to the band. Jack watched the bassist's heavily callused fingers pull on the thick metal strings of his instrument. The man's index and pointer fingers were much larger than the others, swollen like an extraterrestrial hand. Jack marveled at just how black the man was, so that he was almost blue in the dim room. The drummer had his eyes closed, his insect arms twitching as he paced the music. He crossed his arms in and out, tapped metallic rain from the cymbals and clamped them silent with his crab claw hands. The sax player whined, wailed, bleated and groaned; he recorded loops from a sampler at his feet and played them back adding layers until everyone sunk into themselves and each other. Jack felt the gurgle of the ice in his drink as he sucked it dry and wanted another.

Twenty minutes later the band stopped playing, and the sax player took the microphone. "We're Aqueduct Lover and that last song was called *Justice is a Piss-Stained Mattress*. Before that you heard *Headless*

Horseman's Truth, and *Labyrinth to My Soul*. We'd like to thank you for coming to see us," he said in his soft, shy voice.

Aqueduct Lover had received favorable reviews in New York, Chicago and San Francisco, but the group still had no label and sold their CDs personally at their shows. The saxophonist, Errol Stone, had a gift and he devoted himself to it completely. Still, he didn't know if anyone understood his message, and it was that understanding that mattered to him. People have to hear our music to understand, he thought. It's not about the money. The money's nice and I can use it, but I won't sell anything I don't believe in. Music is about believing in yourself, trusting yourself to innovate and not being afraid to go where you haven't gone before inside your mind. Yeah, right there. When he was high everything made sense.

The songs they played that night were not like the recordings. The seven and half minute *Justice is a Piss-Stained Mattress* became a twenty-minute piece of intimate history between Aqueduct Lover and the Brando's crowd. The improvisation came and went in those twenty minutes never to be heard again. That was what music was all about. The tracks off a studio recorded disc would always be the same, which was nothing compared to what they could create in front of a live audience. Errol was petrified of crowds; only his saxophone and the music he made with it protected him from their judgments and prying eyes. He was protected because they didn't understand his power to make the instrument talk.

Jack watched the men and women who sat listening to the band, drinks in hand with eyes closed, looking down at the table or enraptured by some quality of the musicians' faces and movements. These men and women of all colors, shapes and ages exhibited a respectful silence not unlike that of a church or a classroom during an exam. It was a mixture of reverence and concentration.

"So how do like the city so far, Jack? Elizabeth tells me you just got here from, where was it, Arizona?"

The waitress came by with her tray and Jack stopped her. He looked to Arnold and saw that he was also nearly finished with his drink.

"Two more gin and tonics. What do you want Elizabeth?"

"Vodka cranberry," she said.

The waitress nodded and negotiated the crowd to the bar.

"I like the city just fine," Jack said. "I just found a job at a restaurant and I'm looking for a room."

"I might know of a room," Arnold said. "I'll call some people and let you know. Don't let me forget to give you my number before we leave."

Jack nodded.

"So what do you do, Arnold?"

"I'm a system administrator. I keep track of information," he said.

The drinks came and Jack paid. He left the girl a good tip. I only tip well now because I survive on tips myself. If I could track money, say, from the pocket of a customer at Amerika, to my pocket, to this girl's pocket, to the coffee shop where she will spend it in the morning, and so on, I wonder how far it would travel? Would it just circulate in the city? I wonder how long it would take that money to cross the state line?

Jack pushed his lime to the bottom of the glass with his straw where it let off a cloud of juice. He stirred it around and sipped his drink. Money is strange, he thought, some people hoard it, and with others it's easy come, easy go. When I have cash in my pocket I feel like spending it. It seems like a lot of money: a hundred and thirty dollars for six hours work. Still, five days a week for fifty-two weeks, that's under thirty thousand a year. What do people do who make, say, twice that? That's a lot of money. I wonder what Arnold makes?

Jack couldn't think of anything to say to Elizabeth. He felt outclassed by her, the club where drinks cost eight bucks a pop, and finally by Arnold in his designer suit, money clip and fancy job.

If a girl judges you on your money, she's no good, Jack thought. Elizabeth doesn't seem that way. Also, she's unemployed and wanting to climb a mountain or go spelunking. No, she's not your ordinary girl. And you won't be a waiter forever. No, one day you'll have a job of importance and people will listen to you. Remember how it was without a job and sleeping with those bums in the park?

"So, Jack, have you ever been to Burning Town? That's out there in the desert."

"Yeah, I went once two years ago. I help build a desert oasis. Also, I wore this alien head around. It was hot but luckily we had put tiny fans inside to keep from suffocating. Here look at this." Jack reached into his wallet and passed Arnold a picture. In it, five people with enormous oversized green heads with large frog-like eyes, small holes for noses, and antennae stood side by side in the desert.

"I'm one over from the left," Jack said.

"I see," Arnold replied.

"You guys look like the Area 51 gang that our government keeps captive out in that warehouse in the desert," Elizabeth added.

"Well, it's interesting you should mention it because there were five of us in costume, and then this other guy shows up and starts hanging out with us. He looked a little different and he didn't talk much. We never saw him take his head off, and when it was time for pictures, he disappeared."

"I'm working on a little project myself," Arnold said. "I'm gonna make a tree out of female busts. Right now I have almost fifty. I hope to be finished by the next festival."

"So, did you like Burning Town," Elizabeth asked.

"Yeah, I liked it," Jack said. "I liked the people running around naked in silver body paint and the art car shaped like a giant head with the brain exposed and the eyes that moved from side to side glowing red; the palm trees of the oasis and the antique chaise-lounges we set up; the water hole we dug and lined with plastic and filled from a water truck, and the pagan baptism that took place there; the runway platform raised ten feet off the ground and winding on itself like a serpentine Paris fashion show; and the lasers that reflected off prisms and colored glass and mirrors on the flat of the desert at night to make giant patterns. I liked how people came and created things in the desert and helped each other and took charge of their reality. I liked not thinking about money while I was there. What I disliked were the drunks, crazies, false prophets and anarchists, and all those people that refuge themselves in illusions and who do not contribute or have any solidarity with others and are only concerned with their own pleasure and excesses. Once is fine and an experience, but I wouldn't go back."

"You're right about that, Jack. There are too many things to do to repeat yourself. I've traveled a lot of places, and some I enjoyed, but most I wouldn't go back to because they've lost their novelty," Arnold said.

"Well, I think it's a sign of the times," Elizabeth said. "Our generation is plagued with boredom. We're searching for originality in a world where nearly everything has been explored, discovered and used up. Family no longer seems to matter. We don't believe in marriage anymore, and no one wants to have children because it will limit their mobility and freedom. When we get a new job, we're already thinking about finding a better one without putting in the work, or we work for a year or two, quit, and travel to another country or move to another city. What's the point of going somewhere where you're just a stranger? I tell you, we're a culture of loneliness, of social cripples and opportunists, easy in-easy out with no stake in anything. How can we expect to have a meaningful experience when we're disconnected from the places we visit and the people we meet?"

Elizabeth thought to herself: everything I say is true. Yet I plan to leave and run away from myself and my routine: the bill paying, the small irritations of communal living and the repetitive bar scene.

The problem is you've lost your initiative to try anything new in the city. How long has it been since you've gone to the theater or an exhibit? No, you've become complacent. You don't particularly care what new band is playing or about anyone's gallery opening; you are thoroughly infected with the malaise of urban living: the apathy, lack of solidarity and desire for pleasure and escape. You are arrogant like all Californians, and living in San Francisco has made you especially so. The irony of it is that we think this is the center of the world and that life can't get any better. All you have to do is look at the weather, the substandard clubs, the idiotic fads, mediocre art, and our false claims of individuality, in spite of status quo homogeneity and politically correct posturing, to know that it's a farce and an illusion. That is the contradiction of the city: everyone lives in the same way; therefore we need to pretend a great difference from everyone else. Thank God for Arnold who is genuine and doesn't care about convention or appearances, except to abuse them. He manages to find the meaning somewhere.

"If I were a good shot," Arnold said, "then I could kill everyone crowding the bar with one clip of my assault rifle. That's pretty efficient. And it's not a moral question at all. If my well-being were threatened, I could kill just like anyone else. Morality plays no part in survival. And right now survival is being able to get another drink without having to wait twenty minutes at the bar."

"Don't listen to him, Jack. He's just showing off," Elizabeth said.

"For what it's worth, I don't think life's any different than prehistoric times," Arnold said. "It's just that we've reached a level of comfort where ordinary people have the leisure to follow their own dreams. I think that's a good thing. I mean what's so important about family anyway? Why not just do away with marriage? We still have sex, which is motivation enough to keep up appearances. Sex is probably one of the few things that allows people to move freely through prejudice and class barriers. As soon as someone is good-looking, it doesn't matter if they are poor, black, white or purple."

"Still, most beautiful girls have to struggle to achieve something in their lives beyond the status of eye candy," Elizabeth said. "Some are fine with that, but for others beauty can be a limitation to being treated with respect and taken seriously."

To Jack there was no point in discussing it. Beauty was what it was. He thought Elizabeth was beautiful, and also the waitress and the brown-haired girl to his left. He was glad for that beauty and would never date an ugly woman. Then Jack remembered Arnold's horrible teeth and felt embarrassed by the conversation. How about ugly people; if it's a limitation to be beautiful, then how about being ugly, that is, repulsive? While for women it was either a sentence to poverty or personal achievement, for men it fostered a drive for power. More often than not, powerful men were homely and nondescript like the average Joe on the street. Without power, they were the kind of men whose names you couldn't and didn't care to remember.

"You want to know about beauty, watch this," Arnold said. "A good-looking guy could never pull this off. Because he's too arrogant and concerned with being cool. But damn, me with these teeth and being overweight, I got nothing to lose."

Jack still hadn't picked up on the joke; like anyone meeting Arnold for the first time, he was off-balance between pity and amusement.

Arnold walked over to the pretty brown-haired girl to Jack's left, pulled a lollypop from his pocket and handed it to her.

"Hi, I'm Arnold. I give lollypops to all the pretty girls."

The girl hesitated to take his gift. When she saw his crooked-toothed smile and his curly woman's hair and glasses, pity took the upper hand. Looking at the red lollypop, she thought: that's so sweet, took it and thanked him. She had noticed him earlier and tried not to stare, though he was the most curious-looking person in the whole bar.

"So what's your name?"

"I'm Christy," she said.

"Christy, I know you don't know me, but I have a proposition to make. Call it a favor. You see I'm an artist, and when I saw you I thought: she's just perfect for my special project."

"What sort of project is that," Christy asked.

"I cast women in plaster. No, there's nothing sordid in it. All the girls that have done it, adventurous girls that they are, confident beautiful girls all forty-six of them, some of them twice, they all say it's a transcendental experience. They feel somehow rejuvenated by it."

He could be a psychopath, Christy thought. He could be, but busts? Me cast in plaster permanently? That is unusual.

"So forty-six women have done this with you?"

"Yes."

"And how's it going to be exactly?"

"Well, I work out of my garage in the Marina. It's a fairly quick process. You take off your clothes, I mold the plaster to your body, we wait until it dries and voila: you've become a work of art. I plan to exhibit in some galleries in the city when I get finished. I'm going to build a tree from the busts at Burning Town next year in homage to female beauty. But I still have another fifty or so to go. I'm set on having a big tree with many branches."

Christy's skepticism was familiar. For this reason, Arnold never asked the girls for their number but always gave them his own. Sooner or later, boredom or relationship difficulties would bring them to call and ask in that hesitant voice, "Remember me, I'm so and so. We talked in the bar. You said you wanted to do a bust?" "Yes, of course, whenever you want. You decide the day and time." And all would be settled. In the end, Arnold was surprised at how many of the girls called.

Sensing her indecision, Arnold said, "Here, I'll give you my number. If you're interested, gimme a call. Do you see that girl over there," he said, pointing to Elizabeth. "She's a good friend of mine and she's done a bust with me."

Elizabeth figured they were talking about her, so she waved and smiled from where she stood with Jack by the wall.

"She's pretty. Do you only do pretty girls?"

"No, I don't discriminate. I do all kinds of women. It's especially important they have unique bodies. You, for example, are very thin. The last girl I did was overweight. All women are beautiful to me," Arnold said, lowering his eyes in feigned modesty. But there was nothing modest about him; he was shameless.

"All I ask is that you give it some consideration and call me if you're interested," he said. "It was nice meeting you."

Arnold walked back to his friends and caught Jack's stare.

"It's the teeth, Jack, they feel sorry for me. You see, you're too good-looking; the girls are intimidated by you. You have to make an extra effort to put them at ease. With me they always feel at ease."

Arnold checked his watch.

"Say, these guys will be done with their set in another hour or so. I've got a friend who's having a party. Why don't we go? Jack, you could stand to meet a few more people. Without connections you can't get ahead in the city. I'm sure you don't want to be a waiter forever."

The comment didn't seem ill-intended and Jack chose to ignore it.

"I don't know. Elizabeth, what do you want to do," Jack asked.

"It's either that or go dancing," she said.

"We'll do both," Arnold said, knocking back his drink and putting his arms around them. "Come on." He marched them out the door and down the block to his SUV, which was parked perpendicular on the sidewalk so that pedestrians were forced to squeeze by the bumper or walk in the street to get by.

"Parking is such a bitch in this city," he said. "You've gotta be creative."

"That's creative parking, all right. I'm surprised you didn't get a ticket," Elizabeth said.

They got in the car. Jack sat in the back and Elizabeth went shotgun.

"Who needs a drink? Jack, would you be so kind as to reach into the cooler in the back and make us a drink? I've got vodka, gin, rum, coke, orange juice, cranberry and tonic. What do you want, Lizzy?"

"I'll stay with the vodka cranberry," she said. "It's better if I don't mix. I might do something I regret."

"That would be a shame," Arnold said, patting her knee. "A Screwdriver for me, Jack. You'll find glasses and a shaker next to the cooler. You guys like circus music? I love circus music."

Arnold turned on the stereo. Hearing the circus organ, Jack thought: this is ridiculous. Who knows how many Arnold's had, but for some strange reason I feel safe, and if it's time to die, so be it. Such reasoning was typical of his twenty-four years. Twenty-four years without any great tragedy. Arnold seemed confident and, without reason, Jack trusted his judgment.

The intensity of the circus organ built, and Jack could imagine the point in which the man was shot from the cannon and how he would hold his hands wide like a bird, do a flip and bounce into the netting. All that was missing now was for Arnold to put on a red rubber nose and large, squeaky shoes.

Arnold drove off the curb and pulled a U-turn over the median. He weaved through traffic, alternatively flooring it and slamming on the brakes, while Jack tried to mix the drinks from Arnold's mobile bar.

"Aren't you worried about open containers," Jack asked.

"You know what, Jack, the way I figure it I can drink up before they get to the car. I expect you guys to do the same."

For Jack, it was a novel experience. Before he had gone everywhere in the city on foot or by bus or cab. Now he was in a private car and didn't have to sit with strangers. Still, he wanted to be alone with Elizabeth, and Arnold had stolen his thunder with the promise of a party. Now Jack felt like he was just tagging along. Perhaps at the party he and Elizabeth could find a place to be alone together?

17

At that hour, shortly after one, Market Street was relatively empty except for the odd tram to the Castro and the late buses leaving downtown. As they drove, Jack stared at the streetlights, the illuminated buildings and the store marquees. He saw the dark figures stooped in the covered entryways of the shops with their shopping carts and ratty blankets, and the men lined up in their sleeping bags by the dead dry fountain of the Civic Center.

They turned up Powell and the engine roared as they climbed the hill. Arnold made several more turns as they climbed higher and higher. Jack sipped his gin and tonic and contemplated the city below through the back window. Eventually, the road leveled out and they came to a dead end by an art deco apartment block with a large glass entryway and a bright chandelier that glowed warm in the night.

"You guys get out and I'll find a place to park. Just go on in and I'll meet you," Arnold said.

"But we don't know anyone here," Elizabeth said.

"Sure you do. Damian and Alex are gonna be there. The party's for my friend Sarah; she's on the eighth floor. Just say you're friends of mine."

They got out and Arnold drove off. There wasn't any parking for many blocks. Arnold would have to walk, and who knew when he would be back. Jack had never felt comfortable going where he was not invited, but now that he was alone with Elizabeth, he didn't want to seem awkward or nervous.

"Looks like a nice place," Jack said. "I'm afraid I'm a little underdressed."

"Oh, don't worry about it," Elizabeth said. "You're just being yourself." She leaned close and held onto his arm. "It's so cold out here."

"Yeah, there's no protection from the wind," he said.

"Let's go inside," she said.

Another couple was standing at the door, and when it buzzed open, they followed them in. The strangers were dressed like they were going to a formal. They got into the elevator. The women held the men around the arm, and the men looked at the wall. The doors shut, and the man and Elizabeth reached to push the same button.

"Are you going to Sarah's," the man asked.

"Yes, we are."

"Friends from school?"

"No. Friends of friends," Elizabeth said, smiling politely.

Elizabeth and Jack were younger and more attractive than the strangers, who appeared better off financially.

"Well, we're very proud of her for having passed the bar," the woman said. "She's going right into her parents' firm."

"Yes, that's quite an achievement," Elizabeth said.

Where does Arnold meet these people? They're like cardboard cut-outs. Why, these two are almost my parents' age. I hope that Damian's there. He should be good for a few laughs, especially if he's been drinking. Not to mention Alex; he always has something interesting to say. He's not afraid to cut the bullshit, which is admirable in this day and age.

The elevator opened and everyone got out. The man knocked on the door of the apartment, and they all stood there silent and awkward like before. To everyone's relief, they didn't have to wait long before an attractive Asian girl in a black evening dress answered the door.

"Sarah, congratulations," the man said, handing her a gift.

"Oh thanks, Bill, you shouldn't have. Hello, Keri." The young woman hugged them both in a quick and superficial way. "Dad's in the kitchen mixing drinks. Here, let me take your coats."

Jack blushed with embarrassment and fought the urge to run. Here we are total strangers with no gift and I'm wearing jeans at a cocktail party. I wouldn't be surprised if she threw us out. This sure is a fancy place. Did you see those marble floors, the wood paneling in the elevator and the polished brass handles? And would you look at this apartment: hardwood floors and glass cabinets full of fine china, not to mention those sculptures and paintings. Everything here seems like an antique.

Sarah looked at Jack and Elizabeth standing in the doorway. She smiled in a friendly way and waited for them to speak. She was their age and, in spite of her gold jewelry, did not seem pretentious. They noted that her face was flushed, either from the heat or liquor, they could not be sure.

"Hello, we're friends of Arnold. You must be Sarah. He's told me a lot about you. I'm Elizabeth and this is Jack."

"Arnold, really, is he coming," Sarah asked. "I was starting to wonder if he'd make it. Some of Arnold's other friends are here already. I'm glad at least some people my age showed up. Mom and dad invited all their friends and all they do is talk about work."

As she talked Sarah wondered: does this girl know about the bust? She probably does, but maybe not. I wonder what Arnold said about me? I wonder if these two are a couple? Jack sure is handsome. A little shy but definitely handsome.

"Well, don't just stand there, come on in," Sarah said. "There's food on the table and drinks in the kitchen. Who wants champagne?"

Elizabeth thanked her and took a glass from the silver tray.

"No, thanks," Jack said. He was already pretty drunk and noticed he was having to concentrate on his speech. He was sure the champagne would give him a serious hangover so he played it safe and asked for a beer. Sarah left and came back with a bottle.

"Is this all right?"

"Yes, thank you."

The apartment occupied an entire floor. In the parlor a fire burned in the hand-carved limestone fireplace. On the floor was a bearskin rug and behind it a hand-planed mahogany table hemmed in by white leather couches. In the dining room, the table was filled from one end to other with food in silver serving trays. On the walls European landscapes, Japanese scroll paintings and modern art competed for attention. A crystal china cabinet displayed Japanese ceramics and artifacts from different cultures, Persian carpets covered the floor, and in one corner of the room a bust of some famous dead Roman patriarch spectated the gathering. A large window ran the length of the parlor and the dining room, affording a panoramic view of San Francisco Bay. The pinprick lights of Fisherman's Wharf below gave Jack a better sense of how far they had climbed.

What horrible decor, Elizabeth thought. Look at this idiotic fake bust of Marcus Aurelius. And those dull romantic period landscapes. What does a French antique dinner table have to do with a modern Italian couch? This kaleidoscope of styles is just plain tacky. Why is it that the rich have no taste? If this were my apartment . . . At least the parquet floors are nice.

Elizabeth studied the guests. The women were clustered together gossiping with their champagne glasses in hand in the dining room, while the men stood in their suits smoking by the fireplace. I don't know how long I can stand being here, she thought. Then she noticed Damian with his vicious smile chatting up some young women across the hall in the game room. Next to and a step back from him was Alex looking bored. Jack had found his way to the buffet and was piling his plate high with baked ham, mashed potatoes, Caesar salad and beef carpaccio.

Would you look at all this good food, Jack thought. God, I'm starving. I haven't had time to eat all night. I even missed dinner at the restaurant. No wonder I'm so drunk. He sat alone by the window and ate and drank and washed it all down with his beer. This is great. You were lucky to hook up with Arnold.

In the game room Damian was talking film. "Digital video is the future," he said. "I'm sure you've all seen *All Dogs Must Die*. Well, that was shot entirely on digital. And the dogs, well, they were shot with a gun. Ha, ha. Anyway, the total cost for making that film was something around a hundred thousand dollars. And it made sixteen million at the box office. You know what that means," Damian asked in a burst of contagious optimism. "That anyone can make movies! All it takes is a video camera, a computer and some editing software."

Alex interrupted.

"You see, it's like the cereal isle, except now there will be even more choices. We all thought it was hard to find quality before, but just imagine when any asshole can make a movie from home. Also, it means increased competition. When it comes down to it, it's all about marketing; even a turd will sell if you put it in a pretty wrapper," Alex said.

He sipped from his drink and gauged their reaction. Not that he wanted them to react but just to think. Damian talked such a line of bullshit that Alex couldn't help but attack his vulnerabilities.

"That's true, Alex, you're speaking sense," Damian said. "Still, I remind you that this new media isn't going to be distributed or promoted by traditional means. It will all be done via internet. Granted, now a lot of digital video is transferred to celluloid for showing in theatres. And that type of production is firmly in the hands of Hollywood. But we're talking about content here. By lowering the overhead on filmmaking, we'll strip away the sensationalism, expensive graphics and special effects that undermine plot. And that means better films. Films about real people like us with non-linear plots where character development and dialogue are paramount."

The problem wasn't that they didn't agree on an intellectual level about film, writing or the arts in general: it was the fact that, though Damian was intelligent, he had no integrity.

Damian believes he can be everybody's friend and give everyone what they want. But that's nothing more than superficiality and empty promises. Again Alex found himself wondering, distant and outside of himself as always, if there were any point to writing what he believed. Yes, he was writer; he had ten manuscripts stacked in his closet, some mediocre, and others he thought worthy of publication. Of these manuscripts there was one he thought excellent, the completion of which allowed him to come to terms with himself and his own ambition. This work had fundamentally altered his perception of reality, provoking a deep estrangement from what he called "the game." This was the game that Damian so fervently played and that Alex was now above and looking down on with contempt. But though he could stand outside of it in his mind, physically he was trapped.

For many, Alex thought, escape from the game entails the most frenetic engagement in it. In an attempt to free oneself, the individual is divested of his identity and drowned by details and appearances until he is no longer able to live according to his nature. By consuming this sensationalism we have become it, setting for ourselves goals that are unattainable. Quick wealth: that is an illusion. If it can be obtained it is at the price of solidarity and community. It represents the commodification of the soul. And I myself would rather live cheap and free to develop the skills and ideas that make me unique, than be forced into a box of mediocrity where my creativity is wasted.

Give it rest, Alex. How is it at the age of twenty-six you've forgotten how to enjoy yourself? Nothing good ever comes from thinking like that. This intellectual rebellion is personal vanity. So why do you keep it up?

Because without intellectual debate life would cease to have meaning, he told himself. To sacrifice reason would be to accept that we are nothing but animals content to satisfy our basic needs. In the end, each individual has to develop their own purpose in life. For some this may simply be the quest for comfort and leisure, but that is an unsatisfying life in the long run, and those that live in such a way are seldom fulfilled. The cookie cutter truth they subscribe to is nothing more than a marketing scheme that plays on their insecurities. A man should never live his life distracted from his creative potential and innate curiosity.

In a world where everyone is greedy for money, I am greedy for knowledge, Alex thought. It would be a disservice to humanity if everyone suspended critique and fell silent in the face of inequity. What a shame then that when you speak your mind, when you cut the crap, so to speak, and talk about truth, everyone's eyes glaze over and they recoil from you in disgust. That's a tragedy, Alex thought. For really, what's the point in engaging at all with people if only to compare affluence? Affluence is like a house of mirrors where a man doesn't recognize himself or others and cannot find his way back to reality.

Alex had learned early exactly what he could and couldn't get away with in idle conversation. He could be critical of society as a whole but he could not speak frankly about himself or others. He couldn't say: Damian, this is how you think and function, this is your survival plan for life and these are your prejudices, though they both knew each other quite well. Their friendship, like most, lay on the frayed string of not speaking to each other with sincerity. It hadn't always been so, or perhaps it had, he could not remember. All these thoughts ran quickly through Alex's mind before he responded to Damian's monologue:

"Overall I agree that the democratization of the media is a positive trend. I'm so bloody sick of the muck they feed us on television and in the movies. Why, I haven't bothered going to the movies in two years. I don't watch movies or television anymore, and I think it's a tragedy that people no longer read. A man who doesn't read is a liability. Still, for some people it's enough to be comfortable, and some even prefer not to think, because then perhaps they might be forced to act and change. They might even perceive their own flaws. I remember the first time I realized I wasn't prefect. That was certainly hard to swallow."

That was the liquor talking. In the morning Alex would no doubt feel embarrassed for speaking the truth, as anyone rightly would. Add to that a hangover, like every weekend, and it wasn't going to be pleasant. Here he was having the same damn conversation as always, and even when he spoke sense, it seemed like the most meaningless bullshit. Nevertheless, he continued.

"Yes, I actually despised myself for my shameless self-promotion, my arrogance and my pedantry. But then that's life, isn't it: the masking of our insecurities through boasting and lies, and the sharpening of our strengths to undermine and damage others. Disgusting really. The worst part is how everyone pretends to embrace equality and justice when the truth is they could care less about those less fortunate than themselves. I mean our whole democracy is constructed upon that one basic lie, and then everyone looks the other way when it's violated every day by our government. Really, we should just embrace hypocrisy and get it over with."

Damian laughed nervously. He could see how the women were made uncomfortable by Alex's monologue. Can't take him anywhere. All he does is cause dissent. Because he's repressed. He never uses his knowledge to his advantage and that makes him dangerous, because you never know when he's going to reveal a secret or throw some truth in your face that you can't handle. Admit it, you admire him for his talent and his righteous morality. You wish you had a fraction of the creativity he does. He's probably forgotten more good ideas than you'll have in your entire life. If he'd just compromise a little and cooperate, you'd make a great team. But he refuses to write for you or share his work. Sure, he's a good writer but he knows nothing about success. What's he working on now? A book discussing the fall of American Empire? Yeah, that'll fly off the shelves. I tell you the bastard likes to wallow in misery. He actually enjoys it. Well, that's fine but it's not the life for you. Either you're too smart, or you're a coward, but comfort is something you don't take for granted.

Elizabeth approached them with Jack in tow, now on his second helping from the buffet.

"Hey, Elizabeth, good to see you," Damian said, giving her a hug.

"How's it going, guys? I want you to meet my friend, Jack. He's new in town."

Damian and Alex offered their hands and introduced them to the girls: Jill, engaged to an older man, manager in some corporation or other; and Lisa, a grade school teacher and friend of Sarah's from the gym.

"I work in the city schools," Lisa was saying, "and I've seen a lot of kids who grow up with nothing, and the education they receive is so poor. We don't have enough materials or teachers. No one wants to be a teacher anymore."

"Because the pay is terrible and it's the hardest work around. I'm sure it's rewarding, but let's face it, feeling good about what you do doesn't pay the bills," Jill said.

"I still remember some of my teachers from grade school," Lisa said. "There were a few who really had an effect on me. Take math for example. I hated it until I had Mr. Brewer in the ninth grade. He actually made it interesting. Since then I've begun to think that the teacher is more important than the subject you study."

"I'm still afraid of math," Elizabeth said.

"I'm also a teacher," Alex said, addressing himself to Lisa. "I teach at Hunter's Point, and the kids don't have it easy there. They grow up in broken homes, their neighborhoods aren't safe and for them drug abuse and unemployment is the norm. Frankly, I'm not surprised they lose hope. It saddens me the way their poverty is marketed. The fast food chains have got them addicted to garbage food and the media teaches them violence without consequence and greed as a virtue. I watch them go around acting tough when really they're just trying to bridge the gap between what they see and who they are. Meanwhile, they lose track of their own identities and live alienated from their emotions. Sometimes I want to tell these kids: hey, this attitude, this aggression and anger you have, they'll use it to bury you. All it will do is land you in jail. I want to show them that what's really "tough" is to think for yourself, respect others and stand up for your rights. But some of these kids have been so hardened they are ashamed to follow their own ideas. They are broken. Now, I don't think anyone here can understand what it is to think you aren't worth anything or you aren't loved, and that you have no future and aren't smart. It's a shame and it breaks my heart. I'm a bloody teacher for Christ's sake. I'm all these kids have. If you want to make a good movie, Damian, then make it about that. Make it about all the shit in this country that no one talks about."

"You write the script and I'll direct and produce it," Damian said.

"You're a producer," Jill asked.

"Yeah, I've got my own production company," Damian said, handing her a business card. "Stopwatch is internet-based. We accept scripts from anyone, but mostly amateurs. If a script is good enough, then we buy the rights. Since we're relatively new, we don't pay a lot. Usually a few thousand dollars."

Damian wanted to impress Jill, and also Elizabeth with her eyes like gems and her greenhorn friend from Arizona. Still, he couldn't speak loose or free because Alex was there, and the truth was that he hadn't produced anything, but only sold scripts onward to Hollywood at a healthy markup. Damian was more an agent than a producer, and he told himself that when he had saved enough money he would make his own film. He didn't know what the film would be, but he wanted Alex to do the writing, and he would film it himself on digital to keep expenses down. He figured he could make an excellent film for a hundred thousand dollars. He was halfway there in his savings, in addition to what he had put away in stocks, mostly new economy tech stocks and B to B, and not the risky consumer market variety. He invested in hardware, not services.

"So, how many films have you made," Jack asked, feeling left out of the conversation.

"Four."

"And they've been in the theaters?"

"Sure. Does *Glass House,* or *The City* sound familiar?"

"Yeah, I've seen both of those. Wow, that's great, Damian. Those are big-time movies and you talk about it like it's nothing," Jack said.

Suddenly, Damian seemed different to him: larger somehow, more attractive and better-dressed, even.

"Well, it's like this: once I'm finished with a project, it's finished, almost like it never existed. The secret is to never look back. Life is short and I plan to make a lot of films before I'm done," Damian said.

Did he really produce those films, Alex wondered. What does a producer do anyway, besides take credit and make money off writers and their ideas? So maybe he did produce those films. So what. I'll never watch them: composite films of two or three others that came out and were successful. The industry takes no risks, he thought. Nevertheless, Alex found himself wanting to rent them to see if Damian's name appeared in the credits.

Damian thought: it's almost the same. I sold the scripts for both those films. If I had known they were going to be made and that they would be so successful, then I would have asked for more money. Still, twenty-thousand on my first try, face to face with those big-shots, nervous as hell as I built it up for them, I guess I didn't do half bad. And now I've sold them two successful scripts, both of which I bought for a few thousand. Better yet, now they know me. I can call up Michael Karen at Solimar and speak to him personally when I've got something hot. I don't have to sneak in like I did before, pretending I'm delivering a pizza. Why, they were going to throw me out, but I talked my way out of that one. In this world if you can talk it doesn't matter what's truth or fiction; it's about building yourself up and seeming bigger and tougher than you are. Just look at how Jack is staring at me. Poor kid, he knows nothing about any of this. What does Elizabeth see in him, anyway? I never pegged her as going for the dumb model-type.

"So how's Arizona, Jack," Alex asked.

"It's like growing up anywhere; the place becomes a part of you and you miss it when you're gone. I'm sure it's the same for people that grow up near the ocean or in the mountains. I'm a great believer in the idea that our natural surroundings shape the way we think and act. Growing up in the desert gives you a different perspective on things. In the desert I learned to be self-sufficient and not to fear being alone with myself."

"When you talk like that, Jack, I picture a cactus with sharp spines: the only living thing in a dry, dead landscape. No, the desert's not for me. I can't bear to do without water," Elizabeth said.

"Still, I bet housing is cheap out there," Damian said.

"Yes, but that's changing. In a few years that won't be the case. You're wrong though," Jack said to Elizabeth. "The desert's not dead at all. It's full of life. All you have to do is look closely. Then you'll see the kangaroo rats and the lizards, the roadrunners and the beetles, and all sorts of plants. Also the air at night when the sun goes down, it's so crisp and clear you can see the stars bright in the sky when you're out of the city. There's nothing like driving the highway at night watching the stars with the music up real loud and no destination."

"No destination, I like that," Alex said. "Still, I prefer the ocean. As far as I'm concerned, California is its own country with no connection to the rest of what you call the United States. This, my friend, is the center of the world; if it weren't, why would you be here? I can't imagine what I would do with myself staring at all that sand and not a single person to talk to."

"We have our cities, too," Jack defended. "And I don't think people from Arizona are very different from Californians, except we're not as arrogant."

"Well, you know what I think . . ." Alex didn't finish his sentence because just then Arnold arrived. He thought Jack likable enough, and perhaps it was the alcohol that was making him argue.

Arnold stooped to come in the room, as was his habit because of his height, and Sarah squealed, "Arnold," and jumped into his arms. He lifted her off the ground, threw her over his shoulder in a fireman's carry, walked up to an older Asian man with thick silver hair and asked, "Is this your daughter?" He turned so Sarah faced her father and she said, "Daddy, daddy, please make him put me down."

"Sorry, Mr. Yokiyama, but I'm kidnapping your daughter and taking her with me to Las Vegas so we can elope."

Mr. Yokiyama looked perplexed. Arnold still wore his wig and he gave a hideous smile with his false teeth.

"Why, who are . . ."

Finally, Mr. Yokiyama recognized him and let out an explosive laugh. His face was red from alcohol and he said, "Arnold, wow, would you look at those teeth. You really need to see a dentist. I know a few wolves that are recruiting for the pack. As for her, I think you better just take her, because she's too much for me to handle. Just look at my hair, why, just a year ago it was black as a crow's wing."

"Oh, honey," Mrs. Yokiyama said, "you know that isn't true."

Mr. Yokiyama turned and gave her a disapproving glance. Why can't my wife have a sense of humor? Every time I want to joke she gets embarrassed.

Sarah was conservative like her mother. She was in love with a young medical student at San Francisco State named Henry Hara. It saddened her that Henry couldn't make it to her graduation party, because she couldn't understand that he didn't love her but only saw her as a convenience. Henry had made all sorts of excuses, such as having to work in the hospital for his internship and later having to study, but the truth was at that moment he was in a bar in Noe Valley playing darts and drinking with friends, saying, "Would you look at the rack on her!"

Arnold thought: Sarah sure is beautiful. It's a shame all she does is cry for that boyfriend of hers. I've met him. He's a real jerk who treats her like shit.

Arnold had his heart set on freeing Sarah from that oppressive relationship by teaching her how to have fun and encouraging her to try new activities. It had taken him many months to convince her to do a bust; he remembered how nervous and awkward she had been, and that was something he found endearing. She was the girl he loved to embarrass. He made it a point to suggest risqué activities, such as nude sunbathing or frequenting the S and M clubs of the city. It was his pleasure to watch her blush because somewhere beneath that embarrassment was a well-founded lust.

Sarah took Arnold to the kitchen and poured him a drink. Then she led him down the hall to her room decorated with fuzzy rabbits, porcelain dolls and floral wallpaper. Arnold saw the pictures of her when she was a girl with a gap in her teeth in a private school dress: plaid skirt and knee-high socks with her hair in pigtails. What a sweet girl, he thought. I'm no good for her. I only want one thing, but that doesn't mean we can't be friends, too.

They sat on the bed. Arnold took a sip from his Screwdriver, and she looked at him and said, "Henry's not here. This is the most important day of my life and he couldn't come." She burst into tears and put her hands to her face. Arnold put his arms around her and held her tight. He felt her tiny frame shake and said, "Don't cry, look at how many people did come, and if he couldn't make it, you shouldn't let it ruin your night. Maybe you need to find someone new."

"But I love Henry. I've loved him ever since the day we met in the library and he asked me for a pencil. He didn't need a pencil at all, he just wanted to talk to me. We've been together two years, and in the last three months I've hardly seen him and he always makes excuses to avoid seeing me. When I say I'm coming over, he tells me he doesn't have time. Oh Arnold, I'm so lonely. I can't stand it anymore. What's the point if I don't have anyone to love me?"

"Don't talk like that. You have a lot of people that love you. Maybe Henry doesn't know how to appreciate you. The truth is people change."

"Well, they shouldn't. People shouldn't change. Every time I get comfortable with life, it goes and changes on me and then I don't know what to do with myself. Now I'm going to be a lawyer but I always wanted to be a dancer in the ballet. I was good, too; see those bronzed shoes on the wall. I danced for twelve years of my life. I was on my way to New York to study and then my mom said, 'We need you here to help run the practice when your father retires,' and I gave it all up for them. So nothing is like I wanted it to be, not love and not the future, and I just want to run away from here and be far away."

"Well, let's go then," Arnold said. "We'll head to Hawaii for a couple weeks."

Sarah lifted her head from his shoulder and sat up with wide eyes.

"Arnold, you're crazy. I could never do anything like that. What would people say about me running away with you to the islands?"

"What does it matter what they say," Arnold said, draining his glass. Though she was sitting still, Arnold saw her face turning around the room like the hand of a clock but, like a seasoned drunk, he spoke clear and sat straight. He could stay that way until he passed out, pretending he wasn't drunk. He could walk and even drive that way and no one would know the difference. What people don't know won't hurt them, he thought. He wasn't thinking about his condition, because that was second nature, but instead about Sarah's ignorance of men and how he was very different from the caring, loving friend she thought him to be. That he was, in fact, a pervert.

People are never one thing in particular and there's no counting on them, Arnold reasoned. Some people lived against their nature and others with it, but the truth was most people were actors playing roles that weren't their own. Even his larger-than-life personality was a lie, because deep inside he was sad. Though he had been with many women, he never felt he had done it sincerely, but had tricked them instead. He was sure that no one had ever loved him for himself, but because he was amusing like a clown.

When Sarah went to the bathroom to dry her eyes, she found the door locked and heard the sound of retching in the toilet.

Jack had his head over the bowl thinking: God, I'm gonna die. He puked and saw the chewed up ham and the white of the garlic mashed potatoes and bits of carpaccio and salsa. All the colors mixed together to a sort of pink, and it came like a faucet straight down. He wiped the spit from his lips and thought: it was those drinks in the car and the mixing and matching. I usually make it a point never to drink hard liquor. I don't know what's gotten into me. Tonight I'm just excessive and I don't care. He looked at his sweaty, pale face in the mirror. You're pathetic. Why don't you take better care of yourself; it's been a long time since you've puked -at least a year.

Jack felt it coming again. His stomach contracted, and this time his throat burned with bile. He spit, washed his mouth out and gargled. He took a bit of toothpaste, rubbed it on his tongue and filtered it through his teeth with water. Then he wiped the rim of the toilet where his vomit had splashed. I hope they don't smell it on me. I hope whoever is outside this door can't hear me, and I hope it's not the father or one of the older guests, and certainly not Sarah.

He opened the door and they stared at each other: Sarah was as embarrassed about her tears and puffy eyes as Jack was about his puking. They were embarrassed for their failure at keeping up appearances.

Making the best of it, Jack said, "Hi Sarah, please excuse me," as he shuffled past. Sarah, following his lead, said, "Sure Jack, I'm just going to freshen up." They did their best to avoid eye contact.

Wow, I feel much better. Just like a machine: go in, puke, come out and resume the party. Lucky no one but Sarah saw me. I wonder what she was crying about?

Jack returned to the parlor to find Arnold surrounded by Jill, Lisa and Elizabeth. Nikki Star's *Naughty Girl* was blasting and Arnold sang so that the veins stuck out in his neck, "I'm a naughty girl, in a naughty world . . . ," waving his arms in the air like a diva and spinning Lisa and Elizabeth, one in each hand, while Jill clapped. Then Damian was on the dance floor behind Jill moving his hips in what was no less than a fucking motion, in and out, in and out, pointing at his crotch, while Alex spectated and sipped his drink.

Jack was petrified of dancing, especially to eighties music. His limited experience consisted of dancing to modern pop and hip hop, where freaking the girls was in order. He had no problem with rubbing up against a girl and grabbing her, but to *Naughty Girl*? No way, he told himself.

Jack walked off to the kitchen where the suits had gathered, including Mr. Yokiyama, who nodded to him. Jack helped himself to another beer from the fridge. I usually don't puke twice in one night. Just pretend you're starting from scratch, he told himself. In spite of being drunk, Jack still wasn't confident enough to dance or grab Elizabeth, or to ask her to come with him to the study with the nice oak desk, bookcase and comfortable couch that he had spied from the bathroom.

Alex wanted badly to dance. He was confident he was a better dancer than anyone in that room. In fact, he did many things better than other people, but he had been raised to be humble and didn't like to stand out, which sometimes made him bitter because he felt restricted from enjoying himself. Now the music and the alcohol were tempting him to lose control. Drunkenness was a familiar condition that he could control and which afforded him the courage to say and do things that normally embarrassed him. This embarrassment was mainly reserved for the body and his emotions. He disliked imposing his lust on women. He was usually happier drunk than sober and now a rare smile split his face. He started to move slow and careful to the music, while Arnold spun the girls around the room and bumped into the furniture.

Alex found the courage to move in on Lisa, the teacher. He didn't want to be rejected and told himself: go on, just put your arm around her and pull her close. He did and it worked: unbelievably, it worked. They were dancing together now, and Alex was no longer calculating and evaluating every detail of existence with his critical eye.

The older men and women also danced. When *Let's Get Down* came on, they didn't stop, though perhaps it wasn't such a nice fit. Jack thought it surreal to see those older women dancing with neck skin flapping, waving their liver-spotted hands and arms, and showing off their varicose veins. He was embarrassed for them. Their balding and heavy-gutted husbands had joined the party, and Jack caught them looking over their shoulders at Elizabeth's breasts beneath her silk top, and also at the other young women. At that moment Jack realized that men never grew up, that money replaced looks as a means to pursue women, and that everything a man did, be it make a movie, write a book, or turn himself into a martial arts killing machine, was for the sake of women. It was especially the latter, the jock like himself, that had the most trouble with women and would take great measures to impress them with physical strength while being petrified to talk to them about feelings.

Why am I thinking of this nonsense now? I gotta dance with her. So Jack walked out onto the floor like any self-conscious male, and before he knew it, he was enjoying himself along with everyone else. Arnold had turned up the music to an ear-splitting level, and now Jack was trying to rub up against Elizabeth. He danced stiff and awkward like most men, but

Elizabeth gave him credit. At least he's trying, she thought. Not everyone is like Arnold, and if they are, they must be gay.

Elizabeth remembered the women she had kissed and how, when she first came to the city, she had been more experimental. Was it age that was closing in now, making her less open and less eager to get involved with other people and their perversions of character? Before she had praised perversion.

A woman kisses better than a man, she thought. If a man kisses well, that's luck, like winning five bucks in the lottery. No, more like winning ten.

Look at the concentration on Jack's face. He's really trying hard. It's nice when a guy tries hard. Most men only come halfway, and if you want me, baby, you've got to go all the way. Laughing to herself, Elizabeth grabbed Lisa by the hand, spun her round and pressed against her. It was not that she liked Lisa, but that dancing with her was safe. Also, she wanted to feed Jack's imagination and make him tense. Because she was going to give it up. Why the hell not? He looks like a fucking cigarette ad with that jaw of his. He's a stud cowboy in those worn jeans and that flannel shirt. He's like a life-sized action figure and tonight I want some action, she thought.

Damian watched the two girls dancing together and thought: this is better than Hotbitches.com where you can watch the girls making out live on the webcam. If there's one thing I love, it's to lie in bed after work and watch women touching each other. My dream, besides putting it in some girl's ass, is to make it with two girls at the same time. But how do you get away with something like that?

Everything that Damian really wanted from women he thought dirty or wrong. He was an adventurous guy and the missionary just didn't do it for him anymore. The fact that you feel guilty and ashamed for wanting to have experimental sex makes the women feel that you're ashamed of them, ashamed of their bodies and the many ways that a man and woman can please each other; you make them feel dirty and wrong, and that's why you'll never live those dreams. I bet Arnold's had all sorts of kinky sex, Damian thought, eyeing him with envy. I'm not bad-looking, am I? Look at Arnold with his glasses and those fucking fake teeth, and the girls just love him.

Arnold had Jill on his shoulder and was spinning her around the dance floor. Her weight set him off balance and that, combined with the alcohol, sent him spiraling out of control. They spun and Jill's head struck the doorframe with force and they fell to the floor. Arnold got quickly to his feet and said, "Jill, can you hear me. Jill, are you okay?"

Jill saw a man she did not recognize above her, a very ugly man with deep concern on his face, who said, "Jill, Jill." She didn't know who Jill was or where she was. She sat up frightened and wondered: how did I get here?

"Jill, can you hear me?"

Sarah was crouching down by her friend and so was Jill's husband, Kyle, who kept saying, "Don't worry, honey, you've just had a blow to the head. Come on and I'll take you to lie down."

Then Mr. Yokiyama appeared with his wife Pearl, whose face was pale with fear. My God, what if the girl dies in our house? Then there'll be a lawsuit for sure. Pearl was a woman prone to hysterics.

"Come on, she can lie down in Sarah's bed. Sarah, go get an ice pack from the kitchen," Pearl commanded.

"I'm so sorry," Arnold said, addressing the husband. "I was just having fun and then I lost my footing. I didn't mean for her to get hurt."

"Maybe that'll teach you to stop clowning around," Kyle said. Then, without the bite in his voice, "Well, you didn't knock her unconscious, so I'm sure she'll be all right. It's gonna leave a hell of a bruise though."

Kyle Newton was concerned for his wife but also relieved to be alone with her and to care for her, because he loved her a lot and couldn't stand to see her dancing with other men. Now certainly the large, ugly man whose name he couldn't remember would stop bothering them because he had embarrassed himself. Kyle made to lift Jill off the floor and Arnold said, "Here, let me help, maybe she's too heavy . . ."

"Don't you think you've done enough already? I'll carry her myself."

Kyle picked her up and felt the pressure in his groin where he had been operated for a hernia. Damn, you should have taken him up on it, he thought. Why are you such a proud cock? Don't you believe the girl loves you and only you? No, because your ex-wife taught you that such logic is faulty. If you want something done right, you have to do it yourself. The thought reminded Kyle of his father, who was dead now, but who had spoken a lot of sense to him. He had never had a chance to thank him for that.

In the bedroom, Sarah put the icepack on Jill's head and asked, "How do you feel, Jill?"

Jill remembered she was Jill again and said, "It hurts, I'm so tired. I just want to close my eyes."

"No," Kyle said. "Whatever you do, don't go to sleep. You've got a concussion. If you sleep, you might not wake up. Now listen to me. I'm going to tell you story, so you listen and stay awake.

"Leave us alone," he told the others.

"Don't you think it's better if we stay and keep her company," Pearl asked.

"Get out, Pearl, both of you get out of here," Kyle told them.

"Where am I, and who are you," Jill asked.

A chill went down Kyle's spine. "I'm your husband Kyle Newton," he told her. "What do you mean, who am I? I'm your husband Kyle and we live in Pacific Heights in San Francisco. This is San Francisco and we're at a party for your friend Sarah who passed the bar and is going to be a lawyer."

Kyle talked to her like that for the better part of a half an hour until slowly she remembered. Her reason came back in bits and pieces, along with her memories and the emotions they provoked, until finally she recovered her humanity. Vaguely, Jill remembered being afraid, but couldn't remember it was because a moment ago she didn't know who she was.

Only Arnold knew how hard Jill's head had hit the wall, and it made him nervous. His previous good humor evaporated as did his desire to dance. You could have killed her; if she hadn't been all right one of these lawyers would have sued your ass for sure. They could still decide to do it later. I wouldn't put it past that worm Kyle. Where do these women find these guys anyway?

The point is you're out of control. Two or three nights a week you're like this. All you do is work and drink, work and drink. What kind of life is that? You need to get some exercise. Look how fat you've gotten. You must weigh close to two-twenty now. Sure, you're naturally big, but all that drinking is giving you a gut. No, you're going to start riding your bike to work. And what about all that fitness equipment you threw your money away on: the Aborator, the rowing machine, the Thighpro (that you bought for your girlfriends to use before foreplay), and the Bowpress? You live too cluttered a life. Just look at the garage. When are you going to sell the bike? You only bought it to look cool and now you're afraid to ride it. Damn straight. Remember that Driver's Ed video with some biker's head scraped down like an erasure to his shoulders on the highway? Or what Alex told you about that guy that came in and took his helmet off in the convenience store, and his head came apart like a jigsaw puzzle? Damn glad I didn't see that. That's just the kind of news you only get from Alex. He loves that morbid shit.

"Whoa, look at this! Watch me do the 'worm'," Alex said. The crowd parted and there he was slapping his body on the floor, rocking back and forth like a saw between two lumberjacks hard at work. He undulated across the floor to the window, hopped up and took a celebratory drink of beer. Damian slid in, spinning on his back with his knees clutched to his chest, before crashing into and bringing down an end table and a vase, which smashed on the floor. He ignored it, or perhaps didn't notice, and broke into some breakdance moves on his hands and knees. He wasn't bad, though certainly it was silly and outdated. Jack tried to do the "smoothwalk," but after a few steps across the floor, he lost his nerve. A circle had formed and people went into the middle to show off, including a fewer older, unattractive people who got caught up in the moment.

This is how people really are, Arnold thought, distant from the recent trauma. All the seriousness is just nonsense. And here's the proof. Acting the fool is the fastest way to charm people and make them your friends. You do what other people only wish they could do. Ahh, the power of alcohol. Without it none of us can escape our own reason.

Jack was drunk and he was not shy or polite anymore. His true feelings were made apparent when he put his arm around Elizabeth's waist and said, "Come on, let's go some place more quiet."

"But I want to dance, Jack. Aren't you having fun dancing?"

"Yes, the dancing's fine, but I want to be alone with you. It makes me uncomfortable to be around all these people. Let's go somewhere where we can talk and get to know each other better. I haven't had a chance to talk to you all night."

"Well, we're talking now. What is it you want to talk about?"

"No, it's not like that," he said. "It's just, wouldn't it be nice if we could be alone?"

Jack took her by the arm and led her off the dance floor. They walked back to the study and sat down next to each other on the couch. He did not know what he wanted to talk about. Really, he didn't want to talk about anything. He wanted to hook up with her, but in a smooth way and without looking obvious. He laughed at this thought. When you do something it's always obvious. Only thinking it, isn't. But thinking and imagination aren't enough. At least not now. I don't know what's come over me. I've lost control.

"I like your friends," Jack told her, ad-libbing. "I've never been to a party like this back in Arizona. And the things they talk about, especially Alex about teaching; now that's a tough job. And Damian, he must be rich. How is it that he's here with us and not hanging out with movie stars?"

"You like the party because this is still new to you. This party's not bad because none of us know Sarah or anybody else here. After you live here a while you'll see that all the parties are the same; it's always the same people. When friends hang out that much and there's no variety, well, things become a bit incestuous. It's not much different than living in a small town. I'm afraid we're all stuck in a rut and as we get older we become less adventurous. Now that were nearing our thirties, the pressure's on to become successful and find love, and it's making us all a little more selfish and desperate. Pardon me for saying things as they are, Jack, but I've never been one to mince words. Words should be whole and have their full meaning, and sentences should be complete and full of intent, not vagaries."

"I suppose you're right," he said, without understanding her. Mainly, he didn't understand the biting tone of her words. When he had seen her dancing, she seemed happy. But underneath her easy exterior was an intense and serious woman: that had been apparent from the beginning. There was nothing easy about her, and that made her infinitely attractive. He thought her better and more intelligent than himself, and was ashamed for being simple and not seeing the way she did. It was an indication of her character that she didn't judge him for his current profession. He felt that even if he were successful like Damian, she wouldn't treat him any different. No, the real girls don't care about the money, they just want to be loved.

"You're very pretty," he told her, not knowing what else to say. "When you were dancing I couldn't keep my eyes off you. How is it to be beautiful like you?"

It was the first time he saw her blush. She blushed and looked away.

"This sure is a nice apartment," she said.

But he wasn't finished.

"I bet it's hard to be a pretty girl and have all those jerks picking up on you all the time without knowing who you really are or caring about what you have to say."

Boy, I'm really talking nonsense now, Jack thought. Still, it's better to talk than to sit in silence. Silence with her makes me uncomfortable. It's not like that with all girls, though. I guess we don't know each other well enough yet. There's still shame between us. Go on you fool, just kiss her. Can't you tell she's waiting for a kiss?

But Elizabeth had become pensive. He's right about the beauty. It prevents people from respecting what I have to say. What I say will always be cute and not have any meaning because I'm pretty. I know I'm pretty, at least above average. That's why it's all the more important to pretend I'm not, especially with other women. Don't give them the chance to tear you down. Be above the game, she thought.

So you're beautiful and that's just luck. Maybe you take it for granted, but the advantage is people do you favors. Yes, you know how to use your beauty, but you prefer not to.

God, Jack is really drunk; it's kind of sad to see a man that way, with all his dignity stripped away, shaming himself and putting his foot in his mouth and talking nonsense, and now his inability to look away from your breasts. He's only got one thing on his mind and that's fine, but don't go fooling yourself into thinking if you give it to him he's gonna give something in return. The giving and receiving might not be any good either. You've known plenty of men like that with no sense of how to please a woman. Because it's about my pleasure too, Jack, and drunk like you are, there's no way. I wouldn't mind cuddling with you but beyond that nothing. How much patience have you got, I wonder?

Elizabeth watched Jack lick his lips and noticed a slight movement on his part as if to lean forward, so she turned her head.

Your opening is gone, he thought. Time is the enemy, and the longer you wait, the harder it's gonna be. The next time she looks at you and can see what you're doing, you plant one on her, understood? Yes, I understand.

When she turned again, Jack leaned forward quick and surprised her with his speed. Their teeth clicked together and he burned with embarrassment. He kept kissing her and pretended it never happened; she kissed him back and it was forgotten. He put his arm around her and pulled her close. He stuck his free hand between her legs and she responded by squeezing them tightly together so it wouldn't fit. He let his hands roam and made a bold attempt to put them up her shirt and grab her breasts. To Jack's dismay, he felt her fingers close around his wrists and pull his hands away.

"Not here and not like this, Jack," she said. "You're too drunk and this isn't the time. We barely know each other."

"Come on, doesn't it feel good," Jack asked, pushing her down on the sofa. With the door wide open, he tried to climb on top of her. Just then Bill from the elevator walked by in the hallway and saw them. Though he averted his eyes, he thought: I can't believe they're going to have it right there on the couch. Keri would never do that. He stopped just on the other side of the doorway, leaned against the wall, and thought about taking another peek. I'm getting old, he thought. I don't have the nerve to ask Keri to do anything dirty or sexy anymore. I've just given up. Bill was the sort to get melancholy from drinking, and Elizabeth depressed him, like all young, pretty women he couldn't have depressed him.

Jack was in middle of groping Elizabeth's fine figure and kissing her, until he found himself in a pile on the floor with her standing over him adjusting her clothes and fixing her hair.

"How embarrassing," she said. "It was that man from the elevator. I wonder what he's going to think of me now?"

Jack sat down on the couch.

"Who cares what that guy thinks. I thought we were having fun?"

Standing up, Jack pulled Elizabeth to him and continued where he left off. Finally, she pushed him away.

"Jack, you need to cool off. You're not a bad guy, but you're looking worse all the time, and the drinking's no excuse. I'm going to the bathroom."

Elizabeth marched off and left him there wondering what he had done wrong. What's gotten into her anyway? I thought she was enjoying herself?

If there was one thing Jack had to learn it was subtlety of word and deed. He needed to have more patience and a better understanding of a woman's perspective, for in such situations, women possessed more foresight and common sense than men.

When Jack returned to the parlor Damian was chasing Pearl Yokiyama around and spanking her with a broom. He had chased her into a standoff behind the dining room table and was drunk enough that he no longer cared that she was the hostess of the party or that her husband might be angry at his inappropriate behavior. But instead of being angry, Mr. Yokiyama was laughing.

"What are you doing? Stay away from me," Pearl squealed. "Oh, my dress! This is an expensive dress and you'll get it dirty."

George Yokiyama, whose real name was Akira, thought it funny to see his wife involved in such a prank. Sarah's new friends are a lot of fun, and they're good for her, since she's always been too serious like her mother. It's one thing to want to be successful, but if I could turn back the clock, I would have tried to enjoy my youth more. That thinking is an illusion, he told himself. You had to work very hard when you came from Japan; otherwise you wouldn't have been able to provide Sarah with a good education or the luxuries she enjoyed growing up.

Perhaps she feels guilty for her comfort, he thought. Her mother has instilled in her a sense of guilt, as if that can somehow balance wealth and success and make it stay. That is magical thinking. And there is no sense in it. Soon I'll retire and then I'll do everything I never had the time for. Like hang gliding, he thought. Imagine flying in the air like a bird. Amazing!

Damian tired of his fun with Mrs. Yokiyama and interrupted a group of men by sticking the broom in Bill's face and saying, "Whoa, big dog, big dog," while poking the bristles at his mouth. The hilarity of this was too much for him and he broke into a laughing fit. It was only when he was very drunk that Damian would revert to himself: that is, a twenty-seven-year-old man who had never grown up.

Bill grabbed the broom and shoved him angrily away. "Get out of here, you brat, or I'll shove that broomstick up your ass."

"You want me to shove the broomstick up your ass," Damian said, twisting the words to his advantage. "Well, come on then, bend over and we'll see how far it goes."

"Why, I'm gonna break your teeth," Bill said, grabbing for him. He was held back by another middle-aged man named Hank.

"Come on, Bill, leave him alone. Can't you see he's drunk? He's just kidding around."

Hank didn't like Bill because Bill was arrogant, and also because he was subordinate to Bill at the bank. He thought: damned managers, making a living telling others what to do when they are totally incompetent themselves. Still, he was forgetting that Bill had been his colleague before he was a manager, and also that he, Hank, had no desire to be a manager because he despised telling people what to do. Now it was with great satisfaction that he saw Bill turn purple with anger and lose his temper enough to make a grab for the young man.

Bill was always cool as ice in the office. He could tell someone to complete the most tedious and disagreeable tasks, while maintaining his blunt, no-nonsense attitude. Hank could never ask others to perform tasks that he despised himself without feeling embarrassed or ashamed; in that way he was condemned to be ordered about by those more aggressive and less compassionate than himself.

How is it people become like that, when once they worked at a desk next to your own? Hank couldn't be sure, but now he had something on good-old Bill Coney that he wouldn't hesitate to throw in his face, if necessary. Go sit on a broomstick, Bill. Hank smiled to himself and sipped his drink to hide his amusement.

Alex went to the bathroom and left the door ajar. It was the custom with his housemates at home; he didn't care if they saw him in the shower while they pissed or vice versa. Though Alex was shy about most things, he was not shy about his genitalia. His timidity came from trying to hide his sense of superiority over others. Unfortunately, his compassion and sensitivity wouldn't allow him to capitalize on the advantage of his intelligence. He was not a survival-of-the-fittest thinker.

Dick in hand, Alex thought: few things compare to the satisfaction of a long piss. It's better than some sex even. He had a strong bladder and he preferred to hold it if the conversation was good. He didn't like to break things off in the middle, not a song playing on the stereo or a conversation. When Alex spotted or sensed a lull, such as happened when people got tired of justifying themselves or clowning for each other's approval, then he would take leave for his physical needs.

Damian walked in on his housemate in the bathroom, threw his arm around his shoulder, looked down at his member and said, "I'll hold yours if you'll hold mine." Given the state Damian was in, Alex didn't doubt the sincerity of the offer.

Scrutinizing Alex's penis, Damian took out his own. Alex made room for him, as there was no other remedy. They peed together and Damian said, "Yeah, swordfight," crossing his stream of urine with Alex's.

It's just like when you cross wires and someone gets electrocuted; no good is going to come of this, Alex thought. He disapproved of the crossing of urine and thought: one of these days Damian's gonna try to plant one on me. He's twisted like that. Well, you thought it, so what does that say about you? Alex remembered the commercial that claimed Fuego tequila was "purer than your thoughts." It probably was if you could compare the purity of a toxin to the toxicity of reason. Advertising, though, was a social ill that undermined quality of life and human happiness. If Alex had more time, he would do some late night monkeywrenching and burn down a few billboards.

When Damian came out of the bathroom his pants were wet with urine around the crotch because he had miscalculated and peed against the open flap of his slacks, deflecting the urine in an embarrassing way to which he was oblivious.

"I think it's time to go. Do you guys need a ride," Arnold asked Elizabeth and Jack, who had his hand stuck deep in his pockets and was avoiding eye contact with Elizabeth. He must have embarrassed himself, Arnold thought.

Elizabeth felt strong with Jack, and maybe she liked him because he wasn't a fake or a bullshitter like other men she had met. He was still green in the city and hadn't learned to lie to get ahead. He's a nice guy and I should treat him carefully so I don't damage him. Her reasoning came from the fact that several men had broken her up pretty bad. When Elizabeth was done a bad turn she wanted to make it right and not pass on the negativity. This was an attitude she had only recently adopted. Before, in her bitter-with-men stage, she had sought out men and invited them into her to crush them and even the score. But there's no point in that, she thought. It just makes me upset.

"What happened to your pants, Damian?" Arnold said, pointing.

"I must have spilled my drink," he said.

"Right in your crotch? It looks more like you pissed yourself."

Damian looked down and sure enough there was a dark stain ringing his crotch. All eyes were down with his own, and mostly it was Elizabeth's stare that embarrassed him. He could feel her gaze burning into him.

"I know I'm drunk. I've had a lot to drink. I must have spilled on myself."

"No, Damian, when you came in to pee with me and had your swordfight, your aim was bad," Alex said.

"What's a swordfight," Elizabeth asked, her eyes going wide. She didn't want to imagine what two men would do in the bathroom together "swordfighting." There's still a lot I don't know about men, she thought.

"Never mind. Come on, let's get out of here," Damian said. "This place is dead. Who wants to go to the Lucky Dime and get something to eat?"

No way am I going to the Lucky Dime with Damian, Alex thought. The last time he almost had us thrown out of there. The devil gets into him sometimes. The way he was insulting that old waitress, God, that was depressing. And then he had to go and throw his sticky extra pancake on the window and write his name in maple syrup on the countertop.

"I'm going home," Alex said. "Anyone wanna split a cab?"

"I'm driving," Arnold said, leaning against the wall for support. Hope they don't sue me, he thought. Her head hit really hard. Good thing they don't know where I live. Surely, Sarah won't tell them? She's got my back, doesn't she?

Normally, Arnold would have been up for the Lucky Dime and a French dip sandwich at three in the morning with a side of pancakes and a bowl of clam chowder. But tonight he had lost his appetite from the incident and thought: you're just a big clown. The only reason people like you is because you make them laugh.

They piled into the car and Jack went in the backseat with Elizabeth; at least he still had the nerve for that. Arnold wasn't much for conversation, so he turned up the music. Jack leaned into Elizabeth and asked, "Do you think I could stay at your place? I'll be on my best behavior. I could even sleep on the couch if you want."

"We don't have a comfortable couch. You're too long for it."

"Well, then I could sleep in your bed. I'll be a perfect gentleman."

"And I'll be a perfect lady."

"That's fine."

"I'll think about it," she said. They were still halfway across town from Noe Valley where she lived.

Jack put his hand on her leg and she let him. He kissed her some and she kissed him back. He was not as drunk as before, but still drunk enough to obsess about crawling in bed with her. So what if you don't have sex? At least you'll get to see her in her underwear or maybe naked, and you'll get to press up against her, against "warm girl." Who could ask for more than that? That way you don't have to go back to that dump of a hostel. All night Jack had been far away from the reality of his life and now it came flooding back, the work he disliked and the depressing room he rented, and made him even more grateful for Elizabeth. She's all you have, he thought. Don't mess this up.

18

Work was a routine Jack no longer valued: not like the unemployed valued work. Now he longed for the time when he could have his days and nights free to do what he pleased. He missed that vague sense of meaninglessness that came with having too much time and not earning one's own way in life. He missed his youth.

As it turned out, Jack was moved to the Imperial Dining Room where his new uniform consisted of a yellow full dress tunic, a white pith helmet with a spike, white riding breeches and gloves, and patent black leather boots with steel spurs as was typical of the British colonial officer in India. He also wore a sword sheathed in a steel scabbard that hung from a dress sword belt under his tunic. A fake handlebar mustache rounded out the costume.

Jack preferred working in the Wild West Saloon where he didn't have to shave and could wear jeans, a cowboy hat, and boots, not of the knee high variety he wore now, but the ones that smelled of freedom and the range, or at least the illusion of it. Wasn't Phoenix once the range? Now it was the fastest growing city in America; either there or Las Vegas, with their subdivisions and strip malls where history had been bulldozed and removed for the sake of progress. Even if the concept of the American cowboy was a lie, Jack still missed the image of the free man, the loner responsible only for his own welfare, the man who kept his feelings to himself and earned his living from the sweat of his own brow. Is that America, he wondered, now that he was lost in a city that was not that way at all, having met all manner of eccentric people and having seen poverty close hand. I don't know, but somehow it's hard to let go of the cowboy in me. I'm proud of the fact that I haven't complained to anyone about the problems I've encountered here in the city. And now that I've got my independence, things are only going to get better.

Or so Jack told himself. Now that he had learned his job, he found that a wave of small irritations replaced his fears of incompetence and inexperience. He noticed that in the Imperial Dining Room the current waiters and waitresses looked on him with suspicion. In such a job he didn't imagine there would be jealousy or pettiness of any sort. All they had to do was show up, serve the customers and go home. He was responsible for tables ten to fifteen, while the other tables were divided between the other three waiters. Everybody was supposed to do their work and mind their own business. Unfortunately, it wasn't that simple.

Ever since his first day, the waitress, Jennifer, had been giving him orders to bring coffee, serve desserts, stock glasses, polish silverware, fold napkins, and set and clear tables. At first Jack did these things, but as the days wore on he realized that she was using him as an extra busser and making him do her sidework when he had his own to manage. He began to resent her. He thought: either I can ignore her when she asks me to do these things, I can ask her to do similar things for me, or I can confront her and tell her to mind her own business while I mind mine. His indignation at her opportunistic and exploitive behavior kept him up at night with such thoughts as: I'd like to cut that bitch's head off. Where does she get off telling me what to do? She's not my surperior. And it's not just me, she behaves this way toward the others as well. She's downright rude to the Mexican bussers, rude to the point of racist. Jack had learned never to respect someone who treated others as their inferiors, no matter who they were or what their importance was in the world. Such people were without class and culture.

So as happened with everything that is felt but not expressed, Jack was to the point of violence with her. I'll slap that bitch to the floor, he thought. I hate her guts. It was another reminder that in everything he had ever done there was always someone or something disagreeable to be surmounted or ignored. He thought: if there are only ten different types of people in the world, or even twenty, I probably don't get along with ten percent of them. Give or take a person. I consider myself fairly tolerant. The only problem is that tolerance is an obligation, not a choice, and that makes me resentful. You need to speak up instead of being petty and playing her game, he told himself.

Jennifer thought too highly of herself. She was blonde and pretty in that generic way that did not interest him. Perhaps this was why he couldn't stand her: because he had no designs on getting her into bed then or ever, and therefore would allow her no concessions based on her gender.

Then he thought of Paul who always got the best tables because he was fucking the hostess, Nicole. It was a classic symbiotic relationship: the more he earned, the more he took her out. Paul was the kind to take orders from any sort of woman. He was easy prey for Jennifer's hair-flipping, pouty lips and gratuitous chest display. He was the sort of malleable male every woman desired for a husband. Jack was not amused. He thought: you are thirty years old and I can see the crow's feet around your eyes. Then he remembered Candy who he had grown to miss because she was a straight-talking girl in no manner fake or petty. You didn't even know how good you had it in the saloon blowing away the bad cowboy and kissing Candy, with Brad, the bartender, serving up free drinks after closing. Now it's just a competition to see who gets the highest sales.

He came into the dining room and Jennifer said, "Jack, we need the empties taken out, and the trash, and also could you stock some wines?"

Jack did these things with the greatest of resentment as Jennifer stood gossiping with Paul. How is it that when I come here last until close, I have to do both the opening and closing chores? Why is it that the most tedious and disagreeable tasks are always left for me? Why can't everyone do a little more than they're supposed to so that everything gets done faster and we can all go home?

At work, Jack wasn't the sort to waste time or shirk his duties through trickery or plain egotism. It takes more energy to be petty than to just do the job, he thought, dumping the bottles in the ally. Jack manhandled the trash and wondered: how is it that taking out the trash became a man's job? Dad always took out the trash at home and then me; Jennifer won't touch the trash and Candy didn't either. How did women get away with that one? Still, I would take out the trash for Elizabeth. If she wanted, I would even do her laundry; if I knew how to cook, I would cook for her. I would do everything for her. Well, there's your answer, cowboy. Perhaps you should get Jennifer into bed and see if you can't get some utility out of her. No, you're not like that. You don't want any confusion. There is only one road for you and that's the straight and narrow, bla, bla, bla . . .

Jack had done his job long enough that he was outside of himself doing it. Long enough was a month of waiting tables. Essentially, there was nothing else to learn. He could tune in or out given the demands of the moment. Sometimes he would look around the room as if seeing it for the first time and think: what a nice atmosphere. This is a classy place. Look at the people having fun and laughing, and also that pretty brunette over in Paul's section. Wow, she's a real knockout.

Then he would be back in the tunnel with three salads up, a bill for table twelve, wine for ten, oh, there's the bell, I hope it's fifteen. I asked for that table ten minutes ago and now I'm losing face. No, don't look at them. Don't let them blame you with their eyes. Jack knew instinctively when the food should come; if it wasn't ready then he felt badly and hoped that the customers wouldn't notice. Thankfully, some people weren't put off by a small mistake, food that was slightly late, or waiting a few minutes for their bill or dessert. Still, some people were just angry at the world and liked to complain. Jack would be the last man standing for such abuse; much like a soccer goalie during penalty kicks, it was his job to shut them down. His recipe for waiting was as follows: when they ask for something, get it; if they complain and it's justified, apologize, but only once; if they complain and it's not justified, apologize and savor your own insincerity; if they prove to be a problem table, keep your distance, perform your job duties with efficiency and turn the table as quickly as possible. Do not, I repeat, do not engage them in conversation; it will only give them an excuse to exaggerate and expand their complaints. If the customer cracks a joke, laugh and reply with something simple and appropriate. Remember, waiter/customer humor is of the most rudimentary and requires no thought, and there's a good chance that when you reply they won't even be listening. That's how important they think you are. Finally, if the customer is funny and friendly, it's okay to talk and joke, and it might even improve your tip.

The style is different for everyone, Jack thought. When I first came I was over-polite and eager to serve. But this is a restaurant where a little attitude is appropriate, even appreciated. If you don't respect yourself, will they? No, he learned the hard way, taking special orders to the kitchen that made Martino furious and caused him to jab his knife into the table an inch from Jack's hand.

"These fucking *Americanos*," Martino said, "they always want to change things and have something taken out, or eat a meal with the wrong sauce because they have no taste. There are twenty dishes on the menu, and that's just in the colonial room, and they cannot find something they want?"

Sometimes Martino would make a special order and sometimes he wouldn't, so Jack tightened up his style and learned to refuse particular amendments and additions that would disrupt the kitchen and result in all manner of mix-ups and chaos. Before starting his shift, Jack would check inventory so he could be certain of what they had and what they didn't. No longer would he go looking for something to make a show of being diligent, knowing full well he wouldn't find it.

What can a customer expect when they come out to eat, he asked himself. They can expect me to be polite, to bring them their food in a timely manner, to ask if their food is satisfactory, to offer them dessert and to get them their bill when they need it. Nothing more simple than that, he thought.

No, not really, except that the customers all came at exactly the same time, and there were three other waiters also ordering food with Martino, not to mention four other rooms. Though the work was repetitive, whenever Jack went on autopilot he would make mistakes. The main problem was that all the customers were different and he had to adapt to and please them all like a politician. It would be nice to stamp them in and out, he thought, but each table is unique; if they were all the same, and the tip was always the same in relation to the amount of the bill, then it would be a boring job. And what if you got paid a salary? Didn't Andrea in section one say that waiting tables in Italy was a professional career and people got paid a salary to do it? That would sure give a waiter less stress, not having to worry about tips. If it was fifty grand a year full-time maybe I'd take it.

That night Jack had some interesting encounters with the customers. On table thirteen, for example, there was an older homely man with a much younger wife or perhaps girlfriend; their age discrepancy suggested certain things to Jack about society and his recent musings on men.

"Good evening, and how are we doing tonight?"

"Fine, just fine. Say, why don't you get us a bottle of Chateau Sur Mer '92? You want wine, don't you honey?"

"May I see some ID," Jack asked. He had been warned by Carlo to always ask for ID.

"Because if they're undercover, it's my ass, understand Jack? And if it's my ass, it's your ass, too."

The girl was clearly underage, and it was possible that the man was undercover, though he didn't look the part. Undercovers liked to be nondescript, and this man was clearly a predator with his naive young date who behaved like she had never been to a sit-down dinner in a nice restaurant. She's shy, but not stupid, since she'll eat and drink for free. Well, I don't like it, Jack thought. It's wrong for a fifty-year-old to be with an eighteen-year-old. I don't even want to imagine the price of this meal for the girl, because everything has its price.

"I didn't bring my ID," Mercedes said.

"She's my daughter," Arthur said. So it's come to this, he thought: lying to keep up appearances. Still, he'd be damned if this worm of a waiter, this self-important cut-out of a human being, was going to spoil his evening.

"I'm sorry, sir, but it's the law," Jack said. "I can't serve anyone who can't prove their age."

"Well, I don't see you asking me for ID."

"No, perhaps that was an oversight on my part," Jack replied, staring him down. There was a certain power in standing over the seated customers, which he enjoyed. This is my turf, Jack thought. If this guy fucks with me, then I will make it a miserable evening.

"Get me the manager. I'd like to have a talk with him about your lack of cooperation," Arthur threatened. He had been embarrassed in front of the girl and regretted not being more important and influential so he could make the waiter squirm. Who would know the CEO of a toilet paper company, anyway? I have three houses: in L.A., Santa Barbara and San Francisco, respectively, and no one knows who I am. If I told them, they'd just laugh. And wasn't that Gerry Lowe from Conscious Net in the front room? That man is a business genius, Arthur thought. No one respects us old industry guys anymore.

Jack's face revealed no emotion. "I'll go get the manager," he said, filing away. Who knew, maybe he had made a mistake. But, if he lost his job for that, for some lecherous old man seducing young girls, then all the better. Now that he had some experience, he could find work in another restaurant. Then he could lose the ridiculous costume and not have to deal with Jennifer or the alcoholic cook Martino.

Carlo came and Jack went into the kitchen and came out with some plates for another table. When he returned, Carlo was saying, "I'm terribly sorry, sir. Jack is new and he is very careful, you must forgive him. I told him myself to ask for ID from everyone, but it is obvious your daughter is twenty-one. And even if she were not, she's under your supervision and I see no trouble with her having a drink. In fact, in my country we have no such strange laws." Carlo turned to Jack. "Please, get the gentleman a bottle of wine. Sir, may I make a recommendation on the wine?"

"Sure, why don't you pick something out for me."

Jack knew two things about Carlo's character: first, when he was nervous he talked too much; second, that he would humiliate himself in front of the customers if necessary. This show of humility always put them at ease. Once at ease, Carlo would take advantage and sell them his most expensive bottle of wine using their trust against them, or he would offer to make them some special dish, which was usually the leftover half-rotten meat or fish that he would charge them twice as much for.

Jack brought the man the hundred and fifty dollar bottle of wine. From then on Jack would serve him without emotion, just serve him and get him out so he wouldn't have to think about him anymore.

The previous embarrassment having passed, and having gotten his way after dropping hints at his wealth and importance with the owner, Arthur was no longer bothered by the waiter. Now he turned his attention back to his young date.

Jack uncorked the wine and thought: don't spill on the tablecloth. He gave the bottle a quick and necessary twist when he stopped pouring. The man swirled the dark bull's blood vintage in his glass; he put his nose in it and poured it into his sunken cheeks, puffing them in and out, after which he set the glass down and gave a Jack serious expression.

Wine drinkers are ridiculous, Jack thought. Nevertheless, he put on his obligatory serious face and kept himself at false attention in a show of waiting for the man's approval, until the man nodded once gravely without looking at him. Jack poured for the girl, who wouldn't know how to appreciate such wine, much as the man probably wouldn't know the difference either, if, for example, Jack switched labels from some other, say, half as expensive bottle and served it to him just the same. That's typical of people, he thought, to value something only if it has a higher price tag. He remembered what Carlo had said about wine by the glass and the fact that the ten-dollar glass sold better than the eight because people believed it was better, though perhaps more because they wanted to show that they were ten-dollar-a-glass kind of people. And many of them didn't care because they had the money.

That's Carlo's rationale for everything: because a person has money he deserves to be ripped off. Carlo considers it his duty. And maybe it's not just Carlo who thinks that way, Jack reasoned, as he refilled the man's glass. It's just like Carlo said:

"Jack, if you think they can afford it, I see no problem with adding a few dollars here and there to the food. You see, Amerika is not like other restaurants: when people come here they don't want to think about money, they want to have a good time."

"But shouldn't everyone pay the same price," Jack asked.

"There's nothing dishonest in it at all," Carlo said. "It's like those restaurants where the menus have no prices and they make them up on the spot, according to how well the guests ate and enjoyed themselves. We're not here to treat everyone the same. The ones we treat better can pay for it. And if you add a few dollars to the bill, you get a better tip, and the bus boys make more money and also the cooks when you tip them out, right? It's like socialism. Perhaps it's because I'm Italian that I think this way," he added. "In my country we have never been able to decide our political ideology."

And you're a regular savior of the people, Jack thought. Paying your Mexican staff under minimum wage and forcing us to give out forty percent of our tips to keep them happy otherwise. And never mind each extra dollar goes straight into your own pocket.

All this advice had come when Jack had moved up into fine dining and was forced to wear white gloves. Silent service was in order, and he learned that a waiter was best not seen or heard. Resentment built inside him for how the customers didn't even look at him when he took their order. That was when he started inventing prices for the food and even adding on strange surcharges that were hidden in the bill to pad his tip. He knew it was wrong. But he excused himself by saying: this is what everyone does. Wasn't Jennifer bragging about charging nearly double for an entrée and getting away with it? He thought of Carlo with all his dishonesty, saying honesty was the best policy. If you talk about honesty, you're not practicing it, Jack reasoned. Then there were the guys in the kitchen that smuggled steaks home in their pockets; Martino, who kept a drink hidden under the bar at all times; and also the odd bottle of wine that would disappear and not be counted for inventory.

Andrea had taught Jack that little trick and had said in justification, "That asshole Carlo is rolling in the dough. He's a nigger from the south of Italy, son of Arabs, he's never been to school and he's *furbo* for marrying Grace, and now they live in Sausalito and have their own boat. I've been on that boat, forty-two feet long," he whistled, opening his eyes wide so the whites showed, "and I'll be damned if they're going to miss a bottle of wine. It's impossible to make any money here when you have to pay these damn lazy Mexicans. Maybe if they worked harder I would pay them more, *ma*, they have no respect and I have to do everything myself."

I suppose my justification would fall along the line of Carlo's socialism hypothesis, Jack reasoned. I like that about spreading the money around, and those who can, paying more to those who have less. Yeah, that works for me.

Jack brought the couple their food and caught bits and pieces of their conversation.

"You know most pretty girls are stupid and I can't relate to them," Arthur said. "But you're different. I knew that when I first met you. Most people would think: look at this old man who's trying for a girl who's obviously out of his league. But it's not like that all, is it? No, because we have something in common, you and I. We're both lovers of life and we're not afraid to try new things, and you don't seem like a person who follows the crowd, know what I mean? No, you need a man with experience. A man who can treat you right."

Jack thought: this guy is blowing it. He's giving away all his secrets and exposing the game, and now she has all the power because she knows where he stands. It's not implied anymore. She may be young but she's a woman, which brings certain advantages.

Mercedes ate like she hadn't eaten in weeks, stuffing her face with the antipasto of meats and cheeses, smearing the tapenade thick on the bread and gulping the wine. The caviar she piled high. She wasn't listening to Arthur and he wasn't paying attention to her, precoccupied as he was with hearing himself talk.

Mercedes had met Arthur in the bank where she worked and had been extra nice to him when she saw the many zeros of his account. When she passed him his receipt their hands touched and she asked, "Is there anything else I can do for you?" So he told her, "Yes, you can come with me to dinner tonight. You seem like a nice girl and it would be my pleasure."

And now she found herself sitting across from him. Though he wasn't particularly good-looking, he wasn't repulsive, nor was he afraid to spend money on her, which sure beat those guys that took her out and scrutinized the check and double-checked to make sure it was right, and who tried each in their own way to dissuade her from ordering dessert. Those men were young and good-looking, but they didn't have money.

Mercedes was still in awe over the class of the place. She felt naked behind her make-up and thought that her dress looked cheap, though she had spent several hundred dollars on it for a school dance. She didn't consider herself beautiful, though she was proud of her breasts, which were an above average 34D. Those breasts were now being forced out the top of her dress and the valley they created she knew was bound to draw some attention. Otherwise, she was slightly overweight. Her main fault was she liked to eat. She was Latina and her mother had always cooked for the family and made sure they were all well-fed. They ate meat seven days a week, something that certain less fortunate relatives in Mexico would marvel at.

Mercedes earned ten-fifty an hour at the bank and she lived with her parents. Next year she would start community college. She was not sure what she would study, something practical, probably. She had no illusions about the working world and no great ambition. Then she met Arthur Mortenson and started to dream. I could marry him and be rich and also help out the family. Maybe dad could finally start his own business?

"A girl like you deserves better," Arthur continued. Look at her tits, he thought. God, wouldn't you love to lick them and squeeze them in your hands? "I don't imagine you'll be working in a bank all your life. Who knows maybe I could get you a job in sales with my company. You'd get a good salary and there are great benefits . . ."

"Do you have many girlfriends," she asked him. "I like you, Arthur, but sometimes I wonder if you don't take a different girl out every night."

Not every night, he thought. No, the opportunity doesn't present itself that often, and I'm a coward with women anyway. This he was smart enough not to tell her.

"Waiter, excuse me, waiter."

Jack tried to walk by and ignore him. He had to drop a bill and recite the specials on a new table. Arthur grabbed him by the arm.

"Get another bottle of wine. Can't you see her glass is empty?"

Jack walked away, angry at the tone. I'll get the wine last, he thought. No, better get it first. The man is spending money. He's probably the kind that tips without thinking about it. No need to be nice to him, just get what he needs and leave him alone. The man obviously has other things on his mind. If it goes well with the girl, maybe there'll be a good tip. Don't think about the money. Work and don't think about the money. That's the best way.

"No, I don't have any other girlfriends," Arthur told her. "I was married once but it didn't work out. She was a good woman but we were too different. She said I never had time for her."

"I'm sorry to hear that," Mercedes said. She reached out and touched his hand on the table. Their eyes met.

I've got her now, he thought. They always fall for that sensitive stuff.

Men are so predictable, she thought. All they need is a sign of acceptance and they'll do anything for you. If he wants to touch me, I'll let him. He's more confident now. If he wants to kiss, I'll let him do that, too. I'll go out with him for drinks later. But I won't go back with him to his place. No, I want to make this last. He has to think I'm worth it; if I go the first night, he'll find another girl. No, I'll make him wait a week, maybe two. I'll go to bed with him and I'll let him touch me but I'll stop him at the last moment and tell him I'm on my period.

Remember your first time in the back of Manuel's car? You didn't want to be a virgin anymore. Manuel was rough with you and it hurt and you didn't like it. That was two years ago. Only one guy you've been with was any good in bed. His name was Rob and you met him in Dolores Park playing Frisbee . . .

Just imagine how she'll be after a few drinks, Arthur thought. She'll be all over you. Did you see the look in her eye when she touched your hand? All women are the same. They're all whores and you just have to know how to make them feel comfortable. Just think of all those years you wasted when you were younger, trying too hard. No, sometimes it takes time. Still, I bet you could get her back to your place. If necessary you might have to be rough with her. Scare her a little. She doesn't have anything else going, she works in a bank for Christ's sake. I see it. I'm not blind. I'm her sugardaddy. Some things are best left unsaid. Let her pretend she's attracted to me. Where is that damned waiter with the wine?

"How's that woman over on fourteen," Paul asked. "She holds herself well, doesn't she?"

"Yeah, she must take care of herself, get plenty of exercise and all that," Jack said.

Jack went by the new table.

"Can I get you something to drink?"

The woman looked at him with an irritated expression and said, "Get me a Long Island Ice Tea."

"A Long Island Iced Tea," he repeated to be sure.

"That's what I said."

"And are you ready to order?"

"Just get the drinks."

Yeah, Jack thought, she sure is pretty for an older woman with her small cat face and that sculpted blond hair, but she thinks pretty highly of herself, too.

Jack brought the drinks and overheard the conversation. The petite blonde spoke in a strong, angry way to her date, a handsome man of about her age that seemed to understand the value of patience. For some reason, Jack thought him kind. The woman Wendy said, "And that's not the worst of it. The Mexican government has expropriated all my property and also the capital I invested in the factory in Tijuana. That's over a hundred grand in sewing machines alone. And all the money I spent building that house on the beach near Manzanillo is gone. There's nothing I can do because I was leasing on government land. Well, they can do whatever they want with it. I don't care anymore."

Wendy was very upset at the injustice of it all. She sipped pensively from her drink. She didn't think at all about the *maquiladora* women she employed who worked in poor lighting for ten hours a day for a few dollars to maintain themselves and their families in the shantytowns on the outskirts of Tijuana. She probably didn't think about it because she had never seen her employees or how they lived. She never visited the factory, preferring to communicate her business decisions to a manager. When she went to Mexico, it was straight to the beach where she could be alone and forget about the nastiness of the world and the injustice to which she had contributed. And now she sat in one of San Francisco's finest restaurants picking at her food altogether distracted by her own problems.

I wonder what his business is? Is he her husband? Probably. Probably the sewing machines are no great loss. If she had the capital to start such a business, it only affects comfort, not survival. Now instead of visiting her own home, she'll pay for a hotel or rent a house for a few weeks of vacation. Still, I should remember that about the insecurity of buying land in developing countries, Jack thought.

Later that evening Jack was serving desserts on fifteen and brought the party of four a flan, a chocolate crème brûlée, and a piece of black forest cake, but forget one of their coffees, and one of the men, the comedian, said, "There goes your tip." Though it was joke, Jack thought there was nothing as crass as someone who mentioned the tip. That was just poor taste. Just like those customers who tip only on food and not drinks, though he had to bring them those drinks, open the wine, refill glasses and clear them away when they were done; or those foreigners who tipped poorly or not at all, as if their accent served as an excuse. One had to be extremely ignorant to not understand that tipping was fundamental to the American restaurant industry, especially at six twenty-five an hour in California, three dollars an hour in New York and nothing in Arizona. Those foreigners know better and especially the Europeans. When foreigners came, Jack added the tip himself so there would be no misunderstanding.

There was a lull in business and the wait staff was back by the coffee station hidden in a nook between tables five and six. Jennifer was saying in her loud waitress voice, "Did you see the guy on seventeen? Man, he really had to go the way he jumped up from the table. When I was walking by the bathroom I could hear him farting and spraying the bowl with shit; it just came out like an explosion. He must have been really suffering. He was in there for a good twenty minutes, and when he came out, you could smell it all the way to the dining room. I had to tell Ignacio to go clean up in there and spray some disinfectant."

When she finished talking, Jennifer noticed the hostile looks from the customers at the nearby tables. Fortunately, they weren't in her section.

There were some things that customers were not meant to hear. But that didn't bother Paul, who had the habit of walking away from tables saying things like, "Fucking high-maintenance bastards," or "White Zinfandel, who the hell orders a bottle of that *shite*? I thought that went out with the eighties and wine in a box?" Oblivious that the customers were not quite out the door, he would check his tip and say, "Cheap bastards. Only fifteen percent? Fucking tightwads. With the way they had me running back and forth for the butter and the vinegar and then some pepper, one at a time, not to mention how they camped out for two hours locking up the table like a chain gang. What do they think this is, their living room?"

Toward the end of the night Jennifer excused herself early from work as usual because she had to binge drink and get fucked by some new date and not remember it in the morning. They were left with her tables, and when she was gone, Benito, one of the bussers with very limited English, came up to Andrea, who spoke a passable Spanish, and asked him, waving the ten dollar bill that Jennifer had given him in his face, "*Más dinero*, how do you say?"

"More money. More tip. I want more money," Andrea said, gesturing with his hand around an imaginary bonbon.

"No, you got it all wrong," Paul said. "It's, bitch better have my money."

"Yes, more money. *La proxima vez se lo digo a esa perra*," Benito said, smiling. If Jack's high school Spanish was correct, this translated to, "Next time I'll tell it to that bitch."

Jack was last in, so he was last out. At the very end of the night he was left alone, while Andrea sat down to a complementary dish with no meat. In Amerika if you wanted meat, you only got it at a fifteen percent discount.

"He's not Italian anymore," Andrea said, referring to Carlo. "He's become an American. Never in Italy did I eat differently from the customers or the cooks or the owners. All the employees, we ate together. Here, it is everyone for himself."

Damned straight, Jack thought, as he raced to cover all the tables alone. How he hated those customers that came in right before closing. If he could, he would have turned them away, but as it was Carlo was sitting at the main bar in the entrance waving them on. Carlo was the sort to split up tables from four to two to accommodate as many as possible five minutes before closing.

That night a couple came in late. Jack told them the specials, asked what they wanted to drink and if they were ready to order. He was tired now and irritable and ready to go home and said, "Actually, we're closed. I'll still bring you your food, but the restaurant is closed." He did not feel the need to add: you are the only people in here and me, Ignacio, Martino, and Carlo are all waiting for you. So you better eat, drink and be merry quick, and leave a good tip because I think some of the rudest people on earth are those that slip into a restaurant at closing and pretend time is a fiction.

"Why don't you get us a bottle of Grand Putain, and we'll have a look at the menu," the man said, giving him a cold look. Jack had made his position clear, and now the customers were aware they were intruding and had solidified. And then it got worse. As Jack was opening the wine the woman got talkative.

"This is the first time we've been here. How long has this restaurant been open? I like the decor. That uniform looks very official."

"About ten years," Jack said. "Yes, it's a nice place, though the owner does have eccentric taste. The uniform is real. It's what the British soldiers wore during the colonial period in India."

"I feel like I'm in Magicland," the woman said. "Remember, honey, all those pavilions from the different countries, each with their own food and special dress? Are you from around here," she asked.

Jack knew her tactic. To cover for coming late and ruining his night by staying on past eleven she was going to create some sort of intimacy; she was going to make him like her and pretend they were friends and that she cared about his life.

"No. I'm from Arizona."

"Arizona. Wow, must be hot out there. We had some friends that moved out to Phoenix. What's your name?"

"I'm Jack."

"So Jack, what brings you out to San Francisco?"

"I needed a change and I've always wanted to come to California."

"Have you ever been to England, Jack?"

"No."

Jack hated when customers got familiar with him. He never asked or wanted to know their names. The man was still hostile and sat glaring at him because Jack had spoken the truth about not wanting them there.

"No. I've never been out of the country," Jack said.

"Well, you should travel. A young man like you. Working in restaurants gives you that flexibility. Just think you can go anywhere and get a job. I remember when we first went to Europe. We were in London and then we went to Paris and Barcelona. Paris was so romantic. I remember I took French in school but I must have forgotten a lot of it because I couldn't understand a word that anyone was saying. Ha, ha."

Will she ever shut up, Jack wondered. Imagine being married to this woman.

"So are you guys ready to order?"

"Yes. I think so," she said. "Let's start with some appetizers. You know what I remember most about France? The countryside with all the vineyards and fields and farmhouses. I remember we drove down to Provence and ate all this good cheese and drank wine, and that sure would be a good place to live. Imagine running a vineyard in the south of France?"

Yeah, how original, Jack thought. An American moving to the south of France to run a vineyard.

"Are you ready to order?"

He knew the importance of cutting the woman short, if he didn't want to be there all night. It was extremely inconsiderate of them to sit like they were in their own living room: the only people in the restaurant with their own personal waiter. It was doubtful they would adequately compensate him for the privilege, like "campers" never increased their tip for squatting on a table for two or three hours when in that time he could turn it three or four times.

No, the desire to be overly kind and fawning for a tip was fading. Jack had no reservations about pulling plates as soon as possible or about interrupting conversation to push dessert or to drop the bill when dessert was first on the table. He made money by volume; as long as he was prompt, there could be no complaints. He had no desire to befriend his customers. He could never remember their names, even when they told him. He would call them "you," "you guys," "the gentleman," "the lady," and he was always polite and that politeness was a formality.

19

For all practical purposes, Jack had moved in with Elizabeth. He came there after work and slept there. He spent his mornings on the internet searching for information and a way out of his current situation. Life is about searching for a way out, he thought, because things are never as they should be. I wanted to be out of my parent's house, done with school and finally out of Arizona. I wanted out of unemployment, being single and now out of waiting tables. And to think you never went to that interview with the marketing firm because you had to work. That's bad form. You have to learn to follow through with things. You have to learn to prioritize, he thought.

Living with Elizabeth was fine, except that they were seeing too much of each other. He had seen her irritable, and that was mostly because she was without direction in life; she was unemployed, bitter and tired of the city.

"I don't know why you came here in the first place, Jack," she said one night while they watched a movie Jack had chosen on her laptop.

The movie was full of inane action and posing on the part of the actors and she was tired of it, especially the women, whom she thought fake. She wondered: is that just because I want to be in their place? Would I be fake, too, if I were on the screen? It's not their fault though, because the scripts are bad. Still, when the director casts herself in her own film? No, there's no excuse for that.

Ali Rush is a bitch and I hate her mannerisms and the way she talks. All because of beauty, she thought. Fucking inane society. I really should do something worthwhile like go help children in India. Deep down, Elizabeth felt that she couldn't help anyone in her own society because it was already lost. Yes, I know it's all relative; I have traveled to other countries and seen the difference, but is this as advanced and civilized as we can get, she wondered.

Jack watched the movie and felt the rush of adrenaline that all men feel when they see someone kicking someone else's ass. He imagined himself roughing up a customer like that to show him who was boss. Violence was the final word in any disagreement; there was always a winner and loser and that was the way it had to be.

"What?"

"I said, I don't know why you came here in the first place," Elizabeth repeated.

"Well, I met you, didn't I?"

He said it with his characteristic sincerity and even gave her a kiss. She could tell he wasn't paying attention to her and that he didn't understand how she felt inside at the time: alone, even though they were together. He doesn't have a clue about women, she thought. It almost makes me blush to hear him talk like that. Sooner or later someone is going to teach him a lesson and it might as well be me. I'm too young to get involved like this and waste my time watching shitty movies. Really, there's nothing there besides his good looks and easygoing attitude. Easygoing men are like corpses, she thought. He's been with me almost a month now and we have never argued about anything. He has deflected every argument that I've ever wanted to start. I'm a bitch, she thought. I can be such a bitch and I know it, and maybe I'll try to drive him away with it?

"It's fine that you stay here, Jack, but maybe you should start looking for another place to live. I don't have any privacy, and my housemates are upset that they have to share the shower and the kitchen with you."

"But I told you I could pay something. It's only fair since I'm staying here."

"That's not the point, Jack. There isn't room for another person in the house. There are five of us already."

"Have they said anything to you?"

"Tina said that you wake her up when you come home from work and that you make a mess in the bathroom."

Jack was in a bad position and he knew it. Whether or not he washed the girls' dishes and took out the trash to do his part didn't matter because he didn't really live there.

"Tina's kind of a bitch, Jack, so don't take it personal. She's bitter with men because her boyfriend cheated on her and dumped her for the other girl when she confronted him. Also, she's getting older and I think, like all of us, she frustrated at having to live with a bunch of strangers her whole life and never being able to afford a place of her own."

"But you've been living with these girls for years. I thought you all got along."

"People come and go, Jack, this is a transient city and we are living in a transient time. Only Janet and I have a history. We know each other from college. The other girls came later and I don't have much of a relationship with them. They serve to make living affordable and that's about it."

"You're right about me looking for a place. I'm sorry for the inconvenience," he said. "I know it must be hard for you to share your space with me and have to explain yourself to your housemates."

"Stop being so bloody understanding, Jack. Anyway, as for explaining myself to my housemates: they can fuck off. Everyone is a hypocrite and I'm not going to apologize for it to others. I lived with Tina's creepy ex-boyfriend for six months. He was here every day and he had no personality and made no attempt to be polite and never offered to pay for anything. This movie sucks, Jack. You have no taste in movies."

"It's an action film, it's not supposed to be complex and say something about the human condition. It's about identifying with the hero and feeling like you can kick ass and save the world."

"And you waste your time watching and then go to bed with delusions of grandeur imagining all the great things you'll do tomorrow to achieve your dreams. Then you get up late, squander your time and make no progress in your life," she said.

"You're cynical," he told her. "Fine, let's forget the movie and go to the beach. Let's go swim in the ocean naked and roll around in the sand and get dirty."

"You're crazy, Jack. It's freezing out there."

"Just what I thought, all talk," he said.

"You don't mean it, anyway. You knew I wouldn't agree to it and now you're free to watch the movie."

"All right. Now you've done it," he said. "Come on." Jack grabbed her by the hand and pulled her off the bed. "Get dressed and get your shoes on."

"It's almost eleven o'clock," she said.

"Neither of us have anywhere to be tomorrow morning."

The water was cold that night when they ran naked into the shallows, splashing and shouting, before diving under the waves and swimming out into the dark and liquid depths. The current threatened to carry them away and they fought against it, as fear and adrenaline replaced the laziness and apathy of another night watching movies, that staple of American leisure.

The ocean is always here, powerful and strong, and to think most people never come to see it, stuck as they are in their routine and resigned existence. What a waste, Elizabeth thought.

They didn't stay in long, perhaps a minute, a minute and half, but that time seemed like an eternity and would burn a memory greater than the weeks and months spent at work performing routine tasks. It felt that way because they'd had the will to do it; it belonged to them and no one else.

"This is how it feels to be a piece of sugar-coated candy," Elizabeth said, rolling around in the sand with her slick wet body.

Elizabeth never succeeded in getting all the sand out of her bed from that night. But then she thought it nice to sleep with a little grit as a reminder. And to think I've been sleeping ten hours a day now that I don't have anything to wake up for. I don't have to wake up for Jack because he's right next to me. We could probably move in together but that's too easy and it's too soon. I need to get away now while I can. Some people think they can never get away. Fools.

20

Jack began his housing search in earnest. He bought the paper motivated by the thought that soon he wouldn't have to make shallow conversation with Elizabeth's housemates. In particular, he wouldn't miss Tina, who was uptight and stingy and had no sense of humor about herself. Living rigid like that was a good way to be splintered by life. How is it that a person could live permanently on guard afraid to open the door to love and laughter? I hope I never end up that way, Jack thought. Just think where I would have been without Elizabeth. Now that I know

I'm not welcome, I'm tempted to throw some money in Tina's face so she'll leave me alone. The money's not important. You make more than you need anyway. Well, more than you need to subsist, but not enough to have a future. But that'll change, and you mustn't be greedy and demand things in life that can only be seen in the movies.

Now it's one o'clock. You've been up for an hour and have eaten an unnecessarily large breakfast to procrastinate. You've been looking through the paper for rooms and it doesn't look good. It's much more expensive than Tucson, perhaps double, and the households are like this one with four or five people sharing one kitchen and one or two bathrooms. The cheaper places are far from your work, in Daly City or Oakland, and that means a commute. Commuting from Noe Valley to North Beach already takes you an hour when you figure it alltogether.

Jack wrote down some prospects. His priority was price; any money spent on rent was money out the window, so he would do good to cut the expense. He tried to find something with few housemates, but for price, he found it was hard to go below three, not including himself. The Marina was out; it was in the seven to eight hundred range for sharing with two or three and North Beach was the same. The Mission was a good possibility. In the end, except for a few choice neighborhoods, he found the price was more or less the same. For five hundred he would live substandard or crowded, and for seven he would live okay. Elizabeth paid six and a half; the house had its problems but it also had a nice kitchen and a balcony overlooking a garden. If it were his house, he would have put in a nice deck table and barbecue, unlike the girls who had done little to make the place habitable. But then what was the incentive to fix up a house that wasn't yours? The place was bare, empty and cold, and made Jack think of ghosts. Sometimes during the day when he was all alone, he felt depressed being inside and cooped up away from the sun and nature.

There were many curious rental ads in the paper. Rent for a room in shared housing started at four hundred and went quickly up to eight or nine. Jack had even seen an ad for twelve hundred dollars. What a waste, he thought. Who the hell can afford twelve hundred for a room, even if it's in a penthouse apartment with a hot tub, skylights and a balcony overlooking downtown in the nice neighborhood of Pacific Heights. The owner was looking for "an independent, young professional with a clean appearance" who was "reliable" and "quiet," but who also enjoyed cooking and was "queer friendly."

Another ad was for a "beautiful Scandinavian-style apartment decorated with original prints by Ben Mendes." Jack had no idea who Ben Mendes was or how Scandinavian style might look, but he liked that it was "spacious" and "well-lit." If only San Francisco were well-lit and not covered by clouds and soaked by rain. Maybe in a year or two you should move to San Diego? Doesn't Elizabeth always talk about the good weather in Southern California? Then you could take up surfing.

Jack found another ad more in his price range, which stated: "No freaks, losers, weirdos or whining. If you're a student, parents make sure the rent gets here on the first of the month, and I'll make sure your kid is safe." Five hundred a month and a nice fistful of hostility and condescension, Jack thought. But there was a washer and dryer and the room had "plenty of closet space" and "classic redwood floors." It was also "cozy." Might as well have a look, he thought. Could be I like the place. I'm not a student and can take care of myself. I don't have any debt to anyone but the government, and I pay my bills on time.

Then there was a "real bargain." "Live with five hip artists in the Panhandle. Central location. Looking for creative, interesting people who are flexible and open-minded." Four hundred a month.

Or he could check out a "Single room with own entrance on bottom floor, kitchen and bath to share with housemates. Good for a private person who is gone most of the day. Use of living room negotiable."

In another posting someone wrote: "Music lovers wanted. We are three members of Fuck the Government, an all-girl punk band. We like to make noise. Drummers, guitarists, DJs welcome. No men please."

Then there was the vegetarian household. "Absolutely no cutting, storage or eating of meat. All foodstuffs brought into house must be certified organic. We will not contribute to agribusiness or monocropping in any way. We have two cats and a small chimp rescued from poachers in the African Congo. Irie housemates welcome. :) "

Fuck that, Jack thought. Sounds like Noah's ark for Christ's sake. Right before it sinks.

He made a list of numbers thinking there were many people he could never live with. Finding the right place was all about luck. Remember, if it doesn't feel right, it isn't, no matter how much you like the room and need the security. Jack could get along with most people so long as they weren't extreme. He wanted to live with moderate, considerate people; he wanted his privacy, and he wanted his living environment to be clean and noise free.

That afternoon he called his list of prospects and made appointments for an open house and two private showings before work.

Jack took the bus down to the Mission. He bought a banana at the local Latino market and got lost in the neighborhood. He stopped in front of a brilliant mural at the Women's Center on 18th Street and stared at the faces and figures and vivid colors and designs, and thought how a city could be very beautiful when people contributed with public art. Since coming to the city, Jack had seen many such murals, especially decorating the *taquerías*. They all told a story; some focused on history and culture, while others were political and economic critiques. For example, the billboard and posters of the man in the sombrero being impaled by a sword with dollars pinned to his back.

Jack found the house from the ad and rang the bell. A young man opened the door. He seemed ordinary enough. His name was Matt and he moved in a slow and deliberate way as if he had just gotten out of bed. It came out that he worked from home as a web designer. He gave Jack a tour of the house.

The kitchen and living room were finished with hardwood floors and adorned with a collection of mismatched furniture. There was a large entertainment center with speakers in four corners of the room. They climbed the narrow stairwell with its worn wooden steps and Matt said, "Watch your head," while Jack ducked to avoid the low ceiling.

"Your room, the room we're renting, is downstairs. I just wanted to show you the roof."

They went up a second flight of stairs as narrow and steep as the first and came out onto a tarpaper roof. There was an assortment of bleached lawn furniture scattered about, a barbecue worse for the wear, a kiddie pool full of greenish water, and a dilapidated parasol with green, red and white stripes.

Across the way, Jack could see the park and the stucco Mexican style church. He liked the place and Matt was emotionally neutral. Corpses are neutral. Exactly, he thought. I would much rather share a house with a corpse than a person with feelings.

"Let me show you the room," Matt said. "It's the biggest in the house and also the most isolated, if you like your privacy."

As they descended, Matt asked him the usual questions, and Jack told him where he was from, what he did and how he liked to live.

They went out the back door and down the stairs to the basement. Where is he taking me, Jack wondered. Maybe he wants to show me the laundry room?

You have your own key and your own entrance," Matt said. He unlocked the door and pushed on it. It stuck and he kicked it open.

"Well, here we are." Matt clicked on the light and Jack noted the guilty grin on his face. The room was a converted garage with a concrete floor and no windows. The beams and nails were exposed, and there was no insulation whatsoever. Jack couldn't help but wonder about the room that was a hundred dollars cheaper over in the Richmond.

"You've got plenty of space in here for some turntables or something, and you can make all the noise you want. I would have taken it myself, except that it's a little too expensive for me. I have a smaller room so I pay a little less."

The truth was they were renting out the garage so they could all shave an extra hundred off their rent. Housing was hard to find and Matt had seen worse rooms and rented them, too.

Jack thanked him and said he was interested, though he wasn't, just in case.

"We've had a few other people look at it, so why don't you give a call in a couple of days. I think we'll have made a decision by then."

The truth was Matt didn't want to live with any more people. Four was enough. Still, rent was expensive and work had been sporadic. He was a mediocre designer and he knew it, though a few months ago it hadn't mattered. Then everyone had wanted their own web page and he had cashed in. He had spent the money on two vacations: one to Greece and the other to Cuba, and now he was broke again. I might even have to get a real job. The thought came and went and he still had a few weeks to ignore it.

Jack left to check out the four hundred dollar room. His burgeoning skepticism was confirmed when he saw that it was little more than a converted closet with space enough for a bed and maybe a desk if they touched and if he didn't want to open the door all the way.

Jack caught a bus to the Haight where they were showing a place just up the hill on Masonic. The street was crowded with people by the bus stop. It seemed strange that nearly all the people who stood waiting were his age. But then he reminded himself that the Haight was a young neighborhood. He walked up the street and found that the line of people snaked right in the door of the address he was looking for.

"Excuse me," he asked someone in line. "Is everyone here to look at the room?"

The young man looked at him and said, in a dry matter-of-fact way, "I'm afraid we are. I wonder who's going to be the lucky winner?"

"Good luck," Jack said and walked off.

A few days later Jack was seated on the couch in a pleasant apartment. He studied the faces of the young men and women that surrounded him and wondered: who are these people and what are they all about? They fired questions at him and Joe, who seemed to be in charge, said:

"We're a mellow household. We don't bring our girlfriends or boyfriends over to camp out. We do our chores once a week, on time, and when we eat we wash our plates for the next person because the kitchen is a communal space. We don't throw any parties and we don't come home drunk with friends and keep everyone else up. We all work and have to get up early."

He speaks sense, Jack thought. That's how people should live, but people are not that way and I don't want to live in a prison. That's why it's so hard to live with other people. You always have to be conscious of them, of not offending them or invading their privacy. He looked at Joe and thought: either he acts tough and is fair, or he's anal, or he sets standards for others that he can't follow himself. Or, if he's human, his behavior varies between all three. While they were talking, one of the girls, Martha, who was very pretty, left several times to use the phone.

"Do you all share the phone," Jack asked them.

"Yes, we do. But if you want you can get your own line. Most of us have cell phones," Joe said.

"You don't have any pets, do you," Becky asked. She remembered the young man who had come with his weasel and spent the whole time trying to convince them what a cuddly and well-behaved creature it was. He even claimed the animal to be as smart as they were.

"See, now he's shy because we're talking about him," the young man said as the weasel forced its way up his pant leg. "Stop, stop, Kokopelli, oh, that tickles."

The group sat and watched, unamused, as the prospective housemate hopped around and kicked his leg to shake the animal out.

Fuck that, Becky thought. There was a reason "weasel" was a pejorative term. Weasels stank and they were devious; if she didn't like people like that, then how about the real thing?

"I had a cat in Arizona," Jack said. "It was a Siamese and it used to sit on my head like this," he said, demonstrating with a pillow. "We would sleep like that. Or she would sit on my chest, and when I woke up, she would be staring right at me with her blue cross-eyes." He indicated with his hand the proximity of the cat and his startled reaction. "But it was my parent's cat and they kept it when I left."

They talked some more and everyone was relieved that Jack didn't have a car because then there would be an extra space in the garage when Luke moved out.

"Well, Jack, you seem normal enough and you have a college degree and you're employed. Who knows, maybe one day you'll even travel. We've had more than a few people come to see the place, and they've gone from bad to worse, so if the others agree then you can move in," Joe said.

Jack thanked them and said he was interested, thinking if he could do better he would. It wasn't the people he had a problem with, he preferred to live quiet rather than loud, but the room, which was a converted closet with a window looking to a wall as was common with many of the Victorian houses in the city.

21

Ignacio made more money as a busboy at Amerika than his father did as a janitor. He gave his mother money behind his father's back because he didn't want to shame him. He knew how much the waiters made because he saw their receipts at the end of the night. There were none who made as much as Brian and none who tipped out less. Ignacio worked in all rooms and put on whatever silly costume was needed. He was young and proud, and he made almost a hundred dollars a night. Some waiters he didn't like because they lacked respect and didn't pay him fairly for his help. For these, he ignored their requests for water or bread or to make a coffee or clear dessert. He was good at pretending to not understand English though he understood it perfectly and used it daily at school. Still, there were many days he ditched school to skateboard around the city with his friends. Skateboarding was one of his few freedoms. It was a way to use the concrete to his advantage and tame it. He moved with a grace over that landscape, flying off stairs and gliding down the handrails of government institutions and multinational corporations. He would fly down the steep hills of the city and jump cars and think: this is what it's like to be God, moving through everybody and everything without resistance.

To most of the waiters and waitresses the bus staff was invisible. The difference in education between the bussers and waiters was great, and that made it more tragic to be a waiter. Brian had a bit of tragedy in him, which either made a waiter proud and arrogant, or humble and small. Brian was arrogant and would take it upon himself to humiliate boyfriends on their first dates by forcing them to buy wine they could not afford, or by correcting their pronunciation of certain ethnic dishes then proceeding to explain their origins. Brian wasn't stupid, though his only skill was to wait on others. He was secure in the thought that no customer knew the restaurant and its food and wines as well as he did. If a pedant came in boasting knowledge of Bordeauxs, or a good vintage of Dom Pérignon, he could talk them to a stalemate because he had read, sold and listened. Most of the rich men and women didn't have a clue and assumed the signifiers of class like one bought a new car. Then came the cheap men who would pretend greatness and order mediocre wine without letting their date see the wine menu. For wine that cost thirty dollars they would act as if it were worth a hundred, and Brian would play along or not, given his mood and the possibility of a good tip. Like most waiters, he had learned to ignore all the pretentious, inane, lewd, crude and/or spiteful conversations he overheard between friends, couples and colleagues over a meal. More often than not, he found the older married couples who sat down to dinner to be either irritable and antagonistic, or unable to communicate with one another. Imagine being married to someone you disliked or couldn't talk to and having to sit through a whole meal with them. Then imagine having to live with them and sleep in the same bed. Then imagine doing that for a liftime. Brian wondered if the company was really worth it.

Sometimes Brian would be so busy that he no longer thought of customers as people. If they wanted to joke or carry a conversation, he would cut them short; it was a bad night, indeed, when an especially talkative regular, perhaps a lonely man, would come in and share his thoughts with the only person who would listen: his waiter.

Waiters are paid to listen, Brian thought. I would much rather feed the customers like animals in a zoo. It would be easier that way. Line them up at the trough and pour in the slop so they can eat themselves fat. No, you're not that cynical. Talking to the customers is what makes this job bearable. You have to be a people person to wait tables: someone who can say the right thing at the right time, put people at ease, give advice or laugh at a joke whether it's funny or not. You need to be prompt and courteous and know how to disappear or appear on command, build a man up to his date, et cetera. Admit it, you like this job. You just don't like it when everyone expects you to serve them at once, or when you're faced with unreasonable people. Still, these unreasonable people don't have courage with you anymore because you can freeze them out by the tone of your voice, or by bringing them everything they need without delay, so that they don't doubt that you know your business. Sometimes it's hard to know who really has the power, Brian thought.

When I work I look down on people; I spend my life looking down on people and the world. When I stand here in this crowded restaurant and hear them laughing, I feel distant and superior. I am a floating omnipotent head: a piece of calm reason in the chaos of customers that cannot see beyond their own table, their house or their office cubicle. And some of these people think you're stupid or less than them for what you do. But this is a service economy, and what difference is an important title when you work a mediocre job? Most of these people serve; they sell things like I sell food, and I would rather stand with dignity in this beautiful marble hall with the elephant Matilda and the gypsy girls and serve the best cuisine from around the world, than sell computers or cell phones or electronics of any sort, or work in retail or banking. Heaven is a bank; it's sterile and empty, people deposit and collect their money, there's never any danger and the robbers are always caught.

That Friday night was busy. Brian had spilled a drop of wine on the tablecloth and excused himself by saying, "In Italy that's good luck," receiving the needed laugh in spite of his mistake. As a waiter he thought of himself as a goalie trying for a goose egg every night, the sterility of perfection, so that he could rise above his humanity. But he had spilled the wine, a hundred dollar bottle, and their laughter wouldn't cure the shame. Then the food was late on another table and he told Martino, "I've been waiting twenty minutes for six," whining a little like all waiters did to the kitchen.

Martino stared at him through drunken eyes; he was like a fighting bull, violent and dangerous and best kept behind the counter with his cutlery. "I bring it when it is ready," he said. There was nothing Brian could do. These damned cooks play favorites, he thought. The girls always get their plates first and my ticket's been pushed back three orders already.

"*No me gusta este maricón*. I don't like this faggot," Martino said to the other cook Pablo, also Mexican, like a good percentage of all the cooks in California.

"Yes, he lacks balls, doesn't he? He'd look better in a woman's dress," Pablo said, and the two of them laughed. They were full of liquor already; they passed the nights full of liquor in a sea of pots and pans, moving them around the stove like playing a strange instrument, looking to the white tags with the waiters' arcane prescriptions. The kitchen crew couldn't understand the Arabic, Hindi or Japanese adapted into English.

They saw them as symbols and not words. And when the writing was unclear, Cleopatra looked like Calcutta, though they were dishes from two different cultures. When they couldn't read these scribbles, they panicked, and a hate built up inside them for the world. They worried perpetually that the waiters would make mistakes and take the wrong order or mix up the tables. Though they hated him, Brian was the most dependable and consistent, and this helped put them at ease during the chaos of the dinner rush.

Brian left the kitchen upset. He was stressed and behind, and that damned Ignacio hadn't brought his salads to table three, and they were out of water on five, and he needed to total the bill for one and get some drinks from the bartender. And what was that: a five-top on two by the window? Look like rollers, he thought. Better get over there.

Brian ranked his tables by tip; those that had the most profit potential got the best service. The lesser tables he would burn when he was too stressed: old couples, rude people, couples with kids, tourists and teenagers out on a date. Still, his section was the best of the best and he could rarely afford to burn anything. Most were regulars who trusted him and didn't need pampering. He knew their personal tastes and how to keep them satisfied. The few regulars who were stingy he would pawn off on his colleagues. He and the hostess, Nicole, had an understanding on this point. She was the only person he tipped well because he wanted to get into her pants. But then she was out of his league and they both knew it. As a result, Brian had to content himself with a mixture of flirtation, imagination and masturbation.

"Ignacio, I need those salads. *Ahora.* I pay you, so you better do them now if you want a tip at all, *comprendes?*"

Brian had him by the arm and Ignacio shrugged him off. He stuck out his chin, looked Brian in the eye, stood up straight and said, "I have a lot to do. I am very busy. Make the salads yourself. And another thing, you don't pay me. You're not the boss. Carlo is the only one who pays me."

Brian felt the blood rush to his cheeks. Why the brat, and didn't he pay him? He had to give him ten dollars a night for his laziness. Mexicans are just lazy, he thought. Brian believed in stereotypes: only by judging and labeling people in one way or another could he understand things and justify himself. It didn't occur to him that most people were lazy when they weren't paid fairly for their efforts. Perhaps he could have followed John's example; John paid his bussers twice what the others did and all he needed was to snap his fingers and the work would be done.

"You lazy brat," Brian said. "I have to tell you everything twice and it's your job to make salads, not mine. I work hard and I expect the same from you."

But by now Ignacio had turned away and was clearing plates for John and had to make salads for John. John spoke decent Spanish, he was easy-going, he smoked *la mota* and had lived in Mexico in Puerto Escondido, where he hoped to open a bar someday.

I'll kill that *gringo*, Ignacio thought, as he made the salads. He is a racist and does not respect me. He had tolerated Brian's abuse for many months now. He knew Brian was Carlo's favorite and that without him much of the business such as issuing paychecks, paying bills and making orders wouldn't be done. Brian was also in charge of the wine, he wrote the schedules for the rest of the staff and had even fired people. So Ignacio moved out of fear and made the salads. Generally, he did what he was supposed to, but always slow to the point he could get away with and not be fired, and he thought he knew that point.

"I need this salad split," Brian said, coming into the kitchen and throwing a plate in front of Ignacio. "I also need two coffees for three and a cheesecake and bread on one. If you can't handle the work maybe you should get another job. Maybe you can come over and paint my house and weed the garden."

It was said with malice that came from table five asking for things one at a time and making special requests on the food, and now Brian would have to humiliate himself for Martino.

"Listen, I know it's a hassle but it's not me that's giving you a hard time, it's the customer, and when I ask for the food a certain way it's because they want it," Brian said.

"Give me two dollars," Martino told him.

"What?"

"I said give me two dollars. I won't make it unless you give me two dollars. You pay everyone else, so now you can pay me for the trouble."

Intimidated, Brian promised him the two dollars, before heading back out onto the floor. Martino smiled at the others: Ignacio and Pablo and Ricardo and Santos, his brother. "One night we will break his *madre* for how he treats Ignacio. I know the way he walks to the bus stop. Then maybe he'll learn some respect."

Martino liked Ignacio because he remembered himself at that age, before he was a cook, when he had done many humiliating jobs.

"Don't worry. I'll take care of this myself," Ignacio told them. "This is goodbye for me, *compadres*. I'm tired of this shit."

"Where will you go?"

"There is always work. I am legal and can find another job. Don't worry for me. You are good people and I won't forget you."

Ignacio left with the salads and Pablo said, "He speaks like he is going to die."

"*Bueno*, for his age perhaps he is a bit serious," Ricardo said.

"If you ask me, he is stupid," Santos said. "How will his family survive without the money here?"

The question was not how Ignacio's family would survive, or what he would do without his video games, branded clothes and shoes, CDs and new skateboards; it was how he could get his revenge on Brian and leave that place with his head high and not look back.

So it happened that Brain was passing through his section carrying two precariously balanced brimming bowls of soup. Ignacio came toward him, his stomach tight and nervous. Abruptly, he slapped the soup out of Brian's hands and the bowls flew and shattered on the floor. Brian's white robes were stained red and the hot liquid burned his face. All eyes focused on the waiter and the busboy. The gypsy girl held her handstand on Matild's trunk. In a loud voice so everyone could hear, Ignacio said, "I fuck your mother, you son-of-a-bitch, racist asshole," before spitting in Brian's face.

Brian was paralyzed by his own shame reflected in the customers' eyes, while Ignacio stood tall in his moment of glory and basked in their recognition. For once, he was a subject they couldn't ignore. In seeing him perhaps they saw themselves and the pyramids of power they had built on the backs of others for their own advancement. Perhaps they felt a gnawing panic at the thought of their own employees doing such a thing: instigating the revolution that would interrupt their artificial world; or maybe they were only laughing at the comic waiter who looked to be on the verge of tears.

Like a courageous bullfighter, Ignacio turned his back on his adversary after the killing blow and walked slowly and deliberately to the door. Brian had never been one to lose his senses, but at that moment, thinking of nothing but the elimination of the object of his hate, he jerked his Arabic dagger from his belt. The curve of the blade flashed death in the lights and the crowd let out a gasp. Brian ran after the boy and it took three men to wrestle him to the ground and disarm him. All the while

Ignacio did not break his stride as he walked out the door and disappeared into the night.

Carlo had seen it all on the camera. He rushed down the stairs and appeared in the spotlight on stage. With Matilda's trunk wrapped friendly around his neck, he said, "Isn't that amusing, my friends, only the best live shows for you at Amerika. What drama, what acting. Brian, please take a bow. Isn't he great?"

Carlo had a reputation as a practical joker. He had paid strippers to sit in the laps of married men eating with their wives, not to mention the showdowns and the mechanical bull in the Wild West Saloon. The regulars thought it just another show, except for the men that had subdued Brian: in particular, the one who had been stabbed in the leg and who had put his foot on Brian's neck to crush his windpipe, before the others restrained him. That man would no doubt file a pricey lawsuit if Carlo didn't implement some damage control: free meals for the next year and VIP seating.

Reluctantly, Brian took his bow and thought: was it really a joke, was Carlo playing a joke on me? The customers applauded, and Brain went to the locker room and sat there not wanting to face the crowd again. Eventually, he left through the back door. I never tipped Ignacio well and I treated him poorly and it serves me right, Brian thought. This life is just injustice and the restaurant has made me bad and I've stolen plenty of money from Carlo because he is a fool and not a businessman. Maybe it's time to change careers?

22

You know that you're not wanted anymore when Elizabeth's housemates don't look you in the eye and slam their doors. It's extraordinary the inability of people to get along with each other. Maybe you should go back to the hostel?

In college Jack had always lived with friends. Now he was with strangers and would soon move into another house with strangers. The only reason for such a living situation was economic; it was something most people resented sooner or later. I even hate myself living here but what else am I to do? I don't leave the room much anymore, I eat out, I sneak to the bathroom and down the hallway, and when I ring the bell and one of the girls comes to open up, they make no attempt at friendly conversation.

The truth, my friend, is that no one cares about anyone but themself, and people hate to be inconvenienced by others. Strangely, I feel attracted to the girl I like the least. In fact, the hate between us is nothing but frustrated desire. You are always polite to Tina, while she makes life difficult for you by walking around in her tights and sportsbra, before and after her forays to the gym. She is terribly fit, but you can never touch her. Barring a relationship or marriage, men should live with men and women with women, because when men and women live together the sexual tension can be unbearable.

Jack had a few leads on rooms. He had made personal appointments to avoid the chaos of lining up with the crowd, rental application in hand, and feeling the competition. It seemed absurd that one should have to compete to pay a premium for a space to rest one's head. Welcome to California at the turn of the millennium. This place is packed with immigrants from the sticks like me, and Mexicans and other foreigners, who you hear speaking their babble of languages on the bus. The truth is there's no more room in this city and be glad you don't have a car. Elizabeth has so many parking tickets that it's like paying her rent twice each month, because she doesn't want to get up at six in the morning once a week and hike five blocks to move her car before they start ticketing. And then there was that time last week when they had it towed. Boy was she angry, and thank God she hasn't gotten angry with you, though you can tell she's getting tired of you because now she makes excuses and is gone most of the day, and you don't see each other except when you come home and crawl into bed at night. Then it's good because you're both too tired to care about being bothered by each other and your particular habits and ways of talking and the irritability that comes with being human.

It will do you good to get out for the day. You never go anywhere in the city. Where is there to go? By the time you wake up, your back and legs aching from standing and running around for six or seven hours a night, it's noon, and then you go get a coffee and breakfast at a nearby cafe and you read the paper or you just stay in and ignore what you have to do, which is find a place to live because you're fed up. It's not just that you have to fight for an expensive room, but that the rooms themselves are substandard. All this in one of America's principle cities: not to mention the number of people down on their luck and the filth of many parts of town. It's hard to imagine that this is the United States. Filth and beggars and people living in closets and basements and in lofts with no walls: three or four people together with no privacy whatsoever. That's what they've done to those South of Market warehouses, and that's the last time you go there looking for housing. The last thing you want is to live in a commune in the urban sprawl. Maybe in the Oregon woods -

you've heard good things about Oregon- or south of the border that kind of living is fine, but in a city with no privacy in the street and then none at home, no way.

When Jack went to see a room South of Market, he walked into a neighborhood with nothing but warehouses. Where do people live here, he wondered. He had trouble finding his way because there were no numbers on the buildings. He stopped in front of a nondescript steel door and knocked. There were such doors up and down the street often with no windows except high up. When he knocked, it rung hollow and empty. He felt lonely and hopeless because he hadn't found a place for himself in spite of his efforts. Still, many were worse off, having lost their motivation, or for financial difficulties: poverty, that is. Jack felt that every man deserved a decent place to live. In the city it's who you know, he thought. It won't always be like this; one day I'll be comfortable and feel secure when I look at people on the street. Then I won't think anymore about who I was: a lonely young man from the interior of this great country, that great empty interior that is being abandoned slowly for the coasts. I don't think I'll ever be able to afford to live in a place I like in my own country, unless there is a great crisis and those with money and power grow poor and lose what they have; only then is there a chance for people like me. Until then I'll feed on the scraps of the rich and with their charity I'll survive.

You shouldn't hate the rich too much, Jack, because they move money and invest and build, which means jobs. That's how this country is in the world; it spends and spends and other countries follow the example to the extent that they are able, selling us what they can, and the dollar is strong and buys a lot. The truth is you don't know anything about the world or how we have become so powerful, but it must be like a rich man who with his money can control other people's dreams.

Just think Elizabeth has a credit card debt of twenty-eight thousand dollars from school loans and it just keeps growing. She's not working and she keeps the same lifestyle as before. You meet her at the bars every weekend after work; she drinks more now than ever, and you can see that she's not going anywhere in particular.

Jack left to look at a room in the Haight. The young man who answered the door had all the identifying markings of the urban hipster. He wore the latest style tennis shoes, cargo pants made from strange slick material with zip-off legs, a futuristic watch and blue-tinted sunglasses that Jack imagined typical of Italian playboys. He wore his hair short and gelled up in the front as was the current style for men. These were the same men he had seen at Snowball when he had gone with Elizabeth to dance to the horrible, repetitive music called trance. He didn't consider those DJs musicians, but thieves, because all they did was reorganize the rhythms, melodies and vocals of others. What skill was there in that? Still, such thoughts he kept to himself; if not, Elizabeth was sure to accuse him of being backwards. They had argued about it before.

"Technology in music is nothing new, Jack. Look at the electric guitar. What do you think they do in mixing studios when a group puts out a CD? And don't forget the Moog synthesizer, a favorite of Stevie Warner no less, and I dare you to say that Stevie isn't a great musician and genius of our time."

"I don't know. It doesn't even sound human. It sounds like aliens came down and brought this music with them. Give me some Classic Rock any day."

"Oh Jack, you're just old-fashioned. If you don't open your mind you're going to get left behind. Electronica is the new classical. Centuries from now, people will treat this music with the same level of respect as the great composers of the past."

Jack heard her out and thought: she's on E. Still, it's nice the way she gets touchy-feely and sexual with me. No, you're not going to take away her candy, though all this seems superficial. You feel silly jumping around to this music, and that's because you're not on drugs.

Jack didn't care much for keeping up with the trends, but the house was clean and quiet and the young man seemed easygoing. Still, one could never count on a first impression.

"Here let me show you the room, Jack," Tony said.

They had made their introductions already and Jack followed him through the kitchen. Tony opened a door to a nice large room with a chandelier. The walls were painted black, of all colors. Why is that part of the floor so dark, Jack wondered. It almost looks like a black hole.

Tony clicked on the light and cleared his throat. There was no use lying about it or avoiding the subject. He would be honest and straight, and it wasn't so bad after all.

"Yeah, there's a big hole over by the wall. It was like that when I moved in. I don't know the story behind it. But there's always a story, isn't there? It could be from a piece of heavy furniture falling through the floor, like a piano, but that wouldn't explain why it's perfectly square, now would it?"

"I suppose not," Jack said.

"Well, the person that's moving out, John, he never had a problem, never fell in or anything, and the hole is flush with the wall, which means that we would have had to cut into the wall to repair it, so we left it. But I wouldn't worry, no big snake is going to come up in the middle of the night and suck you out of bed, and there's no such thing as ghosts, though John did say that on windy days it sounds like breathing when the air comes up from the basement. John always was a little paranoid, though, taping little hairs over the door jam to make sure no one was coming into his room, and balancing books on the door handle so no one would sneak up on him in his sleep. It could be in a worse place, like the middle of the floor, and so long as you don't put your bed over by that wall then it's not likely you'll fall in. You can always cover it with a few two-by-fours."

"Uh-huh," Jack said. He had seen many things before but none as ridiculous as this. Was this guy fucking nuts? Who would live with a four foot square hole in the floor?

Just then there was a terrible roaring from below like the hole was the mouth of some beast; it grew louder and Tony thought: someone will rent this room and I feel sorry for them, but that's just the way it is. I'm not paying for an empty room and none of the others want to either.

"Yeah, that's the garage below; it's only loud for a minute or two at around five when the others get home from work, and also in the morning at seven or eight, but you'll probably be up by then."

"I work nights," Jack said.

"Well, you know, that's what's fun about the city: it's always busy and teeming with life, and I imagine if you wanted silence you'd go to the cemetery, right? Ha, ha."

Jack thanked him and said that he was not interested. It felt good being honest. Even the cold shoulder and resentment of Elizabeth's housemates was better than living with a secret hole to hell in his bedroom.

Next stop was an old lady's house. She loved cats and liked to knit, and every piece of furniture was covered with gaudy blankets and pillows. There were cat pictures on the walls, the bedroom for rent had flowered wallpaper and, "He didn't have to worry because it was already furnished."

"Well, that's a relief," Jack said.

"Do you like cats," Bernice asked him, dragging her walker over to the kitchen where she was putting on some tea. He told her he did and she said, "Well, that's wonderful because I have seven. They are my children."

Jack saw their bowls all lined up in a row in the kitchen, each a different color with a different name: Tiger and Champ, Elvis and Boy, Rosco, Penny and Satan. Jack couldn't help but wonder about Satan. Some of the cats were hanging about and he couldn't help but ask, "So which one is Satan?"

"Oh, that's the black cat. He's always getting into trouble. I found him half-dead in a dumpster. Would you care for a piece of apple pie?"

Jack didn't plan to live with that woman and her cat family, but at the least he could be polite. She was from another time and could probably tell him a lot about the city and how it had changed. So he accepted the apple pie and took a bite and almost choked because she had used salt instead of sugar. The pie was stale and hard like a rock, so that Jack nearly lost a tooth, and he noticed that she wasn't having any.

"I'm not much for sweets," she said. "I'm trying to watch my figure."

He was a handsome young man, and she thought: why is it that when a woman gets old she has to hide her lust for men? A woman's love life is far too short in this world. I was more or less dead sexually when I turned fifty and then came those long years of default abstinence. Men, they're all the same, even the husbands. When they first meet you, when you're twenty and have ten or twenty suitors to choose from, they say the nicest things and buy you gifts and then later they don't like you because you snore or because of cellulite or the bags under your eyes. Men, their problem is that they're visual, but lust is smell, isn't it?

No one had told Bernice how old women were respected in China and other countries with history. Could she expect any different of the United States where they tore down buildings that were ten or twenty years old, especially casinos, like clothing gone out of style; and where plastic surgery was born and models were dropping in age so that the average now was sixteen being passed off as mature, that is legal, with plenty of airbrush. Who knew that perfection could be so damaging for a society.

So there she was trapped in her own decaying body, renting the room, not because she needed the money, but because she needed the company. Not even a hundred cats could take her loneliness away. Loneliness was something people could smell; it went with fear and shame and all other things that people avoided in each other.

"Tell me about San Francisco," Jack said.

Bernice smiled and looked to the street. It was the first time anyone had asked anything of her in a long time and a pleasure rushed through her at having something to say. She wondered: what does he want to know and how do I keep from boring him?

"San Francisco has been through many great events but none like the great earthquake and fire of 1906. The whole town was ablaze then and everything was covered in smoke and ash. Many people lost their homes and had to live in the street until they could rebuild the city, which took a long time, indeed. Many beautiful buildings were burnt and lost, and it's always a shame to lose history. San Francisco was built on the gold rush and the main activities of the city revolved around gambling, drinking and prostitution. Back then the city was full of prospectors and adventurers from all over the world. Most of them hung around what was then known as the Barbary Coast, down off Pacific and Broadway, which was famous for its whorehouses and bars where the sailors drank and fought and were shanghaied to serve as crew on long voyages to exotic lands. San Francisco was once a dangerous, lawless city, but things change with time and people forget."

"Is it so different from how it was," Jack asked.

"Because of the bay it will always be San Francisco, and many fine buildings that remain today were built after the great earthquake and fire. The city, it changes but stays the same; neighborhoods like the Mission were once home to Irish immigrants and now they're full of Hispanics. Russians have come since the collapse of their country, and the Chinese keep coming. If you ask me there are too many immigrants in this country. It's getting so no one speaks English anymore. I tell you if you're going to live in this country, you'd better speak English."

Bernice was living in another time and Jack thought how, like many senior citizens, she was clinging to what she knew and understood and would drown with it. Being old was the inability to learn, grow and accept change, and Jack didn't want to become like that or give off the stink of death like she did.

"I don't understand kids today with their computers and internet. It doesn't serve any purpose, if you ask me. Just a big waste of time. None of them have ever lived through a depression, and that's why they can act and dress and live the way they do. They have never lived the bad times, and this city and America has had plenty. I suppose some generations are lucky and others are not, but I lived through the hard times with my husband and I'm still here. I sure hope you don't see this country like I've seen it in the bad times, because they are very bad. You take for granted what you have."

Bernice looked the young man in the face and saw the restlessness in his glance and the way he fidgeted in his seat and wondered: is it possible that with each generation people can forget so much?

"This is the greatest this city has ever been and probably will ever be, and you're young and smart and will do just fine for yourself," she said.

Jack left her and promised to call, but that was a lie for the sake of her feelings. He had other things to think about besides this old woman living in her time capsule, so he left and walked the streets and tried to imagine the city many years ago when the motorcar first came: how loud it must have been and how such cars had to be cranked to start, and also how people must have dressed and what they did for work. He wondered if this time was any better than the past. It was probably both better and worse depending on how you looked at it. Some things that were good then were gone now, and Jack felt that life was moving very fast, though there was more to make one comfortable for the ride. I wonder what rent was in San Francisco at the turn of the last century? I wonder how much that woman bought her house for? Yes, time was everything for securing a future, and that meant working hard now and saving money and investing for later. Jack couldn't afford to travel like Elizabeth. He couldn't relate to her dreams and he thought her frivolous. Why doesn't she just stop and build a life for herself here? Jack wasn't nervous and restless like her. He liked to take things slow and coffee made his nerves hum, but if one didn't drink coffee then what was there to do in the afternoon?

Well, Jack, you've seen a lot of ways of living that you don't like, you're running out of time and, besides work, you aren't secure.

23

When Jack came home Elizabeth was at the computer. She let him in and went back to her business. Jack lay down on the bed and watched her, wondering what she could be thinking. There were many things he didn't know about her: aspects of her life that had existed before him and the people she had once touched with her words and actions. These were facts that would separate them forever. He loved her for the mysteries of her past and her ability to look toward the future. She was independent of time and place and could walk away from the America he was scared to leave. It occurred to him that he wouldn't know what to do with himself in another country where they didn't speak English.

Jack remembered high school Spanish and the crippling fear of being called on and questioned. Though he was always prepared, it was the possibility of not knowing the answer that made him afraid. In the end it had made him shy; he had always envied those people who could go in front of a group of strangers and speak their minds. But you did know the answers; you were just ashamed to speak up. Then someone else would answer and Jack would breath relief at hearing he was right.

"I looked at a few places today," he told her. "One of them had a huge hole in the floor and they said it led to a secret world like in a video game and that, if ever I needed to, I could go there for an extra life."

Elizabeth didn't laugh. Instead, she felt uncomfortable because there were things she had to tell him that he wouldn't want to hear. She knew it was wrong to put them off -it had always been her weakness to put things off- so she decided to speak her mind.

"I'm leaving, Jack. I'd like to offer my room to you but this has always been an all-girl house, and frankly Tina doesn't like you; it's not fair of her, but that's how it is. I don't know how long I'll be gone, at least a year, I think. I'm off to Indonesia to teach English. I have a friend there who can put me up until I get settled. I already have a job lined up teaching at a university in Padang."

"But you didn't tell me anything about it."

"Jack, I never tell anyone anything about my plans. Call it superstition, but I don't want to boast of things that I won't have the courage to do. I want to be a teacher, Jack, and also I think it will do me good to get away for a while. I tried to live a stable life here and be a part of the new economy, but really it's just bullshit and I don't give a damn about it."

Don't show her you're weak, he thought. Dammit, it feels like you've been fucking stabbed. You're already missing her and she's not even gone yet. You know her and she's not going to change her mind. Damn you want to touch her now and spend every minute with her because she's so beautiful: the way she's hard on herself and the fire in her. It's not your place to make her stay.

"Don't you have anything to say, Jack? Why is it you never have anything to say? I'm leaving. You're not gonna see me for a long time, maybe never again, and if you do our lives will have changed and you won't be needy and loving anymore, like a stray cat, and I'll probably want children and a house, and maybe you'll be married because you're good Jack, you're beautiful, not like me because I don't know what I'm doing with my life. Oh Jack, I'm so fucking miserable in this place."

Elizabeth started to cry, and it was guilt-crying and self-pity crying because she was going to Indonesia to see her ex-boyfriend, Graham: the only man she had ever loved. She loved him because he had left her to photograph death and misery so he could hold it up like a trophy for others to see. Death had crept into his soul, revealing itself in his skeletal body and his haunted eyes. She was attracted to his courage to be absolutely miserable for the sake of humanity. But she was also smart enough to know he did it for the sake of his own manhood and pride.

"Come and lie down with me," Jack coaxed. Elizabeth crept into the bed and he held her in his arms and thought about children and their teddy bears on stormy nights and all the other talismen of safety, like the nightlight and the favorite blanket. For Jack, love was also a talisman.

"When are you leaving," he asked her.

"In two weeks," she said.

"That doesn't give us much time."

"No. There's never enough time. Memories stay forever and there's never enough time. That's something I never understood."

Jack didn't understand, either, but kept quiet. It was the tone of her voice that mattered, not what was said. There were many things he didn't say because he didn't know the words to use or the order in which to place them. Wasn't that always the problem: with Tina, in renting a room, with strangers, and in job interviews. Even if there were things that needed to be said, they might not be pleasant to hear. Jack was afraid of the truth but hated to lie.

His thoughts moved from her to the practical aspect of finding a room; that was a great concern in his life, just as packing her bags and saying goodbye to the familiar was a concern for her. They were now heading in opposite directions after having met at the crossroads of lust and need. The goodbye was a vile thing, a pile of fetid animal dung steaming there, which they tried to ignore by pressing their bodies together and staring into eyes that projected what each wanted to be outside of themselves.

They sat at a cafe in the Haight and Jack drank beer, though it was still morning. Lately, he had taken to coming into work drunk or buzzed because it made it easier; he was more apt to tell jokes and laugh and his tips were better. Am I becoming a drunk like Nick the musician, Jack wondered. No, it's because I hate coffee; I can't imagine a more pain-in-the-ass job than making coffee to suit people's special needs: long and short espresso; mocha and chai with a dash of cinnamon; skim milk, one percent or two; beans from Indonesia, Jamaica and Brazil. What a lot of pretentious bullshit for that shot of caffeine that was everyone's addiction. Just think of Elizabeth in the morning before her cup of coffee; she's irritable and walks around like a zombie. You've learned to stay away from her: to get out of the way and leave the bathroom when she needs to shower. But now she has her cup of coffee, and I have a bottle of overpriced beer and a bagel with hummus, and life is good. I sure am glad I don't have to work during the day, Jack thought.

The phone rang and Elizabeth answered. Jack thought it would be a long time before he knew enough people to warrant buying a phone for himself. There are times when I don't want to be reached at all, he thought. There are times when a person needs to be alone.

"Damian, how are you?"

"I'm fine. We're on location for a documentary. We're filming healing horses."

"Healing horses?"

"Yeah, there's a ranch up here in Petaluma where they treat disabled children to walk again by letting them ride horses. I know some people think animals are dumb, but these horses are trained specialists, you know, like the dogs that sniff out coke in airports."

"How can riding a horse help a child walk?"

"It's the movement. They develop a sense of their legs as the horse walks. I've seen it myself. There's this kid named Jacob that we're using as our focus for the story. He's been doing this therapy for a year now and after riding he can walk for a few minutes without the help of his crutches. Still, it's not all easy. Once a horse reacted violently to having its mane pulled by some kid and it bucked him off and broke his arm. Hey listen, we gotta shoot in a few minutes. I'll pick you up a hat or a t-shirt or something. Say, have you talked to Jack lately?"

"Yeah, he's right here with me. You wanna talk to him?"

"Sure, listen, I don't know him very well but he seems like a solid guy, and the truth is we need someone to fill an empty room in the house. Is he still looking for a place?"

"Yeah, but I don't know if he'd want to live with you guys. You're a bunch of freaks. Anyway, did I tell you, I'm leaving for Indonesia in a few weeks."

"Indonesia. Sweet. You'll have to tell me all about it. I wish I could get out of the city. We're working on travel documentaries so it might be sooner than I think. Anyway, I'll talk to you later."

"Bye Damian." Elizabeth passed Jack the phone. "It's Damian. He wants to talk to you about a room."

"Jack, hey buddy. How's the city treating you? You're a lucky guy, only been here a month and you've already got a girl, and guess what? We got an empty room in our house. You said you were looking for one, right?"

"You bet I am. Wow, that's great news. I was getting desperate."

"Well, it's a five bedroom and your room is only four hundred dollars. Cheaper rent is impossible, Jack. You'd be living with me and Alex, you remember Alex, and Henrik, this Swedish guy who spins trance at the local clubs, and then there's Julie. Now she's young and hasn't learned how to live with other people yet, but you have to take the bad with the good, right? Anyway, the house is nice and it's in the Haight and we've got a deck and a view and I think you'd fit right in. Why don't you come by tonight and check it out?"

"I can't, I gotta work."

"Well, then how about tomorrow night?"

"Sorry, I work every night except Sunday and Monday."

"Well, why don't we do this, we can all go out together for drinks when you're off and then you can meet everyone. I'll give you a call later this week, say Thursday, and tell you where we're gonna be."

"Sounds good. Thanks Damian. I appreciate you helping me out."

"Don't mention it, buddy. No, no, the black horse, he's better for the camera. Who wants to see a calico? No, not over there. By the barn. I want the company logo in the picture. Sorry, Jack. I'll talk to you later."

24

"This beat will take you to the stratosphere. Race two thousand light years into the future. Dance with me star children."

The DJ spoke with a slight accent, adding additional humor to the statement. He was German or Dutch or Finnish or Swedish, from one of those countries in the North, anyway. The music came hard and pulsing, and the crowd convulsed like orgasm or seizure. The club was called Chameleon, and the lights raced around the room and cut across faces and chests and burned into the walls. Jack's view of the dance floor was obscured by a wall of smoke.

"That's Henrik," Damian said. "He sure likes his music. He's partied and spun in places like Ibiza, London, Ios, Paris and São Paulo. Do you like techno, Jack?"

"Not particularly. I find it superficial and repetitive."

"Well, maybe you're right, Jack, but it sure is fun to dance to and the girls like it. And whatever the girls like, I like, even if it's a movie about a woman who loses her daughter in a car crash, or a mother dying of cancer," Arnold said, pushing his glasses up his nose.

They were seated in a booth by the dance floor, the six of them, including Alex and Julie. Julie was pretty; her hair was brown and her skin very white and she had small cat eyes and nice bones in her face. Otherwise, she was extremely thin and agitated because she was on speed. She sipped from a Cosmopolitan and stared at Jack. Because it was dark and Julie wore make-up, Jack didn't notice the dark smudges under her eyes from lack of sleep.

Arnold sat like a mob boss with his arms stretched wide and resting on the back of the sofa. He wore a white suit with a metallic gray dress shirt and was larger than Jack remembered, inflated but not necessarily fat. Jack realized now that the joke had been on him about the wig and fake teeth when they had first met. Under Arnold's coat was a holster and in it, a handgun, of what make Jack could not be sure. He's got a fucking gun. Why is he packing a gun, Jack wondered.

"I don't mind crying," Arnold continued. "I'm a sensitive guy and seeing a stray cat in the rain, that gets to me. Just because a man is big and tough doesn't mean he can't be gentle like a lamb."

"What the hell are you talking about, Arnold," Alex asked.

"I'm talking about gender relations and the fact that I don't think women are more sensitive than men."

"So anyway Jack, this is Julie, and you already know Alex and the others, and when Henrik is finished with his set, you can meet him, too," Damian said.

They all shook hands with Jack. Now that she was drugged up and agitated by the flashing lights and the music, Julie felt like life had no limits. Normally, she was oppressed by her own shortcomings and insecurities. She had TMJ in her jaw already at twenty-one from clenching her teeth with worry at the question of her beauty. She was from Missouri and ashamed of the way she talked, so she tried to speak as little as possible.

In spite of her rural origins, the city had transformed her. Julie loved to be out on the town and she felt now that she was at the center of the world. She was too young to know any better or to be able create her own center. When she wasn't out at the polished clubs with strangers in their hip clothes and big talk, she was sleeping late, missing class and borrowing money from her parents - like many pseudo students- for her big city adventure as a mature, independent woman. She was taking her classes over again because she had failed them the first time. In spite of her shy nature, Julie believed people would do her favors for the sake of her beauty: a reasonable assumption given the society in which she lived. Julie's nervous energy was perceptible to anyone who came into contact with her; it was apparent that she felt threatened by the outside world.

Elizabeth looked at the others and thought: I'm tired of this. There's no point to it. I would much rather live in a small village in Indonesia, ride my bike to work through the jungle, keep a diary, and take pleasure in cooking and eating and living small like people should. Look at all this useless crap and artifice to keep us distracted. There is nothing original to be said anymore. I don't have a damned thing to say to these people. And they're my friends. I thought they would be my friends forever, but that's an illusion. The only reason we're friends is because we live in the same city and no one can stand to be alone with themselves: that is the disease of urban life. Christ, what I wouldn't give for a bit of privacy.

Two weeks and I'm outta here, Elizabeth thought. Then it'll be like none of this ever happened. But there've been some good times, too. A good party or some handsome young man you saw passing in the street and never forgot, though the two of you never spoke. Sometimes the best memories are those that long for things you never had, she thought. Memories like those you had before you moved to the city and had idealized it. Los Angeles and San Francisco are different, but overall California is a superficial state. People here want everything new all the time; they want to be eternally hip no matter their age.

Alex wasn't much for the nightclub or the bar, except that he liked to drink and needed to get out of the house every now and again. He knew if he didn't get out of the house, he would go insane, though every time he was out on the town he grew irritable. He was the sort who needed to complain about everything; no matter what he had, he was never satisfied. Perhaps that's why he was a chronic bachelor: because women inevitably found out what a pain in the ass he was. And that particular evening was no different. The mediocrity and futility of being human was on glaring display in all directions, and he was not one to keep his mouth shut for the sake of decorum. So Alex did what he was best at and stirred the shit.

"Sometimes when I sit down in a place like this, full of posers and lost souls worshipping the god of hedonism, I understand why we are unable to progress to a more equitable world," he said. "We are content to sacrifice the lessons of history for entertainment. That's the problem with too much leisure."

"What are you talking about," Arnold asked.

"Don't encourage him," Damian said.

"Let me give you an example. There was a time during the Roman Empire when certain slaves were given their freedom, either through merit payment or goodwill. Some of them came to be very powerful and started behaving like their Roman masters; they adopted the fashion of the time, surrounded themselves with fine possessions, had lavish parties, and imitated the speech and behavior of the ruling class," Alex said. "But in their quest for wealth and status in a foreign society, they sacrificed their origins. They were too eager to give up their history and traditions. They simply copied the rich, but that did not give their lives meaning. That's how I see us now. That is the history of the United States with its Wild West and Gold Rush, and the poor immigrants that came from the rest of the world to get rich so they could return home to a better life. But most of them never returned. Most worked hard for a meager existence and died in anonymity; some found success through reputable means and remained to enjoy their newfound comfort and influence, while others built their fortunes through monopoly, corruption and exploitation to become the great leaders of our nation.

"The absence of history made it possible for the most creative, ambitious and optimistic to achieve their dreams in America, but these dreams were primarily economic in nature; we have yet to see a flowering of the arts in this country similar to that of other empires. There was not, nor has there ever been, a concerted effort to create an American culture, except among the urban elite of our great cities. Our culture came about as a byproduct of development: culture was the highway, the motorcar, dams and tract housing; culture was branded consumer goods sold to the masses to make life convenient and comfortable; culture was entertainment in the form of movies, sports, popular music, and the cult of personality of movie stars and the beautiful. The unofficial culture, the culture of the poor and marginalized and the obscure, has had to go through the meat-grinder of economics; all artistic and social movements of any worth in this country have come about as a protest against the cultural vacuum of America. And it's typical of America that once a unique perspective or form of expression is recognized, in spite of the obstacles, then those who scorned or ignored its value are all to eager to hold it up and proclaim it as American and a common heritage. That's the foundation we're building on. We've built the infrastructure and the economic base, but we still have a long way to go in achieving quality of life in America," Alex said.

"Maybe what you say is true," Damian said. "But America is the future, we are the great innovators and dreamers, and you'd better believe that the world is better off because of it. Sometimes people have too much time on their hands to think, and I've always believed that thinking too much is no good."

"I recognize your point," Alex said. "But our actions must be founded on reason. An individual who develops his character based on the lies of others, for the sake of comfort and acceptance, is a fool. It's precisely the attitude of not wanting to think that's the problem. Apathy is the refuge of the coward. As I see it, progress is only possible through communication, action, and subsequent reflection on what one has seen and done. How many people reflect on their daily experiences or make any real effort to learn from and understand people different from themselves? It doesn't seem to me that our model of economic growth embraces community activism or philosophical debate. As for American dreams, they are by and large personal and exclusive dreams in which the success of the individual often comes at the expense of the community. Unfortunately, sustainability and equity do not form part of the American definition of success. The problem with this country is that subsequent generations of Americans have lost sight of the values of their immigrant ancestors. The American bias for convenience, comfort and privacy makes for a lazy, apathetic citizenship with little capacity for critical thinking and compassion for others."

Damian disagreed with Alex's thesis but he didn't want to keep arguing. Alex was always bringing up that heavy shit out of the blue when they were trying to have a good time. You're just as much a part of this as I am, he thought, and it's easy to take the moral high ground, but you live just as I do.

It was not in Damian's character to focus on the negative. There were many men and women out there that, with skill, knowledge and creativity, were working to improve the world. There were plenty of people that worked to help others. And he wasn't exactly the devil, was he? He had produced some documentaries and promoted a meaningful film or two. Was it his fault if he didn't want to occupy himself with the world's problems? So long as he made his own way, it wasn't anyone's damned business. Because philosophical bullshit aside, economics was the only thing that could vindicate or negate an ideology. Stomach first, then lofty ideals. Stick to that adage and you'll be all right.

When Henrik joined them after his set, Jack thought: look it's fucking cyberpunk with his hair spiked and rings in his nose, and what the hell is that in his neck? Why, his neck is ringed with little bumps like an extra pleasure style condom.

Henrik held up his fist, grimaced and punched the air to the beat of the music.

"Yeah, isn't it great? Did you hear that set, man," he said, slapping Damian on the back. "That's original sin, brother, that's what it was in the garden with the snake and the apple and all that. That's the spider eating the fly, dead fish in the river and cannibals swinging severed human heads."

"Henrik, this is Jack. He's the new housemate I was talking about," Damian said.

"Right, Jack. Nice to meet you, mate. God, I love life," Henrik said, holding his arms in the air and thrusting his hips forward and around in a circle. "It's fast and fresh and never the same. Just you wait and I'll take you on a ride through passion and hummingbirds, and the sweet sick smell of rotting tropical fruit and decadence like being naked in the snow with your genitals on fire."

The waitress came by and Henrik grabbed her by the arm. "Mia, why don't you get a drink for the DJ? A Red Devil and vodka, and a round of tequila for my friends. Thanks sweetie," he said, winking and slapping her on the ass.

Henrik's a pervert, Mia thought. A British techno trash pervert. Still, the club scene must be great in London. He's got a nice set of hips, doesn't he? All thin and wiry and full of energy.

Henrik plopped down on the couch and said, "The audience here, they're a bunch of stiffs, man. It's nothing like the *fiestas de espuma* in Ibiza with everyone covered in foam and the babble of five languages humming in the air."

Henrik ignored Julie, but sometimes when he was drunk, and whatever boyfriend she had wasn't around, he would climb into her bed, and they would have sex and not talk about it in the morning.

Henrik was thirty-three and living on borrowed time. Chameleon didn't pay well and many of the places he said he had spun in the world, he hadn't, but he could lie about them because most Americans didn't know the difference. He had been to those places, even if only as another party guest, and many years ago at that. He was native to Stockholm and had lived in London, working in bars and playing private parties and sometimes this or that second-rate club. He made a point of keeping his British accent, though he could speak like an American, too, and particularly a Texan when he wanted to make fun of American provinciality and ignorance. Still, like many Europeans he envied the Wild West and the freedom of the States, where one could get in a car and drive across the empty desert and feel like anything could be accomplished. So there he was trying to make a name for himself in the city with his music. He had his image to rely on; he was trying to sell himself, and there was nothing wrong in that. When he went home to Sweden Henrik was envied by his old friends. Captalizing on the myth of his fame, he went with all the girls who never wanted him before. He told them lies that bloomed in the cold of winter. They imagined his life in the California sun with a big house and a swimming pool and a convertible sports car in the garage. He wasn't going to be the one to tell them otherwise.

The tequila shots came and Henrik held up for a toast, "To Jack, I hope he survives us. Ha, ha."

Jack smiled and they clinked their glasses together and poured them down the hatch. Jack didn't know what to think of Henrik with his rose-colored attitude. He wondered about places like Ibiza, London and Paris, and his mind started to swim. He felt small and jealous of Henrik. He disliked the way Henrik looked at women and Elizabeth in particular: staring at her breasts, licking his lips and smiling like a wolf. If I could read your mind, I'd knock your teeth out, Jack thought.

"So you're from Sweden," Jack said.

"Yeah. Sweden. Where everyone's blond. Yeah, Sweden is nice and clean and the state pays for our health care and also unemployment. We have good public transportation and there aren't any poor on the street like there are here. Poverty in the United States is just appalling, the cities are ugly and you have no history."

"Well, if you don't like it, you foreign bastard, then why have you stayed so long," Arnold asked. "All you do is complain about this place and criticize and then you go home to Sweden for a week and come right back. The grass is always greener, isn't it?"

"I can say what I want about this country. You Americans, all you think about is money and making your shitty movies and music, and your club culture stinks."

"And you're telling me that if you could sell some of your shitty music and make a buck, you wouldn't? Fuck off. You're an opportunist, Henrik. You want to talk plain and criticize; well, you're not making any money, you don't have a name in Europe, and you don't even know the names of the clubs in Ibiza because I've been there and you made them up. There are no clubs named Nightwatch or Casbah in Ibiza. Before you start lying, know your audience," Arnold said.

"He's talking nonsense," Henrik said. "You know how he likes to talk nonsense. Clubs come and go and I tell you the Casbah and Nightwatch were in Ibiza when I was there and I've spun at both of them. This fat clown is just in a bad mood," he said to the others. "You buy someone a drink and this is how they behave."

Arnold pulled out his handgun and pressed it to Henrik's forehead; if he was in a joking mood, he sure had a strange sense of humor.

"Fuck you, you Swedish prick. Do you know what'll happen if I pull this trigger? It'll blow a chunk of your skull about the size of my palm, but more irregular like crushed eggshells, out the back of your head along with a good portion of your brain."

"What the fuck are you doing, Arnold? Put that away before someone sees. For fuck's sake," Alex said.

Henrik had turned white. He was thinking about death and how well he did or did not know Arnold. Just about anyone can snap when the pressure's strong enough, and I've been there several times myself; I've wept like a baby after a night of drugs, he thought.

Arnold threw his head back and laughed. "Gotcha. You thought I was going to do it. Man, you're crazy, Henrik. Ha, ha." Then he pulled the trigger anyway. The gun clicked and Henrik jerked in his seat: a shock that took a year or two off his life and sowed the seeds for his first gray hair.

"Chill out. It wasn't even loaded. Do you think I'd carry a loaded gun?"

But the gun was loaded. Arnold always kept the first chamber empty because he knew himself. He could be rash. There was no sense in having an accident.

"Fucking hell, man. You're crazy." Henrik said, shoving Arnold's gun brandishing arm out of his face.

"I'm crazy. You're the one talking about spiders and flies, dead fish and human heads."

"Whatever, Arnold. You better watch out 'cause I'm gonna get you back, and when I do, you won't know what hit you. Now if you'll excuse me everyone, I've got a set to do."

Henrik stopped off in the bathroom. Arnold had really shaken him up and he needed a fix. Henrik set a small mirror on top of the toilet, emptied a quantity of cocaine onto it from a plastic baggie, tapped out a line with his ATM card, rolled a dollar into a tube, inhaled and felt his head explode. He was hyper-alert and smiling viciously now; he felt strong and invincible with every muscle tense and his jaw tight with euphoria.

Henrik checked himself in the bathroom mirror. He looked at the large silver cross around his neck, felt the synthetic balls implanted in his neck and thought: maybe I should get some horns? I could get horn implants. I can do anything I want to this body. Just think if I came back to Sweden with horns? I could also cap my teeth to make them long and sharp.

Fucking Arnold, he doesn't take me seriously, but I'll show him. He thinks he's big with his gun, and I can never tell if he's joking or not. Still, I gotta put up with him because he's friends with Damian and Alex. He's nothing but a clown. But more the serial killer variety. I don't believe his jokes. The guy's disturbed.

Henrik went back to his turntables, found some Bossa Nova, threw some break beats over it and added some Arabic chanting, before shifting to the baseline of reggae dub. He felt the music moving from continent to continent, telling stories of the human experience on earth through a web of different cultures. He liked to mix heavy beats with harmonious and peaceful melodies. He sampled traditional acoustic instruments and vocals and applied keyboard effects and distortion to create ever-changing loops that kept the ears curious. The music went with his mood, and with it Henrik took everyone into his own mind.

For Henrik, music was a way to travel to places he had never been. More accurately, it was an addiction. He spent most of his waking hours at the turntables and on his computer compiling sounds. He was in the process of creating an album that would trace the history of man on earth; it was to be the audio bible of conscious man. He had already collected and mixed over fifty hours of sound that he would boil down to a twenty-four hour continuous mix. The project was consuming his life to such an extent that he no longer knew the city during the day. He spent his waking hours in his room with the blinds drawn archiving sounds and recording every mix he made. He considered sleep a luxury. He was in the latter stages of his artistic development and believed that creating songs with a definitive beginning and end was a waste of time. He preferred to record in real time and tell stories like people lived, from minute to minute. He had three massive hard drives always running to store the sounds for posterity. There was no way back from where he was going; if he wasn't obliged for economic reasons to spin in the clubs and mix popular tracks by famous DJs, his experimental techno might have brought him to the brink of insanity. Though he hated spinning commercial music by mediocre artists, the club scene fueled his social life and his drug habits. His musical obsession was unhealthy and alienating; nevertheless, he felt it was the only way he could communicate his message to the world. Ironically, his discordant and particular creativity served as a firewall to keep people from getting near him. As a result, he felt extremely misunderstood.

"What's that in his neck," Jack asked.

"Plastic," Alex said. "Henrik's made himself into a bit of an experiment. His entire upper body from his sleeves to his waist is covered by one large tattoo. That tattoo tells the story of the Han dynasty when China was invaded and conquered by the Mongols; it's a picture full of bloodshed and death, but it's also very beautiful. He's also got tattoos of Viking symbols on his scalp underneath his hairline. I think while many of us change inside, Henrik observes and honors these changes by physical marking and self-mutilation. Perhaps there's nothing strange about it. I mean we all have those marks in our minds left by others, scars that shape our character and that we try to hide so we're not exposed and discriminated against. Henrik, on the other hand, is trying very hard to be noticed. He likes to shock."

"What the hell are you doing carrying a gun around, Arnold," Elizabeth asked.

"I have a right to bear arms. It's in the constitution. I'm not gonna use the gun, I just like to have it around. I want to be able to defend myself if I have to."

"You've seen too many movies," Alex said.

"Can I hold it, Arnold? I've never held a real gun before," Julie said.

"Neither had my girlfriends until I took them to the shooting range."

The club was dark and vast and there was no visible security. Arnold reached into his jacket and passed it to her. Julie held the weapon in her hand and pointed it at her reflection in the mirror. There was an electricity to the object: a temptation and a promise in the feel of the trigger against her finger. She held the gun at arm's length and leveled it with one eye closed at two young men walking by on their way from the dance floor to the bar. They did a double-take of the petite girl with the silver gun glinting in the strobe lights, noting that she was training the weapon on them as they walked. She was smiling.

"Bang," she whispered. "Bang, bang, you're dead." The two men watched her mouth the words.

"Come on, Julie, it's not a toy," Arnold told her, taking the gun back and sticking it in the holster underneath his coat.

"Did you see that chick with the gun," Justin asked.

"Chicks with guns are hot," Scott said.

"She was aiming right at us."

"It was probably just a squirt gun. You know how these clubs are. It's like a costume party. The girls bring all their toys: pacifiers, juggling balls, pet snakes, whips and chains. Don't you remember the fire jugglers a few weeks ago?"

"Yeah, that was wild, especially when they caught the curtains on fire."

"I don't see why you need to bring a gun around," Alex said. "It's like nuclear proliferation. You bring a gun to the club and then somebody sees it and does the same, to protect themselves, and then somebody cuts in front of somebody else at the bar or tries to pick up on their girlfriend without knowing she's taken -because that shit happens- and then somebody's on the floor with blood pumping out a hole in their body. It's just not a good idea. And it's illegal. You can't carry a concealed weapon."

"Actually, I can," Arnold said. "I'm a private detective. I've gone through the proper training and I'm licensed."

"Well, I still remember that New Year's before the armageddon of the new millennium, and there we were in a family-run gun shop in Reno buying rounds for your Glock and asking a thirteen-year-old girl to hand us semiautomatic assault rifles that we aimed around the store and at a mannequin of the President in army fatigues," Alex said. "Not to mention the World War II memorabilia. The only thing that was funny about that place was the mounted jackalope on the wall. What wasn't funny was that family selling army surplus weapons illegal in California. I wonder how their two daughters will grow up?"

"Come on, weapons is just a business like anything else," Arnold said.

"I think you do it just for shock value," Alex said.

Arnold frowned.

"No, I do it because I like guns. I like to go shooting at the range and feel the force of the weapons. It's very satisfying to put bullets in the black head area of a target and to know that I can if it ever comes to that. Because all this is just a veneer. This civility, I mean. Civilization is just an illusion. I also like to hunt and I can't stand these peace-loving, hippie types that say it's cruel. Where do they think their food comes from, anyway? It doesn't come sliced and nice in foam containers covered with plastic out in the wild."

"Who taught you how to hunt," Jack asked.

"Well, let me tell you. Once I went on a hunting trip up in Washington with my uncle Jim and his friends, and my two cousins. We were staying at my uncle's cabin, and one morning we packed a lunch, my uncle gave me a rifle and we set out for the woods. According to uncle Jim, deer were really hard to find; they startled easily and sometimes you wouldn't see one for days. We could count ourselves lucky if we had a shot at one.

"That morning, when we set out, everyone went off on their own. I had shot a few times at cans with my cousins, and that was fun enough, but I didn't really care about hunting deer and didn't think I would find one anyway because I didn't know how to look. So I walked off into the woods and found a nice tree where I sat down to wait. The time passed and I got hungry and ate the sandwich I had packed. Then I fell asleep. When I woke up a big buck was standing in the middle of the meadow with his head low eating the grass. He was calm and hadn't seen me. He was a beautiful animal with a rack as wide as my arms," Arnold said, demonstrating.

"Well, here's my chance, I thought, picking up the rifle, slow and careful. I aimed and fired, and the buck tensed, staggered and fell over in the grass. I was excited about my good luck and surprised at how easy it had been. It became apparent that he wasn't dead when, snorting and weezing, he made several vain efforts to stand up. When he had exhausted himself, he lay there thrashing his legs with its eyes wide and alien with fear; he was clearly suffering with his whining, choking, moaning pain, and I was ashamed and embarrassed at what I had done. I had made a mess of it, but now it was too late and I had to finish the job. My hands were shaking so much with fear and adrenaline it took me several more shots to finally kill him. Then I threw up my lunch."

Arnold sipped from his drink and took in his audience. Julie doesn't look so good. Alex, though, he's a sucker for this morbid shit.

"Well, the problem was I was all alone and didn't know what to do with the animal. I knew he had to be dressed but had no idea how to go about it. I thought: shit, look at this beautiful creature I've wasted. It was then that my uncle came jogging through the trees and stopped by my side.

"'I heard the shots. Jesus, Arnold, that's quite a kill. Congratulations. You're a real hunter now,' he said, patting me on the back.

"I should have been proud, but mostly I felt hollow and empty.

"My uncle asked me to give him a hand, and we rolled the buck onto his back, while he sliced him open from his genitals to his rib cage. Then he carved out the diaphragm, reached up inside the chest cavity, grabbed the esophagus and sawed it off with his knife, pulling out the lungs, heart and intestines all in one and leaving them to steam in the cool open air of late afternoon.

"Back at the cabin uncle Jim skinned the buck. He cut the legs off at the knee with a powersaw. Then we hung the animal and he cut around its neck, grabbed the hide and tugged it down, working with the knife where it didn't separate properly from the flesh, pulling and cutting and pulling until it reached the tailbone, which he sawed off, before pulling the hide away in clean sheet. Then I helped him carve the carcass into manageable pieces, starting with the backstrap and tenderloins, before removing the front legs and backquarters, all of which we put into an ice chest. It was a lot of meat, and he told me it was best to butcher it little by little: that way it would age properly and seem like less work.

"All the while I thought how it wasn't a clean kill. The buck died slow and painful; he had seen me and his flesh had been ruined by fear. Fear ruins everything," Arnold said. "I wonder if human meat is like that too? Anyway, we were both covered in blood by then and stank of death. I saw my uncle's arms and face smeared with blood and thought: so this is what it's like to be a hunter. This is where it comes from and how we get it. I was fifteen then."

25

Each day it was the same routine. Jack would wake up and count down the hours like a man going to the gallows. The hate and resentment of his work would fill him, and he found that those leisure hours, if they weren't wasted sleeping, were certainly not used for anything productive, like securing a better future for himself. He was at the pivotal age when he could still work such a job and have his self-respect. Because it was a lifestyle, after all. He would make his tips and feel that cash burning a hole in his pocket. It felt like more money than it was, because he didn't have to wait for a check.

After work Jack would go out to meet Elizabeth and the others. He was becoming a part of the group and counting the days before he had a room of his own. The night Jack met his future housemates he had gone back with them for an afterparty at the house. Inevitably, Damian became unruly and threw a cup of water at some particularly lowbrow sitcom on television. Jack noted then that his future room was small like the other closets he had seen for rent. Still, the rent couldn't be beat, and he didn't plan to spend much time there aside from sleeping. There was a backyard, too, but it was nearing winter and already the city was perpetually shrouded in ominous clouds, buffeted by chill winds and soaked by abrupt and frequent thunderstorms that made the pavement slick and black, encouraging Jack's melancholy. The weather irritated him on his walk to North Beach; the wind mussed his hair and the rain sprayed him sideways and turned his umbrella inside out.

It was one of those stormy afternoons, and Jack sat in the parlor watching the rain streak down the windows. For once he was secure about his freeloading. Elizabeth was leaving in less that a week and the girls would soon be free of both of them. People came looking at the room, and Jack saw in them the same anxiety he had felt at not having a place to call his own. It's amazing how quickly I forgot those times after Damian offered me a place to stay. Now I'm cool and calm and full of resentment toward my obligations, instead of feeling useless like the unemployed or the homeless, of which I have been both.

It occurred to Jack that waiting for work was much worse than the work itself: as perhaps death was really nothing but the fear of it stretched as far as one's imagination. When you're working, you don't think about anything but being polite and efficient and doing the work well so no one has to wait. When you're done there's that feeling of having contributed something of yourself for the benefit others. Later, when you go out, you can spend and laugh and talk big about the world because you have a job. There's nothing wrong with hard work, Jack told himself. You work like everyone else, and every job is the same with both benefits and drawbacks. Still, you mustn't get too lazy about these six or seven hour shifts with every day to yourself. Just look how you waste your time now. You could have gone and found a better job or learned something new, yet you just sit here and waste your life away. Jack wondered: was there ever a time when a man accepted his work and did not feel himself better than others and that he should not have to work to live on earth? Your father worked very hard and you never heard him complain about it: that's the example you should follow. Since coming to the city, Jack saw how many of humanity's problems stemmed from laziness and that, if he could get away with it, a man would have others do his work for him. This was a strange concept for Jack who hadn't grown up in the city and had learned to do things for himself. He still held the philosophy that if you wanted something done right, you had to do it yourself and not pass it on to others who didn't have a stake or interest in it.

Jack always got ready for work an hour and a half before he had to be there. If anything this daily ritual provided a distraction from his thoughts. He showered and shaved and looked at himself in the mirror and thought: how strange that you do this every day. His eyes answered him: yes, it is strange, but for the time being I don't know what else to do. I'm afraid I've lost my rudder. He combed his hair and felt the bristles massage his scalp. I'm glad my hair is still thick, though perhaps one day it will fall out. Nothing like a haircut to make a man feel like new. Jack put gel in his hair and styled it to his satisfaction. When it was perfect like a Japanese cartoon, he smiled.

Jack no longer changed or showered at work. He liked to spend this time at home. So he slipped into his British officer's uniform, put on a slicker and went out into the rain to catch the bus. The closer he got to work, the greater the revulsion became. Once inside, that feeling evaporated to be replaced by the fake veneer of cordiality he would maintain for the rest of the evening, which would no longer be fake once he forgot about it. Like breathing, Jack could think about it or not and it would be the same. Soon he found himself joking with the customers and concerned about the food coming on time and doing a good job. It did him good to be at work, instead of staring out the window of Elizabeth's bedroom at the wet street, ruminating on life. He still believed the point was to one day have a house like his parents and raise a family. I will only do that if I can properly support my children and give them a decent education, he thought. It saddened him to think that a man could no longer build a comfortable life for himself with hard work at an ordinary job.

26

Jack thought that working together with others was the only thing that built tolerance. Though they lived their dreams separately, a certain comraderie existed among the wait staff at the restaurant: they joked with each other to pass the time and talked badly about the customers that paid their rent; they discussed their favorite bars, shows they had attended, vacations they planned to take, and their political views and cultural preferences. Beyond work they had little in common, offered no assistance to each other and demanded none in return.

Jack remembered when a friend had invited him to Mexico with a church group to build houses for the poor and he hadn't gone because he wasn't mature enough to help those less fortunate than himself. He had learned from his father to work hard and take care of himself and not be a burden, and he expected that of others as well. Because Jack had grown up as he did, he didn't understand that some people were born into deficits from which they couldn't free themselves without the goodwill and assistance of others.

Now Jack had become a mercenary working a job where he could earn the most money for the least amount of hours and maximum free time. They all shared that philosophy: some as a means to pursue their dreams, others for laziness or lack of imagination. If work is work, then I'll get in and get out as quick and painless as possible, though I might well be pushed to the breaking point of stress and still have to keep a blank face, and I can't ever forget to be polite. Waiting tables was for the lost wayfarers of America, drifting from one place to the next by choice or adversity, content to bring food to a table for money. It gave one gray hair like Brian, though he was only at the start of his thirties. It made one an insomniac and caused indigestion, because it was a job of stress and uncertainty.

At work they weren't people any longer but machines; it was only in their leisure time that they could be human and free to pursue their dreams. Italian Andrea was saving to build a hostel on his family's beachfront property in Calabria; Brad the bartender was studying to be an engineer; Nick would be the next great rock and roll star if only he could be discovered. He played in bars and coffee shops for free beers and fifty or a hundred bucks a night, and drank heavily to keep from shooting himself. Still, among them, Jack had made one friend to whom he talked about himself, but mostly to whom he listened.

Martino's brother, Santos, had wisdom beyond his years in spite of his lack of education and dead-end future. Santos was soft-spoken, kind and not prone to drunkenness. He managed Martino's accounts because Martino himself couldn't handle money and would just as soon spend it on whores and alcohol, than rent and diapers for his son.

That night they were in the locker room talking before work. Santos stood at the back door to the alley smoking a cigarette and watching the rain.

"Perhaps I have changed, Jack, but I do not like this weather. In the city the rain means nothing, but at home it means good crops. Where I am from it is very dry and drought is a problem."

"Most of your family is still in Mexico," Jack asked him.

"Yes, my mother and two sisters are there, and also my aunts and uncles and some cousins."

"Don't you wanna go back?"

"Yes, but if I leave I do not know if I will be able to come back again. I am not legal. Though I miss my family, it is good that I am here. Without this, things would be very hard back home. I work hard and I send them money, and in this way they know I am thinking of them and that I love them."

Jack thought about how he missed his family, and that it had been wrong of him not to call; he had wanted to seem independent and strong and didn't want to bother them. It was the farthest he had even been from his family and he couldn't imagine leaving for another country and being trapped between his heart and economics.

"I remember leaving my home in Arizona and coming here and how it was hard for me because I didn't know anybody. I can't imagine how it must have been to come to a place with a different language and culture," Jack said.

"I was the first of the brothers in my family to leave Mexico. I went alone without friends to help me on the other side. Perhaps if I had known how difficult it would be, and the many humiliating things I would have to do, I would not have gone. But you must understand that we had heard many stories about this place, magical stories, and I was a young man then, full of dreams. Yes, I had a lot of imagination and I dreamed of being like Enrique Sanchez from our village who had left for many years and come back in a big new truck to throw a party that lasted many days with everything we could eat and drink. I still remember how his mother was unable to hide her pride, and she was a very humble woman. Enrique built her a fine house and invested in his farm and lived a comfortable life. He told big stories, and now I know he said things that were not true about his experience and the people he met here in *El Norte*. He was a storyteller, and I think he made things bigger than they were because that's what we wanted to hear, and perhaps also to forget the difficult times he experienced. Now that I have come here I know how he must have felt separated from his family and the village and his friends. Maybe he did us a service lying and seeming bigger than he was, I don't know. It made me believe I could do it, too. Enrique did not have more education than myself when he left and he spoke no English. I imagine he worked washing dishes like me or cooking food like my brother or perhaps cleaning up garbage. These are the things a man can do here without English. Still, even though I speak, I cannot get real work because I am not legal. I am not legal and the boss pays little but much more than in Mexico. The dollar is worth something there. It buys a lot of pesos. This is why I work six days a week. With me and my brother, we will soon have enough to expand our pig farm. We have some pigs already but we want to have more. It is a good business."

While speaking to Jack, Santos thought about sitting in the dark and quiet of the desert by the wall next to the aqueduct that they would have to cross, and also of the sharp, alert face of the *coyote,* Esteban, who was to lead him and six other men across. Esteban was a thin man with bulging eyes and large teeth that he displayed often. It was not a smile but the grin of a lesser predator trying to survive and not get eaten by what was larger than himself. This man had taken a thousand dollars from each of them. Santos hated him greatly for selling out his people, but he also needed him, and if the man could get them across safely, it would be worth it. Santos knew that all of their lives hung in the balance.

He remembered what Esteban had said.

"I will not wait for any of you, so do not fall behind. If you get lost or hurt, I will leave you. It is possible that one or more of us will be shot, myself included. Understand that if this happens you will be left to die. If we hesitate, none of us will make it across alive."

Esteban did not tell them of the large police trucks that circulated on the bluff across the river, nor of the officers' infrared binoculars or automatic rifles. He did not tell them that for *la migra* this was sport like the hunting of animals. Also, he failed to tell them of the towers where the border patrol looked down on their prey. They were to cross in an area upriver that he knew to be relatively safe. It was sheltered from view and not exposed to the floodlights. They would only be seen when they were first on the other side.

In that moment, Santos remembered he was in possession of nothing but the stars above his head, the crisp, empty, clean smell of the desert, and the silence that filled his ears. He thought about his mother and sisters, and how they had cried when he left, and the knife his brother had given him as a gift. It was long bladed knife that Martino had made by hand. During the crossing, Santos touched his side and felt the weight of it on his leg, and it was as if his brother were there next to him giving him strength to calm the panic of his beating heart.

None of this he told Jack because he felt the boy would not understand. He liked Jack and understood that Jack saw him as a person and not a color or race; still, Santos knew that they were distant from each other, though they stood in the same room. One day Jack would move away and up to a better place that he could not reach. Santos had given up on his dreams of America and its promise of wealth. When he saw the customers through the round kitchen window, he thought of fate and knew that he could not ask for more from life than he had already received. He had land in Mexico and a farm, and one day he would return to take care of his family and tell stories of his adventures in *El Norte*.

"You have land of your own where you're safe and no one can bother you," Jack said. "Here a man can't afford such things. Sometimes it makes me afraid to think that when I'm older and can't work like I do now, for lack of health, I won't own anything and I'll end up forgotten on the street. I think this is the great danger of this society. Maybe you're luckier than me for having something to go back to and for your family, which is large and takes care of itself. In this country family doesn't stick together but divides and spreads where there is work to be found."

"When I first arrived I lived with many strangers in a house," Santos told him. "We were nine and slept three to a room, and the owner was also our boss. I was building houses then. It was a lonely time and I drank, which is not my nature. During that time, my brother came with his wife and we moved to an apartment and they had a child. In this way, it was easier to live. Though I have lived here for many years, I have never become an American. The life here is strange and it is an empty place. Many people are without God here. This I do not understand. How can men not believe that God is watching over them? Yes, life is hard, Jack, but we are not alone and our suffering does not go unnoticed."

Jack didn't tell him he was a nonbeliever, and Santos didn't ask, though perhaps he knew. Perhaps it would be better if I did believe in something beyond myself, Jack thought. It would be easier to be relieved of that responsibility. But like many, I am only a continuation of my parents. I have been taught to believe what they believe, and though I have fought to think and act for myself, I carry them inside me. That's also how culture works, he thought. Culture is shaped by practice and ritual, like going to church and repeating certain words and listening to sermons; it's like commercials and keeping up with the latest fad. God, for many, has become a golden calf; he is there in a new pair of shoes, a cell phone or a car. And to worship that god I need not think. Still, like all of us here, I must work very hard to afford him and to raise him up for others who do not believe. Perhaps that's not the god for me. No I prefer a god of the senses: the god in eating and drinking and new experience, but still I'm afraid. Because in thought and feeling there's nothing tangible.

"Though you believe in your god and I believe in my own, which is not a Christian god but something personal, I don't believe our gods contradict, except in formality and ritual," Jack said. "So long as one lives in balance, supports himself and treats others with respect, then religion doesn't matter. Do you understand me?"

"I understand that you are my friend and that you hear me when I speak. We are men and one day we will die, and hopefully in life we will have been generous and forgiving and understanding as people. This is all we can hope for and for that I will pray. But now we work."

Later that evening, Jack and Jennifer were by the coffee station. Jack felt uncomfortable with the silence between them and said, out of curiosity, "Jennifer, if you have a Master's degree, then why do you keep working in restaurants?"

"Because I don't like responsibility or stress, and I don't have to think about this job when I go home. Forgetting to bring a bottle of wine to a table doesn't keep me up at night. This is quick, easy money, and I can still have my free time."

"Well, you can't do this forever."

"No, I can't, but right now I value my independence more than anything. Carlo likes me and lets me go away for a week or two on vacation whenever I want, so I can't complain," Jennifer said.

"But you serve food, there's no challenge in that. Don't you want to be challenged?"

"No. The only reason I work here is for the money. That's the only reason I work: for the money."

"Money isn't everything," Jack said.

"For me it is."

Jack thought how there were many such people who didn't want to challenge themselves or do something useful with their lives and were content to drift through life in the pursuit of leisure. That was Jennifer's lifestyle. After work, she would put on her tight skirts and tops, makeup, boots and bracelets and go out to meet one of her many men, when those men weren't coming to pick her up in their fancy cars. She was a free spirit, like Candy in the American bar, using her tits and ass to get by. Because of her beauty, Jennifer got her food first from the kitchen; even Jack had to admit that, when she took off her uniform and got into her civilian clothes, she had fine legs and a nice ass. Though her face was pretty, crow's feet had developed around her eyes and wrinkles had formed around her mouth. Her eyes no longer sparkled like those of a young girl, but had hardened with knowledge of how to satisfy her desires. It was then that Jack thought about old diner waitresses with gray or blue hair and no joy whatsoever in their eyes, and no men in their lives either. No, time did not wait for people who didn't challenge themselves.

27

Jack didn't have any furniture for his new room. Damian was good enough to give him a foam mat in the meantime. Jack put it on the floor and thought how it wasn't much different from how he had slept with the homeless in Golden Gate Park. He kept his clothes in his duffle bag and didn't have any pictures to put on the walls. There was no sense of permanence about the room, and that lack of permanence was something he had learned to embrace since he came to the city, especially now that Elizabeth was leaving.

When he took her to the airport, Elizabeth was already far away from him in her journey forward. Jack felt that she was going to a better life and he was being left behind.

"Well, Jack, it's been fun. I hope you understand that this is probably it for us. I won't be back for some time and I don't expect you to wait for me. You're a handsome guy and I'm sure you'll find someone else to make you happy."

"Will you write me?"

"Yes, as soon as I settle in, I'll write," she said.

"I would love to hear about your trip. It would be a way for me to forget about life and escape the routine here and the things I'm used to and find boring. I think it's important to have something to look forward to."

"Just because we won't be seeing each other doesn't mean we can't be friends," she said.

Like many former lovers, they both understood that such a friendship wouldn't last. Though Elizabeth was sincere about writing and Jack sincere about keeping up with her life, distance would cause them to change and not need each other any longer. Neither of them knew how long it would take to forget the other, but somehow it was necessary to forget and move on and they would be better for it.

"I hope you'll be safe there," Jack said. "I know many people get sick when they travel abroad, or they are subjected to violence or have an accident. I don't want any of that happening to you."

Elizabeth listened to him and thought how good and naive he was. She had enjoyed taking care of Jack and opening his mind to the world.

She knew how to handle herself and was vaccinated against most diseases. She knew that he was more nervous than her, even though he was going no farther than the airport.

Jack's imagination was strong and he thought of all the terrible things that could happen to a defenseless woman out in the world. Though Elizabeth had studied Jujutsu, Jack did not place much faith in the martial arts skills of women.

"I have a friend there I can stay with and I've already found a job teaching English. You don't have to worry about me. When I'm gone, you must live your own life and try to do great things. I know you're a hard worker and you'll have learned a lot by the time I come back."

Jack felt those words close to him and he wanted to believe them. He thought: she is ashamed of what I do now; it's lazy of me to drift along in my job without acquiring new skills and finding new opportunities.

"Here, I bought you something," Jack said, reaching into his pocket and handing her a small red box tied with a yellow ribbon. Elizabeth opened her gift and inside found a silver snake bracelet with a gap between the tail and the head. She put it on her wrist and held it up to admire the patterns on the snake's body.

"Thank you, Jack. It's beautiful." She held his face and kissed him.

"It's meant to keep you safe," he said. "Maybe you don't believe in such things, but now at least you have something to remember me by."

In the waiting room Jack put his arm around Elizabeth and she rested her head on his shoulder. They sat like that and watched the people come and go. There wasn't much left to say. Jack knew the city wouldn't be the same without her. It would be empty, though it was full of people worth knowing, while he remained a stranger. How ironic that in cities it could be so hard to meet people. He thought this was because people were suspicious and they lived fast and couldn't be delayed from the obligations, appointments and events of their lives. Jack had met Elizabeth early and approached her in a simple way. Now that he lived in the city, he had learned its shame and the rule of leaving people alone and minding his own business. Slowly but surely, he had lost his small-town innocence; he had grown defensive, and that was because of the uncertainty of his new life, sharing a house with four relative strangers and working a job with no future. For the first time, Jack felt the gravity of his situation and realized that he wasn't much different from many other young people trying to make a life in the city. He did not feel unique or superior any longer; his heart was being extinguished by the mundane reality of daily life. He was occupied with catching the bus, buying groceries and going to work. He was resigned to his routine and no longer took the time to explore beyond it. In that way, the city had become small and oppressive like a prison. If I had brought my car then I could have gotten out of town on my days off and driven the coast and discovered some hidden beaches or done some hiking. Jack thought how he would like to work less, maybe four days a week; with his cheap room he could get away with it, if he stopped going out three or four nights a week. I spend at least twenty dollars every day and often more. Every time I go out on the weekends it costs me at least eighty bucks. No, you can't live that way. You must save some money and then you can take a trip of your own.

Jack carried Elizabeth's bag and walked with her to the departure gate. They stopped there and she put her arms around him and tried not to cry. The mass of his shoulders and body felt good to her and she wanted to hold him tight for a long time. You have to move on, she told herself.

Jack smelled the shampoo in her hair and the perfume of her skin and he kissed her and felt her let him go, and he let go, and she wiped her eyes on her sleeve. The tears did her good; they were a mixture of sadness and joy to signal an important transition in her life. It was not every day Elizabeth had an excuse to cry.

Jack did not cry. Perhaps he could have cried but he didn't see the point; it was not as if she were dying. She was starting a new stage in her life and he promised to be happy for her.

"Goodbye, Jack. Take care of yourself."

"Goodbye, Elizabeth, and thank you."

"Thank you for what?"

"For helping me when I didn't have anyone, for making this city familiar to me, for your laughter and your words of wisdom. I don't think I've ever met a girl like you," he said.

"I hope you never change, Jack. I hope the city doesn't scar you or make you small or break you, and that you don't forget your heart. You have a big heart."

Elizabeth turned and walked through the gate. Jack watched as she got smaller and smaller, until finally she was gone. The bustle of the airport reminded him that he was no longer alone with her. He watched the people come and go and wondered about their lives. Periodically, the hum of voices and movement was interrupted by the loudspeaker announcing new arrivals and departures. Jack thought about his room and the fact that it was empty. The loneliness came rushing back as he made his way through the afternoon crowd.

Part II

1

Quincy Jenkins was a ninth grader at Hunter's Point High who lived with his father in a tract of government-subsidized housing for low-income families. His father, Marcus, worked construction, leaving early in the morning and coming home long after Quincy was supposed to be back from school, usually around eight: an hour or so after Quincy would make a beat home from wherever he had gone skateboarding that afternoon.

Quincy traveled fast on his skateboard. It didn't matter if he found himself downtown or in the Mission at seven or even seven-thirty, he knew the shortcuts through parking lots, over fences and down alleys between houses; he knew his neighborhood and the city well from the hours he spent after school cruising and wondering what to do with his life.

When his father came home, Quincy would be at the kitchen table with his books spread out in an exaggerated way, papers everywhere and the television tuned to the music channel, to which his father did not object, since the young man had his nose in a book.

Quincy hated English class; he was confused by the terms for the different parts of speech and verb tenses, and the grammar rules that everyone ignored in daily conversation. He already knew English; what did he need to study it for? He felt that the many rules of English limited his expression.

"It's important that you learn to write properly," his dad told him. "Writing is important, and you want a job where you work with your head and not your hands like your dad."

"Why do I need to write when I can talk to people? I know how to talk to people and I wanna do business," Quincy said.

"There's a lot of reading and writing in business. If you wanna go to college, you're gonna have to take tests and the tests are written. Even I gotta take tests like that and study if I wanna get my contractor's license."

"What do you need a contractor's license for, dad?"

"I need it so I can manage my own projects, hire people to work for me and set a price for my services; it means that I'll finally be making enough money so that we can move to a better neighborhood. This neighborhood ain't no good for you to grow up in."

And so, after work, father and son sat and studied together. Quincy liked math because numbers made him think of money, and the larger the numbers, the more he liked it. I'm gonna be a businessman, he thought. I don't wanna go to college. I don't need any college education to make money.

I've raised a smart boy. Quincy's good with numbers. He can multiply and divide anything just in his head, Mr. Jenkins thought, as reviewed building regulations and answered the questions of the practice test in his manual. Then he played his game with Quincy.

"679 divided by 36."

"18 almost 19. It's not a whole number."

"1,346 times 78."

"104,988."

"Amazing. Maybe when I'm a contractor you can come work for me and get some experience," Marcus said. "I could use someone with a head for numbers like you. Measurements are important in my business."

Quincy didn't study much, just the hour or two after dinner and before his father went to bed. He thought he was smart and didn't need to study. Still, his writing was bad, and when he read, he fought with some of the words because they didn't look like they sounded. He knew it wasn't cool to study and that if he wanted girls to like him, especially Aisha, then he needed money. You don't make no money working at the burger joint, he thought. There are a lot easier ways to make money. Like dad said: you need to work with your mind and not your hands.

2

When Alex Green first moved to the city he worked as a copy editor for a technology magazine: something he liked to call writing by the numbers. He started without experience beyond the use of Word, but after a few weeks of studying the current and popular magazines of the industry, he was familiar with the language of end-users and programmers alike. He knew acronyms ad infinitum, understood computer hardware and the countless programs and software that he had pirated over the internet from shareware sites.

Alex did not consider tech writing, writing at all. In fact, in regard to terminology, it bore little resemblance to the English language. Aside from editing, he wrote user manuals, which was some of the most tedious work he had ever encountered. It had made him pessimistic about the future of literature and the ability of people to reason at all, being that writing had turned to utility and, in the process, lost its meaning and power of critique. After several months of such work, he had quit and lived off his savings. He locked himself in his room and returned to his project of the last three years: *Pax Americana: The End of Empire*, a monumental work about the imminent decline of the United States as a superpower and democracy. Though Alex tried to eat little and had stopped going out, his money was quickly running out.

Like any experienced writer, experienced with being unable to make a living that is, he knew that many people might not care about what he had to say. He knew that most of what men did to satisfy their ambition or justify their place on earth was of little consequence compared to, say, life on other planets or the big bang. He knew that to go completely into his mind was the height of vanity and that, until a large audience could read his words, he was of no use to anyone: not for mirth or knowledge or truth, or anything else human and incomprehensible. It's as if I don't exist, he told himself. The proof that what I'm doing, this mental masturbation, is ridiculous, is the fact that I'm starving to death and have lost fifteen pounds. That's no way to live.

Slowly the idea fermented that he should give back, that he could somehow be an inspiration to others, though he had lost faith in himself. Maybe I can inspire someone else to take up where I have left off and failed in my work?

So he decided to be a teacher. He took the required tests and got his fingerprints to prove he wasn't a hardened criminal or a child molester. All of this cost him several hundred dollars that the state did not refund, though the schools were in desperate need of teachers and especially substitutes. So, not having any money of his own, he charged it to his credit card. Due to government bureaucracy, it took nearly three months before he was employed.

Alex had never been one to talk to large groups, especially not venomous high school and middle school students. Still, he had chosen them above elementary and preschool, which was not teaching but social conditioning and babysitting. He wanted to work with minds and thought that seventh grade was the time students either studied or rebelled and chose to be cool, when being cool meant drinking, doing drugs, making money and showing off for the girls. Being cool was not writing good poetry, knowing the rules of grammar, The Bill of Rights, algorithms, or the atomic weight of the element neon.

Alex understood that he had been idealistic about his intentions when he got hit in the face with a walnut-sized spitball in class. It occurred to him that his role was more that of drill sergeant than teacher, and that he had to hold the reigns tight to keep the students under control.

He recalled a certain math class at Potrero Hill High when a group of young men began beating their fists on their desks in increasing tempo and shouting: Uprising! Uprising! It started with one student drumming lightly and then another until, like Nazi Germany, everyone began to pound their desks with violence, including the girls. There was safety in numbers; none of them could be held responsible for their behavior, because they were all collectively guilty.

Alex watched it happen and let them pound on the desks until they grew tired. They could only pound so long, and he saw no point in yelling or getting angry. Instead, he said, in a calm voice, kicking his feet up on the table:

"Listen, no one is forcing you to be here. I am not the man or the oppressor. You can either get an education or you can work for someone who's educated. Bang on the desk all you want, it doesn't matter to me. It's not going to solve the injustice of the world, or make life any easier. In fact, enjoy it while you can, because life's just gonna get harder. Frankly, I don't mind if you study or socialize, but the assignment has to be done either way."

The students fell silent after that. They settled in and talked quietly in small groups, which he considered a reasonable compromise. Alex knew that such displays boiled down to peer acceptance and that most of these kids were insecure about themselves and hadn't as yet developed their own character. He wasn't going to sweat them for it.

Sitting at the teacher's desk, Alex thought back to all the disrespectful and juvenile things he had done to substitutes in his high school career. In particular, he remembered the time that Tom Cornelli had brought a twelve of beer into history class and how he, Alex, had helped pass them out under the desks so the old female sub with the glasses wouldn't notice. She was hard of hearing, so they popped the tops of their beers while she explained the events of the Civil War. When she wrote on the board, they tipped their beers to their lips; when she turned to face them, they sat ramrod straight with blank faces and attentive eyes with the beer under their desks. Every time she turned to the board or looked at her notes, they drank. The five of them drank in time with each other while the girls giggled. When the hall monitor passed by, what she saw she thought to be her imagination.

They drank until the twelve-pack was empty. It took nearly the whole period, and when they were finished and pleasantly buzzed, they returned the empties to Tom who put them carefully back in his backpack, along with a new veneer of cool and popularity. Yes, Alex had also been one of those obnoxious, young men. Thinking it over, he decided this was a strength and not a weakness.

I understand these kids, he told himself. They're cocky and selfish and worry about appearances. I must teach them citizenship and respect, and free them from the judgment of each other. Life will come hard and fast, and I must prepare them for the blow so it will not crush them and smother their will and make them cowards. I must try to keep them from growing bitter and mean with each other. I must teach them the value and necessity of hard work, and strip away its false romanticism. Perhaps one student in this whole class will do something great with their life, while the rest will drift without direction always searching for a suitable balance between good and evil.

Twenty-five is a rough year, he thought, in regard to his own age. These kids still have the potential of youth, even if they choose not to use it. There is an average time to jump through the necessary hoops in life, and a young man or woman at twenty-five must be on their way through the hoop of career, or studying for a Master's degree with clear vision of the end of the path. You chose a clear path well before this, but you know now that you can't support yourself through writing, that it is in fact a hobby, though you feel it does people more good than, say, collecting model trains or putting a boat in a bottle with tweezers. As a writer, you challenge people to think for themselves and use their imagination.

Alex had found a means to survive and it wasn't so far off what he enjoyed. Now he was in a position to disseminate his knowledge to the young. Soon, he would start reading to them from *Pax Americana: The End of Empire*, chapter by chapter, so that they understood properly to which country they belonged and the cultural blindness in which they lived. I need to teach these kids to face life and challenge themselves. They need to take on new responsibilities and not be afraid to learn new skills, no matter how scary it might seem, or how foolish they may look in the beginning. Because in the beginning everyone looks foolish, Alex thought. In the beginning, I was scared to death to talk about my beliefs to strangers. I was ashamed of my own thoughts; more importantly, I was too considerate. Yes, the right to think and speak is not given; it must be taken and held tightly. I'm tired of living in a world where people don't speak the truth or listen with sincerity. Truly, that is mediocrity.

Such thoughts spun in his head like a centrifuge. Alex felt the emotion; his eyes would water at the beauty and nobility of his own ideals and he would think: yes, I can do so much more. I am a great individual and I will achieve my dreams and inspire others. But then it occurred to him that anyone with a shred of comfort would think in such a way because they were above the troubles of mere survival. Even for the fortunate, how suddenly adversity could appear and smother one's dreams!

Sometimes Alex would lie awake for hours, unable to sleep, thinking of all the great things he would accomplish in the near future. When morning came, however, he would fail to act on his grand schemes, allowing the day to trickle away like so many others, squandered. Could he help it that the exhaustion of teaching overwhelmed him, or that his body would not cooperate with his mind? What's more, he was still afraid of greatness. He still felt too much guilt and obligation to others. Perhaps it's wrong to have such ambition, he thought. I just want to share my knowledge and live in peace. I know myself now and I have loved many possibilities in life; if I did not pursue them, perhaps it was just infatuation and not love. Infatuation is love without pain; dreaming is living without the work or responsibility.

3

Alex worked for several months as a substitute. It was a gypsy-like existence; he was a wandering fortune-teller and performer, appearing in this or that classroom with his well-preserved stories, beef jerky salted and cured stories: the one's he had lived or heard in a bar or read about. He came with his notebooks full of poems, he played music and juggled: all this from a young man who had spent most of his time locked in a room with his nose in a book or hands at the typewriter because he was afraid of people. And now he found he could talk at length about all things: that in fact he was a talker and a whirling dervish spinning endlessly for attention. He spoke straight to his students and told them shocking, vulgar and outrageous stories about real life because he believed that nothing humanity had done could be inappropriate to discuss. And with these stories, he lied, but they were lies from which a truth could be traced.

Alex taught and entertained children thick with dreams and immortality; he was growing younger and lighter in his heart by the day and there was a new sparkle in his eye. Alex had learned to laugh at himself and he no longer preferred isolation; perhaps he had never enjoyed it, but thought of it as a sort of punishment for consciousness. But such a thought was born of that isolation and it no longer held any worth for him; it was a useless invention, patented and left to gather dust on an empty shelf.

Alex became a collector, gathering lives in fragments and adding them to the incomplete picture in the frame of his mind. He no longer believed in the purity or perfectability of man, but rather sought to live life to the fullest by interacting with others and shocking them into accountability and consequent action. In this way, he protected himself from the melancholy that came from seeing his own mortality and limitations. Those children were his layer of blubber; they were the nuts in his cheeks and the fish in his belly. He thought: I believed myself to be different from other people and that's why I was unhappy. I was also unhappy because I didn't have a voice, and without a voice I couldn't share and laugh with others.

Sometime later that year Alex was offered a position at a high school in Hunter's Point. It seemed the last teacher had been stabbed in the neck with a pencil by a student, and that was one pencil too many for her patience.

Alex knew the school and its students who had been educated in domestic violence, drug addiction, hate and fear. They were children without love, Alex thought. They were starting life at a deficit and had already received a hard education. They had the real-world knowledge it had taken him twenty-five years to acquire, after he had graduated from college and had to provide for himself. While he had learned the hard way that college didn't necessarily translate into success and wealth, it had taught him how to think for himself, control his desires and live within his means. Alex thought: I've learned the value of saving a quarter of every dollar I earn, to buy only what I really need, and to not drug myself, though I do drug myself, but not with the hard stuff; I drink myself into oblivion religiously two nights a week. Even I understand how hard this shit is to take without an outlet.

Knowledge comes from example, it comes from community, and a person develops according to what he or she is exposed to, Alex thought. Many of these kids can't count on family and friends to give them the tools they need to build a better life: that's why they need a good teacher. And let's not pretend that everyone is equal. Just look at the difference between where you live and this old shipyard with it's oil-slick water and toxic air, lack of community, and idle young men and women on the streets whose parents are gone morning until night. The children here are all unique. Some are smart and play dumb, and others are damaged by violence and carry that violence like a rash that infects everyone they touch. The shy and kind are crushed, while others retreat inside their shells and wait to die. Out of the many, a rare few manage to find a decent life and perhaps some success and happiness in work and family life. Still, they will never forget where they came from, and they will resent it, as all people who have less resent those who have more. The talented and intelligent suffer the most, Alex thought, because they see the violence and egoism in both themselves and others, and are paralyzed by it. Then there are those who react by destroying their lives just to prove they're not worthless or weak. In the ghetto trust is a luxury and there's no room for weakness. This is a place where individuals think for themselves in the short term and learn it's best not to stand out from the group.

Alex had a large class, thirty-eight students, and that was too many. Much of what he had thought about education turned out to be nothing but idealism. The classroom was not, as he had believed, a sterile environment with minds like blank paper where citizenship, respect, trust and hard work could be stamped onto each individual so they could get on with the world and each other. These were children of laughter and sorrow, like any children in any school he had worked in; they had been shaped by experience, not factual information. The classroom was not the world, it was theory, like fiction, outside of which Alex could not survive. In that way, the children were older and stronger than he was. They grew up on the street and had accepted life at face value. Many were unable to perceive the abstraction of knowledge: knowledge as separate from action and incubated and refined to fit and enhance experience.

4

Gavin sat in the back row and slept. Often he forgot his books and he seldom did his homework. It occurred to Alex to abandon him to his fate. Gavin didn't care about learning because he was making his own money, represented by his gold chains, designer jeans and the sunglasses he wore in class so no one could see his eyes. He had a cell phone that he put on top of his desk to mark his territory.

"Hey Gavin, wake up," Alex said.

"Hey, why you gotta be touchin' me?"

"I want you awake in here. This is my classroom and I want you awake. I don't care if you listen or not, but this is my time and you sleep on yours. What do you do all night that you're so tired?"

"I got a lot of responsibilities, people to see, things to do, why I gotta be stressin' wit' dis school thing?"

"You don't have to be stressing. We're learning English here. You just have to be stressed enough to know your grammar and vocabulary, and to be able to write a logical essay."

"I ain't never seen nobody git no job by writin' no paper. I make my money and I be supportin' my mother without writin' no paper. I know my English already without all them fancy words you got wit' it that don't mean nothin'. Words ain't nothing, teach. In this world you gotta have product, somethin' to sell, and you can't sell words."

Damned straight, Alex thought. Gavin's right, but he should still learn to read and write properly.

"Just do me the favor and pay attention. Take off your glasses so I can see you. First thing's first, for respect you look someone in the eye. Respect means something to you, doesn't it? I bet you look your friends in the eye, and also your mother, right?"

Gavin took off his sunglasses and laid them on the table. He gave Alex a hostile look. He didn't want to go to school at all. He did it for his mother, who knew where his money came from and didn't want money like that, but didn't have a choice, either.

Gavin made three or four thousand a month dealing drugs, and they all knew he was a dealer or rather a runner for Walter "Mr. Pain" Biggs. Once when Gavin was short of money, because he had smoked some product and given it away to friends, he had come to class with one tooth less and a swollen face; that day Alex did not ask him to take off his glasses.

Either the kid can sell drugs until he goes to jail or gets killed, or he can work a regular job, but that'll never happen. This kid is going to fly high and crash and burn bright and early. I'd condemn him completely, but he does support his mother and he's not a bad person. In this place it's the best thing going, and that's only because drugs are illegal. Still, I don't want to come to class one day and have that seat empty and think of his mother crying over his dead body. This is laughable, Gavin makes more money than I do and I'm his teacher. But then again he spreads addiction, while I try to build minds and give these kids hope. We're working against each other.

As it stood, the young men and women in the classroom were much more concerned with Gavin's wad of hundreds, his brand name clothes and his connection to Mr. Biggs, with his nice ride and designer suits.

Gavin's prosperity was no match for Aisha's beauty, though. It was only a year ago that she had transformed from an emaciated grasshopper into a ripe piece of fruit. Aisha still didn't know what to make of it or how to handle the stares of the young men and her father's football friends that were always over for the game, most of them married and in their forties. There was something in their eyes that frightened her. Once, on the way to the bathroom during halftime, one of them had tried to force himself on her in her bedroom and she had kneed him smartly in the groin. He had managed to lurch back to the living room couch where he sat down with watery eyes and hands folded tightly in his lap. He didn't look at her again after that; it was their little secret.

Somehow Aisha didn't fit in herself any longer or understand her body and how it had changed. Instead, she copied her older sister, Clarice, and put on fake nails and had her hair straightened and highlighted red. She painted her lips and started to wear platform shoes that she promptly fell in and skinned her knee walking down the front steps.

It was then that the other girls began to call her a hoochie mamma saying, "Look at Aisha, girlfriend think she all dat wit' them wacked out styles. She look like she be walkin' on crutches and shit wit' them shoes."

Those other girls were afraid for their boyfriends because Aisha Clark was on everybody's mind; when the young men of the neighborhood were stroking it or "gettin' busy" with their girls, it was to her image.

The result of all this unwanted attention was that Aisha stopped talking. She felt the trap her body had become, and even the teacher, Mr. Green, whom she had never thought to be very human, looked at her in that hungry way.

Aisha was beautiful, but she was also a girl with a stuffed bear named Marley that kept her safe at night. The most important man in her life was still her father. She liked to curl up with him on the couch and watch movies. She liked music and dancing. She was in the color guard and thought that when she got to college, she would try out to be a cheerleader.

The boys in her class made her insecure because they didn't talk to her and couldn't look her in the eye. In fact, very few people talked to her, except Mr. Green, and that was because she always did her homework and knew where to put the period or the comma; she knew about run-on sentences, sentence fragments and the dangers of the passive voice.

Quincy sat behind Aisha in English class. The smell of her hair and the smooth line of her exposed neck kept him in a permanent daydream. He thought that when he had money he would ask her out. Sometimes, when Mr. Green passed out papers or returned assignments, Quincy's hand would touch hers and their eyes would meet and he would feel his heart accelerate. It filled him with despair when she would turn away. Was that love: feeling uncomfortable and like you wanted to die in the moment and never live again?

They had known each other for a long time, though now they never spoke. Years ago when Aisha was a tall and awkward girl, taller than all the boys, they had played basketball together. Sometimes they would be on the same team, but now everything was different. Quincy didn't think of her in that way anymore. Now he thought of her in the way of the videos he had found under his father's bed, with the women on all fours, or on their backs with their legs in the air, and the men handling them and pushing against them in relentless repetition. How do I get her to do that with me, Quincy wondered. If I take her out and buy her shit, will she do it?

It was a time of great changes and sometimes, while daydreaming during class, Quincy would feel a tingling and increasing pressure in his groin. He was glad then to have baggy jeans that allowed him to hold his erection down discreetly with his hand in his pocket. Occasionally, his Aisha fantasies came late in the period and he worried that the reaction they provoked wouldn't go away before they got up to pass. He was particularly worried about Taresa because she was a troublemaker and a loudmouth who would never let him live it down if she noticed.

Though he wanted Aisha to be like the women in the videos, he also wanted to kiss her and be with her and hear her voice in his ear in the dark. She was a sweet girl. He had yet to see her with any men and she was not at all like the video girls that said, "Harder, faster, give it to me big daddy," like it was something they desperately needed, heads thrown back and squirming with their wet lips and hungry teeth and eyes shut tight to keep them from exploding. No, he wouldn't imagine Aisha like that. She probably knew nothing of those videos. Sometimes Quincy wished he had never seen them because they made him nervous around women. If he wanted to be a pimp, then he would have to do those things the men did, and that wasn't possible with his squeaky voice. He wondered how long it would take until he had facial hair and could say, "Yeah baby, you a nasty bitch, girl," in a baritone without the women laughing. With a voice like that no one would laugh and you could say anything and get away with it.

The videos had also changed his view of his father. When he spoke to him about an education and a future, Quincy saw his father like in the videos, where before he imagined him like a bull pulling a heavy load day in and day out. Then he thought about his mother and imagined both his parents in the video, wishing again there were things he hadn't seen. It seemed the more he saw, the less sure he was of himself and life, which he thought he understood when he was younger. Now there were too many things stuck in his head to balance and think about, like Mr.

Green's stories. Though the stories were funny, there was something in them that made him uncomfortable and afraid.

One day a young man Quincy had never seen picked up Aisha in the school parking lot. The stranger drove an imported car: new and red and shiny with tinted windows and silver rims. The image of Aisha's smile and her long black hair blowing in the wind as they drove off pierced Quincy's memory and sank his heart.

Mr. Jenkins came home and found his son staring despondently at the television and asked, "What about your schoolwork," to which Quincy replied, "I don't feel good." As long as Aisha belonged to no one, there was still a chance. But she had gone with the young man who was, no doubt, familiar with the videos. Quincy was worried for Aisha and thought: if he does anything to her, if he hurts her in any way, I'll kill him.

5

Aisha met Duane for the first time at the Nordworth Center. He was trying on jackets when he caught her in his smile. To save herself from the confusion of emotions the handsome young man provoked in her, Aisha turned and walked away. It was the first time a young man had stared unwaveringly into her eyes. His glance was an invitation that she would have accepted if she could have done so in a smooth and easy way. Instead, she felt nervous and ashamed. If he talks to me he won't be interested anymore because I have nothing to say and my life is boring, she thought. I'm not confident and clever like my sister, or elegant and sexy like women in the movies.

Duane watched the girl leave and pondered the fact that, even as he got older, he continued to prefer young girls. He had hoped that he would like girls his age but they were not free or easy; they were all about money and a future and they played games. He wanted a young girl that he could control. This girl, who was perhaps eighteen, was just right for him; she was beautiful, and he could tell by her behavior that she was inexperienced.

Duane Bowen was a man obsessed with appearance who had never gotten over self-love. When he was home alone, or knew no one was watching, he would stare at his reflection, be it in the bathroom mirror or a car window; he would be seated in a restaurant or a bar facing a mirror and he would stare at himself, smitten by his own appearance. Sometimes at home he would dance naked in the mirror. He would wink to himself and smile and look deep into his own eyes and say, half-joking, half-serious, "If I could, I'd fuck you. These girls must be crazy not to want a piece of you."

Duane was too handsome for his own good, except for his crooked erection. So far none of the girls had had anything to say about it, because they weren't preoccupied with such details, whereas dick shape and size were subjects that weighed on a man's mind.

The fact he had wasted many years frozen in the contemplation of his own image, kept women from loving him. He never approached women but expected them to come to him, and when they did, he found them to be either plain or obnoxious. After a time he thought: serves you right, now you're getting older; soon you'll be twenty-five and it's all been downhill since twenty-one. Now Duane was trying to make up for all the time he had wasted, his undercapitalized early-twenties, particularly the last eight-month drought. In addition to his desire for conquest, what attracted him to Aisha was her innocence, something he hadn't possessed since he discovered his own beauty. Now he wielded the weapon of his good looks to serve his own desires, with the knowledge that the most valuable beauty was ignorant of itself, free and uncorrupted by intent. It was just such beauty he desired in the girl, so that he might increase his own stock.

Aisha was infected by his smile. A smile like that comes from a good heart and I would like for him to hold me. I would rest my head on his chest and feel the beat of his heart and the mystery of him and his life. I wish I could read his thoughts through his eyes.

Aisha lingered in the shoe department while Duane purchased a few dress shirts and the jacket, which he put on. To her, everything he did seemed free and easy. She thought: he must have a clean and flawless life, and I would like to be a part of it to escape my own that is empty. She was lonely and thought he could take her loneliness away.

When Duane walked by, he smiled at her again and she looked at him.

"Hi," he said.

"Hi," she replied.

"My name is Duane."

"I'm Aisha."

"Aisha, that's a nice name."

She thanked him for the compliment and surprised herself by saying, "I like your new jacket."

He touched the collar self-consciously and said, "How old are you, Aisha?"

She hesitated. "Eighteen," she told him. That seemed to be the right answer, and he didn't seem surprised at her lie and acted as if it were true. Do I really look eighteen, she wondered.

"Did you find what you were looking for," he asked.

"What?"

Duane smiled.

"Did you find a new pair of shoes?"

She had her hand on a pair of tennis shoes she liked and the tag read one hundred and forty dollars.

"No, I don't like this style. I'm just looking," she told him.

But she did want the shoes; she thought it might make him like her if she bought them. It still hadn't occured to her that he might like her as much as she liked him. She thought: he can't possibly know how I feel now, how my heart is beating and how his eyes make me nervous like being in the color guard when I started, and now he's talking to me and he said I had a nice name!

The silence made her uncomfortable and she said, "Are you going home?"

"I'm not in a hurry. I've got the day off and don't have anything planned."

"Me neither," she said, too quickly she felt, and to cover it up she continued with whatever came to mind, just to keep him there.

"I'm done with school and I decided to go shopping because I was bored. I like to come downtown and people-watch. When I see people I try to imagine how they live, and if they are lonely or sad with life, but with most people I can't tell because they hide behind their faces," she said.

"I don't think it's ever really possible for one person to know the thoughts and feelings of another. But at least we have our smiles to show our good will," he said.

She noticed that he spoke in a proper and polite way, not like the men and boys from her neighborhood, and she tried to speak that way, too. Really, she didn't like most slang, especially the cursing and insults, and mostly spoke it to fit in. She hated to be called a hoochie or a skank or a ho, and that was how Gavin talked, though she knew he wasn't like that because they had grown up together. When he was younger, Gavin had been polite and kind, because his mother had raised him that way, and still he never cursed in front of her. Aisha had never seen a black man talk or act or dress like Duane except on TV, and she felt inferior.

By her look and behavior, Duane thought she must be poor. Still, it didn't matter where she was from or what she believed in. He was going to do her a favor and show her a good time. He liked her and wanted her and knew that such feelings would fade and then he would forget her. Now all he could think about was the red of her lipstick and her fake lashes, her painted toes and artificial nails, her tight capri pants and top, platform shoes, youthful beauty and uncommon curves. Fearing rejection, and worried that the game would suddenly turn to his disadvantage, Duane asked, "Are you hungry? Why don't we get something to eat?"

Aisha agreed to go with him and wondered: is he going to pay? Of course he is; still, what if he doesn't and finds out you don't have any money? Then he might be angry. He probably thinks you have money. Well, it's too late now because you've agreed. You just said yes, without even thinking about it, and that must be intuition, because this is one of those moments when it just feels right, and you feel comfortable with him. Still, you've lied about your age, and if he found out you're sixteen what would he do? He's older than you, but you need a mature man. Quincy and Gavin don't even talk to you in class. They're afraid of you ever since you changed and stopped playing basketball and started wearing make-up.

Duane wasn't rich. He worked as a talent coordinator for corporate events. He was paid by event and received no salary. His company Carl Price had offices nationwide. He worked conventions like the one in Florida for Bentley Bank where he dressed the CEO and other top executives up in drag with wigs and had them do disco covers. He would teach them the necessary dance moves and the men would get on stage in front of lower management and humiliate themselves. Then he would be in San Diego for a pharmaceutical event, and this time he would dress the stiffs up as rappers with fake gold chains, sports jerseys, caps and sunglasses.

He would make those mostly white, middle-aged, fat and balding men strut around, point their hands at their peers in the form of a gun and thrust their hips in a suggestive manner to the beat, and so on and so forth for other white-collar businesses around the country.

After three weeks of straight conventions, sleeping four hours a night and living on the convention room floor, he would come home and sleep for two days straight and then go out on a long drinking binge. Once

Duane had wanted to be a musician or an actor, but now he was stuck in the corporate conference circuit and the only future there was to be a director of corporate video, which he couldn't stomach. No, he was tired of writing rap songs about "Triptopsychophan rockin' the house," "hangin' tough with the patent crew," "hardcore rollin' with diversified assets," "pimpin' those fools at Dosharden Chemical," and "robbin' market share."

It was laughable, but he needed the work. After a heavy summer of events there would be two or three months in the office pushing paper. Perhaps he couldn't complain too much about these companies and their rhetoric and team building conventions when he was allowed to bring in African drummers from Burkina Faso, pass out instruments to three hundred executives and see how happy they were beating the drum without rhythm. It was then that he saw how poor such men were in culture and how their careers had locked them in a box and taught them how to talk and think and act. What a relief in the professional world to be able to joke and laugh and clown for a change, and the only place for that was the corporate convention.

I suppose those stiff execs are just as trapped in their corporate world with all its rules and regulations as blacks are in shitty rap and the gangster image that keeps us down, Duane thought. I bet Aisha knows something about that. She's got the city inside her; she's fed on media hype, and you've got to be strong to resist that.

Perhaps you feel sorry for her: sorry that she's so beautiful and also so ignorant and without direction. You could see that already when you met her in the store. She was overwhelmed by choice and the illusion that those new shoes would help her fit in and make her happy. You're trapped in it, too. Don't pretend it isn't essential that you look good for other people. She likes you because you look good and don't forget it. At least you look good. That's all that matters.

Duane was not an urban black man; he was an insulated mulatto raised in small town affluence. He had attended high school in Carmel and undergrad at Berkeley, his friends were mostly white and so were his last three girlfriends.

Duane's father, Samuel Bowen, had grown up poor in the South and enlisted in the Army as a way out. Captain Bowen had spent many years stationed in Panama and there was much he had participated in that he couldn't talk about. After many tours of duty around the world he had settled in as a Spanish instructor at the Defense Language Institute in Monterey. He was a quiet man who knew too much and could kill if necessary; as a father he had raised his son with the same military discipline he could not live without.

After college, Duane's mother, Kendra, had joined the Peace Corps and was sent to Panama where she met Duane's father in a bar. Back in the States they got married, and Mrs. Bowen enrolled in graduate school in Monterey where she earned an MA in International Policy. After a brief stint in Washington, working as an aide for a California congressman, she returned to Monterey and won a seat on the city council. Duane was born a year later.

It had occurred to Duane that his parents were strong individuals who had raised him well. Still, it came as shock when he moved to San Francisco after college and had been forced to work in jobs he disliked: first as a bartender; then as a secretary at Carl Price. After several months in the position he asked if he could be a part of event planning. He had seen many of the conference videos and thought: at least I'll be able to work with small-time talent, and also write lyrics and skits and organize shows.

These thoughts were in his mind as he walked with Aisha along Market Street and hailed a cab to his favorite restaurant, *Ochente!*, a Brazilian bistro in the Marina. That part of the city reminded him of the picture perfect sterility of Carmel and the house he grew up in with its collection of African and Latin American artifacts, designer glassware, and paintings, none of which ever acquired any dust or meaning, but were rather like that whole town: a collection of sterile beauty separated from suffering, stored safe and dead like in a museum.

Ochente! isn't that expensive, he thought. Maybe it will be fifty bucks all together and I can just charge it on my card.

Since leaving his parents' house, it had been hard for Duane to get used to the drop in standard of living. He also missed the peace and quiet of their house and not having to share anything, being an only child. In his family everyone kept to themselves, had their own projects and obligations, and were polite if not distant from each other when it came to an exchange of real feelings. Still, he missed the privacy and his studio bedroom with the separate entrance.

Ochente! specialized in dishes from the Northeast of Brazil: the blackest, most musical and superstitious part of that great and varied country. Duane was particularly found of the *moqueca* stew with prawns and fish, and it was the *dendê* palm oil that made it so tasty. He had wanted to buy that oil to cook at home, but it was very hard to come by. He had a weakness for *caipirinha*; at *Ochente!* they sold it by the pitcher. They're not going to card her at this time of the day, he thought. I come here a couple times a month and they know my face. When they know you, you can't be an undercover, and that's the only point of carding anyway.

"What's that," Aisha asked, pointing at the cloudy, lime-filled, sweaty cold glass pitcher.

"*Caipirinha*. It's made from *cachaça*, or cane alcohol, mixed with lime and sugar. Simple, but very good. I wish they sold this stuff in the stores."

"Cane alcohol?"

"Sure, like sugarcane," Duane said. "Every country has their own alcohol: Russia has vodka; Japan, sake; Italy, grappa; France, pastis; Spain, sherry; and Portugal, port. I guess alcohol must be pretty important. In each country they use whatever's handy to make it: potatoes, rice, corn, grapes and sugar cane."

Duane offered her a glass. Aisha had never drunk alcohol before; it reminded her too much of her father and his friends on football Sundays and their fat bellies and burping, and also of stale pizza and the smell of burnt barbecue. In short, it reminded her too much of a reality she wanted to forget.

But the *caipirinha* was good; it was sweet and tangy like lemonade and she couldn't taste the alcohol. She drank her glass quickly and Duane poured her another.

"Once at a conference," he told her, "we had a CEO from an insurance firm come swinging down from the scaffolding dressed in a tiger skin. He was supposed to end up right at the podium over the kiddie pool full of water with fake palms and an inflatable alligator. Now either he didn't let go in time, or the rope was too short, because he went flying out over the crowd and fell into the front row. We thought he had killed himself, but sure enough he jumped off the floor, climbed the stairs in his primitive toga, wiped the blood from his head, tapped the mike and said, 'It's a jungle out there and only the strong survive. Accidents happen and we provide insurance for people to deal with the unexpected.' Well, the associates didn't know what to make of the boss on the big screen dabbing the blood from his forehead with a napkin. They didn't realize that he wasn't supposed to go swinging into the crowd. 'I hope the production team is insured,' he said. 'because I expected a softer landing.'

"We were shitting in our pants for fear of a lawsuit, but the guy had a sense of humor, so I guess not all insurance guys are stiffs. Anyway, it just goes to show that you can't trust the grips or the PA's. I've seen my share of accidents, especially with the pyrotechnic guys. Yeah, at a lot of these conferences they want explosions and lights and fire. Once a guest speaker was supposed to come up through a trap door in the stage floor after an explosion, but it turned out the guy caught on fire and we had to put him out with fire extinguishers. Once again, the crowd wasn't sure if it was an accident or part of the show."

"Do they ever have dancers?"

"Sure, once we had some flamenco dancers, and we have bands all the time, local bands. They make more money at the conferences than in bars, even if the crowd sucks."

"I can dance and sing," Aisha said. "Do you think there'd be some work for me?"

"Sure, I don't see why not," Duane said, flashing a smile.

Imagine if I could travel around and perform and make my own money, Aisha thought. She felt very lucky then. It was one of the best days of her life, and the first time she had been drunk, and she was glad to have met Duane.

Later Duane invited her home and showed her his room with its nice stereo, big screen TV, computer, and his bed that was large and soft. He asked if she had heard of Project Brother, and she said she had and that she liked their music a lot. He put their latest album on the stereo; he was talking a lot now, more than before, about the house and the rent and how he needed a vacation and was thinking about Jamaica because he loved reggae music, more than hip hop, because hip hop was just a byproduct of reggae anyway.

They sat side by side on the bed and she was so nervous she couldn't speak; she wanted him to touch her, but she was nervous about it because she didn't know what to do and didn't want him to know that she was inexperienced or that she had never kissed anyone before.

What more is there to talk about, Duane wondered. You should just shut up and make your move because she likes you and you know that. Just say anything, and when she turns to look at you, when your eyes meet, that's the time.

"I've gotten so many parking tickets here that I have to factor them into my monthly budget. There's street cleaning once a week and I have to move my car from one side of the street to the other and back again, and sometimes I'm away at a conference. It's a real pain. You know, I like the Mission a lot more than the Marina. The Marina is superficial and there's nothing to do there but shop. The nearest good club is Benny's. Where did you say you lived?"

"Hunter's Point."

"Hunter's Point, where's that?"

"South of Market," she said. Just how far south she didn't tell him.

It occurred to him that he hadn't asked her any personal questions. It was easier not to know anything about her; that way, he could impose his own feelings and ideas on her and make believe that she shared them and understood him. He was happy then; it was a self-fabricated happiness to which she had contributed no interesting conversation or laughter. No, she was quiet and shy, and normally he would have been bored by that.

"Have you ever been to Alcatraz," he asked her.

"No."

"Neither have I. Why is it that people never take advantage of the sites where they live? When the tourists come what's the first thing they do? They go to Alcatraz and then they walk around North Beach and Fisherman's Wharf. Okay, maybe the tourists aren't that ambitious, either. There isn't much to do in this city anyway, other than eat and drink."

She turned to him then and he stuck his lips on hers, put one hand on the back of her neck and the other on her uncommonly hot leg. He thought to push his hand up under her skirt, and with the help of the *caipirinha,* he did, and with the help of the *caipirinha,* she didn't stop him. He tasted her mouth and wondered how it felt for her to kiss him, or rather how it would feel to kiss himself.

"Let's lay down," Duane said.

He felt smooth then, so he pushed her down on the bed. Amazing, you can get away with just about anything if you believe it. The problem is when you don't want something enough. Wanting is dangerous, and women are dangerous, but she wants someone to tell her what to do. That's why you like young girls. Shame has no place; you can't be ashamed of wanting to caress, kiss, lick and fuck this girl. If she sees you're ashamed, then she'll be ashamed; shame is not caring enough, it's seeing the faults and the futility of passion, and women they live for passion and men's lust. This is something you must do. In ten years you may not be able to get away with this, with money perhaps, but then it won't be the same. With money, it means you're not clever or smooth or good-looking enough to be desirable, and that's shameful.

Aisha felt the pounding of her heart, but Duane's smile and his eyes made her relax as he eased himself on top of her and put his hands on her body. He was a child then delighted by the flesh of her breasts in his hands and the heat that burned through her underwear. The only thing that matters, he thought, is the euphoria of lovemaking. Why is it that as one gets older there is less time to feel this way? Are you talking about less time or less justification? You are at your strongest and best; how can you let that go to waste? Oh Aisha, you beautiful stupid little girl. Aisha, you probably think none of these things. You do not calculate age and think that time is running out. Life is not fast for you, but rather an eternity.

Aisha looked to the bedside clock; it was after six and her father would be home soon. She had to help fix dinner, so they could sit down *"like a decent family and eat together, not like those gangster kids on the corner that ain't got nowhere to be and ain't got no job."*

She had to go, but she felt good with Duane and didn't want to leave, ever.

"Duane, I gotta go. I'm late and I gotta be home," she said.

"Shhh," he told her, "doesn't that feel good?"

"Yes."

"And this."

"Ooh, Duane."

"Here, why don't we take these off? No, no. Leave the heels on. I'll just slip them over the ends."

"Wait, wait. Shouldn't we use a condom," she asked.

"Don't worry, baby. I'll be careful. The condom breaks the feeling. I want us to be together."

"It isn't working. Duane. It doesn't fit."

He had only one thought on his mind and he wasn't going to stop now; he was going to make her his and add her to the list.

"Come on, we'll take it slow. Just relax. Oh, there it is, just a little farther. Oh, you wonderful beautiful girl. Yeah, let's just stay like that-connected."

The mission was complete. Now he could relax and enjoy himself and not worry about the results, facts and statistics he measured his life in, but only the pleasure and things that could not be evaluated. She was trapped. He had won the game and it had cost him so little. Now, for the first time, he was with her and not against her, and he wanted to stay like that forever: to watch her squirm and feel her nails in his flesh. He thought, looking at her contorted face, that pleasure was much like pain and that the human being was a creature that needed to be shamed and abused to find meaning in itself. He kept his eyes open, watching and savoring his power over her. But the power was hers, because she had drawn him from a great distance until they lay together sweating and pushing and gasping to become one.

Duane knew it couldn't last, and perhaps she did not, and that would be her lesson. Duane looked down at where they came together and damn, damn, he was too excited and it was ending, damn, it was ending and the world was returning, the loneliness and the frustration, and just a little longer. Wait, no, you have to stop, stop now. I know it feels good, but stop. Just one more, one more, one more, one more, oh, oh, oh, that's it. Ahhh. And he did not think of her in the same way again.

6

Jack was improving his Spanish joking with the busboys on the floor and Santos in the kitchen, but never Martino, who hated him and all other *gringos*. The wealth of the customers in the restaurant had driven Martino to bitterness. He didn't see them as people, but thieves, and thought: these *gringos* are squeezing my people in their fist and living off our blood. He was disgusted to see the piles of food that the waiters threw away. When the kitchen door opened and he saw the patrons seated at their fancy tables eating and drinking like pigs, he brooded over the jail of his own existence. Even at home there was no escape because he had two extra mouths to feed. Martino was a reckless man, and if it weren't for his brother Santos, he wouldn't have been able to support his family and save money for the farm he did not expect to return to in Mexico.

Martino hated the wait staff, except for the girls who he leered at and boasted he would *chingar* in this way or that, and *chingar* them until they knew who was boss, and *chingar* them to show that white, black or Chinese, they were all whores.

"*Te gusta la verga,* Jennifer? Oh Jennifer, I know you like the *verga.*"

Jennifer knew *verga, chorizo* and other phallic expressions in Spanish, but because it was not her language, she played dumb. Jennifer didn't rightly know herself if she would like Martino's *verga,* if she could have it with no one the wiser. Alternatively, she thought: that son of a bitch would rape me if he could get away with it. Thank God we're at the restaurant and not on some dark deserted street. Men, they're all the same, though certainly some are more desperate than others. Well, he can dream about fucking me all he wants, as long as I get my food on time.

To Martino, all the waitresses were worth a lay. He didn't have any preferences: any *gringa* was a good *gringa,* attractive or not. They were different from his wife, and he was both afraid of and attracted to their glacial demeanor. He thought of such women as witches and wanted to screw one so he'd know for sure. I am a man and I must prove they are like any woman, though they act like men.

Jack was afraid of Martino, though he tried his best to hide it. Goddamn Martino, there's always a Martino to ruin things: Martino like Tina, Elizabeth's old housemate; and Tina like Julie, who's always on the phone and never picks up after herself or pays her bills on time, whose friends are always over and who spends more time in the bathroom than in bed. Julie: strong candidate for worst housemate ever.

Martino sensed Jack's fear and exploited it. His favorite pastime was to humiliate others and drag them down to his own miserable condition. It was because of Martino that Jack had begun to dislike his work. It seemed in any job there were always those individuals that thrived on making things difficult for others. What made Martino especially dangerous was that he had nothing to lose.

"*Andale, andale cabrón*, the plates are getting cold," he would say, and Jack would run out of the kitchen with his tail between his legs, because a cook was harder to find than a waiter. Without Martino there was no food, and an unhappy Martino, Martino as the enemy, meant burnt food and late food and mixed up orders, which meant humiliation for Jack on the floor and apologies and concessions, like a free dessert that would come from his own pocket.

Martino had the hate any cook had for a waiter. Waiters didn't have a proper respect for the food they served; they didn't write clean and neat; they brought too many orders at a time and were demanding. Martino resented this lack of respect and the waiters' privilege of chatting with the pretty girls. Many times he had seen Jack in particular making the girls laugh: Jack, who glided around the room like a prince in his fancy clothes, counting his wad of twenties. Martino thought waiters were nothing but slaves and dogs jumping through a hoop and humiliating themselves for the customers. Look at them, full of lies and false smiles. I could never serve people in that way. No, I prefer to stay here in the kitchen and cook, because people need to eat, even these bastards without respect. How can I cook when they come with order after order and there is no more room on the stove? Their writing is bad like my English. If it weren't for the alcohol to dull the senses and my brother by my side and also Pablo, who is a big drinker and a good friend, and the rest of *la raza* here, it would be too much.

Each night of work Jack worried about making a fatal mistake. He had made them before from exhaustion and haste: like the time he forgot to charge two meals on a table and it came out of his pocket; or, more egregiously, that bottle of hundred dollar wine. That was the first time he had ever been dishonest, discarding the empty bottle in a nearby dumpster on his way home, so that he wouldn't get caught. For that small act, he still lived in fear. It was then that he thought of murder and how a murderer, left to himself and free from justice, would often be consumed by his own guilt. He thought: maybe it isn't right what I did with the bottle, but a hundred dollars is plenty, and I'll never make that mistake again. Another time he had forgotten to put in an order for salads, and when the food came, he didn't tell Martino, but instead apologized to the customers whose salads would never come. Then there were the minor mistakes a waiter could make, like forgetting the sugar or a drink, or throwing out some food that was meant to go, and even the odd clumsiness of a spilled glass of wine or the dropped fork. All of these things transformed into strange nightmares: a dropped fork would become a highly sensitive explosive charge; forgetting the sugar implied missing the last boat from a deserted lonely island from which one could never escape. Jack had many nightmares about missing planes and being late, of running out of food and being unable to find some vital medication to prolong his or his father or mother's life, and for all of this he was to blame. He feared greatly the large mistakes and had learned that with mistakes it was best to pay up front and not try to hide from them. For that reason the hundred dollar of bottle of wine haunted him. Jack dreamed of the police coming to his door and searching for some article, some proof of crime, and many times he was to the point of confession, but still he did not confess.

You didn't steal the bottle of wine. It was the customers who drank it and didn't remind you to put it on the bill. They are the true thieves, he told himself. But how about the free glasses of wine and the salads you gave to Arnold and Damian when they came to eat, in exchange for a large tip? The wine and salads cost almost nothing compared to the price on the menu. Perhaps a few dollars at cost for the wine, and the salad, a few cents. Carlo pays five seventy-five an hour for your labor and then shaves a few hours off your paycheck, or inflates the tax. That was how Jack justified his mistakes: one theft warranted another. As for late food and forgetting the sugar, it wasn't because he didn't care about doing a good job, but rather that he wasn't perfect and it would have to stand at that.

Still, the day came when Jack picked up a second plate for his table and forgot to ask if it was his, because Martino inevitably started to yell when he was asked questions. Logically, he took the plate to where he had deposited the first, made sure the couple had enough wine, wished them a nice meal and went to total a bill. Presently, the woman waved him over and said, "This isn't what I ordered. I had the chicken, not the lamb."

Sure enough, Jack had brought the wrong food, which meant there was another table that wouldn't get their food on time, and a chill went down his spine because she had already eaten from the plate and it couldn't be salvaged. Someone wouldn't get their lamb and Martino would have to make it again. Jack returned to the kitchen and thought: well, here goes nothing.

"*Oye*, Martino, *desculpa*, but I think I brought the wrong food. I thought this was *mesa* twelve."

"What's wrong with you? You are always making mistakes. You don't look. How long have you been working here and still you don't know how to do your job."

Typical of the chef to always blame the waiter. Martino should have had both plates ready for the table, instead of one at a time and then out of sequence: one for twelve, one for four, one for twelve, and so on. This time it was Martino's mistake, that is, if he hadn't done it on purpose. Jack didn't need to hear the abuse, but Martino liked to create conflict, and in the restaurant business people quit or fought or were fired over a side order or a missing appetizer. Martino gave the waiters a hard time in hopes that they would do something foolish that would get them fired, or that they would get angry enough to quit.

"Listen, I just need the chicken reheated and then you can make another lamb for the other table. It's not that serious. They haven't called it yet. It's Paul's, *mesa cuatro*. Sorry Martino."

"But why in the goddamned hell can't you take the right plate, *maricon de mierda*? Now I see what an education does; it makes lazy, stupid waiters that can't take the customer their food. How difficult can it be, *buey*, you bring the food and they give you the money."

"You have no idea how difficult it can be with assholes like you," Jack said. You have no idea how hard it is to make sure everyone gets everything they want exactly when they want it, even if several people want it at the same time, not to mention all the customers that are rude or unreasonable, and the bad stomach its given me and my insomnia and standing on my feet for seven hours at a stretch and making small talk and repeating the same list of specials over and over again in a noisy room, totaling bills and having you fuck up my orders, he thought.

Jack was fed up with the work and he was angry. He had made a mistake and now Martino was playing it to his advantage. From the corner of his eye Jack noticed Santos, who did his best to keep quiet and look away from his brother and Jack, who was his friend.

"You chose to be a cook, and it's not my fault that you hate your work and your life," Jack said. "When I come in here and ask for the food, it's because the customer wants it, and without the customer we don't eat. I know that you burn my food and bring it late and put my tickets last when I ask for them. I'm not the only one who makes mistakes. You've made plenty yourself and I've kept quiet about them. You've been rude and abusive, and I've taken it, and the waitresses have taken your sexist remarks. The truth is that without Pablo you'd drink your family into the street and your child would starve. When are you going to take some responsibility for your behavior? You're a disgrace."

Jack had said too much by then, and it no longer mattered if he got the food anymore. This was a confrontation. He stared Martino in the eye and he was not going to back down.

"You should have kept your mouth shut, *gringo*. No one talks about my family or me. I shit on you and everyone like you. What do you know about life? What do you know about me or what I have done to get here? You can come and go, but I will be here forever. You don't take this job I have in the kitchen. You don't cook. Cooking is the best job I have, and still it is a bad job, a very stressful job, and you come and order me to cook this or that like I was a machine, and you make a mistake like it was nothing and I have to cook again. That is not right and I will not make this food again. You can tell the customers sorry but you made a mistake and now they will not eat."

Martino crossed his arms and smiled malevolently under his thick black moustache.

"If you don't cook the food, then you won't have a job," Jack said.

"How about I break you mother?"

They were to the level of the mother now, and it was all innuendo about fucking someone's mother and about someone's mother being a whore. Those were fighting words, and Jack provided a convenient target for all the hate Martino held inside him at the humiliation he had experienced in America and his shame at having to serve Americans.

"Fuck your mother," Jack said. You want me to take the line, I'll take the line, he thought. "Fuck your mother, you Mexican bastard."

"Jack, don't speak like that," Santos told him. "It's not a good idea and I know you don't mean it. Let him be. He gets in these moods and it's best for you to walk away. Walk away and bring Carlo."

Jack ignored him as he and Martino glared at each other tense and ready for conflict. They stood separated by the kitchen counter calculating how they could hurt each other.

"Come on, *gringo*, I know you hate me. Come on and hit me."

"*Por favor, hermano, no lo hagas.* Jack has done nothing to you. It is just his job."

"This is not your business, Santos. You know much, but this is not your business. He must learn respect and I will teach him," Martino said.

Jack noted that Martino held a knife just beneath the table. This is getting serious, he thought. Martino knows knives and makes them by hand. I'm okay to go a few rounds bare-knuckled, because we both need it to respect each other, but the knife is something else. We're both too proud and a fight is something we need, but the knife is unfair. I don't stand a chance with the knife and maybe I'll die, Jack thought. It's too late to run now. Pablo, Santos and Umberto, they're all watching you, and you can't back down without losing their respect. Santos is ashamed of his brother and the others are scared of him.

Jennifer came into the kitchen and said, "Martino, *cabrón*, where is table six? I need table six now."

"Shut up, bitch," he told her.

Jennifer saw Martino with the knife and the distant look in his eyes, and Jack with his fists up, and said, "What the fuck is going on? Are you guys nuts?"

Jack tried to capitalize on the distraction by taking a swing at Martino; instead of catching him by surprise, Martino avoided the blow, the knife flashed, and Jack noticed that his arm was bleeding. Then Martino jumped the counter and advanced on him.

I will not kill him. I will cut his face and make him bleed, but I will not kill him.

Jack backed away, grabbed a nearby pan and splashed the contents, an inch of hot oil, in Martino's face. Martino let out a howl of pain and, slashing blindly with the knife, put his free hand to his face. Jennifer screamed and pressed herself to the wall as the blade cut the air by her throat.

Sensing his advantage, Jack barreled low into Martino's midsection and slammed him to the wall where, pitting their strength against each other, they proceeded to fight over the knife. Given his size, Martino appeared to have the advantage, but Jack was young and full of muscle and held on as Martino tried to sink the blade into his back. It was apparent to Jack that the fight, begun over a misplaced plate of food, had taken on a new significance to the proud Mexican, and that all Martino's pent up anger and frustration was being channeled to destroy him, whatever the consequences. And until Jennifer smashed a plate over

Martino's head, allowing him to knock the knife away, Jack began to have serious doubts about his future.

Martino shook off the blow, and with surprising speed, head-butted Jack to the floor and proceeded to kick at his head and body, sometimes connecting and sometimes not. Jack rolled and covered as best as he could and, in a clever move, scissored Martino's legs out from under him. On the floor the two men grappled with each other. Jack attempted to subdue Martino in one of the many wrestling holds in his repertoire, but Martino wriggled free. Both men scrambled to their feet where they stood out of each other's reach, bruised, burned, bleeding and gasping for breath. Abruptly, Martino rushed Jack, who, with a careful step and concentrating everything on the timing of it, redirected him head first into the glass rack. The shelves collapsed on Martino's back and knocked him to the floor in a shower of popping broken razor glass. He did not get up.

"*Mataste mi hermano.* You killed him, Jack," Santos said. "How could you do this? Martino, *respondeme, abre los ojos, no mueres, si mueres que voy a decir a mama? Y a tu mujer y el niño?* Martino, answer me, open your eyes, don't die, if you die, what will I tell mama? And your wife and son?"

Santos was by his brother's side and now the other waiters appeared in the doorway and then finally Carlo, who said, "*Porco dio,*" and threw his hands into the air. Santos set about removing the irregular glass shards and wine stems buried in his brother's flesh.

"*Mamma mia, che casino,*" Carlo said. "If Martino dies, there will be big trouble. The police and Grace must never find out about this, *mai.* Andrea, here are the keys to the convertible. Put a towel down. I don't want any blood on the seats. Get him to the nearest hospital. Here is my credit card. I don't care how much it costs. I don't want any confusion."

In another place and another circumstance, Carlo thought, I would give Andrea a gun and tell him to take Martino to the ocean and make him disappear. *Ma, in America che cazzo se puo fa'*? But in America what can you do?

"He's dead. Jack killed him," Santos wailed. "Oh, my brother, you were so misunderstood, life was hard for you because you were crazy. You have always been crazy, may God forgive you."

"Get a hold of yourself," Carlo told him. "He's strong as a horse. He will not die. The glass is not in his heart. See how he breathes? What are you waiting for," he told the others, "there's nothing more to see here. Whoever wants to keep their job better get to work. We have a restaurant to run, and Jack you're fired. This never happened, and I don't want to see you again. Paul, you cover Jack's section."

Then Carlo, the master of crisis; the magician who had learned from his mother to turn half-rotten tomatoes, stale bread and pasta into a three course meal; the policeman who had been kicked until his lung collapsed by the mafia thugs, and whose forearm had been shattered by gunfire at close range by unidentified men, went behind the counter and cooked in Martino's place because, like many Italian restaurateurs, he had once been a cook and also a waiter.

"I don't want anyone one to know about this." Carlo said. "This does not leave the kitchen, understood? If anyone asks about the noise, say someone slipped and knocked over the plates."

Jack covered his bloody arm with a towel and made to walk out the front of the restaurant. Carlo said, "Jack, where the hell do you think you're going? You go out the back. Go out the back and I will pay to fix your arm. I will give you your paycheck and your tips. You don't have to worry about that bottle of wine you never charged for; yes, you think I'm a fool, Jack, but I see everything," he said, opening his eyes in that creepy way of Italians from the South and also Greeks from small superstitious villages, where it was an effective practice to ward off evil spirits. "I have a whole system of cameras to document everything that goes on in this place. I saw you sneak wine behind the bar, eat off the customers' plates in the back and screw Candy in the locker room; she sure was after you, *cazzo*, what a lusty bitch. Still, this is of no matter. Martino is a mess but he cooks, and you understand why I have to let you go."

"I understand," Jack said. "I never liked this business, anyway."

"I know, Jack, it's a rotten business and most of these customers are pigs without class. Still, one has to make a living. Don't think that I have the easy life like that good-for-nothing Andrea would have you believe. Yes, it's true I am rich, but look at me Jack, I am in the shit just like you. Look at this shit people put me through every day. Sometimes I think I would like to return to the life I had when I first came and had no responsibility. But you can walk out that door. I know you're good at heart Jack, so no hard feelings. You can do better than this anyway. Twenty-four is too early for gray hair."

"Martino's a crazy son of a bitch. He's no good, and I don't know why you have people like that working here," Jack said.

"Martino is loyal, and a good chef is hard to find, especially one who will work for five hundred a week. A waiter I can find anytime. Anyone can be a waiter, but few people want to cook. Jack, you have never cooked, but it is hell. It is like being in hell, and I do not wish it on anyone."

Jack stood at the bus stop. His arm had stopped bleeding. When he investigated the wound, it appeared deep enough to warrant stitches. In the morning he would go to the Free Clinic in the Haight and have it checked out. Thank God for the clinic, since he didn't have any insurance. Jack didn't place much faith in Carlo's promise to pay. And how about Martino? He was awful sorry for Martino. He didn't want it to turn out that way, he just wanted to protect himself. Would Carlo take care of Martino or would he put him on the street? Jack got on the bus with the bloody towel pressed to his arm and his shirt stained pink and sat down. No one spoke to him, and at subsequent stops the seat next to him remained empty, though the bus was nearly full.

7

Of all Jack's housemates Julie was the biggest homebody. Now that Jack was unemployed and spending more time at home, their relationship had rapidly deteriorated to the point that they spent most of their time in their rooms with the doors shut, and did their best to avoid each other in the kitchen, hallway and bathroom. They didn't have much in common, and Jack found it difficult to humor her. He remembered their early conversations when he had gone out of his way to be polite and had yet to formulate an opinion of her.

"Hey Julie, how's it going?"

"Hi Jack."

"I'm pretty hungry, so I thought I'd cook a little."

Jack had long since noticed that Julie was the unresponsive type. She didn't make small talk and only spoke when she was questioned. She showed little interest in getting to know him better, and Jack found it a struggle to learn more about her and find some common ground.

"So where's Greg," he asked, remembering her boyfriend. Julie's face was drawn and haggard, and it appeared there was no happiness inside her when she replied.

"I'm sick, Jack. I'm waiting to get my tests back from the doctor to see if I've contracted a VD. Have you ever been tested?"

"Sure," he told her. Her disclosure and the invasiveness of her question caught him off-guard. He still knew nothing of her values or her dreams, but now he could assume she had contracted a venereal disease, which was more information than he wanted to know about her.

"Just because you have some infection doesn't mean you got it sexually," he said, in an attempt to be polite.

"What do you know about it, Jack? Who said it was any of your business?"

"I thought it would make you feel better to hear it," he said.

"Greg called me today and asked if I've been fucking anyone else. Since you're so interested in my business, then you might as well know that I probably got it from Henrik. Henrik's a whore, he hooks up with all the groupies at the club, and I've been fucking him, too. Oh God, Jack, what am I doing? I'm so scared. I don't want to get sick."

Julie started to sob, and Jack patted her on the shoulder and said, "It's okay. Wait until you get the tests back. There's no sense in worrying about it now. Most VD is treatable anyway."

Jack remembered the time when it hurt to pee and he had gone to the doctor. The man had stuck a cotton swab up his urethra, which made Jack's mind turn bright white and was up there with eye operations in things he did not like to see or have done to him. The man had given him some pills and then it was gone. From that experience, Jack learned that the key to life was to deal with problems immediately, instead of waiting for fear or shame. Now he wanted to go to the dentist for a check up. He was worried about the tingle in his lower left lateral incisor when he sucked a deep cold breath or ate something sweet or cold. I sure don't want teeth like those bloody British, he thought. When he got a job with a dental plan, then he would go. He didn't imagine he would be going any time soon.

Julie went to her room without answering him. She lay on the bed thinking how she was alone in the world and that nothing anyone said could change the fact that she'd had sex with Henrik, both anal and the normal kind, many times and without a condom, because when it came time neither of them thought about their health or safety. At least she was on the pill, even though it made her weak and turned her skin yellow.

Julie had yet to be touched by life. She lived on her own and never mentioned her promiscuity, tattoos, drinking or drug use to her parents. This was all a part of her new and hip life, while Missouri and her pregnant, married, high school friends were a distant memory. She thought often of her best friend Jill Hartely who had gotten pregnant in high school and ended up marrying, and now lived in a rundown apartment in a Saint Louis suburb where her husband worked as an electrician. Julie had promised to visit for Christmas break, though the thought of the small apartment with filthy brown carpet, the stinky dog smell of their golden retriever "Bounty," and Jill's complete lack of style that was typical of the Midwest, made her think twice, so she came and went without a visit. She did not plan to see Jill again. She wanted no ties with her past life and felt deeply ashamed of her childhood swimming in the muddy river and going without shoes in the summer. She had been so naive then, so sated with life. If it hadn't been for television, Julie might never have known of California and the infinite possibility that existed there. She would have never found her own town boring, or been ashamed of her accent or her childhood.

Julie had one friend who had moved to San Francisco. That gave her the courage to follow and find a place of her own, though her parents still paid the bills. She was a clever girl and only feared when her parents would stop paying and she would have to make a living herself. Though the city was beautiful and infinite, she couldn't quite determine how she fit in. She had long since noticed that Californians were arrogant, and did her best not mention her past.

Since her arrival a year ago, Julie had been content to indulge her senses through heavy drinking, recreational drug use, bar hopping, clubbing and compulsive shopping for the latest music and clothes. In that lifestyle she found a mentor, Henrik, who was older than her and who had introduced her to a part of herself that she didn't know existed. She was no longer the shy girl in school with nothing to say, nor did she feel the need to go and sit by herself when she was confused about the world, like she had in the field behind her house when she was younger. Or so she believed. For each morning that she awoke after those delirious nights of excess, she would feel more lonely and alienated than ever, full of guilt for the disrespect she had for herself and her body. Julie lacked self-esteem and would have preferred to hide away in her bedroom because she felt unloved and incapable of accomplishing something special in her life that would be remembered. She knew she had come to California to prove to her family and childhood friends that she could achieve great things and be successful on her own terms. She wanted most to be a movie star, but didn't have the courage for it and lacked the vital knowledge of how to control men and bend them to her will. So she decided to become a designer. She had taste and a sense of style, and if only she could get down to studying, she'd be fine.

The house was mostly empty during the day until Alex came home from work. When Jack was working, he would pass Alex in the hall on the way to his shift and envy Alex's satisfaction at having had a full and productive day. But then Alex had to wake up at six in the morning to get to class by seven-thirty, and when Alex came home from work, the first thing he did was lie down for a two hour nap before dinner. When Jack came home at night after his shift he would hear the battle fire of Alex's manual typewriter. Sometimes Alex would leave the door open, because writing was a lonely profession and he liked to be interrupted, or at least seen, even if his work wasn't read. Jack often wondered how he could stand to sit there for hours a day, typing. How is it that some people have so much to say and others so little?

It took all of Alex's will to sit down at his typewriter after dinner and he often procrastinated and found chores to distract him from his work. To Alex, food was nothing but fuel, and for dinner he usually prepared something quick and easy, usually in the microwave or from a can, or he would call for takeout. Alex liked to have a bottle of whiskey on hand for writing. It was a romantic indulgence that did not help his work, but if he couldn't enjoy the process, what was the point? The "process" for him was getting drunk; once he got past the "psyching out" and the cleaning and trimming of his nails and shaving and showering and anything else that could be a distraction to the clean working of his mind, he could proceed with the justification of his own existence, which was serious business. To do it well he couldn't second-guess himself. Once he had a rhythm, he had to keep it, and much of the rhythm was the sound of the keys. He thought the computer an impersonal way to write. He didn't believe that thoughts should be cut and pasted. He was a dinosaur and did not care much for modern technological innovation such as e-books, palm pilots, cell phones or the surveillance cameras that had begun to appear at busy intersections. He thought most of it to be at best a distraction, and at worst a violation of privacy and civil liberties. To him nothing was more powerful than the word. It came before all of these things and was their reason for being.

Only after everything was in place did he sit down to write.

Chapter 3: The Role of Media in Modern Empire

The mass marketing of the American Dream globally through film and television is a subtle form of imperialism that does not persuade through force but in the guise of entertainment. American movies and television programs distributed abroad all too often misrepresent life in the United States, and are not relevant to the reality of the developing world. In order to understand how and why certain images are presented in favor of others, we must first understand the purpose and function of mass media.

What is understood by the term mass media is that it is popular, deals with universal themes, and is readily accessible and palatable to the public. Its purpose is to universalize a specific reality and ideology at the expense of alternative ways of seeing and interpreting the world. In order to understand how our media functions, we must first understand what it means to be an American.

The American economy relies on high levels of consumption both at home and abroad. This consumption is facilitated by credit, i.e. imaginary money. The consumer model is a closed system: the more people consume, the more they need to produce; the more goods produced, the cheaper they become, and the greater the purchasing power of the individual. That, at least, is the general idea. Like the chicken and the egg, it is unclear where the process begins and ends. Such is the relationship between consumer society and the mass media. While this consumptive model may work in the short term to produce comfort for the masses, in the long term it increases the gap between the developed and developing world. Also, it sets a standard and pace for growth that is unsustainable and that ultimately undermines quality of life by reducing social services and creating social problems resulting from an unequal wealth distribution.

We are a visual society where image rules over substance and appearance is superior to content. What is represented or "seen" is valued; all remaining identities and realities, conversely, are rendered invisible and therefore, worthless. Those in control of the means of communication inevitably represent themselves in the most favorable light. Those that have the power to represent are the elite of the social hierarchy. Through conglomeration, mass media has become elite media to promote and consolidate the economic goals of the powerful at the expense of social equity and free expression. While ideas remain free, the right and access to their presentation and distribution is valued at a premium, and therefore severely restricted by media networks. Those who are able to pay this premium do so because it provides them with the opportunity to increase their influence. As a result, mass media provides no forum for social change and intellectual debate, but rather a marketplace where individuals seek value through consumption of products and services. Without equal access and participation in media there can be no critique of, or reflection on the values promoted in a society. In this way, humanity stagnates and becomes corrupted. One has to question, then, the value of a media that serves primarily as a marketing tool for the business elite. Cleverly and covertly, a few privileged individuals have smothered the creative, critical and productive impulses of the masses with the comfortable blanket of consumption. This comfort is an insatiable addiction in disguise. Like all good marketing, it succeeds by creating need where it didn't previously exist, and charging for that which was formerly free. The search for identity, substance and meaning that was formerly accessible through social interaction, compromise and debate, can now only be satisfied through material goods that claim these values and are soon replaced by new and "better" values at a higher price tag. In this paradigm, the best values belong to the rich because they can afford them. To be poor, therefore, is a sign of moral emptiness.

With few exceptions, to watch television or visit the cinema today is to willingly engage in a process of consumer acculturation. While economic prosperity is important for the success and stability of a nation, the absence of forums for debate in mass media has reduced the creative force of America. Above all, it is the media that has transformed the United States from a productive to a consumptive nation. Due to the co-option of the media by business interests, American children grow up with little capacity for critical thinking. They do not have the old-fashioned concept that once material needs are satisfied, one can devote time to development of the spiritual and intellectual pursuits that make life worthwhile. The Unites States is a land of those who will never satisfy their consumptive needs. As a result, the average American citizen will never attain a higher level of achievement in the form of philanthropy, social equity, sustainable living or artistic innovation. In the midst of the boundless wealth of the few, lies the immeasurable cultural, ideological, emotional and economic poverty of the many. In the religion of insatiable material hunger, businesses use mass media to gain control of individual souls. This new religion is not based on faith in a great creator or in a quest for truth in spirituality, but rather in earthly comforts and the pursuit of excess. God has become an act of consumption; the host wafer and wine of communion, the body and blood of Christ, can no longer sate our hunger. Religion has become an ornament without substance that we wear like a brand logo.

Media production that is not rank advertising, the so-called "content" of television programs and films, presents consciously or subconsciously this new world view. Consumer culture is nothing more than a cult of gluttony. In our cinematic ideal, our idols are not the righteous or just, but the privileged and wealthy. The poor and ugly are cast as criminals, while the real criminals are rich and beautiful. Beauty is valued over intelligence, and easy money is everybody's primary goal. In our media fantasy, it's given that everyone lives in a nice house and owns an expensive car. And though most of our media idols live in the height of luxury, it is not enough. When the characters of film and television are unhappy, it is usually because they want more beauty, power and wealth, and seldom because they wish to be better human beings.

This cultural regime is absorbed by the masses at the expense of their ethics and basic humanity. The public would be happier if it did not watch television or go to the movies. By not worrying about what they don't have, they would be free to focus more on each other and to develop values that better conform to their reality and their community. The media elite, movie stars and the like, depend on the support and approval of the public in order to maintain their privileged position, while ordinary citizens benefit little from the hours wasted following the mainstream media and would do better to pull the plug. The dreams presented on television or the movie screen are seldom accessible to the masses. Most Americans cannot afford the lifestyle of media fantasy; many do not have power, beauty, or money, though they may be respectable human beings. It would seem logical, then, for these individuals to reject unrepresentative media ideals that feed on mediocrity and/or misery. No doubt it is hard to turn away from the drug of comfort. Who hasn't wanted to escape for a while into a charmed life instead of settling down to some hard work to change their condition, or to the hard work of helping others? The illusion of wealth and the equation of wealth with happiness promoted by the media leads to idleness as people lose faith in themselves and hope for a change in their condition.

Our nation is threatened by the emotional sickness produced by greed. Not surprisingly, this problem is rarely addressed in the media. You will not see a surgeon general's warning on the back of a fashion magazine stating: this advertisement uses sex and beauty to market its products; nor is there a rating system indicating that the images and information contained in a blockbuster film may be damaging to one's self-esteem and may lead to feelings of frustration, jealousy and depression for not having a better life. The only way to get off the drug of want is to cut consumption and invest in spiritual and cultural pursuits.

While the material wealth in the United States is greater than in any period in human history, it has led to a decline in quality of life on many levels. Average Americans work longer hours and have considerably less vacation time than their European counterparts. A substantial percentage of Americans live without health care. American children perform worse in school than children from other developed or developing nations. Teachers are not paid fairly, divorce and poverty are on the rise, use of non-essential prescription drugs has skyrocketed, prison populations are swelling, public transportation is neglected or non-existent, most Americans are in debt, and many Americans are oblivious to legislation and policies passed by their government that erode their social and economic rights.

The average U.S. citizen has the false belief that America is superior to other nations on all counts, while remaining largely ignorant of world affairs, and the politics, culture and values of other nations. The ideological isolation of America and false sense of superiority keeps our nation from progressing. We have no objective point of reference from which to view ourselves and perceive our shortcomings as a people. We let the media dictate our beliefs and fail to see that material shortcomings are not the true issue at hand. Since there seems to be little separation between the market and our morality, we are unable to recover our identity, creativity, humanity, and reason. Meanwhile the commercial media tells us we should be worried about our looks, or concerned about upgrading our material goods.

And what about American culture? Culture can be loosely defined as the traditions, policies, beliefs, geography, and language that unite a group of people. From that definition are we to draw the conclusion that what makes us American is our ability to buy and sell? Some may argue that what makes us American is our form of government that affords each of us with a set of unalienable rights and liberties. While this is true, one must wonder how it is that, from the strength of our Constitution, we have come to live in a society where scholarship and political involvement have taken a back seat to the satisfaction of superficial wants and desires? Are we really that shallow or has comfort made us so? At what point does excessive comfort undermine our morality and humanity? For consumer culture to prosper is it necessary for us to be alienated from the production process and its impacts? Currently, mass media encourages us to think of consumption as a personal right independent from the source of the raw materials and labor used to produce consumer goods, and the environmental consequences of the extraction, processing, manufacturing and distribution of these goods. To compartmentalize the process of consumption is to negate the systemic nature of our natural world, where one activity is linked to a myriad of others, and where individual behavior contributes to how these systems function. The more a system is manipulated for the benefit of the few, the less likely it is to sustain the many.

The line between marketing and entertainment is blurred in the media. Hollywood markets itself through extensive media coverage of its stars on television, the radio and the magazine rack. It celebrates itself through private awards ceremonies, stars are paid to endorse consumer products and services, and these products appear prominently in films. The public is constantly bombarded with new films, video games, music, and television competing for the consumer dollar. In this way, citizens lose twice. First, by spending money on new products they don't need, and second by sacrificing valuable time that could be better applied learning something new, getting exercise, enjoying time with the family, or visiting a new place. Eventually, the public finds it easier to consume than to create their world and enhance their human relationships through positive ideas and actions.

Unfortunately, comfort has left Americans lazy and complacent. Preoccupied by the banal irritations and greater irrational phobias presented on the big screen or on television, Americans allow their civil liberties and quality of live to be eroded by the bottom line of commerce and material advancement. The American film industry contributes to the social decay of the nation by serving up sensationalist and adulterated versions of historical events that strip the public of its history and core sources of knowledge. The silver screen warps reality to reflect values that may or may not be valid. To not question these historical and cultural interpretations of our nation and the world is to allow them to pass for fact. This gives a nation and its citizens a false sense of morality and greatness that is at best counterproductive to social advancement, and at worst a justification for hate and violence. Often the artificial reality of media propaganda masks the American public from the atrocities committed in its name by the government and corporate interests.

Art is the casualty of sensationalism and vested interests. The Hollywood model is unable to advance artistically and intellectually precisely because we Americans no longer seek to question our world, more concerned as we are with securing our financial prosperity. Comfort has rotted us through and through. Because we have learned that money is the measuring stick of happiness, we either spend our lives in a frantic race to collect it or, once obtained, we sit back and assume that we have nothing more to strive for. Because we demand so little of ourselves, our friends and our neighbors, we are desensitized to how art can enrich our lives and open up new paths to self-fulfillment.

Much of the problem has to do with the fact that America is unable to see itself in a critical and objective light. In truth, there is little difference between the media mogul and the common man in that both have been raised on sensationalism, cultural absolutism, and censorship. The former has made a conscious choice to perpetuate this state of affairs for his own benefit, while the latter has chosen to sit back, swallow it, shit it out to feed his children, and gorge on it with his neighbors. So whose fault is it then that America is stagnant with no real plan for progress in the world?

The myth has always been that those who become leaders are the best the nation has to offer in terms of intelligence, knowledge, education, *and character; however, history has shown that people more often choose the leaders that most closely resemble themselves. What does that say about the American public when their leaders are often cynical, superficial, uncompromising, and corrupt? It is far too simple a conclusion to state that poor leadership is a top-down affair; rather, it is a vicious cycle of mediocrity facilitated by lack of information, in terms of choice, distribution, and access, which starts with an American childhood.*

The simplistic themes and plots of modern American cinema are in part responsible for this endless cycle of cultural and intellectual poverty. The movies we watch create our worldview and Hollywood is in large part responsible for our false perceptions. The constant violence in film makes people fearful and suspicious of their fellow citizens. The wholesale censorship of healthy sexual relationships in film promotes sexual repression. Rags to riches stories mock the reality of Americans living from paycheck to paycheck unable to get ahead. In America there are few true stories about a good and righteous man who defeats the corrupt men that oppress him unjustly. More often the corrupt aren't held accountable for their actions and the average Joe isn't treated fairly, in spite of overtures and myths to the contrary. Swallowing this kind of tripe on the big screen either invokes laughter or contempt. Finally, some of the most dangerous films are those that project an Americentric view of the world that dehumanizes and demonizes other cultures and peoples. These films are dangerous precisely because the representations and associations they make are presented as subtle truth that is readily accepted by the uninformed.

It would be unfair to say that all mass media is shallow or promotes simple good-bad dichotomies. It is also not the case that the values of our nation are inherently negative and self-serving; far too many examples exist to the contrary.

Hollywood filmmaking is not an intellectual pursuit and makes no such pretense. The success of Hollywood is based on a clever blend of marketing and repetition where themes are changed on the visual level and simplified plots are hidden behind the sound of gunfire, the flash of explosions, and the gods and devils that we would all like to believe exist. While there is a large enough segment of the population to support smaller, more profound, and innovative films, Hollywood is concerned with large-scale productions and the profits that follow; therefore, it does not risk presenting the unique and possibly controversial.

The spectacle is nothing new to empire. In Roman times the blood and gore of life was confined to the coliseum and foreign wars. The need for an outlet to human frustrations and limitations was satisfied by spectating battles to the death in the gladiator ring. Though more cruel than the cinema, it was also perhaps more honest, given the public was aware they were witnessing a reality where slaves and ordinary men fought and died, and that those who survived to fight again were real heroes and not myths or illusions.

The American spectator of violent and sensationalist films, however, is desensitized to violence by being at once separate from it in a dark theater, and by knowing in the end that the fight is a pantomime performed by actors and not real men. Therefore, when an actor kills, the spectator cannot take the murder seriously and is not shocked by the death he witnesses. This process of desensitization must be challenged. Film is a powerful medium particularly when it plays on themes of injustice where property, family, and country are concerned, and when the films are set in places that we are familiar with or in periods of our own history. The foreign spectator, however, has a much different impression and perspective on such things. He may believe the illusions and think them as real as a head separated from a man's shoulders in the gladiator ring of a once great empire. He may believe that America is what it has been marketed to be . . .

Alex removed the page and laid it face down on his growing manuscript. This comfort you criticize gives you the freedom to write, he thought. You criticize these things because they matter to you. Even if your life is not as comfortable as it could be, you still have freedom of speech. That's nothing to scoff at. A writer doesn't depend on a good economy or comfort to survive. For a writer, it's always a bad economy. Consequently, when too much comfort exists then art is tamed and stripped of its meaning. As for being able to write, those that have to, do it in any and all appalling and unfit conditions. There are too many examples for that to be mere romanticism. All right then, what about the developing world and American mass media? First off, it has to do with linguistic imperialism. Language is an essential element of culture. Its control equals power. Time to do a little research, Alex thought. Wow, I've been writing for two hours. It's amazing how time passes when you're challenged to think.

His stomach felt hollow; it always did after he wrote. Damn, writers, we have it tough, Alex thought, on his way to the kitchen. We can't have a full time job, otherwise we can't write, we eat more than anyone and have less money. Thank God for eggs. I must go through a dozen every two days. Chicken fetuses, he thought. What if I cracked one and a malformed bird fell out, all curled in a ball with his eyes shut in his disproportionately large head? That reminds me of putting a frog in the refrigerator. Imagine a frog slowed down by the cold. To bad you can't slow yourself down like that. You're a nervous son of bitch and that's why you act calm and move and talk slow. You don't want anyone to know. And also you might just have a panic attack if you went along with it. Why is it that we always compensate for our own nature? Careful, careful, don't burn the eggs.

8

Quincy had skated the car park several times. There were a few good curbs there, slick with red paint, and also the parking blocks and the low retaining wall that separated the asphalt from the sidewalk and the street. Because parking was at a premium in the city, the lot was always full. The people paid into a sealed metal box with slits and a number for each space. It was an outdated system; most parking garages had attendants and issued tickets from machines with exact dates and times. Parking here was eight dollars an hour, about average for that South of Market location.

Quincy liked to skate the car park because no one would bother him or tell him to go away like at the government buildings on Franklin. By City Hall there were stairs and a long sloping wall that was a skateboarder's dream. He thought it a great injustice when the city covered the wall with perfectly spaced bumps and also wires to catch wheels and send a skater crashing to the pavement. The message was clear, but then there was still the handrail and the stairs where you could pull tricks. He remembered filming his buddy Bones doing a nose grind there once. They had done it at night when there was only the occasional rent-a-cop to bother their activities.

Bones was the best skater Quincy knew and that was because he wasn't afraid to get good speed before doing a double flight of stairs, a handrail, a wall or a planter. Skating was about control under pressure and without proper speed most tricks weren't possible. Quincy knew from his own skating that when he failed to get the proper speed, it was because he didn't have the confidence or the desire to pull the trick. Midway through he would kick his board out, being more concerned with not getting hurt than pulling the trick.

That night Quincy sat on the lower step with his back to the wall and the camera aimed up at the railing. From such an angle it wasn't possible to see the approach. The first shot of Bones would be of him flying up from nowhere onto the rail. Ignacio served as the lookout and held up his hand to give the signal. Quincy waited with his eye on the viewfinder until Bones appeared floating in the air with his arms wide like a bird. He stared down at the board stuck to his feet as the truck came into contact with the rail. With all his speed, Bones managed to lift the back truck and balance on the nose as he slid the length of the rail. Toward the bottom his expression changed and the sound of metal on metal reverberated through the steel. Bones's board hung up and he was thrown to the pavement. It was the sort of fall that could not be prevented, like a stone caught in the wheel on a steep hill, or a gap in the sidewalk. Perhaps Bones chose the lesser of two evils when he turned sideways and angled with his shoulder. Fortunately, he didn't fall on his head or neck. Later, when they had a closer look, it seemed that someone had welded metal screw to the railing, just enough to hang up a board; it was for that maliciousness that Bones would spend months with a special cast and harness to keep his shoulder in place. After that he lost confidence in his skating and would no longer try difficult tricks so he could improve. He had discovered his mortality and could not longer fly over the concrete and steel of the city.

At the time they were incensed at the city's anti-skating measures.

"Yo, what do those fools got against us anyway? We ain't hurtin' nobody or robbin' no banks or committing no murder or nothin'. We're just trying to have some fun in this dead place and they gotta go fuck it up," Quincy said.

"Who you think did it," Ignacio asked him.

"Probably one a' them security guards. They all bitter and shit, 'cause they ain't real cops. Shit, rent-a-cop, that ain't even a real job. That's just for lazy fools who wanna feel important."

"Bones, man, you don't look so good. You're all pasty white. Can you move your arm," Ignacio asked.

Bones attempted to move his arm. "Aww, fuck it hurts."

"Leave it alone, man. Just chill and we'll get some help," Quincy said.

"No, man. We'll just get into trouble. They'll arrest us for breaking the law," Bones protested.

"Law, nothin'. They don't want us skating for liability, and to stop us they weld metal to the rail, and you almost broke you're neck, man. How's that for hypocritical? There ain't no law saying how to use a handrail. It's supposed to get you down the stairs, and if that's on a skateboard or walking, what's the difference," Quincy said. "Man, you gotta get to a hospital, but then your mom gonna find out and she gonna toss your board and shit."

"Come on, help me up," Bones told them. He was trying to keep a good face but he was scared. When he noticed the collarbone sticking through his skin, he broke into a sweat. His mouth felt metallic and it was an effort to swallow.

"I'm gonna hail us a cab," Ignacio said. He dropped his board and took off, pumping hard with his leg toward Market Street.

Quincy helped Bones up. Bones's shirt was torn and stained with blood and he held his injured arm at his side like an old-school action figure; it was only missing in his posture that he salute with his good arm.

"You had it, Bones. You pulled it all the way, man. It ain't your fault the screw was there. When we edit this thing, we can cut out the end and it'll be all good."

"Fuck the video. I don't give a damn about the video. They probably won't take it anyway. I've seen guys do handrails twice as long. This is nothing. Mark Goveira does kick flips to 5.0 grinds and can ollie a flight of stairs standing still."

Bones was older than Quincy. He didn't have any friends besides Quincy and Ignacio. He was thin with freckles and insomnia kept him up nights skating the city. In school he would sit in the back row and sleep with his head on his desk. The teachers had long since stopped bothering him. Often he was overcome with a sense of helplessness. He did not know anything about women or being cool, though he watched a lot of television to find out the secret to escaping his own limitations. Many a night, he would lie in bed and think himself small and unimportant and content himself with masturbating to a dog-eared porno mag. When he had had enough of his thoughts and insecurities, when he could not take the sense of failure and hopelessness that was his any longer, he would skate the precipitous streets of San Francisco. He would jump over the obstacles in his path and become one with the video game illusion that he normally experienced by proxy; it was the proximity to danger, the speed and the uncertainty of the street, and the ability to conquer it, that made him forget for a while his limitations. While everyone slept, he skated the empty streets and became one with the urban landscape. He was conscious of every crack in the pavement that could spell disaster, of every opportunity to fly, of the grace and precision of every turn and ollie. He flowed through that hostile terrain with the feeling that one day he would reach his destination and come to an understanding of why the world was as it was.

Quincy saw his friend differently after the accident. The force field of cool was gone. Bones was no longer a superior being whose talent brought him to a state of nirvana he could never hope to reach. No, he became a quivering voice, weakness and fear, and instead of smiling peaceful and omnipotent, he started to cry.

"This place is all messed up. Why do they fucking hate us, man, and treat us like criminals? This is my life and they want to control me and tell me where I can go and what I can do. I'm not like them. Skating's all I've got and they want to take it away. It ain't right, man. And now I'm all fucked up."

Bones was ashamed of his words and behavior, but it no longer seemed to matter. He knew that now Quincy saw him like his peers in school and his parents saw him: as a loser who was intimidated by everyone and everything except for the inanimate, for the concrete and the stationary and safe. At eighteen, maybe he was too old to skateboard. He would never be pro. He should just give it up, get a job and live on his own so that he could respect himself. So long as you can pay your own way, they don't have anything on you.

"Come on, man, you shred," Quincy said. "No one is going to take anything away from you. You've been in magazines, dawg! You're immortal. Shit, I got a picture of you on my wall. You just trippin' 'cause your arm. Man, that'll heal. Remember when I broke my wrist? It'll be just like that and then we'll be right back here doing it again. They can't control nobody. We'll hacksaw that railing and sand it smooth and you'll pull this shit and we'll get it on film."

"I'm never coming back here," Bones said.

"It don't gotta be here. We can go wherever. This scene is wack anyway. No more wall rides or nothin'. We'll do it somewhere else. There are other good spots like over in Pacific Heights. Maybe you can five forty a car on the downhill or somethin' . . ."

Quincy spoke fast and did his best to ignore his friend's emotional breakdown. It was a pretty bad fall, though. Even I would talk like that if I got slammed that bad. Still, behind all his positive talk, Quincy realized that he had lost his idol; he had seen weakness in one he thought to be strong and it had changed him. The thought grew in him that he could not depend on others to get him through life or to prove that things could be done. Bones is scared like me, he thought. It's normal to be scared, but now he has more fear than me and I don't need him anymore.

Bones wasn't listening. Only he knew what he had lost in himself and how he had been scarred. The malice had come from outside to hurt him, and he felt fear and also the loneliness of not being heard or understood, though he spoke with sincerity. This is futile, he thought. How absurd to think you could hit the big time as a pro skater. I mean you were sponsored, but not so you could live off it. No, you've learned the hard way that there are too many obstacles to the dream.

Bones didn't realize it then, but the only obstacle he faced was the defeatism of his own mind. The dream was his and his alone to nurture or abandon.

They helped Bones to the taxi and rode with him to his house. When he got out, they said nice things and made promises to skate when he was better. Bones was himself again; he was distant and polite and didn't say what he thought, though they had heard his confession. As it stood, Quincy and Ignacio, the busboy, never skated with him again. They no longer needed Bones and he didn't need them.

9

Quincy remembered his friend Bones as he skated the parking lot. That day he wasn't particularly interested in skating, so he sat on the wall near the pay box and watched the people put their money in.

The idea had been brewing for some time in his head: he would pretend to be the attendant and keep the parking money for himself. He had even made himself a nametag with that end in mind. He had been watching the parking lot for weeks, trying to work up the courage for his fraud. He knew it was illegal and wrong, but he told himself he needed the money. He didn't believe in the business of paying to park. Skating had taught him to think of pavement as public space, and he didn't believe that someone should control a piece of pavement and charge for its use. This was his rationalization for taking the money. What's more, it was protection money. He made a promise to himself to ensure that none of the cars were stolen, and in that way the payment was justified. Quincy was working for the money.

No more messing around, he told himself. It's time to do this. Resigned to the voice in his head, Quincy put on the nametag and hid his skateboard behind a nearby dumpster. When the first customer came to make a payment, he felt his heart beat fast in his chest. It's all about confidence, he thought. You're a parking attendant and you'll act like one, and they'll believe you because you believe in yourself and your right to survive and make a buck from your own wits. You're a businessman, right? Well, get to it.

Quincy approached the woman and said, "There's been some reports of theft around here, so they've hired me to keep an eye on things. I'm the new attendant. My name's Terence. You're over there in sixteen, looks like. That'll be eight dollars, ma'am."

He folded his arms behind his back, stood straight and watched the traffic in an attempt to look casual. He did not make idle conversation. Liars make idle conversation, he thought. They say too much. She doesn't care about you; you're just the parking attendant. Just let her give you the money and go on about her business.

The woman looked at him and saw his nametag. Quincy was dressed in a pair of overalls and a plain blue cap. She thought: well, it's nice to see a young black man decently employed. She felt motherly towards him, like she was doing him a favor, when she handed him the money.

"Thank you, ma'am. Now you have a nice day. Don't worry your car is safe with me."

When she was gone Quincy took the money and counted it out. I can't believe she gave me the money. I give people too much credit. Still, you saw the way she was looking at you. She felt sorry for you, man. The dumb bitch felt sorry for you. Well, work is work. So let's wait for the next sucker. Quincy felt the particular joy of easy money bubble up inside him. Before that the joy was only in his imagination.

Still, Quincy played it careful. He picked and chose his victims. Some smartly dressed men he found too intimidating and also some women, especially the pretty ones. You're not stealing from them. They gotta pay anyway, he told himself. Your just stealing from the thief that runs this place. I wonder how often they empty the box, anyway? I've been by here plenty and never seen them empty it. Maybe they do it by the month?

Quincy stayed there the whole day when he should have been in school. When he finished he had two hundred and fify-six dollars in assorted denominations rolled thick in his jacket pocket so it bulged. He skated over to the surplus and second hand stores and outlets on Market to find some work clothes. He picked up a pair of pants and a used jacket with a Jesus name patch sewn above the left coat pocket. He could have bought another patch with a more appropriate name, but he didn't bother. He wondered if it was sin to masquerade as Jesus. It seemed to him that certain names should be off-limits, particularly those spoiled by historic figures.

He also bought a hat and decided to have "California Parking" sewn on it in yellow letters like the sign at the lot. He paid and then went to the stationary store and found a receipt booklet that would lend legitimacy to his scheme.

Quincy still had quite a bit of money, over a hundred dollars, and thought to get a cell phone like Gavin so he could put it on his desk for his classmates to admire, especially Aisha. I'm a businessman now and a businessman has got to have his own phone. So later that day he rode home with a new cell phone in his pocket, though he didn't have anyone to call. He liked to hold it up to his ear and make like he was talking to someone important. Next thing I'll do is get some nice clothes and a fresh ride, he thought. How about a convertible? Tomorrow you go to the lot early and charge everyone. Still, you have to watch out so you don't get caught. There must be other places where you can make a buck as a parking pirate.

For dinner he bought himself a few hamburgers at McDoogle's in the Mission, and never had they tasted so good. When he was done with his day, he still had twenty-three dollars to spare. This making a living thing ain't so bad. Dad's always complaining about work but that's 'cause he don't use his head. He never had any ambition, and I'm gonna show him what it's all about.

Quincy skated back to his neighborhood. He felt taller than before, and the older kids smoking on the corner no longer seemed cool. I don't gotta chill with them down and out lazy fools and deal drugs like a bitch. That shit is wack.

When his father came home, Quincy was settled down to his books. His new life and plans were not something he could talk about.

10

Damian was a man tainted by ambition. He had grown up in the San Fernando Valley in Southern California, and much of what he knew about making a living, he had learned from his father who ran a used car dealership. From his father he learned that people were either pessimists or optimists, and if one desired success and happiness it was necessary to be the latter. Nearly everything his father said came back to this rule.

"There is only one life, son, and some people live it reluctantly. These people focus on the bad and use it to justify their unhappiness and failure. We're not that type of person, Damian, and don't you forget it. Life is a fight and you have to fight with all you got. Take the dealership; now I deal in used cars and it's my job to get the most value for each one. The car is both a means of transportation and a tool for self-expression. There are plenty of dealerships out there. Any smart person would shop around like I shop around at the repo auctions. But when they come here you better believe I'm gonna present my vehicles in the best light and not discuss the defects. Sometimes people don't just want a car, they want a new identity. That's the salesman's job: to satisfy the customer's desires and help them improve their image and self-worth. In this life there's no inherent value, Damian. Value is created through negotiation. The value of something depends on how much you want it. In my business, what people see and hear is more important than quality and utility. Maybe this is over your head, son. All I mean to say is that people need illusions to survive. They want to believe that their lives can improve, and if they wish to measure this improvement in a new car, who am I to disappoint them? God knows they're happier for it."

Damian disagreed with his father's thesis of value. True value could not be acquired simply through boasting or image, it was something that had to be proven through merit. A player showed his value to the team through his skill in the game, and so it was in all professions.

At that time in his life Damian believed he would find a calling for which he had a particular talent, and when he did, he would practice until it was mastered. That was the key to success. Though his father was successful in these terms, Damian did not consider it a worthy skill to trick customers into paying too much for second-rate cars or luxury vehicles they couldn't really afford; that was merely dishonesty. Idealistic as he was, Damian believed that to win by false appearances and clever words did not count. In fact, at the age of seventeen, he was in complete rebellion from his father. When his father referred to his taking over the family business, Damian felt his stomach knot in protest and his chin jut in defiance; it was his pride and ambition that told him he was meant for better things. He didn't need his father's help or philosophy to succeed. I'll find my own success, he told himself. To his dismay, Damian was soon to discover that he was one of many born without an inherent gift or talent. In spite of his ambition, he possessed no dreams. And so far none of his interests seemed on the verge of becoming a great passion that gave purpose to a man's life.

At first he had considered a career in sports. He ran track, swam, played water polo, volleyball and soccer. Baseball he found boring, and football he avoided because he didn't like pain. He was quick to learn that besides the physical aspect, there was also a psychological element to sports that he found difficult to manage. Though he was decent at water polo, the hidden underwater kicks and elbows during a match aggravated him. When he served for game point on the volleyball court, his nerves got the better of him and he would hit it long or into the net. When the opposing players on the soccer field spit in his face, cursed his mother and put their cleats into his feet, he couldn't keep his cool and was often ejected for fighting. Soon sport and games lost value to him.

In the classroom Damian earned decent marks, not because he was gifted, but because he had come to understand the institutional formula for success. He was by no means enthusiastic, since he could see no practical application for what he was learning beyond grooming for a sedentary desk job. There was nothing in his studies that directed him toward a career he found compelling. In his opinion, a high school education amounted to little more than social conditioning; it paved the way for resignation to the mediocrity of serving the ruling class. If one wanted to work and make money, one didn't need to go to school. School was for the drones, and any interest he may have had in learning was squandered by the rote memorization and regurgitation of existing information and so-called "facts."

It was at that time that the disillusion spread inside him. He had no idea what he wanted from life, so he preferred not to think about it. He asked himself the question: what is it you really love, and there was no answer. Slowly and inevitably, Damian became like those people his father criticized; he grew negative and cynical and began to live only for the moment. It was then that he turned to the only foundation he had: the theory of the used car salesman who was his father. No one knows how I feel inside, he thought, so I might as well pretend I'm happy. If I pretend to be happy, then I am, because in this world we exist for other people and how they perceive us. So how do I make people like me? How do I get to hang out with Stacey Wilson and all her cute cheerleader friends, and be best bros with Brad Martin, the star quarterback?

11

Peter Hutton noticed the change in his son. Damian spent most of his time after school in his room lying in bed listening to music or sleeping. Mr. Hutton would pass by his son's door and find him staring at the ceiling. Sometimes when he looked at Damian, he was reminded of himself. He remembered all the confusion and insecurities of high school. Though Peter was nostalgic for his youth, he knew that it was a hard time when many teenagers got lost in their own heads. He believed in treating his son like an adult and didn't worry about his future because of the business, which was going well. Maybe I should talk to him. He may want to talk. He might get defensive, but I'll try anyway. He's proud like me, but pride shouldn't matter with the people we love.

"I just thought I'd come see how you're doing."

"I'm fine."

"Is there anything you want to talk about?"

"I don't know," Damian said. But he knew. He wanted to ask his father about life's purpose, and tell him that he was ashamed at not being good at anything in particular and that he didn't want to be a car salesman.

"So, are there any nice girls at school?"

"A few, but I don't really know them. They hang out in a big group by themselves."

Peter smiled. "I still remember the first girl I had a crush on. Her name was Tanya, Tanya Summer. I used to sit and stare at her in math class. She was the most popular girl in school."

"So what happened?"

"What? Oh, nothing. Sometimes things look better from a distance. That way you can imagine the best and have something to dream about. It's important to have dreams."

Peter neglected to tell Damian that once Tanya had to go to the hospital with a beer bottle stuck in her vagina, and it had to be removed surgically, and that later someone had gotten her pregnant and she had to drop out of school. Peter neglected to tell him these things because he didn't want to discourage his son. Nor did he tell him that his wife, Damian's mother, was not the woman he loved most in the world, but that she had been second choice, and that their marriage was a compromise based on respect and tolerance. When he lived in Montana and worked on cars for a living, Peter had met his first and only love. They loved each other passionately and made each other miserable at the same time. Later she left for New York, and he did not go with her. She found another man and married him.

Peter didn't bother to tell his son that he never expected to be a car salesman living in California and married to the woman that was now his wife. Somehow he had ended up there, though his intentions had been different. Still, he was not like those people who wanted to live again and do it differently, because he realized that every path had its detours and difficulties and he had been luckier than most. Though I am not the positive person I pretend to be, I realize it could have been worse. I've always seen the glass half-empty. Still, Damian shouldn't think like that. I hope he has more of his mother than me in him.

"Dad, I've been thinking a lot about what you said. You know about being positive. Well, I haven't been feeling very positive lately. I've been feeling tired. I'm tired of school and sports and people."

"I think you're spending too much time by yourself. Don't kids go to parties these days? And how about the girls? That's reason enough to go to school."

"I don't know, dad."

"How about this: after dinner, you can have a look at my Playboy. That should cheer you up. I'll leave it in the drawer in the bathroom. That way mom'll never know."

It was a kind gesture, Damian realized, but he had already looked at that Playboy, having snuck it from his dad's desk to the bathroom to jerk off. He had come a little on the centerfold but was quick to wipe it off before it stained the paper. He blushed some at the thought that his father might know, but then he thought that jerking off was normal and healthy since he did not know any girls except Brenda in his Geometry class who wouldn't leave him alone. Maybe I should just learn to fuck with Brenda since she's ugly and it won't matter if I make mistakes and don't know what I'm doing? That way I can be good later with someone who counts. No, that won't do, and if anyone found out it'd ruin your image.

"Dad, I've been driving for a year now, and it was nice of you to give me my own car, but like you said, life is all about appearances, so I was wondering if I could borrow the black Camaro that just came into the lot? You know I'm a good driver and I've never had any accidents. I don't just want to dream, dad. I want to impress Stacey Wilson so she'll come with me off-campus for lunch."

Peter smiled and clapped his son on the back. "All right, then. If you think you can handle it, and I'm not talking so much about the car, but Stacey. Ha, ha. Tomorrow we'll head over to the lot and pick it up."

Peter felt good lending Damian a car he could only have dreamed of in his own youth. The thought made him forget his own melancholy. It seemed his son was engaged with life after all.

The first day behind the wheel of that '69 Camaro, Damian's existential crisis was resolved. It's not about being good at anything, he thought. It's about money and looking good. On his way to school Damian studied himself in the mirror.

"Who's your daddy, bitch," he asked himself.

"I am, I'm your big daddy," he replied.

Jesus, listen to that engine. It sounds like a fire-breathing dragon. I bet if I open the hood it's got these big fucking teeth and a hungry black stomach down deep. That's where it all comes from.

Damian got to school early and parked by the front gate where everyone would see him. He sat there and turned the stereo up, not too loud, but loud enough to show off a little. Then he ignored everyone. You can't appear too eager, he told himself. Let them take it in.

Two days later Stacey, Sarah and Jessica, the cool girls, were in his car. They were going off-campus for lunch and it was Stacey who had asked for the ride. Now Damian didn't have do anything but sit back, look cool and answer her questions.

"So what are you doing this weekend, Damian," Stacey asked him.

Damian felt large then and said, casually, "I'm having a party. My parents are gone and I'm having a keg in my garage. Why don't you guys come over? Let Brad and the crew know. I'll give you my number when we get back."

Later in fifth period econ, Damian wondered what he had gotten himself into. Mom and dad aren't going out of town. Where the hell am I gonna get a keg of beer? Meanwhile, Mr. Lawson said:

"There is an opportunity cost and a trade-off for everything we do. Can anyone tell me what the opportunity costs and trade-offs are for skipping college and going straight to work?"

"When I get done with high school I'm gonna work construction for my dad. I can make good money and pay off my new truck and then, if I stick with it, I can take over the business," Todd said.

"College is expensive, and when you get done, you have a lot of debt, like my brother, and you can't get a job anyway," Jason said.

"I wanna go to college to be a doctor. Doctors make good money and they help people, too. My dad wants me to be a doctor," Lisa said.

They all have a point, Mr. Lawson thought. Many people in this town are self-employed and that gives them freedom. Still, owning a business is hard work and one never gets a rest from it. And college is expensive. I went because I thought I was meant for greatness, and when I came out, there was no work. Then they told me to get a Master's, but I wasn't buying it. Now I have a teaching credential and I'm right back where I started: in high school. Still, I'm here because I think I can make a difference. I wonder if Lisa really wants to be a doctor? It sure sounds nice to be a doctor but getting there is hard work and you have to have a passion for it. So what do I tell them about the real world and what do I omit? I don't want the students swallowing any of my cynicism. I had too many cynics for teachers.

I want to be popular and friends with everyone, Damian thought. And there is only one way to do that: by telling people what they want to hear. I'll invite everyone to the party and make friends with them so they'll like me. If a man is liked then he'll be successful.

"I want you guys to write down your primary goal on a piece of paper and explain what it means to you and how you'll go about attaining it," Mr. Lawson said. "Also, I want you to set a deadline for when you will reach your goal and then sign and date it. I'm going to look at them and then I'll give them back for you to keep."

Damian stared at the blank page and thought: what kind of work could I do that would make me famous? I would like to be an artist but I'm not. I would like to be an actor and have everyone know my face. If not an actor, then maybe I could make movies? It'd be cool to film the party with dad's handycam. The question is how do I get mom and dad out of the house? Maybe if I ask, they'll leave. Dad's a cool guy. He was probably a lot like you when he was your age. He let you have the car without any questions, right? Why not a party? He's worried that you aren't meeting any girls. You don't have much time so you better talk to him today.

"All right, let's hand them in. Just because you picked a certain goal today doesn't mean that you can't change it tomorrow. The point is to dream and to dream big," Mr. Lawson said. "Now that you have a dream, it's time to start planning how to reach it because time passes faster than you think."

When the students left, Mr. Lawson sat wondering what had happened to his dream of becoming a rock star. He had spent many years struggling in Los Angeles playing his music in bars and clubs. He had a box full of CDs in his closet that no one had bought. The truth is you weren't cut out to be a rock star, he told himself. A man has to follow his own nature, and you're a much better teacher than a musician. Sure you can play, but there was never anything special about *The Marsupials*. You never struck the universal cord that is necessary with all art for it to be successful. No, music was just a hobby for you. You are not a showman no matter how much you wanted to be one. The problem is you don't have anything to prove and you never did. You weren't made like that.

Mr. Lawson let the thoughts run in his mind. In spite of his lost dream, he was content. Many years had passed and he lived a settled life. He no longer worried about the future or panicked at the passage of time, like he once had. You did play those bars and you knew many women and no one can take that away from you. You are content because you pursued your dream. At least you had the courage for that. And when the dream collapsed, you did what you were good at, which is teaching. Who would have ever thought that you would get paid for hanging out with high school kids? If only they knew how cool you really are.

12

Damian and his father became co-conspirators against Mrs. Hutton. To free up the house, Peter planned a romantic getaway with his wife. He rented a room on the beach in San Diego for the weekend and ordered the keg himself. On Friday morning they picked it up and surreptitiously moved it into the garage. They put it on ice in a garbage can and hid it under a tarp.

"All right. Just a couple of ground rules," Peter told him. "I don't want anyone sleeping in our bed. The door to our bedroom stays closed. The same for my office. No one, I repeat, no one is to go in my office. I want you to lock it before the party. Also, if you're going to turn up the music, close the windows so the neighbors don't complain. If anyone is too drunk to drive, they sleep here; otherwise they get a cab. I have no problem with you drinking and having fun. But be responsible. Don't invite any jerks over. Also, you owe me eighty-five dollars for the keg. You can work it off at the lot."

"Sure thing, dad. Don't worry, I'll keep everything under control."

"And the girl you like, is she coming?"

"You bet. I gave her a lift the other day," Damian said.

"Good man. Here, one last thing. These might come in handy. It's better to be safe." Mr. Hutton pushed a strip of condoms into his son's hand. "Honey, you all packed," he called upstairs.

"Just a minute." Momentarily, Patty Hutton came down dragging a suitcase.

"Where are you going with all that? We're only gonna be gone for two nights."

"I'm not sure how the weather will be, and I brought a few nice outfits for when we go out to eat and also a few pairs of shoes and my make-up kit. You men sure appreciate when we look good but you don't want any of the inconveniences."

"I appreciate everything you do to look good," Peter said. "I was just teasing."

"Have you told Damian everything he needs to know?"

"Don't worry, mom. I'll see you Sunday. Have a good time. The house is safe with me."

"Well, I've made a little list so you don't forget," she said, handing it to him. It was two pages long, front and back.

"Don't forget to turn off the gas when you cook, and if a stranger comes to the door, don't open up, and don't forget to feed the cat and water the ferns, they need a lot of water. I wrote down the phone number of the hotel in case there's an emergency."

"Sounds good," Damian said.

"He's a mature young man, Patty. He can handle himself just fine."

"Yes, I know, but I worry since this is the first time you've been home alone, Damian. One last thing. No parties. I don't want any drinking or strange people in the house. Understand?"

"Anything you say, mom."

Damian and Peter gave each other a sidelong glance and tried not to smile. His dad's voice came back into his head, "*I think a party is a great idea! We just can't tell your mother. What she doesn't know won't hurt her.*"

When his parents left, Damian walked off to the garage, removed a red plastic cup from the hundred-count bag and drew himself a pint of foam. He poured it out into the ice and tapped until it was more beer than foam, drank and thought: this stuff tastes terrible but at least it's cold. Then he went late to school.

Most of the school came out for the party. Cars were parked up and down the street, and right on cue at ten o'clock, the cops came and said the neighbors had complained about the music. Damian locked the garage and told the drunks to shut up. He stood in the door seeing four policemen instead of two and said, "Yes sir," "No sir," "We'll keep the music down, don't worry, sir," and "Thank you for letting us know, sir."

The policeman shined his light into the side yard and tried to look inside the house and said, "I don't want to have to come back. If I come back, you'll be cited for disturbing the peace."

The music was turned down and everyone was crowded in the garage like a rabbit hutch nibbling at their cups. When the police left, the music was turned up again.

Shortly thereafter, two guys from the skater crowd found Mr. Hutton's handgun in the study and emptied out the bullets but forgot the one in the chamber. Then the one called Kenny held it to the one called Ryan's head, laughed and said, "Bang, you're dead," and pulled the trigger.

It was a hell of a party. The music was so loud that no one heard the gun go off in the closed upstairs office. Damian hed managed to get away with Stacey Wilson to his parents' bedroom, but he was so drunk that he couldn't get a hard-on and Stacey vomited in the bed. Oops.

Meanwhile, Kenny slipped out the front door white as sheet and ran down the dark and empty suburban streets knowing he couldn't run away from himself and what he had done. He thought of going back so he could stick the gun barrel in his mouth and have all his problems disappear. Only later did he come back for his car, remembering that he had driven and that it was too far to walk, not home but to Arizona. So he got in his car and drove six hours to Phoenix where he put up in a hotel and was not heard from until he called his mother three days later and, sobbing for a stranger on the street, confessed to having "blown Ryan's brains out."

Well, the party was a big success, especially since Kenny had had the foresight to drag Ryan's body into the closet and shut the door, and also to make the appropriate selection of a maroon towel from the bathroom linen to wipe up the brains and blood from the hardwood floor. Still, he had left the gun with his fingerprints in the closet, along with the towel, when he had fled and nearly bowled over Jessica, the "cool girl" he had a crush on, coming down the stairs. It was not like him to be rude or to ignore a girl with tits like hers, but he was living in fear then and not lust, and she was an obstacle to freedom.

The body wasn't discovered until Sunday evening when Mr. Hutton went to put some papers in the closet safe. He opened the door and clicked on the light and there was the body of a young man unfamiliar to him with his pale, blood-crusted face, shattered skull, gaping mouth and staring eyes. Then he was hit by the smell. He shut the door and opened it again and the young man was still there, unfamiliar and dead. Peter was overwhelmed by a fear so powerful that nothing he felt from then on would compare because the stiff dead boy was in his closet. Then it occurred to him: Damian knows nothing about this. There is no fucking way anyone can keep a straight face about something like this. What the fuck, does he think I'm not going to notice? Did he plan on getting rid of the body later?

There is a fucking dead teenager in your closet, Peter. Yes, it was getting serious now. He was addressing himself in the second person in that formal calm and rational voice he used only when things went really wrong.

After a brief search Peter found the gun. Take it slow now. Don't put your fingers on it, Peter. You can get out of this yet. So what exactly happened here? You're the detective; now tell me what happened. Jesus, you're talking to yourself, Peter. You're losing your mind. Take a deep breath. Go on, get a drink from the liquor cabinet, lock the door and think this through.

Mr. Hutton got himself a drink, sat down and put his feet on the desk. From the corner of his eye he could see the young man with the scream trapped in his throat and was forced to get up and shut the door.

The boy committed suicide. You know how it is with kids these days: they're full of existential problems; they have no direction, and this one, well, he couldn't take it anymore. When he found the gun, he pulled the trigger. God, how could he do it? This is the only time you can have those young girls, fairly anyway. He should have waited until he was my age: now that's a good time to pull the trigger. Christ, Peter, you are really in the shit. The shit is above your head and that whole bottle isn't going to help. Still, you deserve another drink. The condemned man must have all his wishes fulfilled. So here's to the dead boy in the closet. Here's to you, yes, here's to you, little man.

Peter lifted his glass and poured the vodka down his throat where it burned right. What if the boy was murdered? If Damian doesn't know and the police haven't been here since the party, then no one knows and it's probably a suicide. Maybe I can stuff the body in the car and get rid of it? Perhaps I could burn it or put it in a bag in manageable pieces and sink it in the ocean? Or maybe I should tell the police and leave things as they are. Yes, that is what you should do. It's my gun, but it was under lock and key in this drawer. Yes, except you left the key in the lock. That was your mistake. But then it was also Damian's mistake to overlook point number three in bold print on mom's checklist: *Stay out of dad's office!* The reason being that Peter kept alcohol in the cabinet there.

Unfortunately, the gun had been overlooked to cause disaster, like an iron left on during a vacation to the Caribbean. Mr. Hutton liked to keep it handy so he could point it at the wall and pretend to blow people away that he didn't like, such as customers who had gotten the better of him, this or that politician, faceless enemies, or the neighbor next door with his fucking dogs barking all day because no one was ever home to care for them.

Peter thought long and hard about what to do with the body, but before he could make a decision, the police were at his door. They had a warrant and he showed them the body. They said a boy had confessed to the killing. They did not elaborate. They questioned Mr. Hutton and took photographs of the victim. Peter imagined them picking up the body and doing a few turns with it on the parquet floor to Argentine tango with a rose in their teeth, cutting in on each other for the next dance. The police were very serious, though they probably felt like he did that it was a ridiculous situation, and that the boy might as well have been a civilian corpse in a foreign war. It made Peter think, like he had thought before, that life was pointless and futile, and that one day death would take them all. Death was a silly thing when it happened to strangers.

Later, Mr. Hutton was called in for questioning, as the firearm was registered in his name and the body found in his house. After a protracted court case he was acquitted of any criminal wrongdoing. Kenny Moore for lack of witnesses, good lawyer, and perhaps because of his disreputable skater appearance, was found guilty of murder, punished as an adult under a new California sentencing law, and condemned to live and die in a maximum security prison.

Damian never told his mother about his father's involvement in the party. Nevertheless, the father and son trust they had established evaporated along with their friendship. They no longer spoke about girls or parties or sports or any of the things that fathers and sons talked about. They did their best to avoid each other's presence and eyes, and when this wasn't possible, they greeted each other with reluctance and thinly-veiled hostility. Meanwhile his mother's usual good nature withered and she became a recluse, locking herself in the bedroom to watch dramas about cancer, car crashes, AIDS, natural disasters, overdoses, and many other painful and tragic subjects that permitted her to mourn like the mother of the dead boy and atone for her guilt.

Between his father's resentment and his mother's depression, Damian no longer felt welcome at home. To add to his difficulties, when he returned to school he was ostracized. It wasn't long before he grew angry with the injustice of his situation. He thought: I didn't even know Ryan Meyer. I had nothing to do with his death and now that's all people remember. Ryan Meyer dying ruined my life. All those people came to my house and drank and had fun. Then, when the trouble started, they all abandoned me.

Damian felt bitter towards his peers, especially Stacey, who wouldn't talk to him anymore because he was connected to the tragedy. Anything to do with the event was to be ignored in silence or covered up with a plastic smile as if it never happened. He found that people couldn't look him in the eye any longer, and this included his parents. When his peers abandoned him, he learned a valuable lesson about the false and opportunistic nature of people in general. He decided that when he graduated he would move away to prove himself and his worth. You are alone in this life, he told himself; everything you do, you must do for yourself and not other people. Your mistake was wanting to impress others. But this was a mistake Damian would continue to make.

Damian was alone and confused when he set out for Los Angeles. He rented an apartment and cut all ties with his family and the past. He started to work in movies as a PA, getting coffee and driving around town for random props and supplies. He worked as a grip and then learned sound because the pay was better. Eventually, he found himself standing off-camera in warehouses in the valley holding the boom mike over naked women sucking dick and getting fucked in every hole on cheap sets made to appear like suburban tract homes or corporate offices. Many of the women were foreign and didn't speak English. It was there that he learned another of life's lessons: that people lived off each other like parasites. His initial hard-on went limp, first with boredom, then disgust at seeing so many naked women who were also bored and disgusted with the repetition of commercial sex. During this time he was lonely and in need. Still, he did not feel right about trying for the porn girls, seduced as they were into spreading their legs off-camera for the producer's empty promises about their future careers: how, soon, they'd be starring with Dirk Larkin, the famous Hollywood actor, and at most have to show their breasts or appear in lingerie or a bathing suit, thanks to the hypocrisy of American morality, where censorship of popular culture depended on the reality of a thriving porn industry.

Damian made a decent living in sound, enough to embark on a career in alcoholism, but he knew there was no future there. In his spare time he wandered around the various neighborhoods and bars of Los Angeles documenting, with his digital camera, the odd confession of a barfly about the glorious or unfortunate life that had since slid into the gutter. He filmed the LAPD performing field sobriety tests with nightsticks and verbally abusing drunks trying to get a little shut-eye on the luxurious pavement. In his late night wanderings Damian came across all manner of social oddity. Injustice would present itself in a group of gangbangers kicking and beating a lone and unfortunate rival in an alley outside a club, a deranged homeless man smashing up a luxury sedan with a crowbar, the occasional twisted car wreck off Highway 101 with CHP lights flashing and the jaws of death grasping, and the jewel-bedecked head-dressed transvestites servicing their customers at the fast food drive-thru. As a whole, these scenes presented a reality without plot or purpose. That is the mark of an honest film about LA, Damian thought: that it is completely nonlinear and unintelligible.

Soon he had a documentary archive of urban events that he would play at all hours with the sound off and the stereo blasting, while drinking whiskey on the couch or watching the traffic stream up and down Hollywood Boulevard from his balcony. At such moments he told himself: you gotta get the hell outta here. You live like a fucking dog, everyone here does, clinging tight to a piece of tinsel hoping one day it will turn to silver. If he had had too much to drink by then, Damian would think about suicide like some people thought of chocolate, a favorite flavor of ice cream, Hawaii, or a certain make and model sports car. Certainly, some people dreamed bigger than others. If he hadn't yet had enough to drink, he would tell himself: you just need to get laid. You spend too much time watching this shit and it's making you crazy. No matter how much you wallow in this chaos, it doesn't mean you know how to make use of it to create a future for yourself. Let's face it, you may have to wait a long time before you get there, wherever "there" is because you don't even know, maybe all your life, and then you'll be there, right where you wanted, because you'll be dead.

His dissatisfaction with work and leisure grew intolerable, so he signed up with a small production company that specialized in corporate video. He made a fake resume claiming he was familiar with the Avid editing system, which he had seen but not used, and when they hired him he studied night and day to learn it through the internet. He was glad they had given him his own key so he could sleep in the office and finish the work he was too slow to do during his shift.

His experience in Los Angeles taught him many skills. He had also been able to save a great deal of money because he didn't go out and had no girlfriend to maintain. He never took any trips, not even to the beach, in spite of its proximity. He found corporate video mind-numbing and had made no friends in his new work.

Damian thought of the veteran editors that were his colleagues with pity and disgust. The work had mutated them. Have you seen how their eyes bug out of their heads from staring at the screen? They are emaciated machines with sunken cheeks that have forgotten their own physical needs. They work at night and sleep by day like the undead.

No, his dream was to make movies. Not those Hollywood trash movies but something based on experience: something real that people remembered and made them think about themselves, the meaning of their lives and the reality of their deaths.

During his stay in the urban desert of Los Angeles, Damian lived, ate, and slept film and video. He spent eighteen hours a day editing, watching movies and filming, and all the while the idea of his own film eluded him. All I need is one good idea, he thought. That idea can come from anywhere; I just have to keep my eyes and ears open. I have to get out of this town and meet new people. The industry here is closed and limited. Maybe you should get in with a big production company? But then you'll have to work on movies you don't like. If you really want to make money and a name for yourself, you have to do it on your own, like dad and his car lot because *nobody makes any money working for someone else, Damian.*"

You need to surround yourself with creative people. To be successful you have to surround yourself with successful people. But then you know the dilemma because the "real" comes from misery and pain, like how that guy looked after those thugs jumped him in the alley and you found him there. Remember how you lay down on the ground next to him and filmed him in a puddle of his own blood, urine and puke before calling the police? Now you replay that footage again and again in your living room because, like everyone, pain and misery fascinate you. Just think: you're life only became real when that dumb-ass Kenny Moore blew Ryan Meyer away. That was probably the best thing that ever happened to you because now you have a will of your own and are no longer content with mere comfort. In your familiarity with and study of discomfort, comfort has become an alien concept.

It's fine that you have the experience now to tell a real story, but you still need to learn how to direct and you need actors and a good script. Maybe with the money you saved you can buy your own prosumer camera and ditch dad's camcorder? You can do the editing and post it on the net. Where's the best place to go for start-up capital for a tech business? That's right: San Francisco.

13

One thing Jack knew about Damian: he was a busy guy. When Damian did come home, it was only to shower and get ready to go out. He did not eat at home or hang out there. Invariably, he would come through the door with his cell phone stuck to his ear making plans to meet friends, colleagues and acquaintances in various cafes, bars, clubs and parties around town. He organized it in such a way that he would spend a little time in each place, so that he could make as many connections as possible. He lived thin, and in that way he and Jack were different. Jack couldn't understand how someone could lead such a frenetic life. Damian pulled it off by locking his bedroom door every Sunday, turning off his phone and spending the day drifting in and out of sleep in the nest of his pricey down comforter. Sunday was always sacred to Damian as a day of rest.

Whenever they went out, Jack was scarcely able to enjoy his drink before they were set to move on to another venue to meet other people. Often, just after Jack was settled into his new surroundings and enjoying himself, Damian would let him know that it was time to finish up because they had to be in such and such a place at such and such a time. And so they jumped around the city all night in search of novelty.

"Damian, I don't understand why we have to rush around all the time to meet up with all these people," Jack said. "We never get to relax and enjoy ourselves. This bar is full of good-looking women and I don't want to go anywhere else. Don't you ever feel like you're in the right spot and that you don't want to be anywhere else?"

Damian looked at him.

"Sure, it's good here. Yeah, the girls are pretty. But I heard from Mark, our cameraman, that Blitz is really going off. If this is good, it can only get better; now that we got a stamp, we can always come back. So come on and knock it back already. I've never seen anyone drink as slow as you, Jack. And to answer your question: no, I'm not satisfied. The day I'm satisfied is the day I roll into the grave, and the day I do that, I want to know I've lived and seen things. Life can always get better and with that attitude you can't go wrong."

Then Jack would doubt himself. He would wonder about Blitz, and the wondering and not knowing was exciting. Perhaps that's what Damian liked about it, too. Every night in the city was different. If there was a good party going on they were sure as hell gonna be there.

Though Jack was unemployed, he continued to live the lifestyle with the money he had saved, but it was not the same as meeting up after work with a wad of twenties. After two weekends he realized he wouldn't make rent if he kept it up and was obliged to stay home.

Though it was not skilled work, he would have liked to have kept his job. Now he had nothing to structure his day. He could just as soon go to sleep at four in the morning and get up at noon, which was nothing new, only that now during the evenings he had no obligations. It was during this lonely time that he thought more and more of Elizabeth. So far she hadn't sent him so much as a postcard. She must be really busy teaching and organizing her new life, he thought.

One evening Jack's mother called and he lied to her and said that life was good and that he had found a nice place to live and was probably changing jobs because the one he had didn't challenge him. When she asked him what he did, Jack told her he worked in "public relations."

"There are a lot of opportunities here and I want to get into a better field," he said.

"Well, don't quit your job until you have something already lined up. People can change their minds and it's nice to have security. You can't take anyone on their word."

Jack told her that she was right and that he never made a move until he had a guarantee. She asked if he was eating well and he told her he was. She didn't ask what his concept of eating well was, and he didn't mention his diet of spaghetti and tomato sauce, two or three nights a week; eggs everyday, sometimes twice a day; and plenty of bagels and cream cheese, baloney and grilled cheese sandwiches.

Mrs. Wild told her son that his sister, Carol, had her first steady boyfriend. Jack had always been protective of his sister and he fought to ignore the disturbing image of a young man in bed with her. He wished he could have been home to meet the guy and judge his character.

"What kind of guy is he? I hope he's not an asshole."

"Jack, watch your mouth."

"Well, I'm just telling you there are a lot of guys like that out there. Believe me I know, mom. You just tell him that if he does anything to hurt Carol, I'll be there to break his legs."

"He's a nice boy, Jack. I don't see why you're so worked up over it."

Because it's the only thing of any interest that has happened to me all week, he thought. Because I miss you guys like hell and especially Carol. Who is this guy anyway? He's a faceless son-of-a-bitch and you might even like him if you got the chance to go out and drink a few beers together.

"So what's his name?"

"Bud."

"You can't be serious. What the hell kind of name is that?"

"So maybe it isn't the nicest name. I don't believe names have anything to say about someone's character," Mrs. Wild said.

So Bud gets to spend time with Carol when I haven't seen her for months, Jack thought. I wish I was his age going steady with some girl and all I had to do was go to school and put in a few hours at the store.

That was the life. Damian and the others don't have a clue about that kind of life. They don't even have time to live.

"So what does Bud do?"

"He plays baseball, Jack. He's a pitcher just like you."

"Yeah?"

"That's right. He's a good boy, though not very talkative. I can tell he likes our Carol a lot because whenever he comes over to the house his face gets all red. Once when he came over for dinner he was so nervous he spilled the gravy all over dad's lap. It was okay, we laughed about it."

I remember when girls made me like that, Jack thought. That's something you can never go back to. There comes a time in a man's life when he can no longer afford to show that he's not in complete control, even though he knows he's not, and that means controlling women and trying to not look stupid in front of them. Unfortunately, it's always been about thinking in results, and not about loving them and paying attention and listening to them. That's why you never cared about any of those girls that came to the frat house. Because you didn't treat them like women.

His mother was still talking when he came out of his thoughts.

"He invited us to his games, and it reminded me of when you were here with us."

Jack did not know what to say to that. He wanted to say: it made me so damned proud when you came to my games; it made me want to play as hard as I could so you'd be proud of me. There was nothing I loved more than hearing the ball pop in the catcher's mitt to strike the batter out and watching you stand up, mom, and clap your hands and cheer, and the way you smiled at me like there was something only we understood.

"Yeah, that was a long time ago," Jack said, though it had only been a year since graduation. "Before I hung up my mitt. I guess I never made it to the big leagues, huh, mom?"

"Baseball wasn't enough for you, Jack. You're an ambitious boy and I know you wouldn't have been happy with a life like that. You're a smart boy, Jack."

When they were done talking, Jack lay on the bed in the cold empty house listening to the traffic in the street. He thought: there are things I miss about growing up, but I remember it was hard, too. I miss it, but I'm glad I'm not near mom because she loves me too much, and when mothers do that they suffocate and ruin their children. I understand her wanting to protect me from this shit but that only makes it harder. I have to take risks, even if it scares the hell out of me and I fail, otherwise I'll only live with resentment.

Jack thought of the people he had met in the city and how he didn't measure up to them: not to Alex and his discipline; or Damian and his charm and ease with people; or Henrik with his hip life, who lived for his music and was a hell of a long way from home, much farther than Arizona.

14

Depression was becoming his housemate. Before Jack was oppressed by doing work he hated. But that oppression at least had its honor, while there was no honor in the depression of unemployment.

Jack found that he would wait all day for someone to come home, except Julie who was a superficial airhead who ran the heater and forgot to turn it off until the house was like a sauna. Each time that heater came on Jack thought of money leaving his pocket. He didn't respect Julie because she didn't work; then he considered his own situation and wondered how long it would be before the others thought of him in the same way: as a burden and one of the weak to be pitied.

So Jack waited for Damian, Alex or Henrik to come home from work. He missed talking to people, since he couldn't afford to go out anymore, except to walk for an hour in the park, where he didn't speak to anyone but just watched people together while he was alone.

When Henrik came home from a day of leisure, he would often fire up his turntables and spin some music to prepare for his gig. On Fridays he would turn it up extra loud and bring a bottle of gin from the corner store.

"Jack, listen to this jam. God, you're lucky to hear this stuff, man. This is the latest and greatest. Normally, you'd have to pay twenty bucks at the club to hear these beats. This is the hottest groove in the city and I'm gonna spin it at Chameleon tonight. Have you ever heard anything like it?"

After months of clubbing and living with Henrik, Jack was beginning to like electronica. Before, he never imagined music could be bent and twisted in such a way; the new and strange rhythms and melodies produced by endless sampling, fascinated him. Aside from the music, Jack was there to soak up some of Henrik's enthusiasm and have a few drinks free of charge. Henrik may have had his faults but he did not lack generosity. He would mix glass after glass of gin and tonic for both of them until the bottle was empty. With the liquor, Jack found his lonely and hopeless thoughts replaced by the thrill of the night. The beats made him think of sex, beauty and success. He thought vaguely how a certain combination of music, drugs and hedonism could bring someone to the same place that hard work, honesty and love could, only faster.

Damian came home after eight. He had been gone since six in the morning filming on location in Marin with a man who was an expert in dog psychology and used his abilities to train and control difficult and aggressive breeds. The man's philosophy that a dog needed to be disciplined firmly and rewarded sparingly with extra food or affection, stuck in Damian's head. Damian thought that people were like dogs and responded better to punishment than kindness. Dogs were loyal and dependable animals that organized themselves in packs with one leader, the alpha male, whose job it was to maintain order in the group. As with all philosophy, information or advice he had heard from other people, Damian wondered how he could use the knowledge to his own advantage. Was he an alpha male, dominating others and bending them to his will? Could he handle the responsibility and danger of such a role? Somehow he found himself admiring the dog handler, while ignoring the fact that the man lived alone in the hills and was divorced from his wife, who he didn't understand like dogs and who had stripped him of his children.

The guy's got several important clients including basketball star Michael Howard's Rottweiler; pop singer Lisa Dawn's Great Dane; and those two Dobermans that belong to Karl Wilkes, CEO of Logo software. Maybe he could get you connected with them, Damian thought. It couldn't hurt to know people like that. The successful all hang out with each other. Once you have friends like that you've got it made.

Damian was glad to be done with work. He walked in the door with his cell phone glued to his ear and waved a greeting to Jack and Henrik. He paused from his conversation and took a sip of Jack's drink. He pointed to indicate that he was going to his room and continued talking.

"Party at your house then, huh? Sounds cool. Where do you live, anyway? Up in Twin Peaks? It's nice up there. You got an apartment or what? A house? Cool. What? Really? That's the set up, living with a lonely professional who's loaded. What's rent like? Not bad, seven hundred for a whole house practically to yourself. Who's gonna be there? Tech, artsy crowd? Sweet. I've got some friends who wanna come. Great. What time you getting started? Around ten? Cool. We'll see you then. Cheers."

Damian liked his housemates but ultimately had plans to move into his own place. Though he envied Henrik's ability to live in the moment and enjoyed partying with him, Damian had the vague impression that

Henrik was going to destroy himself and others with him. Damian liked to be close to such characters but not so close that he would be consumed by their decadence. Henrik's straight out of a music video, he thought. He's great to hang out with because he's super hip and likes to get into trouble. If you can't get into trouble a few nights a week, what's the point?

Jack he liked for the sake of his good looks. So far he had proven himself to be a dependable, honest and clean-living guy. His only fault seemed to be his lack of ambition; his only vice, drinking, but that was not a personal vice, it was the environment. Personally, Damian drank six nights a week, two or three pints on weekdays then the weekend binge with any and all liquor he could get his hands on. Damian liked to party but he didn't like to waste time. He justified the party by mixing it with business. Parties were the best places to network and mine new information because people had their guard down.

Jack seems innocent and kind, but behind that blank face of his he must have some hidden motives all his own. I wonder what he thinks? Damn, he's a good-looking guy. If I had a face like that I'd get into acting. Maybe I'll use him in one of my films?

Damian got in the shower. He looked at his naked body and thought again of Jack, not with reason but something deeper that he couldn't address. I wish my nose wasn't so big, he thought. You mother said it gives you character and that men who are too beautiful are vain and sometimes not men at all. Maybe that's true, but if you were better looking you'd be less insecure. It's important to surround yourself with beautiful people; that's why you invited Jack to live here. The only person you don't care to have living here is Julie because she's young and immature and it turns out she doesn't have any hot friends. The fact of the matter is that there weren't any better candidates at the time.

15

Alex came home with the usual glow about him, content with having filled young minds with his vision of the world. That day had gone particularly well because it was the first time he had read to his students from his book *Pax Americana*, and they had listened in silence and what Alex interpreted as respect. He knew that none of them had ever thought of their country in that way. He thought they needed to know the truth. Some people would call it depressing, but Alex believed that knowledge of injustice and the unpacking of lies made people stronger. I am not interested in painting a pretty picture, he thought. When you taught elementary kids, it was necessary to guard your words and not ruin that moment in their lives. But in high school there must be an open dialogue. You're trying to get them to communicate and voice an opinion. Who would have thought you could get paid for talking ideas and reading from your books?

It was only when Alex had done something useful that he felt free to party. Unlike Damian, Henrik, or even Jack, alcohol didn't make him loose and easy; on the contrary, drinking made him more blunt and incisive in communication. Alex's problem with drinking was not that it made him sentimental like most, but that it opened the doors to his abundant cynicism. Alcohol did not evoke in him feelings of solidarity, but instead made him more arrogant, confrontational and stubborn. He believed that he was better than other people and that his occupation was superior to theirs, regardless of what they did.

Still, like anyone, Alex was searching for approval. He spent many hours a day in total isolation trying to justify himself to strangers. Alex didn't produce music like Henrik, to make women shake their asses; he had given up women because they distracted him from the documentation of his own mind. Aside from his students, he didn't get on well with people and wasn't popular. Except for Damian, Henrik and Arnold, he had no friends. He did not, as yet, consider Jack a friend. Jack was a nice guy, but to Alex "nice" had never been a compliment or a reason for friendship. Alex wanted to elimate from his life all relationships that caused him discomfort or were a distraction. He was a man with an obsession, and obsession was a personal concern. He knew well the consequences of his path. Sometimes a voice spoke in his head and said: Alex, just think how you could have lived. You could have been with many girls and partied and made many friends instead of putting your nose in a book. In college you were a failure socially; you only slept with one girl and the sex was terrible because you were inexperienced.

But now, with the megaphone of reason, Alex challenged that voice that had mocked him and made him doubt himself in the past. Instinctively, he had always understood that what the voice was promising was a transitory illusion and a distraction from the greater purpose of his life.

You started to write because you couldn't relate to people. Your parents always taught you to be above the game; you felt it was beneath you to compete for popularity or girls, or to attend the cool parties to manage your public image. You were made to be sincere to yourself, and that was something you understood early. In college you earned respect in your own way and built your circle of friends based on your character, leaving the provincial popularity contest of high school behind. What you liked about college was that everyone got a chance to start over and amend their past mistakes and prejudices. People go to college to think and question their world and discover their purpose in life, Alex thought. It's a place where diversity and individuality are assets and not barriers.

You had your fun in college; even though you only boned one girl, you kissed many more and had many girlfriends. You weren't a failure because you didn't find love. In that respect you were average. It was too early and you weren't ready for it and you still aren't; it's best to be ready and not lie to yourself so you regret your decisions. Not lying means playing it cool. You were cool in college and you're cool now, perhaps too cool. Sure, it's a defense, but it works for you and allows you to live the way you want. You've never liked people to be too much in your business.

Alex had an overpriced six-pack from the corner store under his arm and offered them a beer. Jack accepted and Alex thought: Jack never contributes anything of his own. He's such a sponge. I'll bet he was the one who ate my leftovers.

Jack felt guilty for drinking Alex's beer. He knew Alex didn't like to share, but did so to be polite; he was always polite. Jack had never seen him lose his cool, ever. Alex had a way of communicating intensely without saying a word. When I have work again I'll make it up to him, Jack thought. We're all on our own here and it isn't right that I can't pay my own way. I should just go and be alone in my room.

Henrik was lying on his bed. He had retired from the turntables and now they were listening to a mix he had made. He had his own website to sell his discs. He called himself DJ Absolut. He had a display of all the flavors of his country's vodka on the shelf above the fireplace, and also a Swedish flag on the wall; if he were German perhaps such nationalism would have been in poor taste. His furniture all came from Ikea. He went once a week to a Scandinavian store in Oakland for pickled herring, caviar in a tube, Swedish flatbread and goat cheese. Every few months his parents sent him three ten packs of Swedish dip, *snus*, the kind with the fiberglass that cut into the flesh on the inside of one's mouth so that the nicotine went right into the bloodstream. The dip was so strong that Jack, drunk as he was, vomited the first time he tried it. Like anything it was an acquired taste. Henrik used two of the little prepackaged pillows at a time; he slept with them in his mouth and they had worn a neat depression on the inside of his jawbone much like a limpet on a rock. It was impossible to tell when he was dipping or not. He used two tins a week.

Henrik couldn't think of anything better than being a Swede in San Francisco. He was proud of his own country and thought that Swedish women were the best-looking in the world. If things didn't work out in the city, then he could return to Sweden where it was clean and there were no beggars in the streets, and where, if he got sick, he would be taken care of free of charge in a public hospital. Still, Henrik knew that if he went home the provinciality of his country would strangle him in a slow and deliberate way.

In the United States, Henrik thought constantly of race and the Swedish ideal he didn't completely measure up to because his hair was brown, not blond, and which he had bleached to look more the part. He was constantly aware of his light eyes and he often compared them to those of Americans. He always wondered about people's origins, especially blonde American girls. He thought proudly of his characteristic Swedish features: the pronounced cheekbones, the small ski slope nose, the high forehead, and his tall and lanky frame. He was hopelessly vain and very average in appearance, objectively speaking.

Sitting on the bed, Henrik stared at himself in the mirror: at his perfectly sculpted hair, tight ribbed t-shirt with the zipper at the chest, slick metallic cargo pants and baby blue plastic sneakers. Julie got them after I did, that bitch. She's always copying me. Henrik liked to be at the cutting edge of style; it was only natural that Damian and Julie had started to dress like him. He should have considered it a compliment.

In that respect, Alex was in another world. Henrik had no objection to his Fifties rebel threads with his jeans rolled up four fingers' width and resting on his black leather boots; the jean jacket and tight, tucked-in, white t-shirts; the wife beaters, sideburns and black hair cut short on the sides and gelled back from his forehead. That's rockabilly style, Henrik thought. Fifties heartthrob. I've seen faded pictures of dad dressed like that in the Swedish woods with his greaser hair and that beat-up motorcycle he used to ride.

Next, Julie arrived and walked quickly past Henrik's room without greeting them. When they were all together, she felt nervous and insecure. Julie was paranoid and always thought people were talking bad about her behind her back. Also, she couldn't look Henrik in the eye any longer since he had infected her with some unknown venereal disease. She walked past them with her head down concentrating on her shopping bags, pretending they were a big burden. Amazing, though she neither worked nor studied, Julie acted as if life was a big burden. She could often be heard sighing, or she would look like she was on the verge of tears. There were always black circles under her eyes and often an angry pimple marred her child-of-poverty face.

"Hey Julie, come have a drink," Henrik shouted down the hallway. "Aren't you coming out with us tonight? I've got a treat for you. Come on in here. Jesus, you look like somebody just died."

"I'm not feeling well," she told them, putting on her helpless face. It was a face she had first used with her father to get her way or to avoid punishment for something she had done. Pity was her tactic for survival.

Julie stood in the doorway, all ninety-five pounds of her, with her face pale like the moon, so that if you shined the light behind her, you'd be able to see the veins through her skin. The guys looked at her and Henrik thought: if I can't get anything else tonight, I'll bone her. What he liked about Julie was that she was shy and he could tell her what to do. Henrik was a pragmatic young man. He had to accept the fact that he was no longer young and that meant taking what he could get.

Alex thought: the girl is stupid. God I resent stupid girls. I wish I didn't have to share my air with her.

Jack thought: she's suffering like crazy. She's unstable and she hasn't developed her own identity and she's easily fooled. Maybe she thinks I told them about her problem? See the way she keeps glancing at you? I hate having to keep this straight face; it's fake and dishonest because there's no communication between us. She's like a stranger. Sure, we didn't choose to live together, but that's the way it is, and there's much to be said for manners and social etiquette. What gets me most is that she's never asked me anything about my life. She'd rather lock herself in her room than see any of us. Perhaps that's why I resent her. Or maybe it's the fact that I'm not fucking her and don't like to put up with a woman's nonsense without a reward. The truth is that she causes a great number of inconveniences for everyone. She is moody and keeps her emotions inside so you never know what she's thinking. Not even Damian, who is blunt, has the courage to tell her that she's in with the wrong crowd. When you don't fit in, it's better to go someplace else and find people that you get along with and that understand you, right? Instead, she just stays here and makes everyone uncomfortable. I wouldn't have this problem if I had money, Jack thought. Then I could live on my own and do as I please.

What a lie it is about young girls, Alex thought. The young girls play games because they are insecure. In life you have to put up with some bullshit and that bullshit is living with Julie. What I wouldn't give to trade her for a responsible and stable housemate. Sometimes everything she does bothers me.

16

Did Jack tell them? No, Julie didn't feel that she was being treated any differently than before, which was as an outsider and second-class citizen in her own house. She knew they disliked her but she liked the house and the location enough so that it was worth tolerating. Also, in the back of her mind, she hoped that one of them would move out and maybe that a woman would move in and even the odds. It was rare to see a woman in that house.

Alex, for example, was a misogynist, and Julie was scared of him. He had stopped talking to her a long time ago except when necessary in the kitchen, "Excuse me, can I get by please?" She much preferred Damian to tell her, "Jesus, Julie, get the hell out of the shower already!" Or, "You're such a pig, when are you gonna do your dishes?" That was something she could respect. Even if he meant it, he smiled at her when he said it, and she felt like she was a part of his life. She knew there were many things she did that bothered them, but could she help it if she was forgetful about the dishes or the bills? She was good for the bills, they knew that, so what did it matter if she paid a week late?

Jack was the strong, silent type and she even thought him a bit dumb, much like the boys she had grown up with in Missouri. He's just a dumb jock. Didn't I hear him telling Damian that he was in a fraternity? But the real problem is he just ignores me. I don't think he hates me, but if he does, Alex put him up to it, or maybe all of them because that's how guys are when they get together. And this is a strange group of guys. Sometimes I think they're all gay. They're suppressed men that have turned gay because they have no luck with women. And now their hatred for women is directed at me. Well, Henrik is normal enough and he wants only one thing, but he knows how to have a good time and also what I like. Henrik's the devil, but I've always preferred the devil to a bunch of monks. The only thing missing in this house are the robes. Speaking of monks, I bet Alex jerks off to porn on the internet. How couldn't he with all the time he spends in that room?

Anyway, Henrik can't keep his hands off you. Your breasts are too small, but you have a nice body, and once you even thought of modeling. Are you pretty enough to model? The problem is no one ever compliments you or flatters you when you change your hair or get a new outfit. It's like you don't even exist. Not even Henrik seems to notice. What is it about Henrik, and why are you attracted to him? It's the fact that he shows his emotion and has weaknesses, in particular a weakness for you that makes him more human. All the others are dead. They are cold, dead, boring men. Only Henrik is totally uninhibited: he is vulgar and rude; he speaks his mind, follows his passion and doesn't think about tomorrow. Most men think too much about tomorrow.

You should never have trusted Henrik in the first place. He has no self-control. It was stupid of you to listen to him about not "feeling you" with a condom and how it was "uncomfortable" and "ruined the moment," well after he got you worked up. You were drunk and the ecstasy made you feel electric then, so you said, "Forget the condom," because you were on the pill. That was stupid. Still, you don't hate him. It's just as much your fault as his, but you can't look him in the eye now because you know something he doesn't.

The city would be pretty dull without Henrik, since you haven't really made any friends. What you like about Henrik is that he makes you feel comfortable about your body and your sexuality. Sex is funny to him and that makes it okay. There have been times when it was nothing out of the ordinary to go with Henrik to such and such a party at someone's house and let strange men and women take your clothes off. You'd just lie there and let them do whatever they wanted while they whispered nice things in your ear about how beautiful you were and how you were kind and full of love like an angel. Julie had heard that flattery before from strangers and seen the lust in their eyes and their desire. From then on she had wanted to be considered primarily as an object of affection.

It was with Henrik that you started making love to women. What a pleasure to kiss and caress a woman that you admired from afar, and to find your desire reciprocated. How different to feel the softness of a woman's lips, the gentleness of her touch and her deep understanding of your femininity. You enjoy intimacy with women, though you still prefer men, because with a man you feel safe and protected: like you're not responsible for yourself. You don't want to be responsible for anything, and that's why you don't want children. At least not now. You want to be passive and let life carry you without effort. But life is hard and soon you'll be on your own. What would your father say about your grades and the drugs and the sex? You're a little slut; you've been with women and men, with and without protection, and you'd better hope dad doesn't find out. Who knows if it really was Henrik and not some stranger that gave you VD? The truth is you've been very careless; some nights you don't even remember because you were so drugged up.

Fundamentally, Julie felt she had disappointed her father and wished she could be his little girl again.

"Come here, Julie. Put those bags down and have one of these," Henrik said, opening a tin filled with yellow happy face pills. He gave her one, took one himself and washed it down with his gin and tonic. He gave the glass to her. As she drank, she felt their eyes on her and thought: soon I'll be happy again, and they won't bother me anymore.

"Where are you going now," Henrik asked, when she turned to leave.

"I'm going to put my things away and change."

"Then you'll come to Chameleon with me and be my groupie?"

"Sure," she said.

Julie liked to go with Henrik to Chameleon because she could drink for free and dance above the crowd in the DJ box with everyone watching. She liked it because that was not how she saw herself when she was alone or how her housemates knew her. She lived as two people: a naive country girl who was shy and lacked self-esteem, and the compulsive hedonist that wanted to destroy her.

17

Damian had more money than any of his housemates and didn't mind spending it. But money was not something he liked to talk about. If someone asked how much he made, or how much he had in the bank, he would lie and quote a modest sum, or parry the question by changing the subject. As the producer of short documentaries, Damian made a good living; what he didn't spend on ski trips and film equipment, he was saving for a personal project. He told himself: that forty grand you've saved doesn't exist. You can't spend that money. You have a monthly budget of roughly two thousand and that's for rent, food and entertainment. The rest goes to savings except for the two hundred dollars that go into your stock portfolio. Because in addition to his savings, Damian was planning for retirement. Indeed, his situation was unusual for a twenty-seven-year-old. In spite of the security and comfort that money afforded him, Damian wished to live more like his housemates, Alex and Henrik, both of whom he admired for different reasons. They were artists and security did not interest them in the least, or so it seemed.

Alex really doesn't give a damn about anything but his work. I mean sure he's a teacher, but that's because it gives him material and allows him to polish his ideas. His students serve as his critics; he can bounce ideas off them and see things through their eyes. That's why you like living with Alex: because he forces you to reevaluate your opinions and question your motivations.

What's startling are all those manuscripts he has lying around. And he hasn't let me read a single one. I wonder, is that because he's ashamed of them or because he doesn't trust me? Or is it just plain indifference? Doesn't he want to publish? He's already done the hard work: now he just needs to share it and get the recognition. He must be dying for it after all the effort he's put in. Well, you did get a chance to read something of his, the first ten or fifteen pages at least, and that while he was in the shower. He's a good writer, and you believe he'll be big some day. He must believe that, too, because he's extremely arrogant.

Damian still remembered the story he had read. The main character was a college history professor whose outlandish, vulgar and irreverent lectures made him a favorite of the students. In particular, the professor taught history like one gossiped, focusing on the moral shortcomings and quirks of character of historical figures, and the underbelly of scandal and insanity that shaped historical events. History, in the professor's opinion, was not about erecting statues in the town square to absolve individuals or nations of their sins; it was more like digging in a graveyard and staring in horror and fascination at the grotesque truths that came to light.

According to the professor, the great figures of history were not products of fate: rather, they were ordinary people who by small steps, faith in themselves, struggle, alliance, luck or deception were able to capitalize on a particular moment in time. And for every individual or event recognized, a hundred related individuals and events were forgotten. For the professor, it was the flow of history that was of interest, not the protagonists or dates of historical events. History was the product of the collective struggle of humanity: a reflection of its needs and desires at a given period in its evolution. That was the professor's message.

As it stood, the hypocrisy and true drama of the story centered on the fact that the professor had murdered a coed some years before and someone had been convicted of the crime in his place. It was this moral dilemma of the professor's own life history that was his burden to bear.

The story gave Damian cause for reflection. If you want to produce something of value, it needs to address and be relevant to a wider audience, he reasoned. History is too concerned with fact and not character. It does not properly describe relationships between individuals, the reasoning behind decisions made or the extent of one's control over such decisions. But then you always believed history to be an arbitrary invention. Is it possible to erase the past if it doesn't suit you? Can you falsify your own character and cleanse yourself of wrongdoing through lies?

Damian found himself wanting to read more. He wanted to know if Alex would search for the happy ending: in this case, the fair ending where the professor confessed his crime and was punished. Most likely it wouldn't end that way. Alex'll probably have him commit suicide.

Though he's an intense and, at times, disturbing character, Alex gives you the desire and inspiration to pursue your own creative projects. Without a doubt, he has had a defining impact on your life. Hopefully, you can do the same for him, because you both need each other if you're gonna make it. It almost breaks my heart to see his manuscripts piled up and forgotten in the closet. You need to help him get the message out.

Damian didn't mind sharing but he wasn't stupid enough to keep beer in the refrigerator overnight. He bought most of his food and drink in bulk at PriceCo and kept several cases of beer under the bed. He liked to drink, and beer was not something he wanted to run out of. He didn't have a sense of humor about it. So, before finishing his phone calls and getting in the shower, he stuck a six pack in the freezer. Now that it had become habit, it was rare that he would leave it to explode.

An hour later, Damian joined the others with a six pack in hand. Damian was always prepared: an umbrella for the rain, an extra jacket or a sweater, a lighter, a bottle opener, he had whatever one might need in an emergency or otherwise. In his room he kept a toolbox, tape, glue, stamps, envelopes, staples, extension cords, blank CDs, chocolate, several lengths of rope, hooks, light bulbs, knives, a sleeping bag, tent and portable stove. Jack had borrowed a great many things from Damian since he moved in and was much impressed by Damian's planning and logistical skills.

"I'm sure glad it's Friday," Damian said. "This Monday through Friday business is nonsense. If I had my way, I'd have a three-day work week."

"But it's your company. You don't have to go every day," Alex said.

"Right. I guess I don't. But then we have a contract with PBS to get this finished by the end of February, and we still have five episodes to shoot. After that it's time for a vacation."

Now that Jack was idle, he envied Damian's industry and the way he talked about work and his obligations. He might complain, but down deep Damian likes to be busy, Jack thought. Being idle is no good for anyone. Now that you don't work, you don't have any energy. You spend more money unemployed then when you were working. That's because you have too much time on your hands.

"I thought you worked on Fridays, Jack? Those are the big money nights, right? Usually you're outta here by the time I get home," Damian said. "Beer?"

"Sure, thanks." Jack took a beer, which did not go unnoticed by Alex.

Why, Jack doesn't seem to do anything at all, Alex thought. How uninspiring. I hate being around uninspiring people. It's infectious. I don't think Jack has ever offered me a beer or anything else.

"No, the truth is, uh, I didn't really want to talk about it, but . . . well, it's kind of a funny story really," Jack said, feeling both anxious and ashamed of himself at once. He had never been fired from anything and the injustice of it made him blush. He thought of Martino full of hate and how it wasn't right for the cook to behave as he did.

"I quit," Jack said. "The guys in the kitchen were assholes and I was tired of all that running around and kissing ass for a tip. Now that I've seen the restaurant business from the inside, it makes me not want to eat out anymore."

Jack knew the others couldn't relate, since they had never done such work and thought themselves above it.

"Well, maybe it was time you got out. I mean, sure the money's good, but from what you've said you bust your ass," Damian said. "And for what? It's not like there's a future there."

"So what are you gonna do now, Jack," Alex asked him.

"I dunno. I haven't really thought much about it. I think I'd work in just about anything so long as it doesn't have to do with food."

"Well, Jack, maybe we can figure something out," Damian said. "Have you ever thought about acting? That seems like something you'd be good at. You should go over to the Film Foundation and get in on some indie production."

"I've never acted before in my life. It never occurred to me. Do you really think I could act," Jack asked.

"Why not. You've got a good face for it. You have a real American face that people can identify with."

"An actor," Henrik said. "Why I'd be a better actor than Jack. Jack's too introverted. He doesn't have the right attitude."

"Well, I think he should give it a try. Attitude can be learned. Once he gets some experience on independent productions, he'll be well on his way," Damian said.

Henrik took a sip of his drink and sulked. Damian had never told him that he had the face of an actor. What bothered him most was that Damian was right. Jack looked like an actor. He had a familiar face: one that could have all manner of emotions, names and identities plastered to it. Maybe if I spoke English without an accent I would have the confidence. There are all types of actors: some always play the villain, others the hero, and then there are all the people who make a living with their unique faces. Henrik looked at Jack and thought: why, he isn't even cool. He doesn't know how to dress and he's plain and boring. Yes, he's boring and never has anything interesting to say.

"The problem with the Film Foundation is that Jack's not gonna get paid," Alex said.

Just then Julie came in.

"Get paid for what," she asked, interrupting them.

"Acting," Alex repeated without looking at her. He felt himself grow irritable and thought: this is going to be a bad night, I'm going to be irritable and I won't want to talk to the girls, I'll drink and then probably insult someone. I hope that doesn't happen. I hate to lose my self-control. That's a sign of weakness.

"Who's the actor," Julie asked. The E was taking effect and she couldn't help but fondle the two thin African tribesman statues standing naked with their oversized genitals and war spears on Henrik's desk.

"Jack."

"Jack, I didn't know you acted. I thought you worked in the restaurant?" Now that she was drugged, Julie didn't feel inferior to them anymore. She felt the urge to run her fingers along Jack's stubble-covered jaw line and into the cleft of his chin. But she resisted. She had always been afraid of good-looking men. I wish he would pay attention to me, she thought. If he made a pass at me, I wouldn't stop him.

"I quit," he told her.

"Really? Why?"

"Because the cook stabbed me with a kitchen knife and then went to the hospital with a whole tray of broken wine glasses stuck in his back."

Alex let out a snort of laughter.

"That's horrible," Julie said. "I don't believe it. You're just saying that because you know I'm sensitive and I picture things. I hope that I don't have nightmares, and thank God I'm not on acid. Still, I wouldn't take acid with you guys anyway."

"Why not," Alex asked her.

"Because you're way too weird."

"Hey Julie, is this bullshit," Jack asked, showing her the scar on his arm. "Eighteen stitches. If he had wanted to, he could have cut me so my guts dropped out of my chest steaming onto the kitchen floor."

"Don't talk like that, Jack, it grosses me out," Julie said.

"Say Jack, you weren't kidding when you said that the cooks were hostile," Damian said.

"They weren't all hostile, just Martino. His brother's actually a nice guy."

"Has anyone ever seen an eye operation," Alex asked.

"What are you talking about?"

"Well, once I was up watching late night TV and came across the surgery channel where they were showing an eye operation. It seems like they have a channel to suit everybody these days, don't they? Personally, I found it extremely unpleasant to watch them slicing into an exposed living eyeball as it quivered and the pupil stared. It made my eyes water like hell and gave me the chills. But, strangely, I found I couldn't change the channel."

"Oh, shut up, Alex. You're nothing but a pornographer and sensationalist. You just say these things to get a reaction," Henrik said, half-joking, hitting him in the face with a nearby pillow.

The down pillow was heavier than expected and the force of the blow knocked Alex's head into the wall so they all heard. Regrettably, Alex found himself wondering: did that Swedish prick mean to do that? And Henrik thought: I hope he doesn't think I meant to do that. Afterwards, they were uncomfortable with each other.

Alex thought: you can get irritable with anyone you want, but please spare your housemates. Please, at least tonight, do not cut into them with sharp words until they can't stand to be with you.

"So maybe I am a pornographer and a sensationalist, but the point is that I get a reaction and force people to think about what I say so they form pictures in their minds like Julie here, who can probably see that eye or imagine her own being cut," Alex said. "Anyway, that's not the point. I would much rather hang out with a bunch of offensive, exaggerated buffoons and argue and talk nonsense all night long, than be with a group of in-crowd celebrities that comfort and media exposure have made soft and vain.

"Aren't those just the sort of people you'd rather be sitting with because that's what you want to be yourself, Henrik? Isn't that the reason for a foreigner like you coming to California in the first place? To see if he can grab a piece of the celebrity pie with some gimmick of appearance and move from poor and strong in conviction, to rich and inane in purpose? I can't blame you because at least the scenery is nicer in a fancy villa or a gated community somewhere in Los Angeles, than where we're living now. The point is people are lazy and there is no easier way to make money than on appearance. But then maybe I bore you; I'm not sure if that's because none of you are really listening, or because it's a futile intellectual argument that stems from not belonging to the in-crowd. Anyway, I've found from past panic attacks that it's a good idea to not follow an argument too far. That's the point in which an intellectual becomes a mystic anyhow," Alex said.

Henrik couldn't think of anything immediately clever to say, but the comment and distinction of him as a foreigner aggravated him and made him retaliate.

"I think the excessive pride you Americans have for your country is just a cover to hide your shame at your lack of culture. America is a mongrel nation that is desperately searching for legitimacy and an identity of its own. The only way you've been able to achieve this is by strong-arming the rest of the world. Oh, I'm following your argument completely, Alex, and I do agree that I came here because this is where things are happening. However, you're greatly mistaken if you believe that comfort and a private villa make up for the lack of meaning and community in this country. I came here as an adventure, but if you think I would raise my kids here, you're crazy."

"You're probably better off not having kids, Henrik, because anyone that's looked around a bit and read a few lines about the condition of the world will find that it's a mess and that the main problem with the earth is this scourge we call humanity," Alex replied. "A good example is to compare, say, the spread of cancer in the human body to the growth and spread of cities on the planet."

"I don't agree with any of it and I think it's just laziness to sit around and complain about the world," Damian said. "Anyone who wants to make some money and build a life for themselves here can do it with a little hard work. We're the lucky ones, and I won't have it feeling sorry for ourselves or for people who don't have the initiative to change their situation. These arguments about the shortcomings of humanity are defeatist and useless. There's as much vanity in celebrity culture as there is within the intelligentsia who choose to criticize it. As for you, Henrik, there's an old saying that perhaps you've heard before: America, love it or leave it. It's as simple as that. If Sweden's so much better, then why don't you go back? People come here from all over the world every day to have a chance at a new life and escape the poverty of their homeland, do you understand? You must be drunk already, you and Alex boozing it up in here, because then America, the big bad wolf, is all you talk about. And what's this about children? What would you know about raising children?"

Damian could talk straight with the people he trusted when he wanted to. He could get away with saying just about anything because they knew he didn't keep a record of what was said for or against himself or his ideas; he was not the bitter type that harbored old resentments. The fact of the matter was that Sweden sounded like a cool place and one day, when Henrik did go back, Damian would visit.

"Yes, I don't know why I'm talking about children. I'll only have children if I find the right girl, and perhaps I am a little frivolous and selfish for that. It's a question of maturity," Henrik admitted.

This was precisely what Julie had meant when she called them weird. It put her off when they talked about things in such a blunt manner, disagreed and seemingly insulted each other. Even Jack was developing the peculiar habit of speaking his mind. It was the worst on Fridays, but really it could start at any time: for example in the kitchen at breakfast or dinner when they were all present. Otherwise, they would ignore each other and not interfere in each other's business or be in any way mean or rude. It was as if a special agreement existed between them that, no matter how they criticized each other's beliefs about women, society, art, popular culture or whatever else came to mind, they would continue to respect each other. Julie wanted badly to be a part of their fraternity, but she knew they didn't respect her. So if they were smart, perhaps they weren't so smart after all because they had alienated her. The problem is they think they're better than everyone, and that's because they spend too much time with each other.

"So what do you guys think of Nikki Star," she asked.

"Nikki Star," Alex said, "is a media fantasy. She's a sixteen-year-old girl, a lolita if you will, that is marketed toward men's sexual fantasies. She has a terrible voice, she doesn't write her own music, and it's common knowledge that she lip-synchs in her videos and on stage."

"I wouldn't kick her out of bed and I might even share her with a friend," Henrik said.

"Sure. And don't tell me, Alex, that you wouldn't sodomize that girl if you could get away with it and no one would ever know," Damian said.

"I probably would because that's human nature and I'm not above it. But that's beside the point. I was criticizing her as an artist. But it's true that men prefer young women. I bet when you were a girl the age of Nikki Star, Julie, men much older than us probably stared at you, men your father's age, and thought of you as a sex object. That is, they probably jerked off to you, or thought of your face when they were with their wives, like men also do with famous and beautiful women. If your imagination is good enough then that's satisfaction in itself."

"You're so gross, Alex. You're going to be one of those gross old men that give women the creeps," Julie said.

"And what about women," Jack asked her. "You know how guys think 'cause you live with us, but what about women? I hear women talk all kinds of trash when men aren't around."

"What do you wanna know?"

"I wanna know what women think about sex," Damian said.

"What he really wants to know is how can he get a woman to have sex with him after meeting her in a bar. I can't even remember the last time you brought someone home with you, Damian. I'm starting to lose hope," Henrik said.

"I'm just more selective than you are," Damian replied, deflecting his comment. "I don't go with just any crack whore I pull off the street corner."

"And it's not getting you anywhere is it?"

"No, especially not when you come up and cock block me and ruin my game after I do the dirty work and make the first move."

"And you don't do the same?"

"Maybe I do," Damian said, smiling.

"But that's the fun part. It's a game, isn't it Julie? I think that the women enjoy it more than the men, and that's because the window is very small for them to play with an advantage," Henrik said.

"Go on and say it straight out, Henrik," Alex said.

"All right. Women play the game hard when they're young and pretty because they know their attraction won't last forever. They're at an advantage because they don't need the proof of conquest like men and are content with flattery and gifts and other forms of attention directed to please them, including violence between rivals. They are collecting memories for when they are old and decayed. These memories are the real facts of their lives. With time they can speculate on past temptations and invitations they didn't permit themselves out of prudishness or fear. I think women ask themselves 'what if' because they are afraid of acting on their desires, while men are preoccupied with 'how' because they want results."

Henrik did not add that he felt sorry for women and Julie in particular. Women were guarded and fearful because many of them had been mistreated or taken advantage of by men. They knew better than men that there were real consequences to desire. Henrik had learned that to be successful with women he had to treat them badly. There was no joy in it, but that's what they were used to. After all, what was more suspicious to a woman than a man who was polite, generous, affectionate and handsome? Better to go with a jerk: that way there were no surprises. Like most men, Henrik didn't understand or appreciate the advantages of being a woman. There was a gender-based abyss of understanding that separated Julie from the men, spanned by the sexual electricity of attraction.

"You guys don't bring any girls over, ever. That's so weird," Julie said.

"I don't have the time," Damian said.

"They're too expensive," Henrik added.

"Love is a fiction," Alex reasoned.

"Girls are hard to meet," Jack concluded.

"I think you guys are afraid of women. I think guys in general are afraid of women," Julie said.

"I'm not afraid of women," Henrik said, "I'm afraid of kids."

"I'm not willing to give more than fifty percent," Alex said. "I'm through loving women more than they love me. If the sacrifice is love, so be it."

"Anyway, the only reason we let you into the house is because we thought you'd bring some hot friends over," Damian said.

"Oh my God, Damian, there is no way I would let you get together with any of my friends."

"Whatever happened to Greg," Henrik asked.

"It's over with Greg," Julie said and thought: either you or Greg gave me a social disease, and if one of you gave it to me, then you've probably both got it.

"Well, that's probably for the best," Henrik said. "Now I don't have to make inane conversation about sports any more. I hate sports, especially American football. What a stupid game that is. The teams line up, run into each other, the play stops, they put in commercials, come back and do it again."

"It's a war game," Alex added. "The blockers are the Marines, the receivers are the Special Forces and the quarterback is the captain. All the orders come from the general on the sideline for plays that have been worked out in advance. The franchise owner is like our president making money off the success of his army. The sponsors are like defense contractors using the game to market their merchandise. It's a military offensive. The players don't have any choice in what they do, except the quarterback who can modify his attack as necessary. And then the team marches down the field trying to conquer territory."

"Have you guys ever played," Jack asked. "It's different if you play. I was only second string on the team, but I played pick-up games on weekends for fun. There is nothing like the feeling of catching a good pass, beating the defense and running for a touchdown. Also, tackling's fun. I think if people don't have the opportunity to get their aggressions out through sports, they end up picking fights."

"I would rather get laid than throw somebody on the ground," Henrik said. "And in that case I'm sticking closer to human nature than you are."

"Go on and say it out, Henrik. You always leave off before you make your point," Alex said.

"I'm saying that guys fight in bars and compete in sports and everything else because they want to impress women so they can have sex with them. The guys that like to fight are the one's that can't communicate with women."

"And all I'm saying is that it's good to get some exercise on a regular basis," Jack said, getting angry. "Since I moved here, I haven't gotten any at all because of all the damned rain. If it weren't for my nightly push-ups, I'd really be out of shape."

Like all of you, he thought. Jesus, what an unhealthy bunch. It sure gets old hearing Henrik coughing up phlegm and spitting in the sink in the morning, and Alex is just plain pathetic sitting on his ass all the time. Still, that's their business.

Once Henrik had caught a glimpse of Jack doing his push-ups in the cold of the bedroom with his shirt off, his muscles tight and ropy, and a blank expression on his reddened face.

Jack is in great shape, Henrik thought. Sure, the girls like it, but you do just fine with your solid conversation skills and a few nice moves on the dance floor. Because the difference between you and Jack is that you know how to have fun. That's the key to getting laid.

"I gotta get going to Chameleon," Henrik told them, checking his watch. He filled his record case and slung it over his shoulder. He slipped some burned CDs into his jacket pocket, swallowed the rest of the gin and tonic, and made for the door.

"Later doods," he said. "You coming," he asked Julie. "I'm leaving right now so you'd better get ready."

"I'm not ready."

"Why not?"

"Because I've been hanging out with you guys. I'll meet you over there later."

"Fine."

Damian shaped his hand into a phone. "Call us later. We're going to a party in Twin Peaks. Maybe we'll meet you at Snowball after."

Henrik and Damian clasped hands and moved through the cool handshake: business-style to arm-wrestling grip, pointer and index fingers locked and snapping off the thumb.

"I'll catch you guys later," Henrik said.

"Sweet," Damian said.

On the front porch Henrik ran into Arnold, large in his designer suit, with his polished leather shoes, military haircut and the usual disconcerting madness in his eyes.

"Hey Henrik. You goin' for a ride," Arnold said, taking note of the helmet. "I'd watch out. It's kind of wet out there. You don't want to lay down your bike and scrape yourself into a bloody mess. Ha, ha."

"I've been riding my bike in the city in all types of weather for years and I've never had any problems," Henrik told him.

"Well, you know what they say: there are two kind of bikers: those who have gone down and those who will."

"Listen, Arnold, I'd like to hang, but I gotta get to the club. Do you mind?"

Arnold was blocking the doorway in his stiff and imposing manner. Henrik still hadn't forgotten the incident in the bar when Arnold had held a gun to his head. It seemed to Henrik that Arnold delighted in toying with the limits of propriety and sanity. Perhaps only his love of material comfort kept him from going too far. He had too much to lose, probably.

Still, Henrik was afraid of him. Arnold liked to turn the world inside out and put people off center. Because somehow he got away with it.

"So, are you going to give me one of your CDs?"

"You know I'd like to," Henrik told him. "But I'm trying to make a living. I can't just be giving away my CDs to any and all of my friends. It's business. You're not hurting for money."

"Sure, remind me later and I'll buy a copy. I don't mind helping out my friends."

"You're not helping me out. This isn't charity. You're buying a professional product. My music's as good as anything at Virgo and I'm easily a better DJ than Beautychild . . ."

"Sure, you rock," Arnold said. "Your music rocks, man. You just gotta keep it real. I'm with you one hundred," Arnold said, giving him the thumbs up. "Peace, brother. Maybe we'll see you tonight at the club."

Arnold walked down the hall, leaving Henrik standing in the doorway. He's just blowing me off. That's the problem, Henrik thought. They all like my tunes, I get them into the clubs for free and they all say they're gonna buy a CD and never do. That's the problem with Americans: they don't want to support anything until it has already been supported. If I were on the shelf at Virgo, they'd all have my disc. It's all just a lot of empty talk, Henrik thought. But there was something he admired in the ease of that talk. Arnold and Damian had certainly mastered that noncommittal, I'm cool and I'll do it at my leisure if I feel like it, attitude. They were both better off than he was, had more connections and seemed happier. That's the way you have to be to be successful in this country. Why can't I talk that way, Henrik wondered.

Back home, they'd call you superficial, selfish and even insensitive if you acted like that. Still, in Sweden there's no opportunity for an artist like you. There you'd just be a big fish in a small pond. Maybe you're not good enough or clever enough for America. Technically, you're a very good DJ, but you don't have the connections, and here that's more important than what you do or how you do it. You've built an image but it isn't convincing and you don't believe it yourself. You're not living it. Arnold sees through you. To him you're just some foreign turnip. What does he know anyway? I bet he's never been to half the places in the world he claims. But then he has money and that pisses you off.

Henrik fired up his bike and made for the Castro. The break lights of the cars melted red onto the wet street and the asphalt glowed toxic in the green reflection of the traffic signal. He felt the helmet tight around his face and also the adrenaline that made his heart beat fast and pumped the alcohol quick to his brain. He rode faster than necessary. The bike gave him a feeling that was impossible on foot; somehow he was better on the bike, he could melt through life's frustrations and glimpse briefly the beauty hidden behind that wall of tedium and frustration.

Henrik watched a lot of movies and had come to see his own life as a film. He wanted to give the best performance possible. He was the main character and the others, the people on the street, his housemates and the girls he met at the club, they were the supporting cast and the stand-ins. At that moment, flying through the slick city streets, Henrik felt that his film, with the right soundtrack, was better than anything he had seen the actor Jeremy Leads play. Imagine Jeremy Leads playing me?

Still, Henrik's obsession, that modern obsession of objectifying one's own life, crippled him in his words and actions. He was not free to make mistakes. He was petrified of the opinion of others. He was careful of how he spoke and didn't dare stray too far from his routine. And because he was a foreigner, sometimes he would get flustered and forget the right lines: that is, the cool, smooth, empty things that Americans said to one another and claimed as conversation. As a teenager Henrik had wanted to talk like they talked in the movies. Whenever he heard a new piece of slang, he would try to remember so he could use it in context later. He was a junkie for slang, but since there were so many ways to say the same thing, he got confused, and then they would laugh at him because he was outdated.

18

Arnold found them all in Henrik's room: Damian in the Iwada ergonomic chair; Alex in the swivel office chair by the glass desk; and Jack and Julie on the bed with the down comforter and the pillows piled against the wall for their heads.

"Hey-hey, it's Friday night. Look what I've got." From the paper bag under his arm, Arnold removed a bottle of greenish liquor.

"What's that?"

"This is absinthe. It's illegal, isn't that great? Well, not in all countries, but in the U.S. it is, and that's what matters. I know this specialty liquor store out in the Sunset that sells it. Isn't that cool? Absinthe, man. This is what the bohemians used to drink in Europe. It's European, dood. You know delirium tremens and all that? It's got something in it called wormwood that's supposed to make you trip out. Anyway, it's strong shit, so let's all take a shot.

"And how is my little Julie doing?" Arnold said, noticing her stretched out languidly on the bed. Her usual tight and nervous face was serene and peaceful. "When are you going to come do a project with me? You're too shy. Come here. God, I just have this unbelievable desire to fireman carry you! I don't know what's come over me."

Arnold reach down and picked her up. She was small and it took no effort. Julie laughed and watched the floor as the blood rushed to her head; it felt good to be held like that. She felt light and fuzzy like a feather. Arnold ran with her down the long hallway to the kitchen and back again while they both screamed and shouted. He collapsed with her on the bed and they were both laughing. Arnold's forehead was beaded with sweat. He took off his white blazer.

"Man, it's hot in here. I'm burning up. But this stuff will really get you hot," he said, reaching for the bottle. "Where are the glasses? We need some glasses and a pitcher of ice water."

Alex went to the kitchen and returned with the typical communal living assortment of mismatched glassware. Then he went back for the water.

"So Jack, how's Elizabeth," Arnold asked.

"I don't know. I haven't heard from her."

"Well, I wouldn't worry about her being dead or anything like that. She's a tough girl and knows how to kick for the balls."

"I guess so," Jack said.

Arnold produced an ornate slotted spoon and a baggie of sugar cubes.

"Anyhow . . . Wait, aren't you supposed to be at work tonight, making the moola? Have you guys ever seen Jack's restaurant? That place is fucking nuts. They have these weird Shiva sculptures, an elephant and belly dancers, and everyone dresses up in exotic uniforms. My favorite is the electronic bull in the saloon."

"What are you talking about, Arnold? Man, you talk a lot of nonsense," Alex said.

"I don't work there anymore," Jack said. "I quit."

"Lined up something better, huh? So what are you into now? What did you study anyhow?"

"Business."

Arnold was talking without looking as he concentrated on filling a glass with the mysterious green liquid. Afterwards, he placed a sugar cube on a spoon on the rim of the glass and poured the cold water through until it dissolved. Everyone watched with interest as the absinthe grew cloudy.

"Show him your stab wound, Jack," Damian said.

Jack held out his arm and rolled up the sleeve to reveal a scar that ran half the length of his forearm. The stitches were still in and the flesh was angry and red.

"Ooh, look at that. I bet you show that to all the girls. Ha, ha. Wait, no, wait -you wanna see a scar? Maybe you've never noticed but look at my hand," Arnold said. "I shattered it into about fifteen different pieces."

The group looked on while Julie held his big hand in her own and ran her fingers along the scar tissue. Arnold watched her face.

"Doesn't that feel good," he asked her.

"Oh yeah," she said. "I love scars. I love the angles and the texture."

"I can't imagine anything better than skin on skin," he told her. "I mean it's the body's largest sensory organ."

Arnold showed them all his hand in turn, and they could see the ridged scar tissue on its surface.

"You think that's cool, well, I can wiggle my ears," Damian said.

"I once knew a guy who could suck his own dick," Jack said.

"How well did you know him," Alex asked.

"That's where the pins were," Arnold said. "They put steel pins in my hand to hold it together. I had to keep them there for three months. There's still metal in my hand. It's a real bitch at the airport. It's like having your keys stuck up your ass. Or something like that. Anyway, Alex, why don't you start us out? Maybe it'll give you some inspiration. I think we can all probably finish the bottle between us."

"How did you break your hand," Jack asked.

"It's gonna sound stupid. Now promise you won't laugh. I broke it punching an ashtray. Wait, wait, I was really drunk, and I didn't know those damned things were so solid."

"That does sound stupid," Damian said.

"Hey, you're next, buddy. The next drink is for you. Man, this shit gives people hallucinations, isn't that cool?"

"So does malaria," Alex added.

"Yeah. Isn't that cool?"

Julie smelled the glass and made a face.

"It's strong."

"Of course it's strong. It's almost pure alcohol. The next best thing to rubbing alcohol. This stuff is eighty bucks a bottle. I mean no one drinks absinthe! It used to be cool and unique to order an *aquavit* or a *cachaça*, but that's old news. This is the future club drink, man. Imagine it mixed with Red Devil!"

"And *guaraná*, caffeine and ginseng," Damian said.

"Ooh, that does sound cool. What's *guaraná*," Julie asked.

"Some Brazilian drink. Never mind. Julie, are you going to drink or just look at it? We gotta get going soon," Damian said.

"Didn't most of those artists die from this stuff," Jack asked.

"No, they died from hunger, but that's not the point," Arnold said. "What's death if you can live forever?"

"That's a good philosophy," Alex said.

"Well, wouldn't you prefer to be dead and cool, than alive and square?"

"You're right on cue with American values there, Arnold," Alex said.

"Yeah, man, just like some junkie rock star drowning in his own puke," Arnold replied.

After some hesitation, Julie lifted the glass to her lips and sipped. She shook her head back and forth and her body gave off an involuntary shiver. She didn't know what to expect. The liquid was hot like tea though it was room temperature. It tasted different from other alcohol; after the bitter burn, it tickled at a distant truth. Julie felt a warmth and softness in the room that was usually absent. She had not eaten for many hours and her cheeks were flushed. The others gauged her reaction.

"Well," Arnold asked. "How is it? How do you feel?"

"I feel warm and easy. It burns like fire going inside me and I feel like I'm melting inside and- yeah, that's it. But I'm also on drugs, so I don't know."

"Come on, Arnold, what can it do? Pour a big one and we can pass it around the room," Damian said.

"Good idea."

Arnold filled a pint glass part way with liquor, and Jack held the spoon for him while he poured the water. When the sugar cube was consumed, they added another until they had a pint of cloudy liquid.

Arnold took it in his hands, drank and felt the familiar furnace blaze in his belly. Such was the nature of it: he couldn't take more than a sip before it was too much. For a moment his brain was blocked with the heat like molten silver. It's so smooth it turns your stomach into a perfect little crucible, he thought. Yeah, that's exactly what it does.

"Woo-hoo! Damn, that's something. Go on Jack."

"I don't know, man. I don't want to mix. I don't like that foreign shit, like Henrik's *snus* or that black licorice vodka. It just makes me sick."

"Yeah, the black pig," Henrik said. "That stuff is great."

"Just have a sip," Arnold said. "One of these is like a six pack, man. Are you working right now?"

"No."

"Right, so it's all about economy drinking. A couple of sips and you'll be the life of the party. Your head will be so choked with alcohol that you won't be afraid to grab all the girls and speak the filth of your mind. If you make a fool of yourself, you won't remember it either. Wait, did I just describe heaven? Whoop, there it is."

Jack didn't particularly care either way. It was just alcohol, after all.

"There's no opium in this, right? I don't want any smack in my liquor," Jack said.

"Not that I know of."

"Well, there isn't any label. Liquor without a label makes me nervous. For all I know they make it in a fucking bathtub in someone's basement."

"No, this stuff requires a lot of equipment," Arnold said. "It's a complicated process. Have you ever seen a whiskey still? Well, it's like that."

Jack took a gulp that was probably too much because it felt like his insides were boiling. Then just as suddenly it was gone and he floated above it. He thought how cool life was in the city, and how it was good that he had left Arizona because there was nothing to do there. Here he was on his own and free to do as he pleased. All he needed now was another job.

Alex drank with the measure of disdain that was expected of him and thought: alcohol's only dangerous in large quantities. Kind of bitter, isn't it? It's a good principle to stay away from hard liquor. I'm lonely as hell, he thought, and without Arnold and Damian and the others I'd never leave my room. Just think, to your students you're an old man. Who would have thought it would come to that?

Damian restrained himself. He liked having to wait for it, like he waited all week to binge drink. He was an alcoholic; he joked with himself about it, but that didn't make him drink any less. It was something he needed because otherwise he couldn't relax with people and would constantly think of their utility. He hated thinking that way because it made him ugly, and he didn't want to be ugly.

The drink provoked a pleasant detachment, and in a nobel voice Damian told himself: when you make it big you'll help out guys like Alex who have a passion and a dream, and hopefully together we can make a dent in the general decay of popular culture. But until then you have to agent scripts and make idiotic documentaries and the occasional infomercial with people you despise.

"I think we should have one more," Arnold said. "One more glass between friends. What do you say, lads?"

"We should get going, Damian said. He felt his impatience growing as he thought of Jenny up in Twin Peaks, who he had met at the video editing seminar: Jenny, the hottie. Later, he would head over to Blitz to meet Mark and see if he'd do some camera work for the car wash rag infomercial.

I'd like to go to the Roost too, he thought, and see all those mounted dead birds and wait for the queer owner to throw someone out of the place for making homophobic remarks, but maybe we can skip that. Then there's that rave up off Highway 1 near Stinson beach; that's always a possibility. We should also take advantage and get a few free drinks over at Chameleon, though with this absinthe shit I don't think it'll be necessary.

"We got plenty of time," Alex said. "No one'll show up at the party until at least eleven. We still got a couple hours."

"Everything closes at one-thirty or two: that only gives us a few hours and I want to get my drunk on," Damian said.

"Right, right. Good thing for the sugar in this stuff. It tastes like grass soaked in gasoline without," Arnold said, as he prepared another batch.

They passed it around and drank. They were sinking into a deep hole inside themselves from which they were safe and not responsible for their actions. Julie was falling asleep, and Jack felt really drunk and thought: I'm not gonna make it. Even Alex was dulled, and Damian felt that rush of happiness and well-being he had been waiting for. Sober, he was generally depressed about life: about how he had lived for the past several years, the alienation he had always felt racking him, his inability to communicate with people, and the paradox of being liked and successful but still completely alone. Now that he was drunk Damian no longer asked himself like a looping track: what is it you care about?

Arnold wasn't a serious person and didn't lie to himself about it. He was thirty and frivolous; he was in debt with a good-paying job, and the only thing that scared him was that sometimes he was in over his head and behind in his projects. Arnold knew himself well enough that he could perform for others. He played the clown to put people at ease. He liked to party, abhorred work and believed, like the poor hoped, that he would one day come into some money: an illusion he shared with no one in the room. His parents were the owners of a successful retail store and pharmacy in San Diego. They gave him a monthly check to do with as he pleased. None of it had gone to paying off loans but instead to travel, new suits, ice climbing equipment, a motorcycle and anything else he thought might cure him of boredom.

"Whoa there, Jack, having trouble with the balance," Arnold said.

Jack stood and the room spun. Most of his energy was now dedicated to appearing sober and to standing straight. Jack was aware that he was the youngest of them, apart from Julie, and he didn't want to make a fool of himself.

"Well, guys, I hope you have good time," Jack said, the feeling of loneliness overpowering the pleasure of his buzz. The last two hours had been a wonderful time. Jack thought with envy of all the places they would go that night and the girls they would meet. And he didn't have the money for it. It sounded like an eighty or hundred dollar evening. He'd be better off reading a good book or searching for work on the internet. He felt his guilt grow; he always felt guilty for drinking or having fun. He wished he felt differently, but then he wouldn't be Jack at all.

"What do you mean," Arnold asked, incredulous. "You're coming with us, aren't you? Don't pull this 'I'm tired' shit on me."

"I can't, really. I've got things to do, that is, I have a job lead and I wanted to edit my resume."

Arnold, the master procrastinator and rationalist, turned to him with a look of surprise.

"Are you kidding, Jack? Tomorrow is Saturday. Even if you get your resume out, they won't read it before Monday. You've got two days, buddy. Hey, you're out of work. Enjoy it. I could stand a little unemployment myself."

"No, really, I'm trying to ease it back. You know, do some reading and stuff."

"You animal," Arnold said, shaking him. "You animal, what have you done with Jack? Where is Jack, the pace car for my drinking?"

"Jack, man, you've been out every Friday and Saturday night with us for almost three months now. It's tradition," Damian said.

Jack knew it was impossible to refuse them. Also, he knew that he couldn't mention money to them out of pride. *If I go out with them, they'll be paying for me all night. I suppose I could charge it, but that's money you don't have. Remember what dad said: don't live beyond your means. I bet dad never lived like this, going out all the time and getting drunk; it needs to stop, but how can you stop?*

"Go and throw on a hip shirt, get your jacket and let's go," Arnold said.

Jack thought: *I'll go to the party and walk home later. There'll be free beer and food, and maybe I can meet someone without spending any money. It's a good thing the party's close by.*

"I'll call a cab," Alex said.

"Don't bother. If you call it'll take 'em half an hour. We'll just wave one down," Damian said.

"I still have to shower," Julie said.

"No shower. You look great. Just put on some nice clothes; guys are over the whole make-up thing anyway. You look better *au naturel*," Arnold said.

Julie liked Arnold the best because he was a gentleman, had a sense of humor, and more importantly she knew he liked her. Arnold was funny, not like Alex's eye operation creepy humor or Damian's teasing, though that wasn't so bad. She was glad Jack was coming out; if he weren't she might have gone down to Chameleon for drinks directly and left before Henrik got off because she didn't want to be stuck with him, that is unless he could get coke or something else. Henrik's ego needs some adjustment, she thought. He needs to be taken down a notch.

As usual, Julie didn't know what to wear. She changed clothes three times and then settled on some metallic pants, a yellow top that said 'Vixen' surrounded by gold hearts, a pair of canvas tennis shoes with thick heels like marshmallows, and a coat with a faux fur trim hood.

They piled into the taxi at Haight and Divisadero. The cabby let them sit four in the back, and Julie timed it so she could sit in Jack's lap.

Jack kept his hands to himself so she wouldn't get the wrong idea, which was the right idea, though he had suppressed it out of consideration for his peace of mind; one house incest was more than enough as far as he was concerned. Julie wasn't making it any easier by grinding her small behind into his crotch. The heat of the alcohol, his virile youth and the seduction of the city lights that blurred by the window were all conspiring to give Jack a hard-on. To check his desires, he imagined having his finger severed with a razor blade.

Julie could feel the bulk of Jack's cock through his jeans and her mind wandered. The problem with Jack was that every encounter with him was awkward and uncomfortable: like that time when she had walked in on him fresh out of the shower and he had turned to face her with his naked body.

He had caught her completely off-guard and her desire shone clear in her eyes. Julie's heart was in her throat and her mouth hung open. She thought madly: just press yourself against him, kiss his lips, run your fingers through his wet hair and love him, because he's so beautiful. She would always remember him standing there with his eyes locked on hers, his hungry grin shaded by boyish guilt, as he covered himself with a towel.

"Jeez, Julie, how about giving me a little warning, huh?"

His words broke her out of her spell and her face turned red. He had his back to her now and was combing his hair.

"Oh, Jack, I'm sorry, I didn't mean to, I mean I didn't know you were in here and, oh my God, this is so embarrassing."

"Don't be embarrassed," he said.

"I'll leave you alone. I'm gonna go now."

Julie backed out of the room and shut the door carefully, while her heart thudded in her chest and her legs tingled. She had spent the rest of the week dissecting the incident. What was he thinking? How was his tone when he said, "Give me a little warning"? He didn't seem upset really; he was even smiling. What did he mean by, "Don't be embarrassed"? Was he just being polite? Was he flirting with you?

In retrospect, Jack thought: I wish I had walked in on her.

In the taxi Julie thought: I hope he gets a hard-on. Wouldn't that change our relationship? Then we'll have secret that he won't be able to ignore. He'll be embarrassed, but maybe not, because no one else will know. That is, unless you tell somebody. Now there's a way for me to deflate Henrik. Henrik acts big, but he's the jealous type. You were bitchy to Jack in the beginning, but that was because of the VD and his indifference.

Damian, for his part, was drunk enough to not care anymore. His tongue was loose and he started in with the cab driver.

"So do people fuck in your cab? I bet you've seen plenty driving around and you probably don't mind looking either. There, through the rear view mirror, you catch sight of a hand on a tit or maybe a dick in someone's mouth. There are few jobs with perks like that so I wouldn't let it get you down, you know, driving a cab and all."

"Don't listen to him," Alex said. "He hasn't had his medication; it's not your fault."

The driver, a middle-aged man of unknown origin, stared ahead and didn't speak.

"He's mute, Alex. Back in his country they cut out his tongue for being a political dissident, and they did some other things besides so that even if he could speak, he wouldn't."

"You are so rude, Damian. Stop being an asshole," Julie said.

"I'm just making conversation. Cab drivers love this shit. Alex, if I were you I'd drive a cab instead of teaching. Just think of all the great stories you'd hear. All you'd have to do is write them down and you'd win the Nobel Prize."

"Fuck you, Damian," Alex said.

"You must be Russian," Damian said to the driver. "I noticed the other day that they have signs in Russian down at Ocean Beach. If you ask me, it's good you got out of that shithole. I mean I realize you must have a Ph.D. in rocket science, and it must be a real bummer to drive a cab, but just think one day your sons will grow up and become millionaires. It's the American Dream. And even some of those Russian whores I used to film down in the San Fernando Valley in garages with cum on their faces will be great movies stars one day.

"I bet you get sick of driving around brats like us that make more money in a day than you do in a week. But then again you have wisdom, while we are superficial and immature, and that must be a great comfort."

"So Damian, whose party is this," Arnold interrupted.

"A girl I met at an editing seminar. And what luck that Henrik wasn't around. I'm not introducing this one to Henrik. He just fucks everything up."

They arrived and the cabby stopped the meter. Arnold gave him a ten for a six dollar ride. That was a good tip, and he hoped it would make up for the abuse. They got out of the car. Damian was sitting shotgun, and when he tried to get out, the door locked on him, and he was stuck with the cabby.

"You, sir, are very rude," the man told him. "I fuck your mother, understand? I fuck your mother and your sister and your father and your brother, and I cut them up into little pieces and feed them to rats. You piece of American shit. You do not know me, but I know you, piece of shit. I find you and then," he drew his finger across his throat, "I kill you, motherfucker."

The man was leaning so close that Damian could smell the stink of tobacco on his breath. He studied the lines in the cabby's face and felt the spray of spit when the man spoke; the hate was so strong in his eyes that Damian had to look away.

"Hey man, it's cool. I was just making conversation. No hard feelings, right? Ha, ha."

"Get out. I tell you just once. You spoil my car with the stink of your rotting soul."

The locks opened and Damian got out, not too quickly, but fast enough. There was a moment when he thought the man would drive him off to some empty lot and beat his face with a pipe until his own mother didn't recognize him. When he was free again, Damian's confidence returned, and before the man drove off, he kicked the door.

The cab came to a screeching stop and the blood drained from Damian's face. The others turned around to check the source of the commotion. The driver got out and came running toward Damian with an unidentified object in his hand, perhaps a bat or a flashlight. Damian stood there frozen before breaking into a run. The man chased him a block or so until he was out of breath.

"I kill you, American devil! I kill you!"

After the cab drove off, Damian rejoined the group.

"What the fuck. Why you gotta be rude like that, man? He's a human being with feelings. We can't take you anywhere. Jesus, what an asshole," Alex said.

"You almost got you ass beat by that Uzbek. Ha, ha," Arnold said.

"What's an Uzbek," Jack asked.

"Nevermind. Maybe he was a Kurd or a Croat or an Albanian for all I know. If he was Haitian, he woulda beat your ass," Arnold said.

"What's with Haitians," Jack asked.

"Haitians are bad motherfuckers, man," Arnold said.

"Yeah?"

"Yeah, they got voodoo and shit. Now let's check this party. None of us knows anybody, right?"

"We know Jenny," Damian said.

"Look at this pad, wow, that is classy," Jack said.

"If anybody asks, we're with Jenny," Damian said.

"Is it her house," Julie asked.

"No. It's her landlord's house."

"Gotcha."

"Jack, man, stop straggling. You look suspicious like that. We all gotta come in together, you know, act like we know what we're doing, because we're super-fucking-cool like that," Arnold said.

They opened the gate and followed the path past a garden with a gurgling fountain. Through the living room window, they spied the vaulted ceiling and large abstract paintings illuminated by track lighting that reflected off the blonde parquet floor. Guests lounged on the black leather couches, while a DJ spun records in the corner by the window. In the dining room, a table was covered with a large assortment of tasty hors d'oeuvres.

It was still early and the party wasn't too crowded. When they arrived the guests turned to scrutinize them, and they stood together protectively and stared back, secure in their hip styles: Arnold in his white suit and black dress shoes with the silver "A" monogrammed buckles; Alex, looking like a Fifties greaser; Julie, a lolita fantasy without the lollipop; and Jack, with his worn jeans, plaid t-shirt and sneakers, just had to be a dot-com millionaire who didn't give a damn.

The guests turned back to their conversations and the group fanned out. Alex and Jack headed straight for the hors d'oeuvres, Damian and Arnold went to the kitchen for drinks, and Julie wandered over to the turntables and gyrated to the chillout mix the DJ was spinning.

"Who wants a mojito," a thin Asian man with a ponytail asked. They watched as he added the mint leaves and sugar to the rum on ice.

"I'll take one," Damian said.

"Me too," Arnold said. "How about you, Jack?"

"No, man, I'll just have a beer. I'm still feeling that ba-sint."

"Absinthe," Arnold corrected.

"Right."

They got their drinks, and the man said to Damian:

"There isn't really any difference between reality TV and sitcoms because the participants of reality television are aware of the cameras, so they act. Whether they're professional actors or not, doesn't matter. I believe if you want truly interesting programming then the subject can't be aware of the cameras. That's the project I'm working on. I've been filming a man with the cooperation of his housemates, co-workers, and girlfriend as he goes about his daily life. I know it sounds boring but I've introduced fiction into the story. That is, I've given the main character a fabricated conflict to resolve, just to keep it interesting."

"Like what," Damian asked.

"Well, I've had several different people, including a bum and an employee at a coffee shop, tell him that he's the chosen one and that they are waiting for his orders."

"That's strange, so what's the point?"

"Wait, it gets better," the man said. He was drunk and his face was flushed. A smile crept onto his lips.

"I also paid a group of men to kidnap him and dump him on a beach out of town after working him over a little and demanding he confess to things he hadn't done. It's all on camera. These men showed him gory pictures of people he supposedly killed. They also called him by a different name and shared several falsified incriminating pictures of him with people he didn't know in places he'd never been. I think it's finally starting to affect him psychologically."

"That's fucked up, man," Damian said. "Say, this is a really good mojito."

"Thanks."

"So, what's your budget? I have my own production company," Damian said, handing the man his card. "Maybe I can help you out."

"Well, I've gotten a grant for it. I'm exploring extreme psychological states of being. Really, the donors think I'm making a documentary on patients at a mental health facility. I'm making that also, but I'm using most of the money for my personal project. I'm hoping to get some private investment to make a feature film."

"A feature film about fucking up someone's life? How are you going to avoid getting sued? I mean, when the guy finds out, you'll be in deep shit," Damian said.

"Not really. You see he's already signed a consent form releasing me from all liability for the inconvenience and suffering I've caused him."

"I don't understand."

"People never read the fine print. The actress who plays his girlfriend got him to sign it. I hired her to date him."

"And what about production? I can get it produced and distributed for you. It sure is original. If you need any help, give me a call," Damian said.

"I'll keep that in mind. I'm sorry, what was your name?"

"Damian. Damian Hutton."

"Mike Wan. Here's my card. I'll be in touch with you," Mike said, shaking Damian's hand.

Perhaps I shouldn't have told him about it, Mike thought, on his way to the living room. Still, no one else has the nerve to do a project like this. And the best part is that there's nothing illegal about it. And who knows, maybe the guy'll be famous one day? But then again, maybe he'll be dead. A man can be made or broken by his circumstances. If he dies, it's gotta look like an accident. I know he won't leave town because of the girlfriend. She's also talked him out of going to the police. He has to believe it's a case of mistaken identity. If I can get him to kill someone then he'll be implicated. Dammit, I wish I could stop thinking about this shit and enjoy myself.

19

"God knows it isn't easy being an artist," Arnold said. Jenny, the hottie editor, stood next to him sipping a cuba libre and nodding her head.

"I mean the market's saturated as it is. And how can one say objectively what's good or bad? I don't believe in those value judgments myself. I make art because it makes me feel good. I don't really care what other people think."

That's bullshit and you know it, he thought, but it sounds good.

"Yeah, you have to do it for yourself. If not then what's the point," Jenny said.

"Exactly," Arnold said, giving her arm a friendly squeeze. "My point exactly. I mean we all have these day jobs to pay the bills, but that's not what we really want to do. Really, all we want is to experiment and follow our imagination. But then imagination can be a dangerous thing. Sometimes I have these crazy dreams, and I want to paint them, but I always forget exactly how they look when I wake up. I dream a lot about cancer."

"Cancer?"

"Yeah. I think I'm gonna of die of cancer when I get older. Don't ask me why but I dream about it constantly, and I've always taken my dreams as a premonition."

"Tell me one of your dreams, not a cancer one, but something different. Cancer's so depressing," Jenny said.

"Well, sometimes I have this dream where I'm running down the street, you know, away from something like I'm being chased . . ."

"Yeah, I have dreams like that all the time, except my feet are glued in one spot and I can't move, and then I try to scream to wake up and no sound comes out," Jenny said.

"No, it's not like that at all because when I look down I only have one leg and I'm hopping along, and then I look into my hand and there are my eyeballs melting through my fingers like egg yolks."

"What do you think it means," Jenny asked.

"That's the problem, I don't know. It must have some sort of meaning though, something about blindness and disability and . . ."

"Do you want to hear one of my dreams," Jenny asked.

"Tell me," Arnold said, sipping from his mojito.

"Well, sometimes I dream that I float out of my own body, and while I'm floating I look down at myself sleeping, and then I'm slowly pulled through the wall by some force, kind of like a tractor beam, and I disappear into the wall, first my feet and then my knees and my waist. I'm watching it happen to me, and I try to resist and reach for something to hold onto, but there's nothing there, and I can't scream. I open my mouth but no sound comes out."

"So what happens?"

"Before I go completely through the wall, I wake up."

"They say if you die in your dream then you die for real," Arnold said. "I've been shot in my dream and stabbed and beaten, but never killed. So whose house is this, anyway?"

"He's a real estate agent. I rent a studio from him. He likes to throw these wild parties with young people. I think he's kind of lonely. Even though he mostly stays in his bedroom, he likes to feel like there's life in the house.

Jack wandered down the hallway looking for the bathroom. He shut the bathroom door and the sound of music receded and was replaced by whimpering and moaning and the occasional slapping of skin. Another door communicated to the source of this strange commotion and, instead of peeing, Jack put his ear to the door.

"Oh yeah, baby. You like that, you like it when daddy hurts you?" Slap. Slap. More gasps and groans.

Jack couldn't restrain himself. He tried the door and found it unlocked. He turned off the light and opened it carefully just a crack. Inside, a naked man and woman were in bed together. The woman was on her knees with her wrists tied behind her back and her head resting on the pillow; there was a gag in her mouth and she was facing the bathroom door where Jack stood frozen by the intensity of her gaze. Surprisingly, she did not announce his presence.

The man was in the process of whipping the woman with his belt. Jack could tell from the way he checked his blows that this was a sex game and that the woman was not in any danger. Jack thought vaguely about pleasure and pain and a girlfriend that used to dig her fingernails into his back until he bled and how that excited him. He couldn't help but stare, and momentarily he had a raging hard-on. He was reminded that he hadn't gotten laid since Elizabeth left. Jack felt ashamed for being excited by what he saw, and to snap out of it, he thought of his parents severe around the television and at the dinner table. He told himself: you have no right to look. But he couldn't control himself. He was quite drunk off the absinthe, so he unbuttoned his pants and started to masturbate. I've never been into this kinky stuff. Why doesn't he just bone her? Boy, if I was him I'd be boning her like no tomorrow, Jack thought, not noticing how the whole time the man's penis hung limp like a necktie under his gut.

Jack masturbated until he couldn't take it anymore before turning to the sink to empty himself out. He closed the door, flipped on the light and coughed to let them know he was there so he could turn on the faucet. When he had soaped and washed himself, Jack wiped himself with a towel. He stepped into the hall and found the man peeking out the bedroom door in his bathrobe.

"There's another bathroom by the kitchen. This is a private bathroom," Neal said. "I don't want anyone in this part of the house." Jack noted the way the man's eyes searched his face.

"No problem," Jack said.

Neal shut the door and walked back to the bed. Jack had made him suspicious. Bastard was probably listening in at the door, he thought.

The girl, Heather, was a dominatrix Neal had met at the Lust Dungeon, who on their first meeting had whipped and peed on him in front of a group strangers wearing masks. He had grown attached to her and now he paid her for private sessions where they played out various sex games involving light forms of physical punishment and abuse, role-play, defecation and urination. In an attempt to cure his impotence, Neal had done everything from dress up as a baby and suckle at her breast, to having her smear him in shit. He believed impotence to be a psychological problem, and that extreme or taboo behavior would cure him of his illness.

He untied Heather and she rubbed her wrists and took off the gag.

"Well," she asked.

"It didn't do anything for me."

"Didn't you get hard at all?"

"Not even for a minute."

"I thought the prisoner scenario would really do something for you, you know, make you feel potent and help you let out some of those repressed feelings you've got inside."

"Don't get me wrong, it felt good abusing you, and I wanted to hurt and dominate you but, God, I just don't know what's wrong with me," he said, hanging his head. "I just want to be normal like everyone else. I want to have a normal sex life but my body just doesn't cooperate. My body is against me, it's fighting my mind, and sometimes I just can't take it."

Neal felt the sadness and alienation wash over him. He was crying now and looking down at his failed genitals. Heather came and put her arms around him.

"Shhh. Shhh. It's okay. Come lie down with me. Come on." She held his head in her hands and they lay there together.

"I don't think women understand how hard it is to be a man. There's always so much pressure to perform, to be potent, to act, to dominate, to create and succeed. But it's not like that at all. All that is a lie. I just want to give someone pleasure, and that can't be done with will alone. God knows will has gotten me far in life. I've failed like anyone, but I thought if only I could be successful then it wouldn't matter that I can't . . . fuck. Even now that I have this house and a good career, I feel empty and unfulfilled because I can't love anyone.

"Just now in the hallway I ran into a young man; he was handsome and I hated him because I imagined him together with all sorts of sensual and delicious women who loved and suffered for him. For some reason, I imagined him like one of those porn stars that could fuck forever and not get tired. I know none of this makes sense. I don't even know the guy, but sometimes I wish I could be someone else," Neal said.

"It's a lie about young men and people and their sex lives," Heather said. "You should know that. You've been to the Lust Dungeon. Modern society doesn't permit the expression of individual desires. We all have to suppress our feelings to be a part of society, otherwise there's chaos. Anyone who doesn't play by the rules is ostracized. That's the way it has to be. You can't just go into the grocery store and have sex with the checkout girl in front of the other customers, no matter how much you want to. Some things must happen behind closed doors if they're to happen at all. Most people don't feel comfortable talking about or exploring their fantasies with their lovers, wives or husbands. For that they need to pay strangers. How does a man ask his wife to tie him up and whip him for foreplay, or a wife ask her husband to dress up like a pirate, rip her clothes off and take her with a knife to her throat? Humiliation, role play and pain are all parts of sex that people are afraid to explore. Let's face it, most men are crummy lovers, and most women are so repressed they can't orgasm because they've been taught that liking sex is bad. If I told you all the bad lays I've had we'd be here all night. Because sex is about communication and practice. Most young men don't know anything about sex," Heather said, "and I think you and I have a lot more fun than most people."

"That's because you make me feel comfortable," Neal said. "I feel like I can ask you to do anything. But it still hasn't helped solve the problem."

Heather knew many men like Neal: successful and middle-aged with all manner of hang-ups and fetishes. If only your mother knew what you did for a living, she thought. But then she had long since stopped being ashamed. Once she was a shy girl who had been raped in that insipid high school, afraid-to-say-no-but-not-wanting-to way, the not-ready-and-not-without-love way, and now she had dedicated herself to freeing people of their inhibitions and helping them to heal by talking with them and doing things with them that weren't possible with their wives, husbands or lovers.

Still, it wasn't just for their benefit. Though it felt good to help them, it also made her feel beautiful and free, gave her confidence and was extremely well-paid. Heather enjoyed herself immensely exorcising the demons from men with a whip or a stream of urine on their backs. While she loved the power of dominance, she also enjoyed being a love object so desired that men wanted to abuse and destroy her, while at the same time needing to please her and bring her to orgasm.

Heather had discovered the beast inside humanity some time ago. Human reason was not strong enough to control primal instinct; repression and perversion went hand in hand, and only by exploring her desires would they cease to have power over her. She understood that most people were lonely; they wanted to love and be loved, and that meant pleasing others and giving to others. What Heather explored in her work was the conflict between humanity's need to reproduce, learn, create and grow, and its desire for humiliation, pain, suffering and, ultimately, death.

It's mostly about boredom, she thought. Boredom produces either perversion or laziness, and I prefer the former. But then I have seen the limits of our sexuality; I am no longer a participant but an observer. Even when I am whipping a man until he bleeds on the concrete floor of the dungeon, I am cold and distant from myself. He is not human to me anymore; he is an experiment. I remember once I whipped a man unconscious and they had to restrain me. I didn't hear the screams anymore.

When they have their hands on me, all sorts of men with different smells and names like a lottery: skinny, fat, bald, and hairy; big dicks and small; when they are inside me, I think about being on the beach on a warm summer day; or I remember in grade school when a friend and I would swing together and get so high that the chains would go slack and jerk us so that we nearly fell out of our seats. We would swing and jump into the sand, and that's how I cut my chin. Or I daydream about wilderness shows where that man with the pleasant voice talks about the Serengeti plain; if ever there were a place I'd like to visit, it's the Serengeti, so yellow and beautiful it makes me want to cry. Then I flash back and the men are fucking me. I feel them inside me pushing, and I think of a doctor's operation or maybe a piece of fruit or anything with the shape of a dick, including tall buildings, and it seems funny to me and

I start laughing. The men never like it when you laugh. That's the only no-no. You can be quiet, or you can make fun of them and say: oh yeah, yeah big boy, teach me a new trick, you rude dog; you're so good, you big-dicked man. They like that a lot; it feeds their vanity and makes them come real quick, but then I can do that just by flexing a certain way and wiggling my spine so it's over lickity split.

And what about Neal? Boy, I feel sorry for him. He's like a broken toy. I'm starting to doubt that he'll ever get well. But then he's a nice man and easy to talk to, and the way he's paying you for these sessions, soon you'll be able to go into business for yourself. Porn is good business; it's given you a comfortable life, and with it you've been able to save a college fund for Rachel. I've known girls who have gone through med school stripping, working as call girls, making videos and posing for magazines; I know others that own their own homes and they're not even thirty. If you use and don't abuse and get out before you lose, then it's not a bad life.

"We have to have another session, Heather. Come up with something new and interesting for us to do. Anything, and we'll arrange a meeting for next month," Neal said.

"I've already got an idea," she said. "We'll go hook up in public somewhere, maybe at the MOMA or at the Nordworth Center, or in some aisle of Wallsteins or something. You can take some Viagra and then maybe well get caught or someone will see us; it'll be such a rush."

"I'm not taking any fucking Viagra. I hate that shit," Neal said. "It turns my dick into driftwood. I can't feel a thing. There's no pleasure in it and it's not me. It's not real."

"Just think about giving me pleasure; all we need is a little Viagra to get you started," Heather said. "You just have to be careful not to overdo it. I remember I heard a story once about a young man who overdosed on Viagra; he had a hard-on for a week straight."

"Bullshit," Neal said, smiling.

"No, I'm serious," Heather said.

Neal wasn't feeling sorry for himself any longer. How pathetic to feel sorry for yourself like that. That's one thing I don't tolerate. Self-pity is for the weak. Oh, boo-hoo, you have a house in Twin Peaks with a view of the whole city and the bay, a timeshare in Hawaii and a beach house in Santa Cruz. You sell houses on your name alone, mostly to the same clients and between the same clients. In your market they change houses like some people change cars, or women their hairstyles.

What you need to do is find a good woman and get married again. You're too old to be living this bachelor lifestyle throwing parties for kids. If you asked Heather to marry you, would she? No, probably not, because you can't fuck, and she knows how fucked-up you are; she wants to change you, but that hasn't been very successful, has it?

"Go take a shower and let's get back to the party," Neal said. "At any rate I feel a lot better. Progress can be measured many ways, and this time, when I was calling you names and hitting you with the belt, I felt a little tingling down there. I tried to masturbate but it wasn't completely hard."

"You know that famous Spanish painter, what was his name? He had a similar problem, well, along with a million or so American men, but he's interesting because his paintings are full of dripping or drooping phallic objects that should be stiff and solid," Heather said. "He was obsessed with bread, and I remember one painting where he had a half-baked baguette in a crutch so it would stand straight."

I've never seen anything like that before, Jack thought, as he returned to the party. Better just keep quiet about it. Mind your own business if you don't want any confusion, right?

"Hey-hey, Jack, where have you been," Damian asked. "Listen, I just talked to some film crew buddies, you know, Mark and Alan, and they're down at Blitz and say it's really great. I'm gonna get Alex, Arnold and Julie."

"But Damian, it's just starting to fill up and there's free booze, and have you seen this pad, man? Check out Julie on the dance floor; she's rockin' out."

"Julie's a fucking space case, nonentity, Jack. I'm tired of that fucking trance close your eyes and trace cool patterns in the sky with your hands and rock back and forth like you're on a boat, shit. I want to meet some bitches. Don't you want to meet some bitches, Jack? I mean how long has it been since Elizabeth left? She's a great piece of ass, Jack, I gotta hand it to you, but she's gone to Indonesia, man, to live with her old boyfriend."

Damn, Damian sure is an obnoxious jerk when he's drunk. If I wasn't past that stage in my life, and didn't live with him, I might just punch him in the mouth. Best cure for a runny mouth is a fist.

"I know it's over with Elizabeth, Damian, and I don't need you to remind me. When a girl leaves and I don't see her anymore, she's dead in my mind; it's a trick I learned. When she returns she can be the center of my world, but that's because I can see and touch her. That's the way it's gotta be with family, friends and girls, too. I'm not a sentimental guy. If that's what you think, you got me all wrong."

"What the hell are you talking about, Jack?"

"Don't worry about it. I'm just talking nonsense."

"Where's Arnold?"

"Maybe he's banging Jenny in one of the bedrooms," Jack said. "He was talking her up about his art and all that. I wonder, how many artists do it because they mean it and need it and because they have something to say, and how many do it to look cool and get laid?"

"That fucker, if he's banging Jenny . . . I wanted to bang Jenny. I was gonna bang Jenny."

"How are you gonna bang Jenny when you aren't even talking to her?"

"Well, fuck Arnold. I called a taxi ten minutes ago. Let's go out and wait."

"I'm not going to the bar, Damian."

"What? Of course you are," Damian said, throwing his arm around Jack as they walked to the door. "We're gonna have a great time, all the ladies and the flashing lights, just think in this city right now there are a thousand great parties going on and we're stuck here. That's why we gotta be mobile, man. We've got to circulate."

"I've always believed in concentrating my efforts on one place, one person, one task at a time. That gets results. When you spread yourself too thin you can't get anything done and people see right through you," Jack said. "Girls don't like players, man. A real player has patience and waits and watches and then picks his victim and attacks with everything. I don't really care about being seen in all the bars with a bunch of strangers. There's too much choice and too much confusion. And then the girls see you roaming around from one to the next, not committing to anything and hoping for the best. You know what I call that: the garbage man. That's the garbage man because all you're gonna get is the trash that'll go with anyone."

"Man, you're trippin'. Don't be so negative, Jack. What a drag. You never talk to anyone and you're always staring off into nowhere. Don't be a downer, man, and come hang out."

"I don't have any money to go out. I'm unemployed and can't afford it," Jack said, looking at the ground.

"Come on, man, it's not that expensive, maybe it'll cost you forty bucks all night. I'll buy your drinks. You're a good-looking guy, we're good-looking guys, we'll get the girls to buy us drinks. That's what gender equality is all about. The girls wanted to be liberated, so let them buy us some drinks. Ha, ha."

When Damian said, "We're good-looking guys," he looked carefully and closely into Jack's eyes to gauge his reaction. Does he think I'm good-looking? Does he know how good-looking he is? Did he flinch when I said "we," even though I pretended to be kidding?

Jack's face remained frustratingly blank as always. It was impossible to know what he knew or thought, what disgusted or pleased him. In fact, this was the most they had spoken together for some time. It was the alcohol. They had been arguing; normally, Jack never argued or raised his voice.

"What about Alex, isn't he coming? He can keep you company," Jack said.

"I told him to get his ass out here, but you know Alex, he doesn't make any compromises. Maybe he'll meet up later, 'cause if he's not here when the cab comes, I'm not waiting."

I just want to be alone, Jack thought. I should just walk home. Then I can get a good night's rest and send out some resumes in the morning.

"Every time we go out I end up spending like eighty bucks. That was cool when I had cash from the restaurant, but now I gotta lay low until I have something secure again," Jack said.

"You'll get a job easy," Damian said. "You could get another restaurant job tomorrow if you really needed to. I know it isn't that great, but it would just be a temporary thing until you could find something better. Just charge some drinks on your card and pay it later. That's what I'd do."

"I don't work that way with money. One thing my dad always told me was not to get into debt. He said no one in this country really owns what they have: all those fancy cars and houses and vacations, it's all on the card. And once you get a big debt, all you pay is interest. You never pay off the balance, and that way you're never really free. I don't want to owe anything to anybody," Jack said.

"Whoa, tiger. You want to be your own man, pull yourself up by your bootstraps, work yourself to the bone, build a family, save your money, and every year increase the farm and buy a new pig or cow? Man, cut the cowboy crap. Debt is essential. The only reason we can live the way we do is because of credit. It's buying power, and without it this country and the rest of the world would lose all the quality of life we've created over the years. Man, without credit no one could do anything. Only banks would be able to build and invest and grow. The key is knowing how to invest. If you manage debt well, then you can make it work for you and pay it off with your profits.

"For example, there's this parking lot I'm gonna buy in the Mission. I got a loan for the downpayment, and with the money I make on parking, I'll pay it off. Eventually, I'll have a money-making asset that takes care of itself. After that, I'll use the money to buy another property, and so on. Isn't credit great? It's what separates us from the developing world. In Chad, for example, it's next to impossible for an ordinary person to start their own business, even if it's a hot dog stand. Too much initial expense. That's just plain wrong, and what's more, it's against the capitalist spirit."

"I don't know. I just can't get used to the idea of spending money that isn't mine. All this talk about the land of opportunity, I'm starting to doubt. We're too late. I don't own any property, I don't have any capital, and now I'm unemployed. Not to brag, but I consider myself a hard worker and a quick learner; I'm disciplined, but I still can't get a decent job because I don't know anybody. Because my father owns a hardware store out in the desert and that's how I grew up."

"Can't you see, it's your negativity that's dragging you down. A man creates his own reality and mine is going to be a rich one and I'll do whatever it takes to get there; conscience and empathy are just an excuse for losers," Damian said.

"You're right. It's the alcohol talking. It's depressing me and filling me with hate. It always has. When I drink too much I end up fighting people. Listen, Damian, it's better I head home. I'm just gonna walk, man. I don't really feel like talking to anybody. How do I get back from here?"

"All right, if that's what you want. The Castro is to the right. We live straight down the hill. It shouldn't be too hard to find. But it's a long walk. It'll take you a good forty-five minutes with all those curves. Are you sure you don't want to go in the taxi?"

"Man, I'm freezing my ass off out here and I still don't see any taxi."

"It should be coming any minute," Damian said. "I could use a cigarette. Maybe I'll go back and bum one inside and grab Alex. He's probably plowing down as much free liquor as he can get his hands on. Take it easy, Jack. I'll see you back at the house."

"Sure thing, see you later."

Jack wandered down the dark streets past the bright windows of the two-story gated homes of well-to-do San Franciscans. Looking at the lights, he thought of the security, warmth and peace that were absent in his own life. He found himself wishing he had a bottle of something to continue his drunkenness and keep him warm. He thought of the bums in the park; they probably had a bottle, and someone was probably telling a good story. That was not the case where he had been. Though there was plenty to eat and drink, good music, fine decor and expensive furniture, Jack realized that no one there had anything interesting to say. The only reason to go there is to hook up, he thought. That's all it's for anyway.

Really, nothing people talked about seemed real. It didn't seem to Jack that anyone actually did anything but drink and party and talk about the future. I want to do something useful, Jack thought. I want to create something to better people's lives, but the truth is I don't really understand this internet thing.

Once Jack had asked Elizabeth about her work and even she had trouble explaining it. The months he spent with her had changed his perspective about the new economy completely.

"Basically, Jack, we offer services for cell phones and PDAs," she said. "We make a bunch of different and confusing payment plans, and if the customer doesn't say otherwise, we charge them for as many useless extras as possible. If you ask me, it only helps to make life more complicated. These so-called organizers are really a way for people to procrastinate getting their work done. They spend their time organizing instead of doing. Mostly, it's about posing and looking important."

No wonder he missed Elizabeth. She always had something to say and was passionate about her beliefs; it was rare to meet a person like that who wanted to know the truth, who talked ideas and who wouldn't settle for conformity. He had to admit she had influenced him. At times, when Jack felt himself to be ordinary and without direction or ambition, he thought of Elizabeth. He would tell himself that he wasn't afraid of what he didn't know or understand, and that he would discover the truth and strip away all the confusion from his surroundings and his life. There was a feeling growing in him that life was not how he had imagined it. He could not explain this feeling or what purpose it served, but it made him uneasy. Jack hadn't yet come to think that there something wrong with his country and perhaps the world: in that way he was like many Americans.

20

Arnold woke up with a tickle in his throat and concluded with some relief that he must be sick. When such a break came, he wasn't one to let it pass. As he did more often than necessary, he called in sick to work.

I work my ass off for those bastards, he reasoned. Anyway, without me, they can't even manage their own database. They need me and that means when I'm sick, I'm sick. Even if I'm not. But really, I feel something coming on. Really.

As he lay in bed, Arnold wondered how he had ever become a system administrator. He had graduated with an art degree. He had wanted to be an artist. No, don't talk to yourself that way. You are an artist. You have almost fifty busts of women in your garage; you paint, draw and make pornographic animated screen savers. Dammit, if I could just have the time to work on my art.

Arnold went to the bathroom and took his morning cocktail of pills: vitamin C, E and B12; Echinacea and a multivitamin, just in case; aspirin for his headache, Prozac for his depression and Valium for his nerves. He went to the kitchen, put on some coffee and got back into bed where he lay fingering the trigger of his handgun and watching TV. He aimed at the reporter who said, "Is the dot-com boom over? Analyst Milton Seevers will give us the inside scoop on how to protect your investment if the economy goes south."

On the screen, a silver luxury sedan followed a winding road through the lush Irish countryside. A clean palatable techno dramatized the scene.

If they were really clever, they'd film a chase scene with a pretty girl behind the wheel. But then it took them years to get with the program and use techno instead of some recycled rock and roll to sell their cars. I don't like sedans anyway, Arnold thought. Really, he was thinking about buying a new SUV.

Arnold was flat broke and had been meaning to call his parents to ask them to send him more money. That was his business for the day. Then maybe he would go shopping for a new kitchen set. He planned to start cooking again. He liked cooking but never seemed to have the time. Yeah, I'll get some titanium guaranteed-for-life pots and pans, and also a new set of knives and a mixer, and maybe an automatic bread machine and new toaster before the other one burns down the house. But I feel like shit. Do I feel like shit or don't I? Since I've got the day off, I might as well make use of it. Maybe I'll take a bike ride over in Marin, he thought. That's such a beautiful area. I've got to get back into shape.

Arnold fell asleep again and missed what Milton Seevers had to say about the new economy.

"What we're dealing with, Steve, is what's called a speculation bubble. When a good portion of the middle class starts buying into tech stocks, that's a good sign it's gonna pop. By the time ordinary people buy into start-ups, those companies, or pseudo-companies, have already failed."

"Tell us about the IPO, Milton. This seems to be a popular capitalization technique for the tech industry."

"Well, like I was saying, Steve, the IPO is just the sort of speculative trick that leaves the ordinary investor with a bunch of useless shares in nonviable companies. Basically, the IPO is an insider trick and agreement to drive up share prices. Once shares hit a certain value, the major shareholders sell out leaving the small investor to foot the bill. Essentially, what they do is create trust in a non-productive or dummy company and then take people's money."

"So what about the future of the dot-coms? Do you think that any of these companies have a legitimate plan to create and sell new products and services?"

"Oh, most definitely. It's just that e-business is such a new phenomenon that many people don't know how to deal with it. It's not like brick and mortar business at all. It has completely different rules. Unfortunately, lack of experience, combined with over-optimism, has caused a lot of people to invest time and money in business ideas that just aren't viable. The sad truth is that most of these companies don't produce anything at all. Ideas have been bought and sold, and large investments have been made, but no one has stopped to ask: how can we make money from this?"

"So before we go to break, do you think we're heading for a bust?"

"Well, if I say it, people might believe it. Ha, ha. No, the truth is these businesses are unproductive and losing money. It's my feeling that most of them will fail and disappear, while those that remain will provide the foundation for future growth. The majority of the companies that survive won't be consumer-based, but what we call B to B, selling their products and services to other businesses. By and large, they will be the main success stories of the industry, that and brick and mortar businesses that already have brand identity and market share and are simply transferring their sales and marketing network to the net. Unlike the S&P,

which has a long track record of success with established companies, the nascent tech industry is volatile. Technology changes so rapidly that companies have to be flexible to survive. But it's that volatility that makes it exciting because it means greater opportunity. The companies you see fail now are simply not competitive or serious business ventures. To put it simply: yes, I think we're entering a recession, but I think it'll only be a year or two before the industry rebounds and begins to take a more serious approach to doing business. The problem, Steve, is we let this one get a little out of control."

Arnold woke up again sometime around one and decided to call his mother.

"Hey there. Just thought I'd give you a call."

"Who is this," Mrs. Kazinski asked. The voice on the other end was strange to her and she hoped whoever it was wouldn't start breathing heavily and listening to her without saying anything. There were so many sick people in the world nowadays. Back when she was growing up no one did that sort of thing.

"Listen, if you're a solicitor I want my number removed from your list immediately and I don't want to be bothered again. Don't you people have any decency, calling people in their homes at all hours of the day and night?"

"Mom, it's me Arno."

"Oh Arno, sorry, I didn't recognize your voice."

"Mom, how could you not recognize my voice?"

"Oh, Arno, it's so good to hear from you. You should be ashamed of yourself for never calling your mother."

"But I call you every week."

"Well, I miss you, Arno, and I worry about you. Are you getting enough to eat? Did you get those recipes I sent you? You're not losing weight are you? Young people are so skinny these days. It must be these modern times. People always running around, moving twice a year, never time to come visit the family, jaded about love. I tell you I worry about your generation, Arno. You're all so unhappy. You're trying too hard and missing the point. No one eats well, no one sleeps well, and you without a girlfriend and unmarried at thirty. You're five years older than your father when he married me."

Arnold was used to this berating from his mother. Really, they were a lot alike: always doing ten things at once and never finishing any of them; always ten things to say and never saying anything at all. He liked to think that they were so full of life there was no point in containing it.

"I know, mom. I'll get married one day, don't worry. There are a couple of girls I've been spending time with lately. I want to find the right one so you don't chase her away."

"She better be pretty, Arno. Don't you bring any ugly girls home and don't bring any dark girls, either. I want you to find a nice American girl with good values that knows how to cook and isn't one of these career women that just looks out for herself. Watch out for girls like that. They'll just take you for a ride."

"I met this girl Jenny the other night and she's real nice and I think I'm going to take her out again."

"Does she like cheese and garlic?"

"I don't know, mom."

"Well, ask her, because if she doesn't like cheese or garlic, I wouldn't trust her."

"Speaking of cooking, I was planning on buying some cookware today. I've got your recipes and I want to start eating better, you know, like at home. How's dad anyway?"

"He's been going around complaining about his arm so he doesn't have to fix the wall or clean up the garden. I can't even find the lawn furniture anymore in that jungle, and the wall collapsed and looks like an old ruin. All he wants to think about is an Allied warplane model he's been working on in the garage. It's got its own motor, and if I know your father, he's going to fly it around the neighborhood and terrorize the kids. That's what retirement will do."

"Well, life in the city has been stressful lately. Makes me wish I'd moved to Italy and become a painter like I planned," Arnold said. "Life here has become so routine; it almost seems like everyone is just going through the motions of living while they wait to die. It's starting to depress me, but that could be the bad weather, too."

"Well, it was you that wanted to go to San Francisco when you could have lived here with us by the beach. It's warm down here in San Diego."

"I know, mom, but I came here to do my art, and you want me to be a great artist, don't you? I came here to go to school, and it's been good for me to live on my own so I'm not so dependent on you guys. Sometimes I think I love you too much, mom."

"You've always been a sweet boy, and I know you have to make your own life, Arno. Do you need anything? Should I send you some blankets or toothpaste or batteries or soap or motor oil? You must be out of some of that stuff by now."

"Mom, I'm kind of in a bind. I've been working on this new project and I've invested a lot of money in materials and, well, normally I'd be fine, but as it turns out the landlord raised the rent again this month. I wasn't going to tell you because I knew you'd get angry. There's no point in talking to him. The phone number I have for him is no longer in service. He communicates everything by mail, and this time he's raised it two hundred dollars because demand's so high. It's the market, mom, this is one of the most expensive cities in the country and that's because of the tech boom. I know you don't understand the new economy, but it's big. Anyway, the other day, when I was on my way to work, I noticed that someone had run into my truck. They didn't leave a note or anything, and the damage was really bad, the whole passenger side door was smashed in, which is a lot of body work. Body work is expensive, but I gotta get it fixed because it rattles when I drive, and I don't know if that's safe."

"Honey, that's terrible. What a bad time you've been having."

"I guess you're right, mom, things aren't so good after all. I've been lying to you. Last time we talked I had this swelling in my tooth and now it's really bad so that I need to take painkillers. The dentist says it has something to do with my tooth tissue being exposed, which means I gotta have a root canal. I mean it scares me to have to do it because you know I've never liked pain, even the slightest little bit makes me pass out, but I didn't plan on any of this in my budget. Then there's the project I'm working for a friend's gallery, which could mean big things in the future. Wouldn't it be great if you could come to the opening in a few months?"

"How much is all this going to cost?"

"I'm not sure, it's all very confusing, but I think maybe between two and three thousand dollars."

Whenever Arnold asked for money from his parents, above and beyond his two thousand dollar monthly allowance that had been provided for school supplies and tuition since his art academy days, but which had carried over and now was a sort of unwritten agreement, he would give two figures and allow his parents to choose the right sum.

Mrs. Kazinski knew she was being fleeced by her son and that, compared to her own childhood, he was so spoiled that he had disintegrated, turned to fertilizer, regenerated, ripened and spoiled again. But it didn't matter because she wanted him to be happy. If he needed some money to take his girl Jenny out, she would give it to him; if he wanted to spend money on his art, then that was fine, too, because she knew he wanted to be an artist, and she didn't want to limit him or tie his imagination too close to reality. One day he'll grow away from me and close to another woman, and by then he'll have decided his path in life. Arno was always slow to grow up, and maybe I'm the cause of it for loving him and protecting him too much. He'll be better for it in the long run. Between me and his father, we have taught him how to respect people, live right and use his mind. That is his advantage, and it makes me sad to think of all the boys and girls who grow up without that love and reason.

Arnold hated asking for money but that didn't stop him. It was the big secret to his lifestyle, which he couldn't admit to his friends who rightly suspected he couldn't possibly afford to rent in the Marina, insure his car, wear Aldini suits, collect firearms, eat out and drink in bars three or four nights a week, manage his fifty thousand dollar school debt, pay his DSL connection and cell phone, and buy video games, DVDs and anything else he might fancy. Arnold was a man living beyond his means. His main sources of income, besides his very average salary, were his three credit cards, each of which held thousands in debt, and more importantly: his parents.

"Arno, when are you coming down to see us?"

"I'll fly down one of these weekends coming up. I'll take a couple of extra days off."

"Well, just let us know the dates and we'll get the tickets."

"Oh, mom, you don't have to do that. I can buy the tickets myself."

"We just want to make sure you come. It's not the same without you. I'll cook your favorite chicken pot pie."

When Arnold hung up the phone he was hungry. His mother had spent the last few minutes talking only about food, and the truth was that living alone he ate terribly. And he was gaining weight: it was all that fried Chinese food and pasta he ate out; the quick burgers and shakes he got on the way home from work at the fast food drive-thru; his late night cravings for candy and junk food that found him in the sterile isles of the grocery store with the other freaks that did nothing but stay up, do speed, play video games and watch porn.

Arnold grabbed his gut and tugged on it in the mirror. So you've put on a little weight, but you're a big guy and it's not too noticeable. If anything it makes you more cuddly, like a big pillow.

Well, now I don't feel half-bad. And to think I was sick this morning. What would I do without my medicine? I should go shopping today. I wonder who's around? I bet everyone's working. I could call

Jack. I haven't seen him much lately. Good guy, Jack, if not a bit square. Jack really needs someone to break him out of his funk. Poor guy's been out of work for weeks now. He doesn't even go out anymore, but just stays behind and waves us off. Blames it on the money, but I think he's losing interest in life. The city's getting to him. Probably dreams about the desert.

Arnold turned on the video game system and put in the killing game he liked. That was the reason he bought the system in the first place: for the killing game. He had it wired to the home theater, along with his computer, so he could play all the music files he had pirated. Now he could hear his machine gun in surround sound stereo when he blasted the enemy soldiers in the dark damp alleys of the medieval castle. The graphics were so real it was unnerving. He didn't want to die, so he burned more rounds of ammunition than a small army battalion. He blew the enemies' heads from their shoulders and turned them into red butcher's flesh steaming in piles on the cobblestone paths. After a while it didn't seem like he was killing at all, there was so much violence. Then murder became a chore and he turned the game off and called Jack.

As he waited for someone to answer, Arnold picked up the Nikki Star action figure he had bought and looked at the various outfit accessories displayed on the back packaging. He decided that he would buy those, too, and not unwrap them because he was a collector. Nikki Star sure was one hot little sixteen-year-old.

21

When Jack heard the phone, he made no move to answer. He had finally learned the house etiquette of letting the answering machine pick up; it was usually one of Julie's irritating pseudo-friends from yoga or step class, some urban deadbeat she had met on the bus and given her number to, or her father with his long-winded messages. If it wasn't for Julie, then it was for someone else other than Jack.

Since Jack didn't have a job, he didn't have any money; since he didn't have any money, he never left the house; and since he never left the house, he didn't have any friends. Slowly, Jack realized how dark and depressing his life had become, and that was when he started to hate the city and see it as a prison. He longed for the sun and the desert. He would much rather lie in the dirt in the middle of the desert and daydream, than be trapped in that dark bedroom feeling sorry for himself. He noticed after several weeks of unemployment that his housemates had started avoiding him and stopped asking him to go out. They are ashamed of me, Jack thought. That's just human nature: when you're down people just abandon you. They don't want to be reminded that life is hard, and they certainly don't want to see others suffer. What they should do is just put a gun to my head and pull the trigger, Jack thought.

The phone stopped ringing and Jack lay staring at the ceiling. It was one-thirty in the afternoon and he was still in bed. His morning routine of checking the classifieds and getting on the computer to send emails had finally crumbled with despair. Jack recognized the futility of sending emails that were never opened or read. He told himself: just swallow your pride and go back to waiting tables, even though you hate it and it insults your intelligence. If that's your attitude, then think how driving a cab must insult the intelligence of Russian neurosurgeons after the collapse of the Soviet Union.

I know he's there, Arnold thought. I don't understand why no one ever picks up the phone in that house. And who's that voice on the machine anyway? Whoever it is, they don't even live there anymore; those guys are so lazy they haven't even bothered to change the message. And I'm tired of having to listen to that played out pop song every time I call. I'll just show up and surprise Jack. He has to answer the door; if not, I'll break in.

Arnold negotiated the difficult cross-town traffic. When he got to the Haight he couldn't find a parking space between all the red curbs, fire hydrants, driveways and cars wedged in with shoehorns, many of which hadn't been moved since the last ski trip. He pulled up onto the curb and parked on the sidewalk between a pair of white alder trees. He considered any form of parking regulation fascism and chose to park wherever he pleased. This included medians, lawns, sidewalks and anywhere else he could fit his car. He took the sign that read "moving" from the back seat and put it in the window, turned on his emergency lights and walked up the stairs of the blue Victorian with the yellow trim.

The door wasn't locked so he walked in and down the long corridor, through the kitchen and into the family room, where he found Jack lying on the couch wearing a sweater, scarf and beenie, unshaven and staring up at the windows that looked out onto the backyard.

"Jack, what are you doing, buddy?"

"Watching a spider," Jack said. "He's mending his web. Though I don't know what he thinks he's going to catch in here. It's too cold for any bugs to survive. I don't think I've seen a fly in two months."

"Don't you guys have any heat in this house? Jesus, man, I can see my breath. Still, I wouldn't take it for granted about there being no bugs. When I was in Thailand that's all there was were bugs, fucking mosquitoes everywhere, and they really liked me. I guess I have sweet blood. The mosquitoes wouldn't leave me alone, so that I couldn't sleep at night: that with the heat, man, it was hell. And those fuckers carry disease; they're full of malaria. Did you know that malaria kills a few million people a year, no shit. There are innumerable varieties from the feverish, achy, mild version to the dead in twenty-four hours type. The tropics are beautiful but I don't miss the bugs, that's for sure."

Jack didn't have anything to say to that. He was in the self-pity, apathy stage of living. He didn't want to say anything at all, he didn't want to laugh or joke, he didn't give a fuck about Thailand or anywhere else he had never been, and the least Elizabeth could have done was send him a postcard, that selfish bitch.

Arnold took a seat next to Jack and flipped on the television.

"I hope you don't mind me saying so, Jack, but you're fading out, man. You're a shadow of the curious kid I met a few months ago with a pretty girl on his arm, always with money in his pocket to have a good time. Jack, the first class drinker. Do you remember when we started wrestling that night and you pinned me in nothing flat? And I'm twice your size."

"It's all technique," Jack said.

"You should take a look at yourself in the mirror. The funny thing about time, Jack, is that when it passes we don't perceive how we change. Do you mind if I smoke? I don't usually smoke when I'm not drinking, but the hell with it, there are always exceptions. We can't always act the same. There are these forces inside us that are always fighting with each other for control, and I refuse to be categorized. In fact, I'll do what I damn well please and not be afraid of it, and you should, too. Now, like I was saying people change, Jack, and they can't tell that they do. Because they have no point of reference. Every year, since I was twenty, I've been taking a picture of myself and then painting a portrait to see the difference. I must admit sometimes the results have been startling. For one, Jack, I don't know if you knew this, but our faces are asymmetrical, that is, if you cover one half and then the other and compare them, you'll see that they're totally different, and that these differences often become more pronounced with age."

"What's you're point, Arnold? Jesus, sometimes I don't think even you know what you're talking about. You're like a CD skipping and looping endlessly, man, repeating the same bullshit."

"You're right, Jack, but then aren't we all. We are all obsessed with something. Most people have one theme in their life, and some have two or three that they stick with to make sense of the world. You're not any different than me, except maybe you haven't discovered your theme yet, or you still can't accept it and live for yourself. We have to live by our own themes, Jack, and not the hopes and expectations of others. I think everyone should do themselves a favor and be a little more selfish."

"Thanks for the advice."

"Anyway, Jack, it's no good to be alone all the time. When friends lose interest in their appearance and in having a little lively conversation, well, I get concerned. Here, look, I've got this little instant camera with me. I'm going to take a picture of you now and another one later to show you what I'm talking about."

Arnold stepped close and held the camera up, first horizontal and then vertical.

"Now, give me a little smile. No wait, don't. Just act like I'm not here."

The flash went off, and Arnold pulled out the thin strip of film and handed it to Jack.

"It'll develop in a minute. Just leave it. Listen, I think it's time for you to get out of the house. Why don't you shower and shave, and then we'll go for ride? Do you have any coffee? No, never mind, we'll just get something on the way. I was thinking we could do a little shopping and sightseeing. There are some parts of the city that you might find interesting. What you really need is a massage," Arnold said. "Nothing better than a massage to put things in the proper perspective."

Jack was frowning and gritting his teeth. Finally, he could no longer contain himself:

"What no one ever seems to understand, not you or Damian or anyone else, is that I don't have any money, man. I'm flat broke. I eat pasta with oil, beans, rice and eggs. That's my diet. I can even afford a piece of meat anymore."

"I know, Jack. I know. Don't worry about it. It's my treat. Money's just money, man, it doesn't do any good to stick it under the mattress."

Jack didn't like people paying his way, but somehow with Arnold it was less offensive, because he never had a problem with money. Arnonomics, they called it. The truth was he really needed to get out, and in spite of his gloomy appearance and his irritability, he was glad Arnold had stopped by. He can see right through me, Jack thought. He is my only friend and I hope I can I repay him for his kindness. I'm sure he has plenty of friends and things to do, but instead he's stopped by to see me. The world is strange, Jack thought. One minute I was thinking there was no point to anything, and in the next I'm thinking about a massage. I wonder if it's just a massage we're going for?

The shopping list was as follows: one-gallon jug of Bella extra virgin olive oil, $11.99; twelve pack of chunk Startime Tuna, $8.99; Savory assorted soup, ten pack: chicken with rice, chicken with noodles, $7.99; Marino Farms two-pound peeled garlic cloves, $6.99; El Gringo super size spicy salsa, $5.99; Di Franzini linguini, eight pack, $4.99; Huevón super size chips, two pounds, $3.99; El Camino burritos, six pack, $7.99; Saltillo pocket pizzas, eight pack, $10.99; Cynthia's Authentic Belgian Waffles, ten pack, $5.99; Original Wave detergent, sixteen pounds, $13.99; Mountain Mist soap, fourteen bars, $8.99; Spartan forty pack condoms, $8.99; Nibblers cookies, double pack, $4.99, etc, etc.

Arnold pushed the oversized cart down the isle of the PriceCo warehouse. Sterile halogen fixtures glared from the ceiling to the concrete floor. The steel-beamed shelving was stacked high with merchandise. From the back, forklifts brought in the pallets of oversized goods.

"I come here once every three months or so to stock up," Arnold said. "Go and grab a case of Texas Teas. I love that stuff. And how about those energy drinks: twelve for eight bucks. Man, that's less than a dollar a can. This place is full of great deals. And of course we need a couple cases of beer. This is the only place to buy beer. Why don't you grab a case of Deutschland and maybe some Sierra Madre? I'm saving at least five bucks a case if I buy it here instead of the store. A couple things you can never have enough of Jack: pasta, beer and salsa, except that container of El Gringo is so big I can barely fit it in the fridge."

Down the isle they went with Arnold grabbing whatever he felt like. "I always make the mistake of coming here when I'm hungry. We should have stopped for a bite first," he said, tossing a box of Glacier ice creams into the cart. "Doodles, right on. I love Doodles. Which one, Jack, the extra cheesy or the original?"

"Extra cheesy."

"That's what I'm talking about, baby."

Jack pushed the cart while Arnold filled it. He felt small surrounded by such vast quantities of food. Each item was much more than a person could eat in a week or even a month. It seemed strange that all they had to do was throw it in the cart. Still, the convenience and ease of it seduced him. Jack walked in a daze as he watched Arnold in his buying frenzy.

The image of sharks came to mind as customers moved hastily about the store with glazed eyes and competitive stares, jostling their carts and pulling items from the shelves.

"How about some *taquitos*, and ooh, curry chicken with rice, that sounds good, and look at this: they've got mini microwave apple pies. Wow. Come on, let's go back and get some meat and cheese and cold cuts. I'm going to start cooking again," Arnold said. "My mom sent me some recipes."

They went back to the long open refrigerators piled with many pounds of different cuts of beef, pork, and chicken in long styrofoam trays: breasts for half the price of the local market; legs and thighs twenty to a package; whole chickens, London broil, t-bones, chops, and tri-tip enough to feed a wedding party.

"A whole chicken seems like a lot of trouble to me," Arnold said. You have to cut it up and it's full of bones, and they have the neck in there and the liver and other gross stuff like that. Hey, how about a salmon filet? Look at the size of that. Boy, what a great color. Why do think it's orange like that, anyway?"

"Must be their diet," Jack said.

"I'll get one of those and this pack of tri-tip and some chicken breast, and would you look at all this good cheese. Yeah, smoked Fonda. Wow, look at this: Swiss Garlberg, that looks good, and how about a package of black forest ham? Cool, they have bento boxes, too. That's a lot of sushi, maybe we should get one for lunch. What do think Jack, do you like sushi?"

"Sure."

"All right," Arnold said and tossed it in the cart. "Isn't modernity great? Everything is here at our fingertips any time we like. Just imagine how it must have been to live in the United States when it was first settled. That's progress for you. Just think when we're old and gray things will be even more advanced then they are now. I'm not sure how, but it's going to have a lot to do with computers and artificial intelligence. Jesus, would you look at the lines here, it's like a bloody circus. Anyway, soon people won't have to do any sort of manual labor anymore, and all that time will be freed up for creativity and leisure. We are not yet an ideological society; we're still practical, and the truth is too much of our energy is wasted on logistics. But one thing's for sure: anyone who isn't down with computers is going to be left behind. Hey Jack, have you heard of those new fuck dolls they make that are heated and extremely realistic with mechanical functions? How's that for technology? If you ask me, porn has pushed the whole tech revolution."

"How are you today," the checkout woman asked.

"Oh, hi, just fine thanks."

Shopping always gave Arnold a rush. Instant gratification was the cornerstone of his spirituality, and he was a sucker for abundance and unlimited choice. At that juncture in history the illness hadn't been properly diagnosed and there was no available treatment for his condition. Like many of his fellow Americans, Arnold was a materialist and a glutton who suffered from a desire to consume, not out of necessity, but to fill an emotional void within himself. As a result, he had bought more food than necessary and some of it would go to waste. Though the food was processed and artificial with all sorts of harmful chemical additives, it tasted good, and Arnold believed it was better to feel good now than to live a healthy, balanced life in the long term.

Arnold tried to charge the food on his card and it didn't work. Undeterred, he gave the woman another, took the receipt without looking at it and stuffed it in his pocket.

I've never spent money like that, Jack thought. Over three hundred dollars in food. In a small way, Jack found himself resenting his friend. Then he thought, like many of the less fortunate who have successful friends: at least I'll get to drink some of those beers and eat some of those chips and that ice cream, etc. In that way, Jack was rather like a dog and not a person at all.

"I hope you don't think I brought you along for the grunt work, Jack," Arnold said, as they loaded the drinks, bags of rice, canned soup and other heavy and bulky items into the SUV. "Let's go to the park and eat this sushi, drop the food at my house and catch a movie."

22

When Arnold said movie, Jack hadn't imagined that he would find himself in one of those Market Street theaters where it didn't matter if you arrived in the middle of one of the three or four films because it was all basically the same: lots of moaning and groaning, slurping and grunting, oh yeahs, oh gods, uhs and ohs.

At first Jack was embarrassed to be there with Arnold. Here we both are with hard-ons sharing an armrest. Then again, maybe he doesn't have a hard-on at all. I imagine it's all about how much exposure you get to this stuff. If I was by myself, you'd better believe I'd be jerking off. Man, this is frustrating. Look at those girls. Fucking beautiful. Tits, wow, yeah, check that out. That's it, fuck her in the ass. She's just loving it.

Look at that guy in the corner just jerking it like he's alone in his bedroom. Well, he paid his eight bucks, so that's his business. Try and pretend that's not how we all are. Still, how idiotic to sit and watch other people fucking. Take what you can get. Even sex gets boring if you do it for a living. Damn Elizabeth. What a nice pussy she had. No better parking place for a dick then a warm, soft pussy. Life can be really sweet. Sweet pussy. I wonder what Arnold is thinking? I can't tell from his face.

"Isn't this great, Jack? Who'd think that something so simple could be so entertaining? I mean you just put it in an orifice, right? Ha, this is great: the primal urge. What some popcorn? Soda? The floor sure is sticky, huh? I used to take my girlfriend here to have sex. It was great."

"How did you manage that?"

"It was her idea," Arnold said. "She liked screwing to an audience."

"Uh-huh."

For Jack, it was the first time in a theater like that. He had never been to a whorehouse, either, though not for lack of opportunity. He found the sex trade dirty and degrading to women, and he didn't like how it excited him in spite of his better judgment. He felt sorry for the lonely men scattered in that theater. Jack convinced himself that this was just for amusement, and that he didn't need it or want it. He considered it just another peculiarity of Arnold's character.

The movie was fine until the men started kissing. Momentarily, they were servicing each other with the same blank-faced professionalism and petrified wood hard-ons they had exercised with the women. Perverts, Jack thought. That's all fags are: a bunch of dirty perverts. If they could get away with it they'd spend the whole day fucking. But then again so would you.

Jack looked to the floor while casting surreptitious glances at Arnold whose eyes were glued to screen while he speed-munched his popcorn. Jeez, you'd think he was watching the final scene of some action thriller, Jack thought.

After an extended and uncomfortable silence, Arnold said, "If I wasn't so conservative and repressed, I might even let a guy blow me if he was good at it. It could be like maid service. Some dude comes to the door in the morning when you're sitting down to your eggs and reading the paper and deep throats your cock. Ha, ha."

He's just trying to shock you, Jack thought. He doesn't mean it. Everything's a joke to Arnold.

Presently, the camera focused on the women who were occupied in their own dildo-enhanced lesbian interlude. Jack breathed easier. The men rolled out a twister mat and invited the women into the game. Wow, I've never seen a twister match like that: just dicks, cunts, tits, tongues, assholes and fingers all over. It's hard to tell who's who. For a guy who hadn't gotten laid in a while, it was riveting. Jack imagined that if he'd been with anyone else he would have felt ashamed: his frat friends, for example, but they weren't really friends, or maybe his dad. If his dad could see him now unemployed in a porn theater in the middle of the afternoon with another guy, why, well, it was better not to think about it. The orgy was a living, breathing organism that fascinated Jack, until the men started kissing again.

"Man, I can't handle this anymore," Jack said. "I'm outta here."

Arnold grabbed him by the arm.

"Wait, it isn't always like this. They change films every week so you never know what you're gonna get. A lot of gay guys come here to hook up, and that's how the owners make most of their money. Gotta supply the demand, right? We just got stuck in the wrong showing. Come on, I think I know something that you'll like. You're too uptight, man. So some guys want to make out and bone each other, who cares? It's a free country."

"Sure," Jack said. "But if all guys went around boning each other then we'd die out as a species."

"Here we are," Arnold said, pulling into a space on a narrow street in Chinatown.

Nearby was a fish market, a restaurant advertising dim sum lunch specials, and an antique store selling Chinese furniture and art. The store entrance was guarded by a giant carved dragon with a ball in its mouth, and a grinning Buddha with his belly exposed and worn where it had been rubbed for good luck. Across the street was a video shop that rented Mandarin and Cantonese titles and sold pop music CDs by the latest westernized Chinese pop groups. On the street housewives and grandmothers with their imploded prune faces, gray-haired and balding, walked heavy with grocery bags. The traffic was congested near the curbside markets where the women handled the produce and haggled. The street smelled of fish, fried food and trash. Occasionally, the Muni would pass by, and Jack remembered how it was to crowd onto the bus in Chinatown: one had to be quick and aggressive so as not to be pushed around by determined elderly women. Everyone invariably boarded the bus through the back as people got off.

School was out now and the Muni was full of smooth-faced straight-haired Chinese children wearing t-shirts with logos of favorite sports teams, cartoon characters and movie stars. The girls and the boys sat separately, listening to music on their headphones, eating candy and gossiping, though they were at the age where they might have wanted to sit together. They spoke Chinese and English interchangeably. These children were American and probably misunderstood by their grandparents who still lived in the past.

Beside the Chinese herbalists, travel agencies, restaurants, bars, groceries, etc. sat concrete tenements where laundry hung out to dry in the gray of the afternoon. On Stockton Street, a mural commemorated the Chinese contribution to the construction of the Intercontinental Railroad. Jack followed Arnold down a quiet side street lined with the stylized roofs and arches typical of traditional Chinese achitecture. They stopped in front of a door with a green neon sign that read: The Green Lantern.

Arnold knocked and a Chinese woman opened a panel in the door. They saw her smiling eyes before she closed it again and let them inside. She was a middle-aged woman with streaks of gray in her hair. She wore a simple silk robe with slippers, and a great deal of make-up caked her face. Jack noticed that one of her eyes stayed fixed in one position.

"Ah, Mr. Kazinski. So good to see you again. I was hoping you would not forget us here. Just today Mei Li was asking: 'What about Mr. Kazinski? Could it be that I offended him in some way and he will not come back?' "

"You know I can't stay away for long, Mrs. Yun. Sometimes the stresses of life become so great that a man must rest. Mei Li has always taken good care of me. Perhaps one day I will buy her contract and we will marry."

"A jewel such as Mei Li does not come cheap, Mr. Kazinski. She is my most popular entertainer, as you must know. She would not be easy to replace."

"Well, then I suppose I'll have to share her for the time being. But one day I just might make you an offer you can't refuse."

"Yes, I am attached to Mei Li, though certainly there are other girls of equal beauty that can be given refinement and education."

Mrs. Yun commanded a lot of respect. Was it her presence or the silence and peace of the place that caused Arnold to speak softly? Gone was his boasting, larger than life behavior. Now he seemed smaller than normal, though he towered over the woman and dwarfed the furniture.

The reception was a desk of polished red teak. Above it hung a painting of a robed man with a long pointed beard sitting by a river surrounded by various naked women. Incense burned in a small brass bowl and the smoke crept slowly through the pores in the lid. Behind the counter were several small monitors that glared gray in the muted green of the room. On the table was a credit card station like the one Jack had used in the restaurant. There were two maroon plush waiting chairs and a table between them with a statue of a scaly humanoid holding a sword, balanced on one foot in a light suit of armor that did not cover his arms or legs.

Above, green lanterns glowed bright and expectant through the thin paper. Jack couldn't help but wonder at the activity in the interior of the establishment, the identity of Mei Li and Arnold's history in that curious world within a world where he found himself.

"I see you've brought a friend. I hope he will enjoy his experience and return to us as often as you, Mr. Kazinski. We take pride in our personal service. Please follow me."

Mrs. Yun pushed the green, gold-trimmed tapestry aside and led them into another room. Inside there were several booths each separated by a thin folding partition and containing a low table and a rug with silk pillows for accommodation.

She led them to the back and Jack glanced at some men lying on the pillows smoking from a long narrow brass pipes. The men seemed relaxed and they made no effort to look at who was passing.

"Would you like something to eat or drink? Should I bring the menu? Perhaps your friend would like to try some special tea? Or maybe you would like to smoke? Would you like the girls to join you now?"

"No, not now. Please bring us a couple of beers and also a menu for my friend."

Mrs. Yun nodded and bowed, disappearing to the kitchen through a curtain of beads.

"The Chinese have certain customs and habits they like to maintain. Mrs. Yun runs a good business here. She offers service for a man's every need: relaxation, gambling, drinking, smoking, massage, prostitution and medical care, all under one roof. Her husband is a doctor of Chinese medicine, and Mrs. Yun is a businesswoman. Everything here is priced at a premium. The girls are all clean and first rate; they are professional masseuses who can recite poetry and play music, make love or sit and listen. Whatever you need that your girlfriend can't do for you, they'll do," Arnold said.

Mrs. Yun came back with two bottles of Chinese beer and the menu, which she handed to Jack ceremoniously with both hands before leaving them again and attending to the other men. Already the smoke floated thick in the dim green glow of the room. Jack thought it didn't smell right and he felt light-headed. Mrs. Yun spoke to the men in Chinese and they responded in low tones.

"All kinds of people frequent this place: local shopkeepers, bankers and immigration lawyers; slumlords and employees of multinationals with business in China; import export dealers and wholesalers of Chinese goods. It's another world, man. And most *gringos* don't even know it exists."

"It's like North Beach," Jack said. "I swear all the Italians in this town know each other. And they got a different way of doing business. When the boss's friends came to the restaurant, he'd tell me not to charge them for anything. The next day, one of them would come by with a complimentary case of wine, or some desserts or olive oil, and introduce his recently arrived cousin. More often than not, they'd be from the same region of Italy, the cousin would need a job and Carlo would hire him, though the kid barely spoke English. They take care of their own," Jack said.

"I remember there was this old Italian guy, Daniele, who would wander up and down Broadway in his threadbare suit and flirt with the girls. He would come to eat several times a week, and when I tried to charge him, Carlo would say, 'Let it go, Jack. Daniele's our friend.' Well, Daniele didn't work, and when he wasn't eating at Amerika, he was down the street at Michelangelo or La Brace or some other Italian place. It was more common to hear Italian than English with all the friends that came to visit, and no one ever paid for anything."

"The Italians know how to do business, Jack. And so do the Chinese, except they go about it in a completely different way."

"How did you hear about this place if only the Chinese come here?"

"It's one of the best massage parlors in town. Expensive but very good, and sooner or later I find out about that kind of thing," Arnold said and winked. "Ever since I went to Thailand I've had this weakness for Asian girls. When I came back to the United States, all the women here looked fat and pasty, like big balls of dough."

"I see," Jack said, unable to avoid looking at Arnold's belly. What business is it of mine if people want to be overweight, he thought. All I know is I only go with girls that are about my size. I don't like them too big or too small, and short girls get old fast because sooner or later they have to take off their platform shoes.

Jack put his nose in the menu; it was written in Chinese and poorly translated to English. There were several soups with ingredients such as shark fin, turtle egg, dried sea horse, tiger penis and rhino horn, all of it very rare and for that reason a delicacy. Jack had to look twice at the prices.

"Don't get me wrong," Arnold defended, taking a drink from his beer, "I love all kinds of women. I've never been one to turn them away, because they all have something to offer, but Asians really are the best. And it's not the stereotype, either. I don't care if a woman is timid or not, but if she has nice hair and smooth skin, I just come apart. I'm not a skinny guy, sure, but then women are the fairer sex. Men that are too good-looking are usually vain, sometimes to the point of not liking women at all, like those guys in the movie, though they were just ugly bastards with big fucking cocks. Boy, what I wouldn't do to have a big cock like that."

If a bowl of soup costs that much, then how much for a massage or the full treatment, Jack wondered, studying the menu.

"Hey Arnold, I just want you to know that you don't have to do this, man. This place looks real expensive, and you don't have to spend your money on me. I'm having a good time just hanging out, so if you want to go upstairs for a while, that's cool. Maybe I should be getting home soon anyway."

"Don't chicken out on me, Jack. Come on, this is one of life's special moments. You're going to remember this when you're in your rocking chair, and I want to be a part of that memory. I want you to enjoy yourself," Arnold said. "You're such a serious son of a bitch. I want you to be happy for once. You haven't been happy since Elizabeth left. Anyway, it's only money, and I know you'll get me back. There are some really pretty girls here and they'll take care of you like you've never been taken care of before. You deserve it. Learn to love yourself. People don't love themselves enough and that bums me out. Glad I don't have that problem. Ha, ha."

23

Mei Li knew there were worse places she could go. Once the girl Xiao Ying ran away by tying her sheets together and sliding down the fire escape. She had money, but after a few days wandering the city, feeling out of place and ignored in her Chinese finery, she returned and begged to be let back with the other girls where she would be safe and warm and cared for. Xiao Ying had discovered that the world outside of Chinatown was foreign and cold and didn't care about her much. Then there was Wei Ci, who they found in the pink water of the bathtub with both her wrists slit, her skin pale like Chinese noodles. She didn't commit suicide for her condition, but for love. She had loved a client who had promised to buy her contract and take her away. Then he stopped visiting her. After many weeks of waiting and hoping, Wei Ci saw him on the street smiling and laughing with his wife, and her dream was broken.

Mei Li learned then that love had nothing to do with a girl in her profession and she had hardened herself against it. Though she made her mind hard, her heart was soft. There were things she loved and cried about, like her parents who had let her go. They were very poor, her parents. She remembered the day the men came to take her away and her father had talked with them and they had given him money. At first she didn't understand. Later she believed they must not have loved her all that much to do such a thing, but in time she thought differently.

Now, looking around her bedroom with the fine linen, stereo and television, her closet full of clothes and shoes, her collection of perfume and the hot tub, she asked herself: how can you be sad when you have so much?

To Mei Li, America was a cage of gold filled with unhappy birds. These birds would die if they were set free because they have grown fat and spoiled, she thought. Such a thought would blend with the pleasant nostalgia of walking through the reeds along the river at dusk in her home village. She remembered the feeling of seeing the red glow of the fire through the doorway of her parent's house at night. Sometimes she would stop and look at the stars before going inside to help her mother with dinner. She was not afraid then. The fear had come later, in the chaotic streets of Shanghai as strange men pushed and shoved her about, and finally the night when one of the men raped her. There was a misery to that time that made her cling to the objects and luxuries of her bedroom. In her nightmares, Mei Li relived the memories of vomiting in the confines of the tanker ship that would transport them across the great ocean to an uncertain fate. She remembered being unable to keep water down in spite of her dehydration, the fever that kept her in the hallucinatory grasp of death, the men's hands that pawed her as she slept, and the humiliation of having to pee in a bucket that was passed around from one person to the next. After several days there was a great stench of sweat and unwashed bodies, and also of vomit, urine and shit. The woman who helped her to eat, gave her a blanket and held her as she slept, glowed like a bright gem in Mei Li's mind and sowed the seed for her survival. Like many people, I have never been in control of my own life, she thought.

Mei Li couldn't help but be grateful to Mrs. Yun who had bought her fine things to wear, taught her English, massage and love-making, and even paid to have her teeth straightened and the rotten ones filled in. When Mei Li first arrived her cheeks were sunken and she had trouble eating, but with time she grew healthy and her beauty returned. Because she was such a disciplined girl, Mrs. Yun favored her with sweets and ordered special foods to be cooked for her. Mei Li did not have trouble being kind and obedient because she had a private place inside her where she was free. One day, she thought, I will go to that place and it will be like walking along the river as a girl.

It wasn't such a bad profession after all. Mei Li had heard stories from the other girls about men and women who had suffocated in the cargo containers, or fallen overboard in storms and drowned. Many girls ended up in the basements of small Chinese sweatshops sewing in poor light for ten or twelve hours a day, while others were sold as wives to violent, overbearing men. Then there were the other immigrants that had their freedom who she saw on the street on Sundays when she was allowed her free day. She thought it strange that a girl from a poor family such as hers should have the money to buy anything she might want in fine things, while the shopkeepers' wives worked hard and barely got by selling their wares. Though the neighborhood was large, most women knew her profession and gossiped about her and her colleagues in their idle time. Mei Li felt sorry for them, more than she felt sorry for herself, because she knew many things they did not about men, and had learned the value of minding her own business. What she knew of scandalous gossip concerning many of the outstanding members of the community could keep all the cooks, waitresses, and shopkeepers' wives talking for years. But that didn't matter to her.

Mei Li was Mrs. Yun's property. She had been sold for the debt of her transportation. The snakeheads profited handsomely from such agreements. Often they could charge as much as ten thousand dollars per person to bring them into the United States. For the average Chinese peasant it was an astronomical sum; one that would take them many years of hard work to pay off.

Mrs. Yun was not completely heartless, that is if one did not disagree with her or break the rules. Lu Li, who liked to drink, Mrs. Yun beat religiously with her bamboo cane so that the wayward young lady couldn't sleep on her backside or sit down for several days after. Mrs. Yun made a practice of looking after her girls, selling them on to suitors when she found it most profitable, and before they were old maids, which was a different practice than the pimps in the Fillmore and other parts of town who drugged their girls into oblivion, fucked them at their leisure, and sold them out or dropped them in the gutter when they were no longer useful.

Mrs. Yun was no saint, but the business had been profitable enough to raise two sons and a daughter. Her daughter she had married off to a prominent import export dealer. One of her sons was a banker and the other worked with computers, which was something she didn't understand beyond that computers meant money. Mrs. Yun took money very seriously, having spent many hungry years in China. She didn't want her children to have such memories. She took care of her girls because they were valuable to her. She knew that there was nothing more profitable than a woman's beauty. She had a profound respect for beauty, and it was her aesthetic touch that made The Green Lantern stand out from the other massage parlors of the city.

Once I was one of those beautiful girls, Mrs. Yun would remind herself, as she stared in her bedroom mirror. Occasionally, she would take up an old picture from the dresser and marvel at herself many years younger with her long braids and simple clothes, standing by a younger, more handsome version of her husband.

I thought I would be beautiful like that forever, but then beauty fades and is replaced by wisdom. Perhaps that is a just compensation, I do not know.

Her husband all but ignored her now in favor of his library and endless scholarship. With time she began to think of sex as a frivolity. I am an efficient, serious woman, she told herself. That is enough. She lived vicariously through her girls, so when Wei Ci was found dead, Mrs. Yun went about wailing and screaming and pulling her hair, and had to be sedated with tea made from dried bees to soothe her nerves before she was put to bed. From then on Wei Ci's former lover was no longer allowed in the club, for Mrs. Yun couldn't bear to lose another beauty to his slick words.

There was a knock at the door, and with all such knocks, Mei Li found herself wondering what sort of man she would be expected to entertain. Sometimes she liked to daydream and think that it was a handsome, kind man who was coming to take her away and marry her.

In reality, this first knock was a warning, though sometimes she would be called on the intercom from the front desk to attend to a surprise guest: most often a stranger who came for an evening of entertainment and then left the city never to return again. Such men could be difficult to handle; often they were drunk and aggressive, making the art of seduction and pleasure difficult and disagreeable. Mei Li no longer dealt with such customers. She was senior to most of the girls, apart from Lu Li, now dangerously near her thirties and known for her raunchy sense of humor and the way she laughed and scratched herself like a man. Ming Xiu, on the other hand, scratched men until they bled. Mei Li had always thought her to be the model of good manners, so quiet that, were it not for her screams during lovemaking, it would seem that her room was altogether unoccupied. Mei Li, for her part, liked to sing aloud into her hairbrush to Chinese pop music and imagine that she was a star.

The knock grew more insistent. Mei Li opened the door a crack to find Mrs. Yun's unblinking eye fixed on her. The glass eye had acquired a life of it's own, and Mei Li often wondered how it felt to walk in the cold streets with that artificial organ: if it froze her brain like ice cream eaten too quickly, and if she took it out at night and put it in a glass of water like false teeth to keep it clean.

"Mei Li, please get ready. Mr. Kazinski is here. Put on some make-up and a nice gown, light some candles and turn on the hot tub. Do you have condoms and body oil and enough perfume?"

"I have everything Mamma Yun. If not, I would tell you beforehand. Is Mr. Kazinski really coming?"

"He is downstairs drinking with a friend. When they are finished I will send him up."

"Did you ask him if he wanted me to come down and entertain? He did not want me to pour the tea or to drink with him?"

"The last time you drank with him he had to carry you to your room. If I did not know that you had more sense than that, I would have punished you. For that you deserved a good beating. Perhaps I have become soft. I am too good to you."

"Yes, Mamma Yun is very kind, but Mr. Kazinski was satisfied. I did everything he wanted, and he was not displeased with me being drunk."

"With anyone else it would have been unacceptable. It is unladylike to drink with such abandon."

"Yes, it is unladylike," Mei Li agreed.

Mrs. Yun was not altogether displeased with the evening that Mei Li had gotten drunk and started singing and dancing for Mr. Kazinski and the other men in the parlor. She had a pleasant voice and the liquor caused her to sway her hips in a way that made the men tingle below the waist. That night Mrs. Yun made plenty of money in liquor. She had coached the girls to only order the best because "they were worth it." The only drawback was that they invariably got drunk. Once one of them had vomited all over a customer in bed, and Mrs. Yun thought best to sell her on to pay her debt with someone else. A good "entertainer," according to Mrs. Yun, knew how to get the men drunk while nursing their own drink for the duration of the evening. Mei Li was her most profitable investment and for this she was allowed certain liberties.

Perhaps I will have her sing in the parlor for the men on a regular basis? Mrs. Yun imagined how beautiful Mei Li would look walking around the room in a shimmering gown with her powdered face, red lips and fake diamond earrings sparkling in the spotlight. No, it would go to her head, she thought, though the men would certainly be pleased by it. She's every bit as good as those singers she listens to. Most of the time I can't even tell their voices apart.

Mrs. Yun made her way down the hall and knocked on another door. In all there were eight girls at The Green Lantern, the youngest of which was a Thai girl named Mali who didn't speak much and seemed too intelligent for her own good. She sees me as clearly as I see her, Mrs. Yun thought. But she's too smart to test me.

"Mali, you have a customer," Mrs. Yun said. "He will be up in a few minutes. He's a handsome young American. Now get ready and don't disappoint him."

Mrs. Yun shuffled down the hall, stopping to adjust a wall hanging before slipping downstairs to the music and laughter. Another of the girls passed down the hall in an evening gown and heels before Mali shut the door.

A young, good-looking man. That would be change from the old, balding men with their bellies, tobacco-breath and their smell, for it seemed that none of them showered. Still, Mali was skeptical as she perfumed herself and ran a brush through her hair. She put on lipstick and eyeliner until another woman looked back in the reflection of the mirror. Gone was Mali, the scared nineteen-year-old living an alien life in a city she had not seen, in a country she did not know, speaking a language that was not her own. Now she looked in the mirror and saw strength. The woman in the mirror was cold, beautiful and deadly. She was a woman that no man could possess no matter how hard he tried.

Let's do this disagreeable thing, she told herself. Let's do it and forget it like the thousand other disagreeable things you've had to do in your life and the thousand more to come. Perhaps one day this will be over, but perhaps not.

Mali knew the only way to escape from her life with that witch Mrs. Yun was to make a man fall in love with her. But she hadn't yet found a man suitable for the task. A man should be a fool, she thought. The ideal man is a wealthy fool who is generous, handsome and good in bed.

In the year Mali had been living in America she had consumed enough television sitcoms and Hollywood movies to erase her country bumpkin past in Thailand. She wanted to wear fine clothes, live in a big house and drive a fancy car. She had seen Asian women who lived like that in America, and she was going to be successful like them. I am much more beautiful than the movie stars on television, and here I am making money for that old witch, she thought. As if being Chinese were any better than being Thai. There is nothing exotic or original about being Chinese. Foreign men don't go to China for sex, they go to Thailand because our women are beautiful.

It was nearing six o'clock, and the group of men that appeared in the parlor were escorted to a large booth in the corner of the room. The men wore suits and were thin with short hair and some carried briefcases. They were in a cheerful mood and spoke Chinese in an easy manner that made Jack think they were all friends or perhaps colleagues.

"I don't know about you, Jack, but I'm ready to go upstairs. So what did you think of the soup? Ground rhino horn is supposedly an aphrodisiac, and who knows what else they put in there. One thing's for sure, Mrs. Yun makes a mean soup. Her husband is an expert in Chinese medicine. He's so good he can cure a man of a bad attitude with some bark, dried mushrooms and a bit of seaweed."

Jack didn't like the soup, but Arnold had been nice enough to order it for him, so he drank it down and tried not to make a face. He couldn't believe that roots and berries, dried dead animals and ground up bone could cure a man of anything. Jack was a regular two-aspirin-for-a-headache kind of guy, but mostly he preferred not to take anything at all if he could help it. The body should cure itself, he thought. Aphrodisiac, my ass. The only thing this soup is good for is separating a customer from his money.

Mrs. Yun came to their booth and said, "Mei Li is ready to see you, Mr. Kazinski. For your friend I have chosen a very nice girl. Mali is perhaps the most beautiful of my girls, though she lacks Mei Li's charms and experience and also her sense of humor. But then she's only nineteen years old. Please, when you are ready, I will take you upstairs."

Arnold knocked back the rest of his beer.

"Come on Jack, let's go."

"Won't it be expensive? I don't have any money and don't know when I'll be able to pay you back."

"Don't worry about the money, Jack. That's what the plastic's for. Charge now and worry about it later, right? Ha, ha."

Arnold stood up, knocking his head into the lantern. He picked up the flowers he had bought leaving PriceCo, and they pushed their way past the bead curtain and up the narrow wooden stairwell.

They were both directed to their particular doors, and when Jack looked for Mrs. Yun, she had disappeared.

Arnold knocked and was told to come in. He winked at Jack before stepping inside. Jack was left alone in the hall. He was nervous and thought: what if Arnold finishes before me and leaves me here? What if I can't get a hard-on? I wonder what she looks like? I've never believed in prostitution. It feels wrong to treat a woman that way. Why, they live like prisoners here.

It was at this point that Jack felt an unexplained pressure and heat in his groin. The pressure built until he was quite uncomfortable, and he found himself knocking on the door with urgency.

A moment later Jack was staring into the black eyes of Mali. She was strikingly beautiful with dark skin and full red lips. She flashed a smile that gleamed white and perfect and made him think of gluttony, feasting and laughter. They stood there staring at each other, while Jack fidgeted with discomfort as if he had to pee.

"Do you mind if I come in?"

"No, please, how rude of me," Mali said.

He looks like one of those clothing ads for men's underwear when Mrs. Yun takes us shopping at Clancy's and the Nordworth Center. When Americans are beautiful, they are really beautiful, she thought. It's no wonder they have such a powerful country with men like this one.

The first thing Jack did when he came in the room was go to the bathroom.

"Excuse me. I'm sorry. I really have to go," he said.

Jack's face was burning and his cheeks were crimson. In the bathroom, he quickly unbuttoned his jeans and inspected himself. His penis was hard as a rock and so red it was almost purple. What do I do about this? I can't just come out there with my dick like this. God, what a beautiful girl. He turned on the tap and splashed himself with cool water.

Then, with resignation, he carefully bent his member back inside his pants, buttoned up and walked out stiff-legged and awkward.

Mali lay on the bed in a silk nightgown embroidered with flowers.

"Come join me," she said.

He came and sat down like he was told.

"What do you want to do," she asked him. "Do you want a massage, or maybe we could go in the hot tub?"

"I'm sorry," Jack said. "I've never done anything like this before. My friend brought me along. I respect you and you are very beautiful and the truth is I have a really painful hard-on and I'm not sure what's wrong with me."

"Well, I'm sure we can take care of that," Mali said, grabbing his crotch. Jack shot up from the bed and paced the room with clenched fists. He bit his lip to keep from crying out.

God, this is what venereal disease must feel like, he thought. They must have given me the wrong dose in that soup and I've reacted badly to it.

Mali looked at him perplexed.

"Come on then, I won't touch it again. Let me give you a massage instead."

"I'm afraid I won't be able to lay on my stomach," Jack said.

"Well, then we can go in the hot tub," she suggested.

"The water'll probably be too hot. No, I'm just going to take a seat here," Jack said, easing himself into the plush armchair across from the bed. "You're very pretty," he said. "It wasn't my idea to come here, but I'm glad I did, even though I can't enjoy the experience."

"What is it that has happened to you?"

"I don't know. I felt fine before I had the soup. I think my friend wanted to make sure I had a good time, so maybe the soup was a little strong. Also, maybe he is playing a joke on me because I don't believe in aphrodisiacs."

"Oh, but you must believe. There is a medicine in nature to cure every illness in the human being."

"Yes, but I didn't need a cure. And now I need a cure for the cure. I wonder how long it will take for this to go away," Jack said, pointing to the tent stake in his pants.

"Why don't you try giving it some air?"

"No, I don't think that's such a good idea."

"Don't you think you should look and see how bad it is?"

"I saw it in the bathroom. It's swollen and purple. Must be a lot of blood in there."

"Don't you want me to call Mr. Yun to have a look at you? I'm sure he can reverse the effects of his cure."

Jack thought about it for a moment. It felt like he didn't have enough skin for all the blood in his penis. He was starting to break out in a cold sweat. What if it explodes, he wondered. It certainly can't get any more painful. Boy, would I like to lie down and curl up in the fetal position.

"Yes, why don't you call him. I'm not sure I can take this much longer."

24

Arnold picked Mei Li off the ground and held her delicate frame in his embrace. He smelled her delicious perfume and ran his fingers through her silky black hair.

"I've brought you some presents, Mei Li," he said.

He pulled out a bouquet of flowers and handed them to her. It didn't matter that they were second-rate flowers; Mei Li smiled with delight, held them close and smelled so hard that a violet petal tickled her nose.

"Let me find a vase," she said, disappearing into the bathroom. She returned and set the flowers on the nightstand by the bed.

"Ready," Arnold asked. Mei Li nodded.

"You have to close your eyes first."

Mei Li did as she was told. She sat on her hands on the bed and restrained herself from swinging her legs like a little girl might.

Arnold took a slender white box from his coat pocket and set it in her lap.

"Well, what's this," Mei Li asked, examining the box carefully. She knew it must be some sort of jewelry and couldn't help but think about weddings. Those were her favorite type of American films: when women got married to beautiful generous men and got to dress up in big white gowns and be kissed in front of everyone. She wondered if she would be nervous to kiss in front of so many people: if she might miss and kiss the man's cheek or fall off the stage, like the actress who always messed up her fortune by being clumsy.

"Well, aren't you gonna open it?"

She untied the red ribbon and took off the lid, and there inside was a gold necklace with a heart on the end. When Mei Li saw what looked like a diamond in the middle, she let out a gasp.

"Oh, it's so very beautiful, Arnold. You are too kind."

"That's to remind you that I haven't forgotten you," Arnold said.

There was nothing Arnold liked more than to live his fantasies. He hoped that his gifts helped Mei Li dream far away from the confinement of her room and her loneliness.

I escape my own sadness by helping others to escape theirs, he thought. What's the price of a necklace for that look on her face?

"Here, let me put it on for you," he said.

Mei Li lowered her head and pulled her hair out of the way to reveal her pale skin. Arnold leaned behind her and clasped the necklace around her neck.

The gifts allowed them to relax. It seemed that they were two lovers meeting together for mutual enjoyment and the promise that their love would grow and become eternal.

Gone was the Arnold who devoured hardcore pornography and talked nonstop about sex to his friends. Now he lay down with Mei Li and they snuggled together. He tickled her so that she fought against him to get away; he held her tight and tickled until there were tears in her eyes.

You did not think you would like Arnold when you first saw him. He was overweight and did not seem to be much of a lover, like many of these American men that come. But then he has given you more pleasure than any man you know, Mei Li thought. He is very gentle and kind. When he leaves you feel lonely and want to tear out your hair because you can't go with him. You want to be free to visit him. You would like to put on a nice dress and go out in public for a romantic dinner like a real lady.

With Arnold it was possible to imagine that she was not a prostitute and massage girl. Inside her lived a small hope that he would come and buy her contract and take her away. But then maybe even Arnold didn't have the money for that.

After they finished, they lay staring up at the ceiling. Arnold said, "Mei Li, I'm afraid I'm going to lose my job. Many people have been fired already, and we've lost most of our clients. The company isn't making any money, and they're cutting the staff to the bare minimum. Really, they can survive without a system administrator. Maybe it isn't so bad after all. It's not a good company and now's my chance to find a better job. There are plenty of jobs out there for a person with my skills. The truth is I'm worth more than that. I'm worth at least twice what they're paying me. I don't like the job, anyway."

Arnold knew he wasn't the best employee; since he was the only system administrator, he took liberties. There were still several projects that needed to be finished, and for that reason they couldn't let him go. Hiring someone else in his place would be costly, and who knew that such a person would be any more efficient?

At the start of each project Arnold worked hard. When he felt he was ahead of deadline, he would relax and pursue his personal interests. When asked to see what he had done, he would show them results from a week before so as to give himself a window of leisure. Then, after several weeks of playing computer games, downloading music and emailing, he would be behind, and the manager, a rude and pushy Texan named Cleat, would come by on a daily basis to bother him.

"This won't look good on your performance report, Arnold. You haven't finished a single project on time. And you wonder why we're having trouble with the company when we can't keep our records straight or keep track of our clients and our income and expenditures, and now the server is down, and all of this is your responsibility."

Arnold didn't bother to explain to him the difficulty of building a network from scratch. When he was hired everything had been in such a mess that he had to start fresh. He couldn't continue where someone else had left off; he needed to follow his own logic from beginning to end. They weren't likely to fire him until he put everything in order. When they did, he would keep much of the important data for himself, like he had with previous jobs. He was certain the information would be useful when and if he started his own business, or for resale to other companies for marketing purposes.

As it stood, Cleat had been fired because managers were less useful than technicians. Lonestar was based in Houston and soon everyone would be going home. Now Arnold wished he had asked for more pay and less stock options. What was the point in having shares in a dung heap? Lonestar, like most of the IT industry, was worthless. Arnold had discovered, like others, that ideas in themselves were not worth anything unless they could be produced and sold as real products and services.

In spite of his precarious situation, Arnold was not one to economize: hence the trip to The Green Lantern, the necklace, the major shopping spree and the designer cookware he planned to buy to start his new healthy life. He also thought of buying some new home exercise equipment. He was tired of his dad's old rowing machine. What was the fun of pulling on those handles, anyway? It didn't even feel like rowing, and it was a pain in the neck. There were many new and less strenuous ways to keep in shape. Maybe I'll get one of those shock belts to burn the fat off my waist and stimulate my abs? I could wear it around the house or under my clothes when I go out.

It didn't occur to him that jogging in the Marina or doing a few push-ups and sit–ups each night would do wonders for his health. No, he wanted to buy a complex machine so he would feel better about not being in shape. Like the rest of the lonely exercise equipment scattered across the fifty states, it would be stored away in a closet somewhere close at hand but blissfully out of sight. Exercise was more of a theory to Arnold than an activity.

"I'm sure you will find a good job," Mei Li told him. "You are a smart person and you know a lot about computers. Computers are the future and I'm not worried for you."

The problem was he didn't know much about computers. He only knew a couple basic programming languages and couldn't build a computer on his own or repair one; all he knew how to do was move information around, locate it when necessary and work programs that other people had written. That was the extent of his knowledge. Really, he was nothing more than an electronic librarian.

It did Arnold good to be with Mei Li because, unlike many of the American girls he had gone with, she built him up and believed in him, perhaps more than he believed in himself. Talking to her made his doubts disappear and gave him a new fighting will.

If mom knew I was gonna lose my job, she wouldn't be understanding like Mei Li. Once again, Arnold thought about marrying a girl completely unlike his mother. I wish I had met Mei Li at the office and that she worked in a different division of the company, like marketing or PR. No, because then you'd find her intimidating and she'd make you uncomfortable. I want a woman who can work in a team and take the bad with the good, not one who will drop me when I fail or use me to further her own career. I wonder what sort of woman Mei Li is? I know she's smart, perhaps smarter than me, because she listens more than she talks and says only what needs to be said.

Arnold thought a lot about women and wondered: is it possible for a woman to be a good wife and mother and also have a successful career? For a woman to be truly successful, she must be both ambitious and supportive. Then there's the question of beauty. Arnold knew that beauty and compatibility had nothing to do with each other. Beauty and laughter were also great strangers. Good-looking women usually don't have a sense of humor or anything interesting to say. That's social conditioning for you.

Arnold considered the standards of appearance placed on women and men and concluded that he was lucky to be a man. If men and women were measured and matched on appearance alone, and if I wasn't paying her for sex, then Mei Li would have nothing to do with me. I'm a typical overeating, out-of-shape American slob.

"Mei Li, do you think I'm too fat? I feel like I'm getting fatter and wonder how you can find me attractive."

"Just as I am small, you are big. A person is not just appearance but also heart. You have a big heart to match your body, and you are not arrogant or conceited, which are the usual flaws of beauty: be thankful you do not have them. Also, you are blond and have pretty blue eyes," she said.

That sounds real nice, Arnold thought, but if she was fat or ugly I wouldn't like her, and then what would she do to survive? It's hard to feel sorry for a beautiful woman.

Mei Li sure has a way with words; she always says just what I want to hear. I wish I knew her true thoughts. I wonder what people are really thinking, and if their thoughts are as dark and disturbed as mine. I'll bet no one has dreams of watching their parents get ripped apart by alligators in the waters around an old island citadel, or of taking a walk in the woods with an old girlfriend carrying a fetus in a jar of blue gelatin, or of getting pinned alive to a giant corkboard like a rare butterfly in a museum collection.

Every consciousness must be radically different, he thought. I doubt any of us have the same visions or fears or preoccupations: the ones we do share have been conditioned into us by popular culture. The only thing we have in common are sitcoms, national news, video games and pop music. And there's no substance to any of it. That's too bad.

"Arnold, what are you thinking about?"

"Nothing. Why don't you tell me a story? Tell me about the fireflies at night in the village where you grew up, and how the moon looked on the river and the way the grass sounded in the breeze, and how you felt to be home and safe with your family. That's a happy story. Well, it's sad, but it's a path back to happiness, isn't it?"

25

Damian lay awake in bed thinking about the following: his investments, Jenny and Arnold screwing, and how he hated editing shitty corporate video; partying in Sweden with Henrik, and the burritos at Dos Tios in the Marina by his office; his dirty laundry, unpaid bills, lack of creativity and fear of getting old; Alex's intense and obsessive personality, and whether he should cock block Arnold and invite Jenny out for a drink; the shitty weather in San Francisco, and his homesickness for Southern California; the desire to skip out on work, and travel, maybe to Mexico; his plan to make a film out of one of Alex's manuscripts; the dog trainer, not being in control of his life, his loneliness, and the fact that his nose was too big; the time he had masturbated to a mental image of Jack naked, and what that implied about his sexual orientation; and his insomnia, hatred of hangovers and addiction to alcohol. Finally, his thoughts came to rest on Alex in particular.

The problem with Alex is he's paranoid. He doesn't trust anyone. There he is complaining about being a starving writer and he doesn't share his work. He's afraid someone will steal it and get rich at his expense. He sure thinks highly of himself and his ideas, which would be tragic and absurd if he didn't have the talent to back it up. With all the challenges and criticism a writer has to face, I suppose it's only natural to grow a pretty thick shell of militant self-confidence, and even arrogance, to protect oneself. The problem with Alex is that he's too reclusive and insulated. He's hiding from his own destiny. Even though you can't write like that, you can recognize good writing because you've always loved to read. You've even got a decent collection of literature in your bookcase.

Damian once made the mistake of asking Alex why he didn't get himself an agent.

"I'm the one with the ideas and I'll be damned if I'm going to let some mediocre son of a bitch make money off my work. No offense, but they're my ideas and the profit should be all mine. The problem with America is that everyone's a fucking leech. Artists are underpaid and undervalued. It's always the middlemen that make the money: the producers, managers, agents, promoters, publishers and labels. Business from biblical times has been a dirty undertaking and I don't want any part of it. I don't want to be marketed. My thoughts are inherently valuable and people will come to understand that."

"And then you'll be just another dead artist that suffered and starved, and for what? Man, you should be living large now," Damian said. "I wish I had ideas like you, but I don't. Don't you think I wanna promote something worthwhile instead of commercial television, budget documentaries and infomercials? You gotta start somewhere. You need to be recognized and the only way to do that is to sell yourself, man. You're too much of an idealist. You can be an idealist if you want, but then someone is gonna have to do the dirty work for you. How about if I represented you? I understand you not wanting to work with strangers, and I think we'd make a good team. I can sell your writing and make you a lot of money. I'd cut you a fair deal. If later you wanted to work on your own, then that'd be your business."

Damian knew he had lost the argument when Alex stopped talking, turned back to his work and began typing away. When Alex didn't like something or disagreed after having spoken his mind, he would fall silent and not give an answer so he wouldn't have to say "no" outright. He wanted to avoid hurting people's feelings, though he often did so anyway by speaking his mind. In fact, after their conversation Damian knew exactly where he stood in Alex's world. He was a mediocre non-artist; someone who didn't live up to Alex's high standards and therefore someone not to be trusted.

In truth they were rivals. Alex, in spite of his spartan lifestyle, envied Damian's material success and the fact that he was working in his field. Damian had been successful marketing small independent films to Hollywood. Alex did not doubt that Damian could sell his work but feared that Damian would eventually sell him out. The mere possibility of it made his mind turn to hate and violence. If he were to exploit and betray me then I'd kill him. That's the only thing I'd kill for: the theft of my ideas and imagination. Alex believed more than anything that friends should never do business together.

On some nights when he did not feel like writing, Alex would scrutinize an old manuscript, rejected by numerous publishers and agents, for signs of mediocrity. Time and again he came to the conclusion that the work was well-crafted, meticulously revised and technically up to his own standards, which were lofty and devastating as much for himself as for others, though more so for himself. With some despair, he thought: if it were published and put on the shelf, then it would sell on its own merit. The fact that no one wanted his work wounded him. The books were his children; they represented both his reason and his fantasy. In their rejection he saw the negation of his own existence.

I have never been accepted, Alex thought. It was that lack of acceptance that wore on him and made him work harder until writing became a suicide mission. Sometimes, when he didn't have the will to write, he would tell himself: they will have to pry my cold dead hands from this keyboard; they will have to starve me, put out my eyes and beat my skull until I have no memory, to stop me. Now Alex wrote to appease the sickness and disenchantment in his soul. Publication was a secondary aim. He was racing to empty his mind of all the poison it contained. He wanted to spread that poison to contaminate the world, so people would understand what it meant to live: be it in misery or elation, lust or disgust.

Life was something Alex knew little about in practice. Because he wasn't really alive, and that was the problem. He was a dream projected onto a chair in a cold empty room from which he could not escape. Every day of his life he spent locked in the solitude of his mind. It was only the obsession that kept him from realizing the futility of his situation. Like anyone, he had to believe he was important; and like few, he was conscious that he was not. The only fear he had greater than death was that of losing his memory. And strangely, though he feared being rendered dumb, he did wish at times for ignorance.

Alex's obsession was obvious to everyone. One saw it in the way he studied people with razor eyes that sliced surgically through the fine layers of social adornment they had so carefully erected. Humanity was his subject of study and no one was spared dissection. Clearly, if he were not a writer, he would be a psychopath for his ability to stand outside of the emotions that made him human.

Damian was conscious of being on the outside looking in on Alex's world. It was clear that, though he suffered and was plagued by failure, writing was something that gave Alex's life meaning. On more than one occasion, Damian had noticed the glow in Alex's eyes after a particularly productive writing session. His gaze radiated elation; it was something you wanted to be a part of, understand, embrace and curl up in bed with at night as a talisman against weakness and fear. In those instances, Damian understood why Alex lived as he did, and he couldn't help but want a piece of that high for himself. It was in these moments that Damian believed Alex saw truth, and for that he was envious. When Alex was glowing and floating apart from everyone, it was Damian's consolation that Alex was a prisoner obliged to spend the majority of his waking hours teaching to pay the bills.

Deep down, Damian did not have the heart to find truth and teach it to others. It was not that he didn't believe it existed, but rather that whether it did or not, he was more concerned with comfort. Still, he wanted to find comfort doing something he enjoyed, and he could think of nothing more enjoyable than making movies. Though he would have preferred to be an actor, Damian planned to pursue his dreams of fame and fortune as a director and producer. But he knew he would never direct without a good story, and once again he found himself frustrated with Alex and his intransigence and elitism.

It was then that Damian decided, tossing and turning in his bed and watching the numbers increase in value on his bedside clock, that he would steal one of Alex's many manuscripts and use it to make a film. He told himself that he would give Alex credit as the writer; if it sold, he would give him a fair cut of the profits. Perhaps in that way Alex could be encouraged to future partnership. If Alex sees a little money, he's sure to change his tune. When we're both famous, drinking beer on the veranda of my villa overlooking the sea, he'll thank me for it. He'll owe it all to me. Damian's feelings for Alex swung from frustration and jealousy, to love and pity. He knew more than anyone of Alex's mixture of discipline, sensitivity and creativity. Those facets of Alex's personality were so strong that he suffered greatly for them in his obscurity. Alex suffered with the ignorant, with popular culture and in public life, yet he needed contact with society to produce his art. That was his dilemma.

Whenever Alex finished writing a book, he forgot about it. It didn't give him much joy to complete a project; he preferred the process to the result. There were times when he had written more than necessary so as not to face the emptiness between projects. But generally he had more projects, and ideas for projects, than time. He had forgotten more ideas than most people would have in their entire lives. If he didn't have to sleep, eat or teach, then he would have gladly spent every waking hour at the computer with an IV in his arm; he would learn to sleep-write and still he would not be able to cover all the wanderings and topics of his mind. He no longer felt the need to leave the house for material, especially with the internet handy to research anything that he didn't know through experience or hadn't heard first-hand. So, as his nature dictated, Alex continued the endless journey into his own mind, always wishing he could go farther and faster than his own words would take him.

It seemed that *Pax Americana* was a project of sufficient scope and ambition to keep him occupied yet certain that he would fail to say what was necessary to cover the subject properly. He couldn't imagine what he would do when he reached his goal of writing the perfect book, and for that reason he pushed on. Could it be that the high of a perfect book would be so strong that he would lose his mind? Could he lose his mind thinking so much? He didn't know. Sometimes Alex felt as if he weren't writing at all: as if the typing of his fingers was a primal reflex guided by the intuition of a higher power. When that happened, he would sink inside himself to a place of such bliss imagining that one day someone in the world might read his words and think: so that's how it is, amazing! It didn't matter if Alex ever met this person; just the possibility of such a thing happening was electrifying. The dancing fingers were a fight against the alienation, violence, injustice and lies that surrounded him. When Alex was writing strong and well, he felt a protective bubble close around him that left him impervious to attack. The words had power; they were myths and magic; they could create something from nothing, and to him they were reality.

Alex was usually the first up and showered, and that morning was no exception. When he left the bathroom Damian wished him a good day and stepped under the shower himself. In spite of a fitful night of discontented dreams, Damian was alert and excited. He showered quickly, dressed and went into Alex's room to find a suitable manuscript. A criminal feeling assailed him, and he worried about being caught. Even if he was discovered, no one could have guessed at his motives.

Damian pulled the cord for the closet light and stacked before him, like a granary or a vault, was all the wealth of Alex's mind.

Damian felt badly for what he was doing because he didn't approve of people going through or borrowing his personal belongings without his knowledge and permission. When he went away on business or a weekend trip, Damian often had the feeling that people were sleeping in his bed. The possibility of friends or strangers sleeping or screwing in his bed was infuriating, though perhaps exaggerated.

It was wrong of him to be in Alex's room digging through his manuscripts, but this was an exception. Instead of this stuff sitting and gathering dust, it could be put to good use, Damian thought. I'm sure I could make a film from one of these books.

Stacked in the closet were numerous manuscripts wrapped in brown paper and tied with string. To each mound of paper was attached a query letter describing briefly the plot of the work. This speeded up Damian's search, and in no time he found what he was looking for.

Inertia

by Alex Green

Martin Allen and Pedro Sotomayor first meet at a Latino community foundation where Martin works. Martin, the son of a corrupt and wealthy businessman, is ashamed of his privileged past and wishes to make a difference in society through social activism. Pedro is a first generation Mexican-American striving for the American Dream that Martin has rejected.

While helping Pedro find work, Martin learns about the human rights struggle in Chiapas, Mexico, Pedro's home state. Their friendship inspires Martin to head to the Mexican jungle to fight an armed struggle for indigenous rights. Meanwhile, Pedro takes Martin's advice and returns to school. He earns a business degree at the community college and becomes a manager at a factory employing primarily Mexican immigrants.

Pedro begins to question his success when he is told to fire a worker who is seriously injured on the job. Meanwhile, engaged in a hopeless struggle for justice in Mexico, Martin is forced to choose between his own life and that of the indigenous minority who see him as an outsider. "Inertia" explores the struggle of two men to improve their lives in spite of the negative forces of their past.

Light as a feather as usual, Alex, Damian thought. Paging through the manuscript, Damian realized that it would be relatively easy to film, and more importantly, it would be cheap. There were few locations, little or no special effects, and plenty of good dialogue. The characters were solid and the conflicts evident and capable of generating the necessary drama. It would serve nicely as a blueprint for Damian to edit to his needs.

Dialogue is undervalued, Damian thought. A good storyteller is worth his weight in gold at a party or anywhere else. Before books there were stories about the hunt or about gods who made the sun shine and brought rain to the crops. It's just like outdoor school when our counselor Skunkweed told us scary stories around the campfire about boys that went into the woods and never came back, and about the girl that drowned herself in the lake after she caught her boyfriend kissing another girl underneath Lover's Tree. Skunkweed told some good stories. The problem is people don't know how to communicate anymore.

Damian realized he had been sitting on the floor of the closet reading for nearly an hour. Julie startled him by peering in the doorway on her way to the bathroom. Their eyes met and Damian stood up abruptly, hit his head on a shelf and dropped the manuscript on the floor, where it came apart. He got on his knees and went about putting the pages in order. Julie did not offer to help.

"Sorry, Damian. I didn't mean to startle you. I just saw the light and Alex is usually at school by now . . ."

"Yeah, I was just looking for a manuscript. Alex was gonna send it in, and he wanted me to proof it for him, you know, to catch the typos. When you stare at your own work long enough you can't see the mistakes anymore. I couldn't remember which one he wanted me to take a look at, but now I think I've found it."

Why was he explaining himself to her? Julie didn't have a clue about Alex or his work and couldn't possibly know what Damian would want from it. She couldn't imagine the rivalry between the two young men and their frequent disagreements on art and commercialization.

"Is anyone in the bathroom? I hope Jack isn't in there. I hate waiting for the shower," Julie said.

Julie walked down the hall, and to her relief, the bathroom was unoccupied. She went in and stayed for the next hour and a half, showering and cutting and dying her hair in the sink. She felt a cold coming on. When she stepped on the scale, she noticed that she had lost several pounds. Also, she had been feeling weak, sometimes experiencing chills and fever dreams. Julie attributed her poor health to late nights, heavy drinking and the ecstasy that left her neck and jaw tight and achy the next day, though the night before she had been caught in the rain and gotten a chill that tore through her whole body.

All I need to do is take plenty of vitamins and drink lots of water. I sure would like to have some of mom's chicken soup. Julie remembered the times she had been sick as a kid and how safe she felt lying in her bed when her mother came to check on her and attend to her needs. Now when she was sick, Julie felt more alone and vulnerable than usual. Her housemates didn't bring her favorite magazines, sit on her bed and stroke her hair, or feed her. Even after she dyed her hair from black to red and cut it short, the girl inside felt terrible, and Julie started to cry. After a few minutes she wiped the tears away from her swollen eyes. She felt better. Men should cry more, she thought. That's why they're such assholes; they never give themselves any sympathy.

Damian decided to skip work. They weren't shooting until tomorrow anyway. He fired off an email to the office, piled his pillows against the wall and sat down to read the manuscript in its entirety. Shortly before Alex was expected home, he put it back in the closet where he had found it. The next day he would photocopy it at work so he could read in peace and set about translating it to script format. The novel was a great deal more complex than the film he intended to make. Damian planned to remove many of the subplots and concentrate mostly on the friendship between the two men and their mounting differences. As he saw it, like many relationships, the characters Martin and Pedro were separated by background, before growing together and then apart again based on ideology. It was to be a film that explored friendship, a subject that had always troubled Damian, since he had never felt particularly close to anyone. It was his opinion that people came and went. When people were useful and one could learn from them, there was friendship; when these same people held one back or grew dependent and needy, then one would have to remove them like a cancer.

It was Damian's curious position to be respected, yet without any close friends. If I got sick or failed them, they would all abandon me. You can never tell anyone your true thoughts because they will use them against you when convenient. Would he do the same? Damian tried not to ask himself such difficult questions. Philosophy did not interest him.

26

Sometime in the early evening Jack returned from The Green Lantern. Arnold was spared part of the bill for the mix up of herbs that caused Jack's unfortunate swelling. Though Jack had enough of a sense of humor not to be angry at the incident, he did regret leaving the massage parlor with his desires unfulfilled. The excitement of the day, and the love and friendship he had felt while in Arnold's company, soon faded when he was left alone with himself in his dark and gloomy bedroom. Outside a strong wind foreshadowed the coming storm. Jack was glad to be indoors. He lay down on the bed with his head underneath the covers in the fetal position.

Arnold had taken his picture again on the way home. Remembering, Jack got up and fished it from his coat pocket. He set the "before" and "after" photos side by side on his desk and compared them. They appeared like photos of two different people. Jack was alarmed by his derelict appearance in the "before" picture. He was once again conscious that he was not living a life that suited him; in the photo he appeared depressed and without hope. Jack realized that if he were to die in that moment, he would never discover his purpose in life. He thought of Arnold and his adventures, and the mysterious girl in the bedroom at the party. Am I a conservative, he wondered.

Was it true that he lived his life according to other people's standards? Was he afraid to stand apart from the group? He realized his college years had been lived in ignorance. The fraternity was ignorance incarnate. Then he had been nothing but a sheep; he was still that same sheep. He did not have the courage to be great: to stand on his own actions and opinions and to open himself to novel experience. It occurred to him that hypocrisy was present in all people, and that if a difference existed between what he did in his private and public life, then he was not free. I wonder how much smaller I can get? I am humbled and humiliated and alone. Jack hoped that he would hit definitive bottom soon, so that he could start to rebuild his life.

One morning, while still in bed, Jack heard the voices of his housemates from the kitchen. His name was mentioned several times and he could not help but listen. He lay there stiff and straining hoping that it would help his hearing. With the pessimism born of unemployment, he expected them to be slandering him.

"I don't know, Damian. I know the job market's tight, and God knows we've all been there when it comes to hard times and paying our dues, but I must say I have trouble being around him," Alex said. "He's negative, man. And this is coming from me. I'm supposed to be the negative one in this house. Next to Jack I feel like a bonafide Harikrishna. I just don't want to find out that he can't pay his rent and that we've gotta cover for him. He can't expect that of us."

"I don't understand it," Damian said. "Here's this good-looking, straight-talking, all-American guy who just folds when he has a little bad luck with work. It doesn't make sense to me. I mean Jack pulled Elizabeth; she's a hottie and sharp as a razor, and they were an item until she left the country. Sometimes I just want to shake the guy and tell him to snap out of it. Still, you can tell people whatever you want, but they have to deal with their own shit in their own way. I'm not gonna be anybody's keeper, moralizing or cracking the whip."

"Well, I think if he doesn't pull it together soon, maybe we should start looking for a new housemate," Alex said. "After I come home from work the last thing I wanna see is someone moping around and feeling sorry for themselves. I gotta bust my ass all day and then come home and write. I'm over living with uninspiring people. I want to live with people that have projects and interests and goals, not losers. Sometimes I feel like I'm in quicksand around here. And damn, where are my eggs? And yesterday it was the rest of my milk. One thing I hate is when other people eat my food. That ain't right. I want to make some eggs and now there aren't any. And where's my cheese?"

"Uh, I ate your cheese. I'll get you some more," Damian said.

"That's cool. Do you think I could borrow a couple of eggs?"

"It's all you. You don't need to borrow them, you can have them," Damian said.

Kick a man while he's down. I'll show you fuckers, Jack thought. He considered confronting them, rushing in on them and giving them a real piece of his mind. It hurt to hear them speak that way, but then he had never really felt a part of the house. It wasn't necessary for them to say it for Jack to know what they thought of him. Because he was poor, they didn't respect him. He was certain that Alex thought of him as a lower life form.

Jack was aware that he wasn't doing everything he could to find work. It seemed that he would have to go and work in a restaurant again, after all. It was beneath his dignity, but he didn't have a choice. As it stood, he couldn't cover rent and would have to ask for it from his folks. No, instead he would ask Arnold. Or he could get a job tomorrow and save for the next fifteen days and cover it. It would be tight, but he could do it.

Lying there, he knew that he would never forgive Alex for his harsh words. Those words had burned him, and Jack thought it extremely disrespectful for them to talk about him that way when they weren't sure if he could hear them or not. Now he would be unable to hide his resentment.

Then he thought: they're right. You're good-for-nothing. You're a loser. What's happened to you? You used to be strong and a hard worker, and now you huddle in your bed like a fetus in the womb afraid to face the world. What would Elizabeth say if she saw you now? You should be ashamed of yourself.

Fuck Alex. I wash his dishes every day and keep the kitchen clean, and he's extremely stingy and never gives anything to anyone. Remember the way he looked at you when you asked him for a beer, and how he cringed when you took it? He wanted every last beer for himself because if you drank it then it was wasted.

People never see their own faults, but only those of others, Jack thought. So just wash the dishes and keep your mouth shut and don't touch any of Alex's food again so he doesn't have that against you. Then maybe you won't get kicked out because you don't have anywhere to go.

Jack had many negative feelings about his housemates, though he had tried his best to put them aside. During the time he was hating them, Jack didn't stop to think that they might be having the same trouble with life. He was unable to trace back to the roots of their character to understand their problems and fears. In particular, he had never asked himself what was behind Damian's veneer of sociability and productivity. Damian made a thousand phone calls a day and never spent more than a few hours a night with anyone. He was always running. He had money but seldom time to sit down and enjoy his apparent success.

To Jack, Damian was the sort of person who was all talk and no action. Didn't he once tell you that he would look into getting you some work as an actor? Well, I wouldn't count on it. What's gotten into you to ask favors of and depend on other people, anyway?

Unfair treatment made Jack uncooperative; when his feelings were hurt, he preferred to suffer it alone. Of course they don't like living with you; you can't communicate, and when things piss you off, you just keep them bottled inside until you wanna burst. Back in college you got into more than your share of fights. Sure, you won most of them, but you were still fighting, and now you can't even remember what you were fighting for. You've never had anything to fight for until now. Now you have to fight for yourself or shoot yourself: those are your options. Shooting yourself is always going to be an option, so no hurry there. If you lose the great fight, the only fight that really matters, then you can shoot yourself. Thankfully, you're no romantic who would shoot himself over a girl or an ideal. Also, you've got parents and sister to think about. Suicide is nothing but self-pity, so put it out of your head.

The truth is you're a coward. I'm ashamed to be inside you and to have to see your face in the mirror everyday. What is life about when you can't even afford to take out a nice girl and get in bed with her? Don't you just long for a blow job where you can pull a girl's hair back and watch her mouth go up and down? No, don't think about that now. Better not to think about it if you can't have it.

Tomorrow you go find a job. I'm not gonna take any more of this shit from you. Lazy bastard. You deserve the good life every bit as much as all those grinning idiots you see on TV who contibute nothing to the betterment of the country, and who have forgetten the meaning of hard work in favor of personal vanity and popularity contests among their peers. That isn't a life, Jack thought. That's like that version of heaven with the angels and harps and nothing to do all day but sit around with your thumb in your ass. It's such idiotic, puerile visions that make religion the farce that it is. You'd think that people would have more imagination than to think in such polemics. Black and white, God and the Devil. Well, the world looks pretty goddamned gray from my perspective.

Jack couldn't imagine anything more disagreeable than being on display twenty-four seven like a peacock with no privacy whatsoever, while strangers, lacking a purpose in their own lives, formed opinions about him. Jack had never understood the cult of personality of the famous. When he was younger Jack had admired athletes, but never actors. He still admired businessmen, mostly for their power, but also because he believed they created products and services which bettered people's lives. Jack's admiration of the businessman was founded on a lack of understanding about the business world and the moral compromises that material success often demanded.

Jack was one of many Americans who believed that a good idea and hard work were enough to pave the way to success. God knew it took plenty of research, development and marketing to create a new product or service, but even a great idea couldn't be developed without the proper funding. Lacking both ideas and resources of his own, Jack thought a business degree would suitably prepare him for the world of commerce. It was a good choice because in his major he found men and women like himself who lacked the innate ability to buy low and sell high, create demand for new products and anticipate consumer preferences. For the majority of students, a business degree was a hoop to jump through on the way to a secure salaried desk job managing the business of others without a share in the profit. This was not to say that a business degree didn't teach one some useful skills, such as budgeting or accounting, but then these could be learned on one's own. Because "business" was the default degree for people without a purpose in life, Jack found the competition fierce when he set out to find entry-level work in the private sector. Like many, it had been his plan to gain a little experience before setting out on his own; and, like many, he probably would have become dependent on his paycheck and habituated to the comfort of a nine to five life. So perhaps it was for the best that Jack's initial efforts had failed, because now he was forced to use his wits to survive. While Jack understood that the only way to make money was to work for oneself, he had yet to ask himself the difficult question of whether he was the sort of person who could handle the risk and responsibility of being self-employed. He feared the answer to that question because he felt that those who couldn't, ought not to complain about serving others. As it stood, Jack was having enough trouble surviving on the margins of the capitalist paradise into which by chance he was born, to consider the bigger picture of his future.

Like the rest of his generation, Jack had hoped to make his money fast and retire early to enjoy the rest of his days in leisure. It was this dream of quick wealth that contributed to Jack's confusion about what advantages a formal education had to offer, and what, if any, his contribution to the world should be. But Jack did not have any power, capital or connections of his own, and it soon became clear that the dream was a lie that mocked the misery of his current reality. So like anyone living anyplace, Jack's thoughts, hopes and fears turned to himself and his near surroundings. Being idle was no good for anyone, and Jack realized that all the years he had worked in his father's shop, he had never felt hopeless or empty like he did now when he first started to chase the carrot of success.

27

It was only after Elizabeth arrived in Indonesia that she realized she was in over her head. Had it not been for Graham meeting her at the airport, she would have been completely overwhelmed. In spite of her reputation as a tough, independent woman, change scared her. But then she could not live her life in fear. Even if she was killed or died of some disease in that place, it was better than the meaninglessness of her existence in the city. The fear of the new and foreign was less than that of mediocrity, or as she told herself: better to die than be mediocre. Elizabeth was still unclear if she was afraid of being mediocre for what others would say, or for herself and her future. Sometimes she feared that it was the former, and that if she weren't so worried about other people's opinions, she would do nothing at all. Truthfully, she saw herself as a girl without ambition. Elizabeth was more aware than anyone of the contradictions between her public persona and her private mind.

None of us are what we seem, she reasoned. If anything we are the opposite of what we appear to be: the beautiful are often arrogant and shallow; the ugly -humble and kind; the rich are poor in friends, love and trust; the poor are rich in their solidarity. Yes, that's how the world is: for every advantage there's a liability.

Jakarta was a dirty city. Elizabeth hadn't expected otherwise, but it still came as a shock. All her senses were assaulted when she first stepped onto the street. As it was, both from lack of sleep and the company of the man she loved, she felt distant from the chaos, crowding and pollution. Jakarta was a modern capital with polished high-rises and major thoroughfares. It was the collusion of east and west that left the greatest impression. But then it was the nature of major cities to be cosmopolitan and have a face to the world; in that respect Jakarta was no different.

In their time apart, Graham had developed new lines in his face that Elizabeth attributed to the challenges of his new life. Graham was a renegade freelance photographer and reporter who had documented the struggle for indepedence in East Timor and the rioting that ignited Jakarta in the not so recent past. The lines in his cheeks and his forehead were products of fear and worry, and perhaps also a sign of hopelessness. In the two years that had passed since his departure from the city, Graham's eyes had acquired a new depth that she found alarming. They seemed to look through her and beyond her to oblivion. His smile was no longer warm and seductive, but that of a vicious rabid animal.

When they met at the airport, she half expected Graham to bite her, such was the expression on his face.

Graham didn't live in Jakarta. In so many words, he told her that the city had been too much for him. Graham referred to himself as a ruralist. It was his belief that mass migration to the cities provoked by industrialization had not provided opportunity for the rural peasants, but instead was responsible for the increase in poverty of the developing world. Over dinner, in an upscale part of town, he explained his views:

"It's clear to me, having traveled half the world, that a peasant is much better off with his own plot of land where he can grow what he needs and trade for what he wants from others. I don't believe man was ever meant to live in large cities. These cities are the product of economies of scale, which undermine the individual's autonomy and deprive him of his property and independence."

"But you do agree that many of the comforts we enjoy come from mass production? It sounds to me like you're arguing for a return to an agrarian society, but I think it's pretty clear that just isn't possible," Elizabeth said.

"Let's look carefully at what you say about comfort. Now let's be clear on this, a comfort is not a need, and too many people take their comforts for granted and refuse to live without them. The problem here is two-fold: first, individuals don't realize that much of what they have, they can do without; second, in order for goods to be affordable for the average consumer, the cost of production must be sufficiently low. Since one of the greatest expenses of any business is labor, it's not hard to see that for certain groups to live in comfort, many must work at or below subsistence wages to supply the demand."

Elizabeth hadn't intended to involve herself in a political or economic discussion so soon after her arrival. Though she was aware of

Graham's obsession with such matters, she would have preferred that he make love to her. Nevertheless, she did her best to promote the discussion, with the though that it had likely been a long time since he had been able to talk freely with someone he trusted and respected.

"Well, if what you say is true, then why don't the peasants go back to living as they did before?"

"It's a lot more complicated than I've made out. Many of the peasants were working on large farms and didn't own their own land. It's not surprising that they came to the conclusion that life in the city couldn't be much worse and was probably better. Only after they arrive do they realize that the prosperity the city promises is largely an illusion. The more I learn about life, the more I realize that we are trapped by our illusions and that we must struggle to be rid of them. Once I had an illusion about being an international journalist; it seemed like a romantic life, and I imagined it would be tremendously rewarding. I'm not saying it isn't, but the truth is as a journalist you have to enter the most terrible hellholes on the planet and see humanity at its worst. You have to live under the constant strain of death. I've seen horrible things, and there's no romance in that."

"Have you ever thought about doing something else? Maybe you need a rest, Graham. You can't save the world alone and getting yourself killed is no solution."

"I can't quit. In a way I'm attracted to the horror. I seek it out and I'm not sure why. Please don't tell me it's because my mother didn't love me enough, that I don't feel I'm worthy of an ordinary life or that it's because I'm trying to prove my manhood. I'm a great lover of peace and life, and through my work I try to understand what brings people to commit horrible acts against each other. I suppose there's no explanation as to why people can't get along, but I still keep looking for the answers somewhere in the misery."

"I think that without someone to document injustice, it would continue to occur unchecked," Elizabeth said. "By bringing reality to people's attention, those same comfortable people you've mentioned before that have never known violence or injustice, you open their eyes to something greater than themselves. The jury's out on whether or not they'll do anything about it."

"For images to have any resonance they have to be presented in a sociopolitical context and not just as proof of the general horror of the human condition," Graham said. "No one can really identify with faceless peasants piled into a mass grave, though they may be fascinated by the sight of it. Unfortunately, people are obsessed with violence. Death is a common heritage, but there is a great difference between facing your own death for speaking out against a corrupt government, for example, and watching someone get gunned down cold and clean in an action film. The latter is pure romance, and perhaps romance is the product of alienation and passivity, I don't know."

Graham had no illusions about his character. He was abrasive, opinionated, stubborn, negative and cynical. He hadn't always been that way; it was learned behavior that he preferred to good humor, which he could no longer justify given what he had seen. In a way, he had tried to incorporate the misery of the world as a penance for his upbringing in a well-to-do wine growing family in Napa Valley. If he had wanted to, he could have learned the art and business of viticulture, but something, perhaps boredom or an overactive imagination, had driven him far away from his home and his loved ones.

Seeing Elizabeth again moved him. With her, Graham felt free to release all his bitter sentiments about the condition of the world. He respected Elizabeth as his intellectual equal, though he believed she lacked the courage to completely separate herself from comfort. Over the last few years he had made countless appeals for her to join him so they could live out their lives in exile. He didn't intend to return to the United States for anything other than business. He had purchased a small plot of land on the outskirts of Padang, on the island of Sumatra, where he had built his house and cultivated a garden. In the end, he had resigned himself to the fact that Elizabeth would not be coming. She was too comfortable with the pseudo-hip, cosmopolitan lifestyle of the city to be drawn away to some third world outpost.

In the last few months Graham had gotten familiar with a local village girl. She was his student, and he often gave her a lift home from the university where he taught English between assignments. Soon it became clear that the girl was very much in love with him. She was young, and he was reluctant to take advantage of her. After all, wasn't he her teacher and mentor? With time, however, Graham's isolation, and her beauty and favorable disposition, got the better of him, and he seduced her. Though he told himself it was a one-time affair, Graham found it so agreeable that it became habit. All the while, he couldn't rid himself of the image of fat Europeans, Australians and Americans with their young whores -male and female- in Thailand. He had done an exposé on the sex trade there and now was he any better? He had very little in common with the girl beyond desire, but then he had never had an easy time with women, and certainly not in a Muslim nation where they were hopelessly off limits.

Perhaps a month after the start of his relationship with Merpati, he received a letter from Elizabeth announcing her plans to come to Indonesia to live. She confessed to being unemployed and generally unhappy with her life in the city. Could he find her some work at the university as a part-time English teacher?

The novelty of Elizabeth's arrival overshadowed the dilemma of his lover. Elizabeth was as she had always been, and Graham was pleased at the prospect of her coming to live with him. But what would she do when she came home and found Merpati, who now worked for him as a live-in maid to facilitate their affair and quell the suspicions of her family? Elizabeth was a sharp girl and she was bound to figure it out.

With their love affair rekindled, the couple spent a few leisurely days in Jakarta sightseeing, eating and relaxing. Graham wanted to make sure Elizabeth was rested before they journeyed to Padang. It had been Graham's idea that they take the ferry to Sumatra and then travel overland so Elizabeth could appreciate the beauty of the countryside outside of the congested capital. What surprised Elizabeth, however, was that Graham had opted to take the bus.

"Wouldn't it be better to rent a car? That way we could have more privacy and we could stop wherever we want and see things we otherwise might not see."

While Graham agreed that to have private car was the most convenient, he explained his decision.

"Driving here is not like back home. There aren't really any traffic rules. There's certain flow to traffic, and if it gets interrupted, then bad things happen. Worse things happen if you are a foreigner and you interrupt the flow of traffic. Here they have no tolerance. For most Indonesians life is difficult, and they don't need any further inconvenience. When someone needs to get to work, they need to get to work, and there are no excuses. You can see that between the buses, taxis, *bajaj*, motorcycles, private cars and trucks, there is little room for error. Pedestrians, for example, avoid crossing the road indiscriminately. Cars don't stop for pedestrians."

"I'm sure it can't be as serious as you make it out to be," Elizabeth said. "You make it seem as if driving here were some sort of life-threatening, chaotic activity. There must be some sort of order to it like anywhere else."

"They don't recommend that foreigners drive in Indonesia and won't insure you if you do. If you cause an accident or kill someone, then you're in serious danger. If you're injured, you'll find that even with a very good private insurance policy, you won't find good and readily available medical care.

"I don't consider myself a bad driver. I've even bought a car to make my commute to the university. But then I live in a relatively unpopulated area, and when I go to the city, I leave my car on the outskirts so I don't have to deal with the tremendous congestion."

"If you want, I'll drive," Elizabeth said. "I've studied the map and I'm sure we'll be fine once we get over to Sumatra."

"I know you're not afraid of anything, and I shouldn't have talked it up or talked down to you. I know you've jumped out of planes and climbed the Golden Gate Bridge. I know you're a courageous girl, but this is different. Indonesians are a very generous and relaxed people, but not when you make them upset. Let me tell you a story that I hope will change your mind.

"Once there was a woman traveling by car somewhere in a neighboring city near Jakarta. She was the wife of a U.S. State Department employee and she was sightseeing with her six-year-old daughter. As she was driving through a village, a local woman was crossing the street with her son. Perhaps the American was driving too fast. Or maybe it was a blind corner. Whatever the reason, she ran down the boy, who was about the age of her daughter. He died instantly. The American woman stopped the car uncertain of what to do. One can only imagine the thoughts running through her mind: if only I had been paying more attention; if only I had watched the road and not the landscape; if only I had slowed down in the village. But by then it was too late.

"In the United States, such an event, running over a child on a suburban street, would have resulted in the suspension of one's license and a prison term. But in that village far away from American law and custom, justice was exacted differently. Instead of driving away as fast as possible, like she should have, the woman sat in the car in shock over the event. Meanwhile, the local woman gathered her dead child in her arms. Her wailing was interrupted only by angry gestures and curses. Though the American woman couldn't understand her, certainly she sensed the meaning of those words. A number of villagers, some of them bystanders and others drawn in by the commotion, had gathered in the street. The crowd fed on itself and soon it wasn't satisfied to curse and shout any longer. The American woman found her car surrounded by bodies and could hear fists pounding on the roof. Then her back window was smashed in. The crowd was maybe fifty strong now, and she was walled in on all sides. Though it probably crossed her mind, she could not have run them over. Perhaps she realized she was going to be killed.

Understanding the gravity of the situation, her daughter began to cry and cling to her mother in desperation. When the hands reached in to pull the girl away, both mother and daughter were screaming hysterically, much as the Indonesian woman had, holding her dead son. Then the crowd threw the girl on the ground and beat and kicked her until she was dead. After spitting on the foreigner, pulling her hair and cursing her, the crowd dispersed just as quickly as it had formed. The mother was then left to drive home, smashed windows, dents and all, short one daughter but with her life intact."

At the end of his monologue, Graham took the opportunity to finish his whiskey.

"How did you hear about this," Elizabeth asked. "It's absolutely horrible. Get that smirk off your face. How can you possibly smile at that? It makes my stomach turn. How could a group of men and women do that to a little girl? I'll bet you just made it up to shock me."

"One of my students told me the story," Graham said. "Also, it appeared in the paper. Maybe I've embellished it a bit, but the facts are that the American woman killed an Indonesian boy and then her own daughter was killed by a mob. There was never any court case and no one was found guilty of anything. That's a pretty efficient justice system, if you ask me. In many ways, I can see how it's much more humane than putting an innocent man on death row. Also, it's relatively guilt free. The American need not feel guilty about the boy, and the crowd need not feel guilty about its justice. After all, they stopped short of killing the woman. That would have been unfair. As for my smile, I don't think I'm the only one amused by death. Death is something to be mocked. You can cry about it or you can laugh. I choose to laugh. Only by laughing can you strip death of its power and make life viable in tragedy."

"You like to shock, but you're a coward like everyone else," Elizabeth said in irritation.

"Yes, I suppose I am," he said. "I don't like pain. If tortured, I would betray my own mother. You know, what surprises me most about the violence and death I've photographed is the fearlessness of people when they're fighting for their rights. I don't have anything that I believe in that strongly. I have been very lucky not to be hurt or killed in my work. Heck, I haven't even been jailed. I have this recurring nightmare where I am shot to death by a group of soldiers. I place great faith in this dream and believe that is how I will die. I'm not sure what I'll feel when I'm in such a situation. I'm sure the fear will be enormous, but then it will all be over. After death, those feelings won't matter anymore."

She studied his face. Does he really believe that or is it just talk? Elizabeth did not believe in fate. The path her life had taken was the result of the decisions she had made. She had come to Indonesia in order to give her relationship with Graham a second chance. She had become increasingly unhappy with her life in the city, and Indonesia seemed to offer the change she was looking for. She though that only by separating herself from the familiar could she grow as person. Though she did not like to depend on or place too much trust in others, she felt that Graham was the only one who understood her situation, and who could help her discover her purpose in life. And now here he was talking about his own premature death as if it were a foregone conclusion. I don't want him to die that way. But then if a man continues to put himself in the path of danger, he can only expect misfortune. She knew why he was doing it. They both possessed a great fear of mediocrity, and for Graham danger was an escape. He could be great by documenting the horrors of life, certain that it was a path few people would follow. Elizabeth wondered how it might feel to court danger in such a way, and she entertained the idea of joining Graham on his next assignment.

"I think it's a self-fulfilling prophecy. I think you want to die but don't have the courage to kill yourself. You want to be murdered," she said.

"That's nonsense," he replied, laughing. "You're talking the most absolute nonsense."

Graham felt a warmth rush through him. Elizabeth was beautiful and true, and he wondered what would come of her visit. I will enjoy it for what it is. Everything comes and goes, and when it doesn't work anymore, it's time to move on. I don't want it to work out. If everything worked out, then what would you have to be upset about? You like being upset. You like to be angry at the world, and see how you've mellowed since Merpati has come to live with you? You've even turned down assignments for her. You were always scared of the work, but now the fear is getting the better of you; you have the softness and love of a woman to thank for that.

Two women can only mean trouble. Elizabeth's a straight-talker and perhaps you should confess, though really it's none of her business. But then you're afraid she won't fuck you if you tell her. No better wait until she fucks you. You don't have to tell her until the end of the trip. We'll take our time in getting back to Padang. You don't love Merpati anyway. It's Merpati that you have to talk to. She's the one that won't understand. You don't understand her and she won't understand. No one understands.

"How about some dessert," Graham said, to change the subject. He felt Elizabeth come close to a place he had no control over, which revealed itself when he drank: like the time he had been in the car with Merpati and had forced himself on her. Had she wanted to then? Was she really encouraging? Did she have any feelings for him at all, or was it just personal vanity?

They ate rice pudding and drank sweet Indonesian coffee to help the digestion. They took to the streets, and Graham put his arm around Elizabeth. The whiskey made him feel optimistic about the city and excited about the night with all its lights and bustle. This was the good life. He had decided to splurge for a fine Western-style hotel with a view of the main avenue. The city was hopeful now that he had the protection of a familiar face. He remembered when he had first arrived there alone. He thought of the many places he had gone alone and how every face seemed sinister then.

They wandered along the busy avenue and hailed a *bajaj*. They sat in the back under the plastic canopy and listened to the whine of the tiny motor of the three-wheeled vehicle. Graham preferred *bajaj* to buses for getting around in the city. He liked to smell and hear the street and feel the wind in his face as he traveled.

They cruised the city for hours like that, hitching a ride whenever they were tired: from cafes to busy pedestrian streets; from Western-style outdoor malls to the quiet tree-lined avenues of wealthy neighborhoods. The city architecture was a mixture of sleek skyscrapers of glass and steel, offices and residences in the Dutch colonial style, *kampung* slums and modernist buildings, including the Istiqlal mosque.

In that teeming city, like in the jungles surrounding it, the inhabitants had to be resourceful to find their niche. Because of its favorable climate, life in the tropics was abundant and diverse, but it was also competitive and cruel, as individuals and groups competed with each other for space and resources. In such a place, people lived within the limitations and challenges of their environment, without needing to isolate themselves from it.

Elizabeth's mind wandered to Alaska, Siberia, Greenland and other northern latitudes. She thought of the absence of parasites and viruses in such places during the winter. If it was cold enough, it was impossible for a person to catch a cold. That was sterility. Sterility has never been a positive condition, so why was it a goal for modern Western society? Suburbia, gated communities, golf courses, cosmetics, fast food, chat rooms, chain stores, video games, pesticides, pharmaceuticals: all of that is death. Homogenization is not progress, it's a liability, though it may seem safer and easier to manage in the short term. All I know is the equator is where it's at for humanity. Give me some natural abundance, even if it's dangerous, in favor of artificial comfort.

They drove through Thamrin-Sudirman, the main artery of that bustling city, and watched the blur of lights as the traffic flowed like easy electric blood. It must look different by day, she thought. The night hides mystery, the lights cover up the sores, and the empty and forgotten places. Aside from the humidity, Elizabeth found the pollution, traffic and sprawl of the city familiar and reassuring because it reminded her of L.A. Still, she looked forward to discovering a new environment outside of the city, which, with any luck, would change her from the person she was and had grown to dislike in the recent past.

Ultimately, Elizabeth's impression of Jakarta was favorable, especially after their wonderful meal and the calm and ease of her host and lover. The thick humid air felt good on her skin as their driver negotiated the traffic that merged and divided to fit the mutations and curves of the road. In spite of the chaos, there was an order to the city; it was alive and unique, and Elizabeth felt glad to be there and secure in the back seat with Graham's arm around her, while they traveled through the night, oblivious of their destination.

28

He was going to rise and shine like a rock star and bring his message of truth to the people. It was only music that could speak truth, because it was deeper than reason. Alex may have thought himself to be the bearer of truth, but he was wrong. Henrik believed more than anything that it was a mistake to place too much value on human reason. I have my proof, he told himself. Alex has nothing but his words to create meaning, but those words separate him from life. Music is the collective; it is a universal vision compared to the subjective bias of writing and film.

Don't try to analyze it because you can't and it's a trap. Alex's trap. What your music means to you is totally different from how it's perceived by others. It's not like a camera with a frame or a novel with an argument. When you were in school all you wanted was to get away from that analytical cause and effect empirical thinking. What a shame your dad forced you to waste two years of your life in business school. The last thing you want to do is analyze anything. You want to reach right to emotion and tap into people's hearts.

Henrik had been studying music for some time now, particularly music related to religious ceremony wherein the devout reached a higher consciousness through music and dance. He was a lover of gospel, soul and the blues. He was in regular attendance at a black church in the Fillmore where the pastor preached in song to the melody of the organ as he sheparded his faithful to group catharsis. Time and again, Henrik watched the faithful rise from their seats and break into song metered by exuberant clapping. He was sure that they possessed a secret truth beyond the scope of his own reason. It mattered little what was sung, or if it made sense, because they were all connected then, not in words, but through rhythm and melody. It was not unusual for women and men alike to faint from overexertion as they sang and danced and clapped.

Once he had gone to speak to the preacher after his sermon. The man had so exhausted himself that he didn't have the energy to reply to Henrik's questions. Instead, he stood there glassy-eyed and absent, before gathering his things and stumbling to the exit. The parishioners didn't seem bothered by his abrupt disappearance; he had taken them to a sacred place and for that they were grateful.

To Henrik, these ceremonies were a mystery. He always felt like an interloper while in attendance, though he was a familiar face and often exchanged pleasantries with the other churchgoers. Certainly, with his strange appearance, he had drawn some attention. But then those people were polite enough not to stare; mostly they were oblivious to his presence, absorbed as they were in their religious fervor.

This sort of church has nothing to do with God, Henrik thought. Or rather, they've discovered that God is only rhythm and melody and doesn't belong to anyone in particular. The black church in America has fused Christianity with something pure and primal. Its strength is founded on tribal custom and continues today.

Henrik was not a casual observer. He sat in the back row with a digital recorder and microphone in his shoulder bag documenting each sermon. Later he would take these samples home, load them onto the computer and search for patterns in the graphs. He was convinced that there were certain frequencies of melody and patterns of rhythm that, when combined, would invariably bring the listener to a higher consciousness. He felt no guilt at recording these sermons and using them for his own purposes. Trance, as a religious and cultural practice, was not confined to one group of people, though certainly the salient examples were found primarily in the developing world where Western-style capitalism had yet to erase the past. Industrialization had forced the developed world to ignore, bury and forget their cultural and spiritual roots in place of economic progress. Modern society all too frequently dismissed these roots that connected man to both his community and his environment, Henrik thought. Modernity limited man's spirituality, causing people to lose touch with the meaning and purpose of their lives.

Henrik believed that religion was not morality or custom, which divided people; but music, which in its pure form promoted solidarity.

Music was fundamental to human society since its origin. It was practiced by every race, nation and creed, but in most places that music had lost its connection to the human spirit. It is a luxury more valuable than diamonds to be set free by music, Henrik thought.

Henrik had devised a theory that popular music in its basic form primarily reflected a society's morality, customs and cultural bias. In the intermediate stage, music was used to advance a political message that challenged the status quo. In advanced forms, music not only brought people away from ritual practice and religious custom, but also their reason. A song might be part of a ritual with clearly defined lyrics and choreographed steps before expanding into convulsive chaos with no boundaries or rules beyond the physical capabilities of the body.

Henrik saw religion in music and wanted to make music to free people from the jail of their reason. In primitive societies music was used to communicate with the gods; it was the primary path to a higher consciousness beyond primal needs. The collective act of making music brought individuals together and broke the suspicious silence between them. It was and remains the most direct way to communicate the joys and pains of living. How could these sentiments be shared in the modern world where music was a commodity to be enjoyed passively in isolated venues? How could people reconnect with their spirituality if they could no longer create music together and channel their emotions in collective dance?

It should be humanity's primary goal to seek nirvana, Henrik reasoned. When religion diverged from paganism, the musical paths to our spirituality were lost. Forever after, music was forced to serve the demands of religious ideology, as much in the call to prayer of the muezzin or in a Christian hymn. Rhythm and melody became nothing more than a background for the oral repetition of religious texts. The majority of the world's major monotheistic religions chose to venerate reason and pass shame down to the body. In this way, man was logically blocked from attaining higher consciousness through the body's free and uninhibited movement in dance. The brain put chains on all the sensory organs it depended on for information. And when the brain misbehaved, it invariably claimed to have lost control of its subjects. Nonsense, Henrik thought. Even the mind depends on the steady rhythm of the heartbeat. Henrik knew that in order to find the path back to spiritual enlightenment he need look no farther than the pulse inside his own chest.

In Henrik's opinion, organized religion was nothing more than a clever invention of the mind to legislate and moralize the activities of man. Slowly but surely, man's ability to dance his world and feel a part of it, as opposed to an individual apart, was lost. Clearly, man's disrespect for his environment and his fellow human beings was a sign of his inability to feel in the simple way that skin feels heat or the eye perceives light. Henrik did not consider it naive to say that when people danced they forget their differences, their worries and fears, as well as their own humanity, given that humanity had been irretrievably polluted by the moralizing of religion. Not even the Buddhists got it right, he thought. It's not about eliminating desire through the rational effort of forgetting. And what do the Taoists say about non-action? Yet even in non-action there is intellectual discipline and choice. There's a time when the individual must be free from even the pressures of choice.

In his quest for the roots of trance, Henrik studied Candomblé, Umbanda, Voudon and Santería. These syncretic religions had combined animist traditions of African origin with Christianity. Henrik found that in spite of different gods, rituals, and ideology, music played an important role in all forms of worship in bringing individuals into a trance state. From his research he made two conclusions: first, that naming and ritual were not essential to inducing trance; and second, that religions which failed to catalyze a higher consciousness beyond body and mind were incapable of freeing humanity from its earthly limitations. The examples were too many and too varied to disabuse his thesis.

Henrik realized that it was a revolutionary time for humanity; technology had advanced to the stage that one could research and preserve basic trance rhythms and melodies; furthermore, these rhythms could be manipulated and enhanced in such a way that it might be possible to put a man immediately into a trance with the right musical formula. The applications of such a formula were limitless. Extensive studies had been undertaken to prove the curative effects of music on patients suffering from various types of mental illness. No doubt frequencies could be developed for curing the mentally disabled; music could be used to hypnotize psychiatry patients and connect them to the subconscious that had oppressed them for so long. Ordinary people could be freed from daily stress by floating in a state of bliss for as long as they pleased. People could be cured of their inhibitions through trance therapy.

Sometimes Henrik wondered if he wasn't playing God when he manipulated sound files on the computer. He recorded all manner of ambient noise including city traffic, ocean waves, construction machinery and eggs frying in a pan; in addition, he dubbed television and film dialogue, and the conversations of his housemates and strangers in public. Who knew what combination of sound could be useful in triggering the powerful emotions of memory.

Henrik attended as many concerts as his free time and money would allow, sneaking in his recorder and bringing home the new data to add to his compositions. Live music was important because it allowed him to gauge how the crowd reacted to imperfections and improvisation in the music. Much of it was of inferior quality, but he soon realized that even with this inferior music there were moments when the musicians and the crowd fed off of each other until the music and dancing bodies moved as one. During such moments, he would take extensive notes on crowd size, logistics, decibel levels, equipment, etc. Ultimately, it was improvisation more than technical mastery that transformed a band into the spiritual guide that would liberate the crowd.

Henrik was assailed with doubt. Was it possible to capture this feeling and reproduce it artificially? The fear that trance states had to be produced and enjoyed live, in the collective, prevented a good night's sleep. Sometimes Henrik would be found pacing the floor of his room even before Alex got up for work, chain smoking and yellow from lack of sun and sleep. Perhaps in our individualism we have cut ourselves off from the joy of the infinite, he thought.

One sleepless night, it occurred to Henrik that to enter into a trance, a person needed to be removed from their natural environment. In clubs this effect was created by the flashing lights, dark corners and unusual decor, which encouraged people to behave differently then they would, say, in the office or in public where their freedoms were restricted. Crowd dynamics allowed the more timid to feed off the more daring and provided a certain level of anonymity not available at home with friends or family, or at work with colleagues. Live music was rough and imperfect and always different. Maybe that was the missing element in trance? Modern electronica was overproduced; perhaps an element of randomness, a slight margin of error, or a progressive alteration in tempo, pitch or tone was necessary to trigger euphoria? Even the traditional African drumming of various nations and tribes, while observing set patterns, constantly evolved with the mood of the musicians and the response of the dancers.

Soon Henrik began to record and sample only acoustic instruments and organic sound. He did not use standard equipment or computer-generated beats. Instead, he manipulated his real-life samples with homemade synthesizers containing built-in imperfections, which guaranteed that no two recordings were alike.

Equally important to his work was the human voice. Chanting was an important part of traditional trance rituals. He preferred the collective chants and call and response of tribal ceremonies, drawing much of his inspiration from Native American, Amerindian and African traditions. He realized that in many rituals the words were repeated enough so that rhythm eventually superceded meaning. Often he would isolate individual words and word fragments and manipulate them until they were unrecognizable from their linguistic source and cognitive meaning.

The task of creating music overwhelmed him, but Henrik didn't see value in anything else. His project dwarfed all other life concerns. It was his intention to create an audio bible that would allow people to connect with a higher consciousness. Nevertheless, he questioned his own intentions. How could a human being create something from his own emotions and reason that would take man beyond his humanity? But then Henrik really wasn't creating anything new. Man never actually created anything new. All his invention was nothing but a manipulation and restructuring of the biological world. Man depended on his environment just as any other living organism, and it was his great deception to use technology to create a barrier from biology that he labeled civilization.

Henrik was looking ahead and bore no illusions about returning to a more primitive past. He wanted to take what was useful from the past and mix it with the sound of modernity, in hope of bringing humanity some enlightenment in its journey. Of one fact he was certain: man was alienated from himself and his fellow human beings. He avoided free and spontaneous expression of emotion out of fear of being judged and ridiculed by conformists and the ignorant. In the modern industrialized world, dance was the unwitting victim of these fears.

Henrik had read much on the subject of dance and its importance in various cultures. In traditional Indonesian culture, certain gifted boys were raised from an early age to be dancers. Their bodies were trained to channel their emotions. They were taught how to express themselves with a rapid blinking of the eye or an abrupt turn of the head. Without words, they could communicate their innermost passions. Such children hadn't been taught that dancing was shameful or frivolous. Instead, they were the caretakers of tradition: each contributing their own character to preserve and further a universal and ancient form of expression.

Mostly, Henrik was interested in how men, mainly in Europe, North America and Oceania, had been estranged from such a form of self-expression. In his home country, Sweden, the men did not dance unless very drunk and then only in a clumsy and awkward way. Sweden was reputed for its sexually liberated and progressive-minded population, yet when it came time to dance, his countrymen were so uncomfortable in their own bodies that they looked like corpses put there on the dance floor to be shifted about by invisible strings. They danced much like a child would make an action figure dance. Henrik was embarrassed to belong to such an awkward people. He believed that there was an inverse correlation between suicide rates and dancing. Sweden, along with Norway and Finland, had the highest suicide rates in the world per capita, while dancing nations such as Brazil, Cuba or Venezuela barely figured on the list, despite their great poverty and social inequities. Certainly suicide had much to do with the weather, and perhaps even the boredom that came with living in a welfare state, but to Henrik both of these factors seemed a good excuse to dance. When the weather was bad, one could dance away their troubles, and in Scandinavia the troubles were less because of a supportive social network that made sure no one would go hungry. So why weren't people dancing?

The first time he went to Italy, Henrik was shocked to find that Italians didn't dance either. Reputed to be a vivacious, hot-blooded people, he was startled to find that Italian women were some of the least coordinated, most unnatural women he had ever met. They weren't even comfortable walking on the street. When he went to the discos, he had to keep from laughing at the strange attempts that Italians made at dancing. Italy, he learned after a semester exchange, was an extremely rigid superficial society. By concentrating so much on appearance, Italians had forgotten to be comfortable with their bodies. Italian woman, with some exceptions, were content to stand around on the dance floor and inspect each other's shoes and handbags amidst the pulsing music, while Henrik could think of nothing but sex and writhing his body about like a snake. In Italy, the women preferred to be objectified, instead of enjoying the freedom of their bodies, and for that reason it was not a country to visit. What a shame then that Italian women were so beautiful.

In most countries in Europe women danced for fun, and the men did so to meet women, but only reluctantly and after a few beers. In Spain, the stereotype of the Spanish lover didn't hold water. Gypsies aside, Spaniards couldn't dance.

When he was younger, Henrik would often vacation with his family in Malaga. He remembered one incident when he and a friend had gone dancing at the local disco. After a few minutes, they noticed the Spaniards imitating them. As a joke, they started to make ridiculous movements on the dance floor, and even these moves the Spaniards copied for lack of their own. Still, despite his judgments, Henrik did not wish to exclude that suave group of Spanish men who danced *Sevillanas* in the cozy bodegas with their proud black-haired women; to them he would tip his hat and give the most solemn bow. Those were men and women he admired.

In Japan, they did things differently. They turned dancing into a video game. In that way it was possible to compete and determine a winner. Once again his theory held true. Japan suffered from a high suicide rate and not enough dancing.

In the United States men were so afraid of embarrassing themselves dancing that women could only coax them onto the dance floor by bending over and allowing themselves to be dry humped. In the United States "freaking," or that blatant pantomime fucking with no formal steps or artistry, was dancing; American men only engaged in it when very drunk, that is, when they were no longer in control or even conscious of their actions. Not surprising then that American women were so receptive to the hip-shaking precision and confidence of Latino men, heirs to a different tradition.

For the most part, American men weren't comfortable with their bodies, except perhaps black Americans who somehow had preserved that connection. American men were concerned with being tough and independent and wouldn't permit themselves any measure of grace, refinement or sensuality because such traits had somehow been identified with women, or homosexuality. Well, that certainly wasn't the case in the Middle East where men as well as women belly-danced.

But now a new culture was sweeping over the Western world. It was dance culture: a product of the comfortable middle class in Europe that had grown tired of philosophy and tradition and had chosen electronic music as its messiah and savior. Because the history of Europe and the United States was one of religious shame and existential crisis, those postmodern youths needed to follow the messiah through designer drugs. Hedonism was the most direct route to the new god. The young and hip of the middle and upper classes of Europe, the Americas, Japan, Oceania and developing world capitals were simply dancing away from the disintegrating and increasingly inhospitable world of their parents. From the bleak, white expanse of the Arctic Circle, where the summer sun never set, to secluded islands in Southeast Asia, the young gathered in endless rave parties to escape from themselves and a world they disliked but were too lazy to change.

Henrik had been there, and now, more than ever, he was aware that such a lifestyle represented the future. DJs were being elevated to the elite of society. They were superstars, and the best of them, the ones with the greatest congregations, made as much as the professional class. Ideology could not feed or satisfy a man forever, and Henrik was certain that the next viable faith existed only in music. The subculture was increasingly more connected; it had its own independent values and existed globally through internet radio and a network that linked clubs and events live via satellite. It no longer mattered that the participants were separated by race, geography, political affiliation, color or creed. The electronic revolution had done more for international relations and the promotion of democracy than a whole century of nation-state diplomacy.

More than anything, Henrik longed to play his music on seven continents simultaneously to giant stadiums packed with all manner of people. It didn't bother him one bit that rave culture was elitist and yet another stage of Western imperialism that was eroding traditional values, fracturing and warping language, and cutting people off from their origins.

Still, what was the use of diverse musical traditions if they couldn't be sampled and combined to produce a unique vision for the future? Was electronica unifying the world or rendering it unintelligible? Was it simply another tool for economic advancement? Sure, Henrik wanted to make money as a top DJ, but he also believed that good electronica should be free for everyone, as music had always been free for whoever had the talent to produce it. There is no turning back now. Everything that is organic will be copied and reproduced artificially, and that goes for music as well as human biology. We must learn to find what is original inside us through artificial means, Henrik thought. There is no other way.

29

Julie wasn't feeling well at all. She had missed the last week of school, and when she went to the doctor, she discovered she had the flu. All week she had ordered take-out from Phuket, a local Thai restaurant. She ate soup and spent her time watching old black and white movies starring the strong-minded actresses of Hollywood in its heyday. Her favorite films were set in the twenties during prohibition when women cut their hair short and behaved like men. She admired the femme fatales of a bygone era: the iconic women with their sharp wit, poise and grace. She wished that she, too, could dominate men and bend them to her will like she had seen in the movies. But times had changed; there weren't any female role models to look up to anymore in the movies.

One afternoon of her convalescence she collected the mail, one of the few activities that broke the monotony of the day, and found an envelope from the Women's Health Center. A few weeks before she had been diagnosed with herpes. Given her sexual history, the doctor had suggested a blood test to check for HIV. Now she held the envelope with the results of her test. She hadn't wanted to get tested. She thought: if I really have HIV, isn't it better not to know? She was mature enough to realize that to avoid testing was irresponsible and dangerous. Well, you're going to have to open it sooner or later. Don't be a coward. So she opened the letter and it was confirmed: her death sentence printed out and delivered to her door with the morning mail.

On TV, the heroine continued smoking her cigarette while ignoring the attentions of her handsome suitor. Julie couldn't bear to watch any longer. It couldn't have been further from her own reality. From one minute to the next, her life had been turned completely upside down.

She felt sick like she could vomit, and nearly urinated from fear, before becoming angry with herself and her own stupidity. Hatred gripped her at the thought of Henrik and his hedonistic lifestyle, which had proven irresistible. She hated her father for how she had been forced to rebel at the planning of her life. She felt miserable then and started to cry, and strangely that misery was something that she didn't want to let go. It was all she had besides defeat and oblivion. She could spend a thousand days bedridden or maimed, she could be blind or ugly, it didn't matter, as long as she didn't die. Everything she had believed in, and that had occupied her every thought until that moment, was suddenly irrelevant. She didn't care about the color of her hair, or if she had any at all. She was no longer preoccupied with maintaining her hip city girl image. Her obsession with fashion seemed absurd. And she blamed herself; yes, she blamed herself for leaving her home and family. Dad was right: you should never have gone. If you hadn't left, this would have never happened.

From then on Julie would know no peace from her deadly secret. She was officially on death row, and the thought of death so close to her was almost intolerable. Almost, because even in that moment there were beautiful things that she had already begun to miss terribly. Suddenly, the world was so profoundly beautiful it was as if she had never seen it before. She knew then that her future was to be radically different from what it might have been if she had continued as before, wasting her days in the belief that her youth would last an eternity and that there would always be a tomorrow to realize her dreams.

She wondered how many years she had to live. HIV wasn't AIDS, it was only the precursor, but then she had other problems. Her health was so precarious that she thought: I won't last long. And if I don't last long, then maybe I should live the rest of my days doing what I want. There's no sense in studying any more for a future that isn't meant to be. Why should I bother finding love or making a life for myself, if my time is short? I suppose I can go back home and live out the rest of my days with my parents. But a fire inside her told her no. Somewhere in the tragedy she had found an unknown strength. Her misfortune had destroyed the last vestiges of her timid and uneventful life, and from it Julie was reborn a woman with nothing to lose.

Because she was shy, naive and insecure, she had started using drugs and allowed Henrik and others to take advantage of her. She knew there were many other young women out there like her and thought: no, the next thing you'll do is volunteer and make yourself useful. You've been a victim, and the best you can do is to use what you've learned to help other people. You never believed in anything before, but now you believe. Knowledge of your own death has made you believe very strongly in life, when before you could barely get out of bed and you drugged yourself to escape reality.

The hate came rushing back, and she thought: I'll kill Henrik and sit out the rest of my time in prison. That fucking bastard with all his filthy, degenerate friends.

If only it had never happened. If only Julie had admitted to herself that it was a lie and that her environment had been nothing but a predatory free-for-all of selfish hedonists without accountability. Some people have to grow up faster than others, she thought bitterly.

She remembered a time when she had stuck a needle in her arm. She remembered having unprotected anal sex with Henrik and other men. She had enjoyed being used. She had been taught to be used all her life. She had been talked down to and belittled. She had been ignored. And sex had become a gateway to finding her own identity and power. Its stigma was an emblem of achievement. She had been taught all her life that everything that was fun was wrong. But that had only piqued her curiosity. She had needed to discover the world for herself. How could they have expected her to know the consequences, when they never took the time to talk to her? No one ever told her: I know you're going to try things like we did at your age, and it's best you know how to take care of yourself. How could her father have expected that there would never be men who would take advantage of her: who would talk nice to her and give her things for sex? More importantly, how could he expect her not to enjoy sex and actively seek it out?

You live your life believing that you're not gonna be a tragedy, that tragedy is something that happens to other people, and then comes this absurd letter that says you're gonna die. No one ever told me life was hard like this; no one ever told me that I would die from enjoying myself, she thought. But then it never felt right, and you knew there was no love there. The men couldn't care if you were a vegetable so long as they could stick their dick in you, and it probably wasn't the dick but the needle. It was probably a dirty needle that helped you get out of your head. It felt so good that you never thought to ask if it was clean. You hoped that ignorance would save you, but ignorance doesn't save anyone, ever.

Julie wouldn't tell the others; if she told them, they might kick her out of the house or start treating her like a contagious invalid. She couldn't afford that. She needed time to think. It's for the best that you quit your studies because you'll probably be dead before you finish.

You're no good at graphic design anyway. What's more, you don't even like it.

It's time to get a job, maybe at the Women's Health Center where you can talk to women about the risks of sex. Sex is wonderful, and I don't wish celibacy on anyone, but people need to know how to protect themselves: especially junkies and the poor. You need to get condoms and clean needles out to the people who need them.

Julie remembered reading in the paper about the epidemic in Africa, and how, in certain countries, a significant percentage of the population was HIV positive like herself. Previously, such information was of little importance to her; it was just another statistic. Everything's a statistic until you become one yourself, she thought. Now she realized the devastating impact of AIDS and the need for proper drugs, which most people could not afford.

AIDS was a stigma that people preferred not to talk about. Julie had the virus now and was torn between silence and the need to tell Henrik the news. Because if she had it, there was a good chance he did, too. She was not sure how he would react, or if he could be trusted to keep the secret. Would he even bother to get tested? Henrik was reckless. He was living the celebrity lifestyle, having fun now and not looking to the future. Perhaps it would be for the best if he died in excess and debauchery instead of wasting away like an invalid? If Henrik was HIV positive, he would probably only accelerate his lifestyle and take more risks. That was his nature.

30

Nearly every day when Alex woke up for work, he considered calling in sick. He was not the sort to call in sick or be late for anything. When he had an obligation, he met it, and he disrespected people who were lazy, like Jack, for example. He hated that Jack would not accept reality and get back on his feet.

Still, Alex couldn't help but consider shirking all his obligations, staying in bed all day, and ignoring the world and its problems, and the endless amount of work that awaited him until the day he died. It was a game he played with himself at six o'clock every weekday morning for the five to ten minutes he could afford. It was a way for him to steal back his freedom, if only in his own mind.

On the other hand, he had grown accustomed to those quiet mornings standing at the bus stop and sipping on his thermos of coffee, with a gaggle of other early risers. The city was different then, somehow more humane and less sinister than its afternoon counterpart. His two favorite parts of the day were the early morning and the late evening, mainly because those were the times when he could be alone.

Often the thought of facing his students, and having to argue with and discipline them, left a bitterness in Alex's mouth as he rode the bus to work. At such times, he felt trapped in his life and irritated that he couldn't focus on his talent. He knew that he was a better writer than a teacher, and that if he could share his work, he would do much more to influence people and change their views than he could in a classroom.

But unlike many who are forced to choose a career alternate to their dreams, Alex was lucky that the classroom was a place where he could discuss his ideas and test theories before committing them to paper. He had never been one to conform to the teaching standards imposed by the state bureaucracy. He did not believe in standardized testing, but in producing freethinking citizens. It's funny, he thought, how so many people boast of their passion for teaching, and the first chance they get, they move into an administrative position where they work less and get paid more to have no direct contact with the students.

Public education in the United States was underfunded and understaffed. The students lacked study materials, and curriculum was outdated and ill-suited for the globalized information economy. Students in poor neighborhoods remained neglected, minimal efforts were made to integrate immigrant students, and creativity was squandered by a brain drain of teachers looking for greener pastures. College graduates were discouraged from the profession due to a lack of respect, fair pay, classroom overcrowding, increased school violence and excessive bureaucracy. New teachers were required to spend several hundred dollars of their own money to become substitutes, without any health benefits whatsoever, to receive their paychecks several weeks after the beginning of the month when rent had to be paid, and for pay equal to that of the service industry that did not require an additional six years of undergraduate education. It was foolish of the government to believe that there were enough individuals willing to devote themselves to such a difficult profession given such conditions, especially when the current administration set a poor and hypocritical example, concerned more with self-interest than an educated and literate population.

Our President is a bloody fool, Alex thought. If such trends of big business and greed continue, then life in America will become increasingly inhospitable. The one perk of teaching, Alex knew, was the freedom to stand up and speak his mind to the young. Grammar aside, he was a preacher. He was educating the young to be critical of their nation and its leadership; he wanted them to understand that much of what they saw and heard in the media were lies, that freedom in America was an illusion, and that materialism was a disease that kept them comfortable and passive in the face of the global injustice and inequality that were the byproducts of their culture.

He knew that most of his students would never receive his message. They were born with few comforts, so to preach to them to renounce what they had never had was futile, if not elitist. He knew that some of them even thought him ridiculous for his ideas. They couldn't be expected to know the marginal nature of his own life, or the difficulties he faced as an intellectual in America, where intellectuals lost elections and had their ideas sidelined to university talks, local bookshops and small print magazines. How can I prove to them the value of reason above commerce, Alex wondered.

It was ridiculous to think of revolution. A few years down the road when he had a stable job, probably outside of teaching, when he was married with children, then he would not think as he did now. Like most, his thoughts would slide from idealism to practicality; he would move from liberal to centrist to conservative. Jesus, would that also happen to him? At a time when he fantasized about shooting the President, Alex found it unlikely that his views would change any time soon. Granted, he would never shoot the President, but the idea gave him freedom, as did the thought of not going to work to face the difficult task of motivating a bunch of disaffected children into believing they could do something in the world. Why, even with the support of his parents and a college education, he wasn't able to find comfort or success. And what of shooting the President?

I suppose that's desperation. Certainly in this political and global climate of terror, such a statement would land a man in jail or make him mysteriously disappear. And if men did disappear for making such a joke to blow off their frustration, it would prove that it was no longer a free country. Though murder was never justifiable, a strong case could be made for the removal of a corrupt and oppressive government. At any rate, the President was not the problem, but a merely a symptom of a broken and abused system. Shooting the President would be a futile act, indeed, in a country where government was just a front for big business. Voila, the hypocrisy of the rich and powerful: the President and his staff can set policy and implement programs that result in the murder of tens of thousands of innocent civilians in foreign wars, with the dubious claim of promoting democracy, and not be held accountable. That was precisely why the United States had refused to join the International Criminal Court: because it did not wish to be held responsible for its own criminal actions. Imagine: the land of freedom and justice for all won't join the rest of the world in establishing an international court to prosecute terrorists and war criminals for acts of genocide, torture and other extreme antisocial behavior that violates the UN Declaration of Human Rights. And they call this a democratic nation, Alex thought.

There's a lot to be learned from the biblical story of David and Goliath, and the many empires that have come and gone on this earth, most of which have lasted much longer than *Pax Americana*, which, in this international climate of civil war and genocide with nation-states fracturing at the seams, is certainly a misnomer.

In any case, you can't shoot the President or brain him with a pipe, because that's murder, and murder violates human rights. But then these rights seem only to apply to the domestic population of a nation-state that feeds its economy with violence and murder outside its own borders.

The truth is you're scared. You don't feel free to speak your mind anymore about politics in mixed company, though it's become common currency to mock, curse, defame and vilify the President and his administration for policy failures, corruption and self-serving agendas.

Free speech is little more than recreation and entertainment when it's not turned into action that influences political debate and decision-making, Alex thought. Man is promoted by self-interest; therefore, it is all the more important that Americans demand accountability from their politicians. Ignorance, apathy and material comfort are the conditions that have led Americans to take their democracy for granted; people have forgotten that democracy is an obligation and that eternal vigilance is necessary to maintain the hard won rights they currently enjoy. Democracy is self-rule in which the people dictate to their representatives the laws and policies that will best help them govern their economic and social activities. Since the interests of citizens are not all the same, democracy is a necessary tool for compromise. Ultimately, what Americans needed was a refresher course in civics. Contrary to the magical thinking of many, there was no invisible hand to protect their political rights from market interests.

People often say that they dislike or aren't interested in politics, and that they don't want to get involved in political debate; such people are both fools and cowards, Alex thought. They are fools because they wish to ignore that politics permeate every facet of human existence, and they are cowards for relinquishing their agency over the decisions that affect their lives and their welfare. Contrary to popular belief, politics is not confrontation and dissent, but rather cooperation and consensus.

It didn't take a student of history to be alarmed at the current political climate in the country, just an informed citizenship. Alex, and freethinking individuals like himself, represented the front line in the fight for political freedom and justice in America. Alex was a citizen-patriot of the first order defending the core values of American democracy, which meant he was in direct opposition to those that used the system for personal gain. For those individuals with vested interests, he would be labeled a radical and considered a threat. What made Alex so threatening was that he had no stake in preaching truth, beyond the fact that it would do good for people to hear it. Clearly, these were bad times, and like anyone, Alex felt that oppression.

31

That week in class Alex began a segment on human conflict where he grouped his lessons into the following categories: the world wars, regional conflict, civil war, colonial conquest, genocide and domestic riots. He provided a case study for each that included one of the following criteria of difference often employed to justify conflict: ideology, social class, religion, race, color, creed, nationality and territory.

After exploring the history of violence, Alex discussed the international community's attempts to address human rights through legal and diplomatic means. To Alex, the drafting of the Universal Declaration of Human Rights by the United Nations had had little effect on human behavior, for as statistics proved, conflict and violence between individuals and groups persisted. It was Alex's opinion that the recognition of human rights was nothing more than image marketing for the powerful, and a guilt-tripping strategy for those situated on the lower rungs of the hierarchy of needs. Alex suspected that the problem lay in the fact that human beings were lazy and hypocritical, desiring for themselves benefits that they would withhold from others. Add to that the corruption that came from excess, and a distorted sense of self-worth otherwise known as vanity, and it was no wonder humanity was unable to govern itself. He decided it was for the best not to share such thoughts with his students. Instead, Alex would do his best to present the facts and let them draw their own conclusions. He suspected that his students would have an even more cynical and Darwinian outlook on human development than his own.

Ultimately, it was his intention to show that in modern times, under the influence of capitalism, and in spite of international lip service promoting human rights, the world was not a safer place than in the past.

He explained to his students that this was a direct result of the increased poverty and hopelessness of the world's population, for what else could explain the bitter struggles that had erupted between different ethnic, political, and religious groups with a history of coexistence within national borders? Endemic poverty and dwindling resources had strained relationships to the point of violence. The concept of nationality was slowly being eroded with the help of intolerance and the increasing economic power of multinational corporations. No longer were people satisfied to be a part of nation-states that disregarded their rights, gave away their resources and enslaved them for the profit of their leadership and foreign interests. Perhaps it had been a mistake to show the poor and miserable of the planet the wealth of capitalism, while forcing them to perform mindless underpaid labor that insured they would never be able to achieve such dreams. American capitalism was at best a mixed message, and now the most desperate of the poor, marginalized and oppressed had adopted terror to achieve their goals.

When people are no longer served by civil society, government institutions and the rule of law, they resort to terror to protect their interests and ensure their survival. Terrorists aren't primarily concerned with destruction, Alex thought. They don't all wish to bring the world to anarchy or ruin. Many of them simply want a home to call their own, or demand equal representation by their respective governments; most importantly, they wish to live with dignity and respect.

I wonder what are the true rights of man? Does he have a right to his own land where he can grow his food and organize himself into a mutually beneficial trade of goods and services? Well, with all the land in the world, it's certainly possible for each man to assume this right, if it does in fact exist. Not in this city though, where teachers can't afford to own a home; or in this country, where many are forced to beg or slave for the benefit of others to survive.

Well, you're living that dead-end dependent life, too.

The draw of terrorism is clear: in what other way could a peasant exact justice for living in misery than cutting the boss's throat? Just like the French Revolution, just like any revolution. The problem with revolution, though, is that it only changes the faces of the corrupt, because the oppressed don't have the imagination to set up an alternative form of government. Take that Cuban dictator, for example. Sure, he achieved almost total literacy for the entire population of Cuba, but he did so with strong-arm tactics, just like the United States strong-armed the puppet dictator before him. The revolution suceeded in making the country self-sufficient and more egalitarian, but in the process, opposition leaders and political dissidents were jailed and public gatherings of three on more people were prohibited, which meant no more dominos with your friends.

Alex brought a notebook with him everywhere he went. His best ideas always came to him when he was far away from his writing desk; the smallest incident or bit of conversation would send him writing frantically. That's it, the next part of the book! I just need to do some research. In particular, Alex wanted to explore in greater detail Islamic extremism, the Maoist revolution in Nepal, and the recent independence of East Timor, which had finally cast off the chains of Indonesian occupation.

Each Monday, Alex went to his classroom early to prepare his lesson. That week, he photocopied information about Columbia and the U.S. involvement in and support of the drug war, along with several articles regarding legalization of marijuana. Alex hoped to start a polemic in the classroom, especially with Gavin, who had a bit of a mouth and who lived off drugs, and who was also Alex's favorite student. Gavin was smart. He had a head for business and he worked well with people. Because Alex thought Gavin could do better for himself, he challenged him and made his life difficult.

Arrogance never leads anywhere, Alex thought. Gavin hides in relative success, but the truth is he's insecure, and there are no good role models for him to follow. Mr. Biggs is certainly no role model, but at least he has the sense not to come around the school anymore to show off. It's funny how when a man has a little money, he uses it to pretend superiority over others. A man will go so far as to believe that he doesn't have to think or educate himself so long as he can make money. People don't seem to recognize the inherent value of education. Meanwhile, Mr. Biggs strips the community of its strength by turning smart kids like Gavin into dealers, by poisoning his people so he can buy cars sold by white men and listen to rap produced by white men, too.

One thing I can say for consumer culture is that all races have been marketed and exploited; when a buck can be made, people forget about color. Alex remembered the music videos with black men and their fancy cars, branded sports clothes and blatant jewelry and thought: we are certainly living in a hip hop culture. So what does that mean? Does it mean that disaffected urban black youth can sing about their oppressive reality and have voice despite their poverty, or is it simply a marketing tool for the branded world? Are those young men and women really seen and heard, or are they nothing but a circus act?

We've all bought into it; rap sure is popular in white suburbia, because hip hop, like any black cultural movement before it, has captured the soul of America. Commercial hip hop, unlike its politically conscious underground cousin, has become nothing but a bandit philosophy: take what you can get and run, work only so that you don't have to, show off to those that are less fortunate than yourself, disrespect women and those who are different from you, and act tough to hide your weaknesses and insecurity, because you are unable to communicate your true feelings. Almost overnight, hip hop had become the musical genre that most accurately mirrored American values or lack of them. In the hip hop world, the flash of possession ruled over the essence of thought. The lyrical distinction that made rap great was being steadily eroded, recycled and dummified, rendering the genre repetitive and inane like modern culture, so someone might make a buck. And now this rap of illusions was the soundtrack to the movie people wished they were living and invented inside themselves to blot out their failures, producing the blindness and misunderstanding between individuals whose terminus was alienation.

Since no one can relate anymore these days, Alex thought, they should have public booths where one can go to speak their mind freely and not hide behind false façades and material possessions: a sort of modern confessional of consumer angst.

Do you remember when Julie was near to tears for the dent in her leased sedan? I could die and that bitch wouldn't care, but if her car gets a dent, then it's the end of the world. It's absolutely amazing how some people believe they exist through their possessions: as if, say, their cell phone were somehow their arm. Ridiculous.

Alex was working himself up into a rage that he could only let out in the classroom, and that he had gotten tired of sharing in public, or with his friends, because he knew they didn't particularly care. That, a mortal blow to his heart and mind, he had shrugged off. He had shrugged off a lot of things in his life and learned to live for himself, but this was his classroom and inside it he would say what he damn well pleased.

How ironic that you're back here where you started many years ago. The desks haven't even changed. It's as if nothing has changed, well, except you. When you were their age, you didn't care either. If you could just get through to one of them, then you'll have done your job. Then you can sleep well knowing that there is at least one decent person on the street: the kind that you would like to run into and chat with as you go about your business.

The students filed into the classroom and Alex felt better already.

"Hello everyone. All right, let's have a seat."

In the classroom, the actor and performer inside him took over. It was a part of his personality that he didn't address when he was alone with himself or in public. Then he concerned himself with being cool and quiet so he wouldn't make mistakes. But here he couldn't run from the powerful voice inside himself. He spoke easy and free like he wrote. He had no trouble telling them what to do. He was not self-conscious because talking was not like writing. Talking, one wasn't held responsible for the words; they might have their effect but could also be shrugged off. Standing before his audience, Alex knew what tone to take with them and could change his approach to suit their mood. In your books you have to speak straight, but in the classroom you have the full range of options, from subtle persuasion to threat. You can be their friend and joke with them and make the enemy a third party, or you can put the fear of authority in them.

"Sit down, please, and let's be quiet so we can get started."

The students sat down and the bell rang. A few students trickled in late, and Alex eyeballed them and filled out the detention slips; any laxity on his part would be interpreted as weakness. Every day was a struggle for power with the students. If he made concessions on assignments, on attendance, on talking, or anything else, then the students would expect them as rights and press their advantage.

Instead of valuing knowledge, they seek to assert themselves as individuals. They do not know how to fully take advantage of the material and your knowledge and experience, Alex thought. If they did, this class would be enjoyable and you wouldn't have to stick as heavily to the text.

"I've got a few handouts for you. As usual we're going to take the first few minutes of SSR to go over them. Most of you don't have anything to read, anyway, so you might as well be reading something that concerns the world you live in."

Alex looked around the room and called role. Aisha had been gone for more than a month. Rumor had it that she was pregnant. Before her body began to show the signs of supporting not one, but two, she was gone. Alex did not expect her back in school. As happened with so many single mothers, she would have to struggle to support herself and her child, leaving no time to get an education.

A good education starts at home, Alex thought. It is built on love, trust, communication and respect. These days it seems parents aren't doing a proper job in raising their children. Instead, they expect teachers to provide students with the discipline they haven't received at home, in addition to an education. The low pay and lack of prestige of the teaching profession in the public eye; an unstable, overly-permissive or unsupervised home life; and a lack of accountability for one's actions promoted by television and video games, which often served as surrogate parents for children, resulted in a classroom environment of student disobedience and disrespect that made teaching difficult. While this was no longer the case with his class, for Alex treated his students as he expected to be treated and demanded of them their best, it remained a vivid memory from his substitute days.

It's not that parents don't care for their children, Alex thought; it's just that many don't understand the tremendous responsibility and time commitment of raising them properly. And these are the parents that wanted children and were prepared financially to support them. For those that had children by accident, so to speak, it could be much harder. Especially with poverty in the picture.

Alex couldn't blame parents working two jobs or more for not spending quality time with their children. And for children that were unwanted and neglected as a result, someone had to give them a chance and some tools for survival. Generally, children assume the values and follow the example of their parents, he thought. But then it was also true that all his students were individuals and had the free will to decide how they would react to the challenges of life. For example, Aisha was a smart and considerate girl, while Taresa produced poor quality work and was notorious for deprecating others. Was that the result of parenting, or due to personal character?

Alex moved down the list and checked off the names. Ah, yes, Michael Thurman, a talented student who was always busy writing in his notebook and never paid attention, and who Alex would bother because he was bothered when talented students didn't live up to their potential.

"Michael, if you pay attention to the discussion you might learn something. But I guess you got it all figured out already, don't you, and you don't need us anyway."

"Yo, teach, chill, a'ight. This English Lit thing is wack. Why I gotta worry about some tired-ass British folk talking about love? Man, that shit don't speak to me. It's all played out."

Michael first started to pay attention when Alex introduced the work of famous black intellectuals, writers and poets.

"You see how H- uses everyday speech and real life experience in his poetry to convey his message? You can look at rap like that. It's poetry that talks about everyday life in a way that everyone can understand, whether it's the Romantic poets of England in their time or H- that was rhyming long before FunkDMC were conceived in their mothers' bellies. The purpose of studying this stuff is so that one understands the history. Rap is the offspring of reggae and was popularized on the East Coast with the whole breakdance movement. Breakdancing itself can be traced back to *capoeira*, a martial art practiced by plantation slaves in Brazil with its roots in African ritual dance, principally from Angola. The point is that it's all connected, and only by knowing origin can one innovate. Because rap, like any art, builds on itself. Think of the word "original." What is original? It's a starting point, but then nothing can ever start on its own. There is no immaculate conception. You were born of your parents into a community and culture, and you are a legacy of it; it binds you, but you can also change it. When you do something original you're really drawing on the past and adding to it. Michael, you've got a talent for this stuff. You write lyrics and you freestyle; I've heard you in the schoolyard. Then you come into my class and close your mind, mouth and ears. Now I want to hear what you got. Who wants to hear Michael freestyle?"

There was some commotion in the class and a few encouraging voices.

"Go on Michael, show Mr. Green what up."

"Yeah, fool, flow some of that poetry of the mind, yo."

Then, as often happened when teaching, Alex had an epiphany. He saw how he would connect them with language and make them appreciate poetry.

"Why don't we do this: anyone who wants to can write a rap about something going on in their life and present it instead of doing the essay on the Romantic poets. Because, like Michael said, we're not in the Romantic period. We're in the hard motherfucker period, and bitch better have my money and fuck all-you-all period. Am I right, or am I right?"

Alex noticed the way the kids looked at him when he cursed. The students laughed, and he saw a smile twitch on Gavin's lips. Only Quincy remained straight-faced, staring blankly at his notebook. He seemed distracted, and Alex put two and two together and thought that he was missing Aisha. Yep, he's got it bad. I imagine he doesn't like it one bit that Aisha's with that other guy.

Anyway, when he cursed the students paid better attention, because then he was real like them. He was talking like friends talked, and not distant and alien and full of theory that they didn't want to hear.

These kids want reality. I understand how they can't relate to the Western literary canon. The problem is that their roots have been almost totally erased.

"Yo, Mr. Green, if I bust some freestyle can I skip the assignment?"

"If you write it down after and turn it in to me."

"I'll write it down, but it ain't gonna be the same," Michael said. "Freestyle's about the moment and writing rhymes is more planned out 'cause you got time to think. So you wanna hear it or what?"

"Any time you're ready," Alex told him.

It was different rapping in the classroom in front of the teacher than on the street with his friends. Though Michael liked to rap, he was shy about it. And the classroom was so quiet it made him sweat.

"Yo teach, I gotta have some music. Can Turrel put on some beats?"

"Fine."

Turrel pulled his stereo out of his backpack and set it on the desk. The class was suddenly awake and expectant. They had never been allowed to rap in class before. Rapping was for the street. It was full of cursing and insults, and what would Mr. Green do if Michael started to really throw down with profanity?

Michael cleared his throat and got up in front of the classroom. Turrel put on the music, and Michael started to pace around the room and wave his hands for momentum:

This is for all the hunters in the Point

When I could breath I was smoking joints

Nothing but pain to hit the books

Wanted to have the cash without the work

To live the good life like on TV

With everybody lookin' up to me

Started dealin' at an early age

No reason to play the game

The rules they excluded us

Designed to make us give up

And pick up the chains

Substitute our names for the generic
Playin' endless games of logic
To confuse us into thinkin' like them
Sittin' in classrooms that decay
To learn how little we're worth
In the cynicism, hate, and oppression
They claim for truth

I don't believe their lies
I still got my pride
I won't stand workin' them slave jobs
Unable to afford a decent life
To live in rented box and eat their trash
While they force on us their sterility
To forget our culture and our roots
A cup of petty alms don't teach a man
Nothin' but a dependent life

I earn my own money
The best I can
Wanna stuff yourself with poison
It's your own damn fault
Don't go moralizin' on me
When your silver spoon children snort it up
And shoot in their veins
Everyone's got a free choice
In this country
I ain't sold out nobody
Like I been sold out
Before I was born

Never givin' us the right to be decent
You make money on these drugs too
You keep us down with them
When we sell it to get by
And we make it rich
Rappin' about our plight
You take your cut and complain
Of the problems we create
That are your problems too
Is that justice or are we just entertainin' you?

You sell us fancy cars and houses
Pretty women with plastic smiles
When you rollin' they come runnin'
And want a piece of the action
To get fucked and forgotten
Can you blame them for seeing gold?

Ain't no love or loyalty in the hood
We use each other up down here
Where everything's dark
You step on our backs and make us bleed
You wonder why I'm violent and why I deal
When my friends and family die
Where we kill each other for a little advantage
For the ability to stand above you
Just once looking down
With your fancy things in our possession
To say
Is this what you been bragging about?

Fuck that, because to us it ain't nothin'
Built on so much misery

You absorb our culture
Because you have none
You fear us because we are terribly strong
To be bigger than this upside down world
Where corruption is merit and lies are truth
The rich are noble and the poor deserve it
Frozen in your morals and manners
Dead paper devils playing human
Admiring our music and our skills
Desiring our bodies
Turning them safely into myth
You cannot accept what you have created
You cannot see the damage
Of our greatness that is your illusion

How does a black man seek a life?
Walking with weights on his limbs
In submerged dreams
Impotent like a warship
Salvaged from the seafloor
Plagued with the disease of poverty

The children I father blow away
without roots in the wind
While your offspring laugh in the garden
Watered by our tears
My son gets his education
Like his father before him .

From the street

This hostile environment you've created
On divisions of labor and fortune
Where some people are poisoned
By cost cutting measures
Where the sick weak and needy
Are destroyed by individual greed
Where one nation under God
Means one nation for the rich
And one for the poor
And never the two shall meet

You taunt us with images
Success and happiness in private life
Presented on the silver screen
To make us whither inside
You show us abundance
We cannot possess
And wonder why we despair
At the abyss in our hearts
Propaganda and reality tearin' us apart

Our neighborhoods tell a different story
These concentration camps
where the children played hide and seek
From their identity
Their dreams turned dusty and dirty
Like an old book that spoke the truth
That somehow you forgot to burn
They see in your resentful eyes

The color of their skin
And wish it were like paint
So they could add another layer and look like you

That disgrace is what you hoped for
To maintain this lie we call the American Dream.
Keepin' us begging here
In a thousand ghettos like Hunter's Point
Stretched out across the fertile plain
Where some Americans don't matter
For the benefit of others
Do you know the cost of that waste?
Gettin' more expensive every day

My dreams of escape
Remain impossible like the lottery
My desire for things to be different
Does not right the wrongs committed
By men unnaturally small and alien
Because I am black and poor
Do not assume my ignorance
I've been paying attention
To what's happenin'

Now I think in solutions
No longer occupied with revenge
Or pity for what reality has been
I realize there are still good men
To look up to and I want to join them
Like Mr. Green been preachin'
To get ourselves an education

I admire his optimism

And his courage to throw down words

In place of fists

To inspire us to move ahead

Before I wanted to make a life alone

To be the fittest and win the prize

Like in a race or competition

Only to leave my compassion behind

I forgot the help of others

That brought me here and kept me safe

That dried my tears when I failed

The world I knew was strange to me

So many years spent wanderin'

With no vision to see where I was goin'

Until I returned to my community

Surprised to find it destroyed

By selfishness like mine

I wish to build it up again

To renew the life that began

Right here in the Point

When Michael finished, Alex started clapping. The class joined in and there were some shout-outs. Michael pounded his fist to his chest out of pride. He went to his seat with his chin high; his feet scarcely touched the ground as he walked. On his way he high-fived Turrel, Gavin, and few of the other cool kids.

"You go, Michael, that was fat, yo."

"You tell it, Michael. That's where it's at."

"Bustin' the mad rhymes, G."

"That was hella tight, M-dawg."

"Yeah nigga, you be flowin' solid."

Damn straight. Michael knew what it was about and he represented. Someone had to represent. Without it, who would know they mattered?

Alex signaled for Turrel to turn off the music. There's a fine line between learning and letting these kids take liberties, he thought. I bet they'd like to bump the music for the rest of the period and forget all about English.

Michael couldn't see them when he was rapping. Pictures floated in his head and he trapped them in words. Imagination was the place no one could touch him. Nothing could take his words away or strip them of their meaning in his mind. No longer was he sitting in a school desk wondering at greatness or seduced by a distant success.

He was vital. He had expressed himself and was higher than he had ever been on joints. He thought that rap, the ability to talk his feelings to music, was the key to his success. The only way anyone will listen to what you gotta say is if you make it flow, Michael thought. It's hard to be smooth and natural when you freestyle. You're always afraid you'll freeze and be unable to finish a thought. That's why you stopped smokin' the chronic. You can't be smokin' chronic and battling. You can't afford that humiliation.

It was an understatement to say that Alex was impressed. What incredible use of language, and all off the top of his head. I could never do that. The boy is a thinker. He's got a social conscience. He's a potential revolutionary, and damn it's great to see him motivated.

"There it is, our own Michael Thurman. You saw it here first. I just hope he doesn't forget us when he's a big star," Alex said.

A smile played across Michael's face and he kept his eyes low to carry the flattery. The mood in the class was expansive, and a feeling of hope filled the generally tense and oppressive environment. If they could just believe, Alex thought. If I could just believe.

Michael wrote lyrics in his spare time. When he freestyled he would weave in bits of his old material and add new rhymes where they fit. The rhymes he had already committed to paper served as a template for his creative improvisation.

Sometimes when he rapped his feelings surprised him. He said things that came from his subconscious and would haunt him later and cause him shame. The shame didn't come from a weak rhyme, but from speaking too frankly. There were rappers that thrived on being offensive. Michael was not one of them. He preferred subtlety to insult. He would rather use a difficult word from the dictionary, than some common slang, to illustrate his point. The dictionary was his bible. From it he could mine innumerable raps. Amazing to think the alphabet held the solution to all man's problems. Michael revered the dictionary and took it with him wherever he went. It was the one sure companion in his journey through the unknown.

Gavin found himself wishing he had Michael's talent. One day he's gonna be gone from this place. He'll be on VTV and he'll have tons of bitches and mad cash. If I saved some coin I could fund him to make an album. That's an idea. The producers are the ones making the real money. I could cut a deal and give him a percent.

Gavin's mind was always on the money. Though the class was more interesting than usual, he didn't hear what Mr. Green was saying. Deep down he liked Mr. Green, though he would never admit it or let it show. Mr. Green is wacked out. I can't believe what comes out of his mouth sometimes. He's like a big kid. I mean listen to how he talks. He approaches rap the same way he does anything -with the mind. Man, I feel sorry for the guy. He's trapped in himself. Who knows what the hell Mr. Green does when he gets home. If he's so smart, what's he doing teaching us? If I was him I'd go out and make some real money. He looks just like all those other big shots I see cruisin' the city. Mr. Green's his own man and he don't work for the man.

"So here's what we're gonna do," Alex told them. "Anyone else who wants to write a rap can do that instead of the paper on the Romantic poets. But there is one requirement: what you write must talk about love in some way. Also, if anyone wants to they can compare the Romantic period with modernity. Romanticism valued sentimentality and the expression of intense emotion, which is fairly absent in our cynical society. The Romantics looked to the myths and fables of the past to interpret their world. They looked toward their own history for inspiration, while in America we are in a constant state of reconstruction; the old is stripped away to make way for the new, and the past is intentionally erased. It's from the Romantics that we get our perceptions of love, not the vulgar love expressed in music videos, television and film, but that of setting free our passions in spite of the consequences and our better judgment. This emotional concept of love: that we as individuals are to actively seek the objects of our desire and not suppress our true feelings no matter the consequences, still exerts a strong influence on human relationships today.

"We can't ignore that the Romantic period has had a profound effect on the modern world. The concept of individualism: that any of you can grow up to be who you want to be and shape your own future, was first expressed by the Romantics. That is the founding concept of America: that a poor man today can be a rich man tomorrow. It went completely against the aristocracy and the church hierarchy of the time. The Romantic Movement found its strength in the bourgeoisie: what you would call businessmen today.

"So I suppose it was no coincidence that Romanticism advanced hand in hand with the industrial revolution. The Romantic Movement took inspiration from the objects of everyday life and mystified them; it celebrated popular culture without addressing its inequities, unlike Michael's rap, which is realism that focuses on the experience of ordinary people.

"But the truth is society has changed. We aren't living in an ethnically homogenous place. Immigrants continue to shape what it means to be American, and poverty and inequality, not an idealized sense of national identity, provide the conflict and inspiration for young people trying to understand the world today. But then Romanticism comes again to disrupt the order of things by creating the hope that one can escape the harsh reality of daily life and with money rise above the ghetto, travel and be free of the routine. Our romantic legacy is that things are always better somewhere else, even if that somewhere else is a stereotype of our own cultural design.

"It's interesting to note that the Romantics were the first wave of artists that weren't totally dependent on the support of kings and nobles. They made money on their own selling their work to the growing merchant class. That's not to say that they lived well. Most of them endured great poverty to express their thoughts. Either that or they were rich and had the freedom to produce art. Unlike today, when anyone with a little talent willing to take risks can become a big star, even if they were born poor. In the early Nineteenth Century, the farmers and artisans were slowly absorbed into factory work, but either way, they were very poor. Capitalism was just getting started and we hadn't learned how to manage it yet. I guess we still haven't. Anyway, it would still take many years befor the artist achieved celebrity status."

"But it's not like that at all, teach," Gavin interrupted. "Times ain't better today than they was before. Working full time at a fast food joint, a brother can't get by these days. It be like with the farmers in Europe with feudalism, and it's gettin' worse. It ain't as easy to make it as you think. It's just luck, man. It's who you know. Just like the kings before. If you knew the king then you was all right. Now, if you know the producer you got it made. But they still a lot a' cats that be working hard on their shit and they ain't recognized. And the guys that be makin' it, maybe they was good before, but then they start talking trash and they all full a' hype and not connected no more. Man, hip hop's not about talkin' pretty and makin' things seem better than it is. It's about what's wrong with shit; it's about people be sufferin' and wonderin' where the love is at," Gavin said.

Alex didn't care about cursing in his class. He wanted his students to speak their mind, whether it was pretty or not. He cursed, and if someone wanted to curse, let them. So far none of them had ever abused that freedom. They didn't curse for its own sake, but to stress a point.

"I don't think that the Romantics just wanted to say nice things without any meaning," Alex said. "They had a lot of criticism against their society and the Classical period that came before them. I think that's what rap's all about, right? Making a critique, but in a creative and intelligent way that sounds good."

"I don't care about makin' mad cash if it means I gotta lose my integrity," Michael said. "I just wanna be free to say what I want. But more than that, I wanna be recognized. Recognition is more important than money. Because when I die, I wanna know that what I've said had an effect on people. I'm sick a' people frontin' when they don't got nothin' to put up."

Damned straight, Alex thought. Life is all about respect and recognition. Call it what you want. In class the kids want to be listened to and respected. The problem with poverty is that the poor don't feel that they're seen, and if they're seen, then they're certainly not heard. It sure is hard for a man to live if he thinks he's invisible. It's hard to live without love. I don't work this job for the money, but for the reward of knowing I've been heard, and also to teach others to listen. Thank Michael for starting this discussion. He doesn't know what he's started, but now it's too late. I feel the truth bubbling somewhere, and I'm gonna root it out with the scalpel of reason.

"Exactly, Michael. You got it exactly right about integrity. It's got just as much to do with the Romantic poets as it does with modern rap. What we're talking about here is art; when art is forced to conform to the consumer market it gets watered down and loses its meaning. If you look at the Romantics, either they were wealthy themselves and bored, or they were commisioned by a king or a nobleman to paint vanity portraits to flatter and write verse to entertain. Inevitably, they had to avoid biting the hand that fed them. Of course, there were other artists who worked for themselves and the public, who weren't rich. They could create whatever they pleased and were by far the most critical of their society. Still, most of them died in misery, though they may have produced good work. If that's the case, we'll never know, because they weren't recognized. The question is, how does one reconcile the opposing forces of the market with individual creativity?"

"Everybody sells out sooner or later," Turrel said. "It's human nature. You wave enough bills in front of somebody's face and he be doin' whatever you say."

"That's true and it isn't, Turrel. Sometimes artists place their ideals above money. In fact, when a man succeeds in expressing his emotions and thoughts in his work, time and the physical world almost seem to fade away. They become details. That's what you call passion, and that was at the heart of the Romantic Movement. Art, I think, is essentially the physical proof of a desire to be loved and understood; it serves people who can't communicate through normal social avenues. That's why even if there's no money, recognition is so important. No one likes to feel they don't exist. Still, there's clearly a bit of vanity in it. For people that are excluded from the power and prestige occupations in society, art, sports and beauty seem to be the only way to have a shot. Because even if they take everything away from you, they can't take away your talent or your biology. And if you're one of the few to taste success, then you get to stand above everyone and be recognized, when before you were ignored and disrespected. It's a high stakes game, but I think people choose that path out of necessity. So is someone foolish to do something that might not pay off, but that they believe in, instead of being practical and making money?"

"Any man who don't take an opportunity when it comes is a fool," Gavin said.

"And if no opportunity comes?"

"Then he's gotta do something that's gonna make him successful. He's gotta study something or get a skill in something that's useful," Quincy said.

"And what if he is misunderstood by society, poisoned by its hypocrisy, disenchanted by its predictability and would live a life of boredom in material success?"

"Then he's gonna go down," Turrel said. "No two ways about it. You gotta have some serious luck to be able to do what you want. I've been working since I was in the eighth grade and it's got me what I need. That's the most anyone can ask for. I've seen people in a bad way, and I don't wanna go there. Not for ideas, anyhow. If I'm all hungry and cold, what good is a poem?"

"Yet people die for their art," Alex said. "They kill themselves over it. The Romantics were notorious for their emotional suffering and producing art was often their only relief."

"Well, being a star is a job too, right? I mean people gotta work for what they got, and if a businessman don't get lazy when he be making money, why should a rapper or movie star? Everybody wants to do a good job and get paid, right? I think people work harder when they know the money's comin'," Yolanda said.

"Yolanda's got a point. 'Selling out' is something that the competition says about you when you're on top. And when you're really on top, then you can do whatever you want. What we can't get away from is that art is always dependent on commerce, and commerce is meaningless without art. What is the value of a product if it hasn't been fashioned with care and creativity," Alex asked.

"Can't somebody live the good life and have some positive rhymes that uplift the people? There's nothing wrong with that. Some people's just jealous, like when they see a black man rollin' in a nice car and livin' in a fat house on his own merit," Jamil said.

"You're right. And life's not all work and ambition, after all. There are times when a person just wants to take a break. There's nothing wrong with that. The problem is that here in America we are expected to work around the clock. Everyone needs a vacation sometimes to regain their energy, so that they can come back stronger and do better work. A month break or so every year, like they got in Europe, would do wonders to the morale of the working class of this country. It would also rid us of the popular myth of getting rich quick, so we can spend the rest of our lives doing nothing. That goes against human nature; it goes against our desire to be respected, and respect comes only from doing something worthy of respect," Alex said. "No one respects the idle man. They may envy him in the moment, but they don't respect him.

"So what happens when some rapper makes it big? Does he get lazy and take his success for granted? Does he forget where he comes from and what made his rhymes good in the first place? I think that happens in any artistic medium. When you finally make it and have the money, you get carried away. Because stars aren't treated like other people. I imagine it can be easy to get carried away when everybody looks up to you," Alex said. "There's quite a bit of vanity in it; after the vanity, I guess, comes the greed of wanting to be an even bigger star, to have more money, and so on. Then you lose inspiration and produce something that looks or sounds good, but is empty inside and doesn't really move people. And while it hits the charts on star appeal, it has no staying power. I think a lot of popular artists struggle with losing touch. Art must be in dialogue with life to be viable. So my question to you guys, who know more about it than me, is what's up with hip hop these days? Where's it going, and is it still important? What do you think, Michael? This is your scene."

"Yo, I ain't got no more to say about it."

"Come on, man, don't hold out on me," Alex said. "You're just dying to talk about it. I bet you think it's going the wrong way, don't you? And that must piss you off."

"There are some good rappers and stuff," Michael said. "Some of them be makin' it big and are still solid. But then there's also a lot of wannabes. All the stuff that talks about rollin' and pimpin' the nice ride, that's a dead-end rap. Hip hop needs to criticize, it needs to be a thorn in your side, it needs to make people stop and recognize. I think that hip hop's gotta turn around and battle itself freestyle. You can't get up on stage and talk about bling bling in a duel. You need to break a man down and prove he's frontin'. For hip hop to get back to the roots, all them big shots with the record deals gotta come back to where they started and battle the new cats, school and get schooled by them, and inspire and promote them. They can big up the next generation by recruitin' from the hood.

"Hip hop shouldn't be just about economics, but politics. Not just the government, but the politics of community and race, and the politics of economics, and not economics as truth," Michael said. "That ain't art, that's just being a bitch. To rap about "making it" don't make sense. That's just poverty unless you talk about how you got there, how hard it was, who got your back and who tore you down, and what that means for other people. Hip hop gotta be about reality, not a television fantasy 'cause that shit is wack."

Alex left school that day feeling much better than when he had arrived. You learn a lot from these kids, he told himself. You need to speak the truth for their sake. You need to keep it real, whatever the fuck that means. The truth is what comes out when you don't sweat it. It's what you feel down deep that you hide from others.

32

Jack had finally hit bottom or what he thought bottom to be. The bottom had turned out to be much deeper than he imagined, and yet, instinctively, he knew it could be deeper still. The bottom is more than you can take, he thought. Or is it the absolute point when you can take no more? From the bottom will I rise up stronger than before? Will I hold that bottom in me as strength?

He wasn't getting any exercise, and the one window in his bedroom never received any direct sunlight. They were at the tail end of winter, but he still wore his full-length thermal underwear in the house. When it wasn't raining, it was either overcast or windy and always bone cold. His Arizona roots hadn't prepared him for that sort of climate.

Once again Jack asked himself: why should I keep living like this? You'll live like this until you can't take it anymore, then you'll change, he told himself. That's what bottom is: when one follows a path that leads to nowhere for a very long time before deciding to abandon it altogether. It's like that with girlfriends. You follow the girl, stick by her, make concessions for her, always with the hope that it will lead to some peace of mind. And then, if the girl gives you no peace, if you are always reacting to her and trying to make her happy and worrying about her messing around, and finding yourself angry and jealous when she has a life of her own –that's the time to pick a new path. It's the same for women, I know; it's the same for men and women, not just with each other, but for work and play and anything else a person does to make their life worthwhile. If it isn't working, then you gotta change.

Jack's problem, besides unemployment, was that he didn't have a single person who really cared about him, besides his family and particularly his mother. At least most mothers love their children, even if they are rotten or damaged in some way, he thought.

His isolation was apparent in how his housemates talked about him. Now that he was weak, they were all ganging up on him. He lived in constant fear of being kicked out. They shut their doors so they didn't have to see him. Even Henrik had his door shut, including Fridays. Jack didn't drink with them anymore because he had lost his self-esteem. He knew that Alex hated his freeloading. Jack couldn't stand to be in an environment where everything was strained, so he kept to himself.

He had taken to wandering around the neighborhood at night, especially on weekends, so as to not make his housemates uncomfortable with his poverty. He was on the outside looking in on a world he didn't understand. He walked by the bars and restaurants with his hands stuck deep inside the pockets of his shabby coat, the collar up to protect from the wind, watching the more successful animals bare their teeth in laughter and success. He watched the fine, sleek women in their black clothes with their shiny hair and bright white smiles, knowing they were out of his league. He doubted he could even look those girls in the eye. He was one of the weak males: the lion without the mane, so to speak.

It's not physical strength, but money, that implies power in civilized society, he thought. Without money, you are weak; without money, you don't have the right to mate. At least I no longer believe that I have to be tough and strong to attract a nice girl. Girls like brawn, but they prefer brains because brains often equal money. Either that or revolution, as in Alex's case; he could be successful, but he's nearly as bad off as I am.

The truth is, except for Damian, none of us are doing particularly well. We are living dead-end lives, and I'm the only one without an excuse for it. Well, me and Julie maybe. Alex and Henrik have art, that is, they have a passion, and sometimes that's enough to make life bearable.

Jesus, Jack, how could you be born without any talent? Still, you played baseball pretty well; maybe you should have pursued that? But then mom and dad didn't want you to be a baseball player. They thought you were meant for better things. Imagine how ashamed they would be to see you like this, lost and hopeless: a broken man.

One night, Jack's solitary wanderings took him to the park where he had met James and the other homeless. He was hoping to run into James. If there was anyone he could talk to, it was James, who had lived a life, been broken and continued to live. How can he live like he does, Jack wondered. How can a seemingly intelligent and respectable man choose to live in poverty?

That evening Jack surprised many beggars asking for James. If Jack had thought himself shabby compared to the twenty-something tech set, then he could only imagine how the men and women of the street saw him. He noticed how they recoiled from him when he approached and how their eyes were hard and distant, until he asked for James, who they all knew.

At one point, Jack was offered a drink of some cheap low-quality liquor, which he accepted without hesitation. He didn't wish to appear superior. No, in truth he was looking for a little company. Though he didn't smoke, he accepted a cigarette from a shabby hand. It gave him something to do as he went on his way deeper into the park. Jack wandered along the narrow paths hoping for some novel encounter, until finally he ran into James. He stood by a garbage can with fire burning in its belly at the edge of the trees. There was a shed in the clearing and a tractor at the foot of a fire trail. It was a clear night and colder for it. Jack watched the flames flicker in James's face as he approached the group.

Will, Doc and Mary were present, as well as two men Jack didn't know. Once again, the group stiffened and grew tight as he approached.

"Mind if I join you," Jack asked them, stepping closer to the warmth of the fire. He wanted to put them at ease; police and troublemakers weren't in the habit of asking permission to join up.

Jack looked James and the others in the eye and waited. They probably don't remember me. They have more important things to think about than some fool kid. I mean if it doesn't work out for me then I can always go home to a safe place and recover. These people are far gone from having anyone but each other, and that kind of networking will get you nowhere. Sure, they help each other, but they also drag each other down. I guess that's no different from any human relationship. It's the same in college when your buddies want you to skip your homework and go party, so that you're as hung over as they are the next day.

Will was the first to recognize Jack. His first reaction was to freeze before lowering his eyes. He probably remembers his stealing and feels ashamed: not for stealing, Jack thought, but for being caught and then lectured by James, who he respects.

James seemed not to notice Jack, probably thinking him just another body in the night looking for a little warmth. Certainly, the faces came and went with such frequency that to remember was a waste of time. James was distracted and seemed smaller and weaker than Jack remembered. Did he look that tired last time? Perhaps I am only seeing what I see in myself.

"Cold night, huh," Jack said. The group mumbled and some shifted their weight while others rubbed their hands together in reply.

"It's been colder," Doc said. "I remember one winter a few years back when it was so cold there was frost on the ground in the morning. I'm not as young as I used to be and I can't take cold like that anymore. It stays in my bones and makes me stiff."

"That's nothing compared to the Northeast. You fall asleep out there in the winter and you don't wake up," Charlie said. "Say, mister, I haven't seen you before. You just come into town?" Charlie was hoping to hear some news from other cities. He knew many people in many places and often wondered what had happened to them: if they were jailed, dead or missing.

"Oh, no, I've been here a while," Jack said. "I don't spend much time in these parts. I was just out for a walk."

"Just out for a walk?"

"That's right. I didn't have anything better to do, so I thought I'd take a walk."

"Say, you don't look like you're in bad way at all. It looks like you got your hair cut yesterday, and your face is clean and smooth. I get the idea you're makin' sport of us," Fred, the other stranger, said.

"Yep, just like that young man come said he was gonna make a movie about us and help us out. He said if people saw how bad we had it, they'd wanna help. Why, he didn't have a clue did he, James? Thought poverty was some sort a' fashion statement or political agenda. Man, poverty's just poverty. We ain't never seen a penny for helping him make his movie. We shoulda made him pay to film us. Even if it was just a fiver, we shoulda made him pay," Charlie said.

"Well, look at it this way, Charlie, you're famous now. Your face has been all over the big screen, and people have paid to see you. The same people that ignore you, paid to see your miserable face," James said.

"Well, I'll be damned -the fools. Why would anyone do something like that?"

"It's a sickness," Doc said. "They like to sit pretty and masturbate to the misery of the world. It's like going to the zoo. We're animals, and they like to watch us from behind the protection of the screen, as if they was different somehow, but their people just like us. They get drunk like us, they like to have a piece of ass like us and at least we ain't slaves like them. I may be poor, but I'm free, and in this country you can only be free if you don't have any money. Ha, ha."

Doc's hoarse laughter filled the night, and then he broke into a cough that doubled him over: a remnant from a case of pneumonia, which was now more or less a permanent fixture of his deteriorating health.

"But you're wrong, Doc. That kid making the movie was trying to show us intimate-like so that people would see us as individuals and not just some anonymous garbage," James said. "We all told our names and our personal stories. That should count for something."

"The people that go to watch are a minority," Doc said. "Most people don't wanna see us, because to see us means to have to think about how we got here, and also to know that we're human. Not many people want to spend their free time being upset and put out. No, they want to be entertained and taken away from their routines. They want to believe that life is essentially good. The truth is, it's neither one or the other."

"Goddamn, everything is neither one or the other," Fred said, spitting.

"Well, I think you got it better than we do, mister with the warm jacket," Charlie said. "Why, I bet you don't even have a cavity. Wait, wait, let me see those hands," he said, grabbing Jack's hands in his own.

"Ha! Not a single blister. I bet it don't feel nice to have my grubby hands all over you, does it? I bet you wanna run away from me in disgust. Well, go on and git if you don't like it."

Charlie stared him in the eye and Jack felt uncomfortable. He was close to the abyss and wanting to fall and fail and be together with the losers. Charlie's poverty was built on resentment, and anything that was beautiful he wanted to destroy.

"Let him alone," James said, acknowledging Jack for the first time. "So, you've come back. Didn't go as well as you expected? Kid, you're not like us, and I don't want you comin' 'round here no more."

James was disappointed to see the young man return. He felt ashamed; he had hoped to never see Jack again. What the hell is he doing here? He shoulda gotten out; it's no good for him to be with us, and especially not Charlie, who's full a' hate. Charlie's the kind of guy who destroys a man to feel like he's worth somethin'.

"It's like I said, I was just takin' a walk. Anyway, I'm doing all right. I came 'cause I wanted to see you, James. You helped me out before and I just came to talk. I got a lot on my mind."

"Hey, I remember you. You're the kid with the computer that Will tried to steal," Doc said. "Why, you was as green as could be when you came out. Your lucky we didn't strip you bare. Say, I forgot your name, anyhow."

"Jack."

"Listen, Jack, you wouldn't happen to have a bottle, would ya?"

"No. I don't. Maybe I'll bring you one another day. How's that?"

"That's sounds just great, Jack, but a rain check isn't worth much to me. I need a drink now and don't know about tomorrow."

James walked off from the group and Jack fell into step beside him.

James thought: I wonder why I never became a thief? Probably because, though you live like this, you still subscribe to status quo morality. That and you're a coward and could never hurt a man for fear of being hurt yourself. Not to mention your fear of jail. Jail would kill you. You're not a man to be locked up and boxed in. That's why you're out here in the first place.

"So what's on your mind, Jack?"

"Well, what I said back there, you know, about being okay? Well, it isn't true. I'm not okay at all. I got to thinking about it and remembered how you helped me out, and since I don't have anyone to talk to, I thought I'd come see you. I know what you're thinking: what's this kid complaining about, and why doesn't he just go back were he belongs, like you already told me. The truth is I don't know where I belong. Man, James, I had a job, then I got stabbed at work and fired, a girl I liked left me, and now I've been looking for work for a long time and don't get any reply because I don't have any experience. I don't wanna work at some menial job, just like none of you wanna work that way. Let's just say you made an impression on me, is all."

"Most jobs suck, Jack. People are lazy and most jobs suck. You don't seem like a lazy kid to me. You've got a trustworthy face and, what's more, you're young and can afford to make mistakes. Youth is all about making mistakes. My advice to you is to try a few different jobs and learn what you like and what you don't. You'll be surprised how one opportunity will lead to another. The worst thing you can do is isolate yourself. The problem with us out here is that were all isolated, and that's the same as a death sentence, Jack. Chicanery and greed aside, a man still has to create his own opportunities. Just because you were born with a little fortune don't mean you get to keep it. Because for every man who has a comfortable life, there are a hundred more who will kill him to take his place. Some people motivate with threats, and others, with subtle persuasion. I'm not sure which is your suit, Jack. Go get a job, get laid and play the game. You've got all your life to be a wash-up like me."

"Why are you out here, James? I mean, it can't be easy to live like this."

"I'm out here because I dislike people. I'm a misanthrope. I'm out here because success is overrated. I'm out here because I'm an idealist who doesn't want to spend his life adapting to being a bastard, like our politicians and business leaders are bastards. Sure, I'd like to be rich like everyone else, but the price is too high. I mean don't get me wrong, Jack, it is possible to have work that's meaningful where you're not screwing anyone over, but the truth is I never found any work like that. I didn't have enough courage or imagination to look for it. Like most people, I fell into my work."

"What did you do?"

"I was an insurance salesman. Isn't that insipid? Now there's a business. Insurance, like a bank loan, is only given to people who don't need it. I think it's terribly ironic to pay for security. Few people ever experience the great calamity they're covered for. Life insurance is the real kicker. Imagine paying to insure your children if they should die, or your wife or husband for that matter, just so you can capitalize on their death. I remember a guy I worked with, he was crooked all right. His house burnt down once. You'd have thought that he'd have been upset, but it didn't take him more than a week to buy a new one, bigger and nicer than the last. He threw a Christmas party and I remember thinking: how can he afford a place like this? That's what fraud is all about and it usually happens from the inside. Just look at our government."

As they walked, James thought about his son. You're a fraud, he thought. What kind of kid is that going to be who grows up without a father? Why, he probably hates your guts by now, the way you disappeared. That's the thing about women: when the going gets tough, they don't run away. Christine was a good woman, but you didn't love her. You did everything too early and didn't get to enjoy your freedom and youth. That's why you live like this now. Because though you were successful, you didn't have a clue about what life was like for most people. Why, there was a time when you envied Ben Daughton for his new house, even though he was a criminal and a cheat. And how about Jack? Maybe the kid's too good. They say being young is carefree, but that's not true. These kids got more pressure on them than my generation. They're more ambitious and their world is more insecure. They're not interested in family, just their own success. Just think, women these days don't even need to marry anymore. They've got the money and the freedom to be whoever they want, no strings attached. The truth is, though he is younger than me and better-looking, I feel sorry for the kid. I'm glad I'm gonna die before things get really bad, because they will. Imagine, Jack has to come all the way out here and talk to the likes of me for companionship. I don't know what's going on in this country and this world, but I don't like it. I don't like it one bit. Everything that is good and true is going through the wringer.

"I don't know, James. I feel like I want to do something. But I don't know what to do or how to do it. I want to be great, but I'm starting to doubt it's gonna happen. Before I always thought I was the center of the world, and now I feel like I don't even exist."

"Don't talk like that, Jack. Don't talk yourself down, because words are more powerful than we think, and what we say has a way of coming true. The question is: who are you trying to measure up to? A man should only try to measure up to himself, otherwise he won't fit. You should live the way that best suits you. If you do that then you can consider yourself a success. Too many people choose to live against themselves and for the benefit of others. The truth is most people live the way they do because they're afraid. Fear is the controlling factor in most people's lives and that, along with laziness, is a dangerous combination. If you don't like the life you're living, change it. It's as simple as that."

He's right. Maybe the city's not for you. Maybe you should find another place to live, with people who care, and try to meet a nice girl and stop thinking about Elizabeth. Maybe you don't like business at all, and what about trying to work with Damian? Doesn't everyone say you should be an actor?

Each person needs to make their own mistakes, James thought. I can say anything I want to Jack. Maybe it'll make him feel better, but he's still gonna make a hell of a lot of mistakes, like all of us.

James felt lonely. As he walked, he thought that Jack, too, would leave him, live his life and do many things. While at times James wished for death, he also wished he could live life again from the beginning and do it better.

I wonder how many people wish that? I wonder how much of life is chance and how much comes from personal initiative? Perhaps I don't really want to know, James thought. Certainly, some people are born without hope, and others, with great fortune. Still, I do believe that a man can change his own life, and part of that has to do with participation. Opportunity comes from other people, but no one likes to kiss ass for a break. That's the dilemma.

Jack did not feel as lonely as before. He was no longer stuck inside his own head, but thinking about what James had told him and trying to imagine James's past life with a family and a stable job. Walking next to him now, that reality seemed impossible.

James's words clicked in his mind. Jack was tired of living as he did and he would no longer stand for it. His newfound inspiration came from the most unlikely of sources: the poor hermit beside him. They walked together for a time, each in their own thoughts, until they made it to the ocean, where Jack stopped at the corner store for a bottle.

"What are you drinking, James? Anything you want."

"No, really Jack, you don't have to do that."

"What are you drinking?"

"All right. Fine. How about a bottle of whiskey?"

They lay against the dunes at Ocean Beach and the wind whipped at their clothes and hair. They could hear the crash of the waves on the shore while they got drunk, and soon they were laughing together.

"Do you really take your showers out here," Jack asked. "Seems pretty cold to me."

"Yep, I try to go when there ain't no people. I don't think the surfers would like it much if I came in the afternoon, stripped my clothes off and started soaping up. I tell you, Jack, a shower sure does wonders for a man's dignity. After a good shower, I feel a few feet taller and don't have any trouble looking people in the eye. There are a few things a man has to do to keep from losing himself completely, and cleanliness is one of them. Since we have so few possessions, it's important to keep them in good condition. That things deteriorate can't be helped, but one thing's for sure: we use everything we've got until it turns to dust, and we don't ever throw away anything useful. You'd be surprised what people throw away in this city. These tennis shoes, almost brand new. I found them in a dumpster on the Haight. And you learn where to go, too. Some of them used clothing stores put the clothes they can't sell in garbage bags on the street. Pizza places throw wrong orders nicely packaged in their boxes out the back. That's good food and easy to get at."

It occurred to Jack that a clean-thinking man like James could be saved. If he wanted to he could return to the world that he had rejected. Jack thought about bringing him home, giving him a real meal and a hot shower, and letting him sleep on the couch.

No, Damian, and particularly Julie, would never put up with that, especially as things stood. Also, at the back of Jack's mind was the thought that James wouldn't want such charity and that maybe he wasn't altogether to be trusted. Jack hated to think that way, but even he wasn't above the prejudice that surrounded James's appearance and condition. Why, for all he knew, James could be a liar about all the books he had read and his past life, but then again, probably not. After all, James had never asked Jack for anything, whereas others in his position might have. During his time in the city, Jack had learned that very little came for free. Even a beer between friends was expected to be repaid with the next round.

Part III

1

When Graham left Padang he did not tell her where he was going or when he would return.

"Merpati, you can stay here while I'm gone if you like. It might be a bit lonely, and I understand if you want to be with your family. I will give you some money to last until I return."

She feared he was leaving for good and did not have the courage to tell her. But if that were so, would he offer to let her stay in his house?

He was a good man and had always treated her with kindness. Beyond that she knew he was preoccupied with work. She did not know much about his work, except that it was dangerous, and she worried he would be killed.

She loved him. How could she forget the attention he paid her in class: how kindly he spoke to her and how patient he was with her English mistakes? Thanks to Graham, she had learned to speak English well, especially after she moved into his house. However, it was only after lovemaking that he spoke to her with any candor. Then he would ask questions about her family, religion and Indonesian culture. She felt he had great respect for her when he asked such questions. Whenever he experienced any practical problems with the house or the banks or the bureaucracy, he asked her advice. What's more, he followed it.

Still, it bothered her that he never spoke of himself, his family or his country. If he had innumerable questions about Indonesia, so did she about the United States. Merpati had heard many things about his country, and the movies she had seen made her wonder: why does he come here if his home is so rich? Why does he wish to live in the countryside? Even though he didn't say it, she knew Graham was a simple man with simple pleasures. He spent his free time gardening, reading and fishing in the river that ran by the property. He was eager to learn from her about cooking, and she knew that before her arrival he had been self-sufficient, washing his own clothes and preparing his own meals.

He is lucky to have me. I don't understand how he could live without the company of a woman. Do other Americans live this way: each one separate from the next, never receiving visits or visiting their friends and neighbors?

Merpati was sad that her parents could not visit and see her living with Graham as his wife with all honor accorded. What good was the respect she received from him if no one was there to recognize it? What did it matter how well she took care of him if no one could see that he was well-fed and that his house and clothes were clean? She knew he appreciated her and loved her, but she longed to show others how happy she had made him. Also, she wanted children. Sometimes she grew sad at the thought that they would never have children together and never be married. Her family would never accept a non-Muslim. She knew that he would never change his faith and become a believer. During Ramadan he did not fast, he drank alcohol daily and to excess, and she did not like to be with him then. She did not like the smell of his breath or how the alcohol made him reckless and violent and also sad. Once, by accident, she had come upon him crying at his office desk, and he had showered her with abuse and profanity to make her leave. She knew he did not mean those things and that it was the alcohol that made him that way.

They were living an indecent life. It was a dangerous life, and she hoped that no one would discover their secret. If her family found out, then she would be disgraced.

Merpati was afraid he would grow tired of her. He was her teacher and she respected him greatly. He was an important man who had traveled the world. Who knew all the things he had seen and done? So what does he want with an ignorant girl like me? What can I give him besides my flesh, and my love and affection?

The treasures of his knowledge and experience he guards closely in his mind, while I am wrapped protectively in the traditions of my culture and the dreams of my youth. We must share and learn each other's secrets. Perhaps one day you can convince him to accept your religion. Even if he does not believe, he can live like a Muslim and respect our rituals and faith. With time he will learn to see their value.

After he had gone, Merpati returned to her village. There she lived with her parents and her brothers and sisters who were not yet married. During this time, she tried to hide her sadness at his absence. Her father, sensing that something was wrong, told her, "Don't worry, Merpati, soon you will be married and have children. Don't despair. Your beauty will earn you a fine husband." This did little to cheer her up, for she knew that soon her father would find her match, and she would be forced to marry and leave Graham forever. Even then, she imagined escaping with him to a foreign country where they would not find her: if she ran away, she would disgrace her family; if Graham stopped loving her, she would be left with no one. She would end up a beggar or worse: she would be forced to sell her body to merchants and foreigners in the city.

During Graham's absence, Merpati had not known a moment of peace. Only the daily chores of washing, cooking and cleaning kept her from fearful and anxious thoughts. I am so afraid, she told herself. What will happen to me if he does not return?

When Graham finally did return, he was accompanied by a woman who was so striking that Merpati forgot herself and stared. She noted the ice blue of the stranger's eyes and the way she stood, not with her head bowed, but with her chin raised. Merpati was surprised to hear the woman insult Graham in her presence, and she noted how sometimes he could not look the woman in the eye. Why does he not punish her for her lack of respect? Imagine a woman talking that way. But then Merpati had seen this same submissive attitude in her father when her mother mentioned the family finances. That was the shame of being poor, and it was her mother's right to ask about money that had been wasted gambling.

"Elizabeth, this is my maid, Merpati. Merpati, this is Elizabeth, a friend of mine from America. She will be staying with us. I want you to make her as comfortable as possible."

Elizabeth shook the young girl's hand and felt the delicate bones rub together in her grip. Merpati let out a small gasp and pulled her hand away, startled.

I bet he's fucking her, Elizabeth thought. Look at that guilty shit-eating grin he's got on his face. He's fucking her, all right. I bet it turns him on to fuck that young exotic girl. I bet she lets him do anything he wants and is too afraid to ask a real woman. Still, it's not her fault. Don't be jealous because she's younger than you, has beautiful hair and is very sweet.

This must be his wife, Merpati thought. He has been away from her for a long time and now she has come to him. She is beautiful like him, tall and pale and with those sharp clear eyes that cut me like a knife. I do not wish to make her angry. I hate her, but I do not want to fight with her because she will destroy me.

After Elizabeth's arrival, Merpati's life changed. She was forced to sleep in the guest room that had been empty for so long. That same evening, after Merpati had cooked and cleaned for them, she excused herself. If Elizabeth was his wife then she did not wish to make her suspicious.

"Come on, Merpati, why don't you join us. You can tell Elizabeth a story, like the ones you tell me."

Merpati felt that it was not her place to sit with them. She saw Elizabeth's eyebrows form an angry line above her nose, and watched her jaw grow tight.

"No, I am tired. I must go to bed. Do you still require my services?"

"No, thank you, Merpati. You've done enough," Graham said.

"Yes, thank you, good night," Merpati said.

"I could use a drink," Elizabeth said, as Merpati turned to leave.

An uncomfortable silence ensued. Rarely did Graham order her to do anything.

"Yes, um, Merpati, could you get us each a whiskey," Graham told her.

"On the rocks," Elizabeth added.

Merpati went to the kitchen and took down the bottle that said whiskey. Normally, Graham made his own drinks, and she had no idea what "on the rocks" meant. She filled the glasses and brought them out.

"I said I wanted it on the rocks," Elizabeth said.

"Oh, sorry, she doesn't know any better. I usually make my own drinks. Merpati is a Muslim and doesn't drink alcohol. I thought it best to not have her serve it, either. But no matter. Merpati, could you put some ice in her drink, please?"

Merpati was greatly embarrassed at the situation. She did not even know how to make a simple drink. Certainly, Elizabeth knows about our indecent relationship. That is why she is shaming me. Because I have shamed her. I have lain with her husband.

With a mixture of guilt and sadness, Merpati crept into the darkness of the master bedroom and quietly removed any signs of her presence. He is very foolish bringing her here without warning. He should have dismissed me, yet he does not. He feels sorry for me because I am poor. But I am not to be pitied.

That evening, lying alone in bed, Merpati thought that she would leave him and not come back. Clearly, her father would be angry at her for leaving her job. With Graham's money, and the money her father made selling textiles, the family had been living comfortably for the first time in many years. No, perhaps she should stay on and do her work. She did not have to love him. She could change the feelings in her heart.

For Merpati, it was a sleepless night. Elizabeth's obscenities and shameless shouting and moaning kept her awake. Curiosity forced her from the bed. She went outside and approached the bedroom window.

Shrouded in darkness, she watched them make love until tears ran down her face. Perhaps it was best that she drown herself in the river? The pain was great and then it subsided and became a cold resolve. Perhaps I will kill her, she thought.

"Am I as good as your maid fuck slave? God, you're such a pig, Graham. Preaching to me about the injustices of the world when all you want to do is fuck helpless little girls from developing countries."

Elizabeth was on all fours as Graham clung to her hips and repetitively jammed his torso up against her backside. She pushed back in time to the rhythm and felt his hand tighten its grip around her neck, strangling her. Her mind was a supernova of pleasure as she imagined him fucking the maid and her own experience with Jack. Though Jack was better-looking, Graham was a much better lay because he never got tired, had no inhibitions, and could come or not come according to her needs. And he always let go of her throat before she went unconscious.

"Oh yeah, oh, that's right. Fuck me, you asshole, fuck me. Oh, that feels so good. You feel so good."

"I haven't been fucking my maid at all," Graham said, short of breath. "She's like sixteen years old and Muslim, and even if I wanted to I couldn't because she wouldn't let me. She's very chaste."

"Oh, oh, yeah, uhh, uhh, right. You're paying her and she lives with you and she's not gonna fuck you? I bet she does anything you say. Oh God, yeah, right there, oh God, I think I'm gonna come."

Afterwards they lay back on the pillows together and smoked a joint.

"I could care less what you've done with that girl," Elizabeth said. "But now that I'm here, I don't want you fucking her at all. In fact, I want you to send her home. Either you kick her out, or I pack my bags and put up somewhere else. You decide."

"Merpati has been a great help to me. I don't think we can do without her, unless you're willing to cook and clean. I don't have time for that shit. Anyway, you'll find it very useful to have her around, and what's more, you can practice Indonesian with her," Graham said. "And of course I'm not going to fuck her while you're here. I invited you here because I wanted to share my life. I still love you and you wouldn't be here if you didn't still need me."

Elizabeth grimaced and looked toward the window.

"So you admit you fucked her before," she said.

"Yes, I fucked her before."

"How many times?"

"What difference does it make?"

"It makes a big difference," Elizabeth said.

Irritated, Graham said, "I've fucked her every day, sometimes twice or three times a day, since she moved in about three months ago."

"Thanks for your candor. This isn't going to work if you lie. If you had said three or four times a week, or just once a week, or even twenty times since you met her, I'd have called you a liar."

"Well, what do you expect me to do? I live in the middle of nowhere for Christ's sake. It's lonely as hell out here, and I can't just as well fuck the livestock, can I?"

"You don't need to justify yourself. Just don't fuck her again."

"Fine. Do you want another drink?"

"No, I want a cold shower. I'm sweating like crazy. I'd forgotten what real heat was living in the city. But then I do prefer heat to cold. Cold stresses me out."

Showering, Elizabeth had to admit she was happy. Who else could boast of living in the middle of the jungle on several acres of land by a beautiful river in one of the most exotic countries on earth? I hope I wasn't too hard on him, she thought. I just can't stand it when people aren't up front. He should have told you about her before you came. You did the right thing in confronting him. No way are you going to be just another mistress.

With both women around, the house was no longer peaceful. Elizabeth was strong-willed, and she had no qualms about turning things upside down to suit her preferences. She was rude and condescending to Merpati, ordering her about and forcing her to serve her every need. It wasn't Elizabeth's nature to behave that way, but somehow it appeased her jealousy. That and she could get away with it. After a few weeks Graham was no longer as enthusiastic about her visit. The novelty of their relationship was fading fast. Elizabeth was accustomed to her new home and took it for granted. She realized that she would have to start teaching to pay her way. She did not like to depend on Graham, like his slut maid.

With Elizabeth gone teaching in the afternoons, Graham found he could get back to work compiling some of his favorite and most provocative photos. He had recently met with a publisher in New York, and given his reputation as a photojournalist, they had agreed to publish a collection of his best work. Graham had been in a quandary for weeks over which photos to include. The black and white images spread out on his desk contrasted sharply with the peace of his surroundings: the bright green of the jungle, the sound of the river, and the isolation of his property and home.

In the photos, tight-faced youths brandished sticks and hatchets in the smoke-filled streets of besieged neighborhoods; looters emerged from shattered shop windows, eyes bulging with adrenaline and teeth clenched from fear; soldiers savagely beat defenseless civilians into the blood-soaked dirt; mutilated bodies of the dead lay in mass graves dug by the living; hateful children fired automatic rifles at faceless crowds; patients with amputated limbs and terminal diseases filled decaying hospitals; refugee camps swelled with emaciated moony-eyed children, skeletal broken men and stoic mothers staring into eternity.

Graham's study faced the garden and he would often catch himself daydreaming out the window. One day, while he was working, he spotted Merpati hanging laundry. She saw him, waved and flashed her bright smile. Elizabeth didn't measure up to Merpati's smile. She didn't smile as often or with as much sincerity or enjoyment. Seeing Merpati's smile left him needy. Graham could not deny that he cared for her deeply. She had worked her way into his heart and a void was left when Elizabeth replaced her in his bed. Perhaps that was why he invited Elizabeth out: to see if it was true that Merpati was the woman he loved. Graham had lived so much of his life without love that he was incapable of recognizing it, except through contrast. And now Elizabeth was here to stay for an indeterminate amount of time. He couldn't just as well tell her to leave, or send Merpati back home to her family. During this difficult period, it was his only consolation that Merpati was nearby and they could express their affection in subtle gestures and kind words.

Graham watched as Merpati washed her hair in a bucket, wringing it in her hands and twisting it into a thick coil that she draped down her back. Her batik had gotten wet and it clung to her chest and the curves of her body. Was she just being playful? If so, her face did not betray her.

The violence and misery of the images on his desk collided with the idyll of Merpati, with her bright smile and silky fathomless skin, washing her hair with graceful movements. The desire was unbearable. Nothing mattered then but to make love to her.

Graham walked out into the garden and reached out and ran his fingers through her wet hair. They watched each other in silence. Then Merpati splashed him with water and broke the spell. She ran into the garden and he chased her. She was laughing and he was desperate.

Eventually, she let herself be caught and they collapsed together in the grass. Graham kissed her, squeezed her flesh and tore at her batik. She did not laugh anymore. His eyes were glassy. He was distant and outside himself. The playfulness and warmth were gone, replaced by blindness and oblivion. Graham clung desperately to her naked body, hoping that a bit of her innocence would rub off on him. He wanted to reach her soul with his dick and inoculate himself against the crippling loneliness and fear that haunted him. He was in radical oscillation between Merpati's care and protection, and Elizabeth's passion and irreverence.

When Elizabeth came home from work, the house was quiet. She went to the bedroom to shower and change. Looking out the bedroom window, she discovered them lying together in the grass. Such was her shock and fascination that she only remembered to put down her things after they were finished.

She had known from the beginning. The desperate struggle before her was proof of the love that did not exist between her and Graham. Her life had become a play in which she was only a supporting character. Elizabeth had blinded herself with her own vanity and given Merpati nobility through her abuses. She was a fool with only loneliness for consolation. She could not compete with the girl's youth and innocence. Though Elizabeth was only twenty-six, the years had made her bitter and cold.

What do I do now? Do I pretend I never saw it? Do I pack up and leave? Elizabeth did not yet have the confidence to set out on her own in that foreign place, though she had a job. She knew that she would be lonely in a culture she did not fully understand. In no way would she fall for an Indonesian man who would treat her as an inferior. That was something she could not tolerate.

2

Henrik was hired as the in-house DJ at Virgo Records on Market. It was his first nine-to-five job in six years. Though it was a relief to have a steady paycheck, he didn't like to get up early and work an eight-hour shift with an unpaid one-hour predetermined break for lunch. Nor did he enjoy promoting mainstream music at the expense of artists like himself.

Aside from the legendary musicians of the past, who had gained notoriety based on their originality and talent, the popular music industry had mostly to do with the marketing of image and recycling of rhythm and melody. One didn't buy music because it was pleasant to listen to, but to assume an identity and keep current with the latest fad. Music had become something to collect, consume and throw away. CDs were bought for one hit track and not enjoyed from beginning to end. Their lifespan had turned from turtles to flies. Whatever artist or song the major record labels put their money behind would be a hit. The studios saturated the market with their latest stars, and when the public grew tired of the repetition, they engineered the next big act by making a few adjustments to the old formula. Most of that music wouldn't stand the test of time.

It was Henrik's opinion that there was very little mainstream music of any redeemable value currently being produced in the United States, and plenty of quality underground music being blocked by corporate domination of the industry. Shitty music only serves to degrade one's quality of life, he reasoned. Nikki Star was a clear example of the corporate approach to music sales. She was the pretty face that studio executives had turned into an icon. Her songs were written by third-party songwriters with the imperfections of her voice mixed to sterile perfection. It was no longer a question of talent.

As a DJ for corporate America, it was Henrik's job to make the garbage flow as smoothly as possible. It was a tactical move; he would make an okay salary, but more importantly, he would gain access to the industry. Not only would Henrik use his creativity to mix music, he would surreptitiously include some of his own tracks in the licensed playlist that Virgo Corp wanted to promote. He was certain it would create interest. If people asked about his songs, he would supply them with his own home-burned CDs at the bargain price of ten dollars a pop.

Henrik planned to play enough of his music so that even Virgo would sign him. The job was a weigh station, like most jobs were for the ambitious and often deluded. In time, Henrik would play his masterpiece, *The Audiobible*, in its entirety. But he had to be careful. He didn't want to ask permission prematurely and be refused. He had been given the job based on his victory of the San Francisco leg of the World DJ Tour just two weeks ago. And now it was time to prove his worth. Wasn't he the best that San Francisco had to offer? Yes, in his particular niche, he was the best. He was a master of mixing music from different cultural traditions with raw ambient organic sound. What the others lacked was a global vision. Their music lacked depth.

Henrik knew that he wouldn't have been hired if he had played music his way. To win World DJ: San Francisco, he took popular beats and mixed them with some very rare and hard to find international records, to successful results. He had given the crowd a slice of the exotic and unexplored in an easily digestible commercial package. He had given them exactly what they expected from the modern evolution of electronica: tribal chanting, traditional instruments and foreign languages to seduce the modern urban hipster without the discomfort of the truly foreign. Henrik was aware of the irony of his work: let's serve up the exotic and turn it into a consumer product to get people tuned in. But doesn't that strip the music of its cultural underpinnings and context, making it common and bland? Is there any other way, he wondered.

Perhaps the enchantment and beauty of the world could be preserved in the purity of sound? But then you don't believe in the purity of anything. The history of the human race on earth is not one of purity. There is no master race, there is no ideal earth that is clean and good, ruined only by man's flaws. There are no untouched indigenous tribes that live in harmony with everything. Yet, ironically, it was possible to make music that allowed people to dream of harmony and that which was pure, free and good. Only by mixing influences that did not fit historically or culturally, could one learn to appreciate what was unfamiliar and foreign; by manipulating the past, it was possible to invent the future. Because everything down to individual thought contained an element borrowed from somewhere else.

Through sound, Henrik expressed what he considered to be a superior vision of the world; nevertheless, he bore no illusions about the originality of his thoughts, or more precisely, his music. His compositions were the unique products of his own consciousness, but their origins could not be ignored; every new creation was connected to the past with innumerable roots that were impossible to completely expose or comprehend.

Henrik wondered: if nothing is original, then is the novelty of my music enough to make me stand out from the competition? Without recognition does my work have any value? Does quality matter if it exists in a vacuum?

What Henrik desired most was to escape his own mortality. He needed an affirmation that what he did would matter to others in posterity. Meanwhile, his doubts and insecurities fought with his stubborn will to succeed. Unfortunately, he had something to prove.

Often, in despair, he told himself: just keep going. No matter how hard it may be and how unjust, just keep on going, because without this you have nothing. Without the music everything is black and empty, and that's when you want to destroy yourself with sex and alcohol, and destroy others with you. *The Audiobible* is your savior, Henrik. That project is your life's project. If you fail, there's no point in continuing this farce.

3

Henrik had been working at Virgo for several weeks before he decided to play his own music. There was one track in particular he thought would be a hit; it sampled Alex ranting about U.S. hegemony, along with the sound of revving engines, screeching tires, and the crunching metal and shattered glass of car wrecks, set to a tribal drum beat with a spacey keyboard melody heavy on the echo effects.

He played other tracks as well, which included fragments of speeches by civil rights leaders, sounds of flowing water, crashing waves and birdcalls. In one song, a human heartbeat served for the baseline, while Alex unwittingly supplied the lyrics, "We have lost our solidarity, our knowledge of the connection between things, their interdependency."

Henrik had crafted a call and response between Alex and his friend Natasha, the Brazilian bartender at Chameleon with the sugar-coated Portuguese and sexy accent. "*Mas, você não quer gozar da vida?* But don't you want to enjoy life? *Você não quer me tocar?* Don't you want to touch me?" Fighter jets shot across the sky to a hip-hop beat, and Alex weighed in, "How can we expect to find meaning in life when they spoon feed us status quo morality and repress our ambition? Well, I don't buy it . . . don't buy it . . . buy it," and then Natasha, "Don't you want to touch me . . . love me . . . touch me . . . buy it . . . don't love me, touch me . . . buy . . . me . . . status quo morality . . ." Henrik mixed in the high-pitched yelling of Bedouin tribesmen, machine gun fire and an ecstatic violin.

In another track, he supplied some round base punctuated by a searching jazz trumpet, while Alex and Natasha continued their conflicting dialogue of reason and passion. The artificial and smooth beats were accentuated with howling Arctic winds and melancholy piano. Natasha said, "Life is too short to die for an ideal. I believe in emotion. Politics and economics, what does it matter? I'm in love. What's the matter, can't you love?" Alex responded, "Love is a fiction and the product of circumstance." "What's the matter, can't you love?" "Love, like hope, is the illusion we need to cope with life." "No, love is simple: I love you and I want you to love me, too."

From his booth, Henrik watched the crowd mill about the CD racks. He watched them watch each other. He thought: people will buy anything if they think it will make others like them. They will assume any image if it will get them accepted.

Henrik had played three of what he considered his best songs. The question was would anyone notice and appreciate his talent? A knot had formed in his stomach. Henrik was afraid of rejection. In his mind there was little separation between himself and his music: if the public didn't like it, then what would he do?

It had always amazed him that he could work on a project for weeks or months, one song, and when he played it for others, maybe Alex or Damian, they would say, "Cool tunes," and it would be just as soon forgotten. All the time he had invested and it meant so little to everyone else. Or maybe Alex would make some sort of criticism, and the words would sit in his head for the rest of the evening. "Don't you think the polka band is a little over the top? I mean, it's funny, but what exactly are you getting at?"

Alex cared as little for music as he did for reading and writing. Henrik hadn't read a book in he couldn't remember how long. Reading didn't matter to him. Was that how it was with everyone? Were they all caught in their own world unable to see beyond their own reason, personal interests and needs?

Henrik had expected some reaction to his work, but no one in the store seemed to notice or care. Disheartened, he moved on in the playlist. To his irritation, someone came and asked him about one of the popular songs; they had forgotten the name of the artist. Henrik thought to ask if they had heard his music. Instead, he kept quiet. He wouldn't grovel for compliments.

Over the next few weeks Henrik's frustration grew. He was tired of playing the same songs over and over again. No matter how much mixing he did, those songs would never be any good. There was a reason he no longer listened to the radio. That and all the commercials. He responded by playing more of his own music and omitting completely the songs he didn't like from his set. Surprisingly, no one seemed to notice.

Maybe the playlist was only a guideline? Maybe the management doesn't really care what's played? I mean all the policies and procedures come from corporate headquarters, anyway. Most of the people who work here are . . . losers like me? Fuck that. I'm stuck with these teenage losers on their first job, and college grads who have met the wall called reality, but I'm different. Anyway, what do they care what I play? They don't get anything out of it.

It was bitterness and contempt that drove Henrik to play less and less of the playlist. He might sample some commercial tracks only to mix them like a face is mixed when it hits the windshield at, say, sixty. He began to play all of his disc, *Chameleon*. He wasn't yet ready to start playing *The Audiobible*. As it stood, that production was now in its eighteenth hour. He had six hours left for his twenty-four hour masterpiece. Was it idealism to think that someone would listen to it non-stop? Idealism and idealism. Soon people would have radios in their heads and such daily soundtracks would be common.

Then one day it happened: someone came and asked about a track from *Chameleon*. Opera, a xylophone, syncopated clapping, rain, lots of smooth lounge beats, piercing brain tickling highs like baklava pastry: yeah, track seven.

"This is what you heard," Henrik said, handing him the disc.

"What section is it in," the young man asked.

"You can't find it here. I'll give it to you for ten bucks."

"Is the rest any good?"

"I've played three tracks off it. If you want you can wander around and I'll play a little more."

"I really dug that last song. Opera is touchy, when people sample it they usually put too much in. And they always set it to hard trace instead of lounge."

"The key is variation," Henrik told him. "I'm a big fan of variation. People have a tendency to get bored. The music has to change enough to keep the imagination going."

"Is it your disc?"

"Sure is."

"Well, it's better than most of the stuff here. It's too bad you can't get it on the rack. But then again, once it's on the rack, it won't be cool anymore. I'll take it."

Henrik took the money and gave him the CD.

"Listen, put the disc in your bag, so they won't see it on your way out. It doesn't have a security chip, so the alarm won't go off."

"Right."

"If you like that, I've got something else I'm working on. It's a monumental twenty-four hour mix called *The Audiobible*. I'll be playing it next month sometime. Then you'll be able to buy it from my site. The URL is on the back of the disc."

The man left, and though it was only ten bucks and one CD, Henrik felt like he had sold a thousand. *It's better than most of the stuff on the rack.* Damn right it is, and it's good to hear someone say it.

Henrik sold a few more copies of his disc before one of the customers was hassled by the door guard. They came back to the booth: the guard, the floor manager and the unfortunate customer. The manager, Jim, knocked on the glass and Henrik opened up.

"He says he got the disc from you. That you gave it to him."

"That's right. He knows me from the club. He wanted a copy of my set."

"All right," Jim said. Henrik shut the booth, and Jim turned to the customer, "Sorry about that. We've got to be tight with security. Kids come in here all the time and make off with CDs. You wouldn't believe the amount of theft in music retail."

"I don't appreciate at all being humiliated like that in front of other people," the customer said.

"Well, you did have a CD in your pocket that you didn't pay for, and the real shame is that people steal at all. Listen, come with me and we'll get you a gift certificate for a free CD. No hard feelings, huh?"

At the offer of a free disc, the young man lowered his voice and grew less hostile.

"What you really need to worry about is all the music that's stolen every day on the net. If you ask me brick and mortar music retail is a thing of the past. You guys need to go on line and sell MP3s," he said.

It was not the first person Jim had seen go back to talk to the new DJ. What was his name again? Definitely something gay and European. He has an accent, anyway. Jim had his suspicions that the DJ was selling CDs on the side. Still, he did do some pretty cool remixes of Nikki Star.

Jim went back to the booth and knocked on the glass. Henrik saw him coming and feigned irritation. Really, he was nervous about being caught. He had twenty copies of his disc under the counter.

"Hello again. Sorry to bother you, Klaus?"

"Henrik."

"Sure, anyway Henrik, I hope you know that you're working for Virgo and it's detrimental to business if you sell your CDs on the premises. Also, if you were to be caught selling stock under the table for your own profit, then you'd be fired."

Henrik didn't like Jim. He was just the sort of mediocre American who produced nothing and made his living off people more creative than himself. He was, simply put, a lower life form. Without musicians where would this clown be? Why, I bet he listens to Nikki Star of all things.

"Listen, I'm here to spin music," Henrik said. "I've got a few demo discs that I've been giving out."

"Yeah, I can see them. You've got more than a few. It almost looks like you've got a little side business. I hope you're not selling those discs."

"Listen, man, you're cramping my style. You've come and interrupted me twice now, and I can't work like that. I'm the one that makes this place flow. Go and do your job and I'll do mine."

He's an arrogant son of a bitch. I knew I didn't like his face, Jim thought. Fag European that uses his accent to pull chicks. All these DJ types are the same. Fucking pervert junkies. What talent does it take to put together other people's music?

"You just watch yourself. Guys like you are a dime a dozen. There's nothing original about being a DJ."

Henrik waved him away disrespectfully with his hand. Wave, wave, go away, lackey.

Jim had already decided to tell the store manager. Fuck him. If he had been cool, fine. I understand him wanting to promote his own stuff, but he shouldn't have been rude. Jim was a man who prided himself on his hard work and also his manners. One thing he disliked were rude people, and of course the rich. If I were rich, I would probably be rude, he thought. This job sucks. I started to work here because I liked music. That's like working in a toilet factory because you like to shit.

The next day at work there was Jim again knocking on the window. Henrik had barely started the set. He was still sipping from his cappuccino. The morning was when he plowed through the playlist because he was too tired to be creative.

"Listen, I can't work like this," Henrik said, flinging the door to his booth open. "I don't work for you. I'm not one of your stock boy slaves. So fuck off, you cunt."

He'd had a little too much to drink the night before and it wasn't helping that Jim was such a pain in the ass.

"Mark wants to see you in his office. And if you ever call me a cunt again I'll break your freak ass in two," Jim said.

Henrik saw that he was angry. He didn't doubt that Jim was capable of following through on his threat. Until then, he had thought of Jim as spineless. Yesterday, he had even seemed smaller. Now he began to resemble a college football player in size and build. People take things too personally. Henrik was used to insulting people and then groveling his way out of it. To him, groveling was not offensive, but a clever social skill. Groveling and arrogance were two sides to the same coin.

"Whoa, Jim, chill out. Hey, I haven't had my coffee yet. I can be a real bitch without my coffee. Just ask my housemates. They tell me to fuck off. You should do the same."

"Fuck off, and Mark wants you in his office," Jim said.

"Good, see how easy it is," Henrik said. But Jim was already across the floor.

Did you see how his eyes grew wide when you threatened him? You're kind of a bad ass. You play it off, but you know you're a bad ass, Jim told himself. But then you were out of line. That little punk got under your skin, all right. No one gets under your skin like that. Not even mom.

This could be an opportunity. It was stupid to think you could sell your own CDs under their nose, but this could be an opportunity, Henrik thought, looking at the CD in his hand. *Chameleon*. What a disc. If he were stranded on a desert island and could have one CD, it would be *Chameleon*. Henrik no longer enjoyed listening to other people's music. The only purpose of other people's music was to appropriate and adulterate it to make it his. Piss on it, so to speak.

You should have delivered the disc to customers personally, or gotten their address and sent it in the mail. If you keep your job, then that's what you'll do, he thought.

"Ah, Henrik. Yes. Sit down, please."

Mark Grear was a handsome man in his mid-forties. He wore glasses and was stylish in that unoriginal San Francisco way. He was the sort that looked more intelligent with glasses than without. Some people would argue that everyone looked more intelligent with glasses, but that's not true, Henrik thought. Some people looked retarded with glasses.

Mark got right to the point.

"Jim told me that you've been selling you own pirate CDs in our store. Is that true?"

"Not at all. I imagine you're referring to the incident when they accosted a customer to whom I had given a CD? Anyway, I had promised him a CD when I was working at the club."

"According to Jim, you had a stack of your own CDs in the DJ booth."

"Well, not exactly a stack, but I do keep a few copies with me for promotional purposes."

"Listen, no harm no foul, Henrik. I just want you to understand that you can't be doing any side business on our time. If you want to sell CDs, open your own shop."

"Yes sir, I understand." Why not throw in a "sir?" These guys love that shit; it makes them feel important.

"Apropos, I've brought some copies of my disc. Here, why don't you help yourself," Henrik said, sliding a stack across the desk. "I'd really appreciate it if you gave it a listen. Tell me what you think. If you don't mind me asking, do you have any kids?"

"I'm not sure what you're getting at," Mark said.

"Well, my music is geared more toward the younger set. Teenagers and hip twenty-somethings. Let your kids have a listen and . . ."

"Right, thanks for the CD, though I'm not sure I need ten to myself."

"Oh, I've got plenty. Go on and take them."

"Well Henrik, I just wanted to make sure that we understand each other."

"Perfectly. You can be sure that I have not and never will sell my CDs privately while on the job. Oh, and Mr. Grear?"

"Yes?"

"If it wouldn't be too much trouble, well, what the hell. It's not always I get the chance to talk face to face with the San Francisco branch manager of Virgo records. If it wouldn't be too much trouble, could you send these copies out to wherever they need to go? I want to get signed to your label. And if that's not possible, maybe you could give me a contact address, and I could send them myself with a note saying that you've asked them to look at my work?"

"Listen Henrik, it's not that easy. You seem like a nice guy . . ."

Yeah right, what if he came to ask your daughter out? Look at the bumps in his neck, Mark thought. What the hell is that? And those cat contacts. If you want to be successful in life, you can't wear cat contacts and look like an alien.

"Henrik, I can't just tell the guys at the head office that I've discovered the next big thing. We've got talent guys for that. People who know the market. There are thousands of artists like you out there that want to get discovered. I mean your stuff could be great, but it could also be mediocre, and if it is, I'd have to tell you. Also, you may have to live with the fact that the market is suddenly more geared toward hip hop, for example. And who's to say I'm the best judge? I may hate it. That's why I'm not a talent scout or an agent. I'm a jazz guy. I don't like most modern music if it's not jazz, and the jazz I listen to is mostly from dead musicians."

An uncomfortable pause followed this confession.

"So what kind of music do you play," Mark asked.

Henrik smiled. "Well, it's what I like to call Eurotrash Cemetery Fusion Pop."

Their eyes met, and Mark smiled until he couldn't hold it anymore and then he laughed, he laughed and laughed, and Henrik laughed with him.

"That's the stupidest thing I've ever heard," Mark said.

"I know, isn't it ridiculous? They laughed some more, and then Henrik grew serious. "No, really, I play Israeli Breakbeat Bagpipe Tango."

They laughed again, and Mark said, "Are you sure it isn't Cambodian Mariachi Celtic Swing?"

"No, it's more like Mafia Square Dance Afro-Cuban Rock."

"Is that really different from Russian Banjo Lounge Punk?"

"No, it's kind of like Nigerian Heavy Metal Folk Lambada."

Ha, ha. Ha, ha, ha. Ha, ha, ha, ha. They laughed until they had tears in their eyes.

"People don't have a fucking clue, do they? I guess that's the reality of modern music. Woo hoo, that was a good laugh. Anyway Henrik, I'll have a listen to this, whatever it is, and see what I can do. I hear a lot of dead air out there. You better get back to it."

"Thanks, Mr. Grear. I appreciate it. And if you like that, I've got some great New Wave Afghani Hip Hop Porno Groove."

"I'll bet you do," Mark said.

Henrik went back to his DJ booth. Yeah, motherfucker. Yeah. I got you now. A little laughter and it's all mine.

He loved you. Didn't he love you? Eurotrash Cemetery Fusion Pop, indeed. I'm glad he has a sense of humor. We could have just as well cried about it. No telling where a little nonsense will get you. Fucking Jim, what a schmuck. Trying to get me fired. He's just jealous.

4

The good thing about it was that Arnold had three more weeks of severance pay. They had given him six weeks total. Compared to Jack, he'd been lucky. Jack stopped getting paid the day he got fired, and he had never gotten any benefits.

Well, now Arnold had pissed away three weeks doing nothing in particular. He'd bought a new suit and a complete set of titanium pots and pans that he planned on returning. He still hadn't taken them out of the boxes. They were stacked by the kitchen table.

I really should start looking seriously for work, he thought. But the truth was Arnold didn't miss work. In fact, he never wanted to work again. He liked to joke with his friends, saying, "I'm allergic to work. I break out in this angry rash at the mere mention of it. Uh-oh. Better change the subject. Ha, ha."

It's so goddamned expensive in this city, he thought. Just the rent alone costs me fourteen hundred. That's like seventeen grand a year, just to sleep.

The truth was, in spite of all his joking, Arnold was prone to depression. He was a manic-depressive pill popper. His mother was a pharmacist and had raised him on pills. Every little pain or problem he had growing up was solved with a pill. He was a Ritalin boy. And now he took Prozac, Valium, and Xanax, or a combination of all three, to get him through the day. The only stable thing about him was his family and his work, and now he no longer had the work to keep him in line. He was gaining weight. He didn't exercise or cook healthy for himself, in spite of his new pots and pans. How does Jack keep in such good shape, he wondered. That's right, Jack doesn't eat. He can't afford it. I should try that.

Arnold began to have thoughts of moving back home to live with his parents. I can clean out the garage, paint it and put in a window. That way I won't have to pay rent and then maybe I can save for a trip. The truth was he needed a change. But he didn't have enough imagination to know what that change should be.

One afternoon, Arnold sat cleaning his World War II German assault rifle. The barrel had finally been sent from a private supplier in Alabama. That was the last time he would order firearms over the net, at least from Alabama. He began to think they had stiffed him. But after two weeks it came: the highlight of his day.

Arnold was meticulous in cleaning and assembling the respective parts of the rifle, methodically lubricating the mechanisms as he proceeded. When finished, he took cover behind his bed and aimed the weapon at the window of the opposing apartment block; he felt like a soldier waiting to pull the trigger and liquidate the enemy. Life was easier when there was an enemy. Still, it wasn't exactly the right weapon for a clean and quiet murder. For that, he needed his sniper rifle with the silencer. How idiotic that in the movies silencers sometimes made a chirping nose, or a "pffth." Didn't people know silencers were silent? And who had ever heard their fists in a fight? Fists seemed like steel in the movies. Who would have thought that one could break their knuckles or render their fists a bloody pulp? Such movie theatrics had seduced him into believing that war and espionage were romantic subjects. As a result, Arnold had become a collector of weapons and a practitioner of martial arts.

The phone rang. Startled, Arnold squeezed the trigger and put several rounds through his window, and into the television, couch and wall.

"Shit! Shit!"

He grabbed the phone, put his back to the wall by window and looked to the street. It seemed he hadn't hit anything important. The angle must have been too high and the rounds had gone over the second story of the adjacent building. Either that or they were buried in the stucco somewhere. Imagine if he had killed someone? Or if he had put a few holes in the neighbor's car? Then he would be fucked. Luckily, it was the middle of the afternoon and the neighborhood was empty. It occurred to him that the distance from being happy to being fucked was measured in seconds and inches.

"Hello, who's there? Who is it?"

He was confused and wondered for a moment if it wasn't the police. Arnold was petrified of the police. Somehow his excessive obedience to the law justified his breaking it. If anyone should own firearms, it was Arnold, who would never think of using them. In truth, he was a peace-loving individual to the extreme.

"Arnold, this is you mother. Are you okay? You sound tense. I hope you're not working too hard. You know it's good to have some fun, too. Why are you home? You're not sick are you?"

"No mom, I'm fine," Arnold said, trying to control his voice. God, what an idiot. Why didn't I have the safety on? Why did I have it loaded in the first place?

"I'm working from home. I work from home two days a week. I've got the computer here, so there's no point in going to the office."

"I'm surprised you're able to get anything done. You've always been a distracted child."

"Mom, that was when I was ten. I'm thirty now. Twenty years can do a lot for a person."

"Well, I've lived fifty and haven't changed one bit. I could live fifty more and I'd still be the same. You can't change character, after all. You can change the details and fool strangers, but your family you can't fool. Change is overrated anyway," she said.

"Working from home? That's like going to work for vacation. It doesn't make sense. Your generation, Arnold, doesn't know how to work. You're lucky that when you grew up, you learned to work. We put you to work for your own good. So you'd have your own spine. Most people don't get that lesson."

"So how's everything back home, mom?"

Arnold didn't feel like talking to his mother. Her words stung him, especially about work. Work and change. He was aware of the irony. He knew he was no different from his generation, and he was sure his mother was criticizing him. She had a way of criticizing through praise. Still, the tone was not enough to be sarcastic. She probably felt sorry for him. As for change, he wished he weren't the same nervous and insecure boy that had always depended on his mother to protect him from the world. He was a spoiled brat. But then was that his fault? No, it was his mother's for being too strong-willed.

"Well, it's good you should ask," she said. "You know me, I'm not one to exaggerate. I think it's best to say things straight out. Even if no one wants to hear it."

"What are you talking about?"

"I don't want you to worry, Arnold. Don't let anything I'm going to say worry you. God knows you've got enough to worry about. Like getting married. Well, here it is plain and simple. Your father had a heart attack in the garden. He was trying to remove a tree stump and the strain must have been too much for him. He collapsed. I called an ambulance and now he's recovering in the hospital. The doctor says that he's going to have surgery, you know, to clean out the pipes. I told him not to eat all that bacon and corned beef, but you know your father, any chance he gets there he is eating grease, fat and salt."

"Jesus, mom, are you kidding me? Why didn't you call me when it happened? A heart attack?! People die from heart attacks. I don't want dad to die. How does the doctor know that he's gonna be all right? People die in surgery. Hospitals are the leading cause of death in the country. What kind of surgery is it?"

"It's double bypass surgery," she said flatly.

Don't let your son know how scared you are. It's a good thing he can't see you with your red eyes from all the crying. About the only thing that's keeping you from losing it, is trying to keep your son from losing it. He's always been such a sensitive boy.

"Oh wow. Oh man. Well, I'm coming right now. I'll be on the next plane down."

Double bypass surgery. Arnold wasn't exactly sure how it was done, but he knew it had to do with clearing the veins of fat to let the blood flow. Well, he'd heard of single, double and triple bypass. And if it was anything like a cheeseburger, then a triple was serious business.

"Arnold, I don't want you to worry. If you come, you might start to worry more. Maybe you should just stay home."

"What if dad dies? Jesus, what if he dies and I don't get to have that last talk with him, you know, to tell him I love him and all that."

"Shut up. Don't talk nonsense. Your father's not going to die."

Her voice was strong now. It was magical thinking to believe that a strong voice could change fate, but she was willing to give it a try.

"We'll be fine without you. He's going in tomorrow. You won't make it in time. You'll miss work . . ."

She wanted him to come and hold her hand. She had always taken care of her son, but now she needed someone to take care of her. She had been so used to her husband's company that she didn't know what she would do if he were gone. She would probably have to do a whole lot of things to keep from thinking about him. Even if he made it, the security was gone now, and she would always live in fear of losing him. It was like the time she had been in a serious car accident and had come out without a scratch, thanks to the airbag and seatbelt. Even if she still had her health, she was not the same after that. Death seemed closer. She knew then that she would die, and that she could die in a foolish and accidental way. Still, it was only the rare few that died spectacularly. Most died of things like heart attacks, cancer and old age. God, she thought too much about death. It wasn't healthy to think that way. Drowning, she had heard, was a horrible way to die. Imagine the body going livid like a fish on a hook as it inhaled large quantities of water. Slow death is the worst. Burning: that too must be terrible. But they say after the nerves are burned you don't feel it anymore. I guess you never know until you know; and then it's too late.

"Are you listening to me, mom? I'm gonna be there tonight. The job's no big deal. Actually, I don't have a job. I got fired. So you don't have to worry about that."

"You got fired from your job? What are you going to do now? You have to support yourself."

"Don't worry about it," he told her. Arnold held the phone in the crook of his neck, while pulling clothes out of the closet and throwing them into the duffel bag. His heart was pounding fast; he was having a panic attack. I better take some Xanax, he thought. The panic attack was similar to the one he had experienced in Thailand when he had reached into his pocket to pay for a drink in a beachside restaurant and found his wallet missing. In any case, it wasn't pleasant. It was the panic of impending doom: of being fucked.

"Mom, I'll call you from the airport when I get there. Tell dad I love him. I love you."

For some reason, Arnold had always believed that his parents would never die and would always be there for him. He believed that they were stronger than he was and never made mistakes, and that as offspring he was flawed at best.

Shit, why did you tell her you lost your job? Stupid. Stupid. If dad does make it through, I'll never hear the end of it. You weren't thinking, is all. I mean how often do you fire an automatic weapon inside your apartment and get a phone call that your dad is dying? It's like a bad film. If this really was a film, then who would play my part? Maybe Jeremy Leads. You do look a bit like him. The same jaw and eyes. You need to lose a couple of pounds, but it wouldn't be a bad match-up. How would Jeremy Leads deal with this situation? He would certainly have that defiant frown etched into his features, like when something doesn't go his way. He would speak in a flat voice, take action and ask questions later. Jesus, I'm scared. I wonder if Jeremy Leads has ever had to deal with heavy shit in real life. I mean heavy beyond a messy break-up heavy.

Arnold put on his best suit and a pair of black patent leather shoes. He tried to do everything slow and deliberate so he wouldn't hyperventilate. Then the Xanax kicked in and everything felt easier. He made sure his hair was okay. He grabbed his bag and went to the street to hail a taxi. Outside, it was that same San Francisco shit weather that everyone pretended didn't exist. Shoulda brought my umbrella, he thought. This city sucks. Maybe if I had lived closer to home, dad wouldn't have had a heart attack.

5

Damian signed the final papers and was now the proud owner of so and so many square feet of parking lot in the Mission. It was a clever investment. In the city there were more cars than parking spaces, which meant the lot would never be empty. Damian estimated that in five years it would pay for itself. If he'd had the capital, though, he would have bought a house. But in the city that was more or less out of the question.

Even he could see the humor of it. He had spent nearly all his savings for a down payment on a strip of oil-stained pavement. If he paved over a patch of inland desert, it was as good as worthless, but in the city that pavement might as well have been gold.

Even if it was just a parking lot, it was still exciting. Maybe later he could rezone it for housing? Or he could have parties there. He could turn it into a cool club. No, clubs are bad business. No point in owning a club when you can go to one. Sooner or later, you'll grow out of clubbing anyway. Well, later than sooner, that is.

Another perk was that he would always have free parking in the Mission. It was best that his friends didn't find out or they would want free parking, too. He planned to advertise monthly parking in the Chronicle. He would put up a new sign, repaint the lines on the asphalt, and remove the old-school pay automat with the slots, which was all rusted through and looked cheap.

When Damian arrived in the afternoon, the lot was half-full of cars. He pulled into a space, and to his surprise, a young black man in a uniform approached him with a ticket book in hand.

"Day parking's twenty dollars, sir. Otherwise, it's eight dollars an hour."

"Excuse me?"

"Are you parking for the day or the hour? We also got weekly rates."

Quincy looked at the man again and realized that he had made a mistake. He could tell by the man's attitude that he didn't plan on paying anything. Shit, maybe he's the owner of the lot? Well, if worse comes to worst, you can run. It's good thing you got this hat on for anonymity, and that your skateboard is just over by the wall.

"I just bought this lot. Haven't they told you? I didn't know they had a parking attendant."

Poor kid, he's going to be out of job, Damian thought. I can't believe they haven't told him. Well, they probably had other things to think about. For the price of the lot, they must have had some serious money issues.

"No one's told me anything," Quincy said.

"Well, I don't need you anymore. I imagine they're still paying you if you're still here. So you've got today off and you're gonna get paid for it. But before you go, I want today's earnings for those cars. The lot belongs to me now, so if they wanna know where the money is, they can call me. They have my number, but here it is again." Damian took a business card from his wallet and handed it to Quincy.

Quincy wanted badly to keep the money. He thought to say that he couldn't give him the money until he got the okay from his boss. By the time the guy found out he'd been played, Quincy would be long gone. But then he thought better of it.

"Let's see," Quincy said, taking a wad of money from his pocket. He had begun to keep receipts. He realized that no matter what business one was involved in, professionalism was important. The receipt book put people at ease and lent legitimacy to his front, and even hustlers needed legitimacy. That's the difference between small and big time, he thought.

"I got twelve cars in, two at a week rate. That money's been paid already. They came on Monday. Then we got five on the day rate and two by the hour. For the hour rate I have them pay the first hour, and if they stay longer I collect the rest after, or I have them put it in the box if I'm not here. But then you can never trust someone on their honor. That's why you need me. The box isn't reliable. So that's a hundred and sixteen dollars. Here you go."

Damian took the money and counted it out. Before putting it in his pocket, he gave a five to Quincy.

"It's too bad I won't be needing you anymore. You seem like a good kid. If I were you, I'd call the guys at California Parking and see what's up."

"Yeah, I'll do that. Have nice day, mister. Good luck with the lot. I'm gonna miss it."

Damn right you're gonna miss it, Quincy thought, now that you're broke. At least he came early and you didn't stand here all day for nothing.

Quincy was anxious to leave. He had gotten off easy and learned something in the process. Say less and listen more. He could have put himself in the shit if he'd talked too much. By waiting, he'd let the man invent his own story for the strange situation.

Damian opened the cash box just for the hell of it to see if any money was there. He found fifty-six dollars. He changed the lock and went back to his car. It was startling how easy it was to make money with property. For too long he'd been on the wrong side of the deal, paying rent. Now that he had his first investment, things could only get better.

As he drove, Damian thought about the parking attendant and what he'd said about the box. How could he be sure that people paid if someone didn't patrol the area constantly? Damian had hoped that he could just come and collect the money, but now he realized that wasn't realistic. Also, the sign only had an hourly rate posted, which meant all the day and long-term business would go somewhere else. That's probably why they'd hired the kid: so he could charge by the hour, day and week and make sure people paid. But then Damian would have to pay him a wage, which would certainly cut into his profits. And what if the kid skimmed off the top? In a couple of days he would check the box again. If there was a good chunk of money there, fine. If not, then he would have to take action. Too bad he hadn't gotten the boy's number. But then again, it wouldn't be hard to find someone to replace him.

6

The truth was Alex didn't really have the energy. He told himself it wasn't a choice but an obligation. After a day spent fighting to get students to open their minds with marginal success, he had to write. The injustice of the world, and the U.S. Government's role in that injustice, was too much for him to bear. If he didn't lighten the load a little each day by putting his pessimism down on paper, then that pessimism would turn to something worse, perhaps apathy or depression.

Like the majority of Americans who hadn't voted for the current president, Alex was extremely upset about the direction his country was taking. So much for democracy, he thought. And we're definitely not winning any popularity race abroad with our economic bullying and preemptive military action. With that thought in mind, Alex was ready to get back to work on the manuscript:

Chapter 12: Individualism and Inequality in America

The greatest danger we face today as a society is our loss of solidarity. This phenomenon is a direct result of economic prosperity. We are too successful, materially speaking. Many perceive this as a great achievement. Such a view is not without merit, provided one forgets that much of the wealth accumulated in the United States is the result of theft, usury and speculation, subjects discussed further in Chapter 14: Economy of Illusions.

Economic prosperity only appears positive if we consider it independently and not in relation to other factors, such as social welfare. Natural law illustrates that nothing in this world exists for and of itself. Only the fool believes he can separate himself from society by acquiring material wealth without properly caring for the human and environmental resources on which he depends. That is the philosophy of cultural poverty.

In modern America we can see the result of such thinking. Corporations feel no obligation to promote the public good or to preserve environmental resources. Big business profits from the privatization of public goods and the externalization of the costs of production. Market capitalists often claim that waste reduction or resource conservation is prohibitively expensive and would prevent them from providing products and services to the consumer public at competitive prices. Clearly, these costs should be factored into production, a portion of which could be passed on to the public. This would be preferable to having the public pay all the costs, as they do currently with respect to environmental pollution, compromised health, and the loss of the amenities the natural environment provides. As resources dwindle and are valued accordingly, only companies with a closed cycle system of production will be competitive. The wasteful production model of today is based on a false belief in infinite resources; as these resources are consumed or polluted, so will wasteful companies cease to be competitive and drop out of the marketplace.

A parallel reality exists in the social sphere. When a wealthy man sees a poor man living in the street, he is quick to absolve himself of culpability for the man's situation. He rationalizes that the man's condition is the result of lack of personal initiative, discipline, etc. That is often an incorrect assumption. What the wealthy man fails to see is that success depends on a stable family, access to education, food, clothing and shelter. Should any of these factors be lacking, a man may not succeed and will need assistance from his community. Poverty and wealth are often inherited, as are the sentiments of superiority and inferiority relevant to each condition.

The capitalist system encourages individuals to pursue their own best interest with the goal of achieving comfort and leisure in their lives. The byproduct of economic affluence is often a loss of compassion and decreased civic involvement. Because wealth isolates the individual from much of the suffering and difficulties of life, it becomes easier for the wealthy to justify the exploitation of others. Without checks and balances in such a system, human relations are ruled by the fear of exploitation, and not the meaningful interaction and desire to cooperate that is essential to our emotional and social well-being. This feeds a vicious cycle in which the wealthy feel a sense of entitlement and superiority over employees who generate their wealth. As a result, they may see fit to pay their workers less and compel them to work more; they may cut costs by illegal or harmful business practices; they may lobby government and pay for favorable legislation from sponsored elected officials; they may speculate in stock, buy companies and sell them off piecemeal, causing widespread unemployment; they may drive stock prices up through insider trading with other wealthy speculators and then liquidate their assets, leaving the average investor with the losses. In other words, they will promote greater inequality by taking money from the hands of the less fortunate.

Our degraded national fabric is due to a wholesale lack of compassion and sense of fair play. From the corporate boardroom to the city street, the level playing field is just a fiction of a fear-driven economic system. Most Americans subscribe unquestioningly to the ideology of selling-out. Selling-out implies compromising moral and ethical values in exchange for material and social benefits. Because resources are limited, the individual seeks to outcompete others to secure his own prosperity. To achieve his goal, he will employ any means necessary including dishonesty, betrayal, oppression and violence.

Successful people, in these terms, seek to come into contact with the social space as little as possible, believing it to be populated by corrupt and dangerous individuals such as themselves, or by those they have abused and dominated. The poverty of the vanquished is particularly upsetting to the so-called successful man because it represents the poverty of his own actions, and more importantly the inseparability of wealth from poverty.

The individual who has acquired wealth through disreputable means lives in a jail of his own making; he finds his only comfort and relaxation at private clubs and exclusive restaurants; he lives in gated communities with armed guards; he cannot go anywhere in a public fashion, but must employ limousines with tinted windows and fly in private jets to arrive at his destination. By hording excessive wealth, the wealthy promote the decay of society. We know these individuals, but we do not see them. They perform their economic activities in closed meetings and by proxy; they avoid exposure to the media to maintain their anonymity. The more wealth such people acquire, the less generous they become. They are consumed by a competitive drive with their peers. The solidarity that exists among the poor, and which helps them to survive, is a fiction in the world of affluence. The rich are primarily preoccupied with comparing amongst themselves the heights they can reach by standing on the backs of the poor and miserable.

One solution to the lack of community and social responsibility in America is the establishment of mandatory community and/or military service for all young Americans. There should be no exceptions or exemptions to such a policy. Rich children would have to serve alongside the poor. It would be a start in setting the nation back on track to solidarity and cooperation. A society that exists without cooperation cannot succeed. If private interests continue to be promoted over public welfare, the United States will become an increasingly unequal and inhospitable place to live.

To build a strong nation it is important to help those in need. Economic assistance, however, should not be confused with charity. Charity is a random act of vanity. Assistance is a planned action to solve an economic or social problem. More than a hand-out, it requires the provision of skills and knowledge, trust, and true concern for the welfare of others. Though a large part of success comes from personal initiative, cooperation is essential to building a strong community. No matter how cynical the individual, there is a subconscious need for him to feel connected, respected and esteemed by others.

Charity provides a convenient outlet for the selfish and greedy to atone for their guilt and pretend they are making a contribution to the greater good; what makes charity attractive is that it requires no long-term emotional investment, and the sums given are relatively small. For maximum effect, charity is best given in the presence of friends and strangers. By giving, a charitable man demonstrates his superiority over the poor and needy. Charity is a self-serving and primarily middle class concept and activity. It is a mixture of loneliness, guilt and the fear of being poor, and has nothing to do with the cynical, tax write-off charity of the rich. It is a mistake to think that charity can cure the pervasive social ills caused by individualism.

Individualism, in truth, serves as a catalyst for social disintegration. It is responsible for the high incidence of divorce in the developed world, has made the young ambitious at the expense of their conscience, increases job stress and insecurity, loosens family ties, makes people more shallow and less prone to engage in meaningful dialogue, and causes individuals to choose comfort over meaning. One wonders if that is any way to live.

The internet has filled the gap of loneliness left by economic and emotional individualism. It has become the preferred channel for human interaction in modern times. It is now possible for two individuals in different parts of the world to communicate more readily than they would with their respective neighbors. A lack of public space, parkland, and civic and cultural events, coupled with the disorganized Wild West lateral growth of American cities, continues to promote an individualist reality that is synonymous with alienation. We can thank the oil companies and the auto and tire industry for our decentralized city planning and consequent cookie-cutter suburbia. Is it possible to develop community ties when the average America moves every three years from one sterile planned development to the next?

The next victim of individualism is love. More and more, lonely individuals are paying online love brokers to provide them with relationships that before they would have developed through social interaction. In the modern world love is hard to find because no one is willing to make concessions. All too often, the individualist asks him or herself: what can this person do for me? Instead of: what can I give or share with them? Love, it should not be forgotten, is a partnership in which sharing and caring for one's partner is the cornerstone. Love is not a networking opportunity; nor should it be a speculative activity where one upgrades to a better model when possible.

Today, the young are less prone to get married, have children, etc. because they do not wish to be compromised. Not having children makes them ambivalent to the care and education of children in general.

The capitalist promise of material affluence distracts modern man from discovering his purpose in life. Modern society focuses on success and disparages poverty, weakness, and failure. How is the individual to recognize his own humanity if the illusion of perfection serves as his only example? In such an environment, is it possible for the individual to progress if he does not understand himself and his spiritual motivations, particularly in adversity? For it is clear that man does not improve with *the endless pursuit of pleasure. On the contrary, the pursuit of pleasure as an end in itself only leads to debauchery and waste.*

In our quest for comfort, we have developed globalized economies of scale to lower the cost of production of material goods. While many tout the benefits of globalization, few point to the consequences of this market capitalist philosophy, particularly in the regard to the apathy and alienation it creates: apathy about our own lives and the society we live in, and alienation from our individual character, the goods and services we consume, and our communities.

The extent to which material comfort has made modern youth less creative, informed, and engaged in their society is unknown. Certainly, it would be unfair to say that all of today's youth are satisfied with the status quo. In order to escape what they perceive as a homogenized society devoid of meaning and culture, many young people are traveling to peripheral destinations in the developing world to gather new knowledge and experience. The irony of this practice is that these same individuals bring their cultural poverty with them to the "pure" destinations they visit, thereby marginalizing local values and practices. For it is nearly impossible for affluent youth in the developed world not to bring their economic bias with them wherever they go. Tourism is often an exercise in vanity: a desire to have a unique experience in order to claim superiority over those who have not traveled. More accurately, tourism is the extension of domestic laziness and mediocrity, given that the novel experience of the tourist seldom involves any contribution to the community he or she visits, other than the purchase of goods and services. As a result, the tourist learns nothing of value that can be put to use back home. The United States remains a sociocultural backwater because it is trapped in a cycle of escapism and apathy that comes from convenience and the desire to work, not for meaning, but for leisure at home or abroad. Ironically, by focusing on today's comfort, Americans imperil their quality of life in the long term.

Our current stage of human development is not sustainable. We are entering an epoch of tyranny whose principle marker is a lack of communication and understanding between people, and a clear disconnect from the environment in which we live.

Chapter 13: Scientific Materialism and Humanitarian Ethics

Technology has been given much of the credit for improving our quality of life on earth. While this is true, it is also responsible for the greatest tragedies of modern times. Military science has made it easier and more efficient to kill. We have seen the proliferation of biological weapons, the atom bomb and a nuclear arms race during the Cold War which made it possible to exterminate mankind with the arbitrary push of a button. It is a moot point whether technological advancement has made life better or worse. The creative and destructive forces in man have simply been enhanced. While it is not popular to argue that technological advancement should be limited, it would be beneficial to slow development out of precaution for the unknown and unproven consequences of our supposed advancements. The great error in man's defense of technology is the belief that no matter what the negative effects of new inventions, it will always be possible to mitigate the problems they create. This nearsightedness is an integral part of the capitalist ideology. It is, above all, a sign of man's inability to take responsibility for his actions until the damage is done.

Modern capitalist society has been shaped by an artificial division between the humanities and science, wherein science has taken precedence over the humanities, or the emotional, spiritual, artistic, and social activities of man. In other words, the quantitative bias of science has displaced qualitative cultural values. Consequently, the value of the individual is determined by the quantity of the things he owns, produces, or sells, and not the quality of his work, participation, or ideas. In Western culture, ideas are not valued until they can be turned into marketable commodities. Modern capitalist man no longer takes the time to question his actions and motivations for the sake of moral or spiritual improvement. Unlike his forefathers, he is not a philosopher searching for meaning on earth. How is it that we can so quickly cast aside philosophy, which has formed an integral part of classical education since before the advent of the nation-state in Europe? The split between the humanities and science has limited the modern world's social, spiritual, and cultural advancement. In essence, we have lost our ability to think beyond the static formulas and cause and effect of the scientific method.

With its youthful exuberance toward comfort and excess, the United States has forgotten history's most important lessons; it has chosen to ignore a great body of classical scholarship and traditional knowledge in favor of new and often scientific solutions for humanitarian problems. Seldom is it that the new world scientist asks himself: how can I improve the quality of life of the earth's inhabitants? Instead, he concerns himself only with the creation of abundance. Unfortunately, our quest for material abundance all too often damages the cultural foundations and value structures of developing nations that are forced to conform to an Americentric globalized agenda. The United States, founded by immigrants, is among the youngest nations on earth. Native Americans apart, it is younger in tradition and culture than the most recent of nations whose citizens, with their long history of habitation, have simply had borders drawn and redrawn across their backs. The problem with globalization today is not that it seeks new ways to promote the trade that has always existed between nations, but rather that it attempts to impose Western and particularly American culture and values on the rest of the world. The problem with this globalization model is that culture in the United States is synonymous with consumption. American culture requires that traditions and values be sacrificed for the sake of short-term profit. We compel the world to follow our example because we feel threatened by nations that have taken care to preserve their history and culture. But capital can never atone for the crisis of identity and sense of inferiority that many Americans suffer, given that American identity can be obtained with little more than a plane ticket, gainful employment on American soil, and regular trips to the local strip mall. Since everyone can be American by the force of their labor and consumption, is there such a thing as an American identity? Is the American identity any more than a billboard for consumerism?

The American bias towards economic advancement has made it difficult for Americans to construct a viable culture identity. The American consumer model discourages human interaction and exchange of ideas, artistic production, creative, philosophical or intellectual activity, leisure and recreation, and love and compassion when these have no commercial application. The ultimate goal of American culture is to create a world in which human beings live entirely in the material plane in a physical environment that has been standardized for the sake of maximum convenience and profit. Ideally, all emotion, creativity, and uniqueness of character would be erased and the class hierarchy would be maintained, thereby ensuring a manageable society of passive and obedient workers so that the nation's leadership may be largely idle or free to indulge in cultural and intellectual pursuits prohibited to the masses. This seems to be the vision of those Americans who invariably believe they know what's best for others, and whose ambition and cynicism often vaults them to power where they can exercise this notion of the perfectibility of man, where perfectibility refers to the mechanization of his actions and the standardization of his beliefs. Such a vision is flawed at best, for who finds happiness in a homogeneous and impersonal world where material wealth is put over thoughts and feelings? One might argue: why not work a little less for oneself and give a little more to others, not in terms of money, but time? While money can provide a comfortable living environment, it cannot provide a sense of community or the deep connection between individuals that comes through personal interaction. It has been said that the best things in life are free; they are benefits that cannot be justified through economic theory, empirical science, or market forces.

Scientific materialism is essentially a partnership between big business and science. The pharmaceutical industry is a prime example of such a partnership. While profit incentives are necessary to drive research for new drugs that manage human health and cure illness and disease, it is also a moral imperative to provide essential medicines at an affordable cost, and free of charge to the poor, to protect public health and welfare. Ideally, this would occur through a national health care system or, alternatively, through specific government programs. Due to corporate price gouging in the Unites States, it is no surprise that Americans prefer to buy their medicine abroad in Mexico or Canada. Pharmaceutical giants have addressed this threat to their business model by securing protectionist legislation, without which they would cease to be competitive in the free market. The same principal applies to medicine supplied abroad. Frequently, Western pharmaceutical giants refuse to license patents of essential medicines to developing nations for the production of cheaper generic substitutes. Greed thus condemns many human beings to unnecessary illness and premature death, which is not good for business, even if seen through the cynical lens of market capitalism. Surely, it is possible to make a profit and still have compassion by tempering scientific advancement with humanitarian thinking. Unfortunately, corporations do not share this perspective.

The pharmaceutical industry has cleverly repackaged the difficulties of daily life into clinical emotional and mental health problems to be medicated. Consequently, people have internalized, as biological illness, problems stemming from their environment and the choices they have made. Instead of taking responsibility for their lives and finding organic solutions to their problems, individuals are sold a quick fix in the form of a pill to ease their stress, fear, anxiety, and depression. While some individuals may have legitimate mental health problems for which medication is required, for many, non-essential perscription drug use is only an avoidance technique, which gives them a false sense of well-being. Such drug abuse is yet another facet of an esacapist consumer culture that prefers the flatline of comfort and convenience to the challenges of a life well-lived. But then would life really be worth living without the rollercoaster of our humanity? Do we really wish to drug ourselves into complacency?

Much of the raw material used to produce medicine today originates in nature. As a result, private industry seeks to patent genetic material and biological processes to create new consumer products. This privatization of biodiversity, and of food crops in particular, is a direct threat to human survival. It prevents the poor from feeding themselves off the land and with the sweat of their labor. While it is useful and even desireable for private companies to develop new drugs to cure illness and disease, or provide health benefits to human beings, the patenting of the biodiversity used to make these drugs should be prohibited. While an individual plant or animal may be someone's private property, the plant or animal species and the biological characteristics and processes that make it unique belong to the earth. Allowing corporations to overstep their bounds and privatize ecosystems and the organisms that they contain, and which we depend on for survival, is a slippery slope that ends with the commodification of the human spirit. To expect biopirates to hold the biology of the human being sacred is naive at best. As the desirable genes of plant and animal life are privatized, so too will the human genetic code be sliced up and sold piecemeal to the highest bidder. It is impossible to imagine a world where the marketing of genetic material would not promote discrimination and inequality. Such human meddling in evolution can only lead to destructive ends. The more we come to resemble one another genetically, through commerce of preferred genetic traits, the greater the possibility of our extinction.

These alarming developments in profit-driven scientific research have found fertile ground in the university environment. Increasingly, universities are not independent institutions where students are taught to think for themselves; instead, they have become businesses financed by large corporations where students are exploited as cheap labor and indoctrinated in market capitalism. In such an environment, innovation is limited to what is profitable and little weight is placed on the negative results of research and development of new drugs. Worse still, academic independence has been greatly undermined. Professors who disagree with scientific findings financed by corporate interests are not supported by the university, as they were in the past, and may lose their jobs for publishing negative but accurate research results. Simply put, the sale of higher education to big business is highly detrimental to free thought. What can be said of our institutions of higher learning when businessmen have greater say over scientific results than the scientists themselves?

University curriculum is being streamlined to prioritize the sciences at the expense of the humanities. Important subjects such as history, literature, language studies, sociology, fine arts, and philosophy have found their budgets cut for not turning a profit. Because society doesn't value or offer fair pay for a humanities education, parents encourage their children to study business, computer science, engineering, biology, and chemistry. Without a background in humanities, it is questionable whether or not the next generation will be able to make balanced decisions and place science in a sociopolitical and cultural context. This is another case of quantitative shortsightedness. While the benefits of literature, history, fine arts, and philosophy are sometimes difficult to quantify, ultimately their study contributes to creating a conscious, ethical, and responsible citizenship. It is reasonable to assume that a society with this social capital will be more equitable than one that focuses on economics and science alone. People may ask: what is the benefit of a humanities education? Unlike science, which at the BS level focuses on rote memorization of pre-established laws and theorems, a education in the humanities teaches a man to think for himself, to be critical of his world, and to ask difficult questions. With science that is slave to big business, students have little or none of the ideological freedoms that are necessary for a healthy society.

Profit-driven science does not value moderation or balance. It leads one to think of the world as a set of independent variables that can be altered without consideration for how this might upset the balance of the natural system in which they function. If we don't perceive the holistic nature of knowledge, we risk falling out of balance with ourselves and our environment. Science divorced from the humanities may lead to technological innovation, but only ethics, morality, and culture can determine if its contribution is ultimately beneficial to humanity. All scientific innovation must obey nature's time-tested laws and methods of evolutionary design. The form and function of nature informs the aesthetic sensibilities that give our lives value. The desire and struggle to engineer beyond the limits of biology is doomed to failure. Greed is not above the law of conservation of matter and energy. To increase individual wealth one must inevitably decrease the wealth of others, their laughter, their natural resources, their time, and their freedom. What is lost through scientific advancement for the benefit of the few, is quality of life and environmental health for the many.

The scientific materialist bias in America has had damaging consequences for Americans and the world at large. As big business continues to interfere in the academic environment, we will experience a stagnation and single-mindedness that will be far from profitable in the long run. When students are silenced early in their careers, what can be *expected from their future efforts? The technocrat led agenda to eliminate a humanitarian education in favor of economic productivity has created a nation and world that lacks citizenship, solidarity, and an ethical compass. We are less happy as global citizens today because we've been told that art, spirituality, philosophy, intellectual debate, and cultural traditions come second to our function as producers and consumers. No matter how greatly the political, scientific, and economic elite may disparage the humanities, particularly when their interests are at stake, even the most contemptuous of them would not contend that the world they are creating would be worth living in without such a rich and varied field of knowledge. For things to change we must demand of our government that it fund and set policy to encourage a multidisciplinary approach that links the humanties and science in education. There will be no significant improvement in the human condition until the humanities and sciences have an equal influence in dictating the development of our nation and the world. Quantity means nothing without quality.*

Alex couldn't write anymore; it made him ill to think about it. Why do I dwell on this stuff? Because someone has to, he told himself. Because people don't know why things are the way they are. It's your job to tell people what's really going on. There are too many people that don't want to do anything with their lives. They just want to be comfortable. I've seen the way people get upset when I talk about these things. I'm sure many think I'm sick, but really I'm the only healthy person around. Because I know what's real. I know that most of what's around me is a fantasy and a lie. I will not be seduced by comfort into giving up my own reason and character. I would rather die than live that way.

The individual who doesn't question his world and work to change it for the better is useless. Not everyone needs to be a revolutionary. Revolution doesn't work anyway; it just replaces one oppressor with another. Not everyone needs to fly to Africa and hand out food to the poor, either. There are plenty of less dramatic and equally righteous ways to affect change. Social consciousness starts at the local level by contributing to your community and working to inspire your family, friends, peers and neighbors.

Have you done that?

Alex didn't know the answer to his own question. As a teacher, he helped his students. As a friend, he was often negative and moody, and that had much to do with the fact that he wasn't successful. But then he set higher standards for himself than for others. Maybe his world vision was the cause of his failure? Still, it seemed ridiculous to say: I will be successful. He hoped that later he would have the knowledge and experience to say it with confidence. Or forego saying it. But that was still a distant reality. Alex wanted it to come naturally. And that meant hard work, no matter what the fast and easy culture told him.

This culture paralyzes the average man into apathy and stagnation, Alex thought. He sees so much success around him that he is unable to understand how he can be successful in his own way. He dreams of greatness but doesn't see the thousand individual steps it takes to arrive at meaning. He is unaware of his talents and unsure of his purpose. He thinks in results. He tells himself: I would like to be a movie star so I can have all the things a movie star has, and then doesn't put in the work to arrive at his goal. He chooses dreams that are incongruent with his nature, and in that way he is unhappy. Instead of tending to his own needs, he seeks to satisfy others. Yes, in this society we live for others, or more correctly, for how we appear to others.

Don't you remember when your brother told you that you should have more fun, that there's no point in being serious all the time, and that sometimes it's nice not to think at all? Well, he's right, but the truth is you've always felt guilty about it, being that so many people aren't having fun. Now that's an understatement.

Still, let's not pretend that a large part of human existence isn't shallow. But that's also because we're too comfortable. Don't you have fun when you sit at your desk and attempt to document the time you're living in and your relationship to it? That's fun, right? Why, you've even laughed out loud here, by yourself. By yourself, that's right. You should get a girlfriend. Ha, ha. But then isn't that like what you were saying about being a movie star? It's not something you just do and feel better. It's work. And the problem with a girlfriend is that you can't talk as well to her as you can to yourself.

Still, Alex had to admit he was happy. He had written well and said what he had wanted to say; he had brushed the slippery fish of truth with his fingers, and that should have been enough. It seemed wrong to ask more of life.

7

It had been one of the happiest times of her life and now it was over. When she first found out she was pregnant, Aisha didn't want to tell anyone. Instead, she locked herself in her room and buried herself under the covers with her stuffed bear, Marley, and cried. Her father was at work and didn't know that she hadn't gone to school. Most of all, she was scared of her father, though he had always been a gentle, soft-spoken man. She knew that he wished only the best for her and her sister and would do anything to make them happy. Part of this was love and the rest a consequence of the ongoing competition between her parents for their children's affection. Both Aisha and her sister were guilty of playing their parents' insecurities to their advantage. Aisha felt badly about it and, with time, had learned to curb her opportunism.

Her father, Howard Clark, was the co-owner of an auto shop in the Mission. He was a simple man without much education who wanted more than anything for his daughters to have the opportunities he did not. Still, he wasn't the sort of man to sit down with his children and talk about sex. It would have embarrassed him to even think about it. He hoped that by not talking about sex, it wouldn't be an issue. Perhaps that was because he grew up in a time when a man treated a woman like a lady and a queen, like he had treated their mother. But then their mother, Sandra, saw things differently. After eighteen years of marriage, she told him that she needed a change. She wanted a little romance back in her life, like the old days when they went out to dinner and dancing on a regular basis. Well, Howard tried to take her out more, and he bought her flowers every now and again on his way home from work, but these efforts soon faded. Running the business took nearly all his time and made him rather single-minded. He told her that when he came home he liked to relax. So Mrs. Clark changed tactics and brought up her husband's football Sundays with his friends.

"I don't like your friends," she said flatly. "They make a mess and they eat us out of house and home. Why is it always you who has to buy the food and drinks, and why do they always have to come here?"

Then one day Sandra asked flat out for a divorce. She was kind about it. She said he was good man but that she needed a change. She had always been a polite and decent woman, but in that moment he had wanted to curse her to hell and throw things.

Cool off, he told himself. Don't make this ugly after all the years you've spent together. Then he found the courage to ask about the children. How are the children gonna grow up right living between two parents? Think about the children. She said that the children were old enough to understand such things if they were explained properly.

Howard knew that to argue was futile. It had always been such that when Sandra was decided there was no changing her mind.

"Maybe if we live apart for a little while. That way you can think about it and maybe later you can come back?"

"I don't think so, Howard."

Sandra was aware of how hard it was for him to listen to her words. Harder than it was for her to say them. Much harder.

In the end, Howard put his head in her lap and wept, while she patted his hulking frame.

"I don't know what I'm gonna do without you, baby. I love you so much. You know a man can't live decent without a woman. You're everything to me."

A year later Sandra remarried and Howard was still alone. He didn't see the point in marrying again. He wasn't ready to move on. To take his mind off it, he worked harder at the shop. Deep down, he suspected that she thought him too simple. Her new husband, who he had met several times but avoided at all costs, was overly cheerful and, he thought, fake. Nothing like his football buddies or the guys at work. No, the man was full of fine ideas and thought cars and sports common subjects. Howard began to suspect that Sandra had divorced him because he wasn't rich enough. The new husband was a bank manager who wore a suit and tie to work. Sandra lived with him in an apartment in the Marina, while Howard continued to make his living in oil-stained overalls in the Mission. Though Howard was the boss, he knew that his workers wouldn't respect a man who didn't get his hands dirty. Many of the young men that came to work didn't know enough about cars, and he would have to teach them himself. If people see that you bust your ass, then they've got no excuses, he thought.

I wonder if he makes more money than I do? I wonder if it's the money? No, it was because he didn't have a college education. She was a smart woman and better than him, and he was a fool to think he could keep her.

So Aisha felt like she, too, had betrayed her father. He was such a sensitive man. Despite his size and his rough edges, he was a sweetheart.

She always wanted to do the best for him. She and her sister competed for his approval in everything from grades to color guard to playing the piano. They wanted so badly to make him proud. And now she had failed. Her sister would go on to college and become a doctor or lawyer. Aisha, for her part, had made a mistake and gotten pregnant. There was no competition there.

The pregnancy paralyzed her. She didn't know who she was more afraid to talk to: Duane, her father or her mother. But down deep she knew the answer. Her father and mother would love her all the same, even if they were upset. But Duane? Strange that she was most afraid of the person she loved the most.

Duane. He was so classy, so intelligent; he could talk endlessly about anything. He knew so much about the world. He knew the populations of different countries and had strange theories of how geography and climate shaped national character. He talked about how European modern art was inspired by African tribal art. He knew all about Italian cooking and had a passion for Latin dance. He was the most interesting person she had ever met. And she never said a word about him to her father. She knew that her father would feel betrayed, not only because she hadn't told him, but because she had gotten pregnant and ruined all the dreams he had for her.

Her father had always made her feel safe. When she was young he seemed like a large predator that would fight to the death to protect her. Aisha remembered when he would grab her and scrape his stubble on the smooth skin of her face while she struggled to escape. She was aware that she had laughed more with her father when she was younger. Now he didn't smile as much and kept his distance.

If Duane takes care of me, then I've got nothing to worry about. But what if Duane doesn't want the baby? The truth was Aisha didn't have much confidence in Duane. Anything he wanted to do, she did. She even waited for him at his house when he went out drinking with his friends. She thought that he would have invited her along if she weren't underage. Given her sixteen years, it would be longer than he thought before she joined him out on the town.

Aisha wondered what Duane's housemates thought of her. At her insistence, Duane had made her a copy of his key because it embarrassed her to have to ring the bell and explain that she was going to wait for Duane to come home. For some reason, it embarrassed her more to talk to Carrie than to Ben or Tyler. Carrie, she was a real woman. Aisha felt very small compared to her and couldn't look her in the eye. When Carrie invited her to eat or watch a movie she would usually refuse. It was only with time that she got over her shyness. Carrie was always so nice to her, sharing her dinner and asking about her life. Aisha had lied to her, too, about her age. She said she was in her first year of college and that she was eighteen. Carrie seemed more at ease then, or was that just her imagination?

Usually Aisha came over before Duane went out so they could spend time together. Spending time for Duane was having sex. Spending time for her was lying in bed after and listening to Duane talk about his day or where they were going to go or what errands he had to do over the weekend. Sometimes he talked about trips they would take together to far off places she had never been. Occasionally, he would invite her along to a private party provided that, "she behaved herself and didn't drink too much or act immature." The warning wasn't necessary; at parties she usually sat quietly next to Duane and listened to his conversations and his laughter. He behaved differently at parties with his friends; he seemed happier than otherwise, though she thought he drank too much.

On such nights when he was at the bar without her, Aisha couldn't help but wonder if he was with another woman. There had always been so many beautiful, mature and interesting women at those parties. Maybe he used his night out with "friends" as an excuse to meet other women, like she used her friend Jackie as a convenient excuse for why she wouldn't be home on the weekends. After she met Duane, she spent nearly every weekend at "Jackie's." Even if he was out with friends, she had plenty of reason to worry. What did friends do out on the town, anyway? They got drunk and looked for women. Even if Duane wasn't looking, he might be drunk, and maybe he would get carried away with the situation and then, well, she didn't want to think about it.

One reason Aisha stayed over at Duane's when he was out was to make sure he came home at night and that he came home alone. She was possessive and extremely jealous. She hid it poorly and that fact amused him. When she got angry with him about it, he would laugh. It irritated Aisha that Duane treated her like she was a little girl. It also irritated her that he didn't want to meet her father. Every time she mentioned it, he told her it was too soon. Was she forgetting that they weren't even boyfriend and girlfriend? No, she hadn't forgotten. But she didn't see why they shouldn't be, since they spent every weekend together and he picked her up from school several times a week and took her for a drive to the beach or for a walk in the park or home to bed. Maybe it didn't matter that they weren't officially boyfriend and girlfriend. Maybe that was old-fashioned. Now the popular phrase was "hanging out." When Duane talked about her to his friends, he said they were "hanging out." And when he introduced her to the others, he said, "This is my 'friend' Aisha."

If Duane's weekend escapades were difficult, his business trips were worse. Then she would sit at home and sulk with her father in front of the television and eat lots of rocky road ice cream, which she knew wasn't good for her figure.

With Duane gone, it was the end of the world. Aisha made him promise to call her at least once during the trip. It was not unusual for her to disappear from the couch for an hour at a time when the phone rang. Then she would miss most of the movie, and her father would have to tell her what had happened.

Aisha knew the real reason Duane didn't want to meet her father was because he was eight years older than her and she was underage. He knew that no father would appreciate that. But then she thought her father would understand that Duane cared for her, had good intentions, and was a successful and intelligent young man.

Aisha wanted the two men in her life to meet, get along and be friends. She couldn't think of anything better than that. Well, except marriage and moving in with Duane permanently. But then he would have to move. She didn't want to live in shared housing. They would need a place of their own. Like many young girls first in love, she dreamt ahead. She imagined all the possible permutations of their relationship. In her mind they had done everything together and she couldn't wait for those dreams to come true. And now she was pregnant. How could she have been so stupid?

Insecure as she was, Aisha blamed herself for what had happened. She should have made sure he used a condom, but she was afraid he wouldn't like her like that. Now everything was all wrong. She hadn't even finished high school. But she wouldn't get an abortion. The child was a product of both of them and she would be proud to have it. But what would Duane say? Certainly, Duane would stand behind her. Even if he could be cold and distant, she knew that he needed her. Sure, she had fallen for his image. He was a proud young man who kept his chin high and depended on no one. He was an individual among individuals. But privately, she also found that he was shy and kind, that is, unless she asked or told him about his feelings. Then he would close tight like a shell and there was nothing she could do about it. That was when she understood that, though men were intelligent and brave, they could also be stupid, vain and childish. She had seen parts of Duane that weren't smooth and easy, such as his impatience. Of his character, she knew plenty; of his heart, she worried that he didn't love her enough. It was that fear that held her now. Maybe he will feel trapped? Maybe he feels that he can do better? After all, who am I? I'm just a girl without experience with a lot to learn about the world. There are lots of girls like me.

Life had been good to him lately. Aisha had come to him at a time of low self-esteem. Though Duane was still young, he looked to the past with the nostalgia of the elderly. Somehow, he had forgotten how it was to depend on his parents for money and the limitations that came with such dependence. He convinced himself that his youth was an easy time and that love had been easier then; he'd been free to act on his impulses and he hadn't over-analyzed his emotions. Much of that was true, but then he had forgotten what a closed environment high school was. He and his peers hadn't yet developed their own character, but instead followed the trend so as to not stand out and be vulnerable to attack by the group.

No, looking back on his youth, Duane forgot all the worries of that time: getting good grades, his future and his fear of girls. Instead of talking to them and letting his emotions show, Duane feigned indifference, especially to those he liked most. He had never really gotten over that shyness. He still tried to play it cool so people wouldn't perceive his insecurities. By being afraid to try new things and make mistakes, especially in love, he had atrophied.

Once Duane had been in love, but after junior year his girlfriend Vanessa had moved to Michigan, of all places. After she left, they communicated every day. The calling was divided between them. They were both eager to talk to each other: her for being alone in a new place; and him for having been left behind. She would talk about school, a new friend she had met, or her trip to the mall, and he would be jealous of it all. In his life nothing much had changed and he had nothing new to tell her. With time she called less, their conversations got shorter, and often when he called she wasn't home. Still, Duane wasn't willing to let go and replace her with someone else, so for Christmas he took the initiative and bought a ticket to Michigan.

When Vanessa picked him up at the airport in Detroit, a young man was driving the car. Though she presented him as Matt, without label or title, it was clear he was her new boyfriend. For the next two weeks the three of them went out together. It was two weeks too long, and though Matt was nice enough, Duane felt bitter and betrayed. When Matt dropped them off at night after a party or the movies, Duane would go to the guest room, and Vanessa would say good night, go to her bedroom and close the door, and he could have sworn he heard the click of the lock. He didn't have the courage to try the door, though the thought had spun in his head endlessly during those sleepless nights.

It was extremely awkward for him to sit down to meals with her family and Matt at the table. Duane thought he saw pity in her parents' eyes. After all, hadn't he known them for three years now? Whether or not her parents sided with him was of no consequence. He was old news. Duane told himself then that he would never get involved in another long distance relationship.

That betrayal of his first love stuck with him. Though Duane had been with a few girls since, he hadn't gotten involved with any of them in a serious way. Now when he dated he made sure the girls liked him more.

Duane felt that Aisha was helping him to recover his wasted youth. He found her non-threatening. He realized that she loved him like he had loved Vanessa, blindly and with total faith. He felt sorry for her. He was a good-looking young man and vanity compelled him to date attractive women. He had become completely superficial with love and perhaps that was his great failure. Duane did not choose women for their character, humor or kindness; he chose them on appearance alone.

Aisha was his trophy. They were not boyfriend and girlfriend, and she did not make unreasonable demands of him. If he wanted to be with his friends, she would wait for him. It pleased him to bring her around and show her off to his friends. When they asked what she did, she said she went to school. Aisha looked older than her age and they naturally thought she was referring to college. They would ask what she studied and she would reply that she hadn't yet decided. Most of them didn't press her further; it wasn't unusual for college students to be uncertain about their path in life.

That they lied for each other was proof enough that their relationship was flawed. Sometimes a great guilt would wash over Duane at the thought that he was taking advantage of her. He wanted her youth and beauty enough that he was willing to make concessions. It wasn't that she was stupid, just that her sixteen years hadn't given her enough time to form her own opinions and develop her own character. She depended mostly on him for her beliefs. She agreed with everything he said and, in the long run, that was something Duane couldn't tolerate. If he found a girl of similar beauty that had more to say and was closer to his own age, he would let Aisha go. Until then he would enjoy her as a body and not a mind.

It never occurred to Duane that, in spite of the facts and opinions he had collected in life, they were an even match emotionally. He was an immature young man, and intelligent women who spoke their minds intimidated him. What he wanted was a girl he could control. Even if he told himself that he wanted to find true love and a more experienced partner, it was far too early. He was like many young men of his time: an opportunist and a predator looking for the weak so that he could take from them what he did not have inside himself. He was waiting for a goddess to come along, a Brazilian supermodel with a Ph.D., and it would take him a long time to reconcile himself to the reality that such women were rare indeed, and that they could care less about a young man like himself.

One day when Duane thought that he was happy and had life in his hands, Aisha called. She had been sick for the last week and he was anxious to see her.

"Hey Duane. I miss you. Do you miss me?"

"Of course I miss you. Are you feeling better? I was thinking maybe you could come over and we could watch a movie. I rented *The Precipice*. Jeremy Leads is in it. That guy sure is smooth. He can say anything and get away with it."

"That sounds good. Listen, I've got something to tell you. I haven't really been sick. I don't know how to say this, Duane. Sometimes it's so hard to talk to you. I just wish you would understand."

"Come on, what are you talking about?"

Aisha had been thinking about it for a long time. She knew what she had to say and she would say it. It was the first time in her life when she had a real obligation to do something, and while it petrified her, she also felt a resolve that was cold inside her and that she could use to say things that would change her life forever. It was that sort of moment and everything was clear, slow and deliberate.

It dawned on him. Oh my god. She's gonna dump me, that bitch. Just who does she think she is? Does she really think I care that much?

"So what's so important that you have to tell me? Listen, I'm gonna put on the movie. I don't really feel like having a deep talk about our relationship, if that's what you're getting at. I told you I wanted things to be easy. So what did you wanna say?"

"I'm pregnant."

A long silence ensued.

"Duane, did you hear me, I'm gonna have a baby. It's your baby."

Duane had several thoughts. What if she's been fucking someone else and it isn't your baby? She can't be serious. You really fucked up,

Duane, how could you trust the pull-out method? She's got to get an abortion because there's no way that I'm putting my life on hold to raise a kid. She's gonna squeeze you for all sorts of money and you'll have to pay it to her or you're the biggest asshole that ever lived. Her father is gonna kill you if you don't face up to it. You don't owe her anything, just drop her, you didn't ask for any baggage like this. Why wasn't she on the pill? Why the fuck didn't you use a condom, you asshole?

"So what are you gonna do," he asked her carefully. "What do you want me to do?"

Aisha felt like crying. The way he spoke now was cold and distant. She felt that it would never be the same between them: that he wasn't there for her and didn't care for her. It was a lot for her to swallow.

"I'm gonna have the baby . . . I thought we could have it together."

"Listen, if you wanna have the baby, that's your choice, but it's not something I can handle right now. I have too much to take care of in my own life. You're too young to have a baby. You should think about your future. There's no point in raising a baby if you don't have any money. It's better not to have the baby at all if you can't give it all the opportunities it deserves. I'll pay for the abortion. I'll schedule an appointment and we'll take care of it. It's the best decision for everyone involved."

"I don't wanna have an abortion," she said between sobs. "I wanna have this baby. It's our baby and it's alive in me and I'm not gonna kill it. Why do you gotta act this way? I love you, Duane. I'd do anything for you. I promise I'll be the best wife you could ever think of. We'd be so happy together. We'll have a family and everything, and if it's a boy, I bet he'll look just like you."

It was his worst nightmare come true. Duane felt like he was drowning. While he knew supporting her was the right thing to do, he also felt like running away and never looking back. Sure, it would weigh on his conscience, but having a baby, and with a low class girl like her? What would his parents say? Why, what kind of child would that be? He made enough money now so that he could afford a vacation once a year, new clothes and a night out on the town whenever he liked; all of that would be gone if he settled down with her. He had learned the importance of education from his parents, and Aisha, she wasn't even done with high school and now she would have to drop out. The kid would be a born failure. Dammit, why can't she see the sense of an abortion?

"I don't wanna marry you," Duane said. "We don't have enough in common. We're not on the same level. I thought you understood this was a casual relationship, you know, just to have fun. I enjoy spending time with you, but we're worlds apart. I don't wanna get tied down. I have too much left to do. Can't you understand that?"

He was the biggest asshole in the world and he was going to abandon her to her fate, whatever it might be, because he could. There was no law saying that a man had to stick around and take care of a child. That was up to her. Her family could take up the slack.

Duane felt sick at his own cowardice. But he did not love her. If he had loved her, it would have been different, but as it was, she was entertainment.

Aisha felt like killing herself. She didn't understand how he could say the things he said or treat her that way. He had crushed her heart with his words and it would never be the same again.

"I never wanted this to happen, Duane. I'm so sorry it happened. I don't know what to do. If you don't help me, then I don't know where I'll go."

Listening to her sobs, Duane knew he would never be able to respect himself again for his failure to take accountability for his actions. His reaction was something he had no control over; it was as if that child being born signified his own death and the death of all his freedoms. In his selfishness, he could not contemplate the joy of it because, fundamentally, he did not believe in life and did not wish it on anyone.

"I don't want to see you again," he said. "Please don't call me unless you've changed your mind about the abortion. I'm sorry, Aisha. Goodbye."

Duane got in the car and took Highway 1 to Santa Cruz, an hour and a half south. He drove on the lonely highway and felt sick in himself.

Life has not gone the way you expected, he thought. Everything that ever meant anything to you, you've lost. Who are you, Duane, and how can you do the things you do? How can you be so heartless? You have never been there for anyone when they needed you. But then can they expect you to live a life you don't want for one little mistake? No, you'd never do that. You must put yourself before others in this world or you'll never make it through. You can only count on yourself.

9

One day when Jack was moping at home, he found a curious ad in the paper:

Vision Corp is looking for volunteers to participate in the testing of revolutionary virtual reality software. No experience necessary. $500 per session. Must be between 18-30 and in good physical health. Interested parties should contact Vision Corp at 1 (415) XXX-XXXX.

Test virtual reality software. That seemed easy enough. Jack imagined putting on gloves and a headset and moving around the room picking up objects. He wondered if it was like a video game or if it was more practical than that. Well, if they wanted volunteers, then it was probably intended for the consumer market. They probably needed to work the bugs out. Five hundred would cover his rent for the month and just in time. It certainly couldn't be any worse than waiting tables and it paid better, too. How long was a session, Jack wondered. It occurred to him that the ads at the back of the paper were not always legitimate. They dealt in the sale of sperm, something he was too embarrassed to do; acting classes, medical marijuana, massage and envelope stuffing from home for up to twenty-five hundred a week. You have to stuff a lot of envelopes for that, Jack thought. Almost around the clock.

After some deliberation –the time it took him to eat his breakfast- Jack called the number. He was worried that they wouldn't need any more volunteers, for certainly there were enough young and desperately unemployed men and women like him in the city.

Jack told them who he was and that he was interested in participating in the tests. The woman on the other end of the line replied that he could come in tomorrow at three o'clock.

The next day Jack met up at the Vision Corp office in a warehouse south of Market. In the lobby, other young men and women sat furtively watching each other. They must be here for the same reason I am, Jack concluded.

A young man came out of a door next to the office with a man in a suit and tie, clipboard in hand. Jack peeked inside but didn't see anything but an empty room.

"We'll see you again tomorrow then, Mr. Colburn?"

"Right on, man. That's some sweet stuff you guys are working on. When that hits the market, Game Star and Illusion are going to go out of business. Flat screen video games are old school. Man, I thought I was gonna die in there."

The man with the clipboard smiled.

"See you tomorrow at one-thirty," he said.

"Jack Wild?"

Jack stood up and the man shook his hand.

"I'm Simon Norton. Would you come with me? We have a few formalities to take care of before we get started."

Jack followed him into the room. It was clear that everyone in the office was relieved at the young man's enthusiasm when he left.

"So let me tell you a little about what Vision Corp is about. Do you play video games, Jack?"

"I've played video games before," he said.

"At Vision Corp we intend to revolutionize the gaming industry. We've been working on technology that will make reality and fantasy one and the same. The virtual gaming world we have created is as real as daily life. But before we continue, I need you to sign this NDA which prohibits you from discussing anything about your experience with us here today. It's just a formality, you understand. Virtual reality is a highly competitive market and we don't want to give away any secrets."

Jack looked at the paper to make sure it said what the man told him it said, which it did, but in very difficult legal language. Then he signed it.

"Good. Now without going into detail, Vision is a game like any other except, instead of watching a screen, you are surrounded by the action. What makes us different from other virtual reality technology is that we have developed and patented the Vision Suit, which is a full sensory body suit. It's like a second skin; it reacts to the movement of your body and also to outside stimuli. Now I have to inform you that the suit simulates bodily injury and violence via high and low level electric shock, strangulation and chemical modification to the player. Our suit is also capable of provoking pleasure through the same stimuli. But for these tests we are more concerned with pain. If you agree to participate, please understand that any injury that occurs in the game will be felt through the methods previously mentioned. Right now we are perfecting this system. At any moment you can stop the game. But remember, if you do, you may forfeit your right to payment. Do you understand?"

"Yeah, I understand."

Jack had to admit his curiosity was piqued. He had played fighting games before, and it would be exciting to participate physically and not just with his fingers and eyes.

"Could you please sign this? It's a liability waiver to insure that you won't hold Vision Corp responsible for any injuries you may receive."

Jack studied the document.

By signing this waiver, the participant agrees not to hold Vision Corp liable for any short or long-term adverse and possibly life-threatening side effects resulting from malfunction of the Vision Suit, or any neurological disorders that may be provoked by virtual reality simulation. While reasonable precautions have been made to render the Vision gaming experience as safe as practicably possible, the participant recognizes and accepts responsibility for the risk of brain damage, heart attack, seizure, insanity and death that may occur as a result of game operation.

That's a little heavy-handed, isn't it? But I'm sure it's just a formality, Jack thought. They wouldn't make a game that could kill someone.

Jack signed, and Mr. Norton took the paper from him and attached it to his clipboard. He got up from his desk and opened the back door.

"Shall we?"

Inside the warehouse Jack saw what he assumed to be the command center of the game: a large semicircular desk where a man sat with his headphones staring at a wall of monitors while hard drives hummed in the background. Jack followed Norton over to the first of a row of three identical black containers that were about the size of his bedroom at home. Norton punched a code into the keypad and a door slid open revealing a chamber illuminated with a dull blue light. An elongated tapered helmet with a regulator mask and tinted visor hung on the wall by the door. At first glace, there appeared to be a corpse dangling from the ceiling. Norton led Jack to the center of the room. Upon closer inspection, the corpse proved to be a full body suit with a hard outer shell, pistons at the joints, and various loose cables and tubes connected to the helmet. Jack had never seen anything like it. It looked like something right out of a science fiction movie.

"Excuse me, Mr. Norton, how long is a session, typically?"

"Typically, we'll have you in for an hour. If you come back again we'll put you in for two and see how it goes. It also depends on how long you survive. Excuse me, I'll be right back. If you're shy, you can pull the curtain," he said. "Take off your clothes and slip into this plastic sanitation sleeve before you get into the suit."

Norton left to talk to the computer technician. Jack took off his clothes and stepped into a human condom made of thin plastic that covered him up to his neck. The suit opened like a suitcase and was soft and slick on the inside. Jack got in and put on the helmet. Presently, Norton returned to seal the suit and connect the necessary cables. When he was finished, he gave a thumbs up to the technician via the surveillance camera.

"Okay Jack, here's the deal. Once you start the game, you can only communicate with me via radio by pressing the button on the side of your helmet. In the room you'll be all alone. On the floor is a multi-directional conveyer belt. It works much like a treadmill. The slope of the floor adjusts depending on whether you're ascending or descending. The suit itself is calibrated for the weight of objects. If you pick something up, you'll feel its real weight. There are a few tricks to using the suit but those you'll have to figure out yourself. Now, do you see the menu screen?"

Jack nodded.

"All you have to do is reach out and make your selections."

"Have you played the game before," Jack asked him.

Norton looked at him.

"Oh sure, Jack. I've played it. But only in early testing. You're going to test our latest version. This is revolutionary stuff. The guys who designed it are MIT grads who've worked for the Department of Defense. Just between you and me, this system is more advanced than what the military has. We hope to license it to them for training purposes. Anyway, here, it's time to pick a character. We have an archive of two hundred different individuals. They are real people. We have paid for the right to use their image in the game. Some of them you may see again as your adversaries."

Jack flipped through the faces until he found one he liked, a man with a scar on his cheek and two gold teeth. He chose a body a little heavier than his own.

"Remember, everything is calibrated to real life weights and measures. If you go big, you'll be slower. It depends on if you prefer strength to agility."

"Actually, I don't want to be that character," Jack said. "I just picked him because he looked like the kind of guy I wouldn't want to meet in a dark alley."

"Well, just pick someone. It's not that important."

In the end, Jack chose a beautiful dark-haired woman: the kind he'd like to marry. He chose for her a fit body more muscular than he would have liked if she were his girlfriend.

"All right, now choose a location. We've mapped adventures in twenty-three different countries. Remember, the suit is climate-controlled. If you choose the jungle, it's going to be hot; if you choose the North Pole, you're going to need extra clothes."

Jack chose "Desert."

"Now choose a time period."

The choices were "Past," "Present" and "Future."

He chose "Past."

"Now pick some equipment. Remember, everything you pick weighs something and will slow you down."

Jack looked through the inventory of weapons.

"I think you're going to enjoy this, Jack. What better way to spend the day than to go out in the desert and kick some ass. Just try not to get hurt, okay? Ha, ha."

"How much does a suit like this cost?"

"The suit itself is worth several million. The whole set-up is worth tens of millions. Thank god for venture capital and the U.S. Government. So let's plug you in."

Jack looked to where the power cables connected to a series of transformers and generators stacked against the back wall.

"Yeah, it takes a lot of juice to run this one," Norton told him. "The suit is wired for audio and video, it's pressurized, mechanized, heated and cooled, and produces smells from a dead body to chocolate. The olfactory system, in particular, was developed by a team of chemists formerly employed by major perfume companies in France."

And I hope it works according to plan, Norton thought. He seems like a good kid and I almost feel bad getting him into this. But then someone has to test it and work the bugs out. If he knew there were acupuncture needles in this thing that could make him feel the most excruciating pain, would he still do it? We just need to make sure the highs aren't too high. Most people will play on a low to moderate pain level. It's a lot like Indian food, he thought. Never order it extra hot.

Jack took a few steps in the suit. It was like wearing a pea coat and a backpack when you were going hiking and planning on staying out a few days. Then Jack felt the load lighten as Norton activated the various control systems of the suit.

Gravity was simulated by suspension cables that supported the suit and by pistons on the joints, which also permitted or impeded locomotion. The compression system served for cooling, heating, and tactile simulation and consisted of a series of pneumatic sacs that lined the suit. When filled to capacity, the sacs could cut off circulation.

The Vision Suit dealt with injury and death in several ways. If a limb were lost in fighting, the pistons would immobilize it and it would be pressurized until it fell asleep from lack of circulation. In slow death by bleeding or a gun wound, the player would be strangled until he was unconscious. A pressurized ring located at the neck of the suit served this purpose. Finally, in a quick death, the player would be given enough electricity to do the same. This was achieved through a series of voltage contacts inside the suit.

"Remember, unless you push the button on the side of your helmet, communication is only heard in the game and by the other players. If you can hear me, give me a thumbs up."

Jack gave him a thumbs up and, pushing the button, said, "I can't see anything. The screen's all black."

"Just one minute and you'll be in the game," Norton said.

The screen fizzled and then the black disappeared and Jack was in the desert. When he turned, he found the landscape surrounding him and was surprised at how realistic it was. But then that was easy enough. They had filmed it. The question was how were they going to include objects and people that weren't really there?

Just how real is this, Jack wondered, looking down at his body. Noticing his breasts, he reached out to touch them. The pressure pads in his hands filled when they came in contact with the field of his virtual body. When he applied pressure, he could feel it on his body and his hands at the same time. After a certain pressure, the pistons locked to the programmed dimensions of his imaginary bust. It occurred to him then that technology was going to render the world totally unrecognizable. Only man's imagination was the limit.

Jack looked down at his belt and saw the gun. He grabbed it in his hand and the suit reacted to create its weight and substance. He pulled the trigger and the gun kicked as the sound of the shot echoed in his head. He looked at his hand and turned it over. It was a completely realistic woman's hand with thin, fine fingers and olive skin. I never imagined I'd get paid to be a hot chick and kill people, he thought.

Jack walked and the conveyer belt sustained his pace. Everything was quiet except the sound of the wind and his footsteps in the dirt. Presently, a horse and rider appeared on the horizon. As they approached, Jack noted that the rider was a Native American armed with a bow. He had feathers in his long black hair and his face was painted. Jack's amazement at the illusion was broken when the warrior let out a piercing war cry and pulled the bow tight with an arrow. Before he could react, Jack's shoulder erupted in pain and he was thrown to the ground. The horse galloped around him and the warrior continued to shout. Jack looked to his shoulder and could see that he was bleeding. The pain grew dull and incessant. Luckily, it was the left shoulder and not his shooting arm. Jack watched with genuine fear as the warrior pulled another arrow from his quiver. It was clear that there were very real consequences in the game, in spite of the choppy visuals due to processing delay and the blend between film and cut and paste hologram characters that were slightly cartoon-like. Mostly, it was the pain and the sound and smell that made it real.

This guy is gonna kill me, Jack thought. And sure enough, the warrior pulled the bow tight to strike again. Jack rolled in time to hear the arrow snap in the dirt. The rider circled and Jack jerked his gun from his hip, aimed and pulled the trigger. He executed the motion quickly, relying on his experience from the saloon at Amerika. It was a familiar motion except that the kick of the gun put him off target. What would have been a shot to the heart struck his assailant in the neck. The man doubled over on his mount and fell to the dirt. Jack approached him, noting his expression of pain as he held his neck, while blood pumped through his fingers and ran down his chest. Jack felt a pang of compassion and thought: I don't need to kill him. But then again he was set on killing you and it's just a game after all. So Jack aimed and shot him in the head. The man fell back and lay still with death.

Jack's heart was still pounding with adrenaline when he returned his attention to the arrow stuck through his body. He tried to snap it off and almost passed out from pain. You have to do it quickly and with both hands. He counted to three and snapped off the point. Then he pulled out the shaft. Every movement he made with his left arm was accompanied by pain.

He went over to the warrior and took the knife from his belt and his bone and bead necklace. The horse had run off during the fight. Jack set off walking again, unsure of his destination and how long it would take him to get there. What if a war party comes along? Then I'm fucked.

Soon a town appeared in the distance. It was deserted except for some horses stabled outside the local watering hole. Jack went inside. A few men were at the bar, and Jack approached a stool and sat down. The legs in his suit locked and the cables that were attached to the ceiling held his weight suspended above the floor. He felt as if he were really sitting. He found he did not think about the mechanics of the game at all now that he was in it. There were no gaps in the mechanics to reveal reality.

"Why, what's done happened to you, missy? You're all covered in blood," the bartender, Alan, said. "You better go on and git cleaned up. Here's a towel and why don't you pour a little of this on that there wound o' yours."

Alan gave him a towel and set a bottle of alcohol on the bar.

"Thanks mister," Jack said, startled by the female pitch of his voice. He took the towel and splashed it with alcohol. The pressure sacs had filled with cool water in the glove of his suit making the towel feel wet in his hand. Jack pulled the collar of his shirt down over his shoulder, and while the men in the bar stared, he pressed the towel to his wound where it burned.

"Maybe you'd like to go on upstairs and git changed. I'm sure one of the gals could lend you something nice," Alan told her.

"No thanks. I don't plan on staying long," Jack said.

Jack noticed that when the men spoke their lips did not move perfectly with their words. It was an eerie sensation.

"I notice you got yourself an Injun necklace," a man at the bar said.

"I was attacked by an Indian outside of town."

"I'm surprised you made it here alive. They's a fierce heartless people. You lucky they don't done killed you."

"I shot him dead before that could happen," Jack told him.

"Why, I'll be damned," the man said. "I never heard of a lady who was good with a six-shooter. You lucky there wasn't no more of 'um. Then you woulda needed my services. I'da killed 'um dead, every last one, or my name's not Danny the Kid."

Jack wondered how communication worked in the game. In this case, the dialogue of the characters in the bar was mostly scripted from old Westerns or produced real-time by Josh, the staff verbal technician. When Jack spoke, the mainframe scanned a list of relevant canned dialogue for the best replies, remarks or questions, before displaying its choice to Josh, whose job it was to catch any inconsistencies and provide stall dialogue until he worked out an appropriate response. Occasionally, this resulted in minor delays.

"The frontier ain't no place for a lady," Alan said. " It'ad be an easy thing for them Injuns to capture a gal like yourself, and you could count yourself lucky if they took your scalp while leavin' your virtue intact."

Alan smiled and his teeth were nearly hidden by his moustache. He polished a glass.

"Hey Alan, git me another whiskey," Danny said. "And whatever the lady wants. I'm payin'."

Danny pulled out a little bag, produced some bits of gold and put them on the bar.

"You know, Danny, soon that gold's gonna run out," Alan said.

"When it run out, it run out. Then I'll go rustle some cattle from some poor greener, and if he gets in my way I'll kill him. Ha, ha."

At times, Jack wanted to be out of the game. Even if it was more exciting than his own life, he felt disturbed. After the first traumatic incident, he felt that anything could and would go wrong. After all, the point wasn't to be safe and comfortable.

"Say lady, what's your name, anyhow? You sure is pretty," Danny said. "We don't get many pretty ladies in these parts, except the gals upstairs, and they ain't so pretty no more."

In the back of the saloon, a group of men were seated at a table playing cards and smoking. Above them was a balcony that ran the perimeter of the interior. There were doors all along the way, and Jack wished he had chosen to be a man so he could go upstairs and have some fun. I wonder if this suit can do pleasure as well as pain? I'm sure they've got drugs to simulate euphoria and orgasm.

Jack hadn't thought of a name yet, so he said the first thing that came to mind.

"I'm Sally," he said.

"Nice to meet you, Sally. Call me Danny. They call me the Kid 'cause I've got such a baby face. Say, I ain't seen you in these parts before."

"I'm not from around here."

"You got that right."

Jack noticed the way Danny the Kid leaned on the bar. His face was flushed and he seemed to struggle to keep his balance.

"And what can I get for the lady," the bartender asked. "Danny here's buyin'."

"I'll take a whiskey," Jack said.

"Well I'll be darned, she not only kills Injuns, but she drinks whiskey, too. Missy, you sure is strange," Danny said.

Alan served them each a whiskey, and Danny picked his up and said, "Cheers to this godforsaken little town and the law that ain't never gonna catch me."

Jack followed suit. He put the drink to his helmet and a rubber tube filled his mouth with a foul-tasting liquid that he couldn't help but swallow. Meanwhile, a needle injected a percentage of alcohol directly into his bloodstream through a vein in his arm.

They had a second round and Jack began to feel his liquor. He had forgotten that the character he had chosen weighed only one hundred ten pounds, compared to his one hundred eighty-five, and the injections given him were enough to offset the difference.

Danny moved closer, and Jack felt the weight of the man's arm around his waist. He could smell Danny's sweat and the liquor on his breath.

"Say, why don't you give me a kiss, little lady, and then maybe we can take a trip upstairs."

Jack struggled under his arm and pushed him away. Danny crashed to the floor. When he got up again, he was angry.

"Why, you stupid harlot," Danny said, raising his arm to slap him. Jack ducked the blow and shattered his whiskey glass against Danny's head, cutting himself in the process. Meanwhile, Danny was on the floor holding his bloody head in his hands. The other men at the bar looked up and also the men in the back playing cards.

"Christ, what a fiery bitch," one of them said.

"Looks like Danny's got a live one on his hands."

"Yep, sure does."

Danny picked himself up from the floor.

"Y'all just better shut your mouth if you know what's good for you," he told them, before turning his attention to Jack.

"All right, you asked for trouble and now you got it. Normally, I'd just shoot a man dead for that. But since you's a lady, we can step outside and settle it fair and square."

"Don't listen to him, missy, he's drunk. You best run along and I'll take care of this," Alan said.

"You stay outta this, you Irish half-breed," Danny said.

Damn, how could you let this happen? You remember that movie where Danny the Kid kills like twenty people? You don't have a chance, Jack thought. Not even with all your practice at Amerika. This isn't make-believe anymore. What happens if you get killed?

"Leave the lady alone, Danny," one of the men at the bar said. "Only a coward fights a woman."

Danny pulled his gun and fired. The man grabbed his chest and fell to the floor.

"Not in here, Danny. Every time you blow into town, I clean up your mess," Alan said.

"Come on," Danny said, grabbing Jack by the shirt and shoving him forward.

Jack stumbled through the shutter doors and was blinded by the glare of the afternoon sun. He felt dizzy from the loss of blood and the whiskey. I could just turn and kill him now, he thought. There is no way you're going to survive a real showdown. What a fucking nightmare.

Jack pushed the button on his helmet and said, "Norton, Norton, are you there?"

"Yeah, I'm here. Isn't it fantastic? You're going to duel with Danny the Kid. How many people dream about having a showdown with Danny the Kid?"

"Yeah, that's cool and all, but what if I die? What happens if I die?"

"You won't really die, Jack. The screen will just turn black and you'll be done."

"Are you sure about that?"

"Danny the Kid's gonna have a showdown with a woman," a child yelled, running by in the street.

"A woman gonna challenge Danny the Kid," someone shouted.

Faces appeared in the windows and people gathered on the storefront porches. They were poor, plain people and Jack thought: boy, I'm glad I didn't grow up in the Wild West. It's not as romantic as they made it out to be.

"Alan, you take care of the formalities," Danny said.

"All right then," Alan said. "Now listen up. When I say walk, you both start walking at an even pace until I say stop. Then you turn around. When I say draw, you draw. If someone gets hit, it's over. No one's gotta die."

Jack knew from what he had read in history books and seen in movies that Danny never missed and never left anyone alive. Maybe the fact that he was a woman, and beautiful, would save his life. Danny the Kid would have to be a cold motherfucker to overlook that.

Alan stood them back to back. A hush settled over the crowd. Jack felt the sweat dripping from his face.

"Walk," Alan commanded.

To Jack, each step seemed like an eternity. He watched his life play in slow motion through his mind. He wasn't sure what would happen if he were killed. The game was a frightening reality of visceral smells, sounds and emotions with the appearance of a painting in motion. Just think how when you moved to the city you thought you would be a big success. And all you've done is rot. Then Elizabeth left and you haven't gotten laid since, and remember when Martino stabbed you? Well, that was real even though it seems absurd now. What else seems absurd? How about the S & M sex with that woman all tied up in the bedroom at the party? That was real, too. Jack looked to the horizon and thought of his family back home: his mom and sister, and also his dad at the store helping his customers and stocking the shelves. It was an easier life then. When Jack looked up and down the main street in the frontier town where he now found himself, he half-expected to see his family and friends standing there: his mother, with her hands on her face hoping that he would do well, his housemates, and of course Arnold. If Arnold were there, he would probably shoot Danny the Kid in the back. He would have a machine gun and he would blow Danny away without pity. Vision was the perfect game for someone like Arnold. Yeah, a lot of people would get off on it.

"Stop."

Jack stopped walking and turned around. He was maybe ten yards from Danny, scared to death. He felt cold chills and heat run through him simultaneously. He was short of breath. He thought: I hope I can draw and pull the trigger in time. I've done this a hundred times at Amerika. I was the best of all the waiters. But then it's even harder when you aren't sure that the gun's gonna be there. The virtual gun, anyway.

They've got pain down in this game, don't forget that. Soon you're going to feel the pain of a bullet without actually being shot. I wonder how that works?

Jack was sweating profusely. The crowd had fallen silent and Danny looked like the devil himself, even though Jack couldn't see his eyes or his expression. He looked to Alan and back at Danny. When you hear draw, you draw, like your life depends on it. Pain is a much better motivator than pleasure, Jack thought. We live to avoid pain. If we can avoid pain, we're content. But if we're too content, we look for pain again to remind us we're alive. God, I feel so fucking alive right now. Come on, Danny, I'm gonna take you down.

"Draw."

Jack watched as Danny whipped his gun into his hand. Jack was still pulling his gun when he felt a burning pain in his chest. He was thrown to the ground as he heard the report of Danny's gun. He lay there staring at the sky and stuggling to breathe. This is it. I'm gonna die. Norton is a fucking liar. Fuck that, you are Jack Wild and you live in San Francisco and you are unemployed. You are not an olive-skinned supermodel in a showdown with Danny the Kid in 1880. The sky began to fade and Jack saw Alan's face hanging over him.

"It's a shame such a pretty lady's gotta die," he said. "It breaks me Irish heart."

Jack reached up to touch Alan's face and then everything went black.

From the command console Norton was able to monitor Jack's biometric information and adjust the pain levels accordingly. He wanted the pain to be as close to real as possible, which meant stimulating fear, and applying acupressure and electric shock to the player without reducing blood pressure to such a level to induce death by shock, trauma, heart attack, stroke, embolism, etc. As Jack was still alive after the killing blow, Norton considered the experiment a success. An older man would in all likelihood have died from the experience.

"There were only a few glitches here and there where the scenes skipped," Norton said. "We have to get our programmers on that. Otherwise the dialogue flows."

"What about the kid? We'd better make sure he's okay," Josh said.

Norton tapped his headset. "Get the medic over here. We've got a game DOA."

The medic came and they removed Jack from the suit and loaded him onto a gurney. The air smelt of burnt flesh, plastic and shit. Jack's feet were soaking in urine. They wheeled him to the medical lab where they removed the plastic body condom and hosed him off in the shower. His chest was red and blistered where he had been electrocuted.

"He's stopped breathing," the doctor said. "Nurse, get the jumpers."

The doctor grabbed hold of the pads and pressed them to Jack's chest. "Go." Jack's body jerked clear of the gurney. The EKG was still flat. "Give me one more. Jesus, if he dies we're fucked. Just think of the bad publicity."

Norton looked on. This was bad news. Not so much that Jack might die, but for the future of the game. The problem was that people reacted differently to electric shock. They had reviewed capital punishment records and discovered that some individuals were able to resist a voltage that would cook another man alive. That had to be will. Who would have thought a young man of Jack's build wouldn't be able to take four hundred volts? Well, his life wouldn't be lost for nothing. He was a virtual reality pioneer.

There was no telling how far they could go with this. It was a phenomenal program. They would set up Vision Cubes all across the country; soon they would replace movie theatres. Why watch an action hero when you could be one? What was lacking in modern society was real emotion, pain and danger; the average citizen would pay through the nose to take Jack's place in the game.

Unfortunately, Jack wasn't as skilled as the young kid, Colburn, Norton thought. Colburn was a video game wiz. Remember when he played the jungle scenario and annihilated everything he came across, including the wildlife? I guess that says something about the youth of today. They've got a lot of untapped aggression and hate inside.

Some people will like the violence and others will like the sex. It will be a good way to explore their fantasies. I hope Jack lives. I guess we have to cut down on the juice. Strangulation seems to work fine. As soon as he lost consciousness the pressure dropped. Of course liability is big here. But then we'll just make everyone sign a waiver on their life.

Jack came to and saw a man standing above him. He didn't know where he was, but he knew he didn't feel well.

"Well, Jack, you got killed. And now you're back to life. Isn't that great? You're immortal," Norton said.

"Where am I?"

"You're in the medical lab. You've just played a round of Vision, and unfortunately for you, Danny the Kid's just too fast on the draw."

"Unnaturally fast, I think. I've had a little practice at showdowns and I didn't even get my gun clear of the holster. Who's to say you didn't rig it," Jack said.

"It's a probability game. We've timed how long it takes people to draw in the movies and in real life and we took the fastest of all the times and gave that skill to Danny. I mean he was supposed to be the best."

"I thought you only used ordinary people in the game?"

"No, we own the rights to quite a few celebrities. It makes the game more exciting with that star factor. But Danny's a historic figure, so he's open source, so to speak. At any rate, films are starting to use computer models of the famous, so why shouldn't we use them, too? At least until star power is outdated and regular people play themselves to stardom in the virtual world."

"Man, you guys are nuts. This kind of thing could get out of hand."

"When Vision's all the rage, you'll be able to say you were with us in the beginning," Norton said.

"What an honor."

"Listen, Jack, you wouldn't want to sell us the rights to your face and body would you? You've got kind of a classic look to you. You could be a hero in the game."

"No way."

The whole thing was shady. After all, he'd nearly been killed. Then Jack noticed the blister on his chest.

"What the fuck, man. I'm all burned up. I didn't sign up for this. Is it going to heal?"

"That's where you took the bullet," Norton said. "Listen, Jack, we understand if you don't want to come back. I think the game is a little too intense for you."

"Yes, it will heal," the doctor interjected. "We'll give you some cream for it."

"Rest up as long as you like, Jack. Then come into my office and we'll settle up."

"Man, I oughta sue you guys for this. And you're gonna put this thing out on the market? Why, it nearly killed me."

"If you remember, Jack, you signed a waiver before you started," Norton said. "I explained to you clearly the consequences of what you were doing. We're doing these tests precisely so that what happened to you won't happen to the average consumer."

"So you used me as a guinea pig? That isn't fucking right."

"I'll also remind you, Jack, that if you talk to anyone about what happened here, then we'll take you to court. You can pick up your check on the way out. No hard feelings, kid."

Jack lay back on the gurney and felt his head pound. He thought: sooner or later we're going to run ourselves into the ground with all this technology.

10

Elizabeth was in her second month teaching English at the American School in Padang. She had little or no experience teaching and the students' level was so poor that sometimes she wondered if they understood anything at all. Mostly, they sat and smiled at her. None of them had enough courage to answer her question unless specifically called on. There were twenty-two students and, unless she went around the room and put her hand on a specific desk, there was always confusion as to who was being called on. So she resorted to nametags. Her first lesson dealt mainly with vowels. She had them all say their names and then she wrote the English equivalent on the nametags. Some wanted names of famous American movie stars, athletes and musicians, while others wanted nicknames that were beyond her understanding.

During her lessons, Elizabeth performed skits to make them laugh and put them at ease. At first they were shy to laugh, but once they understood that it was okay, they laughed a lot. Later she wrote scripts for them to memorize and perform in front of the class. She had them present in groups so they would feel less self-conscious.

As for the young men, Elizabeth noticed that they paid close attention to her. Mostly, they stared at her breasts. The attention the young men gave her made her feel strong and beautiful. There was one young man in his twenties, Setiawan, that she liked in particular. Setiawan's English was better than the other students. Elizabeth knew he had a crush on her, and she was flattered. She enjoyed calling on him and watching him blush. She did not think she would like Indonesian men. She thought that the predominantly Muslim Indonesians would be sexist. But in fact Indonesians were kind and considerate, Setiawan in particular.

Setiawan had short wavy black hair, he wore collared shirts without a wrinkle and gave his undivided attention to Elizabeth, smiling the whole time. He always answered her questions formally, adding Ms. Brown at the end. His boyish good looks gave him an air of innocence. Even so, Elizabeth imagined that he probably jerked off to her in bed at night. How good is his imagination, she wondered. Part of her attraction to him was the desire to ruin everything that was clean, well-behaved and seemingly naive about him. Part of her desire for him was her belief that he was different from Graham, that stubborn cynic who loved her like a whore. Setiawan's respect for her was charming in its own immature fashion.

While she taught, Elizabeth's mind wandered. Besides Setiawan, the teaching was not very interesting. She would much rather be on vacation eating, swimming, sightseeing and relaxing in Indonesia with all its heat, exotic customs and abundant nature.

Over the past few months Elizabeth had learned some basic Bahasa Indonesia: where, when, what, bathroom, store, bus, car, dog, road, food, water, my name is, excuse me, yes, no, thank you, please, and other such common words. It wasn't a difficult language; she just wasn't motivated to learn because she had decided not to stay. It had long since been her habit to treat everything in a temporary way so that if she failed or was betrayed then she could turn her back and walk away. More than a habit, it was a lifestyle.

After work Elizabeth often stayed in the city to shop for all things Indonesian. She had taken to collecting batiks, which were more comfortable and superior to pants in the heat and otherwise. She now had a different batik to wear every day for a week straight. She enjoyed bargaining in the market and had learned new vocabulary there, such as: how much, small, large, expensive, cheap, good, bad, pretty, plain. She found she could wander for hours looking in the various shops at the fine teak and mahogany furniture and assorted artwork. She shopped for exotic foods and sat at food stalls watching the people go about their daily business.

In the beginning Graham often met Elizabeth in the city for dinner before giving her a lift home from work; with time these encounters became more infrequent. Elizabeth hated to be left alone with Merpati when Graham was away on assignment; when he was home, the thought nagged in her mind that he was fucking Merpati behind her back. Aside from Graham, Elizabeth knew no one; it was only a matter of time before she began to feel lonely.

Her relationship with Graham had become routine. He had always been emotionally absent, more haunted than absent, due to the nature of his work. Though it made him attractive, it also made him seem distant, even when they were pressed against each other in bed. She wasn't sure if Graham was really as he appeared, or if it was just a macho act that, out of habit, had become character. She knew he could have been happier, but perhaps he felt he didn't deserve it.

She had entertained the dream of marrying Graham and building a life with him in exile. She believed that neither was meant for an ordinary life and that it would be hard for them to find someone to match with their particular and divisive natures. On certain issues they would never come to an agreement, each believing in their own reason and experience. We're both too critical and arrogant, she thought.

In spite of her drive for the novel and exotic, for knowledge and some solution to her life, Elizabeth felt herself growing old. She wasn't old, but she was no longer a girl, and girls were what men loved most: innocent, stupid girls with angel faces to be loved, who didn't ask difficult questions. She was more than several years out of that picture.

Elizabeth was feeling the pressure that all women feel to find a decent man who would stand by her and give her children of her own that could carry on her dreams, her beauty and her flaws. She longed to blend herself with another person and create something new and stronger than their individual parts. She was not so much interested in wandering the world aimlessly as she had done in her younger years. Nor was she concerned with solving the world's ills. With time and experience her youthful righteousness had matured into self-interest. By concentrating on her own needs, and the needs of those she loved, she hoped to find some peace in her life. She realized that Graham was not the man to take care of her. Her dream of them making a life together was just the fantasy of a young, romantic girl: the same girl who had alienated herself trying to help and understand others. For the sake of her own vanity and sense of superiority, of course.

It was then that she thought of Jack. Sitting at the food stand, she wrote him a postcard where she lied about her experiences. The postcard she chose featured not Padang, or the village where she lived, but the Singalang volcano: one of two volcanoes located within a few hours drive of the city. She told Jack that sooner or later she planned to climb it. She said that she was happy and that there was little she missed about the city. She told him that her friend had a nice house in the countryside where she was able to relax and think about her future. The postcard was too small and she had to write around the edges until there was barely enough room for her name and a stamp. She realized that she should have written Jack a letter a long time ago. She had much to tell him that she was unable to share with Graham or anyone else. Yes, Jack deserved a good long letter that, once folded, would be hard to fit into the envelope.

No, life wasn't easy in Indonesia and Elizabeth wondered what had driven her to move there. She had always been restless, and perhaps it was the fear of being mediocre that made her do such things. It provided ammunition against the dull, unambitious people one met at parties to be able to say: I lived in a village of eight hundred people in Sumatra. I bought a four-wheel-drive truck and drove it to the most remote parts of the Australian outback and, with the help of some tools and a manual, fixed that truck when it broke down in the middle of nowhere. In my travels I've seen amazing things and spoken to people I would otherwise never have met.

Yes, Elizabeth had her share of stories that made her like a castle: magnificent, impenetrable and cold. The value of those stories was in the pain it took to collect them, the joy of sharing them and the way memory made them better over time. She liked everything that was extreme and nothing in the middle.

One thing she disliked about Indonesia was the public transportation. She hated being pushed and shoved. It upset her that there was no system such as a line where it was first come first served, that they put more people in the bus than could fit comfortably or safely, and that the buses were not on time and did not leave until they were packed full.

Crossing the street was also dangerous. It was not a good idea to run across the street in front of traffic. Unlike America, where drivers sped up if they knew they had the room and would most certainly stop if they did not, Indonesians drove in a way that did not allow for any unexpected pedestrian obstruction whatsoever. If it came, they would not slow down, though they would probably swerve, and that was the cause of many an accident.

One afternoon, distracted in her thoughts, Elizabeth crossed in front of a parked bus. When she stepped past it into the street, two men came on a motorcycle and ran into her at full speed. They were thrown from the bike and Elizabeth ended face down on the asphalt. Her first reaction was to get up, but when she tried to stand, one of her legs wouldn't respond and she collapsed.

The shock made Elizabeth lose her bearings. For a moment she lay staring into the hot black pavement, before trying to drag her body across the street, one hand in front of the other. In spite of the honking horns and the crowd of people that had gathered, she felt lonely and abandoned. No one tried to help her. She had single-handedly brought traffic to a standstill and that was a very serious problem. Drivers shook their fists in anger, a mob of pedestrians gathered on the street shouting, horns honked, and engines roared with impatience at the unexpected delay. The daily schedule had been interrupted by an idiotic, bug-like foreigner.

Elizabeth tried to get out of the road, like the two men who cleared away their bike as soon as they stopped skidding on the ground with their bodies. Only when they were back on the sidewalk did they check their injuries and examine the bike for damages. When they found themselves with only minor cuts and bruises and the bike fully operational, they sped off through the gridlocked traffic. They did not stop to check on Elizabeth crawling on the asphalt slick with her blood, her left leg shattered and nearly torn from her body.

It was infernally hot on the road, and Elizabeth was gasping for air and wetting her lips, wishing for a drink. She was weak with blood loss and tired from her efforts. The world was blurry and slow. Her only goal was to get out of the street.

She had visions of Southern California and the Pacific Ocean. She imagined that soon she would arrive where she was going. She felt light as a feather when two men picked her up and put her on the side of the road, where it was filthy and wet, like a piece of trash. Elizabeth couldn't lift herself and just lay on her back staring at the sky. Her bag and its contents were exploded in the street: her books as well as her wallet and personal effects.

The traffic fought with itself to get going again, but now a crowd had gathered around Elizabeth. Just when the anger of the pedestrians and motorists was about to boil over, a young Indonesian man brandishing a broken bottle shouted them back. What else could they expect from the day but a lunatic standing in the middle of the road?

Setiawan did not waste time. In the confusion, he gathered Elizabeth's things. All it would take was one motorist to drive and he would be caught in a fatal flow of traffic. He got out of the road just as the traffic started to move again. With Elizabeth's bag over his shoulder, he cursed the pedestrians and their mothers for their cowardice and insensitivity; he proclaimed that he would die for this woman who was his teacher. When a group of young men came to shut him up, he swung the bottle at the nearest and they thought better of interfering. Setiawan had broken the spell. Enough time had passed that the event had become sterile history. The crowd was no longer connected in some unconscious way, but competing again to get somewhere that was elsewhere from the stupid foreigner who lay neutralized in the gutter where she belonged.

When Setiawan picked Elizabeth up in his arms he was appalled at the severity of her injury. Her leg hung sideways with the bone exposed. Quickly, he put her down.

He ran about in the near vicinity shouting for the police. "My teacher is dying," he told them. "Please help her, she is dying," he pleaded. But now no one paid any notice to the girl in the gutter as they pushed past the crazy, shouting boy to their destination.

The police came and then an ambulance, a pick-up truck with a canopy: the ambulance of the public hospital. They did not have a proper gurney where she could be placed carefully and secured so that she was not jostled, nor did they have any medicine to give her. They bandaged the leg but did not splint it, so that when they tried to put Elizabeth in the truck, one man holding her legs and the other her upper body, her damaged leg did not cooperate but bent in terrible way that made Setiawan shout in alarm.

They managed to get her in the truck, and Elizabeth was feeling the pain now, so much that she thought she would pass out. She told herself: don't die, don't die, keep awake, that's it, hang on. Setiawan climbed in with her and shut the gate. The truck started with a jolt and they drove fast on the bumpy road like they were delivering sacks of rice or other dry durable goods. Elizabeth slid back and forth and Setiawan had to hold her tight. Setiawan's white collared shirt was stained pink. He had his arms around Elizabeth and was kissing her face, saying in English, "I love you, Ms. Brown, you're not going to die."

Setiawan was scared and sickened by life. He had to hold back the spasms in his throat caused by the heat of the truck, the smell of blood, and the memory of the leg and how it behaved. He thought: Allah, most humble, please do not let her die, she is an infidel but she is a good, kind woman, and there are many infidels that become good Muslims. Is it her fault that she does not know our culture? Please do not let her die.

Elizabeth was unconscious, and in her unconscious she flew in the sky and watched the wrinkled blue of the ocean through her bird's eye. A submerged island floated dark, smooth and peaceful below the crystalline surface. The island undulated in the current, it flicked its tail, and she realized with horror that it was alive. Then her wings failed her and she plunged into the depths of the sea with the knowledge of the predator just underneath her and out of view. She dove with her eyes wide but not wanting to see. Then the primordial beast opened its mouth and swallowed her inside a vast, dark abyss.

The local hospital was filthy; sad women sat waiting, one as sad as the next, some with children, some without. Certain of these children cried, while others were serious as death.

The furniture was cheap, institutional and recycled. There was a notable absence of nurses and doctors and surprisingly little light except what came from the small windows near the ceiling. The paint on the wall was peeling; it seemed that that hospital was every bit as ill as the people who sat waiting inside it.

Elizabeth was put on a gurney and given a shot of penicillin to which she was allergic, provoking an angry rash and causing her to vomit from shock.

Setiawan called Elizabeth's home number, which he had been given in class but had never had the courage to use. Fortunately, Graham was home. Setiawan explained the situation, wondering all the while if Graham was Ms. Brown's boyfriend.

Graham told him, "She needs to get the hell out of that hospital. She's got to be flown to Singapore, immediately. Otherwise, they'll fucking kill her. There isn't a decent hospital in this whole city to deal with something this serious. I'll be there as soon as possible."

Graham had plenty of experience with Indonesian bureaucracy. He spoke decent Bahasa Indonesia and knew that it was better to explain things clearly and politely and not scream and shout and thus shame himself and seem uncivilized. In this way, he managed to secure a helicopter that would fly her directly to Singapore. The only reason that Elizabeth was not dead was because her parents had insisted that she get travel insurance, which they had paid for because she couldn't afford it on her own. Her regular insurance didn't cover accidents in foreign countries where the quality of the hospitals and the doctors and their methods were unknown or of dubious quality.

It was only when the helicopter came that Elizabeth was given the necessary medicine and pain killers, and her leg was put in vacuum cast to make sure the bone would set properly. But it proved to be too little, too late. Her leg was infected and had to be amputated below the knee where it had been broken, where the ligaments and tissues were damaged beyond repair, and where it had received no blood for many hours and served better on the grill than as an appendage.

Graham sat alone in the sterile, modern hospital in the economic hub of Southeast Asia that was Singapore and stared at Elizabeth's face as she lay sleeping, her heart rate terribly low and critical, with all manner of tubes stuck in her body.

Jesus, he thought, looking at the bandaged stump silhouetted underneath the sheets. If I hadn't asked her to come, then this would never have happened. Her life is ruined now. No, you can't go thinking like that. One can't just as well sit at home and not go anywhere or do anything, just to be safe. Why her and not me, like when the hotel was under siege and they shot a glass of whiskey out of your hand with machine gun fire in Haiti? Why not you when you were caught in a riot in South Africa and you lay on the ground pretending to be dead while they walked on your back?

Certainly, you're too healthy to have been in the wrong place at the wrong time so often. He coughed then: a nagging cough that came from prolonged smoking, not enough sleep, a bad diet and heavy drinking. Well, there's healthy and there's healthy; it seems like when a person's healthy they try to ruin it. Is that just boredom? No, it's petty bourgeois pathos.

She'll never be able to walk again. And you had to go and be an asshole and have two women. Why are you so goddamned immature? When are you gonna grow up? All this misery and you're still acting like a baby. Well, it's best that she goes home now. She can't just as well stay here and rot. And you don't want to see her like this, anyway. She wouldn't want it and you don't either. That limb was your relationship and it's gone now in a garbage can somewhere, and when she's gone you'll try to forget her, but you won't be able to because your conscience will itch.

Graham didn't cry. Pity is a luxury, he told himself. If you cry it will only be for yourself, like all tears, for something you have lost. Don't kid yourself and pretend it's for her. She wouldn't want you to cry for her. What you'd really like from her is a slap in the face. That's all anyone ever needs to remind themselves how things really stand.

11

Jack didn't feel well after his virtual reality experiment. When he came back to the house all he wanted was to lie down and sleep. Vision Corp had cut him a check for a thousand dollars: a five hundred dollar bonus for his troubles and some convenient amnesia?

In the hall he met Damian, who said, "Jack, you don't look good at all. You're pasty white, man, and you're sweating like crazy. What's going on with you? You know it pains me to see you like this."

"Not now. It's a long story and I don't want to talk about it right now."

Jack felt the room reeling and put his hand on the wall to steady himself.

Jesus, I wonder if Jack's into stuff? He's been disappearing a lot at night, and if that's the case, then I'd better watch my shit. What if he ODs in the house? Wouldn't that just be the worst luck?

"All right, Jack, we'll talk later. Hey, it's not so bad. All you need is a little break. I hope you're not sniffing or using needles or anything like that?"

"Damian, you know me, do I do that shit? No. Henrik and Julie are the junkies. They're the fucking junkies, all right?"

Jack was ill enough to have lost his patience. He felt his energy ebb and thought about lying down in the hall if Damian didn't stop engaging him in an endless stream of babble.

"Listen, I need to lie down," Jack told him.

"Yeah, that's probably a good idea. We'll talk later and see what we can do to remedy your situation."

Jack turned his back. He didn't have anything else to say. He walked to his bedroom and shut the door behind him. Damian was left standing in the hall, perplexed.

I don't understand it: here's a good-looking guy with an education, and yet he's got no self-esteem and no charisma, either. I wish I were good-looking like Jack, Damian thought. Then I wouldn't have to work so damned hard. I wouldn't have to smile and joke all the time and try to fit in and entertain and satisfy other people. No, I could just sit back and wait to be noticed and appreciated, like Jack. I don't buy it that he doesn't see how the girls look at him, and the guys, too.

Jack had a high fever and in his dreams he talked to Danny the Kid saying, "Danny, don't kill me. Danny, I deserve to live. I'll do better, I promise."

But Danny just smiled and lifted his gun, laughed and fired. Jack convulsed and writhed in the bed as he felt those bullets rip through his body. He had a series of nightmares where he was attacked with various projectiles, including one where a group of irate troglodytes showered him with rocks. Jack tried to scream and wake up, but the rocks kept hitting him and his feet were frozen in place. He slept for many hours and awoke the next day exhausted and confused with what was dream, reality and virtual reality.

Damian knocked on the door.

"Jack, can I come in?"

"Yeah, sure."

Damian came and sat at the foot of Jack's bed.

"Feeling better?"

"I've got a headache."

"You should drink water. You want me to get you some?"

"No, I'll get it myself."

Damian felt sorry for Jack. It was clear that he was really lost. Some people just aren't built to handle this world. I've been there, in L.A. We've all been there before and we'll be there again. He probably thinks life is a total waste and fantasizes about killing himself. Though I don't think Jack's the type to do it. He's not suicidal, he's just depressed. He hasn't had a girl since Elizabeth left. But then neither have I. After Danielle and all her drama, you're tired of women. You just want a little sex now and again and no trouble. You don't want to grovel and worship a woman just for a little piece of sex. And that seems to be what they all demand.

Relationships are just a farce anyway: a status quo pantomime. Two people can never completely understand each other and they shouldn't even try, Damian thought. And kids, forget about it. What did someone tell you once: if you absolutely don't want kids, don't have sex. Well, you could always fuck men. It's more practical, and you should probably stop lying to yourself: you're finding men more attractive by the day. You're a freethinker and you're curious. These taboos, they're old fashioned and you're above them. Why should you worry about what other people think?

So, you're not much better off than Jack, except you have some money to keep you going and can take a vacation when you need it. Because you're the kind who needs that security. You could never live like the rest of them.

"Jack, I'm gonna help you out," Damian said. "You need to get back on your feet. After the incident at the restaurant, I understand why you don't wanna go back to that kind of work. You're too educated for that anyway. Don't you have a degree in economics or something? Anyway, as you know, the market crashed. Everyone was buying stock on margin and now the bubble's burst and the price dropped out of all those start-up tech stocks that weren't making any profit after their IPOs. So, as often is the case, the uninformed got stuck with the bag. But I guess it's not such a big deal because most of the profits were on paper. We were just too greedy, I guess, and that clouded our reason.

"Anyway, you might have noticed how hard it is to find a job these days, even in clerical because all the techies have gone there. Restaurants are closing and people are buying less, traveling less, etc. And I got screwed like everyone else. I know all of you think I'm some sort of bigshot, but the truth is I had to sell my stock at half value a couple weeks ago, and it's good I sold it then, because now it's worth almost nothing."

Jack thought: is he going to get to the point? Everything is a discourse in this house.

"So I've lined you up with a job," Damian said. "I called some people last night after you went to bed and hooked you up with a PA gig, if you want it. I know it's not the best work, but it'll get you into the industry and from there, who knows? It's all about connections anyway. So, if you want, I can have you working by the end of the week. You won't make as much as you did in the restaurant but it gets your foot in the door."

"What's a PA?"

"A production assistant. It sounds kind of fancy, but it isn't. Basically, it means that when someone needs a cup of coffee or a sandwich, you get it. It isn't boring work, though. In film and video production things always go wrong and as a PA it's your job to fix the problems. They'll run you around like crazy. That's something you have to be prepared for. I've done PA work. It's a good way to learn the business. You learn what you can and move on."

"The stuff I'm talking about isn't the movies," Damian said. "You'll be working mostly with corporate video and commercials. You're not gonna meet Jeremy Leads or Nikki Star or anything."

It had never occurred to Jack to think about meeting anybody famous. He didn't plan on becoming famous. He wanted to live a decent life, get married, buy a house and have some kids. And he wanted boys. Sure, he would love his girls if he had them, but it wasn't the same as having boys and teaching them to play ball and ride motorbikes like he had done with his dad. And girls had to be protected from all the assholes out there.

"Sure, I'll give it a try. It can't be worse than the other jobs I've had," Jack said, climbing out of bed and walking across the room to his desk. He was naked, and as he pulled on his boxers, he noticed Damian staring at him.

Well, Jack caught me checking him out and I wonder what he thinks about that? Jack's no fool. It's certainly awkward, but it's happened, and there's nothing you can do about it now, Damian thought. Jack's good at ignoring things he doesn't understand or doesn't want to understand.

Jack plopped down on the bed in his boxers and put his hands behind his head.

"What are those scars on your chest," Damian asked.

"Oh, I went in for an experiment. You know, one of those ads in the back of the paper. Turns out it wasn't such a good idea. I got paid but I almost died in the process. I should've sold my sperm instead. What do I care if some woman I never met has my kid? Hell, I'm even helping her out; if her man's sterile, what's she gonna do?"

"Hey Jack, I feel bad that we haven't hung out for such a long time," Damian said. He was smiling and he patted Jack's leg. It took all his will to touch Jack and look natural about it. Jack didn't react.

"Hey, I understand, man. I'm a fucking loser. It's cool. I understand you not wanting to hang out with me."

Jack's voice was flat and he looked Damian in the eye. Damian was not sure if there was irony there or not. The tone was neither ashamed nor accusing.

"You're not a loser, man. You've just had some bad luck. You've got a lot going for you. Don't you notice the way chicks look at you? Chicks dig you, man."

Don't tell him he's good-looking, Damian thought. If you tell him, he'll know that you're ashamed of your own looks and think he's better looking than you are.

"Yeah? Well, where are all those chicks now? Chicks, they just want fucking money," Jack said. "I haven't so much as flirted with a girl since I was working at the restaurant. I can't afford women anymore."

"It's all about working the system like with anything else," Damian said. "There are chicks out there that would pay your way if you gave them a lay every now and again."

"I don't like ugly girls or old women. I'm not the kind of guy that goes with a sugar mamma. Fuck that if some girl is gonna support me," Jack said.

"Hey, no need to get hot about it. I'm just giving you the facts."

Jack smiled.

"Hey Damian, thanks for letting me live here and for finding me a job. I've been in a bad space lately. I've been feeling sorry for myself for not doing what I got to do to find my way. That's my fault and I don't hold it against you."

Damian smiled at him. His heart hurt then. Jack was so beautiful Damian wanted to lay down with him and kiss him and be beautiful like him, though he knew that nothing he could do would make it so.

"Hey, man, don't go getting sentimental on me. I just offered you a shitty job, that's all," Damian said, grabbing Jack by the feet and pulling him off the bed. Jack got up and put Damian in a headlock.

"Oh yeah, is that how it's gonna be? Are you forgetting who was all-state high school wrestling champ?"

"You're a pussy, Jack. You hear me? Pussy."

In spite of being pinned to the bed, Damian was laughing. He struggled under Jack's weight and laughed and said pussy and felt so good close to Jack. Jack was so simple and clean. He wished he could be simple and clean like Jack.

Jack was smiling his broad smile with half-closed eyes and slapping Damian in the face.

"Give up?" Slap. "Give up?" Slap. "Say Jack is God." Slap.

"Pussy."

Jack tightened his hold and Damian found it hard to breath.

"Jack is God," Damian gasped.

"Say I am a worm and Jack is my lord and master."

Even Jack couldn't help but laugh now.

They were both laughing and Jack relaxed his grip on Damian and pushed him away. Jack's muscles were tight from exertion and his veins were visible in his biceps. He lay down again on the pillows and Damian watched his six-pack rise and fall as he caught his breath. The reason Damian didn't try to kiss him then was because he felt inferior to Jack. Even though Jack was poor, Damian thought him a better man.

You, my friend, are dead in your emotions and your words, Damian told himself. You are nothing but a machine repeating the same operations to insure your own survival. There is no love there. You've never loved yourself enough, and you don't let other people love you either. Dammit, Jack, that this moment will soon be gone.

12

One day after school Alex was called into the principal's office. Alex liked principal Taylor because he felt they shared a similar vision of wanting to help the students be successful and escape the endemic poverty of their neighborhood.

Wallace Taylor was a successful black man who had served and seen combat in Vietnam. He had a Master's degree in education and had worked for ten years as an educator, the last four as principal of Hunter High. With his stubborn determination and iron will, Mr. Taylor had made the transition from killing on command to a career in public education, without becoming disillusioned, bitter or burnt out. The work had carved authority into his face, made his posture rigid and his manner blunt. He commanded respect without saying a word. Mr. Taylor was also an accomplished poet, and this had earned him Alex's admiration.

In other respects, Wallace Taylor was conservative with an old-fashioned approach to education. He believed in discipline and good Christian values, and he set the same standards for his son and daughter as he did for his students. He considered high school the training ground for responsible, hard-working citizens, and he greatly disliked what he called "the commercialization and stereotyping of the American Negro."

"Come have a seat, Alex," Wallace said, taking off his reading glasses and setting them on the table.

Alex did as he was told. He was in a good mood, the day's lesson having gone well, and looked forward to preparing a nice meal at home, maybe even a steak, and sitting down to plow through another chapter of *Pax Americana*.

"Alex, I have no doubt that you are one of the hardest working teachers on our faculty and that your interest in the success of our students is genuine. I know that you are also one of the most popular teachers at this school. But then teaching is not a popularity contest. I have never been popular, but I have given our students the skills they need to survive in the real world. You and I know this is not an easy world to live in. Especially not today when education is a lifelong process and technology leaves many people isolated and impoverished because of their inability to adapt. I don't want to leave our students unprepared. Now there's nothing wrong with producing a critical-minded student body, and creativity is an important part of that process. But then I think that creativity and criticism are more appropriate for higher education. Let me get to the point, Alex."

Wallace was sweating. He did not dislike Alex. On the contrary, he thought the young man exceptional in both talent and sincerity, but then he was also a radical and that made him dangerous. Social change, in Wallace's opinion, came from the inside, gradually and with consensus, not conflict.

"Alex, I've just gotten back the results from the SAT 9 and our students are doing worse than last year. We are in second to last place in the state. What is of interest is that they stand worse off in English than they do in Math. Now, as you know, the worse we perform, the less likely the state is going to continue funding programs at our school. If they see that the money is not producing the desired results, they will simply cut us off. These scores reflect directly on me; I have to answer to the school board and explain why my students are failing. I don't like to have to do that."

"Well, in truth, Mr. Taylor, I don't really believe the SAT 9 is a valid way to measure student performance. I think that the whole system of standardized testing needs to be re-evaluated. In many ways it's discriminatory," Alex said.

Wallace's eyes narrowed. What did this privileged white boy know about discrimination?

"Those tests, Alex, have been a practical way to measure knowledge and performance in public education for quite some time. There isn't another test out there to replace them. And it simply isn't possible on a bureaucratic level to apply and administer a personalized test. Personalization and specialization belong to higher education."

Wallace was curious to hear the reasoning for and philosophy behind Alex's unusual teaching methods. In his opinion, the students weren't performing because Alex was too lax with them, trying to entertain instead of educate. He didn't conform to the texts but used them only for reference. Was it unusual then that the students weren't performing? By not sticking to the standards, Alex had put them at a disadvantage.

There was very little that Alex liked about bureaucracy. It had nearly deterred him from becoming a teacher. As far as he was concerned it was time to do away with outdated materials and irrelevant tests, and provide greater autonomy for teachers to produce their own lessons and encourage student creativity.

"I don't think we're doing anyone a favor in America by creating a society of young men and women who conform to the minimum standards of English," Alex said. "They must be better than the minimum, that is, they need to be freethinkers. If you treat all students alike and teach them that all they have to do is pass a test to succeed in life, then you're doing them and society a great disservice. What I've been trying to produce is a freethinking student body. I am trying to show them that they get out of education what they put in, that education can be fun, and that they can pursue whatever they like and be successful. I'm not interested in creating drones. American society is in trouble. No longer do we educate the young to be open-minded, creative citizens with a sense of responsibility to the community. Instead, we are satisfied to produce a herd of low-level service workers who are forced to accept low-paying jobs with no benefits in hopes that they may one day work their way up to manage other low-paid workers in an overtly unjust system. We need to reject that system and give students the tools to integrate themselves politically, socially and artistically in their community. My students are not numbers, they are individuals, and it's important they know how things really stand."

"I believe, as the expression goes, that you are putting the cart before the horse," Wallace said. "If our students can't measure up to the basic standards of English then they will never be productive, successful members of society. There is a certain language to success they must learn. These children are poor, and like anyone, they desire material success. As it stands, they do not have the comfort to consider ideology. I am aware that you have been encouraging them to rap, that you allow them to curse in class, and that you do not provide the discipline they need and is expected of good citizens. Your discussions of race are biased and unhelpful at best. I am also aware that you share with them suspect literature, including your own work, which is highly opinionated and radical. These children don't need a revolution, Alex. They need a steady job and decent housing in safe communities where they can raise a family and live a Christian life."

Alex took a deep breath. He was reluctant to discuss race with Mr. Taylor. Like many white Americans who had grown up after the civil rights movement, Alex felt guilty for what had happened to blacks in America. This guilt was also attached to the realization that he was incapable of seeing without color. People were colors: that was a difference he was aware of, though he didn't wish for it to be a barrier to his understanding of character.

"Well, I think that these kids should know what they're up against," Alex said. "It's unfair to tell them that they're like everyone else and that if they just work hard enough they can succeed. Pardon me for saying so, Mr. Taylor, but being black in America is a disadvantage, and I think it's my responsibility to discuss race so that they can better know how to fight prejudice and find pride in themselves."

Mr. Taylor was a patient man. Patience was necessary to deal with the ignorant.

"Alex, I'm glad you're interested in the plight of the black man. That's very noble of you. I don't know what exactly you discuss in your class about race, but I think you'd better leave the discussion of what it means to be black in America to black Americans. It's a subject better suited for scholars of Afro-American studies and something that students can pursue in higher education, if they so desire."

He's misunderstood me, Alex thought. I've offended him and he's misunderstood me. I mean for Christ's sake, what am I doing trying to discuss this with a man who grew up during the civil rights movement and whose poetic work deals primarily with black identity? Well, probably because it interests me. Probably because I've never been able to discuss it with him.

But then Alex was cowed. It was the guilt again and perhaps the fear that prejudice was a part of being human. Everyone looked out for their own, be the affinity race, color, creed, or social class. Clearly, such loyalty had been the cause of a tremendous amount of injustice and violence in the world.

"Alex, it's clear to me that you're better-suited for teaching at the university. Public education isn't for everyone. It's hard work that deals mainly with mechanics, not ideology. I am not opposed to creativity, unless it undermines the learning of basic skills. And as for race, yes, it is an important issue. But I don't believe that dwelling on it helps anyone. A man needs to show his worth on merit. If a man has merit then he will earn respect and find prosperity. I am living, breathing proof of that philosophy. I am not a successful black man, I am a successful human being. Alex, you are also a man of merit. You are an inspiring young man with a sharp mind, and I'm sure you'll do just fine for yourself. But you do not share the philosophy of this school and that's why I have to dismiss you. I hope there are no hard feelings."

"No, Mr. Taylor. I understand," Alex said. They shook hands and Alex left the office. It was humiliating to be fired. It was all the more humiliating because he had been fired for his beliefs. Alex was angry but mature enough not to direct his anger at Mr. Taylor.

Wallace Taylor's story was, in many respects, typical. From the hopeful days of his youth, necessity had forced him to the middle, and success had made him a conservative. He was a man with something to lose who stood on precarious line of race and refused to be categorized by it. Each man fights for that balance in his own construction, Alex thought. Individual identity is always in dialogue with the status quo. I wonder how that relationship is in black skin? Certainly, it can't be easy. Alex felt the melancholy overtake him; he was saddened by the inability of human beings to understand and make peace with one another.

Wallace sat in his desk and thought about the black men he hated: the sports stars that made money and gave nothing back to their community, choosing instead to pose for paparazzi in select nightclubs with the rest of the famous deadbeats; the movie stars that played gangsters and drug dealers or clowning cops because they were never given any serious roles; and the rappers that made a buck talking about their money and acting like gangsters. They were all a bunch of sellouts. Nothing new in that, he thought.

Wallace was upset that the students were encouraged to rap in class. He saw hip hop as the degeneration of black culture; it was black music divorced from its roots. Most of the students knew nothing of the blues, which was the true expression of the Afro-American reality in America. Blues, jazz and soul.

But then Wallace was an old-timer who found hip hop threatening. Perhaps he didn't understand that the form of black music had simply changed with the times. Whether or not these were good times for the black heart and soul was irrelevant to popular culture, and popular culture was irrelevant to putting food on the table for one's family. Wallace still firmly believed that the opportunities for success in America, for blacks and whites alike, had never been greater. As a result, he considered many of his students to be lazy, looking for an easy solution instead of putting in the hard work as he had before them. Perhaps it was his age and position that caused him to forget that at one time he too had been frustrated by the very real discrimination and lack of opportunity in his society. Was it any wonder then, with so many obstacles to overcome, that his students would join gangs to earn respect and deal drugs for easy money? After all, not everyone was as tough as Wallace Taylor.

13

Julie began working at the Free Clinic in the Haight where she met a group of people who were dedicated to helping others. She had never been around such people before and was skeptical of their kindness. She thought with time that the façade would crack and expose the egos and self-interest that everyone carried with them. They're just working here because they haven't finished their nursing degree. They're here because they can't get residency at a real hospital. Still, the cracks never appeared.

Dawn, a lesbian who had spent several years working at the clinic, was careful to show Julie all the details of record keeping, and educated her about their various services such as planned parenthood, clean needles, counseling and the suicide hotline. At the clinic they gave vaccinations, routine check-ups and other forms of basic medical care. Julie wished she had come into contact with the clinic when she first arrived in the city. Perhaps then her life would have turned out differently. Instead, she had accustomed herself to hanging around negative, abusive and predatory people: people who were troubled at heart, lacked self-esteem and lived in fear. Maybe it was no accident that she had been drawn to that environment. Until now, she had been unable to see her life and relationships objectively. And God knows, her housemates had never made her feel good about herself. They had been condescending and discriminatory, treating her like a child.

Dawn was the first person to show a true interest in Julie as a friend. In spite of Dawn's tough appearance, and her characteristic explosive laughter chapped by cigarettes, she was soft-spoken, kind and helpful. Like most people worth knowing, she was a contradiction. More and more, Julie was aware that people were not as they appeared. Dawn wasn't just a dyke: she was also a nurse, an administrator, a part-time political activist for animal rights and the environment, a mountain biker and a lover of Italian opera, among other things that weren't immediately visible or hadn't yet come to the surface in conversation. Dawn rode her bike up and down the streets of San Francisco with arias blasting in her headphones. If she had lived in another time and smoked less, she might have been an opera diva.

Julie was hired as a receptionist, a job with which she had previous experience, having worked for various private companies whose values she did not share. What she enjoyed about the clinic was that the work was meaningful and the job positions were not fixed. Since they were understaffed, she was asked to counsel young women or men on various issues including drugs, venereal disease and pregnancy. At first she didn't want such responsibility. She thought: who am I to give advice when I have ruined my own life? It was Dawn who convinced her and made her see another side to her personality.

"You're such a good person, Julie. You're so easy to talk to. What these people need is someone to talk to. Sometimes all people need is a reference point in someone else's supportive presence."

Julie had wanted to cry then. Sometimes, and especially now that she had started to think of death, her emotions would run riot in her frail body. She wanted to tell Dawn about her condition but didn't for fear that she would be discriminated. Even if she didn't intend it, her attitude toward me would change, Julie thought. Maybe they wouldn't want me working here any longer if they knew. Not even as a secretary. Because my blood is toxic.

Counseling proved to be her salvation. Julie had experienced many of the same problems as her patients and that gave her the strength to give them advice. She used herself as an example and created a bond between her and people she would have otherwise never known had her own life not changed so drastically. The counseling was a process of self-healing. She came to understand that she wasn't alone: that many young men and women had gone through difficult periods in which they abused themselves physically and mentally. Julie realized that the relationship between counselor and patient was mutually beneficial. Before she couldn't have conceived of a job where one learned about oneself every day by helping others. She realized that everyone had moments of weakness, fear and hopelessness. Now, instead of being closed inside herself with fear, her heart reached out to others. Her connection to her patients gave her life meaning. She thought: Alex and the others could learn a lesson like this as they sit feeling superior while comfortably detached from the world.

Julie realized that she had been mean to Jack because he was beautiful, and since she couldn't have him, she had wanted to see him suffer like she had. Is it foolish to believe that people will do their best if only given the chance? Is Henrik the jerk I've made him out to be, or is he just confused and lonely for something he can't find? He can't be so different from me because otherwise we wouldn't have been together. We helped drag each other down and now we're both HIV positive. We fucked the same people, and we fucked each other and used needles.

At work, Julie met many interesting people. Sometimes she would see them again in the streets of the neighborhood and they would stop to talk to her. They always seemed glad to see her. She wasn't accustomed to the attention, and somehow their friendly chatter made her sad.

It was death making her sad: the waiting and the certainty of it. Well, everyone has death waiting for them, she thought. Is it any different now? You're just going to die sooner than the rest and sooner than your time. She tried to be cavalier about it, but words that were convincing for her patients rang hollow in her own mind.

The clinic ran a suicide hotline that Julie worked at night. That was the time for that kind of thing, that is, when people felt the loneliness crush its cold, alien hands around their hearts and minds, and their problems swelled to blot out the hope that kept them moving through life.

When Julie started, she didn't know what she was in for. She thought that it would be like health counseling. She couldn't have been more mistaken. In her life she had never had so much responsibility. She was unprepared for the intense psychological pressure that such work involved. She began to carry the weight of the unfortunate lives of others inside her: those who had been born face down in the muck of broken families; the physically and mentally abused; and individuals whose emotional landscape was strewn with barbed wire and shattered glass. She felt the angst and fear in their voices as it poured black and thick into her mind. Though the work was difficult, the belief that she could make a difference kept her going.

Julie's own personal history made her a pragmatic counselor. Her advice was no longer the upbeat "be sure to protect yourself," or the informative "there's nothing wrong with telling your boyfriend to use a condom." Instead, she was blunt: "You just ask your boyfriend if he wants to have a kid or get AIDS." There was power in that kind of talk. She was in control listening to the litany of frustration and despair of her callers through their sobs and tears. It was her job to let them talk, to ask them helpful questions and allow them to empty themselves completely of the poison inside them. She was the last line of defense before death. She was the gatekeeper, and because she was sick and dying, her anger at them, at their arrogance, turned her into a righteous champion of life. She found she could turn any negative to a positive. She was a magician; when she spoke her exuberance for life was contagious.

It was only later that Julie started to record the conversations. In the recordings she could hear her words again and be inspired by them. Though it was ethically wrong, Julie told herself that the recordings were for her own benefit and that she didn't intend to share them. It was only by listening to the conversations that she became aware of a new strength in her voice. Before she had spoken softly and without confidence. She often didn't finish her sentences, or she would let herself be overpowered in conversation. Now she was the voice of hope in the battle for survival waged over a phone line in the forgotten hours of the night. She was constructing a positive world for herself and others from which everyone would benefit.

Julie spent many weeks documenting and archiving the best conversations for her nightly listening. Though she no longer drank or used drugs, she was emaciated because she forgot to eat. She had always been thin and Dawn, with her professional eye, could spot an anorexic.

"Julie, you need to start eating more. You look like a corpse. I could refer you to friend of mine. He's a therapist who specializes in eating disorders. You better promise to go. Because you've got a problem. Do you admit you've got a problem?"

Julie didn't know what to say. Dawn was definitely on the other end of the scale. Julie didn't think she had a problem, but Dawn wouldn't have said it unless she meant it. To avoid confrontation, Julie admitted, "Yes, I've got a problem." The words sounded strange to her, and only in speaking them was she able to weigh their truth. You've been wrong about so many things; only now are you seeing the problems in your life. Could it be that you're anorexic, too?

"I want you to promise to see my friend," Dawn said. "Do you promise? For me?"

"I promise."

But Julie never went. Instead, she reported that the sessions were helping. Until one day she collapsed during work and had to be taken to the hospital. Later, Dawn called her therapist friend and found that Julie had never made an appointment.

14

School was out and Quincy was cruising campus on his skateboard. At an opportune moment, he popped a 180 on the smooth pavement and turned it around off the curb. Riding a skateboard was pure grace; it made the city seem fluid and easy and allowed Quincy to speed along the pavement, and jump and weave like a rare animal. When Quincy was skating, he was smiling, because in that moment life belonged to him. I'll get where I need to go in my style and at my speed, he thought.

Gavin stood at the end of the parking lot with the senior crew talking in their cell phones next to somebody's ride blaring some fuckbeat rap: "Uh uh, gonna take you down baby, uh uh, gonna show ya 'round baby, 'cause we're the underground, turn around and I'll show you down, uh uh, get down, baby, get down." Real smooth West Coast rap: smooth like paint jobs, electronics, jewelry, brand logos and shades so no one could see the soul through the eyes.

It was a typical scene: the girls jiving the guys in their urban lingerie, and the guys fronting with their baggies, jerseys, caps and chains; the girls flipping their hair, driving by slow in Leticia Jones's convertible, smoking with painted nails and their arms resting casual outside the doors. That car bought by Mr. Biggs who was fucking that pussy. Mr. Biggs, thirty-seven, who fucked all the best senior pussy at Hunter High, and the guys all wanting that pussy, too, and knowing that they were as good as dead if they tried it. And there she was, Leticia Jones, a beautiful leper in her convertible, until Mr. Biggs kicked her ass out of bed. Recyclable girls like Leticia Jones.

Quincy coasted through the lot with his back straight, hands deep in the pockets of his oversized jeans and his hat pulled low over his eyes. Quincy, who wanted to skate right by the politics of the neighborhood and right out of his own skin.

"Hey Q-dog," Quincy felt a hand on his shirt as he tried to skate around the group crowded in the lot. "Hey Q, I'm talkin' to you. Don't you roll by like I'm some chump."

Gavin yanked him off his board. Quincy stumbled and tried to recover his cool. No sudden movements. He wasn't afraid of Gavin. Gavin wasn't yoked or nothing, and Quincy was sure he could school him one-on-one. If it came to that, he would get Japanimation on his ass. Gavin was all image and no foundation. There was nothing hard about him; he was a mamma's boy. He carried groceries for his mamma and walked her dog, too. He did all sorts of humiliating shit for his mamma. But he was a real businessman, better than Mr. Biggs's senior stooges who were looking for a break, who would rip Biggs off, or maybe one day get the idea in their heads to write his tombstone. Gavin was loyal and Biggs had complete control over him. Their relationship was father-son. Biggs's word was law and Gavin was clean; he didn't sniff or smoke the goods. That was the difference.

Quincy had to play it cool for the seniors and the idea of Biggs that loomed over Hunter High and mocked the archaic discipline and morality that Principal Taylor had tried to impose there. Taylor was a military man: at school his rule was iron, but on the street they were in Biggs's world where beauty and dreams were for sale and not earned with discipline and will. Biggs was in charge of short-term seduction. Still, as big as Mr. Biggs was, he hadn't shown his face at Hunter High since the day Principal Taylor smashed a bat through his windshield.

"I'll break you, Biggs. I was fighting for your miserable rights while you were still in diapers. What I've lived would crush a man like you. In the line of duty I've killed better men than you. But then you're not even a man, Biggs, you're a caricature, living off your own shit and poisoning the community. You're nothing but a disgrace, and don't make me tell you twice not to come 'round here no more."

Biggs was smart enough to know where the line was drawn. And what did it matter to him? What was the school, anyway? What was the institution when he owned all that was of value in it: the minds and will and beauty of the young, the buyers and the sellers of the future? It was Taylor that was a prisoner and fool fighting a useless war for the ideals of white men. What did Biggs care about his community if he lived better than white men? Taylor was a fool, a dinosaur. But then it didn't go to be provoking a war veteran unnecessarily.

Quincy didn't have much choice but to listen up to Gavin who was part of a bigger plan. Quincy had never liked being a part of anything. He was independent. He didn't need groups to justify his own existence. He didn't need their obligations or their conformity. He didn't have time for that.

Quincy saw the seniors watching him.

"Whatch'you lookin' at bitch," someone said, giving him a shove.

"Yo, Gavin who is this punk ass bitch? He's all wack. He better get lost before I whoop his ass."

"Make this fool disappear, G. He's ruining the vibe."

"Chill. We got business. Come on Q, let's take a walk," Gavin said, clapping his arm down on Quincy's shoulder and walking him away.

"Yo Gavin, I don't want to leave my board, man. They'll fuck it up."

"They won't fuck it up. They just jawin' so don't sweat it. Listen, you and me, we cool, a'ight. I mean we ain't never had no problems, know what I'm sayin'?"

"Sure," Quincy said.

They stopped by a planter and sat down. Gavin took out a smoke and lit up. He offered the pack to Quincy who held up his hand in refusal.

"Listen, I don't drink or use any of that shit," Gavin said. "You know that. I don't even bust it to pull the hoochies, man. I just smoke 'cause it relaxes me."

"That's cool."

Gavin looked at him carefully and continued.

"You notice how Aisha ain't been to class no more?"

"Yeah, I noticed."

"Aisha's superfly," Gavin said, staring straight ahead at nothing in particular. "Aisha's my honey, man, and I didn't get the chance to tell her. I was gonna buy her gold and diamonds and shit, and then she disappeared with that watered-down bitch with the ride and the plastic smile."

Quincy didn't say anything.

"Yo, don't that shit bother you, man? Don't you think it's strange that she gone all a'sudden?"

"I guess so," Quincy said.

"Listen, man, I know you was groovin' on Aisha, too. I know 'cause I seen you peepin' her."

Quincy looked at him.

"Hey, it's chill. I'm just sayin'. She's fly, you know? The whole class was digging on her. Even them older cats."

And Biggs, they both thought. Biggs had invited her to one of his parties via Gavin, his message boy. But Gavin never communicated the message. Because he knew what would happen. Biggs would fill her full of drugs and use her up. Which had happened anyway, in a manner of speaking.

"You know what happen' to Aisha, Q?" Gavin paused for effect. "That punk ass Milkyway nigga knocked her up and then he bounced."

It didn't surprise Quincy. Maybe he was cynical for his sixteen years, but girls like Aisha didn't last long, and he knew they were beyond his reach.

"You know how I know, 'cause Taresa tol' me. She seen Aisha at the store with her dad buyin' food, and she was thick around the middle, man. And that ain't Aisha, she ain't never been thick."

"So whatch'you gonna do about it?"

Gavin laughed. "A'ight, straight down to business. Cool like that, Q-dog."

Gavin flicked his cigarette onto the pavement and his smile disappeared.

"I wanna know where to find that fool. If anybody knows, it's you. You act quiet, but you ain't been foolin' me. You probably knew all this shit before and you been wastin' my time."

"I can find out," Quincy said.

"Good, then find out."

"It's gonna cost you."

"How much?"

"A hundred."

"Man, fuck you, Quincy," Gavin said, peeling a hundred off his money clip.

When they came back, Quincy found that the seniors had thrown his skate on the roof. He climbed up, kicked up some speed, dropped down onto the dumpser, kick-flipped with the board fluttering around his feet and stuck it flat and solid on the pavement. He skated past his teenage peers posing for imaginary fashion ads and music videos. It was modern urban America that blurred as Quincy cruised down the street on his own power, thinking: Aisha, I'm the only man for you.

15

Jack's first production was a computer industry trade show. Being a PA wasn't the most glamorous job. He loaded chairs, drove them around and set them up where they were needed. He photocopied the program schedules and distributed them to the various booths, and helped direct people to where they were supposed to set up. He went to the store for adjustable straps, touch-up painted some lecterns, helped with catering, brought coffee and withdrew several grand from the director's personal account: money that he very seriously considered splitting with. Jack was glad to find out it was a union crew working with the production team, which meant he was forbidden to help the grips with any of the heavy-lifting or setting up of lighting and camera equipment. In the beginning, he had been quick to perform every task he was assigned. But, it seemed that as a PA everyone was his superior, and the faster Jack worked, the more errands he received. Many of these errands were of the I'm too lazy and important to do it myself, "Would you run to my car and grab my laptop?" or "My car is parked in the tow zone, could you move it for me?" type. The assistant producer, Ellen, even asked him to massage her neck when they were alone backstage. Jack did his best to swallow down his role, plagued with that feeling of being unimportant and outclassed, someone to be used. He knew that because he was a simple PA, the girls on the set thought him stupid and not worth a real conversation.

Still, a PA could gain a lot of valuable experience, and Jack thought himself lucky to have the job. To bolster his pride, he tried to act as if he had seen it all before. But really he was amazed at what went into putting on a trade show: making sure the cameras, lighting and the audio worked and was set up properly; seeing to it that the talent arrived on time, was properly dressed and fed; insuring that the executives knew their speeches, when to come out on stage, from what side and for how long. Not to mention coordinating all the events, along with the special effects, seating arrangements for the conference delegates, the printing and distribution of the conference schedule, and, of course, security.

Jack found the endless hours of work and bustle exhausting, so he got in the habit of disappearing to the stairwell or the bathroom to power nap and recharge his batteries. He was paid a fixed rate that he later found out was half the industry standard for his position. In short, what sounded good, one hundred and fifty a day, ended up being between ten and twelve dollars an hour, since a workday could be anywhere from twelve to fourteen hours and even that odd sixteen hour shift. He was the only one on the production team that didn't have his own room by the conference center. No, he had to catch the bus or a taxi. He was sleeping four hours a night and it showed. He began to detest the work and make himself scarce.

"Jack, you need to be quicker, buddy. You went to pick up some speaker cable and headsets over two hours ago."

"I had to go all over town to find the kind you wanted. They were sold out, man. What am I supposed to do?"

Really, Jack had bought what he needed at a nearby electronics store in a half an hour and then spent the rest of the time hanging out in a coffee shop reading the paper and thinking: yeah, now it's time to get my money's worth. Fucking ten dollars an hour for this shit.

Jack had to get some costumes for the headlining boy band, In Quick. They needed matching vests and turtlenecks, so Jack wandered around the Nordworth Center looking for something suitable. What did he know about fashion, anyway? They had to look kind of gay: that's what boy bands were all about. Tight black vests and some baby blue turtlenecks, or maybe he should just go with white?

It turned out that the lead singer Duke Warren was sick with a bad case of strep throat. Duane, the talent coordinator, was getting nervous because they only had a day to rehearse, and a boy band couldn't have only three people. Duane would have done it himself, but he had a terrible voice. That was the reason he was a talent director and not the talent. Why couldn't he have inherited his mother's voice?

He imagined Bob, the director, telling him, "Just get me somebody, anybody, and teach him the moves and the song. Do it. I don't have time for this shit." Bob wasn't the kind to be understanding.

It was then that one of the band members pointed to Jack and said, "Well, what about him? He looks like he belongs in the band more than any of us."

Jack didn't know what to make of that. Just what is he trying to say? I don't look like I belong in any boy band. I'd never be able to live that down.

But then Seth was right, because they were an aging boy band that had produced one hit song in the early nineties, and now they were in their late twenties and early thirties, and the truth was they weren't particularly attractive in the first place. Seth had a bit of a stomach, Erin's hairline was receding, and though Mark was the youngest and fittest of the group, he was still four years Jack's senior.

They were all looking at him now, even Duane, and that made Jack nervous because Duane could make him to do it. A PA's got to be versatile, right?

"That's a great idea, Seth. Why didn't I think of it before? Jack'll be perfect. I think we can whip him into shape for the show," Duane said.

"Hey guys, listen, I don't know anything about dancing or singing or anything like that. It's just not my thing."

"Jack, you look like a fucking rock star. Don't hold yourself back," Mark said. "The chick's dig boy bands. Man, we could tell you some stories. And we're just ordinary guys. We were just doing this for fun when we got started."

Jack started to back away from them.

"No, man, it's cool. I'm sure there's someone else who'll want to do it in my place."

Just the thought of getting up on stage in front of the entire computer industry and singing love songs, made Jack sweat. There's no way I'm gonna make a fool out of myself like that.

But Duane insisted.

"Jack, man, I really need this favor. If you could do this for me I'd be eternally grateful. There's an extra hundred bucks in it for you."

In the end, Jack agreed. Duane was a friend of Damian's, and Jack had been out with him to the bar after work a couple times. Jack still remembered the night when Duane had gotten drunk and emotional about a girl he had ditched because he had gotten her pregnant.

In spite of his upbeat attitude and the way he animated the talent, Jack knew Duane was a man mired in a deep moral crisis. Jack asked himself: what would I do if I got a girl pregnant? Maybe one of the frat girls had one of my kids and I don't even know about it. But then again those girls screwed every member of Sigma Chi.

So Jack got on the stage and Duane coached him one-on-one. Jack was stiff and awkward and his timing was off. Frustrated, Duane started to dance like him.

"Jack, you look like a fucking action figure without the kung-fu grip, man. Is that how you move when you're with a woman? God, I hope not. You gotta feel the music. Don't you feel that? Let those hips roll. Come on, pull those hands to your waist like you're grabbing some hottie. The problem is you're thinking about it too much. All right guys, take five. Jack, you're comin' with me."

"Where are we going?"

"We're going to my car to listen to some tunes and chill for a few. You need to learn how to chill, man."

They sat in the car and Duane put on some hip hop. Jack wasn't the biggest fan of hip hop but then he had been wrong about things before. When he first came to the city, he had held many opinions that in retrospect seemed narrow-minded.

Duane rolled a joint with some weed he kept in a film canister. They passed it back and forth until they could barely see each other in the car. After a few minutes, they opened the doors and stumbled out into the deserted car park, laughing, before returning to the conference center.

Jack felt relaxed now; everything was smooth and easy, and the dancing was fun. Imagine, people get away with this shit, he thought. They can stand up on stage and clown around and be stoned out of their minds so they don't remember a thing. I wonder how many performers need to get wasted before they come on stage? Remember that band you liked, The Dead Monkeys, that was so popular in high school but never gave a single show because the lead singer had crippling stage fright? It seems like the things you fear most are the ones you gotta face down sooner or later, Jack thought. Life's just like that somehow.

So Jack swallowed his pride and lined up with the rest of the band. Duane stood in front of the group and performed the dance moves he had choreographed: the sliding and stomping of the feet; the dropping to the ground on one hand and the thrusting of the hips; and the kung fu kicks and punches to show how tough they were. Jack followed along and he was on cue now, he was feeling it, especially the punching and kicking; it was actually kind of fun to do something like that, especially when he never believed he could dance.

"All right, Jack, I'm gonna put the lyrics up on the teleprompter, just like karaoke, and you follow the bouncing ball and you'll be fine. How's your voice anyway? Never mind. We might have to cut your mic and you can just lip-synch. Most music videos are lip-synched anyway, and the sound added in later. But these guys are going to sing because they can. Most famous artists can't sing worth shit; they just remix their voices in the studio to make them palatable. It's not about the singing anyway, it's about image, and Seth's right, once we get you into costume, you'll be the man. Then maybe you won't have to be a PA anymore. Man, that's a shit job and I'm sorry to see you doing it. You're better than that."

Jack tried to sing the lyrics and was surprised at his voice when it came out; it sounded different and alien, as if it weren't his voice at all. Kind of like the playback of an answering machine or a tape recorder. Jesus, do I really sound like that? And the group sang:

Travel the desert my friend

And leave the past behind

Where the road has no end

That's where you'll find

An eagle sailing on the wind

Lost in time

These dreams are mine

And you won't take them away

This heart will not cry

For what others will say

When you leave me behind

Lost souls lost souls

Fly away

Lost souls lost souls

To your hiding place

Jack had a nice solid voice with no cracks, though he sang wooden and without emotion. He had no experience singing and Duane had to cut the music.

"All right, Jack, so maybe you won't be in form for tomorrow. Your voice isn't bad, though. You could be a real crooner if you wanted. Anyway, guys, we're just gonna cut the mics and you can lip-synch. It's not like these computer geeks are gonna know the difference."

"So long as the shit doesn't start skipping," Seth said. "Man, remember that concert when the audio started to skip and we tried to play it off like it was part of the song, you know, like scratching, but then they started to boo and throw bottles at us."

"This isn't that kind of crowd. Anyway, they don't have anything to throw. Ha, ha. No, but really man, look who you're talking to. I'm a professional," Duane said, touching his hand to his chest. "I've got this under control."

Erin wanted to tell him that they had played to a crowd of ninety thousand at the Rose Bowl; they had done the VTV music awards and gone on tour with Barry Gold, the voice himself. They had been produced by Virgo records and had sold over a million CDs once. There was nothing glamorous about singing a few songs for some trade show. It was downright embarrassing, but they needed the money. If he had put the money into property or stock, instead of pissing it away, then he wouldn't have been so bitter. Erin realized more than ever that fame came and went and that perhaps they should have managed their career better. They had been a fad band, a one-hit wonder, nothing more. The truth was Erin was tired; he just wanted to get paid and go home. The passion wasn't there anymore.

"Hey Duane, we've sung these songs a hundred times. You've got some good moves, but I think we've got it down," Erin said. "I'm taking the rest of the day off. Jack, I'm sure you'll do fine. Thanks for covering for us, man."

"All right guys, but I want you in here early tomorrow morning for the final rehearsal," Duane said.

The rest of the band left and Duane worked with Jack until he had the steps down. They had the cameras focused on stage, and Jack was on the big screen. Ellen, the assistant producer, said, "Isn't that Jack? What the heck is he doing up there with Duane?" She got on the megaphone. "Jack, we've got a lot stuff to take care of and if you're going to clown around then you can walk today and we'll get someone in your place."

Jack snapped out of his reverie. I don't want to be a PA ever again, he told himself. I have no desire to be a grip, a sound technician or even a director. Jack realized that he could do better, that he could do whatever he wanted because it was his life.

"Duane, man, can you tell her that we need to practice this and that I'm actually saving her ass. Just get me out of doing that other stuff. Have them hire someone else."

So Duane talked to Bob who agreed to hire another PA. Certainly, they could find someone else from the Film Academy to fill the hole for the sake of experience.

"Ellen, we need another PA. Jack is filling in for Duke Warren who's got strep throat or something. I want to you to get on that, pronto," Bob said.

Ellen felt a wave of bitterness wash through her. She enjoyed telling Jack what to do and also she liked flirting with him, and now he was with Duane in talent. Jack was the only hot guy her age on the entire production team, well, except for the odd grip, but then grips were dumb like soldiers. A bunch of fucking orangutans, those grips.

The thought reminded Ellen of a trip to the zoo with her family in San Diego when they had visited the primate enclosure to observe the orangutans, and what seemed like a lazy afternoon turned sordid when a male orangutan came down from the tree, grabbed the female by her ankles and fucked her aggressively while she lay docile on her back watching the crowd. Then, when he was finished, he climbed back into the tree and fell asleep. While some men would certainly consider that ideal, Ellen remembered how uncomfortable she had felt standing next to her parents. How could she forget their silence and how everyone in the crowd looked to the floor to avoid eye contact before shuffling to the next exhibit? She was fourteen then, and that memory had spoiled sex for her and made her frigid. Perhaps if someone had laughed, it would have been better.

16

Jack went home that evening and went straight to bed. He found he couldn't sleep worrying that he would make a fool of himself at the show, though by now he was excited to be a part of it. Even he remembered In Quick, the band they had made fun of in college and called fags, posers and kooks. The insults came from the fact that the members of In Quick could get laid by hot chicks any time they wanted; they were famous, made a lot of money and obviously could give a damn about priding themselves on being real men doing manual labor and fighting for the ladies.

Just think, you're gonna get up on stage with the same guys you talked shit about. Now that you've met them, you know they're not bad guys; they're just trying to make a living. I wonder what they had to do to make it? Jack continued to toss and turn, and to add insult to injury, the bum that lived in the alley under his window came home to his piss-stained mattress and was cursing and carrying on:

"Fuck all you bitches. Come try take me away and call me low-class. Fuck you! All these rich mothas think they know what's goin' on, they can come here and I'll show them what up. Bitch tell me she's too good for me. Gonna get me some drink, gonna rot and die here, you'll see, cold-hearted ruthless motha-fuckers turn me out and call me a menace. You hear me! You all crazy mothas! I know what's going on 'cause I'm the man you just don't know I'm the man I'm so the man, amen. Gonna get me a lady and a smooth ride roll out and show all-you-all what it's all about 'cause I'm takin' over."

Jack could hear him like he was standing in the bedroom. Damn, can't the others hear that? How do they put up with this shit? I mean, I don't mind him sleeping down there in the alley if he doesn't have anywhere else to go, but it's never been like this. Maybe it's someone new? I've seen all sorts of people sleeping and screwing down there on that filthy mattress. Man, if he can't have some respect, he deserves to be taught a lesson. That's it, I'm calling the cops and getting him outta here. I can't take this shit anymore. This guy's like James said: his community's gone and he's lost it. I wonder if James'll go like that one day? I wonder if I'll go like that? Is it just laziness? Dammit. Shut up, shut up, motherfucker, shut up.

Jack gritted his teeth and crammed his pillow over his ears. His lack of sleep, anxiety, and then this piece of misery below his window was too much for his nerves to bear.

"'Cause I'm a bad motha-fucker. Yeah, you bad. You gonna show 'em what up. Y'all don't know it yet, is all. That's right come and get me. Come on ladies, come get your champion lover."

Jack kicked off his sheets and sprung out of bed. He grabbed his bat from the closet, stormed down the hallway and burst out the front door. He came out onto the landing and there was the man swaying next to Damian's car with a bottle in a paper bag, drinking.

"Hey buddy. Hey, I'm talking to you. Don't pretend you don't see me, man. I live in this house and I'm trying to get to some goddamned sleep. I don't mind you sleepin' here if you shut up. But if you don't shut the fuck up, I'm gonna call the police to drag your ass off to jail."

The man swayed and kept talking, "I always been your pimp daddy. I'm your daddy and you betta respect your daddy. I always respect my daddy. He was damned fine man, my daddy, work real hard and raise a family and then he gone died on us. I love you, daddy."

"Man, shut up! Shut the fuck up, or I'm gonna bust your fucking skull open!"

Jack was standing a few feet away and the man paid him no attention.

He must be real far gone, Jack thought. He's so gone he doesn't know what's going on. Still, I gotta get him out of here. In spite of the fact that Jack was in the right, the man made him nervous and uncomfortable. What if he doesn't leave?

"Hey man, I'm talking to you. Look at me. Yeah, it's you I'm talking to. Get the fuck out of here. Fucking go away. Go anywhere, just get the fuck out of my face. I don't want to have to get ugly on your ass. I'll make you wish you never set foot here. Beat it. Bail. Fuck off."

Just when Jack began to think the situation was hopeless, the man abruptly turned away and drifted off down the street. Jack went back into the house to find everyone up and blinking half-asleep in their doorways.

"Jack, what's going on, man? What are you yelling about?"

Jack was full of adrenaline like when he used to wrestle. He was so worked up his knuckles were white from gripping the bat and the veins bulged in his biceps.

"You didn't hear that guy outside? There was some fucking crazy guy outside yelling and carrying on. I can't believe you guys didn't hear that."

They all went back to bed and Jack lay awake thinking how they probably thought him just as crazy as the nut job on the street; he had been shouting just like the stranger because he was tense.

On the way to his room, Alex had muttered to Damian, "Man, Jack's losing it. He's really losing it. I'm locking my door."

To Jack, it seemed his new life was always a reaction to outside forces; it was a balancing act where he was forced to do things against his will, and where he found himself put into strange situations that had nothing to do with his own initiative or sensibilities. How he would have liked a little desert peace and quiet for a change.

That night, Jack slept for an hour, maybe two. It was still dark outside when he got back on the bus and returned to the conference center. He had become one of those strange creatures of the city with dark circles under their eyes and unkempt hair. He was a man with a story to tell. He was aware that he wasn't clean or pure as he had been before: that somehow the lines had blurred until he was no longer sure of his own identity.

The next morning, Jack sat in the dressing room in front of the mirror along with the rest of In Quick and had the circles under his eyes rubbed away and his eyelashes done, gel put in his hair and his face powdered until the wrinkles in his forehead were gone and also the frown line between his eyes that had not been there six months ago. They went to wardrobe and he put on the vest and the turtleneck he had bought. They wore black pin-striped slacks with some thick-heeled boots. Jack saw himself in the mirror and thought again: who the hell am I?

The rehearsal went fairly well; the place was empty and there was no pressure. Later, the band sat in the back waiting, while the doors opened for the trade show and the buyers and the media poured in. Jack found he couldn't eat though he was hungry. He wanted to drink some alcohol to ease his nerves.

"Jack, man, it's a piece of cake. You look like somebody died or something. This is entertainment," Seth said. "Don't take it so serious."

It was almost showtime and Jack thought about disappearing and never coming back, just shining the job and his paycheck completely, because he didn't need the grief.

Then Duane announced to the crowd, "And now ladies and gentlemen, the smooth sound of San Francisco's own In Quick!"

Jack heard the cheers and he looked at the band and saw the glow in their faces and eyes. The ovation transformed them; before Jack knew it, they were running through the curtain. Well, here goes nothing, Jack thought, running after them into the blinding lights. He couldn't see the crowd at all as he waved his hands in the air to the cheers and checked the floor to see the tape where he was supposed to stand. From the shelter of the curtain, Duane gave him a thumbs-up.

Damn, I hope Jack doesn't trip or fall off stage. Please let this go well, please God. Duane rubbed the lucky Indian arrowhead he had found in the forest of Big Sur nervously between his fingers.

There was an explosion and the lights flashed. The band ran toward the middle of the floor and went into their dance routine: Jack dropped for a stylized push-up as planned, and Seth flipped over him in the air. The music slowed to an R&B rhythm and each of them sung a verse of the song. When it was his turn, Jack performed the dance he had practiced so many times. He ran and slid across the stage on his knees, got up, spun and threw his hands wide while the others followed his steps. He put his hand to his heart and then held it to the sky. He felt like he was outside of his own body watching everything in slow motion. For the first time, the lyrics moved him. As he lip-synched, he imagined all the beautiful girls he had seen behind the glass on his lonely walks: the ones that had ignored him because he was poor. He thought of the months he had spent alone since Elizabeth had gone, and the sincerity of emotion seen in his tortured eyes was made all the more beautiful by the sadness of his expression. His face was visible to thousands on the big screen, and while he performed his solo number, camera's flashed. How fortunate for Jack that Duke Warren, the front man for In Quick, had gotten sick.

They sang their big hit *I Don't Want to Cry* and three other songs, including *Lost Souls* from their latest album. As Seth had told him in the dressing room, "Jack, we're making a comeback. We were big once, but then we had some problems with our manager and broke up for a while, but now we're back. We don't usually play these corporate gigs, but this is different. Everyone wants to know what's going on with high tech. We're sure to get our picture in the paper and national press."

After the final number, the crowd wouldn't stop cheering. Several women tried to climb on stage but were held back by security. Jack felt euphoric in the midst of the praise of so many strangers. It was a seminal moment in his life; he wanted to stand there a long time and bask in the acceptance that had eluded him for so long.

When they were finished Duane appeared on stage next to the band and they all took a bow.

"Let's hear it for In Quick," Duane said. "The new album *Eternity* is available in stores now."

The band returned to the dressing room, sat down on the couch and helped themselves to some complimentary beers courtesy of Duane. They were all drenched in sweat.

"Man, what a rush," Seth said. "That's what I live for. I feel like I'm floating above the world. It's not like life at all; it's a dream where you live forever."

"We're playing a trade show," Erin said. "This is nothing compared to how it used to be. We're a bunch of dinosaurs."

"Why you gotta be so negative, man? I thought it went well," Mark said. "The crowd was animated. I prefer this to playing clubs. The money's better at least."

"Say guys, I think we need to hear it for Jack. Man, that solo stuff was great. Even though you weren't singing, it looked like you were really feeling it," Seth said.

Mark patted him on the back.

"Yeah, right on, Jack. How does it feel to be a rock star for a day?"

Jack smiled.

"You know when I was in college I thought you guys were a bunch of fags. No offense. I mean this isn't exactly my kind of music. But now I have to say that it's pretty cool being out there and performing. It was great. I wish I had the talent to be a rock star. You guys were big once. All the girls had your CD. A lot of guys envied that."

Erin smiled. "Yeah, I guess we had it once. We lived our ten seconds of fame. That's more than most can say."

"Come on," Jack said. "This isn't bad, either. They were cheering for you guys like crazy, man. You have a hit song, a classic. It's gonna be played on the radio forever."

It was at that point that the groupies started trickling backstage. They came asking for autographs, and several of them crowded Jack. He started to explain that he wasn't really in the band, but it wasn't necessary. They knew it, but it didn't seem to matter.

"Jack, would you sign my shirt? Oh Jack, can I take a picture with you?"

Jack looked to Erin who just nodded and smiled. Jack put his arms around a pair of twenty-somethings and they kissed his cheeks while their friend snapped a picture. The girls lingered and talked nonstop. Erin and the band played it cool and easy: for them it was nothing new. Seth passed out beers, Mark lit up a cigarette, and the girls sat with them on the couch and said, "We still love your music. The new song is really good. Can we have a copy of the album?"

The party progressed to the band's hotel room where Jack sat on the sofa, drunk and stoned, while some girl chattered in his ear. Seth had disappeared into the bedroom with a girl who could barely walk and couldn't stop laughing; Erin was mixing drinks; Mark was passed out in a chair on the balcony; and Duane was bumping hip hop on the stereo and freaking with the rest of the crowd in the middle of the room.

Project Brother, the other act, was staying down the hall and soon both parties melted together. Project Brother were some hard-smoking black men from L.A. with a sizable fan club of their own. They shook Jack's hand and the one called Da Bomb said, "Yo man, your shit's smooth. The girls they be diggin' that lover's rock."

Jack wondered: didn't I see these guys on VTV? He didn't follow along much with pop culture and was overwhelmed by the party. He had smoked too much of Project Brother's chronic and he went to the bedroom to pass out. Later, he woke up with a girl asleep in arms. In the bed next to him he heard people fucking. Carefully, Jack slipped free of the girl, found his clothes and put them on. His head was pounding as he took the elevator down to the lobby. He stepped out onto the street, hailed a cab and, before he knew it, was home in his own bed.

Some hours later Henrik burst into his room.

"Hey Jack, man, check this out. You're on the front page of the entertainment section of the Chronicle. Look, man, it's you," Henrik said, jabbing his finger at the half-page head shot: Jack with his headset mic and his mouth open, his eyes wrinkled from the strain of singing, or fake singing, sweat on his forehead.

Jack felt like shit. His head was pounding from a pot and alcohol hangover, and when he first looked at the picture, he felt nauseous. Then something like excitement began to tickle in his stomach and mutated into guarded pride.

"Wow, that's me, isn't it?"

"Yeah, it sure is," Henrik said. "I don't get it, Jack. It says you're a member of In Quick. Since when are you with In Quick? I mean I hate that kind of music, but they were huge in Europe and still are. They were just on tour last year and they even stopped in Sweden. My sister has a poster of them on her wall."

Henrik's feelings were a mixture of jealously and awe at living with the newest member of a world famous pop band. And just when he had given Jack up as a total loser. Jack had been a nonentity as far as he was concerned. Now Jack's face was on the cover of the entertainment section of the Chronicle. When he first saw it, Henrik thought: why he's a fucking rock star and he's been hiding it all along. He must have great connections. And to think I never really paid much attention to him. That's what happens when you judge someone at face value.

"Damian hooked me up with a job working the Bay Area Tech Conference," Jack said. "Duke Warren got strep throat and I had to take his place in the band. It wasn't even my idea."

"Man, Jack, I didn't know you could sing. What a fantastic break. God, just listen to this guy – *'and I had to take his place.'* Yeah man, what a drag. Shit! Always so modest. It wasn't even your idea. Ha! Jack, you're so modest, you're almost dead."

"It's not that big a deal," Jack said. "I only got paid a hundred and fifty bucks plus a hundred dollar bonus for the day. The band isn't even that big anymore."

"Oh yeah? Did you read the caption? Listen up, I'll read it to you:

'Pop legend In Quick opens world's largest technology fair at the Civic. Singer Jack Wild electrifies crowd with classic hit I Don't Want to Cry.'

"Man, with that kind of publicity you've got it made. You can't buy publicity like that."

"Hey man, it doesn't matter," Jack told him. "I'm not really in the band. I was just filling in. Duke's coming back when he gets over his virus."

"But you've got to be in the band now. I mean they would be stupid not to ask you to join up," Henrik said. "You've got the face they want. You can be like the fifth member or something. Man, Jack, if I were you I wouldn't blow this. This is the most important thing you've done in your whole life."

What a lucky bastard, Henrik thought. What a lucky break. Can it really be that arbitrary? What if you never get that break? Damn, Jack doesn't even have any talent. It's just his face they want. Just like Jeremy Leads. But then I guess he's an okay actor.

Is this really the most important thing I've done, Jack wondered. All I did was stand up on stage and mouth the words to a song someone else wrote and do some dance moves that Duane choreographed. No, the best thing I've done was help take us to the conference finals when I played baseball for U of A. Even though we lost, it was still an achievement. But I suppose that doesn't matter much to anybody else.

"I don't really want to be a part of the band. I was just doing them a favor," Jack said.

"When you find out how much they're going to pay to use your face, you'll change your mind. If I were you, I'd get on the phone and call In Quick, like now, and negotiate a contract."

Henrik was stressing him out. All Jack wanted to do was go back to sleep. He wanted to sleep a long time. He wanted his privacy.

"Tonight we're gonna go out and celebrate, Jack. Now that you've got something going, you can go big and not feel guilty about it like you always do. It's been forever since we've gone out. I've missed you, man. I'll talk to the guys and we'll get it sorted. I gotta go work at Virgo but I'll be off later. You got my cell so just give me a buzz, okay?"

"Sure," Jack said, certain that another night of the same would kill him.

So once my face shows up in the paper Henrik wants to be buddy buddy again, when before I could have died in here and it wouldn't have made a difference. What a superficial son of a bitch. This whole bloody culture is superficial.

Lying there, Jack felt very small in relation to the forces around him. He began to wonder how much of a man's life was fortune and how much was will. It seemed when he tried his hardest to find a job and be successful he came up empty. And now what was going on? Was Henrik exaggerating?

When Jack looked at his picture in the paper, he felt uncomfortable. Now he couldn't avoid being recognized on the street. He had become a face without character: a caricature of himself. I wonder: have these so-called friends of mine always seen me that way?

It had been exciting to be on stage at the conference, but Jack doubted he could make a life of it. It embarrassed him to be the center of attention. Truthfully, he was rather shy. When people watched him too closely, it made him nervous. He couldn't imagine a life under scrutiny without time to himself.

Everything was out of balance. Jack felt distant from his family, and without love and true friends. He was paralyzed by his new life. I am just a small fragment of a large chaotic formula. Wouldn't life have been better if he'd married his first love, stayed in his hometown and taken over his father's store? Life would have been easier, anyway. Jack missed his mother's cooking, playing ball, camping and riding dirt bikes with his dad. And he worried about his sister and the guys she dated. He thought: maybe it's time to take trip a back home.

17

"Hey Alex, what are you doing home," Damian asked. "Is it another holiday? Man, you always complain about the hours you work but then you get a week off for spring break, two weeks for Christmas, and two months for summer: not to mention all those other holidays. What is it, Flag Day or something?"

"No, I got fired from my job. Now, finally, I have time to get some work done."

Alex was sitting in the kitchen with a pen and a stack of paper. He held his head in his hand with his fingers filed into his unkempt hair. He was doing revisions of *Pax Americana*. He wore an old brown robe and his horn-rims and looked every bit like a father putting in a little work on Sunday morning.

"You got fired? What for?"

"The principal seems to think I'm a Marxist revolutionary. He's got the idea that teaching people how to think for themselves is dangerous. He's a military guy, what do you expect? He wants the students to be able to sit, roll over and play dead. Anyway, it's all good. I'll just consider this a vacation."

"I'm sure you could find a job at another school."

"I remember once you suggested that I be a taxi driver. I just might take you up on that. I think it would be good for inspiration. I could work nights and write during the day."

"Talk about being underemployed," Damian said.

"You know what the problem with this country is? People are judged by the status of their job and not on their creativity, intelligence or citizenship. It bothers me how people assume that anyone who works an ordinary job is uneducated and worthless. A job is not necessarily a profession. For most people, their job conflicts with their chosen profession. I don't believe that people should be defined by their jobs, if the prime purpose of that job is to pay the bills at the expense of their unique abilities and talents."

Damian felt sorry for Alex. Poor guy just never has any luck. He works damned hard and he's very proud and can't get any recognition.

"Maybe you're right," Damian said. "What are you working on, anyway?"

"I'm editing."

Jack came in.

"Damn Jack, you look like shit," Alex commented. "Had a rough night? Were there any more crazies hanging out in the driveway?"

"No, I've just had a long weekend. Friday I was at some hotel party with Project Brother and In Quick."

"Yeah right, you were chillin' with Project Brother. And I took Nikki Star home with me last night," Damian said.

Alex thought to himself: man, I hate all that commercialized pop music and hip hop. What a bunch of trash. Music was never as good as in the Fifties: the good old days of rock and roll. You can't reinvent the wheel. Boy, I wish I could have lived in the Fifties when America had style.

I'm not going to make a big deal out of it, Jack thought. Still, these guys never give me any respect. I've always been the outsider. He put the paper Henrik had given him on the table with the entertainment section face down.

"I'm making some eggs. Who wants eggs," Damian asked.

"I'll take some eggs. Do we have any orange juice?" Jack opened up the fridge and peered into the chaos. Something was rotten in there somewhere. "Out of juice. I'll go to Habib's. Anybody want anything?"

Jack was over the fact that the corner store was a rip-off. If I were better at planning, then I wouldn't have to go there at all, he thought. If I bought everything in bulk like Arnold, but then I don't have a PriceCo card.

Damian scrambled some eggs and sat down to the paper.

"So what are you working on these days," Alex asked him, without looking up from his work.

"I'm working on this script I'm gonna pitch. But this one I wanna direct myself. Wow, did you see this, I can't believe it. It's boy wonder himself," Damian said, showing Alex Jack's picture.

"What the hell. Lemme see that," Alex said, snatching at the paper.

"Hang on. You'll just have to wait your turn. I thought you didn't like this kind of superficial stuff?"

"Whatever. What's it about, anyway?"

Alex felt the jealousy build. What was Jack doing in the paper? Why, all he did was mope around the house and now he was a superstar? Goddamn America, land of shit. There had to be some logical explanation.

Damian laughed.

"Oh, I know what this is all about. I hooked Jack up with a PA gig with an old production company I used to work for. All kinds of unexpected things come up during these shows, and it looks like Jack had to fill in for the band. You have to admit, he's got the face for it. I never thought they'd get groups like that for a trade show, but then again it was the tech expo. Project Brother, they're way into tech. They do concerts over the internet and build their own synthesizers. They play like they're hardcore from the hood, but they're really Orange County college grads. I saw them on Phat Pads on VTV last week. Man, you should see how those guys live. They've got this huge two-acre ranch up in the Hollywood hills with an Olympic sized lap pool and their own bar and private nightclub. I bet they're growing pot out there somewhere, too."

"I could care less about how a bunch of people I don't know who make music I don't like, live," Alex said. "I don't care how they live because it just reminds me that I live like shit, like most everyone else in this country. If I had a lot of money, I'd be quiet it about it so as not to offend people."

There it is, Alex thought. Celebrity culture. That's my next chapter: *Celebrity Culture and Exhibitionism*. Well, it seems like the day wasn't wasted after all.

"That's the problem with the United States," Alex continued. "Instead of keeping quiet about our wealth, we flaunt it. That's why the rest of the world hates us. Because we're show-offs. Hasn't history taught us anything? One of these days we'll go bankrupt and all our power and wealth will be gone and we'll be ridiculed and humiliated. Whatever happened to humility?"

"You're just jealous," Damian said.

"Of course I'm fucking jealous. Let's just compare our show-off culture to the French Revolution. What's preventing me and people like me from invading Project Brother's "Phat Pad," looting it and cutting their heads off?"

"Because they're cool. Anyway, you got it wrong, Alex. Project Brother are just a bunch of guys like us who've made it. They're an effect not a cause. For every Project Brother, there are bigshots behind the scenes taking a cut for their talent. That's just how it works. I look at a guy like you and I think: he's got talent. He could write an award–winning screenplay if he wanted to. But then he's got his priorities all wrong. The thing about you, Alex, is that you live to oppose things. But where would your discerning intellect be without superficiality and injustice? And what if you just went along with it? I see a bunch of guys with a fat pad and I think: cool. Good for them. Why can't you think that way? Because you're upset that everyone else isn't upset like you."

"Maybe you're right, but then I'm a product of my circumstances," Alex said. "I just want you to understand my argument. In the United States today we rely on mannequins to tell us what we should value and how we should live our lives. As a result, our culture becomes nothing but a pantomime of appearances in which individual identity and character is erased. The average person is made miserable in an endless attempt to acquire the changing appearance of success. This individual will never feel that his life measures up to that of a movie star, because his humanity has been erased. The small pleasures of life become bitter when one is confronted with the excesses of fame and success. The cult of personality in our culture is so insidious that even the mannequins don't feel they are beautiful or successful enough. Many of our celebrity idols suffer from an identity crisis caused by attempting to live up to their falsified image, while hiding their faults and neglecting their intellectual and emotional development. For individuals who are critical of the shortcomings of our society and culture, and who work to improve themselves as human beings, life in the United States is comparable to hell. So I repeat that I couldn't give a damn as to what this or that celebrity does or how they dress or live. I take the greatest liberty in saying they have no bearing on my life; they are nonentities. I value what is close to me and what I can influence through my own efforts. I sincerely wish others would share in my philosophy by developing a meaningful identity and finding a purpose in their lives irrespective of popular culture. If this leads to stardom, so be it. I don't claim that all stars are superficial profiteers of image culture. And if it leads to friendship, understanding and the respect of one's peers, even better. A man must not make himself and others miserable through excessive ambition."

At some point in the conversation Jack returned with the juice.

Damian said, "So Jack, are you gonna become a superficial profiteer of image culture?"

"No, I hadn't planned on it," Jack said. "Are these eggs for me?"

"It's all you, brother."

Jack sat down and started to eat.

"So we saw your picture in the paper. The PA gig wasn't all bad then, was it? The party with Project Brother must have been pretty crazy. Man, Jack, when stuff like that happens, you gotta call us," Damian said. "You help me, I help you, know what I mean?"

"Yeah, I'm sorry. I didn't think about it. I was pretty fucked up."

"Well, this is good news, Jack, I must say. Sometimes I think life is all about timing," Damian said. "How would you like to be an actor?"

"Sounds good to me but how am I gonna do that? That PA job, In Quick appearance aside, was pretty lame. I'm not interested in that at all."

"I know Jack. It's bullshit. No one ever makes it in the film industry starting as PA. You got to get their attention somehow. Anyway, the idea just came to me that you could be in my next film. I'm gonna pitch a script to Solimar Productions, you know the one that does all the foreign and indie flicks, and I think you'd be perfect for it."

"What's it about?"

Damian cast a quick look over at Alex who had his nose in his manuscript.

"I can't tell you yet. First they have to accept it. And what's more they have to agree to let me direct it. My key selling point is the ridiculously low budget. Here's the drawback. Since we want to keep it cheap, I can't pay you that much, maybe a couple of thousand at most. But if we can get it into some film festivals, people will see your face, and that's your key to Hollywood. And never mind what Alex tells you about Hollywood. He's a purist, and in this world you gotta be practical. Admittedly, a lot of mainstream movies are childish and inane, but then it's better than working some crappy restaurant gig, right?"

"Like I said, sign me up," Jack said. "I don't know a damn thing about acting, but I'll give it shot."

"Acting's just like anything, all it takes is a little practice."

"And remember you've been practicing all your life," Alex said. "Just harness the energy from all those times that you've thought one thing and said another. It's the basis of our whole society. Crocodile tears and plastic smiles."

"At any rate, it'll be fun," Damian said. "We'll get to hang out more and you won't be broke and bitter."

"I don't know that I've been bitter. Mostly, I've just been depressed," Jack said.

"It happens to the best of them," Damian said.

18

With a hundred dollars to spare, Quincy decided to make his move. He thought: just do it, man, you got nothing to lose. Her dad's probably at work. You know she's having a hard time, and it's not like you're a stranger. Actually, why don't you go to the store and buy her something nice? No, better play it cooler than that. You don't know what she needs.

A half hour later he was outside Aisha's apartment. Man, just make a move. You be looking all stupid and shit standing here without doing nothin'. Quincy approached the door and, for a moment, thought about running away and never coming back. But then he surprised himself and rang the bell.

Aisha was lying on the couch watching television. Next to her was a half-eaten pint of rocky road ice cream and a can of soda. She was wearing pajamas, the pair with the multicolored bears on them, and her ponytail was wound tight on her head in a purple hair tie.

I wonder who that could be? For the past two months Aisha had been cut off from her friends. If it weren't for her sister and dad, she would have only had the television for company. In all that time she hadn't heard so much as a word from Duane. She was trying her best to erase him from her memory. Still, she knew he would never be completely gone. One day their child would want to meet its father. And where would Duane be then? Was it possible for someone to just disappear? Sure, if they wanted to badly enough.

She looked in the peephole and saw Quincy Jenkins standing there with his hat pulled low over his eyes and his skateboard in his hand.

Oh my God, Quincy, what's he doing here? And then Aisha realized that she was too ashamed to see him. She told herself: I just won't answer and wait 'til he walks away. She felt ashamed for what he would think of her. When she was with Duane, she began to think the young men of her neighborhood uneducated and without culture. She had felt superior to them. She ignored everyone in class and dreamt of being far away from the poverty of her community. And here was Quincy who she'd always considered strange for how he kept to himself and didn't talk much. She had sat in front of Quincy for most of the year and he hadn't said more than a few words to her.

Aisha's curiosity grew and she wondered if Quincy didn't have something important to tell her. Finally, her desire to escape from the endless days of limbo and self-imposed house quarantine forced her to open the door.

This was not the Aisha he remembered. She seemed older, her eyes were tired and her body had ballooned.

"Hiya Quincy. Whatch'you doin' here," Aisha said, trying her best to be cheerful.

Quincy tried his best to hide the disappointment in his face. What did you expect? She's having a baby and she's wasn't expecting no visit. People look different when they wake up and before they get themselves ready for work and school. She's without all her make-up, but she's still pretty.

"I notice' you weren't comin' to school no more," Quincy said. "I thought I'd come see what happen' to you."

Compared to Duane, Quincy seemed like a boy: the way he couldn't look at her, how his words came out uneven, and the way he dressed. Still, his consideration touched her, and Aisha felt sad wishing that she could return to the innocence of her sixteen years.

"Well, come on and sit down. It's nice to have a visit," Aisha said.

No point in talking about what happened. Thanks to Taresa, the whole school knows already. It's better not to mention it, she thought. No need to make him uncomfortable.

"Do you want a soda or some'in'?"

"No, I'm fine," Quincy said.

They sat on the couch together and watched television for a while without talking.

"Guess what," Quincy said.

"What?"

"Mr. Green got fired. He don't work at Hunter no more. We got some new teacher this week. She's an old lady and she's not funny or crazy like Mr. Green. She sticks right to the book and she's hella tough. Without you and Mr. Green, English class is wack. I don't even wanna be there no more. I'm thinking of droppin' out, gettin' my GED and goin' into business for myself."

"Why did they fire Mr. Green? What did he do?"

"I don't know. He didn't even get to tell us he was leaving. Man, Mr. Green let us write raps and he talked about oppression and human rights and how our government is just a bunch of thieves. Well, you know how he talked. And then he read from that crazy book of his, and I never thought about any of that stuff before."

It was Mr. Green that had gotten Aisha into writing. During the past weeks, she had written extensively and often in her diary to purge her emotions so they didn't rage in her mind and break her down.

"I miss school and Mr. Green," Aisha said. "But then I don't think I'll be back. At least not this year. I got other responsibilities now."

"Maybe you should take the GED, too. That way you could still go to college," Quincy told her. "We could study together and you could help me out. You always been smart and I bet you could be a lawyer or some'in'. I'm good in math but I need help with English and history. I've got a bad memory for history and my writing ain't so good. Won't you help me? I could pay you."

"I'm not thinkin' about college no more. I gotta support myself and the baby. That's just the way life is. College is just for rich people. But I do wanna finish high school, and if you wanna study for the test, then we can study together. You don't gotta pay me or nothin'," Aisha said. "We'll help each other. I need help with math."

"Don't you get lonely sittin' here all by yourself?"

"It's not so bad. I rent movies and listen to music and read. At night dad comes home and takes care of me. I wish this hadn't happened because of dad. He's had it so bad with the divorce. I feel like I let him down," she said.

"You didn't let him down. You just didn't know what you were gettin' into. There's bad people out there that don't feel good about themselves and they'll use you up. They're vampires. It ain't right at all what that guy done to you, and if he was a real man, he'd step up and take care of you. You don't gotta go feeling sorry for yourself for bein' victimized."

"I wanted to live a dream, Quincy. I thought it was a dream just like in the movies. I thought I had found my prince and now I'm back where I started. Sometimes I'm afraid I'm never gonna get out of here and live a decent life and have the things other people have."

"Don't talk like that. That's just nonsense. Like Mr. Green says, they just playin' you making you believe all them things is real. You got to be real to yourself. You got people that love you. You got a good family. And you got friends. And you gonna get outta here," Quincy said.

I'm gonna take you away from here and show you the good life, he thought. 'Cause your my queen and I'd do anything for you.

"I just get to feeling down when I'm alone like this," Aisha said. She had a lot more to say about it but was afraid she'd break down and cry. It had been so long since her emotions had anywhere to go.

"Listen, it's expensive raising a baby. A baby's gotta have stuff. I been working at the car park, you know valet parking and all that, and I been making some money so I can help you out." Quincy reached into his pocket and put the hundred on the table. "Why don't you save this for a rainy day and take some of the stress off your dad?"

"I can't take your money, Quincy. My dad'll take care of me fine."

"Just save it for me," he said. "You don't have to use it, just put it away until you need it."

"I don't know why you're doing this, Quincy. Why do you care what happens to me?"

"I just don't think it's right the way things turned out. We grown up together and I don't want you havin' a hard time. I don't want you workin' at no mini-mart or fast food joint when you got a baby to raise and you gotta study. A baby needs love and attention. Save that money away for college. I got more where that's comin' from. I'm only giving you the extra I don't need for myself. It's no big deal. That's what money's for, to help people out."

"My dad's gonna be comin' home soon. I don't think you should be here. It won't look right you being here," she told him.

"I understand. I'll come back next week so we can start studyin'. I'll bring some books for you," he said.

Quincy thought again about the guy Daryl or Darren or Duane, and then about his promise to Gavin. He's a stupid bitch, all right, but what if Gavin caps his ass? Then it's my fault, too. Still, I already took the money. I'll make him promise just to fuck him up. That would be the best, because that punk-ass sure deserves it. Gavin don't have the nerve to shoot nobody. His mamma gave him too much heart.

Quincy would have to trick Aisha somehow to get her to tell him where he was. She'd probably try to protect him.

"That guy you was with, he was some bigshot, huh? Taresa said he was on TV."

"He was a talent agent for some place called Carl Price. He made a lot of money and he was smart. What a fool I was for thinking he'd want anything with girl like me," Aisha said.

There it was. Quincy had heard the name before. They had billboards around the city. It wouldn't be hard to find the office. He would look it up in the phone book and pass the information on to Gavin, who could use it as he pleased.

"Let me tell you somethin' about people like him. They ain't got their priorities right. They always looking out for number one, themselves, and that's a lonely life. I wouldn't want to be in his shoes and have no heart," Quincy said.

Aisha saw him to the door, and just as he was about to leave, she called his name. Quincy turned around and saw her face all twisted up like dough and then she was crying. Somehow he was holding her. He was holding her and thinking about the future with her. He thought that if he gave her everything he could, she would love him. He felt like he could fly and do anything because she needed him.

"Oh Quincy, I'm so scared."

"It's gonna be a'ight," he said, noticing the difference in his voice. It was deep and firm and didn't allow for argument. It was grown-up's voice, like Mr. Taylor or his dad. It was the voice of a man who knew himself. I know what I gotta do, Quincy thought. Everything else is just hype.

Quincy felt the roundness of her belly pressing into his own and savored the smell of her skin and hair. She no longer seemed old and tired, but like the Aisha he knew, who was sixteen and beautiful and who didn't understand the dangers of the world or her place in it.

19

One afternoon the housemates received a call from Julie in the hospital. She had collapsed at work, but they shouldn't worry because she was better now, just that she needed some things from home like her portable CD player and CDs, her design books, and could they get her a copy of *Woman* and *Her Life*? Also, she needed some clothes because she was going to be staying awhile. "Have Henrik pick out some clothes for me. He knows what I wear." Finally, she wanted her laptop computer, and could they bring her some strawberries?

Damian decided they should all chip in for flowers. They called Henrik at work and he came out on his bike and helped pack Julie's bag, all the while wondering what was wrong with her.

Damian drove them over to the hospital and they met up in Julie's room with the supplies and gave her the flowers. She looked so small and frail. She had a tube in her arm and was more pale than usual. There was a dyke-looking woman there who introduced herself as Dawn and who worked at the clinic where Julie had recently gotten a job.

Damian filled a vase with water, arranged the flowers and opened the curtains saying, "Man, this is almost as dark as that closet you live in back home. Ha, ha."

Julie couldn't suppress a smile. They all gave her hugs, and Alex felt guilty, as if his being mean to her had made her sick, and thought: why are you such an asshole with women? Did it really matter with the heat and Greg staying over every night and the shower and the phone and the dishes? Well, it wasn't easy, but she's a human being, after all.

Jack thought: she looks like she's dying. If she hadn't been your housemate, you might have hooked up with her. Remember the time she sat in your lap in the car and it took all your will to keep from putting your hands on her?

"You have to take better care of yourself," Damian said. "See what happens when you try and party with the big boys. Ha, ha."

Damian could do nothing but joke because ever since Kenny shot Ryan at his party, he had been unable to face death and misfortune seriously. Death was a destructive force that tore people apart, and though Julie wasn't dying, to see her sick made Damian want to joke and laugh and make fun to insure that he was healthy in both mind and spirit. He didn't want to be morose like Alex.

Alex thought: I wonder when my parents will die? They will die one day and you have to start thinking about it now, like you should have invested in mutual funds. You need the emotional insurance of years of preparation for their death. Because then you'll have to make it on your own, not just financially like you do now, but emotionally too, because the safety net of their concern and love will be gone. If you didn't have them to love you, who would? Certainly not any of your peers. Sure, they're your friends and your community today, but they could just as soon abandon you tomorrow.

"So what did the doctor say was wrong with you," Henrik asked.

"He says I have mono," Julie said.

"Oh, man, I've had mono. That's bad," Jack said. "You feel like you can't do anything at all. It takes months to recover."

"I don't think you're cheering her up, Jack," Alex said.

"Well, mono's not the end of the world. I mean it's not like AIDS or anything," Jack said. "It goes away."

Julie avoided eye contact. She told herself: keep a straight face and let it pass. None of them suspect that.

Henrik thought: man, AIDS must be terrible. If I had AIDS, I would take out a big loan, live my dreams and fuck the consequences. I would skydive and race bikes and travel all over the world and then, when I was good and happy on a perfect beach at sunset or on the top of a mountain, I'd blow my brains out. Suicide is all about going out on top at one's full strength and not wasting away in some hospital.

"So you're not going to be around for a while, or what," Alex asked. "How long do you have to stay here?"

"I'm still too weak. They're keeping me here until I regain my strength."

"Hey, you got a TV and a DVD player," Henrik said. "I can come by after work and bring some movies."

Julie forced a smile. You can't blame Henrik. You were a grown woman. You took care of yourself and made your own decisions. You never believed anything would touch you. You thought you were a princess, but you were just a naive little girl. You were living with the wrong people. You were in over your head.

She looked at Henrik again and saw his faults. He was a caricature and not a person at all. He was the ever-changing face of hip with no essence. He was a joker and a fake who was alone, scared and far away from home. Why did I ever go with him? Because you believed in television. You and Henrik, and maybe Jack, all of you from the outside, believed in the illusion of California and its eternal renewable face of hip and cool. So what do you have to show for it now? You're dying and the only identity you've established is as a social worker helping other people. That is what you feel good about. That is your legacy.

Jack felt sorry for Julie, sick and reduced as she was. He felt sorry and didn't know what to do or say. Sometimes people have it hard, he thought. He sat on the bed and put his large hand over Julie's small one. He remembered his sister and hoped that she was happy.

They stayed a while and Alex talked with Dawn about her work, especially the suicide hotline, which he found fascinating. Dawn had participated in the WTO protest in Seattle and he asked her about her experience. Talking to Dawn, Alex realized that he was all theory and no action; that had to change. What about teaching? Okay, teaching. But writing? Then he wondered if activism really could change the course of history. Only if everyone participates, he thought. The same with tyranny. When everyone is apathetic, tyranny happens.

"Look Julie, I raided the newsstand," Henrik said. "I got *Woman* and *Her Life* and *Phat Zine* and *Urban Hip* and *Tech World* . . ." He held them all up for her to see. "The girl on the cover of *Her Life* is so hot. Those Latina chicks are really making it big. It's about time. Daisy Gonzales is such a babe."

"It's all airbrush," Alex said.

"The girl is sixteen," Dawn added. "All woman are supposed to compare to sixteen-year-olds, and you wonder why I'm a lesbian."

Her words made Jack feel uncomfortable. Man, she's abrasive but I guess she's right. Still, I've never been with a girl that looked like Daisy Gonzales, and I'm too old to go with a sixteen-year-old.

Julie felt good holding Jack's hand. Eventually, she fell asleep and they decided it was time to go.

"Hey, did anyone call Arnold," Jack asked.

"He's down in SoCal," Damian said. "He said he had some family business to take care of."

When they tried to leave quietly, Julie woke up again and asked Henrik to stay behind. He didn't have any place in particular to go and didn't mind keeping her company for a little while longer. He sat down next to her on the bed and turned on the television.

"Don't worry, soon you'll feel better and then you can come back to the house," he told her.

"That's what I wanted to talk to you about," she said.

"What's that?"

"Henrik, I'm not coming back."

"What do you mean?"

I'm going home to stay with my parents. I'm really very sick. Just between you and me. I didn't want anyone else to know, but I thought you had the right to know. Promise me that you won't tell the others."

"Sure, I promise."

"Promise whatever we say to each other will stay between us."

"Well, we've kept other things between us, haven't we?"

"Yes, and that's the problem. I'm telling you this because I think you ought to know and also so that you don't hurt other people."

Henrik felt the nervous knot in his stomach and did his best to ignore it. How could anything she told him prevent him from hurting other people? Since when had he hurt other people?

"I'm not sure I understand," he said. "Listen, you're tired and you've been through a lot, maybe you should get some rest and I'll come back tomorrow and we can talk all you want. How does that sound?"

"When they checked me into the hospital here they ran some tests to figure out what was wrong with me. Well, like you know, I have mono, and it's making me feel weak. But that's not the real problem. I found out that I have HIV. Actually, I've known for while now. Ever since I got checked out for VD and found out I had herpes. Both of them I imagine I got from you. I called Greg and he got checked out, and aside from the herpes, he's clean. Which means that it's almost certain you also have HIV. I recommend you get checked out to see for yourself. I know I'm responsible for myself, but I deeply regret having ever been involved with you. You are one of the most irresponsible, superficial and hopeless people I have ever met. In fact, you disgust me. And you've ruined my life. I don't want to ever see you again," Julie said through sobs as tears stained her cheeks.

"You're crazy, Julie. That's all bullshit and you know it. I don't have HIV and I've never had a venereal disease in my life. You're losing it. I'm sorry you're feeling bad, but there's no need to attack me and get nasty. I never wanted to hurt you. You have to believe that. If you even have HIV, you can bet you didn't get it from me."

"And you know for a fact you're clean? You've checked yourself out? You want me to believe that?"

"Right. Yeah. I, uh, got checked a month ago. And that was well after we hooked up for the last time."

"Bullshit. Just get out. You bastard, get the fuck out of my face," she screamed.

Julie threw a magazine at his head and then another, which Henrik deflected with his hands as he backed toward to door.

"Julie, listen to me. It's not my fault, okay? Stop freaking out."

"Stop freaking out? Fuck you. I'm gonna die and so are you, liar. You fucking liar. Get the fuck out of here. Get out. Godammit, get out."

Julie threw her last magazine, and Henrik ran from the room and down the hallway, colliding with a nurse and knocking her paperwork from her hands. His heart was pounding and he couldn't breath. He rushed into the bathroom and threw up in the toilet. Then he went to the sink and splashed some cold water on his face. He was very pale in the reflection of the mirror.

Oh God, dear God, please don't let me have HIV. Just because she has it doesn't mean you do. She's had casual sex with at least three other guys besides me this year, and I never shared a needle with her, though we did have anal sex a lot without protection. Maybe she got it from someone else and you're okay, because it's hard for a guy to get it from a girl, right? Right. You're probably fine. Don't worry about it. What if she's fucking with you? What if she's just playing a game with you to pay you back for using her as a convenient lay? But she wanted it as much as you did. You should have never messed with her in the first place, stupid bitch, but then she was cute, and when she moved in it was too good to be true and too easy, and you were lonely. You had some good times with Julie. And what happened? Maybe you didn't respect her. You didn't respect her for doing everything you told her to do. That's just how it is, right? The naive little girls, you don't respect; and the real women, they don't respect you. They never have. And you can't just be alone. You need to get it somewhere.

For the first time in his life, Henrik wondered if he had been an asshole. He thought of how he treated women and people in general and realized that he had always placed himself before others and didn't care at all about people unless they had something to offer him. Am I really like that? I treat people fair. I have friends.

Alex, Damian, and even Jack, they were his friends, right? They went out and had fun together, and they liked him for who he was. It wasn't like back in Sweden where he never fit in and always had something to prove.

HIV. He was not HIV positive. Junkies got HIV. And he was no junkie. Sure, he'd tried different things, he liked to experiment, but he wasn't a junkie. A couple of times with heroin and always clean. Every needle sterilized, no mistakes. No, Julie must have gotten it from one of those after-hours parties where everyone was on E and drunk and it was custom to trade partners, and everyone ended up fucking everyone, condom or no condom, in as many creative ways as possible.

Henrik didn't want to know the truth. He wouldn't be able to take it if she was right. It was just too much to take to know you were going to die. I mean everyone would die, but not early and painful and in a hospital bed. Don't think about it, he told himself. Don't think because there have been plenty of times when you've been unsafe, particularly with Julie. No, you can't check to see if you're infected. It's better not to know. Shut up, shut up, don't go there. Think of the music, the nice music, think clean and empty and pure like air. God, please let me be okay. Let it all pass away and disappear.

Henrik would ignore her advice and hope that ignorance would solve his problem and make him lucky. But then he had tested luck far too many times. It was nearly miraculous that he hadn't fathered an unwanted child, contracted some social disease, OD'd on drugs, gotten a DUI or killed himself drunk driving on his motorcycle. Perhaps, down deep, he wished for the destruction to come and take him. There was no other explanation for how he had lived his life. Henrik wanted to exit life because he had never found meaning in it and didn't like himself and the role that had become his own almost involuntarily. The sound of music was just an escape from the misery of his thoughts, just as the drugs and the endless hunt for pleasure were escapes from a useless and superfluous existence.

Henrik knew the truth of these thoughts, though he didn't like to bring them to the surface. He wasn't a fool, just a coward, like most. He knew the truth, just as he knew that if Julie had HIV then there was a good chance he did, too. He didn't need to go to the clinic to find that out; he just needed to find a beautiful way to die. He had lived more than most people and didn't wish to decay or suffer unnecessarily. He was too old to change and salvage his dignity and self-respect.

20

One afternoon Alex went with Damian to check on the parking lot. He had already spent the morning editing his manuscript and the rest of the day lay vast and empty like a wasteland before him. The psychosis of unemployment was running him down. Alex needed a little company and Damian was good for that. He was an upbeat guy. *I wonder what tortures Damian at night in his own mind?*

"How long have you had the lot," Alex asked him.

"About a month now," Damian said.

"How much did you put down?"

"Thirty grand."

"What's your mortgage?"

"Somewhere around two and half grand. I figure I'll clear that easily with my earnings," Damian said.

"Can you build on it?"

"I don't know. But I know that I can make a lot more on parking than on rent. And who knows what it would cost to build and get water and sewage hook-ups."

There were apartments behind the lot, and it had occurred to Damian to build some units later when he was more established. But then why not just buy a condo somewhere else and keep the lot for cash flow?

He's smarter than I am, Alex thought. What if I had saved my money and done the same thing? Then I could just spend my time writing and use my passive income to pay rent and food.

"Man, it sucks being poor," Alex said.

"What made you think of that?"

"I don't know. Just in general. I mean, I don't want to be rich but I would like to have enough money so that I don't have to always think about my economy. Just look at food. I'd like to be able to eat whatever I want whenever I want and not have to worry about buying meat that's a dollar cheaper per pound. And I also don't want to have to worry about some unforeseen expense, like a hospital stay, that would put me in debt for the rest of my life. I had a friend with a heart problem who was uninsured. Well, he was lucky enough to get it operated on, but now he's in debt a couple hundred thousand dollars."

"Hey, man, at least he's got his health. That's worth more than money, " Damian said.

They pulled into the lot and parked.

"So this is it, huh? This is your first big investment," Alex said.

"Yeah. Can you believe I paid three hundred thousand dollars for this? If we were in the Central Valley, it wouldn't be worth a damned thing."

"Just wait 'til it fills up out there. You better buy now or you'll miss the boat," Alex told him.

Quincy stood up and walked over just as Damian and Alex were getting out of the car. Damian saw him, then Alex, and Damian said, "What the? Hey, what are you doing here? I thought I told you to get lost."

Quincy said, "Oh . . ," and then, "Mr. Green."

"Quincy –"

Quincy started to run and Damian chased him down the street. Alex ran after, but he wasn't used to exercise, and after a block a stitch in his side doubled him over and forced him to a walk.

Damn, I shoulda grabbed my skate, Quincy thought. Please don't let this motherfucker catch me. Watch out for the pole, dodge the lady, jump the fence into the park. Yeah, over the fence. Quincy was gasping for breath and his heart was pounding in his chest. Behind him, he heard the man yelling, "Come back here, you cheat. You've been ripping me off!"

Damian chased him through the park and across the street. Quincy nearly got hit by a car while Damian jumped and ran over the hood and the driver yelled, "Hey, fuck you, man!" Then they were in an alley and Damian grabbed for Quincy's shirt, missed, and finally caught him. Quincy choked on his collar and stopped. Damian pushed him to the wall.

"Hand it over."

"Hand what over? Yo, I don't gotta hand nothin' over. Man, you're crazy, get your hands off'a me," Quincy said, as he tried to wriggle free.

"Listen, punk. You've been stealing from me, and if there's one thing I don't like it's a thief. That's my lot and I worked hard to buy it and then some punk ass like you tries to rip me off," Damian said.

Man, look how wide the kid's eyes are. He must think I'm hardcore. I wish I had Alex filming this with the digital. Good film is all about real drama. Do I really look that tough?

"You don't know who you're messin' with," Quincy said. "I'm gonna tell Mr. Biggs what you're doin'."

"I don't give a damn what you tell any Mr. Biggs," Damian said. "I know you got my money. Now give it up."

Quincy thought about kneeing him in the balls, but when he saw Mr. Green, he thought better of it, and all his resistance turned to shame.

"Here it is, man, just take the money and let me go. I don't want Mr. Green to see none a' this."

Damian took the wadded-up money.

"Now I'm gonna let you go and you're gonna stay put. If you don't stay put, I'm gonna have the police put your ass in jail. Understood?"

"It's cool."

Damian let him go and Quincy stood there leaning on the wall thinking: how am I gonna buy those books for Aisha if I ain't got no money? How am I gonna help her out now? Man, this is wack. And there's Mr. Green, shit.

"Now if I see you in my lot again . . ."

"What's going on here," Alex asked. "What are you runnin' for Quincy?"

"Yo, Mr. Green, there's nothin' going on. Why you not at school no more, teach?"

"What's going on here is this punk's been ripping me off," Damian said. "He's been faking like he's the parking attendant and pocketing my money."

Damian turned to Quincy.

"You thought you had me fooled. You thought: this guy doesn't know what's up and I'll just disappear and come back when he's gone. That was a dumb idea."

"I don't know what he's talkin' about, Mr. Green. I was working for the parking lot and then he comes and tells me I'm not working no more. I was just doin' my job."

"I talked to those guys. They said they never had anyone working in the lot, you liar."

Damian had him by the shirt and was shaking him.

"Hey, leave him alone, Damian," Alex said.

"What's it to you, Alex? How do you know this kid, anyway?"

"He is, or rather was, one of my students. He's a good student. A good kid," Alex said. "So Quincy, you wanna tell me what's really going on?"

Quincy looked to the floor and bit his lip.

"I was workin' the lot and takin' the money and keepin' it for myself. I didn't take all the money, I left some. I mean I was workin' and needed the money and didn't think nobody cared 'cause nobody ever came by to collect."

"Quincy, man, you're lucky I'm not your teacher anymore 'cause I'd bust your ass for this one. Man, how'd you figure that taking other people's money and lying was the right thing to do? Where'd you learn that?"

"I didn't learn it. I don't know. I saw how Gavin had all that green and his new threads and his cell phone, and I thought I wanted to be that way. I mean, I don't care about all that shit, but I wanted to have money so I could help people."

"Quincy, Gavin's a dealer. You know that. That's why he has all that money. And let's face it, Gavin's gonna end up face down in the gutter with a bullet in his brain for his trouble. Maybe not today or tomorrow but sometime. That's what people do when you fuck with their money. I'm disappointed in you. You should have known better. But then it's your life and your conscience, and what business is it of mine how you want to live?"

"I don't want to live like that, I just don't know what else to do," Quincy said.

"Go get yourself a job like everyone else," Damian said.

"I'm sorry, Mr. Green. It was wrong of me, and I'm sorry for it."

"Don't tell me, tell him," Alex said.

"Hey mister, I'm sorry. I know it was your money and I took it. I'm sorry."

"Listen, kid, you're lucky Alex is a friend of yours. Otherwise, I'd just think you were some punk. So here's the deal, I'm not gonna tell anyone about this. But if I see you in my lot again, you're in trouble. Got it?"

"Yeah, I got it."

"Why don't you give him a job," Alex said.

"What?"

"I said why don't you give our man Quincy a job so he can make good again. It'll be good for his character."

"The hell I will. He ripped me off. Who's to say he won't do it again?"

"He says. And who's to say someone else won't come along and try the same thing?"

"Maybe you're right," Damian said. "But then I'm gonna want an accurate record of all the cars that come in and out of this lot, and I'll be coming by and checking up on you to make sure you're not fucking up."

"How much you gonna pay me," Quincy asked.

"Did you hear that? You got some balls, kid. I'll pay you six dollars an hour."

Six dollars? What a slave driver, Alex thought. But then it's none of my business.

"Ten," Quincy said.

"Ten? You kidding me? Ten bucks to stand around in this lot and collect money all day? Seven bucks."

"Nine."

"I'll give you seven fifty, or you can beat it," Damian told him.

"All right. I'll take it."

The truth was Quincy needed the money and maybe he could skim off the top. He was loyal, but he saw no difference between him skimming what he deserved and the man skimming what he could for parking. Business was all about what one could get away with, and in that sense they weren't so different.

"Quincy, my name's Damian. No hard feelings, huh?"

Damian stuck out his hand and Quincy shook it.

"No man, it's cool. I'da done the same thing if I was you. It's all just a matter of perspective."

On the drive home Damian thought: did I just agree to that because Alex was there and I didn't want to look bad? I wonder what seven-fifty an hour is gonna cost me?

21

If Elizabeth weren't American, she wouldn't have been airlifted to Singapore; if her parents hadn't bought her travel insurance, she wouldn't have been able to pay the hospital bills. After losing her job, she no longer had insurance. Even with the insurance provided by her employer accidents occurring overseas weren't covered. And the company had never paid any of her medical expenses at home because of her high deductible. They claimed to cover eighty percent of the medical costs resulting from catastrophic injury within the Unites States, but now even that sounded dubious. It seemed that when you got around to reading the fine print of insurance policies you were invariably on your own. Thanks to the foresight of her parents, Elizabeth wasn't totally fucked. Instead, she was asleep on heavy sedatives in a clean bed at the American hospital in Singapore.

She had been operated on and was alone, except for Graham who sat in a chair beside the bed holding her hand. Two thoughts ran through Graham's mind: how is Elizabeth going to react when she finds out that her leg has been amputated below the knee; and, I can't wait to get her on the plane home to the United States. She needs to go home and be somewhere safe after this one. I wonder if she'll blame me for the accident and for it not working out between us. I've done the best I could. I called her parents and made sure she got here safe, but it wasn't in time. She's ruined now. She's missing a part of her body, for fuck's sake. Well, she can probably get a prosthetic limb. It's not so bad. At least it wasn't her face.

Elizabeth woke up, saw Graham and asked him, "Where am I?"

"Singapore. You had an accident. You lost a lot of blood. You're lucky to be alive."

Elizabeth was euphoric from the morphine, and the memory of the accident recalled itself in bits and pieces. She remembered vaguely the contorted faces of death and violence in Graham's photographs. She remembered Setiawan's smile. She felt good with Graham by her side with his sad eyes, running his fingers through her hair. She had yet to notice that a portion of her leg was missing.

Should I mention it or let her find out for herself, Graham wondered.

"You had an operation," he said.

"What sort of operation?"

"Your leg. They were fixing your leg," he said. You better tell her a story to get her mind off things, he thought. Preferably something funny. Or at least something with a positive message.

"Remember that mountain near Padang you said you wanted to climb? Well, I'd also had the same idea when I first arrived, and during a school holiday I finally worked up the courage. This was before I had a car, and the mountain was a two-day bike ride away . . ."

When Graham finished his story, he noticed her eyes were closed.

"Elizabeth, are you sleeping?"

She opened her eyes.

"No, I was listening. You were talking about a tiger."

He hoped she had gotten the message of the story: that to have a meaningful life you had to challenge yourself in spite of your limitations. To live in fear of what might happen, and in sorrow over what was lost, was futile. Whether the tiger that had stalked him was real or not was inconsequential for the fear had been there nonetheless. And fear of the unknown, or fear for its own sake, would always be worse than the object of fear, which on appearance presented solutions.

Although the moral of the story was typical enough, Graham didn't find it convincing. Perhaps there had been nothing behind his climb other than boredom, desperation and vanity. If anything, he had hoped to entertain and distract Elizabeth with his words. He wondered: can a story ever really provide any respite from life's misfortunes? Can one individual ever really understand another's tragedy? He had always been the sort to feel sorry for himself, but what was that sorrow in comparison to her own? It was this general torment of the mind that Graham sought to escape when he climbed the mountain. On top of the mountain, looking out over the world, he had found a moment of peace, and that had to be enough. It was the same peace he felt as a photographer, connecting with his subjects without knowing their thoughts. Peace was built on the mysteries that the intellect could not uncover. The mystics had discovered long ago that only the impossible could silence the mind and elevate the spirit.

More than ever, Graham was certain that to find life's true reward it was necessary to risk everything, free oneself from need and attachment, and embrace constant change. Only then were you living in the moment. Elizabeth was the embodiment of that philosophy. It was this shared perspective that had made them friends. And though Graham was saddened by her accident, he was certain she would persevere. There was nothing more he could do for her.

"I have to leave now, Elizabeth. Visiting hours are over. I'll be back tomorrow at the same time," he told her, before leaning over to give her a kiss.

Graham's words had a calming effect on Elizabeth. When she shut her eyes, she imagined herself safe in the comfort of Graham's bed at that house where time stood still on the edge of Padang River; a place that before had bored her and where her only entertainment was being bitchy to the maid.

Elizabeth drifted in and out of sleep. Later, when she felt an itch on her leg and went to scratch it, she was surprised to find nothing there. Just another hallucination. She sat up, looked down at her feet and noticed how one leg stopped at the knee. His first reaction was to shout in alarm. She shouted and thrashed about in the bed and nearly fell onto the floor. When the nurse came she was vomiting, trying to get the sickness out of her stomach.

"What's wrong, please? What's wrong? Calm down, please," the nurse said, as she turned up the morphine drip. Spit leaked from the corner of Elizabeth's mouth and her pupils were dialated.

"What have you bastards done with my leg? My fucking leg is gone!" And then she passed out.

A week later, Elizabeth's parents came and escorted her back to California.

22

"Hello, Mr. Karen? Damian Hutton calling. How are you?"

"Fine, Damian. What's on your mind? I got about two minutes," Michael Karen said.

"I've got a script for you."

"Damian, you know all you gotta do is send it. Your stuff goes right to my desk. If it's anything like *Glass House* or *The City,* then I'm interested. How long has it been since *The City* anyway?"

"Two years. I haven't really come across anything worthwhile until this last project."

"Well, let's hear the pitch," Michael said.

"Okay, you've got two characters: Martin, son of garment industry tycoon Bill Allen; and Pedro Sotomayor, son of Mexican immigrants. Well, it turns out that Bill is ignoring health and safety regulations at his SF warehouse, hiring illegal workers and firing them when they are injured on the job. Pedro's father had the misfortune of being crushed to death in Allen's warehouse loading dock, with his family receiving no compensation for his death.

"Because of his strong social conscience, and as a result of his father's lack of business ethics, Martin decides to make it on his own as a social activist. Working for a Latino community foundation, Martin meets and befriends Pedro, who has dropped out of school to work full time to support his mother and younger brother and sister. While Martin convinces Pedro to study for his GED, Pedro opens Martin's eyes to the poverty and oppression in Chiapas that drove his family to emigrate.

"Inspired by Pedro's story, Martin travels to Mexico on a humanitarian mission. After a brief stint in Tijuana investigating and lobbying to no avail for improved working conditions at his father's *maquiladora* factories, Martin heads south to Chiapas where he contacts Pedro's cousin and joins in the human rights struggle. By lying to his father about a business venture, Martin secures funding for the United Liberation Front, an armed peasant organization fighting for social justice and human rights against the Mexican government. Assuming the identity of Subcomandante Pablo, Martin puts the struggle on the map through internet publicity and support from international human rights NGOs.

When he appears with his ski mask on international television, assault rifle in hand, Martin is raised to cult status.

"In spite of Martin's success in gaining attention for the struggle, the Mexican army attacks and massacres the rebel army in the mountains of Chiapas. In the ensuing battle Martin disappears and is presumed dead. Some months later Pedro is surprised to receive a letter from his friend, penned in exile, in which Martin vows to take the fight for social justice and human rights global, while asking Pedro to keep his identity and whereabouts a secret.

"So that's it. What do you think?"

"I don't know, Damian. I've heard of this Subcomandante guy, but why make a film about him? I mean, I don't think the American public really cares about what's happening to some peasants down in Mexico. Still, I like the idea of this kid assuming a new identity to fight injustice. That has legs. Especially, since he chooses to help people out instead of taking over his dad's business. I like the irony of him using his dad's wealth to good purpose. Why don't you make some corrections and send it out to me, say, in a month? I didn't think *The City* would work, but after we cut the ending, you know, where the writer guy commits suicide and the kid from Kansas never ends up finding the American Dream, after we turned that around, it was fine. I mean a script doesn't have to be depressing to have value. It can be depressing up to the main conflict, halfway through or so, but after that there has to be a little redemption. You know what I mean? How long is this thing, anyway?"

Damian swallowed hard.

"Uh-um, one hundred and forty pages."

"That's too long, Damian, and you know it," Michael said. "No one wants to sit in the theater for two and half hours."

"Actually, films are getting longer."

"Whatever. If you want me to consider it, then it's gotta be at most one hundred," Michael said.

"That seems rather arbitrary," Damian said.

"Maybe it is. But it's ten minutes more than the average film. That ten minutes is for you 'cause you're a good kid and you've never given me a bum script."

"So then your interested?"

"Like I said, send it out to me and it'll go to the top of my list," Michael said. "More I can't promise you."

"Thing is, I wanna direct it myself," Damian said. It was time for the fast talk. "Listen, I wanna do this film on digital. I've already got the actors in place and most of the locations. I can make this film for a tenth of what it would cost you guys to make it. All I'm asking for is twenty percent."

"What's the budget?"

"Two hundred grand. At most two-fifty. Just think of the profit margin on that. For example, what did it cost to make *The City*, five million? And that's cheap because the film wasn't about special effects. And, last I heard, it pulled in almost twenty at the box office. Even if this film only makes a couple million, that would be good money for a two hundred thousand dollar investment."

"And what if it bombs," Michael asked.

"Even if it bombs, you're sure to make back the initial investment."

"I'll give you ten percent," Michael said.

"Fifteen," Damian said.

"Ten. Period. Listen I'm out of time. Take it or leave it."

"Okay, ten," Damian said.

"Good, you make the corrections on that script and then fly down here and we'll meet and work out the details. Oh, and Damian . . ."

"What's that?"

"You got balls, kid. Imagine calling and asking for two hundred grand just like that. You know the favor I'm doing you?"

"Yeah, but then do you know how much money you've made off those scripts I sold you for almost nothing?"

"Fair enough, Damian. Fair enough. We'll talk soon," Michael said. "Call Martia to set up a meeting."

With Solimar's distribution network they were sure to recoup the money. Just think of it as a loan, Michael told himself. He would have given Damian the money regardless. The kid had a good eye for the market, and what's more, his films were cheap to make compared to the thirty million and up action flicks; those were a risky bet. And what was two hundred thousand? It would probably cost more like five hundred. If costs went up they would just have to draw up a contract amendment, with the additional money provided entirely as a loan. Damian had, no doubt, underestimated the costs of filming abroad. Most of the movie would need to be filmed in Mexico, and that meant plane tickets and putting up the whole cast and crew in hotels and feeding them. Anyway, that was Damian's business. It was his budget and his production. And if it went well there would be plenty of profit for virtually no effort.

Damian knew he stood to make a lot of money if the film did well at the box office. Jack, he would pay maybe two or three grand from the original budget. Perhaps he had underestimated the price of the film, but then probably not. In Mexico, it would just be him and Jack, and maybe Henrik for sound, in addition to props and equipment. It would be an adventure, anyway, and the studio would foot the whole bill. Damian was excited at the idea of beginning the project. He still needed to rework the script a little and get the cast together. He would also have to scout locations. Damian needed someone to play Pedro and was unsure how to find him. I'd like to use real actors, but amateurs are cheaper.

This is it, Damian told himself. You've finally made it. It took you years to get that first script through the door. But then everything builds on itself. Without that first script you wouldn't be where you are today. The problem with people is that they want to do it all at once. You have to pay your dues, Damian thought. Sell a good script for nothing, help people out for free, and learn some skills with the camera, sound and editing. Bide your time in television and documentary production and then, boom, one day you pitch your own film and get a bunch of cash to play with. Karen's a good guy. He's got vision and that's why small independent films are the fastest growing segment of the industry. Big budgets are out. Every time the budget gets too big the film turns to shit and studios end up in the hole. When I start producing, I'm gonna go for cheap films with content. We've got to get out of special effects and back into plot.

Damian was the ambitious sort. He was always two steps ahead in his plans. He was already thinking about the festivals and distribution to Europe. And then he had his car park going and quite a bit of stock, the tech portion having long been sold and the more stable Dow stocks at bottom, but then he was young and could wait for the market to recover.

With the money I make on this film, I'm going to buy a house, he thought. Damian didn't plan to send any more scripts on spec to Solimar. Now that he had the money, he could concentrate on his own project. I better sit down and fix that script. Alex has explored every aspect of this idea, and I just have to make some adjustments.

Damian thought most people fools for working nine-to-five jobs at a subsistence wage. He felt confident that he could succeed at anything; all it took was a little nerve. Nerve is something you're born with, I suppose. And most people don't have any direction or ambition. That's the problem. People like that deserve to work meaningless jobs until they're dead. For people like that death is a gift.

Damian had always been a big-talker and an opportunist. Such traits had served him well. He knew himself as the weasel but never imagined that it would get him this far in life. He had just pulled the biggest coup of his career: he had fast-talked a film executive. By projecting success in his mind, he had made it a reality. And when the film was done and successful, he would go farther still. Pretty nice to get a paid vacation to Latin America. By cutting corners on production, particularly by hiring free talent, Damian would have money left over to spend on expensive hotels and nice restaurants. Why rough it if you don't have to? It's not like you're some guerrilla filmmaker who has to sell an organ to fund a project.

23

Arnold's father died in the hospital. He was in a coma and Arnold wasn't able to tell him goodbye. He didn't realize until then how important his father was to him and how it was always an assurance knowing he would be there if times got tough. Arnold found that he was able to live carefree and full of humor because he had strong family support. He knew if he ever failed in what he did, or wherever he went, he could always return home and be safe. Even when he was as far off as Thailand, drinking fruit cocktails and fucking underage Thai girls, he felt that security.

With the loss of his job and the death of his father, Arnold felt like the world was falling apart. Nothing was stable as it had been. The operation to save his father's heart had been very expensive, as well as the many days of hospitalization and care during which he was unconscious and didn't speak a single word: those days of absence until his death.

It fell on Arnold to sort out the confusing world of his family's finances. Because their insurance plan didn't completely cover the medical expenses, they were forced to dip into the family savings and sell some stock at a loss. For Arnold this meant that his allowance was finished and with it his financial security. For once he would have to live responsibly.

Arnold decided to move home and help manage the family pharmacy. He had two younger siblings who were starting high school and it was their future he had to think of. Money had to be put away for their college tuition. In the meantime, Arnold would have to pay rent on his apartment in the Marina. He could cover that by subletting it for a premium and pocketing the difference.

Arnold did not look forward to taking over the family finances from his father. He had never been good with money, which was fine in his own life, but not when his carelessness could affect others.

For the next few weeks, Arnold was occupied with planning the details of the funeral. He and his mother were in disagreement over whether to have his father buried or cremated. Arnold shuddered at the thought of his father being put in a box in the ground where he would rot and be eaten by worms. His mother was of the mind that to burn the dead was a disrespectful, pagan practice. Arnold didn't want to offend her by talking about the worms and decay. When I die my kids better burn me up, he thought. At my funeral I want everyone to party and have a good time. I'll have a keg of beer and some good music. Maybe we could do a funeral pool party? Dad would like that.

Never mind that empty hole in your chest. Forget about the loneliness and the fear that you'll never grow up and be a man like your father, or even some of your friends who already have a wife and family. Forget about it. You're just different, is all. You'll figure it out sooner or later. Doesn't mom always say that life doesn't throw us anything that we can't handle? No matter how tough it gets, you should be able to handle it. Arnold was ashamed of himself. If only I had been there more for my parents, worked harder and made a lot of money so they could be proud of me, he thought.

Mrs. Kazinski had always babied her only son. Perhaps she had spoiled him with so much love, but then love was a blessing to be shared. Still, she had never had the courage to ask him to move home, find a job nearby, marry and give her a grandson. It will all happen in due time, she told herself. But now when Arnold suggested that he come home to stay with her for a while and help with the kids, the business and the chores around the house (she wasn't as young as she used to be), she did not dissuade him. No, she was glad to have her son come home and promised herself she wouldn't be too demanding or meddle in his life or say what she thought of his girlfriends. So long as he didn't bring home any black, brown or yellow girls, it was fine with her. In spite of Arnold's numerous trips to Asia for summer break, she remained oblivious to his multicultural tastes. If anything Mrs. Kazinski was good mother-in-law material: tough and uncompromising with her values properly frozen in the past when people had a little backbone and stomach for misery.

24

Henrik had another meeting with Mr. Grear, who told him, "I don't know what's happening to music these days. It's not like it used to be, but I know my daughter Samantha liked your CD. In fact, she liked it so much she gave the extra copies to her friends. She said she had never heard anything like it. Samantha is sixteen, Henrik. She can't go to the clubs, but she's exactly the market were going for in this industry: high school kids with their parent's money to spend. Anyway, to get to the point, we'll sign you. But we can't put any money behind it. We'll sign you and give you, say, five percent of sales."

Henrik swelled with pride. It was the best news he'd heard in months, though five percent seemed like nothing, especially without promotion. Sure, his CDs would be in Virgo's stores, but no one would know who he was. He told Mr. Grear as much.

"Why would I give up the rights to my music for five percent, especially if you aren't going to put any money behind me? Man, I need a poster or a billboard or something. People need to hear my tracks on the radio. I need my CD in the listening station and it needs to be prominently displayed."

"Henrik, you're asking a lot. You can't just become a superstar overnight. As for the listening station, we can do that. We can send your disc out to local radio, no problem. But a poster's asking a little much. I mean, no offense, but you're a nobody. You can't just expect to have your own poster up in the window or at the bus stop like Nikki Star or Lisa Dawn."

"But you don't understand. If I had a poster, and if you put as much cash behind me as them, I would be the next big star," Henrik said. "You and I both know it's all marketing. I want fifteen percent of sales or no deal."

Mark thought: all these artists are the same. They think they're so bloody important, but what are they without distribution? I'm of the mind to tell him to get lost. Too bad he already works for me, and he's a good DJ, except for that abstract crap he plays every now and again. But then what do I know about it? Samantha's the best barometer of the market we've got.

"You can have seven percent. That's what you'd be getting anyway if you had an agent," Mark said.

"Fifteen up to a hundred thousand copies and then seven after that. I have to make my money, too."

"And you're going to keep working here?"

"For the foreseeable future. Still, this deal and my job have nothing to do with each other. I want that understood."

"Henrik, I'll give you seven percent. We'll put your CD on the shelf, add you to the listening station and get you a poster. But I can only do that for you at this store."

"But you're an international chain," Henrik said.

"The deal is through this store and exclusively through me. First you prove that people like your music and then we'll talk about expansion. And if you want copies of your disc you can buy them at cost, if you want to sell them on the side. That's my final offer."

Henrik knew he had reached the wall. He felt confident about his work but knew that even the big stars only got a small percent of what they sold. But they sold millions of copies.

"I'll take it."

"Great, I'll draw up the contract and have it ready next week," Mark said.

They shook hands and Henrik excused himself. At the door, he was overwhelmed with emotion. He had finally made it. He was being produced by a major record label in the United States. He felt his eyes grow misty and momentarily his arrogance faded.

"Thanks a lot, Mr. Grear. You don't know what this means to me. There are so many guys out there trying to make it and most of them just get buried by the competition. I didn't want it to be that way with me."

"No problem, Henrik. Just doing my job. You make money, I make money, know what I mean?"

"Yeah, I know what you mean."

For Mark, it was just an experiment. He'd run a few thousand copies of the CD to start out. It wouldn't be a big deal to put it in the listening station. If it did well, he might talk to headquarters and push to get it in the national stores. But that was only if it sold in the thousands. And that would probably never happen.

25

Duane left the office after working out the final details of payroll for the entertainment at the tech conference. That was the part of the job he disliked: the enormous amount of paperwork and endless phone calls that were necessary before and after a production. And the San Francisco Tech Conference was the biggest event they had ever done. It was a milestone for the company and the optimism of the higher-ups was contagious. After that it was only a matter of time before they were booked solid until the end of next year. Soon Duane would be heading to Atlanta for a company conference by the telecommunications giant Spirit. They had a lot of money to throw around and were asking for big talent, instead of those B bands that were so common on the conference circuit.

Gavin stood outside the Carl Price building by the convenience store with a soda in one hand and a hot dog in the other. All the standing and waiting was making him nervous. Most people get off at five, don't they? It was getting close to six and still no sign of him. Soon I gotta take a walk or folks is gonna get suspicious, he thought.

Gavin had his hat low over his eyes and his pants were piled up baggy on his white sneakers. He could feel the gun jammed in the back of his jeans under his shirt. The metal had warmed to his body. Maybe you shouldn't be packing. But then he could be one of those karate motherfuckers and you need it so he don't try nothin'. You ain't gonna shoot his ass, you just gonna fuck him up and scare him real bad. You gonna teach that motherfucker a lesson. Yeah, damn straight.

Every now and again, Gavin looked across the street to where his friends were waiting in the car. I hope they don't get restless and leave my ass here. No, they wouldn't do that. I'm in good with Biggs. At first, Gavin had entertained the thought of having Biggs come out and take care of it himself. But Biggs, he didn't like to get his hands dirty. No, man, you gotta deal with your own shit. It's time to take out the trash.

Gavin kept talking to himself that way, building himself up and making it so he wouldn't chicken out and leave. Aisha don't even know you doin' this. You ain't even checked to see how she been. You should get her a present or somethin'. But, man, she's gonna have a kid. You don't want no kid. No, this is for justice's sake. I ain't rich but I got justice, motherfucker. I'm gonna make you responsible for your behavior.

Duane came out of the building and walked with his briefcase up the street. Gavin stuffed the last of the hot dog in his mouth. His stomach was tight and nervous, and he had to wash the food down with his drink because he couldn't swallow it. He threw his trash away and fell into step behind Duane.

There you is. Yeah, you think everything cool like that. You think you gonna go home chill, but I got a surprise comin'.

Duane had parked in the garage a few blocks away. Though he only lived across town, he preferred driving to public transportation. There were too many unsavory types on the bus. No, he liked to stick to the clean and polish of the city and did his best to avoid the riff-raff and the crazies.

Gavin was waiting for his opportunity. He trailed Duane and thought of forcing him into an adjacent alleyway, but then a man came walking and interrupted his plan. On several occasions, Gavin worked himself up for the assault and then someone came along, or there was some traffic, and he chose restraint. I wonder where he's going?

They neared the Stockton Garage, and Duane went inside. They took the elevator together, and Gavin looked at the floor. The elevator was full. Everyone was heading home from work. Gavin and Duane were separated by the bodies.

They both got out on the second to last floor, and Duane walked to his car. Gavin recognized it from the school parking lot when Duane used to pick Aisha up from school. He paused by the elevator and let Duane get a lead. Then he followed after. Duane was putting his key in the door when Gavin came up behind him and pushed the gun into his back.

"Don't move or I'll cap your ass."

"My wallet's in my right pocket," Duane said.

"I ain't lookin' for no wallet, bitch. I don't need any uppity nigga like you telling me what I need. Do I look like a poor motherfucker to you?"

"No, you don't."

"That's right 'cause you're the poor motherfucker, motherfucker. And I wouldn't want to be you right now," Gavin said.

"Listen, what's this about?"

"I ain't got time for this. Get your ass in the car."

Duane did as he was told. Gavin climbed into the back seat and pushed the rear view mirror down so he was not in view.

"I want your eyes straight ahead. I don't want you lookin' at me."

"Where are we going?"

"We goin' to Ocean Beach."

Duane thought: who is this guy? Is he gonna kill me? What the hell have I done to him? He doesn't have his seatbelt on, maybe I should just floor it into the wall?

Duane drove out of the lot and paid the attendant. He thought of screaming for help but worried about the consequences. Is this reality? Everything is moving so slow. As he drove, Duane focused his attention on his surroundings. He thought about how much he loved the city. He took it for granted: especially the ladies. He never did manage to pick up on the assistant producer, Ellen, though it seemed like she hadn't gotten down with anybody for a long time. That's probably why: the longer it goes, the more uptight they get, he thought. Then it hit him: Aisha. This has to be about Aisha. The Point was a rough neighborhood, and Aisha must have enlisted some friends to get even. But she wasn't the vindictive and violent type, was she? Duane wondered how well he really knew her.

Or maybe this was one of the guys in her class who had a crush on her. God knows he had been by the school enough to be recognized, and if he remembered high school correctly, there certainly would have been talk about it. No one knows how to keep their mouth shut in high school, Duane thought. That's something you learn later. Tact. Well, this guy was young and didn't have much tact and probably not much self-control, either, so what would he do? It was kids his age that were really dangerous: still feeling immortal like superheroes and unable to control their emotions. Maybe he was Aisha's old boyfriend? Or maybe he was her brother? But she didn't have a brother, did she? Didn't she have a sister? If only he were a better listener. Damn Aisha. Damn, you should have never gotten pregnant. Bitch.

Never had it taken so long to get to Ocean Beach. They sat in silence until Duane's speculation got the better of him.

"Listen, can't you just tell me why you're doing this? I mean to me? Do I know you from somewhere?"

"This is payback. Everybody's gotta pay sooner or later, rich or poor. Man, you don't know what this is about? Yeah, you all fancy and whitewashed and shit, think you can kick it in the hood and play us like fools. You know damned straight what this is about, or you ain't as smart as you been frontin'."

They stopped at the light and Duane said, "Aisha."

"That's right, Aisha. Your pimpin' come back and bite you in the ass."

"Let's speak frankly. If Aisha's your girl then she never told me about it. I don't mess with that kind of stuff."

Duane felt the pull to talk low and tough: to drop his polite office speech, adapt to the moment, and try and get on the kid's good side through the slang. No, it's not your slang. You grew up in Carmel. You never learned to speak like that. You spoke like a surfer and now you speak like a television news reporter, especially when the information has to be clear.

"And if you and Aisha had a thing going, then is it my fault she went with me? That's just love, man."

"Yo, me and Aisha's none of your damn business. Shut the fuck up and drive the car."

Is this for real? Is this kid really talking to me like he's straight out of a Jackson Black flick? *"Shut the fuck up and drive the car?"* Damn kids these days trying to be hard. Man, this kid's lost and now he's gonna come take me out like he's Jackson Black, ghetto prince?

"Listen, let's talk straight," Damian said. "Don't tell me you never had sex without a condom. Accidents happen, but the girl's gotta take some responsibility too, right? Give me a little solidarity here, you know, man to man. Stick with your gender. I'm sorry it happened, but I offered to pay for the abortion. Some people don't like abortion, they think it's unchristian and all that. But, man, I don't think it's fair for Aisha to ruin her life with a kid. What the fuck is she gonna do with a kid? She shoulda been on the pill."

Gavin sat silent in the back seat. He had been with a couple girls without a condom, like that one time with Desiree when he didn't pull out in time and wanted to talk about it 'cause he was scared, but instead kept quiet hoping it would go away. Luckily, it did.

Dood be talkin' sense. That's women's business, condoms and the pill and shit like that. But then we talkin' about Aisha and the guy was just playin' her. Man, he's like thirty-years-old and he's goin' with a girl that's sixteen, that shit ain't right. Aisha was my girl and he gone ruined it, just used it all up. I hate them niggas that be thinkin' they white, speakin' all polite and shit, living uptown and thinkin' they all that.

"Well, what do you think," Duane asked him. "Doesn't it make sense? Man, if I've offended you in any way then I'm deeply sorry. What can I do to make it up to you?"

"Shut up and park the car, we goin' for a walk. There ain't nothin' you can do to make it up."

It was dusk when they pulled into the parking lot at the beach. In the distance the waves crashed as they rolled to shore.

"A'ight, gimme the keys and get out of the car."

Duane did as he was told.

Man, I haven't been to the beach in forever, Duane thought. The ocean sure is beautiful. I wonder if he's gonna shoot me? Well, it's true I didn't treat Aisha right. I'm a son of a bitch and I suppose I've created this situation. You knew it was superficial and wrong to go with a young girl like that. It was just the way she looked, because a woman never looks as good as when she's a teenager: from there it's all downhill as far as the body goes. It ain't easy being a man with all those magazines with young girls and singers like Nikki Star and those tiny t-shirts they wear that say "Pet the Kitty" and all that. Social living is nothing but hypocrisy. This fucker is going to walk me to the beach and shoot me. Man, people like him shoot each other for nothing because they've learned that life is cheap. What if I had grown up like them? Well, I'm used to the discrimination, too. Even when they try and hide it, you know what they're thinking. Mulattos, man, we're the true outcasts. When I get the chance I'll try and overpower him.

If I shoot this motherfucker, I'll go to jail, Gavin told himself. This ain't no movie. Life ain't no movie, though sometimes it feels like it.

"Get on your knees, bitch."

Duane did as he was told.

It was a weekday in the month of March and the beachside restaurant was deserted. It started to rain and the wind whipped at their clothes. Gavin had his hat low over his eyes and he walked around to face Duane. He pointed the gun at his head.

"Kiss my foot and beg me not to kill your ass," Gavin said, putting out his foot. I'm gonna enjoy this. Nigga think he's all smooth and now who's the man? "That's right, kiss my foot, bitch, then maybe I won't fuck you up."

It's now or never, Duane thought. Quickly, he grabbed Gavin's foot and shoved him backward.

The action took Gavin by surprise; involuntarily, he fired a shot as he lost his balance and fell. When he got to his feet again, Duane was face down on the pavement.

"Oh shit, oh shit, man. I shot him. Shit. Shit.

In a panic, Gavin reached down, rolled him over and held him in his arms. Duane was bleeding from the chest, his eyes were wide, and he was shaking and gasping for breath. With great effort, he said, "Tell Aisha I'm sorry." Then he stopped struggling and died. Gavin recovered from the shock of the moment and dragged the body to the car, where he locked it in the trunk.

That dumbass grabbed your leg. Shit man, it ain't your fault. You wasn't gonna kill 'im. You was just gonna bitch smack him and knock his ass out. You don't wanna go to no fuckin' jail. All that horrible shit that be happenin' in jail. You better get the fuck outta here. Yeah, lose the gun in the ocean, take the car and bail.

Gavin ran across the street and onto the beach. He stumbled through the sand, waded into the water with all his clothes and threw the gun as far as he could. It was the first time he had even been in the ocean. He fell in the current and thought: what the fuck are you doing, man, all this for a ho you ain't barely talked to.

The current was strong and it pulled him off his feet. Gavin tried to stand up again, but the water was too deep. He didn't know how to swim and he went under. He fought to get his head to the surface to breathe. It was dark now and he couldn't see the shore. A wave drenched him and held him down. He inhaled water, panicked and inhaled more. Then the current washed him out to sea.

26

April was a busy month. The news was out that Julie was HIV positive, and one day her parents came with a van to pick up her things. Jack and Alex were home and they helped to move the bed and anything else that was heavy. Mr. Stevens's face was tight, and in spite of his blank expression, his movements were aggressive and spastic. It seemed to Jack that he wanted to get everything out as quickly as possible and never see that place again. Jack wondered if he didn't hate that city for what it had done to Julie, and them, too, for not looking after her. Maybe he didn't think that at all, but there was bound to be resentment; if not for specifics, then for the world in general that had dealt his family a bad hand.

Mrs. Stevens's lips were tight, she was pale and there were circles under her eyes. Her movements were slow and deliberate. When they asked where to put things, or if she could step out of the way to let them by with the bed or the desk, she looked at them like they were ghosts. When they repeated themselves, she would manage a scarecrow smile and say, "Oh, thank you boys, you're so helpful," looking as though she might cry.

Jack found that he was over-polite and eager to help. He didn't want to make it any more difficult for them than necessary. Yes, Jack had social skills when he needed them; during the whole move he didn't mention Julie once, though she was on all their minds. Alex, for his part, buried his acid wit and sarcasm and did everything with the utmost efficiency and courtesy.

These poor people, Alex thought. The least I can do is help them move. When bad things happen they come in waves. Maybe it's for the best that Julie leaves this miserable pit, and maybe I should leave, too?

But there was a lot Alex liked about the city; he didn't think he could live anywhere else, except maybe New York. That was about it for intelligentsia and culture in the United States. Suburbia was not for him. He needed to have contact with the latest news and ideas. Access to information was essential to his craft. The internet was not yet sophisticated enough to provide what he needed; it was primarily a marketing tool and a forum for amateurs to discuss their opinions and preach their specialties. I bet things are better in Europe, Alex thought. I've heard good things about London. I bet they respect a serious author in Europe. But then, if you've learned anything, you know this back to Europe thing is hype. Still, maybe you should take a trip? Yeah, when you finish *Pax Americana* you deserve a trip.

Jack felt badly for what had happened to Julie. Especially after his luck with the In Quick gig when Duane had referred him to an agent he knew who called and asked, "How do you feel about modeling? With that publicity photo in the Chronicle I can get you in some shoots easy, and if you don't think you have what it takes, let me tell you something, honey, do you know how many women wrote in to the paper asking who you were? Also, I got In Quick bugging me about signing you to the band."

"But I can't sing."

"You don't have to know how to sing. You're just there for eye candy," she said.

After news of Julie, and then Duane's body being found in the trunk of his car, Jack had a hard time thinking about singing for In Quick or being a model. Are you really gonna be a fucking model and go around in your underwear and have people take your picture? What'll mom and dad say when they ask about work and you show them some magazine with you and some other guys lounging by the pool in your underwear like a bunch of fags? Then they'll really wonder what you been doing with yourself in the city. You've been feeding mom that line about working in marketing for the past couple months now. Man, what a shame lying to your own mother. It had to get that bad, didn't it?

I wonder what Duane was mixed up in to end like that? And now Julie's gonna die. What the hell do I say to these people? Yeah, I just wanted to say sorry about your daughter dying and stuff. She was a good girl, even though we didn't get along. And what about Henrik, that bastard, there's no way he's showing his face here today. I wonder if Julie's talked about him to her folks? From what Alex said, he got her into all kinds of bad shit. Still, I don't think she told them because then her dad would find Henrik and snap him in two to release all the anger he's got inside. Do you remember Henrik's face when Damian asked about it? I'd be that scared, too, if I was using needles and having unprotected sex with Julie and all those liberal, fuck it, those amoral urban hipsters and groupies with no soul he hangs out with. I wonder if he's gonna get tested? I remember I got tested once and I was scared to death about it. That must be what it's like when you're waiting on death row, Jack thought. Sort of, anyway.

I wonder who we're gonna find to live in that closet? The rent's cheap but, man, it's a crapshoot. It's a pretty important decision because there are a lot of freaks in this town; you've seen them on the bus and everywhere else you've been. Well, Mr. Stevens is a decent guy and I feel bad for making fun of those nervous father messages with Alex. At least he's gonna pay through the month. He even said he understands our situation. Poor guy. I'm even willing to let the rent slide. But then I wouldn't have been a few months ago when I was rotting hopeless in my room. Shit man, why does life have to be so tough? Remember how Julie looked at you when you went to visit her in the hospital a few weeks ago? I suppose you can't know what she meant by that look, but she seemed so alone then. And she said, "Jack, I'm sorry that we didn't get along. I've always liked you. I just didn't think you liked me. I wish we could have talked more. I bet you have a lot to talk about, though you don't say much."

Jack didn't have much to say after that, either, just something polite that he had learned from movies and books and his parents on formal occasions.

Jesus, Julie, why'd you have to go and say that and make my heart hurt like I'm losing my own sister? Why'd you have to go and get mixed up like that, and now look what's happened.

Jack was sentimental all right, but he had built up a hard shell around his softer parts and learned to keep a straight face and not cry. He was the sort to keep his pain and suffering to himself. When it was really bad, Jack stuck it out alone so as to not burden anyone with his problems. But damn, he felt for her. His own problems seemed small since he still had his health; he didn't know what he would do without his health.

In the end, he took Candice Newman as his agent mostly on Damian's recommendation.

"Trust me," Damian had told him, "it's better to have someone else manage your career. They know about this stuff, and she wouldn't have called you if she didn't think you were a good investment. It's impossible to get anything done if you manage your own career. Just promise me one thing."

"What's that?"

"That you'll do this film for me and you won't accept anything else until it's done. Right now you can go and model or whatever and make a little money, but in a month or so I'm gonna need you here one hundred percent," Damian said.

"Of course. I owe all this to you, anyway. If it hadn't been for you I wouldn't have met Duane . . ."

"Yeah, Duane."

"I know, poor guy."

They fell silent.

". . . and the show with In Quick wouldn't have happened and then Candice wouldn't have called me," Jack continued. "Man, anything you need, I'm there for you."

Jack was a man of his word who liked to pay his debts, financial or otherwise. Helping Damian with the movie was the least he could do. If it hadn't been for Damian, then his life might have been a different one altogether. Let's not get ahead of ourselves, Jack thought. All this is still speculation.

"It just seems so strange the way everything has happened," Jack said. "Almost as if it's all connected somehow. I can't explain it. It's not a feeling I'm used to."

Damian smiled.

"Let me tell you something, Jack," Damian said, putting his arm around him. Such it was with Jack that he couldn't resist the temptation to touch him. Call it a weakness. Though Damian knew better, he was getting attached to Jack and doing his best to keep him around and dependent.

"What you're talking about, this feeling of things coming together, once you've got that then you can realize all your goals," Damian said. "The idea is that subconsciously we project our reality. The greater your ability to follow your intuition, the easier it becomes to make the right decisions in your life. You have to learn how you can work and fit together with other people without pushing. When it's supposed to happen, it happens. That's why it's important to come into contact with as many people as possible. That way you increase your prospects and are able to anticipate opportunity. It's the same for business as it is for love. You have to read the signs and act. This is your moment, Jack. Now you have the opportunity to live up to your potential. Deep down, you've already anticipated this. You've known it in your subconscious mind. It led you away from your life in Arizona and the jobs you hated. Jack, you're ambitious, and I bet there are many things you know about yourself that you don't share with anyone because you're afraid of appearing arrogant. But everyone can see it right there in your posture and the way you walk and how you talk to people."

Jack had never thought about himself in that way. Part of him thought Damian was talking nonsense, while another part wanted to believe it was true.

Damian had his own interests in mind. Since the failure of his last relationship, and the lack of passion that ended their sexual relapses, Damian found himself more attracted to men and particularly, Jack. He had always been attracted to Jack but never confident to explore his feelings for fear of failure. It would probably never amount to anything, he thought. Jack was as straight as they came, while his own feelings were probably just the result of taboo and boredom and the fact that the women he liked had never given him the time of day and seemed haughty and arrogant and altogether a headache. Why not just try it out once and see how it is, not with Jack but someone else, someone that you don't know that well who you can make disappear afterwards so it doesn't haunt you? Do you just like beautiful men because you aren't one yourself?

"Listen, I know you have your reservations about modeling," Damian said. "But look at it this way, it pays well and people will see your face. Sure, I know you came here with the idea of working for a company. I know you've got a head for business. It's just you don't have any money, right? Well, take this opportunity to save some up. Save the money and invest in some stock. Milk it for what it's worth, and when it's over, hopefully you'll never have to work again."

"I think you're getting carried away," Jack told him.

"No way. See, that's where you're wrong. You have to dream big. And you have to learn to walk, talk and act like you mean business and that you know exactly what you're doing. That's your mistake, Jack. You've got to cut the modesty."

Then Damian decided to break the news. He had been saving it for the right occasion, like a child hoarding candy, and now it was time to divulge his secret.

"Soon we're gonna be in Mexico, man. I got money for the film and the script is almost done."

"Mexico? What are we gonna do there? Is that where the film takes place?"

"Partly. I'll tell you all about it later. Anyway, it's just gonna be us, man, chilling on the beach for a month or two down there. Sure, we'll film, but we'll also hang out. You've never been out of the States, right?"

"Nope."

"Well, this is going to be the experience of your life," Damian said. "That's synchronicity. Everything coming together and being right. Man, aren't you excited?"

Damian's optimism was contagious. What does Damian see in me that I don't, Jack wondered. He talks like I'm gonna be president or something. Well, he's always been full of crazy ideas. If he wants me to do this movie and come with him to Mexico, it sounds good to me. Sure is a lot more exciting than sticking around here.

27

Arnold sat on the living room floor surrounded by boxes. He was not a man who liked change, and now he was leaving the city and returning to his mom's house after eight years on his own. What had gone wrong? Why hadn't he found the success he was looking for? He blamed himself for his failure.

During the flight back from San Diego, after his father's funeral, he'd had plenty of time to think. He came to the conclusion that if he'd just worked a little harder, managed his money better and taken more risks, then he would have made a life for himself. Was he just a lazy dreamer? Sometimes the thought came to him that he wasn't made for this world; he was far too sensitive. He had grown up safe in the love of his parents and they hadn't prepared him for the hostile reality in which he now found himself.

With time, Arnold had grown suspicious of the professional class in their suits and ties, cell phone babble and accessory souls. He was no longer fooled by their posturing. He knew that many of them didn't live a life they believed in. They were entirely cynical about money and that made them unhappy. When I lived like that I wasn't happy, either, he thought. Arnold saw nothing but hypocrisy in their lunchtime rituals where false laughter mixed with rent-seeking behavior. They have an hour a day to show off and then it's back to the same meaningless number-crunching, marketing of useless products, promotion of unnecessary services, and profiteering on necessary services that had once been free. They were enemies of the social contract, trying to make money while eroding everyone's quality of life.

Arnold thought: I'm through screwing people over by adopting a value system I don't support so I can rub my cynicism and amorality in their faces by showing off to earn their respect and envy. What kind of sick cultural formula is that? It just doesn't make sense when you think it through.

I really should call someone to fix that window. The carpet and the armchair are ruined now by the rain, since you left it that way when you went to SoCal. Maybe you can put a rug over there for whoever moves in?

Arnold packed slow, saying goodbye to possessions that recalled memories of his past relationship and interests. His personal projects illustrated the path his growth had taken. He was reminded of his attempt to learn to play the guitar, his fleeting passion for tribal masks, the women whose busts had formed his fertility tree at Burning Town, and his weapons collection. He studied the photos of friends, old and new, at all manner of social gatherings and events; and those of trips he had taken large and small, like his three-month journey to Asia. He found old notes and scraps of paper with names and numbers of men and women he no longer recalled and ideas for projects he had never started. He considered his dormant exercise equipment, his mediocre paintings (what were you doing thinking you could be a painter?), and his shrunken head collection from New Guinea. Who would have thought human heads could come so cheap? I guess life is cheap. People think life is worth something but it's really cheap. It's the one thing we have in abundance. Too much life makes life hard. Stop thinking like that.

As if it hadn't been enough that his whole life was coming apart, Julie was HIV positive. Arnold had always liked Julie. She is fragile and misunderstood like me, he thought. She was trying too hard to please everyone and forgot to look out for herself. And Henrik didn't help any.

Well, that's their business. There were times when you wanted to strangle Henrik, but then even you have self-restraint.

It took all your effort to cheer yourself and the others up. That's why you always drank so much. They didn't know it, but that day before your visit to see Julie in the hospital, after your trip to see your dad in the hospital, you were drinking all day sitting in this apartment with the lights out and the curtains drawn. You were thinking about relativity and how quickly a life could be altered and destroyed. You thought: there isn't enough time to wait until tomorrow like you always have, because it may never come. Waiting until tomorrow is a dangerous firework trick of hope. You can't afford to sit in limbo any longer imagining that what you were hoping for is going to fall into your lap. Remember when settling down was on your mind? Jenny from the party, she was a nice girl, but that just faded out, didn't it? There must be a reason for it beyond apathy. There must be something fundamentally wrong with your value system. You've got the poison of the suits in you, and now it's time to detox from that status quo, look-the-other-way, not-in-my-backyard, ignorance-is-bliss bullshit. God only knows how painful it's gonna be to try and live like a decent human being and responsible citizen.

It would have been nice to talk about how you really felt for once, but you didn't want to burden your friends with your problems and be a downer. They expected a certain quality of behavior from you. You didn't have the luxury to go moping like Jack, and you couldn't become an opportunistic cynic like Damian, or a misanthrope like Alex. No, they expected you to be happy and to make them feel like life was worth something; as if somehow we were the center of the world, our little group, and that if we stuck together we would make it. And sure we'll make it, but the question is where? Will we make it where we thought we would when we were children? Will we make it to where we dreamed? When was the last time you dreamed about anything but survival? Why, you don't even dream of vacation anymore because life is holding you too tight.

So that's how it is, Arnold thought. Your dad dies and your friend is dying, and there's no way for you to reach either of them or for anyone to reach you. No, it's best to keep quiet about it and carry it with dignity. You were happy and larger than life because you could be. You had that luxury. But now that there's no money, and with your debts, you're in real trouble. It's all coming back to you now. I wonder, without the alcohol and the Prozac, Xanax and Valium, would you have made it through any of this? That's the problem with growing up in a pharmacy. Sure, you were a nervous kid, but they didn't have to go and fill you with pills.

Arnold was drinking vodka from the bottle and packing while blasting his favorite songs on the stereo. After an hour or two, he ordered out for Chinese.

When the food arrived he was sufficiently drunk but trying to stay serious to himself. You're not drunk. If that box weren't in the way you wouldn't have fallen and cut yourself.

Arnold shoveled bits of Szechwan beef and rice into his mouth and thought: after this I'll just take a little nap. Damn, this shit's spicy. I'm not leaving for another week, anyway. I suppose I should have told the others I was leaving. But then, with Julie and all, it wasn't the right time.

I need to drink up all the liquor in the house before I leave. No point in trucking it back home. Mom's got plenty more where that came from. Mom's liquor cabinet has served you well in the past, like when you were in high school and you filled water bottles to take to the party.

I wonder how Jack's doing? Didn't Damian say they were going to make a movie together? I wouldn't mind helping them make a movie.

Eventually, Arnold passed out on the couch. During the stress of the last few months he had put on weight, and now he lay there with his mouth open, snoring, his face damp with sweat. In his alcohol dreams a Chinese girl in a brilliant blue silk gown appeared on the opposite bank of a river and beckoned to him. It was Mei Li, and before he could reach her, she turned and disappeared into the fog.

28

Jack stuck with Mrs. Newman, his agent, and his main thought was money. You need money, and if you can make some now, then things will be easier later because you don't know how long this will last. Experience has taught you that things come to an end, that you have to make the best of them, and that when they're gone you have to let them go and look ahead. Like Damian said: your problem is your lack of vision for the future.

With time Damian had become Jack's mentor. He speaks a lot of sense, and the truth is I owe him everything, Jack thought. He found me a place to live, got me a job, made connections for me and now he's going to put me in his movie. It was hard for Jack not to get carried away. Damian's optimism was spreading.

It really is all about who you hang out with, Jack thought. Alex doesn't hang out with anyone and that's why he'll never make it.

For the first time Jack had a little money in the bank, almost two thousand dollars, and just that fact made him more confident.

Mrs. Newman had hooked him a modeling job with an Italian clothing company called Baducci or Bellini or something like that, and they were going to take some pictures in the studio. Jack was told not to shave and that all he needed to do was show up and the photographer, art director and make-up crew would do the rest.

Jack had only put on make-up once before in his life. Even now when he looked at that picture of himself in the Chronicle, he was embarrassed. He kept the article folded up in the drawer of his desk, and the stack of newspapers that Henrik had bought for him sat on the floor at the foot of his bed. He never told his parents about his experience. Under no circumstance would he put that picture on the wall. The only picture Jack had up was of himself in uniform for U of A with his mitt: the same mitt that hung on the wall above his bed.

Jack wasn't sure what to expect at the photo shoot. He had seen the pictures of men in the fashion magazines that Julie left lying on the couch. He remembered their vacant stares and bored expressions when surrounded by beautiful women. It just doesn't make sense, Jack thought. Hey, what if I get to meet some supermodel chicks? In spite of the women, Jack thought the men looked gay posing with each other in their tight clothes. Benign situations, like a trip to the swimming hole with some buddies, always came out lewd and provocative in a photo shoot for a fashion mag.

I don't know if I can look or behave like that, Jack thought. If they want to take a picture of me and I don't have to look like that, fine, but I'm not opening my eyes real wide, pushing my lips forward or sticking out my ass like those fags.

Jack found himself wondering about the other men that would be there and how they might look. He worried a little about the burn mark on his chest. It wasn't as bad as it had been, it was healing, but if they had to have their shirts off what would he do? Maybe some make-up could cover it up? He stood in front of the mirror flexing and admiring his physique. Before he left, he did fifty push-ups and fifty sit-ups, fast enough and until it burned, and that gave him confidence. I wonder if there'll be anyone there bigger than me? During the bus ride downtown, Jack was preoccupied by his scar and felt that everyone could sense his imperfection.

Jack arrived at the studio and was introduced to the photographer, Yves, with his shaved head, earrings and hip clothes. His face was much like a criminal's with a broad nose, square chin and lumpy skull; his eyebrows were thick and nearly grown together. Jack met the art director, not the famous designer Sergio Baducci himself, but his assistant, Marco.

Sergio? Oh, he was on a yacht off the Emerald Coast of Sardinia. To Jack, it didn't matter, he had never heard of Sergio Baducci or worn any of his clothes; no, he wore jeans, crew neck t-shirts and tennis shoes. Fashion didn't matter to him. He wanted to be comfortable and liked to wear clothes that fit. He wasn't down with the baggy style.

Jack remembered his waiter days at Amerika and how the Italian, Andrea, used to dress like he was going to the theater or a formal dinner when he went out. Marco dressed the same. He was wiry and serious, his hair was black and perfect, he had a hooked nose, and his eyes were very blue and too large for his face. He wore a blazer and a bright-patterned shirt with a flared collar, off-white pants with zip pockets and black pointed leather shoes. It always surprised Jack that men would spend so much time on their appearance when they could just as well get away with putting on whatever was handy. Jack had never cared for the urban hip of the city and now he was going to be modeling it. He would embody the image of urban success for all the laughing faces of the warm and glowing, display-windowed, polished wood and brass bars and restaurants that he had forgone out of shame and destitution on his solitary walks in the past.

"We really have to do something about that hair. Claire, can you cut his hair, please? It's just a disaster. I mean, *veramente*," Marco said in his Italian-accented English. "Make it short, but I don't want it neat, no, I want to look a bit like –well, like a badly trimmed bush. I want it a little uneven and leave the back; whatever you do, don't clean up the back. I want it to look like he's had a long night. He has such a classic face; his solid cheekbones and the strong nose will make up for what is messy and superficial with the hair. I want him to be like a statue that has been marred by the elements but still retains its integrity."

What the hell is this guy talking about, Jack wondered. It was the first time in a long time that he had let his hair creep down his neck and over his ears. Haircuts cost money. Jack liked his hair short, shaved on the neck and clean above the ears. But lately he had been too preoccupied by his future to give a damn about his appearance. The irony did not escape him now and he smiled in spite of himself.

He met the other models, two men and a woman. The woman, Lexi, was a thin yet busty blonde that moved and looked like a cat. Anthony was thin with delicate features and a fair complexion. He had curly blond hair, blue eyes, and was shaped like a martini glass. Paul had dark hair and eyes and olive skin. His bold and exaggerated features somehow fit together in their monstrosity: thick lips, wide mouth, large eyes, and a conical nose. His eyes hypnotized and paralyzed, and one half-expected him to tear into a person with his teeth and pierce them with his nose. His hands were large enough to palm a basketball and his feet were like small skis.

Jack was not oblivious to the otherworldly appearance of the two men. He began to wonder what he was doing there and what people might say of his appearance. He knew he wasn't pretty like Anthony or a playboy like Paul. But I'm in the best shape, he told himself. Paul is bigger than me, but he isn't as cut. And Anthony, he's small and looks like a girl; that was the kind of guy Jack was suspicious about. I'm just an ordinary guy, Jack thought. And I like it that way.

Lexi hadn't done many fashion shoots with men. She was not famous and had never been out of the country, but she had gone to New York twice for big shoots for *Woman* and *Her Life*. She had done an eyeliner commercial for an internationally recognized brand which she hoped would launch her into the lucrative couture market and pave her way from San Francisco to Paris. New York didn't agree with her. She had tried living there for a year and found it stressful; she missed the beach and the laid-back California attitude.

Anthony had come up from Los Angeles for the shoot; it was a break for him landing a job with one of the world's top designers with stores in seventeen different countries. His biggest gig to date was an appearance in *MS, Men's Style*; before that he had mostly done commercials for toothpaste, computers and assorted frozen and processed food. He was trying to be an actor and, in spite of his rare appearance, had a great disdain for modeling and models. He was an expert at picking up on women with feigned indifference.

Paul was a world-class model. He had worked in Europe and was an occasional fuck friend of last year's male model of the year, Milton Verias, the Brazilian. Paul was occasionally straight but mostly gay. He was a favorite of Sergio Baducci, who he modeled for frequently and who was not averse to letting handsome men suck his dick. Paul had built his career by putting out and, consequently, always had plenty of work. He liked to have a good time, didn't worry much about the state of the world and wasn't someone burdened with a mission in life. He enjoyed his lifestyle and he followed his passions, falling in and out of love on a regular basis.

Paul lived in South Beach, close to his mother's native Cuba. It was the only place in the United States with any action. He was a regular at the hottest dance clubs and was often seen driving up and down the strip in his yellow convertible blaring Cumbia, Rumba, Merengue, or any other

Latin genre with a frenetic beat, though he spoke Spanish haltingly having spent most of his adolescence trying to be white. But times had changed and now his heritage was something to be exploited; it was certainly a part of his beauty and appeal.

He liked Europe, but only in the summer when it was warm, and mostly Spain where they knew how to party. Clouds and rain depressed him: depression being a highly unusual and unwelcome emotion for a young man who didn't think much about the future of the world he lived in.

Given Paul's inability to live in Europe, or anywhere else with a bad climate, it was problematic that the industry was centered in New York, Milan, Paris and London. For the fall and winter season he would often opt for domestic gigs with less important magazines and designers, especially on the West Coast, where it was all about sports clothing and bathing suits, which meant the occasional trip to Mexico. But the fashion market was expanding; Sergio was opening an emporium in the Financial District across from his more established rival, Giorgio Aldini. Baducci needed some quick billboard shots and an ad or two in an American publication like *MS*; it was easier and cheaper to use little-known American models and keep Paul to lend the ads commercial credibility.

Paul didn't think much of models, particularly the women. He liked women with curves, not girls that looked better on a stake in a cornfield. As for Jack and Anthony, he had seen beautiful men before and only went with models more famous than himself. He had a particular weakness for artists of any sort, given that he was not creative himself; he made exceptions for famous women, anemic or not; and he courted producers and directors when he was in L.A., because he still held onto the hope of becoming an actor. Paul's sexual opportunism had even earned him a part in a large budget feature film, but when the camera rolled and he had to speak, he couldn't remember his lines, or he spoke them awkwardly and without the appropriate emotion. Truth be told, he had a hard enough time playing himself. In spite of his poor performance, Paul continued to ingratiate himself with the Hollywood scene in hopes of landing another film role. He wanted more than anything to be part of the super famous: the trendsetters. Though he liked the company of beautiful people, he preferred men with ideas and talent who could sit down and talk passionately about subjects he did not understand.

Jack had his hair styled and his make-up done before joining Marco at the apparel racks. Marco put his fingers over his mouth and held his chin. His brow wrinkled and he talked to himself, "No, no, we need something black, it must be simple and honest like a good confession."

Marco walked along the rack and ran his fingers along the fabric of the outfits until he found what he was looking for.

"Oh, perfect. Just what was missing."

Marco draped a pair of slacks over his arm, walked on and selected what looked like a woman's blouse with puffy sleeves, embroidery and a drawstring collar. He continued along the far rack and took out a blazer, frowned, put it back, and took out another, which he held up to Jack's shoulder.

Jack felt like when he went shopping with his sister and she held up all the clothes and asked how he liked them. In the beginning he had tried to be sincere and specific; it was only later that he learned to be supportive and vague. When she tried to trick him with comparisons or ask him don't-you-think questions, he learned to stick to his guns and say he liked them all the same, even though they were different. Now he stood there and thought: well, at least I'm getting paid for my time. He can look all he wants. I'd like to sit down but that might look bad, like I don't care.

Marco finally found the clothes he wanted for everyone, and they all changed in front of each other in the communal dressing room. No one was shy about it; they stood there in their underwear, and Jack found himself counting Lexi's ribs.

Jack put on the pants, extremely tight in the crotch and made of some strange stretch material, then the linen shirt with the puffy sleeves. It's okay, you look like a pirate; it's not a blouse, it's for when it's hot and you're in the Caribbean or someplace like that. Next, he slipped into the black corduroy jacket with the faux fox fur collar and cuffs and gray goat horn buttons. Finally, he stepped into some black zip-up leather boots with ornamental buckles.

They were directed to a set consisting of some palatial furniture in mahogany with crimson velvet upholstery, a maroon carpet with black, white and blue floral patterns and scrolling vine ornamentation, a brass regency chandelier festooned with glass beads and affixed to the exposed steel beams of the bare ceiling, and burnt sienna wallpaper with a tiger orchid motif that ran the length of the wall behind the couch.

Yves, the photographer, positioned Lexi, her make-up thick and whorish, on the couch with her legs folded underneath her and her heels scattered on the rug. Some cocktails were placed on the table and she was told to light a cigarette. Anthony sat on one side of the couch and was directed to look away from her. Paul was instructed to look at the floor.

"Remember, Paul, you're dissatisfied, you're bitter, you hate the woman but you want her all the same time, though you're too proud to admit it," Yves told him.

Jack was ordered to sit in the facing chair with a martini in hand and fix Lexi with a hostile glare as she stared at an undetermined point in the distance.

Yves talked to them constantly.

"Yes, yes, that's great Jack. She's been cheating on you with two other men and you've caught her, and Lexi, listen Lexi, you're ashamed but you're also happy to be making all these men suffer for you. Paul, could you turn your head just a little so the light catches your jaw? Okay, okay, that's good. Anthony, yes, Anthony, unbutton your pants and look at me. Look at the camera like you want to have your way with it."

Occasionally, Yves would get agitated and raise his voice. "Yes! Yes! This is beautiful. Oh, perfect! Hold it, hold it, I'm in heaven. Perfect!"

At other times he was lost in concentration and didn't utter a word so as to not disturb the mood.

Jack wondered how long it was going to last, but soon he forgot about the time and began to think about the scenario that Yves had constructed. It was a sordid love affair and game of seduction. Every instruction was meant to elevate the tension and ambiguity of their relationships: Lexi sitting in Anthony's lap, while the other men stared on with jealousy; Lexi lying on the floor with her blond hair spread out on the carpet with the three men looking down at her from their seats; Anthony straddling her and pinning her arms to the floor with his hair hanging in his eyes; Jack and Paul toasting each other with fluorescent cocktails and taciturn expressions; Lexi on all fours on the couch nose to nose with Jack with her ass in Paul's face; Lexi throwing her arms around Paul and Jack with Anthony kneeling at her feet; Anthony pulling Lexi roughly from the couch; Lexi kissing Paul on the cheek as she is pulled away; Lexi clinging to Jack with her head on his chest as he drinks and stares off into the distance; Lexi, Jack and Paul laughing together while Anthony stands awkward and apart; Lexi with a rose in her teeth dancing with Anthony; Paul and Jack arm wrestling on the table; Paul and Jack with their arms around each other; and Jack ultimately feeling uncomfortable and confused by the false narrative of Yves' camera.

Jack had never paid much attention to appearance. Sure, he paid attention to attractive women, like any other guy, while remaining ignorant to the details of beauty: the tricks of make-up, fashion, and sensuality that all formed part of the package. For Jack, it was a novelty to see men go through this superficial transformation. Before he would have never measured his male friends on their appearance. For the most part, barring deformity, Jack considered them all to be like himself: ordinary guys that could pull an attractive girl if they made the effort and the timing was right. So long as a guy kept in shape, wore clean clothes, and took the time to shave and shower, he could expect to land a nice girl.

That was how Jack had thought before the shoot. It was Yves' camera, the contrived set, and the designer clothes that brought to Jack's attention the concept of beauty and its many subtleties, gradations and variations. Beauty, Jack began to realize, was an act of manipulation. For the flawed masses, being beautiful was the conscious act of enhancing one's attributes and minimizing one's faults; for those who were born with golden ratio proportions, it was about dissimulating perfection so as to avoid both persecution and veneration, or the destructive sides of the dialogue of vanity between the individual and society.

Perhaps Jack was better off being ignorant of the complexity of a system of discrimination based on appearance by which individuals manipulated each other for purpose of their own self-advancement, through offspring or otherwise, and whereby corporations manipulated consumers into filling the gap of their insecurities with material goods. For humanity, veneration of physical beauty was based entirely on the impossibility of its possession through merit, knowledge, discipline or force.

Would Jack forget what he had learned as a boy in the deserts and canyons of Arizona: that natural beauty was the manifestation of a balanced biological system in which every plant and animal played an equally important role in the preservation and evolution of life, and that attempts to control, manipulate, acquire and/or exploit such a system only led to corruption, waste and eventual destruction?

Jack found himself admiring Paul and Anthony's good looks. He was sure that neither of them had to worry about meeting women or making friends. Jack realized that he was attracted to them, not in the primal way he had always been attracted to beautiful women, but because their appearance indicated their success with such women and with life in general. They were the kind of guys you wanted for friends because they made you look good knowing them. It was no accident that attractive people hung around primarily with each other. And with that epiphany, that a guy could be attracted to other guys without wanting to bend them over or suck their cocks, came another: Jack's participation in the shoot made him their peer and equal. He was in fact beautiful, something that he had never seriously considered. Perhaps he had never thought of it that way because it wasn't appropriate or practical for a man to consider his appearance: that was vanity and, in the worst case, a gateway to homosexuality. Now Jack understood such thinking to be wrong; it was okay to be attractive and know it, and it was possible to be attractive without being vain. He had always hated vanity. Finally, Jack was coming to understand the value of his beauty and why people treated him the way they had all his life.

There is power in looking good and being aware of your body, Jack thought. The mind controls beauty and allows us to appreciate it. But then that awareness makes you artificial and insecure, which is a limitation to your freedom.

The strange reality that surrounded him, where image ruled over other concerns, had changed Jack and how he thought of himself. Was this the power Damian had been talking about that would inevitably make him famous? While he had been chosen to represent an ideal for others, Jack was equally aware, from his experience behind the scene, that it was an illusion and that desiring it would make it disappear. Was he disappearing?

He remembered the man and the woman at the party with their sex games, The Green Lantern brothel, Arnold's bust collection and the duel with Danny the Kid, and was once again unable to distinguish the fine line that separated fantasy from reality. Was it true that a person could do anything they wanted if only they had the courage to imagine? That had been his failing.

Jack likened the relatively banal photo shoot to a religious experience. By posing for the camera, he became an image separated from his own suffering and doubt, and was momentarily liberated from the grinding reality of his weaknesses and fears.

Yves used the camera to invade people and discover the intensity of their hidden emotions. He was quick to notice and exploit the tension between Jack and Paul: that balance of attraction and fear between two adversaries who were uncertain whether to fuck or kill each other, or both. His work brought out the lust, jealousy, fear and hate lurking under the surface of their blank expressions. For though the models gave a pleasant face and form to the clothes, they inevitably invested those garments with the emotional drama that Yves manipulated with such alacrity and grace and with which anyone could identify. Yves understood the careful balance between the perfection that individuals aspired to, the decadence they cultivated, and the shame they felt they deserved. It was this formula that served so well to sell clothing. What most people desire in their lives, Yves reasoned, is a little drama; if possible, they prefer to be abused by someone beautiful rather than uphold dull social conventions among their equally ordinary peers.

At one o'clock, the models stopped for a catered lunch. It was hot underneath the lights and Jack found himself guzzling the bottled water. Everyone was hungry and they didn't talk much, concentrating instead on their bento boxes. They were all perfect strangers, though the pictures would have told a different story, and no one seemed to see the point in exchanging superficial dialogue. By now they were accustomed to saying everything with their eyes, faces and posturing, but like abstract painting, they could also be accused of saying nothing at all; it was probably for the best that they kept quiet so as to not ruin the illusion of perfection. Jack had kept his face that way all his life, expressionless and seemingly oblivious, and it had worked out for him. Somehow it had gotten him places; people trusted him.

Paul had seen a thousand young men like Jack. Once, he had been one of them. When he finally learned his place as a commodity, Paul dedicated his life to appearance. He realized that Jack, and young men like Jack, would one day take his place. But he was also aware that Jack was blind to his own potential and lacked the nerve to test the limits of his world. Jack was just the sort of young man he had been: perhaps too good for the world, perhaps confused, struggling with the occult and overt desire of third parties and learning that his own feelings and thoughts came secondary to how people wanted to treat him. There would always be those who would try to hold him down because he was beautiful and others that, for the same reason, would allow him to behave as he saw fit. Jack had the characteristic caution of the beautiful: the desire to not stand out or be exposed to the ugliness and cruelty of life.

Maybe that was Jack, or maybe it wasn't. Maybe Paul was simply looking back on his own life and seeing his own development and the innocence he had lost. For a moment he wanted to mentor Jack and introduce him to that world of illusion and passion without love: to the temporality of the fashion and entertainment industry and its inherent incest and perversion. Or maybe he wanted Jack to discover it for himself and accept it, or walk away a better man.

During the shoot, Paul wondered what he might have become if he had chosen differently. Perhaps my whole life has been a waste and I am good for nothing, he thought. No, that's not it. Thank God I got in and was not left outside like so many others who had the dream and wanted one day of immortality, who suffered with their unfulfilled ambitions, and who stared at my picture with envy and wondered why they hadn't been born beautiful or gotten that job they felt they deserved: all those desperate individuals who kick themselves for not knowing the right people and being lucky like me or Jack.

Is this beauty perfection or a flaw, Paul wondered. Certainly, it can be both. But this is business and I am a professional. I know how to communicate my emotions without saying a word. I can appear vulnerable, innocent or confident simply through body language and the quality of my gaze. That is what separates a good model from a pretty face. You have to know how to carry that beauty: how to share it and withhold it. People expect it of you. They assume grace and beauty are one and don't understand that one can be beautiful and awkward at the same time; one can be beautiful and uncomfortable, one can easily be crushed by beauty and become a slave to it.

To appear natural, Paul thought constantly about how to portray natural emotions. He was more interested in appearance than emotion. By mimicking emotion he had divorced himself from it. Even when making love he was conscious of how he looked. Paul liked to watch himself in the mirror and be outside of himself looking in, thinking: I wonder what this person who looks like me is feeling? He was beautiful with every emotion, and consequently, they ceased to have meaning and became pantomime. In front of the camera Paul was a blank page to be branded by clothing and by his relationship to fellow models. Fear, the one great emotion he had no control over, could not touch him with all the favorable lighting, make-up, fine clothes and that body he worked so rigorously to maintain.

However, fear and time were stronger than the illusion of the camera. Paul was terrorized by the deepening and fracturing of the wrinkles on his face. He would wake up in a cold sweat over nightmares of turning into a prune. His face and his body were his identity. How was it possible for him to change from the strange-looking child that had no friends, the boy who was neither white nor Latino, the boy who had no unique talents or skills to speak of and nothing clever to say, into the young man that was so beautiful he didn't have to say anything to be loved and admired? The wrinkles, Paul feared, would crack that lie.

The shoot was half over and Paul wondered what the billboard, magazine and advertising spread would look like. Though he had hidden the shy curious boy inside, Paul always hoped to find him somewhere staring at him quizzically from the pages of a magazine.

Yves was not shy about burning a ton of film because it allowed him to distill the very best, his so-called immortal images, those that told the true story of human experience. Even though he was taking pictures to sell clothes, he was an artist and a student of humanity; he was searching for meaning beyond appearance. He liked being around the pretty men and women, but they did not stir a passion in him that was viable. His passion resided in the fantasy of his work; he was by trade a voyeur, and no affair or betrayal would ever be as good as the one he could imagine and coach behind his lens.

For Jack, it was easy money. He never imagined that he could get paid for putting on some clothes and having his picture taken. In a day he would make more than in a month of waiting tables. What kind of world is this, Jack wondered. If there was one thing the city had taught him it was that good fortune wouldn't last forever. While Jack thought of what to do with his money –he had always wanted a fancy laptop like Damian's- he knew he should probably save it for hard times, which he had lived since his arrival up to the present moment.

Later, in the street, Jack had a conversation with Anthony, who said, "Modeling is just like anything else, Jack. There are thousands of perfect faces out there. What is it to be good-looking? Just luck, really. I tell you, I'm not much for it. It's not like acting where you can become someone else and have an identity. Just look at Paul. We've all seen his face in magazines, but who is he really? I mean, what will he have to show for himself later when he's old and out of the business? Me, I want to make a contribution. I want to do something I'll be remembered by. You think anyone remembers a clothing ad? The truth is we don't really contribute anything to this world, Jack. We are puppets divorced from our thoughts and feelings. We are exploited for our looks and then discarded."

"I guess you're right," Jack said.

"Of course I'm right."

There was a wild look in Anthony's eyes that Jack didn't understand. It was the product of many years of living in limbo in some ashtray of an L.A. suburb, of wanting to do something great but having no ideas or direction, of being just like one's neighbors with delusions of grandeur fostered on biographies of the famous; it was the realization that one had to use what one was given no matter how inadequate it might be, especially for those that had been given nothing. It was the wild stare of inequity, settling, making do and paying one's dues.

Jack, who had also suffered and been deluded, didn't understand, because his lucky break had given him amnesia. Fundamentally, he wasn't a cynic because he knew that somewhere out in the desert was a family that loved him, no matter what. His roots were in the desert and when times were hard he could return there in his mind.

29

Alex stood on an ice flow surrounded by icebergs that floated stark and white in the metallic ocean. Here there wasn't a single person to distract him and the joy of nothing filled his mind. There was no analysis, criticism, skepticism, judgment or doubt: just a lasting peace, and him another feature of the landscape. He was nothing more than the bright orange speck of his parka on an irregular and incomprehensible fragment of ice floating in that immense, inviting and deadly ocean.

What was he waiting for? The wheels of his mind began to turn. He looked around and evaluated the boundaries of his personal island. He paced to the other side, no more than a few yards. He walked the perimeter and looked down into the depths to where the white sloped out and disappeared from view. He marveled at the clarity of the liquid below his feet, the impervious slate gray of it at a distance, and all the shades, contrasts, and continuities of black and white that made up his world.

Alex studied the raw angles of the ice mountains around him and thought: if I could just get to one of the bigger flows I could step across to solid ground. What are the odds of that? If only I had boat. If only I wasn't alone.

But how did I get here? This ice sheet must have broken off from the rest and now it's drifting on unseen currents carrying me farther away from the mainland. Why didn't you jump off when it happened? Perhaps it was too sudden. Or perhaps you had faith and were tired of where you had already been.

Alex was neither hungry nor cold. Nor was he scared. He was resigned to whatever came to pass. It occurred to him that he could stand there and contemplate his surroundings for eternity. The beauty was astounding. It was better here than on the mainland. It was much better than the filth and crowding of civilization. It was clean and neat and deadly, which was something he could respect and even admire.

Why, this ocean doesn't give a shit about me. It doesn't care what I think, or if I am a beggar or king, for it will kill me all the same. All my thoughts and hopes and fears are nothing but a fragile illusion in this vast ocean. That water will purify me; it will clear my thoughts and show me, once and for all, the truth I have searched for all my life. Was it all in vain?

The water was now at Alex's feet. It crept slowly up his boots to his ankles and then his knees. It was so cold that he no longer felt below his waist. He watched his hands turn pale in the clear liquid; he filtered it through his fingers, captivated by its luminosity and simple beauty. It occurred to him that he had wasted his time on land. He wished he had been born a fish so he could live without the oppression of his own weight.

Soon the water reached his neck. It hurt to breathe and he felt sleepy. Alex looked eagerly at the sharp white mountains of ice from the rippling plane just below his chin. He smiled, overwhelmed by the beauty of all he saw. That's the secret, he thought. You have to see everything as if it were the last time.

Alex sank below the surface, his laughter severed by the great silence. From above an orange speck was just visible on the tiny white canvas. Then both the canvas and speck were gone and forgotten.

Alex sat up in bed. What an absurd little dream, he thought, with a slight smile on his face. Dreams he called them, because he didn't believe in nightmares. I wonder what it means? Perhaps it was just a fanciful interpretation of his general unease at the state of world affairs? Or maybe a premonition of tragedy?

Alex thought of Tarot cards and a friend who had read fortunes in college. To assuage everyone's unease at the appearance of apparently negative cards such as The Devil, The Tower, Death, or the Ten of Swords in a reading, he had explained that each had their positive reversal, and even when that was not the case, a painful event, an abrupt change, and emotional challenges could lead to positive outcomes and personal growth.

30

He had been thinking about it for some time. The idea was built on loneliness and sustained by confusion, until finally it developed into an act of passion: Arnold was going to kidnap Mei Li and take her with him to San Diego. He was going to set her free and for that she would love him eternally. If he ever performed a meaningful act in his life, this would be it. Arnold would contribute to another person's happiness, and in so doing, he would be happy. It was just the sort of romantic act that suited his fantasy.

The question of whether she would come kept Arnold awake at night. He worried that she might not have the courage, or that he was only a customer, nothing more, and that she had been polite for that reason. He worried that he would get caught, or that clever Mrs. Yun would somehow spoil his plan. It's that glass eye that makes her so clever. She only has half her sight, so all her other senses are enhanced.

If Mei Li doesn't want to go, then maybe I'll kidnap her for real. Mei Li's deathly afraid of Mrs. Yun and that fear could make her throw away a beautiful future. Arnold wouldn't allow that to happen.

On the day of Arnold's departure Jack insisted on sporting him lunch. Jack wanted to make good and show his gratitude for all the times Arnold had paid his way in the past. Arnold didn't object. They went to a sushi bar and ate their fill with Jack in top spirits picking up the bill.

Jack told him, "When I was feeling down, you were the only one there for me. I'll never forget that. After living here a while, I've learned that is the exception and not the rule."

Arnold shrugged off the flattery. Jack was a good friend who had never judged him on his eccentricities. It's only in leaving that you realize what people mean to you. Now don't get emotional on me. Jack's a good guy and this isn't the last time you'll see him. You'll come back to the city; it's just that now your mother needs you and you need to think seriously about what you want to do with your life. You've spent too many years thinking you were bigger than you are.

"Friends help each other. That's what friends do," Arnold told him. "I don't think there's anyone out there who can go it alone. I don't want to go it alone anymore."

"You're not going to be gone forever, are you?" Jack asked.

Besides Arnold, all Jack had were his housemates to keep him company. And Alex and Henrik had never really been much company, absorbed as they were in their work.

"No, Jack, I'll come back. I promise you that."

In the street, Jack held out his hand to say goodbye, and Arnold seized him in his embrace, picking him off the ground and squeezing him tight. When he put him down again, Jack was short of breath.

"Sorry, Jack, I guess I got a little carried away."

"Oh, go on and get out of here," Jack said, smiling.

That Arnold: what a character. Some people were just born to break the mold. Jack had Arnold to thank for teaching him not to worry so much about other people's opinions.

Arnold drove to Chinatown. Lunch with Jack had put him in good spirits. It made him happy to see Jack smiling again without that gray cloud hanging over his head. Even his good posture had returned. It was a positive omen to see Jack that way. Jack: now there's a real fighter. He could have given up, but no, he hung in there; that Arizona boy had made it.

Arnold told himself that he would make it, too, that he and Mei Li would be married and that he would work hard to make her happy. Let's not get carried away. Take it one step at a time; if you try to go too fast and do too much, you'll ruin it. Haven't you learned anything?

Arnold talked to himself in this way, scolding himself for his shortcomings and praising his daring and initiative, until he pulled into the alley behind The Green Lantern and stopped the moving van underneath Mei Li's window. It was almost three o'clock and they were expecting him. What if she looks out and sees me in the truck? What will she think? Worry about that if it happens. Fine. Well, here you are. Go on and take a deep breath. There, that's it. Just relax. It's gonna go real smooth 'cause you're a smooth guy.

Arnold checked his hair in the mirror. He dabbed the sweat from his forehead with a handkerchief and got out of the car. He was wearing his best suit, a silver Aldini from when times were better, and he had a bouquet of roses under his arm. He was taking everything very seriously and needed every advantage he could muster.

Arnold stepped into the green glowing den he knew so well, exchanged the usual pleasantries with Mrs. Yun, and lied about a successful deal he had just closed and how he wanted to celebrate with his favorite girl. Mrs. Yun fawned over him as usual because Mr. Kazinski was a big spender. Why, he even gave Mei Li gifts. First the necklace, and now some nice roses. Another class of man that Mr. Kazinski. A real gentleman for a gentlemen's club. She had had enough of the loud businessmen drinking rice wine and arguing over mahjong. Those weren't the sort of men for her girls, but then business was business, and without the support of the local community business would be tough, indeed.

Arnold knocked on the door and Mei Li let him in. She was wearing a nice gown of transparent blue silk with matching underwear. She seemed to have stepped directly from his dream, and he found himself staring at her. Her face lit up in a smile and her melancholy velvet eyes grew warm and inviting.

"Arnold, so good to see you. Please come in."

That Mei Li, always so polite. Arnold blushed and stuck the roses out to her.

"They're so beautiful. You shouldn't have. Let me put them away."

She collected a porcelain vase and disappeared to the bathroom. Over the sound of running water, he said, "Mei Li, are you happy here?"

She thought she noticed something different in his tone and paused before answering. She had learned the art of careful circuitous answers and soft humble questions, and said, an image of Mrs. Yun with her teeth bared lilting through her mind, "What is happiness? When I want to sleep I have a warm bed, when I am hungry I have food to eat, and my circumstances aren't exactly poor. I suppose if happiness were measured in this way, I am happier than most."

She returned with the riot of roses spilling from the vase. Their color and scent infected the room.

"Uh-um, what I meant to say was: have you ever thought about leaving here?"

"It is not my place to think of such things. I was born to be grateful," Mei Li said.

"I wish you wouldn't talk that way," Arnold said.

"You have so many questions today. Come on, why don't we lie down, and you can relax your mind and not think of such things. I am happy that you are here."

Arnold did as he was told, all the while thinking: time is running out, I have to get her out of here. He lay down with his feet hanging off the bed, and Mei Li crouched on the floor and started to untie his shoes.

"No, no," he said, sitting up.

"You can't as well get into bed with your shoes on?"

"Mei Li, I want you to tell me the truth, you hate it here, don't you? You put on a brave face and you smile, but I see the sadness in you. It hurts me to see you that way. I hate to think of you here with all sorts of men, serving them, locked in your pretty little room. What kind of life is that?"

"Why have you come? Don't you want to make love to me? Don't I appeal to you any longer?"

She knew what he was getting at. Just let him say it full out. He's going to offer to buy your contract. He's not a bad man. Perhaps not the best looking, but twice another man in his kindness and generosity. He is a sensitive man and he loves you, perhaps. But then let him tell you that. If he buys your contract you will go with him. Oh, if he would buy your contract! Mei Li looked to the floor to hide her shy smile of expectation.

"Yes, I do, and yes, you do. In every way," he said, getting up from the bed and pacing nervously to the window. He looked down at the street and saw that he had parked too far to the left. Dammit, he thought. Dammit.

"You're a fantastic woman. You're worth more than a hundred girls on the street. I tell you, I'll forego them all just to have you. You are smart and beautiful, and when you sing I get all tingly up and down my spine, until I can't help but touch and get close to you . . ."

Arnold was flushed and sweating in his suit that was too tight. He reached into his coat pocket, pulled out his hip flask and took a deep swallow. Mei Li watched him with wide eyes. Her heart was trying to push through her chest to meet him. Is this really happening, she wondered.

"Mei Li," he said, taking a deep breath, "I want you to go away with me. I am leaving for San Diego today. My mother lives in San Diego and we can stay with her. She has a big house by the beach and she is lonely. I think it will make her happy to have us there."

Run away? Was he crazy? How would she ever get away? Remember what happened to Xiao Ying when she tried to run away? Why, she got thirty lashes from Mrs. Yun until she couldn't sit down again for weeks.

"I could never run away from here," Mei Li said, her face tight as her eyes dimmed with sadness. The ice of fear spread in her chest and mingled with the vain hope of freedom in her mind. "No, that would not be right. And if I was caught. If Mrs. Yun even suspected . . ."

The fear returned. Mrs. Yun's face and the silver fillings in her teeth. Mrs. Yun's terrible breath and her false friendship and kindness. Why, what if she were listening at the door? What if she had heard everything and was waiting to barge into the room and expose their little plot?

Arnold felt the shame fill him. I know what she thinks. She thinks I am too cheap and do not value her enough to pay Mrs. Yun for her contract.

He told her, "If I had the money I would pay whatever Mrs. Yun asked to set you free. Even if you didn't want to go with me, I would like to be able to set you free to live a better life."

The emotion was strong in him. Dear God, don't cry. I know things have been hard lately and you're desperate to do the right thing and be good and not live just for yourself or play games anymore. It's gonna work out, just hold on a little longer.

Mei Li crossed over to the mirror and began to brush her hair.

"I don't care if you have the money. I don't care about money or Mrs. Yun. If I was free, then it is you I would choose, for no one else has ever cared for me or been kind to me like you."

Mei Li clenched her teeth to keep from crying. Was it possible to cry bitter and happy tears at once?

"I may be poor now, Mei Li, but I promise I'll work real hard to make you happy. You don't need to worry about Mrs. Yun. I'll take care of her, if it comes to that. So this is how it's gonna be," he said, touching her shoulder. "I've parked the truck underneath the fire escape. All we have to do is climb down and we're free."

"Is it really possible," she asked.

"Yes. I promise that today we'll leave this city together and drive down the coast of this beautiful state and you'll see where I grew up and never think about this place again."

"The fire escape is below Mali's window. Mali, she's mean. She don't like Chinese. Maybe she'll tell Mrs. Yun and give us away? She don't want to see a girl like me go free and her left behind."

"Don't you worry about her. She won't have time to tell anyone. We'll go in quick before she knows what's happening," Arnold said. "We don't have much time. Get your things together. Your favorite things, what you need, but not everything. We don't have much time," he repeated, looking out the window to the street.

Mei Li filled her suitcases with fancy brothel clothes, jewelry, perfume and her favorite CDs. Eat your heart out Mamma Yun. I'm gonna sing a song more beautiful than you've ever heard. I'm gonna be a big star. Mei Li was so nervous packing her things that she dropped them on the floor, and Arnold bent down to help her. When she was done, they opened the door and peeked into the hall for a sign of the old woman. She was nowhere to be seen.

"Go tell Mali you need to borrow a brush or something. Go on," he said.

"Hey, you don't have to push."

Mei Li felt absurd asking Mali to borrow a brush when they hardly spoke to each other. She knocked on the door and Mali answered without opening. They spoke pidgin to each other.

"What you wan'?"

"I wan' borrow brush, comb hair."

"You got brush."

"Need brush, really, have customer. My brush gone."

"No got brush. I busy."

Please, Mali. You nice girl. Borrow brush, we stay friend."

"Popular girl wan' borrow brush now. You have problem."

Mei Li didn't know what else to say. She stood there and shrugged to Arnold. But then the door opened and there was Mali's face: that beautiful face that held such cold sharp thoughts. Were those thoughts the product of her condition?

Arnold barged in with both suitcases in hand. He moved surprisingly quickly for a man his size, and Mali didn't have time to react. Mei Li shut the door quickly behind her and locked it.

"What happen here? Who you? What you do in my room? I scream and Mrs. Yun come quick and you in big trouble."

"I'm taking Mei Li away from here," Arnold said.

He walked over to the window and threw it open. The two women stared at each other. No, they were not friends, and Mei Li was daring Mali to scream or make a fuss so she could pull her hair out. Just you try it, you Thai bitch, she thought. Thai bitch just jealous because I have talent.

"You leave here, I scream for Mamma Yun," Mali said.

"You say one word, I scratch your eyes," Mei Li said.

"Mali go with Mei Li."

"No."

Arnold put the suitcases on the fire escape and turned to them.

"Yeah, that's a great idea. Mali, you come with and we can take you wherever you wanna go. But let's go already."

"I don't want her coming with us," Mei Li said.

"Listen. Forget about it. She's coming and that's it. She has just as much right to come as you. Now let's get outta here."

Arnold climbed down the ladder and dropped onto the roof of the truck.

"Go on, throw me the suitcases," he said.

Mei Li let one fall and it caught him in the chest and knocked him on his back.

"What did you put in these things, anyway," Arnold said, gasping for breath and getting to his feet.

Mei Li smiled at him and let the other one go.

Mali was packing now, throwing things into her suitcase, anything she could get her hands on. They were leaving soon and she didn't want to miss her chance. Mei Li, you bitch, I could kiss you. Mei Li, if we get away, I will do anything you say. I will worship you.

It just happened at that time Mrs. Yun was strolling the hall and noticed Mei Li's door was open. When she looked inside and found no one there, she panicked and felt the anger build inside her. She went to the window and looked to the street and there he was, that son of a devil, lying, two-time cheat. She had known it all along: those whites, never could trust them an inch. The shame of trying to steal her girls.

Mrs. Yun went with her quick shuffle to Mali's room and put the key in the lock. She had a key to every room for such emergencies. She entered the room just as Mali was stepping through the narrow window frame.

Then Mrs. Yun had her by the arm and Mali was screaming. She bit Mrs. Yun's hand so that it bled, and Mrs. Yun shouted madly in Chinese so that Mei Li's face colored red from where she stood on the roof of the truck.

"Go on and jump, I'll catch you," Arnold coaxed.

Instead Mali's suitcase fell; it was so filled with stuff and so heavy that when it struck the roof of the truck, it exploded in shower of lacy undergarments that fluttered parade-like to the street.

Mrs. Yun was a determined woman. She had her little legs on the window frame and was pulling with all her strength on Mali's arm. Meanwhile, Mali was screaming in Thai, screaming and shouting, and now there were some curious faces in the nearby windows. A few men were milling in the street, their curiosity piqued by the lingerie storm.

Arnold said, "Come on and jump already."

Mali put her foot smartly in Mrs. Yun's face and her big toe flicked the madam's glass eye out of the socket and sent it rolling across the hardwood floor. Then Mali was on the fire escape hanging from the bars until she dropped into Arnold's waiting arms.

"Look boys, that man is stealing all the whores from The Green Lantern," someone in the street said in Chinese to the men standing nearby. "Come on, let's stop him."

Another man said, "Aww let 'im be. I wish I'da thought a' that."

Some men grabbed fruit and vegetables from a nearby stand and started throwing them at the truck. The fugitives piled into the cab: the women in their underwear, and Arnold with his suit stained by tomato. Thin on patience, Arnold pulled out his handgun and brandished it out the window.

Mali said, "What he do? What he do? He crazy. You boyfriend, he crazy."

Arnold fired in the air, and the men lay down in the street and stayed there. The truck roared past them down the alley and was gone.

31

Henrik noticed it for the first time walking to work. On the billboard was a giant Jack reclining on a couch with a beautiful blonde in his arms. Jack was blank-faced and staring off in the distance over the high rises of the city and beyond them, presumably to his destiny.

Henrik stopped dead in his tracks and stood with his head cocked to the side and his mouth open. It was the sort of thing that impressed him. Jack was a monument; he was as real and eternal as any of the buildings below his gaze.

Just what is it about Jack, Henrik wondered. What about that young man with whom he shared a wall but didn't really know? Because Jack was the silent type, Henrik had always considered him a man without opinion or consequence. Jack was not a man of ideas; he was just another dumb American. He was a puppet. He was a byproduct of a country Henrik would never come to understand.

Henrik stood there a while longer with mixed emotions. Though his CDs were on the rack at Virgo, he wasn't satisfied. Jack had beaten him. Of all of them, Jack had become a star. It wasn't enough that Henrik's CD was finally in the stores or that people recognized him at clubs and bars. Jack's billboard was a slap in the face to remind Henrik of his ravenous and unsated hunger for fame. How long was it going to take before he appeared on VTV and did interviews in *DJZine*: before word got out and they wanted him as resident DJ in Ibiza, that island of the beautiful where superstar DJs could make a hundred thousand in a season? No, he wasn't satisfied that his disc had sold a thousand copies. Before he was bitter and now he was frustrated.

Though competition was something Henrik understood, he was growing tired of adapting to a world that was constantly changing. He had come to America because he embraced the survival of the fittest philosophy, but he was beginning to fear that he was falling behind. Perhaps he should have been satisfied that he had been able to follow his passion for making music. But now he longed for recognition of his efforts.

You still have so far to go, he told himself. Why, you haven't even sold enough CDs to get national distribution. You're a regional DJ; outside of the city no one knows your name. I wonder if Jack's billboard is up in New York? Or Italy, even. I mean who doesn't wear Baducci? Why, my shades are Baducci.

Henrik wanted to be happy for Jack, but he was the sort to resent the success of others. What's being a model, anyway? Models are just there to hang clothes on. It's nothing like making music. It doesn't take any talent. Henrik felt better then, having justified himself and put Jack in his place. So what about Jack? It's not like he's a movie star or anything. He's not exactly Jeremy Leads, though he is better-looking.

When Paul heard about the billboard, he threw a tantrum. He complained to Marco and threatened to call Sergio himself out there on his yacht somewhere in the Mediterranean. And he did call, but Sergio was completely and conveniently inaccessible.

Marco explained to Paul that it had been Yves' decision, not his own. Yves was an award-winning photographer and it was his artistic vision that mattered.

Later, when he and Jack were in the elevator, Paul said, "What do you know about modeling? Look at the way you dress and the way you stand. Why, you've got no style or class, whatsoever. You'd never make it in Europe like that. The cowboy look is out, guy. So you'd better just drop the hard face and the stubble."

Jack thought: let it go. He's upset. You could take him, but then he might sue you for giving him a black eye. Fag.

Jack felt badly for having been picked for the billboard. Paul obviously cared more about it than he did. Jack was embarrassed by that photo of him and Lexi together: Lexi, a painted designer whore; and he, her derelict junkie boyfriend. He blushed at the thought of his parents seeing him like that. When they were looking over the negatives Jack had suggested several in which he did not figure prominently. To avoid embarrassment, he preferred to be in the background or absent altogether. Ultimately, Jack just wanted to get paid.

A week later, Jack found himself on the beach south of the city playing a mock game of football in speedos with a bunch of men who obviously did not have much experience with the game. As quarterback, Jack threw what he thought were some great passes, but the receivers dropped the ball time and again, and Jack grew irritable and eventually found himself shouting, "Come on, man, where did you learn to catch? The ball isn't gonna fucking bite!"

The other models stopped and stared, and the cameraman came over and said, "Jack, it's supposed to be a casual pick-up game between friends. You're supposed to be smiling and laughing, not frowning and shouting."

Jack tried his best to check his emotions. He was competitive by nature and this was the strangest game of football he had ever played. The cameraman kept saying, "I want you to look natural. Remember, you're really having fun out there. Just be natural, don't think about the camera, just play." And Jack thought: yeah, real natural the way they tackled each other slow and turned their heads toward the camera. But it wasn't all bad; a few of the guys actually had some skills. Still, when Jack was on defense he had stuck the unsuspecting receiver and planted him so hard that the guy rolled around on the ground with his knees to his chest gasping for breath.

"Hey, man, take it easy," someone had said, getting in Jack's face. "This is a photo shoot. It's supposed to be a game, so just chill out."

Jack shrugged and got back into position. He was grinning now, a vicious grin of satisfaction at his great hit. Damn, I wish I had been better at football, he thought.

The other team connected a few good passes and gained some yards on the ground. Then the QB tried a pass into the end zone marked with the Zip Sports flags, which Jack picked off and ran past the diving players. No, he hadn't made many friends that day and they were after him now. Jack put his arm in the face of a defender, deflecting him to the ground, and ran the whole stretch, juking and stutter-stepping into the end zone where he spiked the ball and did a celebratory dance. Judging by the looks on the faces of his competitors, they did not appreciate his skill. What have these guys done with their lives if they don't know how to play a little pickup football, Jack wondered.

They finished the shoot on the beach and changed into some board shorts. The models were given some multicolored surfboards to pose with and they went down to the water where the photographer joined them with a waterproof camera and took pictures of them paddling out. Jack had never been on a surfboard before, unlike some of the other men, and with the first wave he got swamped off his board. Surfing wasn't easy and Jack was glad when it was over.

After lunch, they played keep-away with the newly arrived female models. Jack was amused when the women tried to tackle him by grabbing and pulling on him from every angle. Finally, he had reason to laugh as he dragged and carried that pile of girls with him through the sand. It felt good to have those girls on him, to feel their sun-warmed bodies against his own. And eventually, out of magnanimity, he let them bring him down into the sand.

Later, he took his favorite on his shoulders and ran her, kicking and screaming and laughing, down to the water where he dunked her in the frigid surf.

Yes, it had been a good day. The girls helped the men relax, and no one was upset any more from football.

It was Jack's first trip since moving to the city. He had never been anywhere in California besides San Francisco and the few cities he stopped in on his way out from the desert. He marveled at the beauty of the coast and wondered why it had taken him eight months to get out of the city.

You're not really a city person, anyway. You like to be out in open spaces and have your freedom. Yes, the city had things to offer, but now Jack wanted to explore his new adopted state and camp and hike and live a simpler life. The truth was he needed a vacation. He began to see how people got trapped in their routine in the city. With time, they stopped trying new activities and resisted new friendships and associations. Jack didn't want to live like that. He was tired of being locked inside himself.

32

Damian secured an Avid system on loan through his connections and Julie's room was turned into an editing studio. With the check from Solimar Productions he bought equipment for the project. Then he convinced Henrik to produce the soundtrack for the movie. They set up a computer with two extra hard drives for storage, and Henrik moved his synthesizer, mixer and audio software to the new system. They had extra monitors, and Damian bought a second camera so they could film simultaneously from different perspectives. Over the next year they would be spending a lot of time locked in that makeshift studio reviewing the footage, and editing and mixing the audio and video. Sure, Damian missed Julie, but now the room was put to much better use. Already, Damian was thinking about the festival circuit and hoping for the recognition he deserved. Finally, they were all working together on a project and contributing their individual talent to something bigger than themselves.

But still Alex held out. His book was nearly finished and he was living off his savings, leaving his room only to eat and use the bathroom. Damian worried Alex would find out the script had been adapted from his novel and oppose it. If so, fine, he could pay him off with a few thousand dollars. Now that Alex was out of work he might be more than happy to take the money. Fat chance for that watchtower of righteousness. He would probably stop the project. Maybe he would even file a lawsuit? Well, that didn't matter because the script was different from the original work. The ending was changed and now Pedro played only a minor role. Really, it was about Martin's transformation from wealthy son to social activist to revolutionary.

The supporting cast was composed of mostly no-name actors: amateurs that came cheap and were easily sold on the project for the opportunity it presented. The SF footage was shot in black and white with a blue filter. It was a relay of grainy images, jump cuts and rapid montage set to Henrik's abrasive beats, as if it were all happening inside Martin's head.

Then Damian disappeared into the editing room and trimmed down the many hours of footage into a neat story that fit into the first forty-five minutes before Martin's break with his father and departure to Mexico. Some of the scenes, those with a lot of dialogue, needed to be shot again, because Jack wasn't the best actor and Damian wasn't satisfied.

To prepare for the trip, Jack read up on Latin American history. He studied the biographies of the region's famous revolutionary leaders and brushed up on his Spanish by watching soccer games and the news on Mexican TV, and by listening to language tapes.

Preparing for the part wasn't as straightforward as Jack might have thought. First of all, he hadn't grown up in a wealthy family and it was hard to feign that slight edge of elitism that formed part of Martin's character; second, rich, poor or average, Jack had never really been much concerned with the plight of the less fortunate, thinking mostly that it was a man's own responsibility to look after himself. Though he felt sorry for James and the other homeless, and knew what it was like to be poor, Jack still had family. He could never really know what it was like to be truly fucked, and even less so now that he'd gotten a break.

Aware of Jack's on-camera troubles, Damian was determined not to let bad acting ruin the production. To help Jack capture the social consciousness the role required, Damian supplied him with a series of profoundly depressing videos. These included documentaries on the Truth and Reconciliation Commission in post-apartheid South Africa, human trafficking in Asia, the landless movement in Brazil, and child prostitution in India.

"Here, you might want to check this out, too," Damian told him, handing him a coffee table book with a black and white photo of an emaciated African girl extending an empty bowl in her cupped hands. "The guy that took these pictures is Elizabeth's old boyfriend, Graham."

This audiovisual and graphic material opened Jack's eyes to a world he scarcely knew existed. It would have never occurred to him to seek out such information willingly, but after absorbing it, he felt that his own past troubles were minor in comparison, and that his former self-pity was cowardly and shameful at best. You don't know what a hard time is, he told himself.

After further study of the script, Jack understood that Martin's desire to make a positive difference in the world was partly due to the guilt he felt at having grown up with privilege. That his father's wealth and influence had been gained through corruption and lies made it all the more imperative for Martin to leave home and discover his moral and ethical compass in the service of those less fortunate than himself. These new insights helped Jack fill his character's shoes as if he were a living man.

It was not as smooth as that, of course. Jack had always been the self-conscious sort and he was never one to pretend. So to stand there in front of friends and strangers alike and feign anger, sadness or mirth, proved difficult. It was one of the few lessons that remained for him: to divest himself of concern for the opinion of others; to no longer try to live careful and without mistakes, never taking any chances or getting ahead.

With effort, Jack learned how to tap emotions that until then had only surfaced in drunkenness. What a relief it was to shout or act the fool for the camera, when before his best and only role had been that of the straight guy: the cool character whose feathers weren't ruffled by anything, not an insult or the attentions of beautiful women. For once Jack was free to shout and throw furniture in anger. He could joke or be silly on the set when he messed up his lines, and such informality put everyone at ease. Over the next few months, he learned what it meant to act and why people did. Jack realized that acting freed him from the preoccupations and routine that shaped his life. He was able to step out of himself and be reborn a stranger.

At night when they sat down to watch the dailies, Jack was hypnotized by his own image on the screen. The camera had changed him somehow; it invested his every word and action with a deeper meaning and lent his emotions a drama that made him larger than life. By some trick of the camera he became more interesting, passionate and important than he felt in his own skin.

In truth, Jack didn't recognize himself on the screen. Certainly that couldn't be him: a social worker and future revolutionary with a temper? The drama and beauty of those images had as much or more to do with Damian's cinematography and Henrik's musical score, than it did with his acting. While before Jack was wedded to his stubbornness and the idea of doing things alone and in his own way, he came to understand that without collaboration nothing would come of the project. It was with this thought in mind that Jack sought feedback on his performance and learned to appreciate the value of critique in making him a better actor.

Sometimes, late at night when everyone was sleeping, Jack went to the makeshift studio and studied his performances. During those nightly sessions he concentrated on his mannerisms, facial expressions, tone and delivery, imagining ways that he could improve his craft. You have to stop touching your face: that's a sign of insecurity. Try to be less stiff and move with your emotions instead of fighting them. Say your lines with sincerity and not like you're reading from a script.

When Jack wasn't reviewing the footage, he was going over the script line by line with a highlighter and making notes in the margins. Finally, it seemed he had found something meaningful to do with his life. I will live on in this movie, he thought. I have helped create something. That feeling was quite different from the fleeting pride of seeing himself on television in the Baducci ad, where he was a silent mannequin wearing someone else's clothes and assuming an image that had nothing to do with his own character. The tape of his first TV ad sat forgotten in his closet. To Jack, it no longer seemed like much of an achievement. Most people would have been satisfied with a billboard, a TV commercial, or a photograph in a magazine. But then Damian's ambition had infected him. Jeremy Leads made it in the movies, didn't he? Well, if he can do it, so can I. He's just a man like me. Someone has to be the star, right?

Jack had been conned by Damian's smooth words. Didn't Damian say that if they got the film into Cannes or Sunfest, they'd be famous? Damian's confidence was all the proof Jack needed. It was amazing what a little confidence and even arrogance could do to change things for the better.

Despite his grand thoughts of the future, Jack hadn't lost his rudder of common sense and small-town skepticism. He was an old-fashioned young man after his father who had taught him the value of hard work and self-reliance. Jack knew his father would consider acting a vain pursuit. When Jack came to the city he had every intention of pursuing a business career that his father could identify with and respect. But everything Jack had seen and experienced since his arrival had left him hopelessly derailed from the stable, respectable life his father had modeled for him.

His father's influence was rapidly fading, along with the values born of his small-town upbringing. Damian had long since become Jack's mentor; Alex had influenced Jack's political views; Henrik and Arnold had stripped Jack of his naivité and exposed to him a world of hedonism and decadence. Jack's adopted social circle had changed his worldview and led him to question the values of his society and human behavior in general. The world was no longer black and white as he had seen it before; it was not a place of absolute truths and empirical laws, but of disparate opinions and ideas all fighting for exposure. It was a world of exceptions and compromise where adaptation and creativity helped a man to survive the rules and limitations imposed on him by others.

Jack had become conscious of the reality beneath the surface of things. He felt that if he just looked hard enough and concentrated, he would perceive the essence behind appearances. The previous balance and order he thought fundamental was really a false veneer to cover the underlying chaos and confusion. With time, Jack had come to the conclusion that no one really knew what they were doing; even his father he suspected of inventing life and assigning it meaning from one day to the next. There was no more to it than that.

Jack wanted a future for himself and he would work hard to earn it. In the process he would hurt no one; in that way, he falsely believed himself exempt from the general corruption and stupidity of the status quo.

The dream of living large, ripe in a young man raised on television and patriotism, overpowered him. Just when he had fallen into despair, luck had brought Jack a prosperity he planned to keep. His economic condition continued to define his status, self-esteem and identity. Now that Jack was looking back from the other side of the fence, arrogance was taking hold of his heart. Equality was a noble idea, fine for those who needed it for their own self-pity, but not when you possessed talent and skill superior to others. Sure, you've been lucky, but the true reason you made it is because of who you are, different and unique from everyone else. No one else can fairly claim your life and achievements.

But then you can't go acting big, Jack told himself. You can't look down on people that have less than you because one day it might all be gone. So many people when they are riding high forget about that, Jack thought. Fortune comes and goes, and the trick is knowing how to manage it and maximize its benefit so that you don't have to depend on it in the future. Most people hang their dreams on a distant and vague hope. That's how it was with you. So don't go thinking you're better.

Jack told himself what so many well-intentioned, average Americans had about the vanity and arrogance of movies stars: if I ever get famous I'll be humble. I just want to eat well, live comfortably, have a house for myself, be able to buy the things I need, and take a vacation now and again. But then how could Jack know how he would act if he ever moved from provincial fame to the big time? He cursed himself for letting such thoughts keep him awake at night.

33

The project was their business and Alex didn't want anything to do with it. He had never been much for TV or movies, devoted as he was to the literary medium.

This book is long past due, he told himself. You've been living it for the last three years. You know what it means to live a project: to go to bed with it and wake up with it resting on your shoulders. You understand and have accepted the responsibility and weight of the work. You know that what you write needs to be said. It may not pay the bills now; it may seem fruitless and brittle and weak compared to the candy images of the movies, the fast easy images that people don't even digest before they're forgotten, but then you have never been one for instant gratification. One day people will understand what you have been working on all these years: the projects that you have put your guts into; the endless pages that have made you cry happy tears and forced you to sacrifice certain joys of youth and carnal desires; the words and sentences and paragraphs that have made you alien with your thin skin and hyperactive imagination. You understand this insanity that makes you laugh out loud in the solitude of your bedroom. It's a logical madness, precise like surgery, with neat channels to navigate. No matter how much you discover, you can still go further. You know the secret is not thinking too much about what you're doing. What needs to be written will be written. The occupation is both vital and pointless; you know that better than anyone. What remains is to write the final chapter and be done with it.

Chapter 18: Our Nation, Our Problem

In the previous chapters, I have examined the ideological and cultural flaws of United States Empire, which, if not remedied, will ultimately lead to its collapse. The problems we experience and the challenges we face as a society today are not new but founded on historical inequities. Finding a cure to the apathy, consumerism, corruption, moral decay, and ideological repression that plagues America today requires a revision of the policies, laws, and practices of our political and legal systems.

Democracy no longer exists in the United States. Fraudulent elections have conceded victory to candidates without a majority vote, or without a complete vote count. Democracy doesn't mean tallying the votes of your support base and invalidating those of your opponents through deceptive ballots, technicalities of document design and format, no-record electronic voting, voter intimidation, and intentional misinformation to keep voters from their district polling station. Democracy is not practiced by allowing business lobby groups to dictate government policy to representatives of congress, which go against the interests of their constituencies. Democracy is defunct when the government engages in criminal activities, represses the civil liberties of its citizens, and drafs legislation the majority of the public opposes. Finally, democracy has failed when the majority does not support a government program or policy, and the administration insists on pushing it through despite protest.

So how did democracy cease to be effective in expressing the will of the people and how can it be restored? First, we need to ask what is meant by democracy. Democracy can be defined as the freedom of the *citizens of a nation to express their political preferences through representative government. This is the most plausible root of the term "freedom" in relation to democracy. Problems arise when freedom comes to mean the freedom to express one's economic preferences while ignoring social and environmental responsibilities. In a democratic nation, the freedom of the individual, group, or corporation to pursue economic prosperity is a right necessarily limited by the obligation to protect and preserve the public good. This includes access to and provision of social services, conservation and sustainable management of environmental resources, and respect for the civil and human rights of fellow citizens. Freedom that does not conform to that definition is tyranny.*

Democracy as representative government does not function today because lobbyists bribe government representatives to support their interests, which, more often than not, conflict with the public good. Furthermore, congressional elections are non-competitive events. Only certain individuals are able to raise sufficient funds to mount electoral campaigns; this funding comes primarily from interested parties seeking favorable legislation, contracts, etc. from the representatives they support.

Historical legacies add to the difficulties of good government. Team mentality is one such obstacle. In the Unites States, notwithstanding the endeavor or activity, there are two teams; this applies as much to the Civil War, Major League Baseball, or the Federal Government. The goal of all American activity, economic or otherwise, is to win. To the winner go the spoils, the ability to tell the story of victory, and the admiration and envy of the public and one's peers. In the quest to win and avoid the ostracism, resentment, and mistrust that are the burden of the loser, the eventual victor, and often both competing parties, will resort to dishonest means to achieve their goal. In this winner-take-all system, the winner absolves himself of any wrongdoing.

The political victor, once in power, sets about changing the laws, policies, and activities of government to favor his own and, by extension, his party's economic interests and moral prejudices. For the public this means that laws and policies created for their benefit and well-being will often be repealed or amended to promote the self-serving agenda of the political leadership. When the opposing party steps into power, this process of destruction and reconstruction repeats itself, while the nation stagnates with its resources squandered along with the faith of its citizens.

Coalition government avoids many of the pitfalls of the two-party system by forcing competing parties to join forces and make concessions in exchange for a role in shaping policy. While far from perfect, multiparty government is more cooperative and more representative than a two-party system in which both parties come to resemble each other by taking a middle road in an attempt to satisfy the majority of the electorate. A viable third party in America would do much to prevent the homogenization of American politics and the force-feeding of undesirable candidates and their partisan politics on the electorate.

The existing systemic flaws of American government have been worsened by the political climate of corruption and impunity created by the current administration. This corruption includes the production of false reports and the denial of facts to justify war, state-sponsored terrorism, and the violation of the human and civil rights of American citizens and foreign nationals alike. Meanwhile, government officials have the greed and gall to take interest group bribes and pass preferential legislation for the benefit of their corporate friends and business associates on the public's tax dollar. If that weren't enough, these same politicians appoint private industry professionals to head government agencies that regulate the corporations where they were formerly employed. Later, these professionals-cum-bureaucrats become lobbyists paid to use their government contacts to secure favors for their former corporate employers. In most cases, these crimes against the American people and their interests, when brought to light, elicit little more than a forced apology from the guilty parties, while summary dismissal from public office and jail time constitute the appropriate administrative and legal responses.

It would seem that, increasingly, political leaders believe that decorum, dignity, and respect no longer form part of their mandate when conducting public affairs. While we are all aware that politics is a balancing act requiring half-truths and unfulfilled promises, what makes democracy work is the effort and appearance of good will, disingenuous or not, made by politicians in performance of their duties. It is the responsibility of a democratic administration to address political concerns, policy mistakes, calamitous events, government scandals, etc. with promptness, candor, sincerity, and good will toward the American people. When politicians exposed for wrongdoing or incompetence hide away and cover their tracks, instead of making public statements regarding their policies or actions; when they lash out with hostility to those who call them to account for their crimes, failures, and shortcomings; when they place blame on others and show their open resentment to the American people for demanding honesty, ethical behavior, and loyal service; when they arrogantly ignore public demands and outcries of indignation regarding their cynical self-serving agendas and continue with business as usual, then we can truly say that democracy is dead.

In the classroom, students are taught a different story entirely about the theoretical America of liberty and justice for all that in practice does not exist. Young minds are brainwashed to believe that the American Dream is something you earn through discipline, hard work, honesty, and fair play. When they are duped into fighting for their country in wars staged on the pretense of protecting freedom, justice, and democracy, their efforts only serve to undermine democracy by protecting the economic interests of the wealthy and political elite. The average American is told to pull himself up by his bootstraps in a society that lacks universal health care, affordable housing, quality schools and a sustainable environment. Meanwhile, the rich and their children maintain their privilege through nepotism, inheritance, tax shelters, bribes, and lies. It's no wonder that the youth of today, and the American public in general, are apathetic about government. It is clearly an example of the "do as we say, not as we do" philosophy promoted by the nation's political leaders who benefit by fixing the rules to suit their needs, and when this is not possible, by breaking them. When exposed, our politicians either refuse to admit guilt or dodge blame through cover-ups and lies, the scapegoating of their subordinates, and the smearing of their accusers and opponents with negative labels and propaganda.

While the United States has no global monopoly on corruption, what makes the American political reality so hard to swallow is the government's insistence on preaching justice, democracy, and freedom to the world when these values are increasingly under threat at home. This hypocrisy could perhaps be tolerated if the nation did not possess a sound political foundation and the wealth and resources sufficient to preserve the democratic values of the Founding Fathers. Instead, our elected officials squander the social and cultural capital of America as they actively work to dismantle the democratic process from the inside and sell it off to the highest bidder. This looting of the nation is made more insidious by the efforts of powerbrokers to distract, confuse, and silence the public with a combination of commercial advertising, censorship, propaganda, and fear-mongering. This is not a conspiracy. It is simply the consequence of a deeply embedded and mutually beneficial connection between government, corporations, and the media that during World War II was commonly referred to as fascism.

The failure of American democracy has as much to do with an apathetic citizenship, as it does with the self-interest of the oligarchy. The general decay of American government is a cycle where the victor mentality, which forms the core of the American value structure, brings the most unscrupulous to power. By not participating in the democratic process, which means being informed on the issues and demanding accountability from our politicians, the American public allows *democracy to become a beauty contest and horse race where gimmick, speculation, and spectacle determine elections. The result is a leadership of appearance and lip service, and not ideas and actions. Americans like nothing better than to enjoy leisure and material comfort while others do the dirty work of producing the goods and services they so readily consume. As a result, Americans get what they deserve: politicians that sit back comfortably and serve their own interests while ignoring the public good. The American politician is the mirror of the American citizen.*

What politicians know that they hope the public never learns is that in a democracy the people ultimately have the power to decide their future. A smart leadership understands that in order to maintain power with the least constraint and oversight it must keep the populous fat and comfortable, and when this does not work, divide it, so citizens are unable to protect their common interest. When citizens are no longer able to address their concerns collectively, democracy is transformed into oligarchy, where the few make the decisions for the many. The oligarchs consolidate power by pursuing policies to turn the average citizen from political subject to legislated object by dismantling and/or eliminating social services, civil and labor rights, environmental regulations, etc.

Citizens, by not being properly informed, or because they have been confused as to their priorities and interests, find themselves beholden to a government that produces no measurable benefit in their lives. For this reason, they perceive taxation as a waste of resources. While they remain legally obligated to pay tax, they are resentful of taxation and vote to remove or limit programs their taxes support. Against their best interest, they abet corporate-influenced government legislation to privatize and/or reduce their health care, pensions, social security, and unemployment benefits, while the government gives the difference away in the form of preferential contracts, subsidies, and tax breaks to corporations and wealthy individuals. Meanwhile, essential public services, including the roadways, schools, and hospitals taxpayers use daily, do not receive proper funding. The public has full right to be incensed by their government, given that the rich do not pay taxes, but rather hide their money behind the legal protections of corporations, and earn their income from non-taxable investments and stock dividends. If all citizens were able to follow their example by hording their money away and living off interest, then the public space in America would become the inhospitable wasteland of polluted and crime-ridden cities and economically stagnant rural areas that is the reality of the developing world. To the insulated economic and political elite, it would make no difference, either way.

Sooner or later some of the electorate wises up. They begin to recognize politicians for what they are: individuals using public resources and institutions for their own advancement. Perceiving correctly that they have little choice in government, the public stops voting for candidates to public office. They have neither the political will, knowledge, or time to invest in democracy. Finally, they fall into apathy and accept the loss of their rights and political agency without a fight. This public apathy permits the whole process to continue indefinitely.

In reality, the average individual is too preoccupied with paying his bills to take political action. To escape the routine and banality of his life, Joe Citizen immerses himself in a fathomless pool of cheap and meaningless entertainment that the Unites States generates in such quantities. The wealth, beauty, and excitement Joe Citizen sees on television, or in the movies, distracts him from his everyday problems and concerns. If he's not entertaining himself in escapist media fantasies, then he's getting into debt on his credit card buying materials goods in a vain attempt to fill the lack of meaning in his life, or drugging himself into oblivion, thereby ensuring his permanent enslavement to a system that has stripped him of his basic humanity.

His environment encourages this cycle of civic, mental, and emotional paralysis. In Joe Citizen's average American town little exists in the form of social activity to occupy the inhabitants aside from commerce. Local-run businesses have been bankrupted and replaced by corporate chains that import cheap goods from abroad and pay misery wages to their employees. When Joe goes about his business, he has no personal connection to the chain store staff, who in turn have no loyalty to the corporation owned by men that they will never see, who live in a different city, state, or even county. These men clearly do not have the best interest of the local community in mind, preferring instead to milk it for profit and extract its resources before moving on.

City, county, and state governments enable this state of affairs by providing tax incentives and free land to encourage corporations to set up shop, while, in the name of fiscal responsibility, eliminating services such as cultural programs and recreational infrastructure projects that would improve the town's quality of life. Meanwhile, individuals like Joe spend their free time shopping and watching television or playing video games instead of contributing funds or volunteering time to organize events and solve problems in their community.

The death knell of community life comes in the form of poor planning and a lack of development regulations, which promote suburban sprawl. As a result, transportation costs and congestion increase along with air pollution, while the amount of open space available for recreation and leisure activities diminishes. Furthermore, the distance between services, housing, and the workplace discourages walking and biking in the community. There is little wonder that Joe Citizen lacks citizenship. Because he does not live where he works, or shop where lives, he spends his free time sitting in traffic instead of interacting with his friends, family, and neighbors. Each week the cycle is repeated, offering no alternative to his poor quality of life.

This state of affairs has come to pass because Joe, and citizens like him, have not invested the time to stand up and demand accountability from the corporations that are ruining their communities and the politicians that favor them out of self-interest. They are unable to see that their desire to pay lower prices for foreign goods hastens a process in which the individual, the community, the business, and the product are being compartmentalized in a way that undermines individual and collective identity. In this formula identity is verified through the act of consumption, and not in thought, interpersonal communication, or creativity. As a result, consumption has become the preferred path for individuals to fill the vacuum of meaning in their lives; however, since it does not satisfy the need for human companionship, or the creative drive that defines humanity, the momentary high of acquiring new material goods quickly turns to dissatisfaction.

It is laziness to seek fulfillment in the possession of objects, but people continue to do so because they've been trained that way and left without alternatives. In a world of infinite consumer choice, citizens have forgotten that they have the choice to think for themselves and be politically and socially engaged. This is the sort of qualitative amnesia that corporate interests promote. They want people to forget that quality of life consists of supporting the local businesses in one's community; paying one's workers fairly and providing them with medical benefits and retirement plans, because a healthy workforce is a happy workforce; finding the time to relax, read, or play sports in the park, because leisure, reflection, and recreation are just as important as commerce; leaving the car at home and walking or biking when possible to reduce energy consumption, while enjoying the sights and sounds of the neighborhood in the process. In sum, we must look beyond our own narrow economic self-interest and have compassion and sympathy for others, and not see them as faceless drones serving our food or working the cash register. We must talk and question, argue and disagree when necessary, and take an active part in shaping community life, with the time-tested knowledge that the best things in life are free if only people will fight to keep them that way. That is an idea that corporations seek to eliminate by marketing everything including our fears, by forcing us into a race with each other for no reward except debt, by creating a social space in which all activity is channeled toward consumption and as little as possible toward creative thought and public discourse.

If Americans continue to be apathetic about the privatization and commercialization of American values and identity; if they continue to complain and shake their heads with each new government scandal and each policy that erodes their communities and destroys their environment, that censors them and strips them of their civil rights; each new and unnecessary war for the benefit of the few that diverts money from the many at home -without mailing a letter, informing a friend, making a speech, writing a book, singing a song of protest, traversing the desert to support an ideal, or enduring violence and imprisonment to defend truth and justice, they will find that the America of the people, for the people, and by the people that they hold dear will slip through their fingers like sand blown by the wind of apathy to be lost forever to future generations.

No one ever said it would be easy for Joe Citizen to take off the blinders and protest policies and legislation that affect the quality of his life, to organize others to his cause, to meet and talk and petition and march, to draw the line when his inalienable rights are threatened, or to be willing to endure suffering to right an injustice or to stop an abuse of power. No one ever claimed that democracy was easy to manage or that it was strong enough to stand alone in words without proper application and adequate participation. Democracy has to be fought for because it is the only viable tool the electorate has in place of money and influence to protect its rights.

People of means perceive democracy as an obstacle to the pursuit of their economic self-interest and seek to destroy or weaken it. Such a vision is shortsighted, even for the selfish, because the pursuit of total economic freedom, independent from the social obligations and environmental duties that tie the individual to his community, is ultimately self-destructive. Such an attitude causes both the community and the environment, from which wealth is generated, to eventually collapse. Men who think in such a way need to be protected from themselves as much as communities need to be protected from their activities.

If we still claim to be a democracy, then it is our duty to oppose the self-interest of the few by participating in public and political life. In our fast-paced society we need to schedule time to be democratic and call to account those individuals who lack ethics and are guided by greed and selfishness, particularly when they are our political leaders, elected fairly or not. We need to ensure that the people as a majority dictate to their representatives the policies and programs they should support; when these same officials do not cooperate, they need to be removed from office.

The Unites States faces very real and challenging threats to its global hegemony in the modern age. The current administration has failed to properly define, identify and prioritize these threats. Where diplomatic solutions and cooperation are necessary, it has chosen armed intervention and unilateral action. This undermines the legitimacy of American democracy in the eyes of the global community.

The U.S. Government has always practiced and supported terrorism in the Middle East; the retaliation by fundamentalist groups is only the mirror of the intolerance of our government and its own inability to separate church and state. Both the current administration of the U.S. Government and radical political organizations in the Middle East have exploited this antagonistic relationship to consolidate their own power, while American citizens and the peoples of the Middle East foot the bill in death, fear, zenophobia, and hatred. Americans interested in the great history and culture of the Muslim world will find that their government has poisoned their image and imperiled their safety, if ever they should wish to visit that cradle of civilization. A more suitable U.S. foreign policy would have concerned itself with education, cultural exchange, and economic support to help developing Muslim nations progress to the ideals of better government, respect for human rights, and a more open, egalitarian society. By choosing to wage war, the U.S. Government ignored its own democratic ideals and squandered the precious resources necessary to improve public services and infrastructure at home. Instead of bringing the Middle East closer to democracy, the U.S. Government met them halfway by limiting the civil rights of its own citizens and ignoring their opposition to its foreign policy.

The U.S. Government has overwhelmingly favored supply side solutions to resource management when demand reduction in many instances would have been a cheaper and more sustainable long-term alternative to promoting American prosperity.

Dependence on foreign oil is the historical strategic weakness of the Unites States, and one that is proving increasing costly to maintain. If we consider the true cost of oil, in terms of the military resources invested to secure its supply, then the development and expansion of rail transportation in and between cities of the nation becomes a comparatively inexpensive alternative. Taxpayer dollars currently invested in the defense budget would be put to much better use by developing a viable system of public transportation that would reduce the demand for cars and consequently the need for costly roadway infrastructure projects. If state-by-state alternative transportation plans were implemented, in conjunction with the development of mixed use communities where shopping, work, and housing were centrally located, we would further reduce the demand for cars and the fuel they require to operate. These communities would ideally be located in existing urban centers, and would help revitalize American cities and reverse urban blight and suburban sprawl. The success of such plans would require that Americans change their consumptive, convenience lifestyle to a sustainable, productive one in which less time is spent commuting and more time is invested in community and family life; this would translate into less pollution, improved air quality, and better health and quality of life for everyone.

In order to solve our energy crisis, government defense dollars used to subsidize the oil industry need to be invested in research and development of alternative energy sources. Money used for defense could be funneled into solar, electric, wind, biofuel and hydrogen fuel cell technology, which would provide sustainable solutions to our long-term energy needs. If this money were invested now, it would help make the United States a world leader in alternative energy, creating new jobs and expanding the energy portfolio available to all Americans.

If the United States wishes to remain competitive in the world it must invest in the education of its citizens. By prioritizing defense and security over education, we are squandering our social capital. The average American receives no tangible benefit from an increased defense budget. A cost benefit analysis would reveal that investment in homeland security to reduce domestic terror threats is a waste of money. Terrorism is nearly impossible to prevent because it is covert, employs materials available to everyone, and can be committed at any time, in any location. Counter-terrorism programs and activities are inconsistent in their scope and application and ineffectual at predicting terrorist activity. Anyone who has been to the airport and noted how one person is searched, arbitrarily, while another is not, would draw the same conclusion. To search everyone thoroughly would require costly increases in security, in addition to producing delays that would paralyze modern life. Providing comprehensive security throughout the nation is both prohibitively expensive and would violate the privacy of every American, reducing quality of life to such an extent that any loss of life from an isolated terrorist act would be marginal compared to the cost of sacrificed freedom. If this is the case, why not put the money back where it belongs, in education?

The United States is an information economy that requires a skilled labor force. In order to hold its place as a leader of research and development, it must continue to invest in producing the best and brightest thinkers in all academic fields. This goal is achieved by *expanding educational facilities, increasing grant funding, and providing scholarships and loans to deserving students. A proper education starts in elementary school; federal and state governments should ensure that K-12 public education is properly funded, free, and accessible to all. Schemes to provide vouchers for private schools only undermine access to a fair education and create a disadvantage for children enrolled in public schools, who find their budget drained by a diversified and competitive educational market. Funding based on property tax needs to be weighted so that schools in good neighborhoods don't unfairly benefit from high real estate valuations, while inner city areas struggle to provide materials and facilities for their students. Anyone who claims that free public education is ineffective and too costly to maintain need only consider defense spending to truly understand waste. As for ineffective, one can only expect to hire and keep talented teachers when they are fairly paid and not required to teach oversized classes with insufficient resources.*

All the issues discussed in this book are related. Ethical behavior, honesty, investment in education, a commitment to democracy and justice, proper planning, civic participation in government, and a respect for freedom when it doesn't undermine human and civil rights or damage the environment, are all essential to building a better United States. The current administration promotes and possesses few, if any, of the above-mentioned values, policies and goals, and therefore represents an obstacle to human progress.

The current American political system is such that citizens are often stuck with leaders they do not support. Many citizens who do support a corrupt administration, do so out of ignorance. Others do so because they are unable to separate church from state and politics from personal choice. Consequently, they perceive values as more important than rights and attempt to impose their values on others, thereby limiting individual constitutional rights. Still others support a corrupt administration out of self-interest. They are the haves, those that have been brainwashed to believe they are the haves, or those that one day hope to become the haves by exploiting others. Though it may be hard to accept or understand, some people simply lack ethics, morality, and a compassion for their fellow man. Thankfully, they represent the minority. It is against these individuals we must protect ourselves. While it is hard to beat a cheater by fair means, we must redouble our efforts before corruption and dishonesty render our society unmanageable. A society built on lies, suspicion, fear, and hatred is in nobody's interest and ultimately leads to anarchy.

If we, as Americans, do not actively work to uphold the traditional values of United States democracy, we will find our days of prosperity

*and preeminence numbered; we will go the way of Rome, consumed by
our own greed, decadence, and hypocrisy, only to be replaced by another
nation that failed to learn the lesson of history. Ultimately, our great
achievements will be overshadowed by our injustices, and our legacy to
the world will be that of the resentment and mistrust fostered by our
leadership. It's time to step back and take a critical look at our present
reality and discard attitudes, behaviors, and actions that prevent us from
progressing as human beings. We must look to the ultimate objective of
creating a physically, mentally, and morally healthful world for all.*

The End

When Alex finished he did not celebrate or call his parents and say,
guess what? He did not go shouting in the halls to the others about his
achievement. Instead, he sat there and stared at those last two words
knowing they were a lie. It was not "The End." Though the book was
finished, it would never be "The End." It had taken him three long years
of painstaking work to earn that moment: three years to find peace in
himself and to come to terms with and understand the world he lived in.
He wanted to savor that understanding while it lasted. He would enjoy it
in private, like he enjoyed most things.

The work had completely exhausted him. While Alex felt that he
couldn't write another line, he knew that after a day or two he would be
back at the computer starting on the next book. He had ideas for so many
books that he would die before he had a chance to write them all.

34

Sometimes somebody on the bus would approach Jack and say,
"Hey, I know you, you're that guy from the billboard." More often than
not that someone was a pretty girl his age: a girl like the ones he had
admired in the bars when he was without money and hope. Their attention
made Jack swell with pride until it threatened to burst through his skin.
He was displeased by this reaction and did his best to suppress his
reckless and burgeoning vanity. Sure, he was the guy on the billboard,
what of it?

"Yeah, that's me," he would reply. He had never been talkative. Not
as a boy and not now. He was the humble type, no better or worse than
anybody else. That was the way he'd learned it and that's the way he
liked it. But a voice inside told him otherwise. It said that excessive

humbleness was only masked arrogance for those who were too lazy or afraid to really stand up and follow their dreams, because in reality they thought themselves too good or perfect to be judged by others.

Usually, the curious interlopers would leave him alone after his cool reception and apparent disinterest. But sometimes they persisted.

"It's a nice picture of you. It must be cool to be on a billboard. What's your name? I'm . . ."

"Jack. Nice to meet you . . ."

The first time it happened Jack was caught off guard and felt embarrassed by the attention. Never did he imagine that pretty girls would ask him the questions. He couldn't help but notice the way they stared at him with hungry and inviting smiles, chests pushed out, and playing with their hair. It was only a matter of time before Jack began to understand that the billboard gave him power over them. Soon his reserve faded and he found himself staring, flashing his winning smile and posing for them like he did on camera: things he hadn't had the courage to do in a long time. When Jack looked those pretty girls in the eye, his mind thought only about fucking them. He did not care what their names were, what they did or what they believed in.

Jack found himself inviting them to lunch on the spot and was amazed, time and again, when they accepted and got off the bus with him at whichever stop he indicated. After lunch it was no trouble bringing them home. In his newfound wisdom, Jack let them do most of the talking. He listened, smiled and sometimes found the nerve to kiss them right there in public, at the cafe, on a park bench or in the street. At home, he stripped them down and took them to bed for the rest of the afternoon. Later, he would invite them to dinner and sometimes home again to spend the night. Sometimes, when they fell asleep, Jack would lie there and study their faces. They always seemed so peaceful, while he felt distant and estranged from himself, as if life had no purpose. He would think of the lies he had fabricated for their entertainment: his years in Paris, the summers in Ibiza; thank Henrik for those fun facts. Ibiza, it might as well have been Atlantis, for all Jack knew about it. He even resorted to naming the famous as his friends.

None of it was necessary. So why did he do it? Sometimes he felt Damian speaking through him. What does it matter if it isn't true? If I believe it, then maybe some day it will be. These girls want to dream. They don't want to know who I really am. They don't want to hear about Arizona, or waiting tables or being poor. They don't want to hear Alex's politics and misery. No, they want to be happy and so do you, and now you are. This pretty girl in your bed is all yours. She is with you and you can have her any way you want.

In the period of a week Jack slept with four women. It was a new record. And that wasn't counting the ones he disdained because they weren't pretty enough. These he mocked and made uncomfortable, much like women had done to him when he was trying too hard. Serves them right, Jack thought, for playing out of their league. I've worked with girls much better than these. I've splashed in the waves and kissed and held some of the most beautiful women in the world, and there are pictures to prove it.

Jack flirted wherever he went. When he felt the women staring he would meet their eyes and smile and watch them blush and look to the floor or turn away, startled. At such moments Jack wanted to laugh. He wanted to guffaw and slap his knee. So this is how women really are, he thought.

Jack was like a blind man whose vision had suddenly cleared. He had been living against himself and his potential. Why, women were nothing to be afraid of, after all.

Sometimes after the day's shoot, Jack and his housemates would go out on the town like old times. Jack had money now, and the project had brought them closer together. Since his lucky break, he and Henrik had become the best of friends. Henrik was the perfect party companion, and to make up for lost time, Jack started going out four or five nights a week. When a new club opened, they were there. When there was an after-hours party, they were on the guest list. Henrik and Damian were both connected each in their own way, and Jack was quickly becoming a known face. They no longer had to wait in line. Jack knew the bouncers at Snowball, Ninja, Tommy Gun, Starchild and many other clubs, personally.

"Hey Jack, when's your movie coming out? So Jack, that model in the Smooth Digs ad, the exotic brunette, did you hook up with her?"

Jack would smile then and pat Frankie, the bouncer at Ninja, on the back as he disappeared into the club.

"Why you gotta be so mysterious, Jack? When are you gonna hook me up with one of those girls, bro?"

Jack was always in the company of women. He went clubbing with his model friends, women he met around town, and the waitresses and bartenders he knew from the hip restaurants and bars. Jack would show up with a girl he had taken to dinner, pick up another in the bar, and leave with a third from the club. Henrik had gotten him into coke and he was drinking as much as he did in his frat days, which was too much. More often than not, the emotions Jack kept inside when he was sober would boil to the surface and he would start a fight in a bar over some minor misunderstanding or perceived slight. For example, that night at Starchild when he punched a guy down for talking to his date and his bouncer friends regrettably had to throw him out. Was that the real Jack: insecure and jealous over the women he thought he controlled? Was it the stranger's fault for being captivated by the beauty of Jack's company, while Jack was busy grabbing another girl at the bar? Did it matter that the model wasn't even Jack's girlfriend?

Jack wasn't a one-woman man, and sometimes people had to be reminded of that. Even if he had to be thrown out now and again, they always let him back because he was the luminary of the in-crowd with his cool, player attitude and hot, drunken temper that made the girls stick to him like glue.

For all the privation he had suffered, Jack had developed an insatiable appetite for excess. He wanted all the pretty girls; he wanted to party and have a rep in every club in the city; he wanted to drink and smoke and snort his way to heaven and bliss; he wanted to be seen and admired and talked about; he wanted everyone to have his name on their lips. There goes Jack Wild, the model and future movie star. So you'd better not mess with Jack.

Henrik, who had a fan club in his own right, could appreciate Jack's magnetism. He admired Jack's transformation from a stoic, silent, Arizona boy to a flamboyant hedonist and cult figure on the club scene known for his fits of violence and joy, glass breaking and fisticuffs, frenetic dancing and ass grabbing; Jack, with his vicious smile and epic confidence, who handled women like produce and was always impeccably dressed; and who could just as likely be found lying on the bathroom floor unconscious, doing a bar dance, or groping some girl in a secluded alcove.

Jack was living life as if he would die tomorrow. He was making up for all the time he had wasted being a quiet and conforming all-American boy who worked hard so as to not think about his feelings. Jack was finally learning to cut loose. He was acting on his emotions, doing what he felt like when he felt like it, without thought of the consequences or what other people would say. Though it was the drinking and drugs that made it possible, the results were the same: he was the life of the party. While Henrik was a seasoned veteran on the scene, he had never really been loose like Jack was now. They made a good team: Jack, with his mixture of charm and recklessness, collected the girls; while Henrik, like a good wingman, took whatever came his way, which more often than not was nothing to scoff at and sometimes something to marvel over.

Often when the clubs closed they would have a private party at the house with friends and the women they had met. They would raid the liquor cabinet, roll joints, do lines, and Henrik would set up the tables and throw on some records for a private session.

One night Alex came out at five in the morning to find them dancing in the living room: Damian, Jack, and Henrik with five girls in their early to mid-twenties and a couple of guys he didn't recognize but immediately disliked. He stood there in his underwear, pale skin and hairy chest watching them, before shouting over the beats, "Fucking shut up already, it's five in the morning. I've had it with this shit. Every fucking weekend you guys pull this bullshit."

But since everyone was drunk and high, all they did was laugh. Alex felt like a deflated balloon, useless and no fun, as he watched the girls laughing with their white teeth and pink tongues, squeezing their eyes shut to hold back the tears. He hated them. The anger and hate twisted his stomach tight in a knot and he felt the acid bath of disrespect burn his heart and soul. And the pretty girls kept laughing; they pointed at him and doubled over and slapped their knees to the rhythm of their mirth.

This is the world you live in, Alex thought. Is it any wonder that no one cares about literature? These stupid girls, what do they care about critical thinking or intellectual pursuits? This is your potential public. No wonder you can't get published; nobody reads anymore. It's all about hedonism: have fun and try to think as little as possible. God, what a tragedy.

With hunched shoulders, Alex returned to his room. The others had already forgotten about him. After he shut the door, Alex sat on the bed and listened to them: to their loud ecstatic voices, their shouts of joy and the incessant delicious pulse of the music. He knew he should put on his clothes and join them. But he didn't have the energy for it anymore. He had been out with them on their weekend city crawls enough to know that he found the experience unfulfilling. Their social circle was becoming increasingly superficial. He thought it a waste of time to go out and have conversations about pop culture or consumer products. He would just as soon stay home with a good book. The individuals Alex considered his peers were either dead or distant in the literature he read. How nice it would have been to meet those literary men and women he so admired and have a meaningful conversation for a change.

The girls' voices and dolphin laughter broke Alex out of his thoughts. He wasn't made of stone, after all. Truthfully, if he could have one of those girls he would, critical thinking or not. But it had always been hard for him to simply take what he wanted: to insinuate and expose himself to the humiliation and need, that damned need that would never go away, no matter how much he wrote.

Alex lay back in bed and recalled the details of the women he could still hear: the color of their eyes, the size and shape of their breasts, their clothing, their haircuts and the shades of their skin. Then he would jerk off furiously to them: to the tall leggy brunette with the fuzzy pink sweater that had pointed to him, to the curly redhead with the big breasts, and to the mulatto girl with the nice ass and full lips. He would jerk off in homage to them; he would have them in his mind's eye, and there was nothing they could do about it. Yeah, that's right, I own you girls, I can do anything I want, yeah, that's right, oh yeah, right there, that's the way I like it, wonderful girls, and his mind would explode and blissfully block out all thought, before returning to its usual surgical self. Then Alex would lie there feeling like a leper and an outcast until he fell sleep.

At those weekend after-hours house parties Henrik and Jack noticed that Damian often paid more attention to the men than the women. They saw how he leaned close to them when he talked, put his arm around them in a friendly way or touched their leg to make a point. Many of them were models that Jack knew or had worked with, some had been stand-ins in the party scene of the film, and they all knew that an up-and-coming director like Damian was a good contact to have.

Damian was not modest. He talked to them about his movie deal with Solimar, the award he would win at Cannes, and his plans for his next big project. There was always a promise in his words: an invitation that hinted at future stardom. Damian, he was full of promises; they gave him confidence where it was lacking with people he thought better than himself.

Damian talked to the handsome men while casting furtive glances at Jack. Jack understood everything then. Damian was searching for approval before he revealed himself completely. For the first time, Jack saw the confusion, fear, and uncertainty of his friend, who he had grown to admire for his business skills and confidence to pursue his dreams, but whose personal life was mired in crisis. Perhaps Jack had known it all along and ignored it: like he had ignored his own character and destiny. Now that he was out of the fog, it was clear: Damian was gay. Surprisingly, Jack didn't care. It did not repulse him. He had been living in the city too long to keep such a provincial prejudice. He remembered what he had seen in the movie house with Arnold and thought: so what if Damian likes guys? What business is it of mine? His admiration of

Damian and the debt he owed to him was too strong. Without Damian there would have been no work, no girls and no fame. It's his life and he can do with it what he wants. Who am I to judge?

So when Damian disappeared into the bedroom with a young model named Rob, no one said anything about it.

The first time he slept with another man Damian woke up disgusted with himself. A voice in his head told him: you're ill. You deviant, now you've done it and there's nothing you can do to go back. You've done all those things and you enjoyed them. Dammit, why do you have to be this way and what will the others say now? Well, Alex has known all along. Alex sees everything. If ever there were a man with tact, it's Alex.

In the morning Damian found that, on top of feeling hung over, irritable, and mildly depressed from his excesses and weakness of the night before, he had trouble looking Jack in the eye, and that when he did, the look was not the same. Of course, it could never be the same. Damian thought: it's best to talk about it. Why can't he just come out and ask me so I can tell him it's true? I can tell him a good story and say: yes, I like men. I don't know why, but I do. I can't help it and I don't want this to change our relationship. When I look at you I'm not thinking of having sex with you, though I know you probably think that's what we think about all the time. No, it's not like that, Jack. We're friends.

But Damian said nothing. When Rob came over, pretty Rob, they would all be polite to him and pretend he was just a friend.

Well, Rob came and went like a season, and Damian settled back into the project. Perhaps it was just a little experimentation? Or maybe it was a reaction to being unable to find a woman he could relate to like his friends? Or maybe it was boredom?

The party days were over. The housemates had used up their surplus of hedonism and it was time to get back down to business. Damian recovered his work ethic and discipline. He bought the tickets to Mexico; they were going to film down in Chiapas and would have to scout locations and hire some locals to put on masks and uniforms for the final battle. They would need to get a hold of some weapons and explosives for special effects and authenticity's sake. Jack's job, beyond playing the leading role, was to act as translator for the group. He had never gotten worse than a B in his high school Spanish classes, and talking with Santos and the rest of the guys at the restaurant had improved his spoken Spanish considerably; now he could cuss with the best of them. Nevertheless, in the weeks leading up to departure, Jack immersed himself in grammar books and language tapes and watched a good deal of Mexican TV, primarily soccer, because he couldn't stand the soap operas.

At night Jack would lay in bed unable to sleep, thinking: I'm going to Mexico, man. I'm going to the land of *margaritas* and beautiful beaches and sun, and it'll be warm again like the desert.

Damian told Henrik that he didn't have enough in his budget to pay his way, though he did, since Henrik wasn't really essential until later when they were finished shooting. Henrik wanted to be along for the adventure and money wasn't a problem; a trip to Mexico would probably come out cheaper than the same time spent in the city clubbing and eating out. He had always wanted to go to Mexico; there was hardly anything more exotic for a Swede than Latin America. He dreamt about Mexican girls and wondered how he could work some ranchera or mariachi music in with some beats, and what the clubs would be like in Mexico City.

There were still several weeks left before the trip. Jack had a modeling job for a mail-order catalogue, but mostly he was killing time. The fun of clubbing had worn off and he was tired of the city. His current modeling gig bored him, though it would be over soon enough. He didn't want to see most of the girls he had met and been with, though some still called him; sometimes on a lonely night he would break down and invite them over or take a cab to visit them. He wasn't better than that.

There was one girl, Caroline, who Jack liked more than the others. She was a nurse and he had taken her out a few times since their first meeting. He had called her more than that, but she was often too busy with work to see him. She was a genuine person, she worked hard and was kind and caring: all traits that suited her profession. Though they talked often on the phone, he never told her about the other girls or the clubs or his drinking, which he had to work very hard to control, especially with company like Damian and Henrik, alcoholics in their own right. She was not a girl one met in the bars. She was marriage quality and that fact alone scared him. He thought: you're only twenty-four. What's the hurry?

In the end, Jack determined that one didn't meet a good woman in a bar or at a fashion shoot. Though he liked the attention and all those pretty faces, he wanted someone that he could talk to and who cared for him and not his image. Most girls went with him because they wanted to be noticed, but not Caroline: she was a nurse and a midwife; she cared for the sick and delivered babies; she was real and didn't wear a plastic smile or pose or worry too much about her appearance. So Jack liked her and would meet her at her convenience. He talked to her about Arizona and told her about his family. She would laugh at his jokes, the most wonderful illuminating laugh, and he would think: she's just like me.

When I'm with her I don't care about those other girls or the drinking, I just want to make her happy. Who would have thought that I would meet her on the bus?

So they began to spend more time together. It was difficult for both of them when Caroline was called away for a delivery. Jack knew it was selfish for him to want her to stay but that was the way he felt; certainly it was worse for Caroline who had to climb from that warm bed into the cold night to help another life into the world.

But so it was and Jack thought: take it slow and easy. You're in no hurry and life is good now; you have money and work and a girl, and she has her life and you have yours, but sometimes you get lonely when she's not around, and that's when you start to think about the other girls, too. You're still young, Jack, and you shouldn't just settle down because it's convenient or easy. What if something better comes along? Nuts to thoughts like that.

Jack hated that call of youth and the lie of it and how it made him hungry and fake like his pictures, and not Jack at all: Jack without his soul that not even his own parents would recognize. No, he couldn't face up to that. You enjoyed it for a few months, the going out and showing off, but now you're nothing but a mail-order catalogue model and people have forgotten you.

35

Then one day Jack found Elizabeth at his door. Elizabeth, glorious Elizabeth, fire incarnate, the world traveler, the radical and non-conformist back from her adventures. Elizabeth, who looked older than he remembered and who smiled in a difficult, uncertain way: that from a girl who seemed to have it all figured out. Elizabeth had been the light that kept him moving in his dark and lonely days. Even though she didn't write him, except a single postcard that he had saved, he still believed in her, like one believes in a theory without logical foundation.

The thought of their meeting made Elizabeth nervous. She had returned from Indonesia broken and ashamed, repeating in her mind the image of crossing the street and trying to stop herself but stepping off the curb nonetheless, oblivious and blind to the danger and impending disaster.

She had moped around her parents' house in some suburb of Los Angeles watching television, reading books and staying in her frozen-in-time childhood bedroom staring at the ceiling. At night when she sat down to dinner with her parents, they were careful not to mention her trip or her disability. No, they tried to be kind and talk about work, her brother Sean -who had just gone away to college-, the weather and current events. It angered her that they were cowards and that she had become a coward like them. She wanted them to scold her and blame her and tell her to get on with her life.

She wanted to shout, "Dammit, don't be so fucking nice. Don't fucking feel sorry for me and pretend that nothing's changed. I'm not home for the fucking holidays. This is my life."

But she never said anything. She wanted her life to be like that forever; she wanted to be safe with her family. Never again would she go far away where she did not belong and where there was no compassion.

Elizabeth spent a few months at her folk's place, unemployed and moping. She knew that they talked about her in their bedroom at night. She heard their voices through the door, and she wanted to listen and feel the burn of their true feelings, but she was afraid. She slept late into the day, and when she was dreaming, she would forget she was a cripple with a plastic leg, until she woke up and felt the strange shortness there insulting her. Though time had passed, the despair still overwhelmed her and made her feel like she was less than everyone else and that everything would be much harder now.

Often Elizabeth sat on the patio overlooking the garden. The sight of the flowers and the hummingbirds cheered her, and she would think about the beauty of nature and how that was something to live for. One day there were some Blue Jays in the yard, carrying on as Blue Jays do, and she thought how ill-tempered and cruel they were compared to most birds. She watched one of them come down and peck at a lizard lying on the patio. She felt sorry for the lizard, small and green and alone as it was on the hot red tile with the large hostile bird attacking it; she watched with horror as the bird pecked its tail from its body and swallowed it. She got up from her chair, limped to where they were and, waving her crutch, shouted with tears in her eyes, "Beat it, you fucking birds. Leave him alone. Goddamned birds, I hate you. You hear me? I fucking hate you."

Crying, Elizabeth bent down to pick up the injured lizard. She had a lump in her throat as she held his small warm body in her hand and felt his panicked heart. She was sorry for the lizard like she was sorry for herself. Her mother watched from the window, bitterly sad for her daughter. The lizard would grow a new tail, but her daughter would never have a new leg.

Sometimes Elizabeth would think about Jack and feel ashamed for having written him only one postcard in all her time away. She thought herself selfish and cold and deserving of her fate for how she had treated those who had cared for her. She realized that she hadn't written to Graham either, to thank him for helping her in her time of need. She had spent a long time hating Graham and blaming him for her accident, but that was just her anger at him not loving her: anger at her naive love and subsequent delusion. She knew that Graham loved her in his own way and that they were too much alike to ever survive together. She knew that.

So there Elizabeth sat in that shit town Los Angeles, in that shit country, in some shit suburb that looked like all the rest, with her life stretched out before her dead and empty like a desert, inhospitable, knowing that before long she would have to get a job and stop pitying herself.

Elizabeth still had friends in the city and she would return to them. If she practiced, she would be able to walk just fine on her new leg. It was a good leg, and if she wore pants it looked like her own, and that was better than losing an arm, probably. Jack was the person she wanted to see. She needed Jack. She remembered how shy and sad and alone he had been looking for work and wondered how he had done for himself.

Handsome Jack. A real American boy who treated you like a queen and would have done anything for you, and you didn't write him more than a postcard. Well, he probably hasn't been waiting around for you. Why, he must have a whole new life, and you're just a memory to him now, if he thinks about you at all. The truth is you really liked Jack but were never willing to give it a chance. Jack was good for you; Graham frustrated and challenged you and that made you want to conquer him. But he's nothing but a miserable loner with his native wife to do whatever he says, and that's fine. Go and be master with your slave girl, you imperialist bastard.

Give him a break, she thought. He's all alone out there and he treats her sweet and probably loves her, too. There's no recipe for love; if there is, you never learned it.

One morning Elizabeth packed her bags, and at breakfast with her parents before work, she told them she was leaving for San Francisco. It took them by surprise. They didn't want her to leave; they didn't think she was ready and said, "Why don't you stay a little longer and think about it. Maybe you could find something here in L.A.?"

"No thanks. You've been kind to me, and I love you both very much, but I'm leaving. I can't sit here and stew any longer."

"How long are you going to be gone, honey? When will we see you again?"

"I don't know. As long as it takes. I can't let this business with the leg ruin my life. I'm better than that," she said.

It was the first time the leg had been mentioned since her arrival home, and they all fell silent as if it were standing among them with its own opinions and feelings.

But it wasn't, and Elizabeth left, thinking all the while about what Jack would say when he found out. Would it disgust him? Would he pretend it didn't matter? It had no doubt changed her. Had life also changed Jack from the man he was?

When he saw Elizabeth, Jack knew that he still loved her. Caroline was warm-hearted and kind, but she wasn't Elizabeth. She was a well-behaved stand-in. Wonderful in her own way but very clearly a replacement for a lost love. He knew that now.

"Hi Jack. Can I come in?"

Jack stood there dumb. Here she was straight from a dream. Just last evening after Caroline had gone home, Jack had dreamt of Elizabeth. In the dream she was crying and he was holding her. They were together and he felt her wet tears on his neck. He told her, "Don't worry, I'm still here." But she was inconsolable.

"Wow, Elizabeth, is it really you? Wow. I can't believe it."

Jack stepped onto the porch and gave her a big hug still thinking of the dream and wondering: did she have a difficult time? She looks tired. Maybe she just got back. He forgot that he was angry with her and all the time that had passed with no communication. The fact that she was there visiting him showed that she hadn't forgotten. She was really back; Jack was hugging her and she was hugging him tight, none of that fake loose hugging that left you wondering.

"Oh Elizabeth, it's so good to see you. God, I've forgotten how pretty you are. How have you been? What's been going on? What have you seen and done? I've got so many questions for you. Wow, I gotta say a lot's happened here. You wouldn't believe it if I told you. Come on, let's go inside."

She noticed that he was happy. He was happy and talkative and wasn't afraid to hug her or hold her hand after so much time. She thought he would be uncomfortable. But now that feeling was exclusively hers. The past is the past, she thought.

"Do you want to say hi to the others?"

"Later," she said.

Jack smiled. "Yeah, later, that's better." He didn't want to share her with them anyway. She was there to see him in particular because they were a team. They had been together and now she had come back to him.

They sat on the bed.

"Arnold's not here anymore," Jack said. "He kidnapped a Chinese girl and brought her down to San Diego and married her."

Elizabeth smiled for the first time and everything that seemed different about her disappeared.

"Why doesn't that surprise me?"

"And that's not all. The girl, her name is Mei Li, is a singer. She sings in bars around the military base."

"How does Arnold feel about that?"

"Well, when I talked to him last week, he told me he'd been in jail for punching a military guy who was feeling her up. Unfortunately, the guy's squad was there and they ganged up on him in the parking lot and nearly killed him. He says he's been sleeping with steaks on his eyes and that his nose is a little flatter now."

"I can just picture it," she said. "So what about you? How are things?"

"Good. Things are good."

"Come on, Jack, don't clam up on me now. When I saw you again I thought how happy you looked. You're still as handsome as ever, you know," she said, pushing her fingers through his hair.

"Oh, come on. Anyway, I guess I've been happy. You wouldn't believe what I've been through since you left," he said.

Just wait until you hear my story, she thought. Just wait until I tell you what I've been through, Jack, because I need to tell someone before it kills me.

"The weather's just been terrible. You sure were lucky to go off there to Thailand and be in the tropics, and I bet you have some great stories."

"Indonesia, not Thailand."

"Right, Indonesia. Man, I almost froze to death this winter. I wore my thermals non-stop, I could see my breath in the air and I lived on eggs, beans and rice. And the economy. Boy, it just kept getting worse. I did an experiment with virtual reality to make some extra cash and I got electrocuted so bad it knocked me unconscious."

Jack was coming to the present and he deliberated over showing her his modeling pictures. He wanted her to be proud of him, but worried she would think him vain. She wasn't like the other girls.

"Anyway, Damian got me this job as a PA, and the next thing I know I'm on stage with In Quick, and I know they're a bunch of fags, but check this out." Jack went to his desk and found the picture of himself in the Chronicle. He collected the magazines he had appeared in, and his portfolio photos, and handed them to her.

"I guess this says it better than I can."

She looked them over and smiled. There was Jack looking handsome and mysterious with his distant gaze and blank face, a man's face, a face that had been hers before. There he was with unfamiliar women in his arms. Elizabeth was jealous and wondered who those women could be and if he had know them well. She wanted to ask if that's why he was so happy: not because he was making money modeling, but because one of those girls was his.

"I guess you must get plenty of attention these days," she said.

"Oh, no. Well, I meet a lot of girls on the shoots, but that's just professional, and most of them live in other places and . . . They're not like you, Elizabeth. I mean they're pretty, but they aren't like you. They don't know me like you do, and most people don't understand that this stuff isn't real, anyway. Even when you're there, it isn't real. I don't wanna be a model for the rest of my life. I mean it's easy money, I feel guilty how easy it is, but if they think I'm right for it, I'll do it."

"You don't have to apologize for yourself, Jack. I've been gone a long time and I'm sure you've met a lot of sweet women to keep you happy. I don't care about that. Do you have a girlfriend?"

"Not really. I mean, I have a friend or two, but girlfriend, no, not really," he said. Before, he would have never been able to lie like that. "Damian and I are making a movie," he said, to change the subject.

"Oh yeah, what about?"

"I'll show it to you later," he said. "We've got the first part done, well, the raw footage anyway."

Jack was looking at her in that way now, the one he had learned on the bus and taken to the clubs. He was hungry for her and he wanted to touch her and press himself against her and be her slave, son and father. He wanted to abuse her and die with her and forget the day with her and return to her after such a long absence. He wanted so much from her and couldn't help but think about her and her body, and how they could be together, and what they could talk about, and their laughter and tears, moans, shouts and sighs. Looking into her eyes, Jack imagined that there was something she wanted and needed from him, too, and he would give it to her, oh yes he would; he would do anything for her. Jack put his arms around her and kissed her. Soon he was pushing her down on the bed and undressing her.

"Jack, please. Stop."

"What's wrong?

"Jack, I've got something to tell you. I missed you so much, and now I'm back, and I want it to be okay between us. I want us to be together. I want you, Jack, and I want you to want me, too."

"But I do want you. I want you so bad it hurts. I want you so bad I'd cut off my finger for you."

"No, Jack, no," she said, her face twisting up. "Don't talk like that, please, you don't know what you're saying."

And then came the fear that she would be separated from him: her only point of stability and the only person that could fill the hole inside her. The emotion flooded out of her: all the fear and anguish and frailty of her life; and there was Jack, a prince like in his pictures, immortal and beautiful and whole, waiting to save her. She had traveled halfway around the world to come back to him where she belonged. But now she was crippled.

"Oh God, Jack, why do I feel this way? I'm weak and I'm damaged, and I've had a hard time. I thought I could do it. I thought I didn't need anyone to be great. But he didn't love me, Jack. I wanted to be great with him and explore the world and face my fears, to look at them and laugh and be free, but I failed."

Elizabeth was crying now, and Jack lay back and held her and ran his fingers through her hair. Hasn't this happened before, he wondered. But how does it turn out? I just can't remember the ending. It's like tomorrow and I don't know what's going to happen.

"He had another girl, and I watched them having sex in the garden, and all he thinks about is blood and death, so he can be miserable. You're much better than that, Jack. You're so good to me. I don't deserve you. I abandoned you."

"Shhh, shhh. Don't worry, I'm still here. You're with me now and not in Thailand."

She was too upset to correct him.

"I don't know what happened there but I imagine it must have been hard," he said. "I mean what do I know? I've never been anywhere like that. I'm not courageous like you. I can never know what you've seen."

Elizabeth sat up and looked him in the eye. Her eyes were angry through her tears. She was upset at herself and the drama. She hated drama, and that she would indulge in it now when it was so important to face it down and say it straight out.

She began to fumble with her belt, "Now you're gonna see, Jack. Now you're gonna see what's wrong with me."

Elizabeth fought her pants down, and Jack saw the smooth skin of her thighs and thought to touch her, but she was so angry, she was seething and violent, and he watched with horror as she removed her leg, her left leg; she took it right off and shook it at him.

"You see, Jack. Can you ever love a freak like me? Look at this. Isn't it absurd?"

Jack had no answer for her. He was in shock. She threw the leg down and it thudded heavy on the redwood floor.

"Make love to me, Jack. Fuck me, even if it's the last time. Then I'll go away and you can be with the magazine girls and forget about me and think about how it once was when things were different."

Elizabeth pressed herself against him and kissed him, and Jack managed to close his face and hide his shock. She was the same now as before; they struggled together and she was crying and kissing him, and he said, "Oh Elizabeth, oh God, you're too good to me, you're so sweet." The feeling of the curious stump of her leg excited him and he couldn't get enough of her.

She's fucked up, all right. This is fucked up. God, this is terrible. What does it matter if she doesn't have a leg? You'd prefer it if she did, but she doesn't, and you can't choose it. It's not like in the magazines, you can't fake it or pretend, you have to take it as it comes with the bad and the good together.

36

Graham woke up in the morning with a bad feeling, and in his business a bad feeling meant death. It was not that he was a courageous man; he was simply accustomed to taking risks. There had been times in his life when he had prayed desperately to a god he did not believe in and literally shit in his pants and urinated in his shoes from fear. Only a person who hadn't experienced it would feel ashamed of that. But this feeling was different. It was a distant and manageable unease like that of an army before the battle. I wonder if it's going to happen today? The army has been talking about an offensive for some time now. They're going to strike the granary, which is full of weapons and not grain at all, if what Mbeki tells me is correct.

Mbeki's a good snitch. It's the only way to be in this place. Work for yourself. Be independent, because no one is your friend. In that way I can relate to him. He can relate to me because I give him money in a country where if you don't join the rebels or the army and get a gun, so that you can rob your friends and neighbors, then you won't survive. I've seen it time and again; in politics and economics it's always ordinary people that get caught in the middle and suffer. It's the children whose schools are riddled with bullets and destroyed, the teachers that are forced to desert, the workers that lose their jobs, and the women that are raped and lose their homes, husbands and children. That's the reality of our world. It's not a place where violence has been erased. Everywhere is the face of death. For the men who have become soldiers, who have taken sides to control this or that diamond mine, who desire to oust the dictator so that they may become him, for them, weapons and belligerence serve to keep the taboo of death at arm's length. They know now, after so much bloodshed, hatred and lies, that the only way out is kill or be killed. For this reason, a neighbor kills a neighbor, a brother and brother, and a soldier, his fellow soldier.

It was unclear to Graham which was better: a repressive dictatorship controlled by foreign interest that paid miners below subsistence wages and murdered the political opposition; or the chaos of civil war between said dictatorship and rebel forces led by an equally heartless, blood-thirsty strongman. It was clear to him that civil war was the logical consequence of colonial power and its politics of inequity; dictators were only removed in such nations by a coup, bloody or not, invariably replaced by clones in the guise of progress and change. The ousted leaders would then flee to live off their amassed wealth in some foreign exile where they might even be fêted as celebrities. No, Graham realized, armed revolution was not the solution.

The northern region of the nation was in rebel control when Graham arrived there from the capital. He was familiar with Dr. K, the rebel leader, since the early period of the conflict. At the time Graham had been idealistic, believing Dr. K to be sincere in his desire to liberate his country from an oppressive government and improve the lives its citizens.

Graham had interviewed him and published an article in the American press documenting Dr. K's rise to power.

At the time Dr. K had said, "What we desire is a democracy such as you have in the West. The people here wish to control their own destiny. We will take over the mines and distribute the wealth to the people. In this way we will build a strong nation."

Now Dr. K did control the mines: not all, but a substantial portion of them. Combining his message of prosperity with diamond revenues, he had built himself an army equal to or more powerful than that of the President. In spite of the progress of the revolution, there had been no improvement in the daily lives of the people; instead, the civil war had brought only death, homelessness, starvation and unemployment.

Dr. K later defended the revolution, stating, "Until we have rid ourselves of this dictatorship, that is, until all government forces have been defeated and run out of this land, the people will see no end to their suffering and need. This corrupt and oppressive regime has left us with no recourse but violence. For justice to prevail and democracy to be established, the people must be willing to die for the cause."

Graham had been granted permission to enter rebel territory and record government atrocities, provided his reports of Dr. K and his army remained favorable. In a telephone conversation, Dr. K had told him, "War is an ugly business, Mr. Ellis, but our war is a just one in which violence is a necessary tool to achieve our aims. It is the government that makes no distinction between civilians and soldiers. For them, we are one and the same: a problem to be eliminated. I remember you from the early days of the revolution. I have not forgotten your face. You have documented our struggle and I believe you are sympathetic to our cause. I hope you will not violate this trust and put yourself in danger."

Graham did not have the nerve to ask Dr. K why he used the villages as arms repositories, or why he stationed his troops next to schools and in private homes. He did not voice his misgivings about the rebel army, or mention the well-founded rumors of Dr. K's secret bank account that was estimated in the tens of millions, fed daily by the struggle. Nor did he ask why that money was not going to help the people.

The novelty of international journalism had worn off. Graham's idealism had solidified into a calculated practicality. He would keep his mouth shut, find a way into the conflict zone and take the pictures that told the truth about both sides. If all went well, he would survive to write the story to be read by those who were safe at home in mediocrity, unclear about the condition of the world.

This time when Graham requested an interview, he was refused. Dr. K was far too busy. The government had intensified the conflict and was planning several new offensives. Graham had access to one of Dr. K's generals who informed him that the likely target was a town on the western edge of the diamond fields. The general then arranged for Graham's passage, at his own risk, on a troop convoy sent to fortify the town.

Now Graham walked the streets of that town with electricity in his spine, tense and painfully sensitive to the smallest details of the moment. It was always like this before the battle. Graham was seeing things for the first time with no thought of yesterday or tomorrow.

It was a town of roughly ten thousand people. The shop-lined main road terminated in a town square that served as the local bus station and marketplace. The square was filled with brightly dressed women, merchants and customers alike: the former hawking grain, spices, produce and livestock; the latter socializing and bargaining to fill the baskets carried on their heads. Rebel soldiers stood in nearby doorways, assault rifles hanging from their shoulders, smoking and staring into infinity. In the upper floor windows of the concrete tenements more troops waited out the day. On the terraces, behind retaining walls, artillery pieces had been positioned to cover the road. Aside from the women and children in the market, the town was unusually quiet. Graham knew why and so did the troops that had been ordered to remain. Whether an assault would come that day, that week or ever, was unknown. Graham knew the storehouse was empty and that many of the local men had been armed by the revolutionaries and paid to fight for them. Whether they would fight or run was questionable. There had been many false warnings; often the intelligence was wrong and a different village would go under attack, or the mines themselves, but there one had to be careful to not disrupt work or risk collapsing the caves with artillery.

In a civil war, Graham had learned, it was impossible to distinguish lies from truth, the enemy from the ally. Every man's truth was another's lie, and often people lied to themselves and were enemies to their friends and friends to their enemies for the sake of their own survival. Morality aside, the government was as likely to retain power as the rebels were to take it for themselves, and those who chose the wrong side would die. Once again Graham would have to trust his instincts to survive.

37

Jack did not see Elizabeth again. In the morning, when she put on her leg, he knew it was over between them. Jack was not strong enough to support her disability; it was a superficial and shameful attitude to have, but it was the truth. Her power over him had faded. He did not think of her as better than him any longer. She had become needy and dependent, and shame and embarrassment prevented them from looking each other in the eye. They could no longer talk to each other with candor. The connection was broken.

Jack turned away as she got dressed. Daylight brought with it the harsh reality of the leg and the sad knowledge that its absence prevented their union. When they said their goodbyes, it was for the last time, despite the promises, excuses and explanations they employed to mask the truth. It was still early and Jack lay in bed watching Elizabeth behind half closed-eyes. She leaned over and kissed him on the forehead.

"Goodbye, Jack."

"Goodbye, Elizabeth."

She stepped into the hallway, shut the door carefully behind her and was gone. Jack rolled over to her side of the bed, stuck her pillow under his head, smelled the perfume of her hair and felt the warmth of her recently departed body in the sheets.

She left early so the others wouldn't see her, he thought. She's ashamed of herself and she's not coming back. It's not because you don't want to be with her, he told himself. No, it's because of other people and what they will say. You wanted to be with her forever when you saw her again. It seemed right then. But it doesn't now. She's not the same woman you loved. She's lost her fire, and you're no longer lonely or poor.

There are plenty of girls that can give you love and affection who are whole and not damaged by life. So why don't you pick one and stick with her? Because now that you've stopped living like a pauper and a slave, you want to enjoy yourself.

Since Elizabeth, Jack had been attracted to and had enjoyed the company of many women. Though he felt he could settle down with any one of them and make it work, he did not feel it was time. Fame had revealed to Jack his innate beauty and charm, and from this foundation he had built a ladder of confidence to higher goals: among them an acting career and, ultimately, financial success. Jack's ego was by now inflated to dangerous proportions and was in the process of destroying his heart. As a result, he had let Caroline go; he was not mature enough to love a real woman. As for Elizabeth, he had become her: vain and self-absorbed, while her star had gone out forever. He told himself that his womanizing was in fact a search for the ideal woman, but in truth he was only loving himself by proxy with each new pretty face.

Now when you seduce women, they bore you. Is that just age? Probably. Part age and part fear of how it could change your life and bring unwanted responsibility. The truth is, you're more interested in novelty than commitment. Like Damian said, you have to use what you've got to get what you want. You want to have fun and know lots of women, and though that's what you'll always want, you can't stay on top forever. So you might as well ride this out as long as you can.

It was only later that Jack realized socializing was a full-time job. If he wanted to be successful with women, he had to focus all his time and energy on their entertainment. Not to mention money. He soon realized that the supply was inexhaustable and that he risked becoming a mere caricature of himself if he continued the game. He had become another predator flashing through the darkness of the discotheque, snapping the jaws of his desire on the elusive mass of young pretty female prey, always desiring what escaped his grasp. What he caught was quickly consumed, yet his hunger was not sated. The hunt could not continue indefinitely. To stay on top of the food chain in the pop culture and entertainment scene required publicity, continued achievement and strategic alliance. The goal was to remain popular and be admired by strangers, at the expense of one's heart, mind and soul.

It was only a matter of time before Jack was no longer a fresh face on the scene. Though he had started acting, he had yet to appear on screen, and it was not certain the film would ever make it to the theater. No, he was a small fish, and he doubted he would ever have the comfort or the energy to engage fully in the vanity of the famous. Jack was not a man prone to envy; he had grown up in a loving family and did not crave attention. Mostly, he was glad to be able to enjoy his youth and the new life he had found with the housemates that had become his close friends. But he was also a man who loved women, and regardless of fame, he was fortunate to enjoy their attention. He would have been a fool to ignore the opportunities that came his way.

Sooner or later, you'll have to choose a woman, and you want that choice to be right for you, he thought. The irony was that a choice, once made, was in fact the negation of choice. Just as it wasn't possible to head two directions simultaneously, nor was it possible to return to the origin of one's departure. With each choice, the future choices would change.

The best girls, the one's with looks, brains and a sense of humor to boot, required complete commitment, and if he wasn't cable of it, there would always be another guy who was. Jack was still unsure if he preferred a practical woman who could care for his needs, manage a household and provide him with comfort, or an adventurous woman who required flattery and novelty in a relationship. In his life, he had known women to fall somewhere in these two categories. Caroline had been the former and Elizabeth the latter. Ultimately, the answer depended on whether it was better to love or be loved.

38

That week Jack didn't have much going so he had lunch in the Haight and took the bus downtown. After a stop at the Nordworth Center, he made his way to Virgo to visit Henrik.

I wonder if Henrik got tested? He puts on a good face but it must weigh on him knowing what happened to Julie. I'd want to know for sure.

Jack stood at the crosswalk in Union Square watching the pedestrians and the traffic. It took him a moment to notice the beggar with the red beard and Giants cap across the street. Jack found the intensity of the man's gaze disconcerting. He experienced a moment of disequilibrium and conflicted emotions. The man was young and Jack identified with him. That young man is me or what I could have become. Who's to say it isn't just chance that separates us? Jack's empathy, coupled with the memory of James, drove him to dig into his pocket for change.

The light changed and the crowd surged across the street. How does a kid like that end up homeless, Jack wondered. It can't just be laziness; like James said, plenty of good people end badly. James, it would be nice to see him again. Boy, if I ran into James, I'd buy him a fancy dinner and make good on what he's done for me. Sure, he didn't give me money or help me get a job, but he talked straight to me. He told it like it was and cut the bullshit; that's worth a lot in this world.

Jack and the beggar met in the street. Jack was caught in the young man's gravity as the men and women of the city surged by unhindered and oblivious. The young man had been staring at Jack a long time with his flinty blue eyes. And Jack stared back, aware of the danger and complicity of a stare in public.

It doesn't matter, Jack thought. You're gonna give him some money anyway, so what if he jabbers at you? Let him talk and then give him the money. Who knows what he'll use it for, but just give it to him and keep walking. Maybe that'll fill the hole and the vertigo inside you. Maybe it'll put you back in place again, and you can feel like you're a good person and that things will go favorably for you because of your good deed. Not that charity does anything for a man. Charity is just so you can feel good. You're giving him the money because you're thinking of James, Doc and Mary.

They were side by side, and before Jack could give him the money, the man said, "I seen you. I seen you up in the sky. Look there you are."

He pointed and Jack, perplexed and uneasy, turned and looked up. Sure enough, it was the billboard. He knew it was there but somehow had forgotten, absorbed as he was in his thoughts. In fact, he had been oblivious to the landscape since he had left the house; it was something that happened when you lived in the city. Not that Jack didn't know where he was, but it was habit that had gotten him there, always to the same places. He no longer noticed the details. The man's words broke through the wall of Jack's thoughts and pulled him from his reverie.

"Yeah, that's me," Jack said. He was going to give him a dollar and change, but suddenly it wasn't enough. He opened his wallet and pulled out a five and handed it over.

"Here."

The young man took the money and stuck it away without looking at it.

"No, but I known you before. From when you was with us sleeping in the park. I know you, man."

He was agitated now and grabbed Jack's arm. The pedestrians turned their heads to stare.

Jack looked at him again.

"Will."

"Yeah, that's me. I'm Will. Now I don't remember your name, never been good with names, but I knew we was familiar. And now you're up in the sky. Would'ya look at that. I'da never believed it. Once we was gonna be movie stars, us in the park, I mean. Someone said they was gonna put us in a movie so they'd know about us, you know, how we's good people and all. But I guess that never came to much."

Almost a year had passed and Jack was startled to see how much Will had aged. His face was a mess of wrinkles, he had grown a beard, and his hair was wild under his hat; everything about him said sadness and deprivation. Jack thought: Will, how did you get here? Who were your parents, where did you come from and why doesn't anyone care about you?

"So how's James," Jack asked.

"Oh James, he's been suffering a cough, and Doc pulled out one of his teeth that was rotten with a pair of pliers the other day. It must'a hurt fierce 'cause James was ahollerin'. And you know James, he ain't one to make a big fuss. What was your name, anyhow? I wish I coulda remember' it. Problem is I forget stuff . . ."

"Jack."

"Right Jack, 'course I remember now. Sure nice'a you to lend me a hand, Jack. Big star like you. Who'da thought I'da known you."

Jack felt a sickness that came from deep inside and was built on experience: it was a sickness for the frailty of the human condition and the knowledge that loneliness and fear destroyed even the best of men; it was disgust at the waste, mistakes, misunderstanding and failure that made life such a difficult journey. And here was Will blubbering about knowing him, the big star, acting small when they were equal. It was too much to take. Whatever you do, don't you cry, Jack. It makes you so goddamned sad, but don't you cry.

If I could only give them some hope, Jack thought. It won't last forever, and it sure as hell won't save them, but maybe it can stop the pain for a while.

"Listen, Will, I'm gonna give you my number. You give it to James and tell him to call me. Tell him it's important. Can you do that for me?"

"Sure Jack."

"Are you gonna get something to eat with the money?"

"Sure am, Jack. I ain't gonna get me a bottle. I like the bottle but all I been dreamin' about lately is blueberry pancakes. Blueberry pancakes just like my ma used to make when we was kids, and the smell of it and how they're warm in your mouth with syrup on top."

"That sounds good, Will. You take care of yourself and I'll be seeing you soon. And don't you forget that message."

Jack stuck out his hand and Will shook it vigorously and said, "Jack, you're a good man and I'm awful sorry about trying to steal from you. I'm sorry about that, Jack. I may be poor but I still got a conscience."

"That's all right, Will. The past is the past and I forgive you."

You're crazy, Jack. You think you're gonna help them out? Get them some clothes and a haircut, take them out on the town and show them a good time? If anything it'll depress them. They'll see how they could have had it if their luck had been different. That might be hard to swallow. Though not much harder than the television dreams we swallow every day.

Just what are you trying to prove, anyway? You aren't exactly made of money. You should be saving that money instead of blowing it on shopping and partying and handouts to your conscience.

I'm doing it because I can and I should, Jack told himself. I want to create a little magic. I've never done anything for anyone and now's my chance. Soon we'll be in Mexico, and now's my chance to give some people a laugh or at least a little comfort, when they haven't had it for so long. It's the sort of thing you do and don't talk about. Fine. Yes, as far as you're concerned people don't do it enough. The world would be a better place if people were more generous. And I'm not talking about money, but in word and deed.

39

Graham sat eating at a street kitchen in the company of laborers, shopkeepers, deliverymen with their carts nearby, and the occasional merchant with his wares in a bag by his side. Graham ate stew with vegetables and bits of goat, bones and all. It was good stew and hot, and he didn't worry about germs. He'd traveled plenty and been sick enough off food that his stomach had developed a tolerance for such things. At any rate, he liked eating what the locals ate. He liked sitting beside them, hearing their chatter and looking into their faces; each of their lives was a unique story of hardship and perseverence. Graham sympathized with those men and was humbled by their company.

The force of the blast knocked them from their seats and showered them with dirt, concrete and metal. When Graham opened his eyes, he saw the same men bathed in blood, some dead and others injured and maimed with eyes wild and full of fear and adrenaline like his own.

The battle had begun.

People were shouting now; the pleasant hum of voices over the lunch table, of men on break from their duties, was gone. The man to his right, with his bright laughter, was lying face down in the dirt. Graham had to crawl over his body to find shelter behind the wall. Under the corrugated steel overhang of the restaurant, arms and legs, hands and feet, pieces of people were strewn about, absurdly fragmented and lonely. The hum was there again, the electric hum that came from death and seeing it and somehow being spared its violence and authority. Ironically, it was this curiosity about death that drove Graham's work and gave meaning to his life.

Graham found his camera bag slung by the remains of the wall. He was relieved to find that his camera hadn't been damaged in the blast. The shelling continued as he checked over and prepared his equipment. Then he set about documenting the carnage. He collected the corpses in his lens, storing them up for posterity, before taking to the streets. He pulled on his white press jersey and joined the chaos. He placed more trust in that white shirt than in any person he had ever known. It was a talisman that was worth more to him than anything he had ever owned or would own.

A rooftop artillery gun was hit with a shell from the incoming tanks, releasing an explosion that showered the street with concrete. Panic reigned as the government stormed the town with tanks and an entire battalion of soldiers. Graham saw the vicious tight skull faces of the army, rebel soldiers, and civilians alike as they fought for their lives. Drugged with fear, soldiers shot down women and children in cold blood. Civilians defended themselves with machetes, rocks, and any implement at hand. In some cases, army soldiers were cornered and overwhelmed, beaten to death, butchered or burned alive. Few Liberation Party troops remained in town and it fell upon ordinary people to defend their homes and families.

The rebel soldiers present, the two gunner teams and the few hundred guards, were decoys condemned to death. Graham realized with horror that the shelling came from outside the town: from the Liberation Party itself. They are sacrificing their own people to ambush the government. If necessary, they will kill everyone to achieve victory. If I don't get out, I'll die, too, jersey or no jersey.

Graham found a secure place where he could crouch with his back to the wall. The scene was apocalyptic: bawling mothers carried their dead, bloodied children through the streets; civilians were rounded up, forced on their knees, and summarily executed; the defenseless scavenged weapons from the dead and shot anything in a uniform and sometimes each other. People looted. Children learned for the first time that they could kill.

Graham skirted the wall and kept to the narrow streets and alleyways. From a nearby window he heard a woman's screams. Peering inside, he saw the military men, three of them: two that stood laughing and unbuttoning their pants as the third raped a woman on the bed. Graham's heart was racing. The sickness had overwhelmed him. It had always been his job to document such things and not get involved. He wanted to float above the misery and protect himself from it by freezing it in time. He wanted to be immune to humanity. But now he wanted to trade his camera for a gun.

Presently, one of the men turned to the window. Graham photographed him, immortalizing the white of his eyes and teeth. After the click of the shutter, the man leveled a pistol at Graham's face and pulled the trigger.

Later, when the men had all taken their turn with the woman and cut her throat, they stripped Graham's body and took his clothes and belongings. They fought over his camera and wallet. One of the men got the camera, and the other two split the contents of the wallet. They were in a good mood then and feeling funny, so they took Graham's naked body and threw it in bed on top of the dead woman.

"It's dangerous to sleep with another man's wife," one man said.

"Stupid white man. Why he come so far to die?"

Those same three soldiers were dead twenty minutes later when the rebel forces invaded the town after leveling most of the buildings and killing nearly all of the civilians present and several thousand government troops. In the end the government army was forced to retreat. Graham's white press jersey was later to be seen on a rebel soldier riding on the back of a tank in the victory train leaving town.

Merpati gave birth to Graham's son, Santoso, eight months later. She would spend many years waiting and hoping in vain for Graham's return. She was a disgraced widow now and her family never spoke to her again.

40

Jack met James, Doc, Mary and Will in the park. He paid their fare downtown and took them to a department store, nothing fancy, but a place where they could get some decent clothes. At first they were ashamed to go inside. Will looked at the floor and they all stuck together. Even James, who was a thinking man, was without his dignity. But that's why they were there in the first place. How could they be dignified without a decent set of clothes? So Jack did his best to help and encourage them. He brought out shirts and pants and asked their preferences, while they shrugged, so alien was the concept of shopping to them. James was the first to show interest in a certain style and color of slacks. Then he found the courage to pick out a shirt on his own. The others soon followed his example. Jack let them shop, conscious of the dirty and disgusted looks they received from customers and staff. At one point, an employee grabbed Doc by the arm and told him to leave, but Jack intervened and explained the situation. He was their social worker and they were entitled to some decent clothes so they might get a job. The young clerk relented. He seemed embarrassed and did not bother them again. They wore their purchases out, but there was still a problem: they were unwashed and needed haircuts.

Mary, more than the men, had been suffering from her appearance. Her new outfit brought a smile to her face; it was the first time Jack had seen her smile. It was not a pretty smile, crooked teeth and all, but it was a smile, nonetheless.

On the way to the barber and the hairdresser, James told Doc, "I bet you ain't looked this good since the high school dance."

"And I still remember the girl I went with. Lola Makenzie. Now she was a real looker, I'm tellin' you."

At the barber's they waited while Will had his hair washed, cut short and parted on the side; they watched his baby face appear when his beard was shaved away. He was a handsome young man, and Jack thought again how they could have been friends; he looked like someone Jack might see at one of the many house parties he went to with Damian and the others.

Though James shaved regularly, his hair was long and unkempt. When the barber finished, Jack saw the father he had once been and wondered what James might have been thinking looking at himself as he was now.

Mary had her hair washed, cut and dyed at the salon, while the men went to the cafe for a cup of coffee. Jack instructed the stylist to give her the full treatment. The young woman did her best to hide her discomfort at Mary's looks. Mary had lived a hard life and that was something people didn't want to know about.

When they were ready, Jack told them, "I've made reservations at a nice restaurant. I'm taking you all there and we're going to eat and drink until we're satisfied. That means I don't want anyone saying they're just going to have a salad, or acting shy about ordering as many drinks as they want. Is that understood?"

"Jack, thanks a lot for the clothes and the haircut. It means a lot to us. But I don't think we can take you up on your offer," James said. "It's not our life, Jack. You can't make us something we're not, or we'll just embarrass you."

"I'm not trying to make you anything at all. I just want to show you a good time for a change. I mean, just look at you guys. You look great. You're ready to do the town. And you're gonna go home? Come on. Doc, do you want to go home, or do you want to go and have a drink and see some gypsy dancers? I bet you've never seen anything like that, have you?"

"Well, Jack, I do have a soft spot for gypsies."

"And Will, how about you? Wouldn't you like to see all the pretty girls down there in Italytown?"

Will shrugged.

"All right, Jack, I get the point," James said. "If you want us to go, we'll go. But I don't want you to think you're doing us no favors. It's your money and you do what you want with it. I guess since you're a big star it's not that important how you spend it. What do I know, anyhow?"

James spoke in his tough, cynical way, but he didn't feel tough or cynical inside. He was deeply moved and he wanted to hug Jack. Walking along the street, he couldn't help but turn to look at his reflection in the shop windows; it scared him to see the man he had once been. He wanted to run away and hide from that man's judgment. James thought him dead, but now he had returned to fix James with his piercing gaze and ask the question: why?

Jack had made his reservation at Amerika. Sure, he had sworn never to return, but that promise was made to be broken. It was nostalgia that brought him back as an older and wiser version of himself. He hoped to measure his growth on the memory of his first experience at Amerika. Carlo, he's crooked all right, but you can forgive him for what happened. And you can't blame Martino for his anger at the world. He's just a working stiff.

They walked down Broadway in the fading light of dusk alongside the tourists and weekend crowds: the young and hip, the families, the businessmen and couples. Why, they could have been tourists themselves.

This could be my family, Jack thought. We could be on vacation from another state. But we're not visitors, are we? We know this city and are aware of its lies and illusions. We know that the people that live and work here seldom come to this part of town; they don't eat clam chowder at Pier 39, visit Alcatraz or ride the cable car, because they're too busy making a living.

In spite of these thoughts, Jack felt good walking with the others. He felt like a tour guide taking them places they had never been.

Will couldn't help his twenty-something eyes from staring at those young women, in groups or alone, dressed to the nines, full of smiles and laughter; for once they were conscious of his gaze and looked away flattered. Will wanted to have one of those girls very badly and felt the anguish of knowing that it would never be so, that he was unwanted and that it was just another fantasy like that warm comfort of being drunk when all problems receded and one felt a sense of peace and belonging again.

Doc walked with his chest out, unconsciously stroking the lapel of his blazer. Doc was a man of experience who had worked hard in his youth before losing his faith in the world. He'd had his share of misfortunes like anyone, until one day he woke up alone on the street with just the bottle for a friend. Somehow, he'd become a broken man and given up on his dreams.

James walked with his arm around Mary; to Jack they seemed like any married couple, old and tired but somehow satisfied with life. Jack noted those small signs of pleasure in all of them and thought that the greatest gift of the poor was the ability to find joy in the details of life. I'm not any happier now that I have some money, Jack thought. I can do what I want, but I'm not any happier. In fact, sometimes when I think about my future I worry that it won't work out, that I won't try hard enough, or that the film will fail and I'll never get ahead. There is nothing worse than just drifting through life, though ambition can make a man sick and blind if he's not careful.

Looking at his friends, Jack thought: it's impossible to see beneath the surface to someone's heart to know how they really feel. Is it all just an illusion like advertisement: a collective effort to pretend we've got it together? Remember Arnold? We all thought he had it together. But then you came by his place and he was desperate; he confessed to you about the debt and the loneliness and all the rest. He was falling apart. And he was someone you admired. It's only now that Arnold's worthy of admiration: since he's stopped living to impress others and started living for his heart. He's seen his own limitations. Or maybe he has created them for the sake of his own sanity. Well, you're not there yet. One day you'll have to face that, but not today. Or perhaps you're just luckier than most.

"Hey, hold up, guys. This is the place," Jack said.

They were nearly out of Italytown, on the border of the Financial District, when he stopped them in front of the marbled façade of Amerika. Jack had returned to the beginning.

The valet pulled up in a black luxury sedan and handed the keys to a man in a suit talking on his cell phone. The man directed his young female companion into the passenger seat and stuck some bills in the valet's hand.

"I don't know, Jack, this place looks pretty high end," James said. "We could just go to the diner and get us some steak and fries and that would be great. I don't think none of us have been out to eat in a long time. It don't matter where we go."

"We've been to the soup kitchen," Doc said. "I reckon that's the last time we was out."

"I don't wanna hear that kind of talk," Jack said. "I know this place. I used to work here and the boss, Carlo, so long as you pay, he doesn't care. That's how it is."

Jack approached the unfamiliar hostess and gave her his name.

"I know who you are. I've seen you on the billboard," she told him, smiling. It was familiar attention and Jack let a brief fantasy of her pass through his mind.

She found his reservation, looked from Jack to his company, and back again. Noting her confusion, Jack explained, "This is my family. They're from out of state."

Though James and the others were dressed nice enough, they were underdressed, and they stood strange and awkward in the doorway. The men and women sitting at the bar and in the lounge gave them looks; like arrogant museum statues, they looked down from whatever pedestal they had built for themselves. They were confused at the juxtaposition of Jack, immaculate in his Baducci suit, with the worn country folk in their ill-fitting clothes and apparent apprehension.

Even if the regular patrons didn't recognize Jack, his appearance made them uneasy. The men touched the bald spot on their heads or patted their swollen bellies, while the women checked themselves in the mirror behind the bar, hoping for a glance they did not receive.

And then Carlo came, Carlo who was not of these people, either; no, he was just a clever Italian beggar who had used his head in America, who knew no shame in spectacle, who charmed people with the lack of manners and outlandish behavior that came with growing up poor and dreaming big.

"*Ma*, what a beautiful sight. I knew it, Jack, that you were going to do okay for yourself. You can judge a man by the women, and the women always liked you. Are you alone? Nice suit, ha? You meet Sergio? That dickhead Milanese. Well, he makes nice suits. He's not Aldini, but hey. Sergio, he comes to eat sometimes, and his nephew Marco, he's always here. Those Northern Italians, Jack, no offense, but they have no respect. But that don't bother me if I can take their money. Ha, ha."

Carlo looked over his shoulder at the rest of the group.

"Kristen, who are these people? How did these people get in here? You're supposed to check the door. We can't have every tourist off the street coming here. If they wanna eat they can go down to Il Romano. I got a waiting list until ten-thirty. There's no space. Sorry people, we don't got no space."

Mary watched the frenetic Italian and felt his eyes burn into her. This isn't right, she thought. Just turn around and walk away. This is no place for you. They can see that you ain't like them. And the dress is ugly. It's not a pretty dress at all.

"They're with me. I've made a reservation for five at eight o'clock. I asked for a window table in the front room. That table over there is mine," Jack said, pointing across the room.

"Listen, Jack, if it was you and your girlfriend, fine. But I've got the mayor comin' here. I've got businessmen and movie stars comin' here. You know, famous people."

"How many times has the mayor come here," Jack asked.

"Listen. We're friends and you're a star and I wanna do you a favor. I can put you in the American bar. That's the most I can do."

"But that table is empty and I reserved it."

"Listen, Jack, it's no big deal," James said, putting a hand on his shoulder. "We'll go somewhere else."

"I can put you in any other room, Jack, but not in the front by the window. You may be in a few ads and a commercial . . . It's nice commercial, in fact. Tell me, those girls, do you know them? Why don't you bring some of those girls here?"

Jack felt his anger build. He wanted to punch Carlo in the face in front of everybody. Instead, he took him aside and said, "This is my family, Carlo. They're from Arizona and they've come out to see me. What if your mother and father came out from their little town in Southern Italy, you know that poor town you grew up in, to see you and all that you've made of yourself? Would you make them sit in the back somewhere? Or do you want to keep kissing ass to all these rich folk like Sergio Baducci or the mayor or whoever else? I know business is business and you want to look good. But I just want to treat my folks to a good meal. I mean, I used to work here and now I'm in magazines. You should be proud to have me here in your front window pulling business."

"You're right, Jack. You're right. I'm stupid. But why didn't you tell me they're family? Family is family. You know, between you and me, I don't give a damn about these piece of shit Americans. *C'é*, but I'm in a difficult situation. They come expecting a table, and if I don't give it to them, they talk bad about my place and don't come back, and business isn't so good these days, Jack. Look, I've got the real estate developer Steven Phillip and his family here. He owns most of the Financial District and they've been waiting for the window. You see my problem?"

After a little more discussion, and Carlo introducing himself personally to Jack's family, the Phillips sat down at the window and Jack and the others were directed to the bar for a free round of drinks. Doc had no problem with that, he didn't need to sit by the window; no, the window table wasn't that important, but to Jack the free drink tasted bitter. That was the tact of being a restaurant owner and Carlo, he was one of the best, being that his diplomacy came from the bottom up, that is, where death and not just the bruising of an ego was at stake.

Brian was still working there. Jack saw him on the floor, his face a blank mask, taking orders and gliding between the tables in anonymity, like the professional he was. It was clear he'd been at it a long time; like anyone with a repetitive job, he had boiled his work down to the essential. He did everything with an economy of emotion: just enough to get the task done. That was fine for a waiter, because waiters could be rude or silent; uber-friendliness wasn't required like in other service jobs where it didn't even earn a tip.

Jack hoped to catch his eye. He disliked Brian for being both mediocre and arrogant. Jack wanted to show him that he had moved on, and that when Brian had assigned him to the worst sections, it hadn't mattered because he had proven he was better than that. Perhaps that was the reason for Jack's return. Because even now that he was better off than most, now that he had lived his fifteen seconds of fame, Jack felt the unease and sickness of becoming what he saw around him: a plastic smile, a character defined by his economic function, an actor and image for other people to hang their hopes on.

"Jack, you look glum. What are you thinkin' so hard about, anyhow," Will asked him.

Will's spirits were up, now that he was at the bar with a drink in his hand watching the dancers and the elephant on stage.

"Nothing. Sometimes it doesn't matter what you think. It makes no difference because thoughts aren't actions," Jack said.

"Wow, I ain't had a whiskey this good since I can't remember when," Doc said, knocking it back. "Bartender, gimme another."

"Hey, you better take it easy," James said. "Just because Jack says it's okay don't mean you have to take advantage."

But then Jack didn't care how much Doc drank. In fact, he also felt the need to drink after his argument with Carlo.

The more Mary looked around at the other women, the more worthless she felt. What do I have compared to them? She couldn't imagine having their lives or their beauty; no, she was just an ugly witch glad for any attention at all from men. She couldn't understand why James didn't just tell her to get lost. 'Cause he feels sorry for you, is all.

By the time they got seated Doc was already three whiskeys in.

"Would you look at this, I must be the prince of Arabia," he said, in a voice louder than necessary, referring to the decor.

Brian handed them the menus and pretended not to recognize Jack. Is he just pretending or can't he remember? Maybe he was relieved that Brian played it that way, because now, in spite of his pride, Jack felt ashamed of his company. He thought better than to remind Brian who he was.

Jack ordered a bottle of wine and some appetizers, and Will leaned over to Jack and said, "Jack, I can't read any of these words, would you just pick somethin' out, somethin' with meat, I don't want nothin' vegetarian. If I wanted to eat grass, I'd be a cow."

"Would you look at this, they've goat on the menu. I don't think I've ever eaten a goat in my life," Doc said. He was talking loud, and at the next table, where the Phillips sat, Mr. Phillip turned and gave them a dirty look.

"So what do you want, Mary," James asked.

"Oh, anything's fine with me," she said. "I'm sure it's all very good."

Sitting there, Jack found himself watching the waiters and the bussers, and thinking about the cooks; he was aware of the arteries of the restaurant and did not feel separate from the staff, like most of the diners who were oblivious and could care less because they would never have to do such work. Jack tried his best to be classy when Brian poured the wine; he tasted it with gravity, took a suitable pause and nodded that it was fine, following the superficial procedure to the letter.

Brian filled their glasses and left. The rest of group knocked it back like it was beer or water, except James who took it slower. Certainly, they could care less if the bottle cost two dollars or seventy-five. Jack wouldn't tell them anyway, because they weren't the kind of people to be impressed by it, and that was fine as far as he was concerned. So after that he dropped the wine and they ordered round after round of cocktails. By the time they were eating dinner, Mary was laughing and putting her head on James's shoulder, Will looked a little green in the gills and Doc felt like talking so everybody could hear.

"You know what this is we're eatin', Jack? I know this is supposed to be fine dining but it looks like pig vomit."

"It's puréed eggplant," Jack said.

"Well, the things people dream up. Whatever happened to a good steak? I tell you people have a lot of money and all they want to eat is snails and fish eggs. What a bunch of crap."

Mr. Phillip leaned over from the window table.

"You're obviously in the wrong place. I suggest you stop by McDoogle's and get a hamburger and go back to your blue-collar existence watching football and drinking domestic canned beer. Furthermore, if you can't keep quiet, I'll have you removed."

"Well, I'll be damned," Doc said. "A man can't even speak his mind around here. Did you hear that, Jack? I was just making an observation and then I've got someone telling me what to do. I thought this was a free country?"

"In your case, it shouldn't be," Mr. Phillip said.

Jack looked over at the Phillip family and saw their rabbit faces nervous, tight and wide-eyed with embarrassment.

"Leave it alone, Doc," James told him.

They ate the main course, and Doc had trouble with a particularly difficult piece of chicken, so he used his fingers, sucking on them and licking the bones clean before wiping his hands on the edge of the tablecloth.

Jack said, "So I've heard there are housing programs and also occupational training courses to help people get back to work. That's something you guys should look into."

"Jack, I don't need no one preachin' to me, thank you," Doc said.

"Listen, I know all this is bullshit and that even if you work hard you'll never get to live the life you want," Jack said. "The good life, that's only for a few, and mostly you have to be born into it. But that doesn't mean you can't get a job and make your own money and have a place to sleep. Especially you, Will, 'cause you're still young. You have a life to live so you can't give up now. Maybe I've invited you all here to say: don't give up. You could go out tomorrow and have some work. You could pool your money and rent an apartment, maybe. You can take it step by step."

"Jack, this life you talk about ain't nothing but slavery," James said.

"Well, you're right in that life is mostly work with a few sweet breaks in between," Jack said. "So if you're gonna work, you want to make sure you're not on the bottom. Then, little by little, you find comfort. When I first came to the city I didn't have much. I got my first job here in this restaurant and I found a place to live. In the meantime, I searched for something better. It wasn't easy, but now I think I've found my calling. I believe a man can go as far as his will takes him."

"You got it wrong, Jack. I get your point, but it's a little different than that," Doc said. "Life's not slavery like James says. It's greedy people and hierarchical thinking that makes everyone slaves. It's some people thinkin' they're better than others and tellin' 'um so that makes life like that. You believe in the good in people and I believe in the bad. People are rotten to core and it's best not to have anything to do with 'um. You hear that? You're all a bunch of filthy rotten bastards!"

James had seen it happen before. With a few drinks Doc's true personality came out: all the negativity and the hate he had to swallow every day, all his shame and loss of hope in the world, and everything that he had to carry for unknown reasons. Why had it gone this way? Was it his thinking alone? Was it laziness?

At the Phillip's table, the woman said, "Honey, please just ignore him. I don't think he's very stable. Oh, this is so embarrassing. I wish we could just go somewhere else."

Brian came by and said, "You're going to have to keep it down. Please respect the people around you and allow them to eat in peace."

"Fine. Fine. We're all right," Jack told him.

They returned to their meal.

"Well, I hope you're enjoying yourselves," Jack said. "I thought it was the least I could do, since you were all so nice to me in the park."

James sat and stared at his plate. He was biting his lip. They were all drunk now. Mary's chin rested on her chest and she lifted it every now and again to fight the drowsiness that was coming on. Jack looked at James and noticed tears in his eyes.

"Jack, you've been so good to us. You've tried to give us a little dignity, and you've given us respect and treated us like human beings. We're not used to that. I'm sorry," he said, wiping his eyes. "How shameful of me crying like this. I'm afraid we've embarrassed you. When you ain't had love or understanding for a while, it can hurt real bad when you get it. It's like a knife in there, all cold and alien. Jack, I'm not gonna forget this. This is the best day of my life."

The rest of the meal went on in relative silence. Jack thought: I'm not going to see them again. Perhaps that's what's so sad: the fact that this is only temporary, and that when the evening is over, they'll go back to their world and I to mine.

"I think I'm gonna have a dance with one of them gypsy girls," Doc said. "Look at the way they shake their bellies. I gotta have me some of that." He got up from his chair and stumbled into the Phillip's table, knocking over the wine glasses.

Mr. Phillip was furious.

"You goddamned low life. Look at my jacket. You've ruined my jacket. I've a mind to throw you out myself. Waiter! Waiter!"

"You son of a bitch. You bourgeois clown," Doc slurred. He took a swing at him, missed and fell on the floor.

"You're a disgrace. Look at yourself. And you wonder why you're on the bottom," Mr. Phillip said. "Oh, I heard the conversation. The world is unfair and you don't want to be slave to the system. That's original. A man's reward is based on his own merit, and you are a worthless, lazy derelict. Why, you'd be better off dead. I don't understand why people like you don't just kill themselves and do society a favor."

James got up so quick he knocked his chair over. No way was he gonna to stand for that kind of talk about one of his own. Mr. Phillip's two sons rose reluctantly to face him; they were young clones of their father, fine strong-jawed boys uncomfortable and unsure of themselves and the situation. Finally, Jack rose to the occasion with the thought that whatever came to pass, he would come to regret it.

"Whoa there," James said. "I'm sorry about your wine. But talk like that, I don't like the sound of it one bit."

"Screw you, buddy. Do you know who I am? I can ruin your life, so you'd better watch your step."

James threw a neat right jab that knocked Mr. Phillip against the window and to the floor.

"You can't do nothin' to me," James said. "I don't have nothin' to lose no more. It don't matter if you throw me in jail 'cause I already been there. I'm not afraid a' jail or death, neither."

The boys, maybe sixteen and eighteen, stood still and watched their father with his bloody nose while their mother ran to his side.

"Oh, Steven, are you all right? Look what they've done to you."

Jack and James stood their ground and the boys sat down.

Brian came and spoke to Jack. There was a hint of a smile on his face.

"Jack, you're going to have to leave. Either you take these people out of here, or I'll have the police do it. Once again, looks like you've made a mess of things."

Fucker, Jack thought. Fucker. Now he knows me, sure. Now that he can look down on me. Go on and punch him. Just punch him. No, you're better than that.

"Like that time Ignacio threw soup in your face, you prick," Jack said. "You sure earned that one."

Brian's face went white.

"What's the matter, don't have anything to say for yourself?" Jack leaned close to him. "It's assholes like you, pretending you're better than everybody to save your broken pride, who make life miserable for the rest of us."

It was the drink again. Reason was getting away from him and Jack was seeing red. It occurred to him to pick up a chair and smash it over Brian's head, until even that look of incredulity disappeared from his eyes.

Then Carlo came. "*Mamma mia*, what's happening? Mr. Phillip, I am so sorry. *Veramente*. These people, they do not belong here and I will have them removed immediately. Jack, you *stronzo*, I should know better then to let you in here. First you fight with Martino and now this? *Porco dio*, Jack. Get out. I've had it."

"But Carlo, the man was being rude and . . ."

"I don't give a shit. Get the fuck out of my restaurant and never come back. You ruin me, Jack. I can't take this shit anymore. I said get out!"

"But what about the bill?"

"Oh yes, the bill. Get them out and we'll do the bill, but then *finito*, understand? The scum you bring to my place. Americans, they have no class," Carlo said, under his breath, as Jack followed him to the register. "*Dio mio*, and I thought you were a good kid."

41

It was early morning and the soldiers sat around the fire eating breakfast and drinking black coffee. The men and women had their masks pulled up so they could eat properly. This was the only time they could see each other's faces, except perhaps before they bedded down for the night. Still, none of them had ever seen the face of the Subcomandante. He ate separately from them, and whenever he was in view, he wore a mask. They thought Subcomandante Pablo was a foreigner from the upper class. He spoke grammatically correct Spanish without vulgarisms of any kind, and his accent was not from their region. He did not speak their native language. They did not resent this difference. He had fought for their rights and made the rest of the world aware of their struggle for land, food and equality against a government that had exploited and kept them in poverty. It seemed little had changed in that country since Zapata, and Zapata, he had been murdered. Would they also be killed? Probably. But then wasn't it better to die fighting than from starvation?

When Subcomandante Pablo first appeared on national television, the villagers had filled the local bar to watch the event. Some of them had even gone with him to the capital to voice their grievances. He was on magazine covers around the world, and now other nations were putting pressure on the Mexican government to address their complaints. The peasants did not ask much: just a return of ownership of their hereditary land so they could grow their own food, clean water and sanitation, and electricity in the more isolated areas. That was all. They no longer wished to work as itinerant laborers for a misery wage on land that had belonged to their ancestors.

Subcomandante Pablo had been effective in organizing the local population and turning them into a political and military unit. Tired of a history of unfulfilled government promises, recruits came from the surrounding villages in the region to join the movement. It was only after the formation of the United Revolutionary Front that the government saw fit to act by sending tanks and armed soldiers to attack the villages and quell the revolt. Now they were embroiled in a guerrilla war with the rebels. The Subcomandante told his men that they must be prepared to die. Many had already been killed, including civilians, especially in San

Cristobal when it was recaptured. Still, the rebels knew the terrain well and had killed many soldiers in ambush. They were outnumbered, yet they survived.

The Subcomandante had trained them well in the tactics of guerrilla warfare. Before that, none of the villagers had ever held a weapon or done anything but farm. Using the Cuban Revolution and the United States War of Independence as examples, he explained that many times in history civilians had defeated the government in spite of limited resources. He told them that the people would always win against the government if they united and fought on their own terms. He told them, "We do not want power for its own sake, we want the autonomy and freedom to govern ourselves and decide our own fate."

At dawn *compadre* Sanchez returned to camp bearing bad news of the death of one of the scouting party. According to his report, troops were gathering in the west for an offensive. Soon they would surround the valley. "There are many troops, thousands," he said, his eyes large with fear.

Subcomandante Pablo called his captains to the tent for a full report. How many troops were there? Did they have artillery? After receiving the intelligence, he laid out the map and explained the battle plan. Then he ordered his units to take up their positions. If the military wanted to take the valley, they would have to pay dearly for it.

It was a primitive guerrilla war supported by technology. After all units were deployed, Pablo sat down to his laptop and reported the situation to his contacts at various news agencies and NGOs. Meanwhile, he kept an open line of communication with his captains via cell phone. With a remaining force of six hundred soldiers, the situation was critical. Hopefully, media exposure of the offensive would stop the government in its tracks before they were all killed. Though, even if the United Revolutionary Front ceased to exist, there remained many sympathizers who had helped in their way with food and supplies, but who did not fight. Not to mention the international donors that provided funding for the cause. This was the new face of guerilla warfare: a conglomeration of international organizations, foreign investors, high technology and rural poor. With such a network it would be possible to start again.

It was not long before the peace of the forest was broken by the sound of gunfire. Fortunately, the camp was hidden, and Pablo was able to monitor his surveillance cameras in relative security. His units reported their movements and the movements of the enemy by text message to their commander and each other.

Though the government suffered heavy losses, in the end its troops were more numerous and better trained than the peasant soldiers. Pablo knew that soon the base camp would be overrun. He took what he could carry and set a timed charge that would destroy the camp. No one knew his identity; soon he would be across the border and on a plane to a safe haven. They had been fighting the war for two years and now it was coming to an end.

Since the revolutionary army had been defeated, Pablo thought it best that he live to fight another day. He was sorry for the men who had died. He had lived with those men and fought with them, and now he would abandon them. Had it been his war or theirs?

42

When they first arrived in Mexico, Jack found the poverty he saw oppressive and debilitating. He had never been outside the United States before and was not emotionally prepared to cope with the reduced conditions in which fellow human beings were forced to live. All his reading and study of the history of Latin America, and Mexico in particular, was just a warm-up for the education he was about to receive through his own visceral experience.

Mexico City, he felt, seemed no different than what he had seen of Los Angeles, where they had stopped for several days before flying south. Both were dry dusty cities with bad air, sprawling cityscapes, noise, congestion and excessive heat. Both had business districts with smooth structures of glass and steel kissing the sky that helped spin the wheels of commerce; and upscale restaurants, bars and nightclubs where the rich and famous appeared in hours of leisure to indulge their lusts and passions, and measure each other's success. Culturally, Mexico outclassed its northern neighbor with its museums, art galleries and monumental ruins of past civilizations.

It was only outside the tourist avenues and international hotels where the desperation and futility of mortality was exposed: on street corners where urban homeless or rural migrants stood in dejection; in the ubiquitous dilapidated vendor's carts that formed the lifeblood of the cities informal economy on which so many depended; with the trash that filled the gutters and blew in the streets; in the sea of indistinguishable cars that flowed through the city like schizophrenic bloodlines; and in the soot-coated high-rise tenements of veined and cracked cement in which ordinary people lived out their anonymous lives.

The chaos made Jack consider the absurdity of social living. Truthfully, it was no different there than in California, or perhaps anywhere, this life of the city that was so desperate yet so ingenious at survival.

Within a matter of days, Jack had coated his tender nerves with a convenient veneer of cynicism, supported by a nightly cleansing of alcohol, so that he might focus on what was good in that city and all that it had to offer beyond what he had known at home. Ultimately, Jack found that his sentiment toward Mexico was one of fondness, and he felt that California was fortunate to have such a neighbor. His experience had given him a new perspective and appreciation of the Mexicans he had worked with at Amerika. Finally, he was seeing their country with his own eyes.

After a week spent in the capital, the housemates rented a car and traveled south beyond the flash, bustle and pollution of the city into the dry cracked landscape of indifferent mountains and brush, past isolated ranches and agricultural plots with their meager fences, which carried on despite lack of water. Jack regarded the countryside with a mixture of nostalgia for his home in Arizona, and the fear of being trapped in the anonymity of rural life. He felt both superior to and humbled by what he saw.

They stopped in small adobe towns with their well-maintained churches, laughing children and taciturn adults. They sat in dark bars with resigned truck drivers, tired laborers, the unemployed who aspired to working lives of monotony and toil, and men that had simply given up and only aspired to the bottle. They ate in the living rooms of family homes turned restaurants where they were served generous helpings of delicious food by kind-hearted women, and watched with unbridled curiosity from behind doorways and corners by bright-eyed children. In larger towns, they wandered through the markets with their ubiquity of human life and commerce. Here they sampled local food, marveled at the sheer diversity of peppers that were the heart of Mexican cooking, and bought cowboy hats, bracelets and knives. The poverty and hardship of the vendors was apparent in the dress and the lines that marked their long-suffering faces. Many of them had traveled far to attend the market and would travel again until they had made enough money to return home to their families in distant anonymous villages. Jack's heart went out to them; he admired their tenacity and willpower.

As they traveled south, away from the *mestizaje* of the capital, Jack noted how the indigenous heritage of the people grew more pronounced with respect to stature, skin color and facial features. They were Maya and other ethnicities that had been blanketed by a pan-Mexican identity and the Spanish language.

The travelers were obliviously cool in that landscape, having left their own routines behind for a while to engage in art, that safe haven of reflection on life's struggle. In tourism, they had the luxury of standing above humanity and looking down at its precocious ingenuity; they were spectators and consumers of the culture in which they found themselves. In Mexico, the travelers were able to say: we are part of a human race that is capable of producing great beauty and meaning, though for the moment they made no contribution of their own.

They came to those towns with their video cameras and designer clothes, sunglasses and cell phones, looking every bit the affluent Americans of global stereotype. They were fresh and new in the old churches and the plazas, safe in the shelter of their dollar bills and credit cards. They blared electronic music from the car stereo to the discomfort and confusion of peasants and their livestock. They got drunk and jabbered in English, passing through everything like an amusement park, seeing but not understanding. They were arrogant and obnoxious and without vision. In spite of their artistic pretensions, they were nevertheless products of America. As a result, it was impossible for them to develop any spiritual or cultural identity that was not directly tied to economics.

They left the countryside and colonial towns for the beach resorts of the Yucatán. They danced in teeming discos with Americans, Spaniards, Germans and Brits; they lounged by swimming pools, drank themselves to oblivion in the swim-up bars, and passed out in sterile air-conditioned hotel suites; they met and got intimate with strangers they hoped never to see again, all under the eternal gaze of Maya descendants dressed in the uniform of Western civilization, who were the hidden and suffering soul of the tourist industry and its respective venues. Those maids, bartenders, waiters, guides and cabbies cranked the wheel for the endless cycle of consumption and spiritual decay of the foreign guests. Jack couldn't help but recall his own servitude and the sore of resentment it had forced him to carry and remember with a wince of pain when it was aggravated. Such it was remembered and such it was forgotten in the moment when life smiled in leisure. For it was leisure they needed after the struggle they had faced to survive and find meaning in the city. They were putting the cynical professionalism of America aside to live large with what they had accumulated of surplus time and money; like good Americans, they had learned to compartmentalize their lives so that the box of fun and the box of obligation did not spill one into the next.

Eventually, they got down to the business of the film. They reviewed the script and discussed logistics. They had been traveling for two months and hadn't yet made it to their destination. Otherwise, they were getting along. Except that night when they came home wasted from the bar in Playa del Carmen and Damian had wanted to get along a little better by crawling into bed with Jack.

"Come on, Jack, no one will ever know. Henrik's passed out. Do it for me, Jack. Just this once and I'll never ask you again. Promise. You owe me, man. What's the big deal?"

"You're drunk, Damian. Get off a me. I'm not into that. I don't like doods, and I don't want to have to get rough with you, so just lay off."

So Damian left him alone and they never mentioned it again. Still, the encounter lingered in Jack's mind and made him uncomfortable; he began to wonder if that wasn't the reason for all Damian's favors, including being given the lead role in the film. If Damian was angry or disappointed at the rebuke, he did a good job hiding it. Jack didn't like to feel like he owed anybody. What had Damian done for him, anyway? Given him a room in the house? Gotten him a mediocre job? Paid his ticket to Mexico? Well, since their arrival, it had all come out of his own pocket. Jack wondered if he would get paid at all for the film, or if Damian was just using him for free labor. Well, even if I don't get paid, it's been a good trip. Fundamentally, Damian's a good guy; he tries to be positive about life, and searches for opportunities for himself and his friends. I guess he's figured out that the secret to success is to have successful friends, and even better if they owe you one. I wish I'd realized that sooner.

Regardless of what comes of it, this trip with the guys has been great. You've had a lot of fun and seen many things you thought you'd never get to see. Who would have thought Mexico could be so cool?

The trip had given Jack time to think about his life back in the States. He realized that since his arrival in the city not once had he taken trip in California, or gone home to visit his parents. When he asked himself why, he realized it simply hadn't crossed his mind; the city and his life there had occupied all his time and energy. Now that he had taken that first step beyond what he knew was safe and comfortable, Jack's fear of travel faded and he began to wonder about the outside world.

The trip had a strange effect on Henrik. Sometimes, when they were visiting some ruin, national park, church or bar, he would rhapsodize on the beauty of life and the necessity of living every moment as if it were one's last. It was the usual carpe diem sentiment, though Henrik seemed to take it pretty serious the way he clenched his jaw to keep his emotions down. Sometimes his eyes would brim with liquid just before tears, and Jack would feel sorry for his friend who was prematurely dying. Still, Jack knew better than to talk about it, for not once had Henrik confided in them about having HIV. It must be hard to live in denial in face of the facts.

Well, this has been an amazing experience and I'm never going to forget it, Jack thought. We've gotten pretty close these last few months, and though this trip will end for all of us, we'll still have our memories. As for Henrik, I guess I'd be pretty sensitive, too, if I knew I was gonna die. It's too bad we're just learning to appreciate each other now.

So Jack and Damian got used to Henrik -in his drunkenness-embracing them, professing his love and making them promise to never forget him. As was custom with pledges of friendship, they ordered shots to make it official. They had no idea that Henrik planned to end the trip with a bullet to the head.

A week later they arrived in San Cristobal de las Casas in the State of Chiapas and set up shop at a small pension. They spent the days driving around the jungle to remote villages. Jack used his ever-improving Spanish to inquire about the revolution, and was met with the reticence and skepticism of the locals. No one seemed particularly eager to talk about those times and what had been lost. No, they were looking to the ground again, at one foot in front of the other to arrive at tomorrow; the *gringos* were at best an absurdity in their daily lives. Eventually, they met a man named Vargas who had fought with Subcomandante Pablo and escaped capture and death in the final government offensive. He told the story of the battle and the Subcomandante's disappearance.

"He lives and will return to help us," Vargas told them.

They bought him drinks and encouraged his story. According to Vargas, Subcomandante Pablo was a Mexican intellectual who resigned his university post and left his family to join the struggle. Other bar patrons were of a different opinion: no, he was a Spanish businessman; no, a Cuban communist; no, an *Americano*. One thing was clear: no one had ever seen his face. There were no known pictures of him without his mask.

From their inquiries, they learned of the location of the village that served as Pablo's former camp. Vargas arranged for them to travel there by truck from San Cristobal and provided them with a letter of introduction that would allow them to stay and make the film. A few days later, they left San Cristobal for the mountains.

The tiny village that had been at the heart of so much conflict made little impression on Jack and the others when they arrived several years after the massacre. For the villagers the arrival of the *gringos* was a novelty rife with suspicion and mistrust. They wondered: why have these young men traveled so far from their families and their homes? Why do they come here where life is hard? As with all things foreign to their community, they expected the worst. However, with Vargas's letter, written in what Jack assumed to be some form of Mayan, the foreigners were accepted into the village without protest and given a house with earth walls and no running water or electricity. They were glad to have followed Vargas's advice to buy a gas generator that they would be so kind as to leave behind.

Through Jack, Damian told Cacoch Soto, the informal leader of the community, of their project. It was Soto who convinced them of the necessity of modifying the story to suit the facts as the village knew them. Soto was instrumental in helping them recruit the local men and women to play parts in the film. Damian offered to pay them each ten dollars a day and found that, while all were eager to play revolutionaries, which they had been, were and would always be in their blood, few wanted to act the part of the government, which they so despised. In the end, Damian had to pay twice as much for a mock government army, in addition to putting up with their complaints.

"My children are hungry, otherwise I would not shame myself in this way," someone said.

In a tone thick with malice, another commented, "It's very ironic, isn't it, dressing up as the enemy? It's like a nightmare that keeps repeating."

Jack promised them that after the filming was over they could burn the uniforms.

"Yes, we will have a party and fill the uniforms with straw and burn them in commemoration of the losses we have suffered," they agreed.

The subject matter and message of the film were not exactly favorable to the interests of the nation's ruling political party. Whether it took place in Mexico, Guatemala, Nicaragua, or El Salvador, didn't matter, for all of those countries had fought internal wars, civil wars, that pitted corrupt governments against their own people. So it was best to secure the weapons and uniforms they needed as clandestinely as possible. This they achieved by giving money to Vargas to bribe soldiers at the military post in San Cristobal. The arms were by far the biggest expense of the film, and Damian grumbled about how he might go over budget, not including the daily pay of two makeshift armies of twenty men each.

One day a man known as El Chivo came to the village claiming affiliation with Vargas. He advised them to buy grenades, and more rifles and ammunition -live rounds, not blanks. His praise for the utility of such items was duly noted.

"You want the film to be authentic, no?"

El Chivo said this in a way that implied consequences. He smiled a lot and drank their tax-free whiskey and said, "Yes, it is good to make this film. We believe in this film and it would be a shame if something happened and it was never finished."

That was when they knew they were in over their heads and that the peasants weren't so simple after all. They had revolution in their blood.

Henrik was of the idea that they should leave.

"Man, we're supplying arms to the revolutionaries. If they catch us we'll be jailed or even killed. This is serious shit, guys. I don't want to spend my last years in jail. That guy basically threatened us. I say we get out of here before this turns ugly."

"Listen, if there was a problem and the government came here and found the weapons, we'd just pretend we were filming a nature show and that we didn't know anything about it," Damian said. "We're Americans. The Mexican government isn't going to fuck with some *Americanos* when they can arrest and throw these rebels in jail once and for all."

But they were all a little nervous after that. Somehow the story became real then, and Jack lay awake at night thinking about Subcomandante Pablo's legend and identity and why he had come to fight for the peasants. How do people find the courage for that sort of thing, he wondered. In comparison all he and the others had done back home seemed inane.

They stayed in the village for many weeks, filming and storing footage. They drank at night in the local bar, and Henrik spun music, mixing the Mexican songs he had collected with lyrics, rhythms and beats the locals had never heard before. That bar had never been so full, not because of the music, which took some getting used to, but because Damian was buying. The locals were quickly becoming big drinkers and they accepted Damian's hospitality with gusto, to the point that it would have been an offense for it to be anything but unconditional. The general festive atmosphere, coupled with the arms purchase that had nearly tapped out Damian's budget, translated into conspiratorial nods and tips of the hat in the street.

Henrik was by far the biggest attraction with his rings, tattoos and the bumps in his neck. They revered him like a god. Even Vargas, who came to visit them occasionally, seemed afraid of Henrik and did not look him in the eye. When they brought up El Chivo's visit, Vargas simply thanked them for their gift to the village.

As it turned out, some women would not let their children out at night for fear that Henrik would eat them. There was even talk that the foreigners be expelled from the village. But Vargas stopped such superstition. He was an educated man. He had been to Mexico City and seen life outside of the village, and was aware of the foreigners' utility. Their money was taking the edge off poverty, they were supplying weapons and they were interested in the cause. Perhaps even Subcomandante Pablo himself had sent them.

Then one night the locals watched with horror as Henrik walked off with one of the village girls.

"Don't worry. *No te preocupes*," Jack told them. "He's not going to eat her. He's not dangerous. It's all artifice. He's a normal person like you and me. I promise." Jack laughed to put them at ease and mask his own anger at Henrik's irresponsibility.

But the locals remained tense and nervous. Lidia must be a witch, they thought. Otherwise, he would not take her. If she disappears, what will we tell her mother and father when they return from the fields? Sorry, but the devil took her. A small sacrifice for all the good the strangers brought with them.

But Lidia came back and did not seem damaged in any way. There were no teeth marks on her, she was not missing any limbs and her eyes bore no evil. She smiled and laughed, and the village breathed easier.

"And if she has a child, will it be a demon," a dissenting voice asked.

"If it is a demon, we kill it," came the response. "There is no other remedy."

43

"Okay, I want you to look relaxed around the campfire," Damian said. "Remember, the day is just getting started and no one is expecting an attack."

Jack translated as best as he could for the men. They nodded that they understood.

"Your weapons are full of blanks, so when you shoot, do it for real. Aim to kill, because no one will die. I want this to be as realistic as possible."

Damian was standing surrounded by the men dressed in their respective uniforms and armed with automatic rifles. I wonder how it would be to lead a revolution? Once the people fought here for real. Their families and friends were killed here just a few years ago. I understand why they don't want to wear the government uniforms. Look at the disgust on their faces.

Damian remembered what one of the men had suggested to him in the bar.

"And if in the movie you make it so we win, *jefe*? That would not be so bad. Then the people will see it and be inspired."

But he couldn't do that. He could promise that it would be an even battle, and that the government troops would suffer losses, but in the end the rebels would be defeated.

"Do you support the revolution," they asked him.

"Yes," Damian said, "if it allows you to feed and educate your children, work your own land and be independent. Go on, Jack, tell him what I said."

Now Damian stood in the jungle, surrounded by the men, giving directions for the battle.

"We've placed charges in various locations around camp and in the surrounding area. All of the spots are labeled on these maps, please take the time to study them," Damian said. "As an extra precaution we've painted the ground around the explosives. It is important that you don't step inside the marked areas."

God, I hope Jack translated it right. The last thing we need is some injury or death during the filming, he thought.

Damian gave them further directions and the men took up their positions. Jack put on his mask, shouldered his rifle and waited for his cue. They had three DV cameras, in addition to several surveillance cameras mounted on actors and in various locations around the camp. Damian would shoot the primary plot-driven footage, while two men from the village, who had been trained to use the spare cameras, would film the general action of the battle. Henrik was in charge of the explosives.

Damian gave the signal and the troops clashed; the government army advanced up the hill and the revolutionaries fired down on them from their positions. Henrik set off charges and men dove for cover. One man fell from a tree onto a hidden mat. Soldiers collapsed in mock death and feigned injury as the camera focused on the eyes behind the masks, the shouting faces and the gritted teeth.

A panicked soldier returned to camp to report on the carnage of the battle. Subcomandante Pablo ordered the remaining troops to take up their weapons and join the fight. Then he armed himself with grenades, ammunition and his assault rifle, and ran off through the trees, followed by the camera. Gunfire rattled in the air and an artillery blast threw him to the ground and knocked the wind out of him.

Jack lay on the ground gasping for breath. This is crazy, he thought. It's crazy what the villagers told us about what really went down. And by that time Subcomandante Pablo was already gone. He abandoned them. And I understand why. If this were a real war, I would desert, too. But then what if you don't have any other choice but to fight, because it's your home?

Jack lay in a prone position and opened fire on the approaching soldiers. His rifle blazed and the men dropped or dove for cover. He threw a prop grenade, and Henrik, somewhere in between, set off a charge that launched one of the men, shouting, into the air.

What if I kill someone with these blasts? They're buried fairly deep, but we're still talking a quarter-stick of dynamite. I wonder if he's hurt? Certainly, he can't jump that high? Then Henrik thought: maybe I should just go stand on a blast myself. If this were a real war, I might just do a suicide mission. My life is going to be short anyway. Why not do something useful for a change? Boy, Lidia sure was a good lay. I think when the others go I will stay here a little longer. Or maybe I will take Lidia with me when I travel. Still, it's stupid to fuck Lidia. It's irresponsible, even with a condom.

Fantastic, Damian thought, as he ran along behind the men and panned in on Jack who was firing like his life depended on it from the shelter of an embankment.

Jack, confident that he had put them on the defensive, made a diagonal run for a nearby group of trees, peppering the enemy with gunfire to hold them off. He made it safely to his destination and crouched with his back against a tree across from the enemy's position. He was aware of the danger of his situation; he was alone and trapped by a unit of between five and eight men. Two, he was certain he had killed. Their bodies lay where he had surprised them on the path that snaked between the trees. If he could make it south past their position, he would be able to loop back around on the lower trail and work his way under cover back to the 3rd Unit that was transmitting via GPS a half mile to the east. Then they could come back and outflank the enemy from behind. Deciding on this plan of action, Jack started to crawl on his hands and knees through the vegetation and detritus of the jungle floor. Despite the occasional opportunistic gunfire from the enemy, he was making good progress. The trees thinned and opened into a clearing roughly eighty feet in diameter, and he was forced to stop or be exposed. Well, it's risky, he told himself, but it's your only choice. He was already past their location and knew that, if he made it across, he would be able to back steadily away under cover with his rifle checking their progress and forcing them to risk death if they chose to go on the offensive and pursue him.

"Well, let's see how your luck is today, *amigo*," he commented to himself. It calmed his nerves to talk to himself this way and made him feel as if his lonely endeavor was somehow teamwork with others depending on him. Company of the crazy, he thought. Spend enough time out here and even the trees start talking.

When the forest fell silent, but for the sound of the bugs in his face, and when Damian gave the signal, Jack threw a grenade in the general direction of the previous gunfire and ran in a crouch across no man's land. The explosion produced a confused and misdirected gunfire, and sensing his advantage and imminent arrival, Jack's nerves began to loosen their stranglehold on his panicked heart. Death had brushed its hands across his shoulders and not taken hold, though it stood in the shadow of his every movement.

But then too late, and in the slow motion of irreversible catastrophic events, Jack noted the soldier, who had no doubt anticipated his plan, positioned against a tree to the southeast with little more than his head exposed and the muzzle of his weapon leveled at Jack's chest. Jack thought: I better make this believable because this is the moment that the old Jack dies and the new is born.

Jack turned to defend himself, but staccato gunfire rang out before he could issue his own. His rifle fell from his clutching grasp, his chest popped with blood, and his body convulsed in a manner that was humble and mortal and anything but exaggerated, before he fell into the earth's comprehensive embrace.

Afterwards, the soldier, Reynaldo, entered the clearing between the trees, came to stand by the fallen Subcomandante and kicked him over onto his back. Jack stared to the sky, a trickle of blood leaking from the corner of his mouth -that wonderful theatrical detail- while Reynaldo peered down inquisitively into Damian's waiting and equally inquisitive lens, his face warped like a curious fish in a bowl, all lips and eyes, and said, "*Puto revolucionario*, it was only lacking that you die in this way," before spitting into the camera that was Jack's face and the face of anyone who refused to accept their place in the world.

The government soldiers gathered in a circle around the fallen rebel leader, the awe and fear in them apparent by their awkward investigative movements, gawking at a man that had become the legend they would never be, perhaps not even believing it true, wondering if he weren't in fact just another peasant or imposter.

"And now we'll see who this *cabrón* really is," Reynaldo said, bending down to remove the mask.

"Is it really him?"

"Hard to say."

"He must be a *gringo*, look how white he is."

"Okay, let's bring the body back to General Herrera. We're certain to receive a promotion for this."

"*Pués*, he's dead," Reynaldo said.

"Yes, we know. Thank God," the other men commented, following Reynaldo's lead with some improvisation of their own.

"All right, cut. It's a wrap, gentlemen," Damian said, repeating in his broken Spanish, "*Muy bien, amigos. Parar película. Vamos para fiesta!*"

Damian was ecstatic over the final scene. The improvised baggies of pig's blood and the rubber bullets worked like a charm, though Jack was certain to be sore after that one. And to think Damian had worried that Jack would overact and pull some dramatic "I'm dying, go on without me," hand on the forehead bullshit. But Jack had risen to the occasion; the film had made an actor of him, and Damian couldn't have been more proud. Even if they shot it twenty times, he couldn't have hoped for a better performance.

It was almost too much to believe that the dream which had sustained him for the last ten years was finally coming true; he was finally directing films that mattered. His first feature was completed, editing and post-production aside, and the future stretched before him replete with promise. He felt like having a big cathartic group hug with the local men and women who had helped make it possible. At the very least, he would thank them by getting their story onto the big screen.

"A real five-star performance, Jack. And I've got a cold beer with your name on it to commemorate the start of a great career and partnership. Man, you were great," Damian said. "Lucky for you, Reynaldo's a good shot, the best in the village, otherwise you coulda lost an eye."

Now that the scene was over, the rest of the cast had gathered and were talking quietly amongst themselves. Frankly, it hadn't been as bad as they thought making the movie, and now everyone was going to see them in the old *Estados Unidos*. It was really too much to believe.

Meanwhile, Reynaldo stood apart from the group and stared from Jack to his rifle and back again. His gaze had the depth and resignation of one accustomed to the weight of timeless oppression. He knew it would be callous to explain to the foreigners that only now could they fully begin to understand the horrors of senseless death and violence that the village had faced. If anything, it would create a bond between them that could never be broken; what was fiction had become reality, and vice versa.

"*Que pasa*, Reynaldo," Damian said. "You're a pretty good shot, you know that? You sure showed the old Subcomandante here who's boss, right Jack?"

Jack made no comment.

"I killed him," Reynaldo said.

"That's right, Reynaldo, you sure did," Damian said, patting him on the back. Now let's get out of here and hit the bar. "*Cerveza para todos,*" he shouted to the cast that proceeded to clap and whistle at the announcement.

All right, Jack, stop clowning and get your ass up," Damian said. "Man, that was so realistic. I could just feel the bullets tearing the life out of you. I mean one minute you're firing away, giving it all you got, and the next you're face down in the dirt like you never even existed."

"It wasn't my fault," Reynaldo said. "I didn't do it on purpose. I swear to God on my mother's grave that it was an accident."

Damian wasn't paying attention, high as he was on the moment, imagining just how drunk they were going to get as soon as possible. If ever there were a time to get drunk, it was now, he thought.

Abruptly, Reynaldo aimed his rifle at a nearby tree and opened fired until a branch crashed to the ground.

"My rifle's loaded, understand? My fucking rifle is loaded! And not with plastic, with real bullets," he shouted. "The *gringo* is dead, *de verdad.*"

Though Damian didn't understand all that was said, his heart lurched in his chest in that way like when he thought he had lost his keys, or when the lights of a police car flashed in his rear-view mirror. That premonition of disaster overtook his good humor and made it a memory.

"Come on, Jack, stop messing around. That shit ain't funny. Get your ass up and let's hit the bar. Tonight we're gonna have a party this town will never forget."

But Jack did not get up.

So Damian dropped to his knees, stared into Jack's unblinking eyes and laid his hand on his chest to feel his silent heart.

"Jack, don't you fucking die on me, man. You can't leave me now. We're a team, you and me. We're good like that. And this is just the beginning. It's just gonna keep getting better, don't you see? All those days of living hand to mouth and having to do all kinds of shitty work are over, man. Don't you get it? We're gonna be famous. What do you think of that? Isn't that what you always wanted? Goddammit, Jack, fucking say something!

Damian shook Jack by the shoulders with hope that there was life in him yet. Then he slumped over Jack's body with his head in his hands and wept. He wept for the death of Ryan Meyer, which had taken away his childhood; for the family he no longer spoke to, for what he'd had to become to survive, and for the great distance that separated him from ever being happy. He wept for those qualities in Jack that he admired and did not possess: the honesty, integrity, trust and sincerity that to Damian had come to signify at best beautiful fictions, and at worst hindrances to success. And though Damian knew the world to be a brutal, competitive and unjust place, he wanted badly to recover a sense of optimism and joy in life; he needed badly to believe in doing the right thing. To see Jack destroyed in such an arbitrary way closed the door with finality on hope. To Damian, Jack represented what was good in men, and he had hoped to present Jack to the world on the silver screen as an ideal to emulate.

All of Jack's character that betrayed that ideal -his faults, weaknesses, contradictions and prejudices- had been erased in death, allowing Damian to cling to the belief that Jack, and people like Jack, made the world bearable. They were the reliable, stoic individuals content with their position in life, and not the predators and opportunists who used others for their own advancement, who never gave anything for free, who were absent when the going got tough, whose friendships amounted to little more than convenience and networking opportunities, and who believed self-interest and personal gratification to be the highest achievements of man. Damian had tried to teach Jack these lessons about the world because he thought him dangerously naive; now he realized he had done Jack a disservice. You can't make someone something they're not, he thought, because they'll always be faking it, and that's not a life. It was because Damian loved Jack and wanted to see him succeed that he had done these things; for those same reasons, he had also sheltered and protected Jack from certain harsh realities, in hope that Jack would come to love him. Perhaps Jack had loved him in his own way, but not in the way Damian needed or wanted. His desire for love and acceptance had seen Jack killed; it would not have happened without his intervention in Jack's life, and the blame was now his to bear. Hope of a better future and trust in others had been Jack's undoing.

Jack's death would be forever on Damian's conscience: it was another scar added to his already wounded soul; a constant oppressive weight slowing him down and serving as an admonition for his ambition and pride, lies and opportunism, and inability to live a life of sincerity and compassion for others. Besides himself, Jack was the only person Damian had truly cared about, and now Jack was gone. Ultimately, he had betrayed Jack by using him to fill a void in himself. By helping Jack, Damian was only trying to help himself. Damian saw clearly that Jack's appeal lay in his innocence and sincerity; consequently, he had appropriated these traits to further his own career.

And now malice had come to spoil his careful plans. Damian had always known his relationship with the villagers was one of utility, and God knew he had done his best to help them. And they had repaid him with Jack's murder. It was a premeditated act on Reynaldo's part, but to what end? Damian thought that the whole village must be in on the conspiracy, but what exactly did they expect to gain from Jack's death? Was it a general hatred of the outsider that had boiled over into violence? Were they seeking media attention for the struggle? Was it a warning from the government, or some other political gambit whose purpose and intent Damian could only begin to imagine? Damian realized that he, too, had been terribly naive believing that they could walk into a conflict zone in another country, appropriate the drama for their own ends, throw some money in people's faces and leave unscathed. And to think he had supplied the village with weapons. He had paid for the bullets that had ripped through Jack's body.

It had been a mistake to help the village, and the only honorable recourse that remained for him was revenge. Damian's grief evolved into anger and hatred, and he was ready to exact retribution for the crime committed. He had always been one to avoid problems and flee from conflict, but now he felt it was his duty to confront and defeat the hostile forces he saw before him. He was no longer willing to pretend what he did not believe, nod in favor when he was in fact in opposition, or humor and patronize others in the interest of self-preservation. Beneath Damian's cheerful and enthusiastic demeanor resided the anger over having the best years of his youth taken from him; it had been a daily struggle to control those negative and destructive emotions he'd held inside since high school. Only in his drunkenness would the veil slip as he insulted others and engaged in random acts of vandalism. Damian had reached the breaking point: the pain had to have an outlet, it had to go somewhere outside of himself and become a material reality; he had to maim and kill and disfigure everything to match the soul within that was long since destroyed with bitterness and loss. He had to act or risk losing his sanity. There was no more room for tolerance.

Damian stared with hatred at the men and women that a moment before he had loved; in his delusion he read conspiracy and contempt in their plain, emotionless faces. He fixed his eyes on the object of his hate: Reynaldo, Jack's executioner, who stood with his rifle in his hands a few feet away. Reynaldo was the source of the pain inside, and Damian would destroy the evil he represented, which consistently robbed him of the things he loved. Damian was beyond reason. At no point did he stop to consider the potentially accidental nature of the event, or rather that the source of injustice was infinitely more complex than a single man, even if he were guilty.

It would have been expedient for Reynaldo to knock the *gringo* out with the butt of his rifle and let him come to his senses, but he knew better than that. There was a time when he had felt the same blind hatred and righteous indignation that he now saw carved into Damian's face. To think that before he and Damian had been friends. But then he had killed Jack. He hadn't meant to kill him; it was an event larger than himself, of what sort he could not be sure, which Damian could not be expected to understand, at least not now.

Reynaldo, who had also lost loved ones to violence and misfortune, awaited the confrontation with the reckless angry youth with the same resignation he reserved for the other hardships in his life. He dropped the rifle to the ground and awaited his punishment. He made no attempt to defend himself.

Damian struck him in the face and knocked him down. Reynaldo did his best to protect his head and groin while Damian savagely kicked and beat him. The villagers approached the conflict but did not intervene. Damian eventually pinned Reynaldo to ground and, clutching him by the throat, pulled a knife from his belt. He had every intention of killing Reynaldo. There's no law here, Damian told himself; the law in this place, like any other, is an invention to give an appearance of order to the general chaos.

Reynaldo struggled under Damian's weight and thought about death. He did not think Damian would be so foolish as to kill him. Indeed, he had always considered Damian a reasonable man. But now he began to doubt, and that doubt turned to fear and panic.

"Don't do it, Damian. It's a misunderstanding," he gasped. "I didn't want to, I swear. *No quería.* Please, don't kill me. I have a wife and children."

Damian knew that even if the rest of the village tried to stop him now, they would be too late. It was a quick matter to kill Reynaldo and be done with it. As for security, a few paces away he had the only loaded rifle on the set.

"What the fuck is going on here," Henrik said, interrupting the scene. One of the villagers had gone to fetch him amidst the drama, and now they came running up the trail together.

Perhaps it was Henrik's voice that broke the spell, or Damian's realization that he could not kill. The panic in Reynaldo's eyes and his fear of dying blended with Damian's own panic and fear at the macabre turn of events. To see people killed was different from death in theory or the sterility of death in a newspaper headline. Looking into Reynaldo's panicked eyes, Damian realized he was telling the truth. There was no malice there; it was a case of involuntary manslaughter. And with that realization his anger subsided and the absurdity of the situation became clear to him. So what was he to do if there was no one to blame for what had happened, no logical resolution to the event and no justice to be had?

Damian surrendered the knife and allowed Henrik to pull him to his feet. Reynaldo doubled over in a coughing fit and wiped the blood from his mouth.

"What's going on here? Man, Damian, I don't know what he did, but you coulda killed him."

"*Estás bien*, Reynaldo," Henrik asked, helping him to a sitting position.

"*Si, si. Estoy bien*," Reynaldo said, sitting up and rubbing his neck.

"Do you need a doctor?"

"No, it's okay. I'm fine. It was a misunderstanding."

"What's up, man? Reynaldo's a cool guy," Henrik said. "You shouldn't take those 'your mother' commments so personal. Everybody jokes like that down here."

Damian looked over to where Jack lay in the dirt.

"Whatever was said, just forget about it," Henrik said, following Damian's gaze.

"Jack, you're giving me the creeps lying there like that," Henrik said. "Why is everybody acting so fucking strange around here? Come on and let's all head back to the *pueblo*."

Henrik came late on the scene and had missed the final drama, the machine-gunning of the tree, the collective realization of what had happened, and the fear of the consequences, both real and imagined.

Henrik walked over to Jack.

"You all right, Jack? You're not hurt, are you? Come on and get your ass up already."

Henrik reached down to pull him up and noticed the gaping mouth and unblinking eyes. Recognizing death, he passed his hand over Jack's face to close his eyes and give him peace.

Jack's untimely death left Henrik cold. Who was Jack Wild? Now that mystery would never be clarified. Perhaps he was just an ordinary guy content to follow the path of least resistance? Or perhaps it was Jack's ambition that had brought him to this spectacular end? Would it have been better otherwise: if Jack had married, produced children of his own and worked until he was old and gray at some nondescript commercial endeavor? Was it better to pursue a life of a few great and ultimately devastating achievements to be remembered, or to live for the small joys of a routine, prolonged and altogether anonymous existence?

Henrik spoke to the villagers in passable Spanish and agreed with them that it had been an accident. He did not doubt Reynaldo's sincerity. He had been their friend ever since their arrival and had helped them with the minor difficulties of adapting to the third world conditions of the village. Clearly, what had happened was larger than Jack, the film and the village itself. For the moment, Henrik was unable to formulate a reasonable explanation, though he was filled with unease and foreboding.

So there they were, he and Damian, far away from home with Jack gone forever. After all the shouting and gunfire and explosions, the silence returned with palpable force. Henrik noted the sun's descent in the sky, the birdsong in the trees, the dead calm of the air and the second skin of humidity. He wiped the sweat from his forehead and caught a whiff of the slightly metallic and acrid odor of Jack's blood drying in the sun.

Henrik was glad to have met Jack and regretted having underestimated him. Perhaps it was jealousy that had made Henrik reluctant to accept him. He had thought, like many think of the beautiful: Jack's got it easy, fortune will smile on him; and for that reason he desired Jack's failure and destruction. But now he knew that, while beauty could be an advantage, it took a strong person to carry it; and beauty without intelligence was a commodity to be exploited by others, like he had exploited Jack after his fame -as a catalyst and hanger-on in Jack's descent into debauchery. If not for the project that had given them a sense of purpose, how low would they have sunk? Henrik had been living low for a long time, the bottom was his habitat, and he was all too glad to hold Jack there in that pit of superficial desires and poisonous addictions of the insecure and anonymous urbanites who lacked meaning in their lives. But even amidst the hedonism, Henrik felt the strength of the compass inside Jack that, no matter how far he strayed, would always return him to center. Perhaps that was Jack's attraction: his magnetic sense of self and consistency of word and deed. Even when he was in a bad way, this was apparent. Ultimately, Jack had won him over, and now their friendship was sealed in eternity.

Henrik had already said his silent and personal goodbye to Jack; in reality it had happened sooner than expected and in the wrong order. Jack was supposed to mourn him. Since they stepped on the plane to Mexico, Henrik had made up his mind never to return to the States. He had taken out a substantial loan and would travel until the money ran out before ending his life. Perhaps he would return to Sweden to see his family, though he worried he would break down and confess to them the truth. He had no desire to be sheltered and mourned until his premature death. He did not plan to waste away in bed like an invalid. In a way, he would have preferred to take Jack's place. Then it wouldn't have been such a waste after all, to die at the completion of the film, forever immortalized on the big screen.

It seemed Jack had unwittingly achieved his destiny, albeit not in the manner he had expected. Otherwise, it might have taken Jack his whole life, if ever, to reach icon status. And now he stood a good chance of achieving it tomorrow. Death had made Jack a better man; he would be a role model for all the dreamers who would gladly pay with their lives for eternal adulation. Be careful what you wish for, Henrik thought.

Even in tragedy, the specter of opportunity loomed with Damian's unconscionable ability to make a buck. Though Damian lamented and suffered now, Jack would forever be his vehicle to success. Damian was not the sort to let failure and loss get in the way of progress; after all, wasn't it the practice of the living to make use of the dead? Had it ever been any other way? After the grief and mourning passed, Jack would no doubt serve his purpose.

Damian had sunk lower than even he could imagine. It was the most miserable thing he had ever done to bring Jack with him and then get him killed in such an arbitrary way. Who would have thought it possible? It was as if the last bit of his heart that was true and good had withered and died; he had lost everything that meant something to him, and that it should occur at this hour when his star was in ascendance. If he had known the true price of success, would he have been willing to pay it again in the same currency?

"Come on, Damian," Henrik coaxed. "There's nothing we can do. If I could change it, I would, but it's impossible. Jack was a good guy and he went out on top. Let's bring him back to the village and make arrangements to send him back to his family. I'm sure they'd want that."

"And say what: 'you don't know me, but I'm Jack's housemate. I took him to Mexico with me to make a movie and things didn't go right, so here's your fucking son, sorry he's coming home in a box' ?"

"Exactly. Because that's where we're at and there's nothing we can do about it. So there's no point in talking about what could have been. Now come on and help me carry him."

They held a funeral and the peasants decorated the village, prepared special foods and brought in a live band from the area. The local men and women gave their condolences for the death of *compadre* Jack and drank to his memory. Damian and Henrik drank heavily that evening to ease their sorrow, and Reynaldo drank with them.

It was never clarified whether the rifle had been loaded with live ammunition by accident or with malice. Nor was it known how the police found out about Jack's untimely death, for they had all agreed not to disclose the event to avoid intervention and possible punishment by the authorities. In the end, they were unable to prevent the police, military, and U.S. and Mexican reporters from flooding the village to uncover the facts. But the fact was no one was talking. According to the account by the Americans and the villagers, Jack had been shot by an unknown gunman.

The resulting publicity caused a stir in both Mexico and the United States and put Chiapas back on the map as a place of conflict and instability. Local and national Mexican news media, and major news media in the United States, published stories on the mysterious murder of American actor Jack Wild during the filming of *Inertia* on location in Mexico.

Damian and Henrik were interviewed and asked about the circumstances and motivations of Jack's murder, his character and their relationship to him, and the plot and future of the film; their opinion of Subcomandante Pablo and the United Revolutionary Front, and Chiapas and the village that had hosted them; and their personal lives and future plans. The story was of the sort that captured the hearts and minds of the public. Jack Wild was once again a cover story, this time with the caption: *Why did he die?* In the United States, articles were published regarding the risk of traveling to Chiapas and other parts of southern Mexico. In Mexico, conservative publications discussed the possible involvement of Subcomandante Pablo in Jack Wild's death, and rumors that the United Revolutionary Front was gathering strength to continue the fight for autonomy from the Mexican government. Liberal publications, for their part, discussed possible government involvement in Jack Wild's death, which would provide a convenient excuse for intensifying their persecution of the indigenous population in Chiapas.

In the meantime, Damian's cell phone rang nonstop. Michael Karen from Solimar was eager to know the status of the production. It was sure to be a blockbuster, particularly since the final scene was real; showing it would cause a lot of controversy, and that was sure to pack the theaters. Karen was relieved that Damian had gotten Jack to sign a work-for-hire contract, which meant that Jack's family couldn't stop the film or ask for compensation from future profits. Meanwhile, the big studios were calling to offer anything Damian wanted for his next project.

To the reporters and police, Damian tried to say as little as possible. He worried about a government investigation and the possibility of his equipment being confiscated; fortunately, the night of Jack's death, Damian had copied the footage onto a second external hard drive and hidden both of them in two different but secure locations in the nearby jungle. When it was safe he would return to collect them. The work had become priceless, both as evidence that could land him and Henrik and the whole village in prison, and because it would make him an overnight success upon release back home.

Damian's initial fear of being jailed as a suspect for the murder of his friend was unfounded. The media publicity had effectively made him untouchable to the Mexican authorities. Reynaldo wasn't so fortunate; he had been arrested as the main suspect of Jack's murder on the testimony of an undisclosed informant. When they asked about the cuts and bruises on his face and body, he had little to say. His life had been such that no matter what absurdity confronted him, he would face it without comment.

Henrik suspected that Vargas, who had sold them the stolen weapons, was a government agent sent to stop their project for the bad press it would generate. But if that were so, then why did he broker the weapons deal through his accomplice El Chivo? Because, Henrik reasoned, the government had planned to arrest and make an example of them for political leverage against the United States. The *gringos* would have been charged on two counts: possession of firearms, and theft of government property, in this case military hardware.

The key to the puzzle remained El Chivo, who had intimidated them into buying live ammunition, grenades and additional weapons. Who was he, where had he gone and where were the arms now? For when the police had come, along with the military, to ransack the village and arrest everyone in it, they had found nothing incriminating; the uniforms had been burned, and the weapons and ammunition were nowhere to be found. When they commanded Damian to hand over his footage, he told them he had already sent it back to the States. When they checked his laptop, they found it had been erased. To make matters worse, the media spotlight forced the army and police to be on their best behavior. Still, it would never do to underestimate the vindictive and resourceful nature of government authority.

In the face of such events, and after the initial storm of scrutiny and interrogation from the authorities had subsided, Henrik suggested they leave as soon as possible. Since they weren't under arrest, they could come and go as they pleased. There was no point waiting around until the authorities fabricated an excuse to detain them, or precipitated another accident that they could conveniently blame on local unrest.

Damian and Henrik paid Emiliano, the bar owner with the prodigious mustache, a reasonable sum for a truck they would use for their escape. Under the cover of night, while the police and military stationed in the village slept, Damian recovered his precious footage, they put Jack in his makeshift coffin into the flatbed, packed him with copious amounts of ice from the bar -so he would stay fresh for the journey- and made for the Guatemalan border. Damian was determined to get the footage back to the States. He felt it was his duty to Jack to get the film released. If everything worked out as he hoped, Jack would not have died in vain.

Epilogue

Alex was alone in the apartment now. It was a strange feeling waking up to an empty house. The silence that before he had savored, was oppressive. It was only a matter of time before he started talking to himself.

"Well, you're done with your book, Alex. Good job, you deserve a pat on the back for your fine service. So what are you gonna do now? Are you gonna look for a job, you deadbeat, or are you just gonna sit here and rot?

"You know, maybe I'll just rot. Maybe I won't shower anymore and I'll order take-out from Phuket and never leave the house again. How do you feel about that?

"Fine, suit yourself. It's your life, if you want to throw it away what difference does it make to me? You're ill, man. Too much thinking is pushing you to the edge. You gotta stop talking to yourself like this."

You're right, he thought. So I wonder when the guys'll be back? If I'd had the money, I would have gone with them. I could use a vacation in Mexico.

One day, Alex's curiosity got the better of him and he sat down in the editing studio and popped in one of the tapes of Damian's new film. It took him a minute to realize that what he was watching was a cinematic version of his novel *Inertia*. He felt the rage bubble inside him. Damian, lacking creativity and a story of his own, had stolen his work. To add insult to injury, he had butchered it, cutting out key scenes and elements of the plot. The film was stylized and choppy to suit the short attention span of the modern movie-going public, and set to what was no doubt Henrik's abstract electronic score. Most surreal of all was the sight of Jack playing the lead and speaking word for word the lines he had written.

In spite of his shock and anger, Alex watched the entire first half of the film. Was it vanity at seeing his words and ideas acted out on the screen that kept him there? Was it hope that his work would finally be recognized? For many years Alex had honed his craft in silence and anonymity. He had sent his work out to countless agents and publishers, applied for writing scholarships and participated in contests, all without favorable response. It seemed that, in his case, talent and discipline weren't enough. What it boiled down to was getting a break, like Jack with his singing gig. In spite of all his effort, it seemed that he needed Damian to get ahead after all. Instead of being angry at the theft of his work, he should have been grateful, because the film was his best shot at exposure. Bullshit, he thought. If the film is successful Damian will reap the reward, while you'll still be stuck here living hand to mouth. Even if your name does appear in the credits, it's not like anyone reads them anyway. No one ever knows who the writer is. And who's to say Damian will even give you credit? Well, I've got a copyright on the book; if he wants to use it, he's gotta get the rights from me. Which isn't going to happen because I'll make him shut down the project. And if he doesn't, then I'll take him to court.

Alex wasn't concerned about compensation, because he knew he would get it one way or the other. What he really found infuriating was Damian's opportunism. What a master of false promises, bullshit, boasting and manipulation. Damian claimed to have sold his first script by impersonating a pizza man; to Alex that said it all. From what Alex knew, none of the scripts Damian had pitched were his own; he had bought them off others for nothing and put his name on them. While Damian claimed to be a film agent, in actuality he only represented himself. When he did help people make connections and find opportunities, it was so they would owe him and he could call in the favor later. And now it seemed he would even sell out his friends.

While Alex had come to accept Damian for who he was, just as Damian might have accepted Alex's less desirable character traits, this betrayal of trust had effectively ended their friendship. It was because of his distrust of Damian that Alex had refused to work with him in the first place. But one thing was sure, Damian knew how to play the game and had been rewarded for his efforts. Didn't he say that the production company had given him a quarter of a million dollars to make the film? That for someone whose only experience directing amounted to car wash rag commercials and the like? Meanwhile, all those years Alex had invested trying to craft quality literature had gotten him nowhere. Instead, he should have just pumped out shallow, clichéd pulp by the truckload and, with pretty packaging and some marketing gimmick, shoved it down America's throat.

What Damian had understood from the beginning was that it all came down to marketing, and that when the system didn't work, you had to go around it and do it yourself. The publishing industry, like most other established commercial activities, was threatened by monopoly. In spite of myths to the contrary, all business tended toward monopoly, and it was the monopoly of distribution that was stifling innovation and creativity in

America. If someone wanted to make money, they didn't waste their time producing content, but focused their efforts on controlling distribution. For those individuals who needed to produce something of value to feel fulfilled, this meant ingratiating oneself to the system and sacrificing one's ideals in hope of getting a break. Essentially, it wasn't about quality, it was about access. Once you were in the system and had a name, then you could work on projects you believed in, provided they made money and did not challenge the values of the system. Therein lay the rub for the writer: for it was the writer's job to expose the truth, no matter how ugly or inconvenient. Though Alex had always been aware of the dark side of opportunity and success, the point was driven home when he sat down to watch the film. He was devastated by what that truth meant for his future. It was quite possible that the only way to make it was Damian's way, by cheating or selling out. But if being an artist was no different than working for a corporation, then what was the point?

Though he understood the game, Alex would never sell out or compromise his integrity like Damian. Alex wrote because he had to, not because it seemed like a fun way to make money. There were things he needed to say and he would say them. He had a purpose beyond that of his own self-advancement. It's not about me, it's about telling stories to both entertain people and help them ask the bigger questions of who they are, why they're here and where they're going. Alex knew there would always be a difference between the story he told and the way it was interpreted by others. That was what made it worthwhile; each individual used his own experience to find meaning in the work. It was the same reason he wrote multiple endings to his books: because he could not cope with the loss of choice and the finality of a single outcome. For Alex, life and the world were about possibilities.

Yes, it was integrity that mattered: without it, no achievement had any value. Alex was sick and bloody tired of creating value in the world only to have it sponged off by opportunists. What was happening now was his worst nightmare; his work was being used for the advancement and benefit of others, while he continued to rot away and starve in spite of his contribution. And to think they had all conspired against him to keep it a secret. Now they were in Mexico making his movie without his permission or participation. They were living it up while he was alone and miserable as usual from his efforts. If he hadn't been so absorbed in his work, he might have seen it coming.

Alex sat alone in the darkness while the light of the television reflected off his face and into his glassy eyes. Watching the film that night broke his heart because he felt that he never had a chance, or better yet, that everything boiled down to chance, and when chance didn't come your way, it seemed you had to lie and cheat to get it. The betrayal made Alex sick. He felt sick and lonely and detached from the world. In his mind there was no greater offense then the theft of ideas. There was nothing lower than that: to take another man's ideas, call them one's own and profit from them. But then wasn't that what middleman America, venture capitalism and corporate take-over were all about? If only Damian had asked, then he might have felt differently about it. As it stood it was theft, and Alex's feelings were sufficiently hurt to warrant a drastic reaction.

Alex drank the rest of the afternoon and into the night. He blared music and danced around the house with a bottle of vodka in hand. He raved and shouted oaths at the top of his lungs. He was losing his mind. He wanted to lose his mind. He didn't want to think any more or try to understand things that would never make sense. He didn't want to maintain control because there was no point to it. He was trapped in that rathole life where only the bastards got ahead, and now they had gone and stolen the only thing he had left: his ideas and the hope they inspired. The rage took him. It was good he hadn't gone down to the bar that night, or he would have found himself regaining consciousness on the losing end of a fistfight he had started.

That evening, when he could no longer take the absurdity of the television he was watching, Alex threw the monitor out the living room window into the garden. He ran down the hall and barged into Jack's room, found his trusty bat, and smashed the remaining video equipment in the studio. When he had exhausted himself, he slid to the floor and wept. He wept for the injustice of life; for the loneliness, misery and despair; for the absurdity and the futility of everything he had ever done, and the fear that ruled him and kept him from realizing his dreams. When Alex was finished, when he had unleashed that pent-up physical rage and purged himself of everything he could not write or say, he looked at his destruction with shame and regret. Only you know the depth of your own despair. That's a secret you can never share with anyone.

Alex lay down in his bed in that cold, empty house listening to his own breathing and wishing he weren't alone, as the room spun around him. He felt a premonition of disaster. The mind is powerful thing, he told himself. What you think and believe will be your fate. The world you have created is not one of happiness and success; you have never been concerned about appearance, leisure, socializing or making love. You could have lived with those priorities, but instead you chose to write about misery and injustice. And in so doing, you paved the way for your own failure and destruction. Ha, ha. Ha, ha, ha. You crazy motherfucker. You don't give a damn anymore, do you? Either that or you care more than you'd like to admit. Like anyone, you want to be accepted; like any American, you want to do something great and be admired by others; like any American, you live for others and not yourself. And you thought you were different. As if it were possible to step outside of your own culture and be independent from it. No, you're not independent. You are in opposition, which means you are reacting, adapting and altogether implicated in the system.

The next morning Alex woke up with a terrible hangover. He had succeeded in finishing up the leftover liquor that no one had touched since the last party. The rest of the day he spent sending out letters to various agents and publishers to keep himself busy and distracted from thinking about his dwindling funds and the need to look for work. He was sick to death of work, given that he worked around the clock without reward.

Later that afternoon Alex heard helicopters flying above the neighborhood, and sirens in the street. Must be a fire, he thought. Every now and again one of the old Victorians would go up in smoke. When he left the house to buy groceries, Alex noticed that the streets were empty except for numerous police cars that came with their sirens wailing and lights flashing. He walked by McLeary's, the Irish bar, and peeked inside. Though it was crowded, there was no music, and people stood silently with their eyes riveted to the television.

Alex pushed his way inside to get a better look. He was just in time to watch a tanker ship explode underneath the Golden Gate Bridge. Amidst the black smoke and the flames of the blast, a section of the bridge collapsed into the bay. The ship was torn through the middle and taking in water, as the deck burned thick with smoke. The cars that had been on the bridge at the time were either scattered and overturned or had dropped with the bridge into the water below.

Footage of the event was replayed ad nauseam. The bar patrons were still deep in the shock of it, thinking it more Hollywood spectacle than reality. It was so fantastic that it was almost beautiful. Again and again, the explosion flashed bright with hot flames and endless smoke that cleared to reveal the broken bridge and the mangled ship sinking in the water.

The reporter's voice was tight and fast.

"You're watching live footage of a tanker ship explosion that has damaged the Golden Gate Bridge. This is a terrorist attack. The mayor is imposing martial law until the security of the city can be assured. The people of San Francisco are asked to keep calm and to remain in their homes. Bay News will keep you informed of the latest developments in this crisis."

Ticker text scrolled across the bottom of the screen: *Attack on America: Terrorists destroy Golden Gate Bridge. Thirteen presumed dead. Mayor declares martial law.*

"We've just received video footage provided by a local resident who witnessed the explosion first hand."

The video was shot in Crissy Filed by the Presidio. The tanker blew up and the cameraman started shouting, "They blew up the bridge! Holy shit, they blew up the bridge!" The camera shook as the anonymous man ran down the street. Around him, people were shouting and looking at each other in disbelief. He ran towards the bridge while others ran past him away from it. Momentarily, sirens could be heard as the police, fire department and several ambulances arrived on the scene. The man was confronted by the police and questioned. Then he was told to turn off his camera.

"Motorists are being rescued from the bridge as we speak. The death toll is estimated at thirteen. So far no names are available. Please stay tuned for the latest . . ."

The power went out and the bar was dark.

"What's going on here? They've cut the power. We're under attack. They're attacking the city," someone shouted.

Though no one knew who "they" were, it caused a panic in the room. Patrons pushed and shoved and trampled each other to get to the door. Outside, people stood in the middle of the street talking in their cell phones, faces white with fear, hugging and comforting each other with tears in their eyes, while others ran to the safety of their homes.

Alex had no delusions that they were under attack. It was an isolated incident, and he felt that the imposition of martial law was unwarranted. The bombing was an act of cowardice, all right, but it had been effective. The terrorists may not have had many resources, but they knew how to make a statement, and they should probably give Hollywood credit for the ideas. There was a purpose to that act; it was not merely destruction for its own sake, but signaled that there were individuals and groups deeply dissatisfied with their condition, the state of the world, and particularly the United States and its politics. They represented an extreme element of a world that was tired of the dark side of American Empire that fed off violence, corruption, exploitation and greed.

The destruction of the bridge was proof in Alex's mind of the wrong path the nation had taken. It was as if the attack confirmed everything he had researched and written about in his book. History had finally caught up with the United States.

Though Alex believed there would never be any attack on America in the military sense, Americans would now have to live with the uncertainty and fear of random violence, typical of the developing world, inside their own borders. It was as if the bubble of safety and comfort had been popped and they were all being sucked into chaos.

What does it say about America that people will commit such acts of voilence against us, Alex wondered. What is it that can engender such hatred, and why does it come as such a surprise? I guess even the powerful are vulnerable and can be called to account for their actions. Certainly, we're no angels. We've been mixed up in the politics of other nations for ages, and there is blood on our hands for our efforts. Denying it won't change the facts. And the fact is, if you act with malice toward others, you should expect reprisal. So I wonder how our mandarins will react to this one? Will they revoke our civil liberties for the sake of our own protection? Will they continue with the politics of inequality that make the rich richer while the poor suffer and learn to hate? Or will they suddenly have a change of heart and realize that everyone has a right to life, liberty and the pursuit of happiness, when individual happiness means not impinging on the rights of others and destroying the environment? Don't hold your breath, Alex thought. Some people simply have no morals or conscience. I know it's hard to believe, but it's true.

As always, the extremely tragic and miserable in life brought a smile to Alex's face. He was smiling, not because senseless death made him happy, but because finally he had concrete proof that his thesis was correct. And while he wished it were not so, it was satisfying to know that the madness was not his own but belonged to the society he lived in, and that, ultimately, the current global order was merely the continuation of humanity's historic inability to govern itself in a reasonable manner.

Alex was positively cheerful when he made his way home. Of course that was because he never stopped to consider that he could have died on that bridge. Just like average Americans never stopped to think about the wars started in their name under false pretenses which resulted in the death of innocent people. Really, the bridge was a small sacrifice if it could serve as a symbol to the American people of the hypocrisy and absurdity of a system they followed with such blind faith.